"This is the most
Christian-fiction series ever."

PUBLISHERS WEEKLY

* * *

"Combines Tom Clancy–like suspense with touches of romance, high-tech flash and Biblical references."

THE NEW YORK TIMES

* * *

"Tim LaHaye and Jerry Jenkins . . . are doing for Christian fiction what John Grisham did for courtroom thrillers."

TIME

* * *

"Wildly popular—and highly controversial."

USA TODAY

* * *

"Call it what you like, the Left Behind series . . . now has a label its creators could have never predicted: blockbuster success."

ENTERTAINMENT WEEKLY

LEFT BEHIND SERIES

LEFT BEHIND · TRIBULATION FORCE · NICOLAE

COLLECTORS EDITION I

RAPTURE'S WITNESS

✠ ✠ ✠

TIM LaHAYE
JERRY B. JENKINS

Tyndale House Publishers, Inc., Carol Stream, Illinois

Visit Tyndale's exciting Web site at www.tyndale.com.

For the latest Left Behind news visit the Left Behind Web site at www.leftbehind.com.

Rapture's Witness: Left Behind Collectors Edition I

Rapture's Witness: Left Behind Collectors Edition I first published in 2009 by Tyndale House Publishers, Inc.

Cover photography of outer space by NASA/courtesy of nasaimages.org.

Designed by Dean H. Renninger

Published in association with the literary agency of Alive Communications, Inc., 7680 Goddard Street, Suite 200, Colorado Springs, CO 80920, www.alivecommunications.com.

Library of Congress Cataloging-in-Publication Data

LaHaye, Tim F.
Rapture's witness / Tim LaHaye ; Jerry B. Jenkins.
p. cm. — (Left behind series collectors edition ; 1)
ISBN 978-1-4143-3485-1 (sc)
1. Steele, Rayford (Fictitious character)—Fiction. 2. Rapture (Christian eschatology)—Fiction. 3. Fantasy fiction, American. 4. Christian fiction, American. I. Jenkins, Jerry B. II. LaHaye, Tim F. Left behind. III. LaHaye, Tim F. Tribulation force. IV. LaHaye, Tim F. Nicolae. V. LaHaye, Tim F. Left behind series. VI. Title.
PS3562.A315R433 2009
813'.54—dc22 2009033780

Printed in the United States of America

15 14 13 12 11 10 09
7 6 5 4 3 2 1

LEFT BEHIND

✠ ✠ ✠

For Alice MacDonald and Bonita Jenkins,
who ensured we would not be left behind

1

RAYFORD STEELE'S MIND was on a woman he had never touched. With his fully loaded 747 on autopilot above the Atlantic en route to a 6 a.m. landing at Heathrow, Rayford had pushed from his mind thoughts of his family.

Over spring break he would spend time with his wife and twelve-year-old son. Their daughter would be home from college, too. But for now, with his first officer fighting sleep, Rayford imagined Hattie Durham's smile and looked forward to their next meeting.

Hattie was Rayford's senior flight attendant. He hadn't seen her in more than an hour.

Rayford used to look forward to getting home to his wife. Irene was attractive and vivacious enough, even at forty. But lately he had found himself repelled by her obsession with religion. It was all she could talk about.

God was OK with Rayford Steele. Rayford even enjoyed church occasionally. But since Irene had hooked up with a smaller congregation and was into weekly Bible studies and church every Sunday, Rayford had become uncomfortable. Hers was not a church where people gave you the benefit of the doubt, assumed the best about you, and let you be. People there had actually asked him, to his face, what God was doing in his life.

"Blessing my socks off" had become the smiling response that seemed to satisfy them, but he found more and more excuses to be busy on Sundays.

Rayford tried to tell himself it was his wife's devotion to a divine suitor that caused his mind to wander. But he knew the real reason was his own libido.

Besides, Hattie Durham was drop-dead gorgeous. No one could argue that. What he enjoyed most was that she was a toucher. Nothing inappropriate, nothing showy. She simply touched his arm as she brushed past or rested her hand gently on his shoulder when she stood behind his seat in the cockpit.

It wasn't her touch alone that made Rayford enjoy her company. He could tell from her expressions, her demeanor, her eye contact that she at least admired and respected him. Whether she was interested in anything more, he could only guess. And so he did.

They had spent time together, chatting for hours over drinks or dinner, sometimes with coworkers, sometimes not. He had not returned so much as one brush of a finger, but his eyes had held her gaze, and he could only assume his smile had made its point.

Maybe today. Maybe this morning, if her coded tap on the door didn't rouse his first officer, he would reach and cover the hand on his shoulder—in a friendly way he hoped she would recognize as a step, a first from his side, toward a relationship.

And a first it would be. He was no prude, but Rayford had never been unfaithful to Irene. He'd had plenty of opportunities. He had long felt guilty about a private necking session he enjoyed at a company Christmas party more than twelve years before. Irene had stayed home, uncomfortably past her ninth month carrying their surprise tagalong son, Ray Jr.

Though under the influence, Rayford had known enough to leave the party early. It was clear Irene noticed he was slightly drunk, but she couldn't have suspected anything else, not from her straight-arrow captain. He was the pilot who had once consumed two martinis during a snowy shutdown at O'Hare and then voluntarily grounded himself when the weather cleared. He offered to pay for bringing in a relief pilot, but Pan-Continental was so impressed that instead they made an example of his self-discipline and wisdom.

In a couple of hours Rayford would be the first to see hints of the sun, a teasing palette of pastels that would signal the reluctant dawn over the continent. Until then, the blackness through the window seemed miles thick. His groggy or sleeping passengers had window shades down, pillows and blankets in place. For now the plane was a dark, humming sleep chamber for all but a few wanderers, the attendants, and one or two responders to nature's call.

The question of the darkest hour before dawn, then, was whether Rayford Steele should risk a new, exciting relationship with Hattie Durham. He suppressed a smile. Was he kidding himself? Would someone with his reputation ever do anything but dream about a beautiful woman fifteen years his junior? He wasn't so sure anymore. If only Irene hadn't gone off on this new kick.

Would it fade, her preoccupation with the end of the world, with the love of Jesus, with the salvation of souls? Lately she had been reading everything she could get her hands on about the rapture of the church. "Can you imagine, Rafe," she exulted, "Jesus coming back to get us before we die?"

"Yeah, boy," he said, peeking over the top of his newspaper, "that would kill me."

She was not amused. "If I didn't know what would happen to me," she said, "I wouldn't be glib about it."

"I *do* know what would happen to me," he insisted. "I'd be dead, gone, *finis*. But you, of course, would fly right up to heaven."

He hadn't meant to offend her. He was just having fun. When she turned away he rose and pursued her. He spun her around and tried to kiss her, but she was cold. "Come on, Irene," he said. "Tell me thousands wouldn't just keel over if they saw Jesus coming back for all the good people."

She had pulled away in tears. "I've told you and told you. Saved people aren't good people, they're—"

"Just forgiven, yeah, I know," he said, feeling rejected and vulnerable in his own living room. He returned to his chair and his paper. "If it makes you feel any better, I'm happy for you that you can be so cocksure."

"I only believe what the Bible says," Irene said.

Rayford shrugged. He wanted to say, "Good for you," but he didn't want to make a bad situation worse. In a way he had envied her confidence, but in truth he wrote it off to her being a more emotional, more feelings-oriented person. He didn't want to articulate it, but the fact was, he was brighter—yes, more intelligent. He believed in rules, systems, laws, patterns, things you could see and feel and hear and touch.

If God was part of all that, OK. A higher power, a loving being, a force behind the laws of nature, fine. Let's sing about it, pray about it, feel good about our ability to be kind to others, and go about our business. Rayford's greatest fear was that this religious fixation would not fade like Irene's Amway days, her Tupperware phase, and her aerobics spell. He could just see her ringing doorbells and asking if she could read people a verse or two. Surely she knew better than to dream of his tagging along.

Irene had become a full-fledged religious fanatic, and somehow that freed Rayford to daydream without guilt about Hattie Durham. Maybe he would say something, suggest something, hint at something as he and Hattie strode through Heathrow toward the cab line. Maybe earlier. Dare he assert himself even now, hours before touchdown?

* * *

Next to a window in first class, a writer sat hunched over his laptop. He shut down the machine, vowing to get back to his journal later. At thirty, Cameron Williams was the youngest ever senior writer for the prestigious *Global Weekly*. The envy of the rest of the veteran staff, he either scooped them on or was assigned to the best stories in the world. Both admirers and detractors at the magazine called him Buck, because they said he was always bucking tradition and authority. Buck believed he lived a charmed life, having been eyewitness to some of the most pivotal events in history.

A year and two months earlier, his January 1 cover story had taken him to Israel to interview Chaim Rosenzweig and had resulted in the most bizarre event he had ever experienced.

The elderly Rosenzweig had been the only unanimous choice for Newsmaker of the Year in the history of *Global Weekly*. Its staff had customarily steered clear of anyone who would be an obvious pick as *Time*'s Man of the Year. But Rosenzweig was an automatic. Cameron Williams had gone into the staff meeting prepared to argue for Rosenzweig and against whatever media star the others would typically champion.

He was pleasantly surprised when executive editor Steve Plank opened with, "Anybody want to nominate someone stupid, such as anyone other than the Nobel prizewinner in chemistry?"

The senior staff members looked at each other, shook their heads, and pretended to begin leaving. "Put the chairs on the wagon—the meetin' is over," Buck said. "Steve, I'm not angling for it, but you know I know the guy and he trusts me."

"Not so fast, Cowboy," a rival said, then appealed to Plank. "You letting Buck assign himself now?"

"I might," Steve said. "And what if I do?"

"I just think this is a technical piece, a science story," Buck's detractor muttered. "I'd put the science writer on it."

"And you'd put the reader to sleep," Plank said. "C'mon, you know the writer for showcase pieces comes from this group. And this is not a science piece any more than the first one Buck did on him. This has to be told so the reader gets to know the man and understands the significance of his achievement."

"Like that isn't obvious. It only changed the course of history."

"I'll make the assignment today," the executive editor said. "Thanks for your willingness, Buck. I assume everyone else is willing as well." Expressions of eagerness filled the room, but Buck also heard grumbled predictions that the fair-haired boy would get the nod. Which he did.

Such confidence from his boss and competition from his peers made him all the more determined to outdo himself with every assignment. In Israel, Buck stayed in a military compound and met with Rosenzweig in the same kibbutz on the outskirts of Haifa where he had interviewed him a year earlier.

Rosenzweig was fascinating, of course, but it was his discovery, or invention—no one knew quite how to categorize it—that was truly the "newsmaker of the year." The humble man called himself a botanist, but he was in truth a chemical engineer who had concocted a synthetic fertilizer that caused the desert sands of Israel to bloom like a greenhouse.

"Irrigation has not been a problem for decades," the old man said. "But all that did was make the sand wet. My formula, added to the water, fertilizes the sand."

Buck was not a scientist, but he knew enough to shake his head at that simple statement. Rosenzweig's formula was fast making Israel the richest nation on earth, far more profitable than its oil-laden neighbors. Every inch of ground blossomed with flowers and grains, including produce never before conceivable in Israel. The Holy Land became an export capital, the envy of the world, with virtually zero unemployment. Everyone prospered.

The prosperity brought about by the miracle formula changed the course of history for Israel. Flush with cash and resources, Israel made peace with her neighbors. Free trade and liberal passage allowed all who loved the nation to have access to it. What they did not have access to, however, was the formula.

Buck had not even asked the old man to reveal the formula or the complicated security process that protected it from any potential enemy. The very fact that Buck was housed by the military evidenced the importance of security. Maintaining that secret ensured the power and independence of the state of Israel. Never had Israel enjoyed such tranquility. The walled city of Jerusalem was only a symbol now, welcoming everyone who embraced peace. The old guard believed God had rewarded them and compensated them for centuries of persecution.

Chaim Rosenzweig was honored throughout the world and revered in his own country. Global leaders sought him out, and he was protected by security systems as complex as those that protected heads of state. As heady as Israel became with newfound glory, the nation's leaders were not stupid. A kidnapped and tortured Rosenzweig could be forced to reveal a secret that would similarly revolutionize any nation in the world.

Imagine what the formula might do if modified to work on the vast tundra of Russia! Could regions bloom, though snow covered most of the year? Was this the key to resurrecting that massive nation following the shattering of the Union of Soviet Socialist Republics?

Russia had become a great brooding giant with a devastated economy and regressed technology. All the nation had was military might, every spare mark going into weaponry. And the switch from rubles to marks had not been a smooth transition for the struggling nation. Streamlining world finance to three major currencies had taken years, but once the change was made, most were happy with it. All of Europe and Russia dealt exclusively in marks. Asia, Africa, and the Middle East traded in yen. North and South America and Australia dealt in dollars. A move was afoot to go to one global currency, but those nations that had reluctantly switched once were loath to do it again.

Frustrated at their inability to profit from Israel's fortune and determined to dominate and occupy the Holy Land, the Russians had launched an attack against Israel in the middle of the night. The assault became known as the Russian Pearl Harbor, and because of his interview with Rosenzweig, Buck Williams was in Haifa when it happened. The Russians sent intercontinental ballistic missiles and nuclear-equipped MiG fighter-bombers into the region. The number of aircraft and warheads made it clear their mission was annihilation.

To say the Israelis were caught off guard, Cameron Williams had written, was like saying the Great Wall of China was long. When Israeli radar picked up the Russian planes, they were nearly overhead. Israel's frantic plea for support from her immediate neighbors and the United States was simultaneous with her demand to know the intentions of the invaders of her airspace. By the time Israel and her allies could have mounted anything close to a defense, it was obvious the Russians would have her outnumbered a hundred to one.

They had only moments before the destruction would begin. There would be no more negotiating, no more pleas for a sharing of the wealth with the hordes of the north. If the Russians meant only to intimidate and bully, they would not have filled the sky with missiles. Planes could turn back, but the missiles were armed and targeted.

So this was no grandstand play designed to bring Israel to her knees. There was no message for the victims. Receiving no explanation for war machines crossing her borders and descending upon her, Israel was forced to defend herself, knowing full well that the first volley would bring about her virtual disappearance from the face of the earth.

With warning sirens screaming and radio and television sending the doomed for what flimsy cover they might find, Israel defended herself for what would surely be the last time in history. The first battery of Israeli surface-to-air missiles hit their marks, and the sky was lit with orange and yellow balls of fire that would certainly do little to slow a Russian offensive for which there could be no defense.

Those who knew the odds and what the radar screens foretold interpreted the deafening explosions in the sky as the Russian onslaught. Every military leader who knew what was coming expected to be put out of his misery in seconds when the fusillade reached the ground and covered the nation.

From what he heard and saw in the military compound, Buck Williams knew the end was near. There was no escape. But as the night shone like day and the horrific, deafening explosions continued, nothing on the ground suffered. The building shook and rattled and rumbled. And yet it was not hit.

Outside, warplanes slammed to the ground, digging craters and sending burning debris flying. Yet lines of communication stayed open. No other command posts had been hit. No reports of casualties. Nothing destroyed yet.

Was this some sort of a cruel joke? Sure, the first Israeli missiles had taken out Russian fighters and caused missiles to explode too high to cause more than fire damage on the ground. But what had happened to the rest of the Russian air corps? Radar showed they had clearly sent nearly every plane they had, leaving hardly anything in reserve for defense. Thousands of planes swooped down on the tiny country's most populated cities.

The roar and the cacophony continued, the explosions so horrifying that veteran military leaders buried their faces and screamed in terror. Buck had always wanted to be near the front lines, but his survival instinct was on full throttle. He knew beyond doubt that he would die, and he found himself thinking the strangest thoughts. Why had he never married? Would there be remnants of his body for his father and brother to identify? Was there a God? Would death be the end?

He crouched beneath a console, surprised by the urge to sob. This was not at all what he had expected war to sound like, to look like. He had imagined himself peeking at the action from a safe spot, recording in his mind the drama.

Several minutes into the holocaust, Buck realized he would be no more dead outside than in. He felt no bravado, only uniqueness. He would be the only person in this post who would see and know what killed him. He made his way to a door on rubbery legs. No one seemed to notice or care to warn him. It was as if they had all been sentenced to death.

He forced open the door against a furnace blast and had to shield his eyes from the whiteness of the blaze. The sky was afire. He still heard planes over the din and roar of the fire itself, and the occasional exploding missile sent new showers of flame into the air. He stood in stark terror and amazement as the great machines of war plummeted to the earth all over the city, crashing and burning. But they fell between buildings and in deserted streets and fields. Anything atomic and explosive erupted high in the atmosphere, and Buck stood there in the heat, his face blistering and his body pouring sweat. What in the world was happening?

Then came chunks of ice and hailstones big as golf balls, forcing Buck to cover his head with his jacket. The earth shook and resounded, throwing him to the ground. Facedown in the freezing shards, he felt rain wash over him.

Suddenly the only sound was the fire in the sky, and it began to fade as it drifted lower. After ten minutes of thunderous roaring, the fire dissipated, and scattered balls of flame flickered on the ground. The firelight disappeared as quickly as it had come. Stillness settled over the land.

As clouds of smoke wafted away on a gentle breeze, the night sky reappeared in its blue-blackness and stars shone peacefully as if nothing had gone awry.

Buck turned back to the building, his muddy leather jacket in his fist. The doorknob was still hot, and inside, military leaders wept and shuddered. The radio was alive with reports from Israeli pilots. They had not been able to get airborne in time to do anything but watch as the entire Russian air offensive seemed to destroy itself.

Miraculously, not one casualty was reported in all of Israel. Otherwise Buck might have believed some mysterious malfunction had caused missile and plane to destroy each other. But witnesses reported that it had been a firestorm, along with rain and hail and an earthquake, that consumed the entire offensive effort.

Had it been a divinely appointed meteor shower? Perhaps. But what accounted for hundreds and thousands of chunks of burning, twisted, molten steel smashing to the ground in Haifa, Jerusalem, Tel Aviv, Jericho, even Bethlehem—leveling ancient walls but not so much as scratching one living creature? Daylight revealed the carnage and exposed Russia's secret alliance with Middle Eastern nations, primarily Ethiopia and Libya.

Among the ruins, the Israelis found combustible material that would serve as fuel and preserve their natural resources for more than six years. Special task forces competed with buzzards and vultures for the flesh of the enemy dead, trying to bury them before their bones were picked clean and disease threatened the nation.

Buck remembered it vividly, as if it were yesterday. Had he not been there and seen it himself, he would not have believed it. And it took more than he had in him to get any reader of *Global Weekly* to buy it either.

Editors and readers had their own explanations for the phenomenon, but Buck admitted, if only to himself, that he became a believer in God that day. Jewish scholars pointed out passages from the Bible that talked about God destroying Israel's enemies with a firestorm, earthquake, hail, and rain. Buck was stunned when he read Ezekiel 38 and 39 about a great enemy from the north invading Israel with the help of Persia, Libya, and Ethiopia. More stark was that the Scriptures foretold of weapons of war used as fire fuel and enemy soldiers eaten by birds or buried in a common grave.

Christian friends wanted Buck to take the next step and believe in Christ, now that he was so clearly spiritually attuned. He wasn't prepared to go that far, but he was certainly a different person and a different journalist from then on. To him, nothing was beyond belief.

* * *

Not sure whether he'd follow through with anything overt, Captain Rayford Steele felt an irresistible urge to see Hattie Durham right then. He unstrapped himself and squeezed his first officer's shoulder on the way out of the cockpit. "We're still on auto, Christopher," he said as the younger man roused and straightened his headphones. "I'm gonna make the sunup stroll."

Christopher squinted and licked his lips. "Doesn't look like sunup to me, Cap."

"Probably another hour or two. I'll see if anybody's stirring anyway."

"Roger. If they are, tell 'em Chris says, 'Hey.'"

Rayford snorted and nodded. As he opened the cockpit door, Hattie Durham nearly bowled him over.

"No need to knock," he said. "I'm coming."

The senior flight attendant pulled him into the galleyway, but there was no passion in her touch. Her fingers felt like talons on his forearm, and her body shuddered in the darkness.

"Hattie—"

She pressed him back against the cooking compartments, her face close to his. Had she not been clearly terrified, he might have enjoyed this and returned her embrace. Her knees buckled as she tried to speak, and her voice came in a whiny squeal.

"People are missing," she managed in a whisper, burying her head in his chest.

He took her shoulders and tried to push her back, but she fought to stay close. "What do you m—?"

She was sobbing now, her body out of control. "A whole bunch of people, just gone!"

"Hattie, this is a big plane. They've wandered to the lavs or—"

She pulled his head down so she could speak directly into his ear. Despite her weeping, she was plainly fighting to make herself understood. "I've been everywhere. I'm telling you, dozens of people are missing."

"Hattie, it's still dark. We'll find—"

"I'm not crazy! See for yourself! All over the plane, people have disappeared."

"It's a joke. They're hiding, trying to—"

"Ray! Their shoes, their socks, their clothes, everything was left behind. These people are gone!"

Hattie slipped from his grasp and knelt whimpering in the corner. Rayford wanted to comfort her, to enlist her help, or to get Chris to go with him through the plane. More than anything he wanted to believe the woman was crazy. She knew better than to put him on. It was obvious she really believed people had disappeared.

He had been daydreaming in the cockpit. Was he asleep now? He bit his lip hard and winced at the pain. So he was wide awake. He stepped into first class, where an elderly woman sat stunned in the predawn haze, her husband's sweater and trousers in her hands. "What in the world?" she said. "Harold?"

Rayford scanned the rest of first class. Most passengers were still asleep, including a young man by the window, his laptop computer on the tray table. But indeed several seats were empty. As Rayford's eyes grew accustomed to the low light, he strode quickly to the stairway. He started down, but the woman called to him.

"Sir, my husband—"

Rayford put a finger to his lips and whispered, "I know. We'll find him. I'll be right back."

What nonsense! he thought as he descended, aware of Hattie right behind him. *"We'll find him"*?

Hattie grabbed his shoulder and he slowed. "Should I turn on the cabin lights?"

"No," he whispered. "The less people know right now, the better."

Rayford wanted to be strong, to have answers, to be an example to his crew, to Hattie. But when he reached the lower level he knew the rest of the flight would be chaotic. He was as scared as anyone on board. As he scanned the seats, he nearly panicked. He backed into a secluded spot behind the bulkhead and slapped himself hard on the cheek.

This was no joke, no trick, no dream. Something was terribly wrong, and there was no place to run. There would be enough confusion and terror without his losing control. Nothing had prepared him for this, and he would be the one everybody would look to. But for what? What was he supposed to do?

First one, then another cried out when they realized their seatmates were missing but that their clothes were still there. They cried, they screamed, they leaped from their seats. Hattie grabbed Rayford from behind and wrapped her hands so tight around his chest that he could hardly breathe. "Rayford, what is this?"

He pulled her hands apart and turned to face her. "Hattie, listen. I don't know any more than you do. But we've got to calm these people and get on the ground. I'll make some kind of an announcement, and you and your people keep everybody in their seats. OK?"

She nodded but she didn't look OK at all. As he edged past her to hurry back to the cockpit, he heard her scream. *So much for calming the passengers,* he thought as he whirled to see her on her knees in the aisle. She lifted a blazer, shirt and tie still intact. Trousers lay at her feet. Hattie frantically turned the blazer to the low light and read the name tag. "Tony!" she wailed. "Tony's gone!"

Rayford snatched the clothes from her and tossed them behind the bulkhead. He lifted Hattie by her elbows and pulled her out of sight. "Hattie, we're hours from touchdown. We can't have a planeload of hysterical people. I'm going to make an announcement, but you have to do your job. Can you?"

She nodded, her eyes vacant. He forced her to look at him. "Will you?" he said.

She nodded again. "Rayford, are we going to die?"

"No," he said. "That I'm sure of."

But he wasn't sure of anything. How could he know? He'd rather have faced an engine fire or even an uncontrolled dive. A crash into the ocean had to be better than this. How would he keep people calm in such a nightmare?

By now keeping the cabin lights off was doing more harm than good, and he was glad to be able to give Hattie a specific assignment. "I don't know what I'm going to say," he said, "but get the lights on so we can make an accurate record of who's here and who's gone, and then get more of those foreign visitor declaration forms."

"For what?"

"Just do it. Have them ready."

Rayford didn't know if he had done the right thing by leaving Hattie in charge of the passengers and crew. As he raced up the stairs, he caught sight of another attendant backing out of a galleyway, screaming. By now poor Christopher in the cockpit was the only one on the plane unaware of what was happening. Worse, Rayford had told Hattie he didn't know what was happening any more than she did.

The terrifying truth was that he knew all too well. Irene had been right. He, and most of his passengers, had been left behind.

2

CAMERON WILLIAMS had roused when the old woman directly in front of him called out to the pilot. The pilot had shushed her, causing her to peek back at Buck. He dragged his fingers through his longish blond hair and forced a groggy smile. "Trouble, ma'am?"

"It's my Harold," she said.

Buck had helped the old man put his herringbone wool jacket and felt hat in the overhead bin when they boarded. Harold was a short, dapper gentleman in penny loafers, brown slacks, and a tan sweater-vest over a shirt and tie. He was balding, and Buck assumed he would want the hat again later when the air-conditioning kicked in.

"Does he need something?"

"He's gone!"

"I'm sorry?"

"He's disappeared!"

"Well, I'm sure he slipped off to the washroom while you were sleeping."

"Would you mind checking for me? And take a blanket."

"Ma'am?"

"I'm afraid he's gone off naked. He's a religious person, and he'll be terribly embarrassed."

Buck suppressed a smile when he noticed the woman's pained expression. He climbed over the sleeping executive on the aisle, who had far exceeded his limit of free drinks, and leaned in to take a blanket from the old woman. Indeed, Harold's clothes were in a neat pile on his seat, his glasses and hearing aid on top. The pant legs still hung over the edge and led to his shoes and socks. *Bizarre,* Buck thought. *Why so fastidious?* He remembered a friend in high school who had a form of epilepsy that occasionally caused him to black out when he seemed perfectly conscious. He might remove his shoes and socks in public or come out of a washroom with his clothes open.

"Does your husband have a history of epilepsy?"

"No."

"Sleepwalking?"

"No."

"I'll be right back."

The first-class lavs were unoccupied, but as Buck headed for the stairs he found several other passengers in the aisle. "Excuse me," he said, "I'm looking for someone."

"Who isn't?" a woman said.

Buck pushed his way past several people and found lines to the washrooms in business and economy. The pilot brushed past him without a word, and Buck was soon met by the senior flight attendant. "Sir, I need to ask you to return to your seat and fasten your belt."

"I'm looking for—"

"Everybody is looking for someone," she said. "We hope to have some information for you in a few minutes. Now, please." She steered him back toward the stairs, then slipped past him and took the steps two at a time.

Halfway up the stairs Buck turned and surveyed the scene. It was the middle of the night, for heaven's sake, and as the cabin lights came on, he shuddered. All over the plane, people were holding up clothes and gasping or shrieking that someone was missing.

Somehow he knew this was no dream, and he felt the same terror he had endured awaiting his death in Israel. What was he going to tell Harold's wife? *You're not the only one? Lots of people left their clothes in their seats?*

As he hurried back to his seat, his mind searched its memory banks for anything he had ever read, seen, or heard of any technology that could remove people from their clothes and make them disappear from a decidedly secure environment. Whoever did this, were they on the plane? Would they make demands? Would another wave of disappearances be next? Would he become a victim? Where would he find himself?

Fear seemed to pervade the cabin as he climbed over his sleeping seatmate again. He stood and leaned over the back of the chair ahead of him. "Apparently many people are missing," he told the old woman. She looked as puzzled and fearful as Buck himself felt.

He sat down as the intercom came on and the captain addressed the passengers. After instructing them to return to their assigned seats, the captain explained, "I'm going to ask the flight attendants to check the lavatories and be sure everybody is accounted for. Then I'll ask them to pass out foreign entry cards. If anyone in your party is missing, I would like you to fill out the card in his or her name and list every shred of detail you can think of, from date of birth to description.

"I'm sure you all realize that we have a very troubling situation. The cards will give us a count of those missing, and I'll have something to give authorities. My first officer, Mr. Smith, will now make a cursory count of empty seats. I will try to contact Pan-Continental. I must tell you, however, that our location makes it extremely difficult to communicate with the ground without long delays. I will try to raise them on the satellite phone. As soon as I know anything, I'll convey it to you. In the meantime, I appreciate your cooperation and calm."

Buck watched as the first officer came rushing from the cockpit, hatless and flushed. He hurried down one aisle and up the other, eyes darting from seat to seat as the flight attendants passed out cards.

Buck's seatmate roused, drooling, when an attendant asked if anyone in his party was missing. "Missing? No. And there's nobody in this party but me." He curled up again and went back to sleep, unaware.

+ + +

The first officer had been gone only a few minutes when Rayford heard his key in the cockpit door and it banged open. Christopher flopped into his chair, ignored the seat belt, and sat with his head in his hands.

"What's going on, Ray?" he said. "We got us more than a hundred people gone with nothing but their clothes left behind."

"That many?"

"Yeah, like it'd be better if it was only fifty? How the heck are we gonna explain landing with less passengers than we took off with?"

Rayford shook his head, still working the radio, trying to reach someone, anyone, in Greenland or an island in the middle of nowhere. But they were too remote even to pick up a radio station for news. Finally he connected with a Concorde several miles away heading the other direction. He nodded to Christopher to put on his own earphones.

"You got enough fuel to get back to the States, over?" the pilot asked Rayford.

He looked at Christopher, who nodded and whispered, "We're halfway."

"I could make Kennedy," Rayford said.

"Forget it," came the reply. "Nothing's landing in New York. Two runways still open in Chicago. That's where we're going."

"We came from Chicago. Can't I put down at Heathrow?"

"Negative. Closed."

"Paris?"

"Man, you've got to get back where you came from. We left Paris an hour ago, got the word what's happening, and were told to go straight to Chicago."

"What's happening, Concorde?"

"If you don't know, why'd you put out the Mayday?"

"I've got a situation here I don't even want to talk about."

"Hey, friend, it's all over the world, you know?"

"Negative, I don't know," Rayford said. "Talk to me."

"You're missing passengers, right?"

"Roger. More than a hundred."

"Whoa! We lost nearly fifty."

"What do you make of it, Concorde?"

"First thing I thought of was spontaneous combustion, but there would have been smoke, residue. These people materially disappeared. Only thing I can compare it to is the old *Star Trek* shows where people got dematerialized and rematerialized, beamed all over the place."

"I sure wish I could tell my people their loved ones were going to reappear just as quickly and completely as they disappeared," Rayford said.

"That's not the worst of it, Pan Heavy. People everywhere have disappeared. Orly lost air traffic controllers and ground controllers. Some planes have lost flight crews. Where it's daylight there are car pileups, chaos everywhere. Planes down all over and at every major airport."

"So this was a spontaneous thing?"

"Everywhere at once, just a little under an hour ago."

"I was almost hoping it was something on this plane. Some gas, some malfunction."

"That it was selective, you mean, over?"

Rayford caught the sarcasm.

"I see what you mean, Concorde. Gotta admit this is somewhere we've never been before."

"And never want to be again. I keep telling myself it's a bad dream."

"A nightmare, over."

"Roger, but it's not, is it?"

"What are you going to tell your passengers, Concorde?"

"No clue. You, over?"

"The truth."

"Can't hurt now. But what's the truth? What do we know?"

"Not a blessed thing."

"Good choice of words, Pan Heavy. You know what some people are saying, over?"

"Roger," Rayford said. "Better it's people gone to heaven than some world power doing this with fancy rays."

"Word we get is that every country has been affected. See you in Chicago?"

"Roger."

Rayford Steele looked at Christopher, who began changing the settings to turn the monstrous wide-body around and get it headed back toward the States. "Ladies and gentlemen," Rayford said over the intercom, "we're not going to be able to land in Europe. We're headed back to Chicago. We're almost exactly halfway to our original destination, so we will not have a fuel problem. I hope this puts your minds at ease somewhat. I will let you know when we are close enough to begin using the telephones. Until I do, you will do yourself a favor by not trying."

* * *

When the captain had come back on the intercom with the information about returning to the United States, Buck Williams was surprised to hear applause throughout the cabin. Shocked and terrified as everyone was, most were from the States and wanted at least to return to familiarity to sort this thing out. Buck nudged the businessman on his right. "I'm sorry, friend, but you're going to want to be awake for this."

The man peered at Buck with a disgusted look and slurred, "If we're not crashin', don't bother me."

* * *

Later, when Captain Rayford Steele was finally able to take a minute from flying tasks, he used the satellite phone to dial an all-news radio outlet and learned the far-reaching effects of the disappearance of people from every continent. Communication lines were jammed. Medical, technical, and service people were among the missing all over the world. Every civil service agency was on full emergency status, trying to handle the unending tragedies. Rayford remembered the El-train disaster in Chicago years before and how the hospitals and fire and police units brought everyone in to work. He could imagine that now, multiplied thousands of times.

Even the newscasters' voices were terror filled, as much as they tried to mask it. Every conceivable explanation was proffered, but overshadowing all such discussion and even coverage of the carnage were the practical aspects. What people wanted from the news was simple information on how to get where they were going and how to contact their loved ones to determine if they were still around. Rayford was instructed to get in a multistate traffic pattern that would allow him to land at O'Hare at a precise moment. Only two runways were open, and every large plane in the country seemed headed that way. Thousands were dead in plane crashes and car pileups. Emergency crews were trying to clear expressways and runways, all the while grieving over loved ones and coworkers who had disappeared. One report said that so many cabbies had disappeared from the cab corral at O'Hare that volunteers were being brought in to move the cars that had been left running with the former drivers' clothes still on the seats.

Cars driven by people who spontaneously disappeared had careened out of control, of course. The toughest chore for emergency personnel was to determine who had disappeared, who was killed, and who was injured, and then to communicate that to the survivors.

When Rayford was close enough to communicate to the tower at O'Hare, he asked if they would try to connect him by phone to his home. He was laughed off. "Sorry, Captain, but phone lines are so jammed and phone personnel so spotty that the only hope is to get a dial tone and use a phone with a redial button."

Rayford filled the passengers in on the extent of the phenomenon and pleaded with them to remain calm. "There is nothing we can do on this plane that will change the situation. My plan is to get you on the ground as quickly as possible in Chicago so you can have access to some answers and, I hope, some help."

* * *

The in-flight phone embedded in the back of the seat in front of Buck Williams was not assembled with external modular connections the way most phones were. Buck imagined that Pan-Con Airlines would soon be replacing these relics to avoid complaints from computer users. But Buck guessed that inside the phone the connection was standard and that if he could somehow get in there without damaging the phone, he could connect his computer's modem directly to the line. His own cellular phone was not cooperating at this altitude.

In front of him, Harold's wife rocked and whimpered, her face buried in her hands. The executive next to Buck snored. Before drinking himself into oblivion soon after takeoff, he had said something about a major meeting in Scotland. Would he be surprised by the view upon landing!

All around Buck, people cried, prayed, and talked. Flight attendants offered snacks and drinks, but few accepted. Having preferred an aisle seat for a little more legroom, Buck was now glad he was partially hidden near the window. He removed from his computer bag a tiny tool kit he had never expected to use, and went to work on the phone.

Disappointed to find no modular connection even inside the housing, he decided to play amateur electrician. These phone lines always have the same color wires, he decided, so he opened his computer and cut the wire leading to the female connector. Inside the phone, he cut the wire and sliced off the protective rubber coating. Sure enough, the four inner wires from both computer and phone looked identical. In a few minutes, he had spliced them together.

Buck tapped out a quick message to his executive editor, Steve Plank, in New York, telling of his destination. "I will bang out all I know, and I'm sure this will be just one of many similar stories. But at least this will be up to the minute, as it happens. Whether it will be of any use, I don't know. The thought hits me, Steve, that you may be among the missing. How would I know? You know my computer address. Let me know you're still with us."

He stored the note and set up his modem to send it to New York in the background, while he was working on his own writing. At the top of the screen a status bar flashed every twenty seconds, informing him that the connection to his ramp on the information superhighway was busy. He kept working.

The senior flight attendant startled him several pages into his own reflections and feelings. "What in the world are you doing?" she said, leaning in to stare at the mess of wires leading from his laptop to the in-flight phone. "I can't let you do that."

He glanced at her name tag. "Listen, beautiful Hattie, are we or are we not looking at the end of the world as we know it?"

"Don't patronize me, sir. I can't let you sit here and vandalize airline property."

"I'm not vandalizing it. I'm adapting it in an emergency. With this I can hopefully make a connection where nothing else will work."

"I can't let you do it."

"Hattie, can I tell you something?"

"Only that you're going to put that phone back the way you found it."

"I will."

"Now."

"No, I won't do that."

"That's the only thing I want to hear."

"I understand that, but please listen."

The man next to Buck stared at him and then at Hattie. He swore, then used a pillow to cover his right ear, pressing his left against the seat back.

Hattie grabbed a computer printout from her pocket and located Buck's name. "Mr. Williams, I expect you to cooperate. I don't want to bother the pilot with this."

Buck reached for her hand. She stiffened but didn't pull away. "Can we talk for just a second?"

"I'm not going to change my mind, sir. Now please, I have a plane full of frightened people."

"Aren't you one of them?" He was still holding her hand.

She pursed her lips and nodded.

"Wouldn't you like to make contact with someone? If this works, I can reach people who can make phone calls for you, let your family know you're all right, even get a message back to you. I haven't destroyed anything, and I promise I can put it back the way I found it."

"You can?"

"I can."

"And you'd help me?"

"Anything. Give me some names and phone numbers. I'll send them in with what I'm trying to upload to New York, and I'll insist that someone make the calls for you and report back to me. I can't guarantee I'll get through or that if I do they'll get back to me, but I will try."

"I'd be grateful."

"And can you protect me from other overly zealous flight attendants?"

Hattie managed a smile. "They might all want your help."

"This is a long shot as it is. Just keep everybody away from me, and let me keep trying."

"Deal," she said, but she looked troubled.

"Hattie, you're doing the right thing," he said. "It's OK in a situation like this to think of yourself a little. That's what I'm doing."

"But everybody's in the same boat, sir. And I have responsibilities."

"You have to admit, when people disappear, some rules go out the window."

* * *

Rayford Steele sat ashen-faced in the cockpit. Half an hour from touchdown in Chicago, he had told the passengers everything he knew. The simultaneous disappearance of millions all over the globe had resulted in chaos far beyond imagination. He complimented everyone on remaining calm and avoiding hysterics, although he had received reports of doctors on board who handed out Valium like candy.

Rayford had been forthright, the only way he knew to be. He realized he had told the people more than he might have if he'd lost an engine or his hydraulics or even his landing gear. He had been frank with them that those who had not had loved ones disappear might get home to discover that they had been victims of the many tragedies that had ensued.

He thought, but didn't say, how grateful he was to have been in the air when this event had taken place. What confusion must await them on the ground! Here, in a literal sense, they were above it all. They had been affected, of course. People were missing from everywhere. But except for the staff shortage caused by the disappearance of three crew members, the passengers didn't suffer the way they might have had they been in traffic or if he and Christopher had been among those who had disappeared.

As he settled into a holding pattern miles from O'Hare, the full impact of the tragedy began to come into view. Flights from all over the country were being rerouted to Chicago. Planes were reorganized based on their fuel supplies. Rayford needed to stay in priority position after flying across the eastern seaboard and then over the Atlantic before turning back. It was not Rayford's practice to communicate with ground control until after he landed, but now the air traffic control tower was recommending it. He was informed that visibility was excellent, despite intermittent smoke from wreckages on the ground, but that landing would be risky and precarious because the two open runways were crowded with jets. They lined either side, all the way down the runway. Every gate was full, and none were backing out. Every mode of human transport was in use, busing passengers from the ends of the runways back to the terminal.

But, Rayford was told, he would likely find that his people—at least most of them—would have to walk all the way. All remaining personnel had been called in to serve, but they were busy directing planes to safe areas. The few buses and vans were reserved for the handicapped, elderly, and flight crews. Rayford passed the word along that his crew would be walking.

Passengers reported that they had been unable to get through on the in-flight phones. Hattie Durham told Rayford that one enterprising passenger in first class had somehow hooked up the phone to his computer, and while he composed messages it was automatically dialing and redialing New York. If a line opened, this would be the guy who got through.

+ + +

By the time the plane began its descent into Chicago, Buck had been able to squeeze onto only one briefly freed-up line to his computer service, which prompted him to download his waiting mail. This came just as Hattie announced that all electronic devices must be turned off.

With an acumen he didn't realize he possessed, Buck speed-tapped the keys that retrieved and filed all his messages, downloaded them, and backed out of the linkup in seconds. Just when his machine might have interfered with flight communications, he was off-line and would have to wait to search his files for news from friends, coworkers, relatives, anyone.

Before her last-minute preparations for landing, Hattie hurried to Buck. "Anything?" He shook his head apologetically. "Thanks for trying," she said. And she began to weep.

He reached for her wrist. "Hattie, we're all going to go home and cry today. But hang in there. Get your passengers off the plane, and you can at least feel good about that."

"Mr. Williams," she sobbed, "you know we lost several old people, but not all of them. And we lost several middle-aged people, but not all of them. And we lost several people your age and my age, but not all of them. We even lost some teenagers."

He stared at her. What was she driving at?

"Sir, we lost every child and baby on this plane."

"How many were there?"

"More than a dozen. But all of them! Not one was left."

The man next to Buck roused and squinted at the late-morning sun burning through the window. "What in blazes are you two talking about?" he said.

"We're about to land in Chicago," Hattie said. "I've got to run."

"Chicago?"

"You don't want to know," Buck said.

The man nearly sat in Buck's lap to get a look out the window, his boozy breath enveloping Buck. "What, are we at war? Riots? What?"

Having just cut through the cloud bank, the plane allowed passengers a view of the Chicago area. Smoke. Fire. Cars off the road and smashed into each other and guardrails. Planes in pieces on the ground. Emergency vehicles, lights flashing, picking their way around the debris.

As O'Hare came into view, it was clear no one was going anywhere soon. There were planes as far as the eye could see, some crashed and burning, the others gridlocked in line. People trudged through the grass and between vehicles toward the terminal. The expressways that led to the airport looked like they had during the great Chicago blizzards, only without the snow.

Cranes and wreckers were trying to clear a path through the front of the terminal so cars could get in and out, but that would take hours, if not days. A snake of humanity wended its way slowly out of the great terminal buildings, between the motionless cars, and onto the ramps. People walking, walking, walking, looking for a cab or a limo. Buck began plotting how he would beat the new system. Somehow, he had to get moving and get out of such a congested area. The problem was, his goal was to get to a worse one: New York.

+ + +

"Ladies and gentlemen," Rayford announced, "I want to thank you again for your cooperation today. We've been asked to put down on the only runway that will take this size plane and then to taxi to an open area about two miles from the terminal. I'm afraid I'm going to have to ask you to use our inflatable emergency chutes, because we will not be able to hook up to any gateways. If you are unable to walk to the terminal, please stay with the plane, and we will send someone back for you."

There was no thanking them for choosing Pan-Continental, no "We hope you'll make us your choice next time you need air service." He did remind them to stay seated with their belts fastened until he turned off the seat belt sign, because privately he knew this would be his most difficult landing in years. He knew he could do it, but it had been a long time since he had had to land a plane among other aircraft.

Rayford envied whoever it was in first class who had the inside track on communicating by modem. He was desperate to call Irene, Chloe, and Ray Jr. On the other hand, he feared he might never talk to them again.

3

HATTIE DURHAM and what was left of her cabin crew encouraged passengers to study the safety cards in their seat pockets. Many feared they would be unable to jump and slide down the chutes, especially with their carry-on luggage. They were instructed to remove their shoes and to jump seatfirst onto the chute. Then crew members would toss them their shoes and bags. They were advised not to wait in the terminal for their checked baggage. That, they were promised, would eventually be delivered to their homes. No guarantees when.

Buck Williams gave Hattie his card and got her phone number, "just in case I get through to your people before you do."

"You're with *Global Weekly*?" she said. "I had no idea."

"And you were going to send me to my room for tampering with the phone."

She appeared to be trying to smile. "Sorry," Buck said, "not funny. I'll let you go."

Always a light traveler, Buck was grateful he had checked no baggage. Never did, not even on international flights. When he opened the bin to pull down his leather bag, he found the old man's hat and jacket still perched atop it. Harold's wife sat staring at Buck, her eyes full, jaw set. "Ma'am," he said quietly, "would you want these?"

The grieving woman gratefully gathered in the hat and coat, and crushed them against her chest as if she would never let them go. She said something Buck couldn't hear. He asked her to repeat it. "I can't jump out of any airplane," she said.

"Stay right here," he said. "They'll send someone for you."

"But will I still have to jump and slide down that thing?"

"No, ma'am. I'm sure they'll have a lift of some sort."

Buck carefully laid his laptop and case in among his clothes. With his bag zipped, he hurried to the front of the line, eager to show others how easy it was. He tossed his shoes down first, watching them bounce and skitter onto the runway. Then he clutched his bag across his chest, took a quick step, and threw his feet out in front of him.

A bit enthusiastic, he landed not on his seat but on his shoulders, which threw his feet over the top of his head. He picked up speed and hit the bottom with his weight shifting forward. The buggy-whip centripetal force slammed his stockinged feet to the ground and brought his torso up and over in a somersault that barely missed planting his face on the concrete. At the last instant, still hanging on to his bag for dear life, he tucked his head under and took the abrasion on the back of his head rather than on his nose. He fought the urge to say, "No problem," but he couldn't keep from rubbing the back of his head, already matted with blood. It wasn't a serious problem, only a nuisance. He quickly retrieved his shoes and began jogging toward the terminal, as much from embarrassment as need. He knew there would be no more hurrying once he hit the terminal.

* * *

Rayford, Christopher, and Hattie were the last three off the 747. Before disembarking, they had made sure all able-bodied people got down the chutes and that the elderly and infirm were transported by bus. The bus driver insisted that the crew ride with him and the last passengers, but Rayford refused. "I can't see passing my own passengers as they walk to the terminal," he said. "How would that look?"

Christopher said, "Suit yourself, Cap. You mind if I take him up on his offer?"

Rayford glared at him. "You're serious?"

"I don't get paid enough for this."

"Like this was the airline's fault. Chris, you don't mean it."

"The heck I don't. By the time you get up there, you'll wish you'd ridden, too."

"I should write you up for this."

"Millions of people disappear into thin air and I should worry about getting written up for riding instead of walking? Later, Steele."

Rayford shook his head and turned to Hattie. "Maybe I'll see you up there. If you can get out of the terminal, don't wait for me."

"Are you kidding? If you're walking, I'm walking."

"You don't need to do that."

"After that dressing-down you just gave Smith? I'm walking."

"He's first officer. He ought to be helping the last passenger off the ship and first to volunteer for emergency duty."

"Well, do me a favor and consider me part of your crew, too. Just because I can't fly the thing doesn't mean I don't feel some ownership. And don't treat me like a little woman."

"I would never do that. Got your stuff?"

Hattie pulled her bag on wheels and Rayford carried his pilot's bag. It was a long walk, and several times they waved off offers of rides from units speeding out to pick up the nonambulatory. Along the way they passed other passengers from their flight. Many thanked Rayford; he wasn't sure for what. For not panicking, he guessed. But they looked as terrified and shell-shocked as he felt.

They shielded their ears from flights screaming in to land. Rayford tried to calculate how long it would be before this runway was shut down, too. He couldn't imagine the other open strip holding many more planes, either. Would some have to try to put down on highways or open fields? And how far away from the big cities would they have to look for open stretches of highway unencumbered by bridges? He shuddered at the thought.

All around were ambulances and other emergency vehicles trying to get to ugly wreckage scenes.

Finally in the terminal, Rayford found crowds standing in lines behind banks of phones. Most had angry people waiting, yelling at callers who shrugged and redialed. Airport snack bars and restaurants were already sold out of or low on food, and all newspapers and magazines were gone. In shops where staffers had disappeared, looters walked off with merchandise.

Rayford wanted more than anything to sit and talk with someone about what to make of this. But everybody he saw—friend, acquaintance, or stranger—was busy trying to make arrangements. O'Hare was like a massive prison with resources dwindling and gridlock growing. No one slept. Everyone scurried about, trying to find some link to the outside world, to contact their families, and to get out of the airport.

At the flight center in the bowels of the place, Rayford found much the same thing. Hattie said she would try making her calls from the lounge and would meet him later to see if they could share a ride to the suburbs. He knew they were unlikely to find any rides going anywhere, and he didn't relish walking twenty miles. But all hotels in the area were already full.

Finally a supervisor asked for the attention of the fliers in the underground center. "We have some secure lines, about five," he said. "Whether you can get through, we don't know, but it's your best chance. They do bypass the normal trunk lines out of here, so you won't be competing with all the pay phones in the terminal. Streamline your calls. Also, there are a limited number of helicopter rides available to suburban hospitals and police departments, but naturally you're secondary to medical emergencies. Get in line over here for phones and rides to the suburbs. As of right now we have no word of the cancellation of any flights except for the remainder of today. It's your responsibility to be back here for your next flight or to call in and find out its status."

Rayford got in line, beginning to feel the tension of having flown too long and known too little. Worse was the knowledge that he had a better idea than most of what had happened. If he was right, if it were true, he would not be getting an answer when he dialed home. As he stood there, a TV monitor above him broadcast images of the chaos. From around the globe came wailing mothers, stoic families, reports of death and destruction. Dozens of stories included eyewitnesses who had seen loved ones and friends disappear before their eyes.

Most shocking to Rayford was a woman in labor, about to go into the delivery room, who was suddenly barren. Doctors delivered the placenta. Her husband had caught the disappearance of the fetus on tape. As he videotaped her great belly and sweaty face, he asked questions. How did she feel? "How do you think I feel, Earl? Turn that thing off." What was she hoping for? "That you'll get close enough for me to slug you." Did she realize that in a few moments they'd be parents? "In about a minute, you're going to be divorced."

Then came the scream and the dropping of the camera, terrified voices, running nurses, and the doctor. CNN reran the footage in super-slow motion, showing the woman going from very pregnant to nearly flat stomached, as if she had instantaneously delivered. "Now, watch with us again," the newsman intoned, "and keep your eyes on the left edge of your screen, where a nurse appears to be reading a printout from the fetal heart monitor. There, see?" The action stopped as the pregnant woman's stomach deflated. "The nurse's uniform seems to still be standing as if an invisible person is wearing it. She's gone. Half a second later, watch." The tape moved ahead and stopped. "The uniform, stockings and all, are in a pile atop her shoes."

Local television stations from around the world reported bizarre occurrences, especially in time zones where the event had happened during the day or early evening. CNN showed via satellite the video of a groom disappearing while slipping the ring onto his bride's finger. A funeral home in Australia reported that nearly every mourner disappeared from one memorial service, including the corpse, while at another service at the same time, only a few disappeared and the corpse remained. Morgues also reported corpse disappearances. At a burial, three of six pallbearers stumbled and dropped a casket when the other three disappeared. When they picked up the casket, it too was empty.

Rayford was second in line for the phone, but what he saw next on the screen convinced him he would never see his wife again. At a Christian high school soccer game at a missionary headquarters in Indonesia, most of the spectators and all but one of the players disappeared in the middle of play, leaving their shoes and uniforms on the ground. The CNN reporter announced that, in his remorse, the surviving player took his own life.

But it was more than remorse, Rayford knew. Of all people, that player, a student at a Christian school, would have known the truth immediately. The Rapture had taken place. Jesus Christ had returned for his people, and that boy was not one of them. When Rayford sat at the phone, tears streamed down his face. Someone said, "You have four minutes," and he knew that would be more than he needed. His answering machine at home picked up immediately, and he was pierced to hear the cheerful voice of his wife. "Your call is important to us," she said. "Please leave a message after the beep."

Rayford punched a few buttons to check for messages. He ran through three or four mundane ones, then was startled to hear Chloe's voice. "Mom? Dad? Are you there? Have you seen what's going on? Call me as soon as you can. We've lost at least ten students and two profs, and all the married students' kids disappeared. Is Raymie all right? Call me!" Well, at least he knew Chloe was still around. All he wanted was to hold her.

Rayford redialed and left a message on his own machine. "Irene? Ray? If you're there, pick up. If you get this message, I'm at O'Hare and trying to get home. It may take a while if I don't get a copter ride. I sure hope you're there."

"Let's go, Cap," someone said. "Everybody's got a call to make."

Rayford nodded and quickly dialed his daughter's dorm room at Stanford. He got the irritating message that his call could not be completed as dialed.

Rayford gathered his belongings and checked his mail slot. Besides a pile of the usual junk, he found a padded manila envelope from his home address. Irene had taken to mailing him little surprises lately, the result of a marriage book she had been urging him to read. He slipped the envelope into his case and went looking for Hattie Durham. Funny, he had no emotional attraction whatever to Hattie just now. But he felt obligated to be sure she got home.

As he stood in a crowd by the elevator, he heard the announcement that a helicopter was available for no more than eight pilots and would make a run to Mount Prospect, Arlington Heights, and Des Plaines. Rayford hurried to the pad. "Got room for one to Mount Prospect?"

"Yup."

"How about another to Des Plaines?"

"Maybe, if he gets here in about two minutes."

"It's not a he. She's a flight attendant."

"Pilots only. Sorry."

"What if you have room?"

"Well, maybe, but I don't see her."

"I'll have her paged."

"They're not paging anyone."

"Give me a second. Don't leave without me."

The chopper pilot looked at his watch. "Three minutes," he said. "I'm leavin' at one."

Rayford left his bag on the ground, hoping it would hold the helicopter pilot in case he was a little late. He charged up the stairs and into the corridor. Finding Hattie would be impossible. He grabbed a courtesy phone. "I'm sorry, we're unable to page anyone just now."

"This is an emergency and I am a Pan-Continental captain."

"What is it?"

"Have Hattie Durham meet her party at K-17."

"I'll try."

"Do it!"

Rayford stood on tiptoe to see Hattie coming, yet still somehow she surprised him. "I was fourth in line for the phone in the lounge," she said, appearing at his side. "Got a better deal?"

"Got us a helicopter ride if we hurry," he said.

As they skipped down the stairs she said, "Wasn't it awful about Chris?"

"What about him?"

"You really don't know?"

Rayford wanted to stop and tell her to quit making him work so hard. That frustrated him about people her age. They enjoyed a volleying conversation game. He liked to get to the point. "Just tell me!" he said, sounding more exasperated than he intended.

As they burst through the door and onto the tarmac, the chopper blades whipped their hair and deafened them. Rayford's bag had already been put on board, and only one seat remained. The pilot pointed at Hattie and shook his head. Rayford grabbed her elbow and pulled her aboard as he climbed in. "Only way she's not coming is if you can't handle the weight!"

"What do you weigh, doll?" the pilot said.

"One-fifteen!"

"I can handle the weight!" he told Rayford. "But if she's not buckled in, I'm not responsible!"

"Let's go!" Rayford shouted.

He buckled himself in and Hattie sat in his lap. He wrapped his arms around her waist and clasped his wrists together. He thought how ironic it was that he had been dreaming of this for weeks, and now there was no joy, no excitement in it, nothing sensual whatever. He was miserable. Glad to be able to help her out, but miserable.

Hattie looked embarrassed and uncomfortable, and Rayford noticed she took a sheepish peek at the other seven pilots in the copter. None seemed to return her gaze. This disaster was still too fresh and there were too many unknowns. Rayford thought he heard or lip-read one of them saying, "Christopher Smith," but there was no way he could hear inside the raucous craft. He put his mouth next to Hattie's ear.

"Now what about Chris?" he said.

She turned and spoke into his ear. "They wheeled him past us while I was going into the lounge. Blood all over!"

"What happened?"

"I don't know, but, Rayford, he didn't look good!"

"How bad?"

"I think he was dead! I mean, they were working on him, but I'd be surprised if he made it."

Rayford shook his head. What next? "Did he get hit or something? Did that bus crash?" Wouldn't that be ironic!

"I don't know," she said. "The blood seemed like it was coming from his hand or his waist or both."

Rayford tapped the pilot on the shoulder. "Do you know anything about First Officer Christopher Smith?"

"He with Pan-Con?" the pilot said.

"Yes!"

"Was he the suicide?"

Rayford recoiled. "I don't think so! Was there a suicide?"

"Lots of 'em, I guess, but mostly passengers. Only crew member I heard about was a Smith from Pan. Slit his wrists."

Rayford quickly scanned the others in the chopper to see if he recognized anyone. He didn't, but one was nodding sadly, having overheard the pilot's shouting. He leaned forward. "Chris Smith! You know him?"

"My first officer!"

"Sorry."

"What'd you hear?"

"Don't know how reliable this is, but the rumor is he found out his boys had disappeared and his wife was killed in a wreck!"

For the first time the enormity of the situation became personal for Rayford. He didn't know Smith well. He vaguely remembered Chris had two sons. Seemed they were young teenagers, very close in age. He had never met the wife. But suicide! Was that an option for Rayford? No, not with Chloe still there. But what if he had discovered that Irene and young Ray were gone and Chloe had been killed? What would he have to live for?

He hadn't been living for them anyway, certainly not the last several months. He had been playing around on the edges of his mind with the girl in his lap, though he had never gone so far as touching her, even when she often touched him. Would he want to live if Hattie Durham were the only person he cared about? And why did he care about her? She was beautiful and sexy and smart, but only for her age. They had little in common. Was it only because he was convinced Irene was gone that he now longed to hold his own wife?

There was no affection in his embrace of Hattie Durham just now, nor in hers. Both were scared to death, and flirting was the last thing on their minds. The irony was not lost on him. He recalled that the last thing he daydreamed about—before Hattie's announcement—was finally making a move on her. How could he have known she would be in his lap hours later and that he would have no more interest in her than in a stranger?

The first stop was the Des Plaines Police Department, where Hattie disembarked. Rayford advised her to ask for a ride home with the police if a squad car was available. Most had been pressed into service in more congested areas, so that was unlikely. "I'm only about a mile from here anyway!" Hattie shouted above the roar as Rayford helped her from the chopper. "I can walk!" She wrapped her arms around his neck in a fierce embrace, and he felt her quiver in fear. "I hope everyone's OK at your place!" she said. "Call me and let me know, OK?"

He nodded.

"OK?" she insisted.

"OK!"

As they lifted off he watched her survey the parking lot. Spotting no squad cars, she turned and hurried off, pulling her suitcase on wheels. By the time the helicopter began to swing toward Mount Prospect, Hattie was trotting toward her condominium.

* * *

Buck Williams had been the first passenger from his flight to reach the terminal at O'Hare. He found a mess. No one waiting in line for a phone would put up with his trying to plug his modem into it, and he couldn't get his cellular phone to work, so he made his way to the exclusive Pan-Con Club. It, too, was jammed, but despite a loss of personnel, including the disappearance of several employees while on the job, some semblance of order prevailed. Even here people waited in line for the phones, but as each became available, it was understood that some might try faxing or connecting directly by modem. While Buck waited, he went to work again on his computer, reattaching the inside modem cord to the female connector. Then he called up the messages that he had quickly downloaded before landing.

The first was from Steve Plank, his executive editor, addressed to all field personnel:

Stay put. Do not try to come to New York. Impossible here. Call when you can. Check your voice mail and your e-mail regularly. Keep in touch as possible. We have enough staff to remain on schedule, and we want personal accounts, on-the-scene stuff, as much as you can transmit. Not sure of transportation and communications lines between us and our printers, nor their employee levels. If possible, we'll print on time.

Just a note: Begin thinking about the causes. Military? Cosmic? Scientific? Spiritual? But so far we're dealing mainly with what happened.

Take care, and keep in touch.

The second message was also from Steve and was for Buck's eyes only.

Buck, ignore general staff memo. Get to New York as soon as you can at any expense. Take care of family matters, of course, and file any personal experience or reflections, just like everyone else. But you're going to head up this effort to get at what's behind the phenomenon. Ideas are like egos—everybody's got one.

Whether we'll come to any conclusions, I don't know, but at the very least we'll catalog the reasonable possibilities. You may wonder why we need you here to do this; I do have an ulterior motive. Sometimes I think because of the position I'm in, I'm the only one who knows these things; but three different department editors have turned in story ideas on various international groups meeting in New York this month. Political editor wants to cover a Jewish Nationalist conference in Manhattan that has something to do with a new world order government. What they care about that, I don't know and the political editor doesn't either. Religion editor has something in my in-box about a conference of Orthodox Jews also coming for a meeting. These are not just from Israel but apparently all over, and they are no longer haggling over the Dead Sea Scrolls. They're still giddy over the destruction of Russia and her allies—which I know you still think was supernatural, but hey, I love you anyway. Religion editor thinks they're looking for help in rebuilding the temple. That may be no big deal or have anything to do with anything other than the religion department, but I was struck by the timing—with the other Jewish group meeting at pretty much the same time and at the same place about something entirely political. The other religious conference in town is among leaders of all the major religions, from the standard ones to the New Agers, also talking about a one-world religious order. They ought to get together with the Jewish Nationalists, huh? Need your brain on this. Don't know what to make of it, if anything.

I know all anybody cares about is the disappearances. But we need to keep an eye on the rest of the world. You know the United Nations has that international monetarist confab coming up, trying to gauge how we're all doing with the three-currency thing. Personally I like it, but I'm a little skittish about going to one currency unless it's dollars. Can you imagine trading in yen or marks here? Guess I'm still provincial.

Everybody's pretty enamored with this Carpathia guy from Romania who so impressed your friend Rosenzweig. He's got everybody in a bind in the upper house in his own country because he's been invited to speak at the U.N. in a couple of weeks. Nobody knows how he wangled an invitation, but his international popularity reminds me a lot of Walesa or even Gorbachev. Remember them? Ha!

Hey, friend, get word to me you didn't disappear. As far as I know right now, I lost a niece and two nephews, a sister-in-law I didn't like, and possibly a couple of other distant relatives. You think they'll be back? Well, save that till we get rolling on what's behind this. If I had to guess, I'm anticipating some god-awful ransom demand. I mean, it's not like these people who disappeared are dead. What in the world is going to happen to the life insurance industry? I'm not ready to start believing the tabloids. You just know they're going to be saying the space aliens finally got us.

Get in here, Buck.

4

BUCK KEPT PRESSING a handkerchief soaked with cold water onto the back of his head. His wound had stopped bleeding, but it stung. He found another message in his e-mail in-box and was about to call it up when he was tapped on the shoulder.

"I'm a doctor. Let me dress your wound."

"Oh, it's all right, and I—"

"Just let me do this, pal. I'm going crazy here with nothing to do, and I have my bag. I'm workin' free today. Call it a Rapture Special."

"A what?"

"Well, what would you call what happened?" the doctor said, removing a bottle and gauze from his bag. "This is gonna be pretty rudimentary, but we will be sterile. AIDS?"

"I'm sorry?"

"C'mon, you know the routine." He snapped on rubber gloves. "Have you got HIV or anything fun like that?"

"No. And, hey, I appreciate this." At that instant the doctor splashed a heavy dose of disinfectant on the gauze and held it against Buck's scraped head. "Yow! Take it easy!"

"Be a big boy there, stud. This'll hurt less than the infection you'd get otherwise." He roughly scraped the wound, cleansing it and causing it to ooze blood again. "Listen, I'm going to do a little shave job so I can get a bandage to hold. All right with you?"

Buck's eyes were watering. "Yeah, sure, but what was that you said about rapture?"

"Is there any other explanation that makes sense?" the doctor said, using a scalpel to tear into Buck's hair. A club attendant came by and asked if they could move the operation into one of the washrooms.

"I promise to clean up, hon," the doctor said. "Almost done here."

"Well, this can't be sanitary, and we do have other members to think about."

"Why don't you just give them their drinks and nuts, all right? You'll find this just isn't going to upset them that much on a day like this."

"I don't appreciate being spoken to that way."

The doctor sighed as he worked. "You're right. What's your name?"

"Suzie."

"Listen, Suzie, I've been rude and I apologize. OK? Now let me finish this, and I promise not to perform any more surgery right out here in public." Suzie left, shaking her head.

"Doc," Buck said, "leave me your card so I can properly thank you."

"No need," the doctor said, putting his stuff away.

"Now give me your take on this. What did you mean about the Rapture?"

"Another time. Your turn for the phone."

Buck was torn, but he couldn't pass up the chance to communicate with New York. He tried dialing direct but couldn't get through. He hooked his modem up to the phone and initiated repeat dialing while he looked at the message from Steve Plank's secretary, the matronly Marge Potter.

Buck, you scoundrel! Like I don't have enough to do and worry about today, I've got to check on your girlfriends' families? Where'd you meet this Hattie Durham? You can tell her I reached her mother out west, but that was before a flood or storm or something knocked phone lines out again. She's perfectly healthy but rattled, and she was very grateful to know her daughter hadn't disappeared. The two sisters are OK, too, according to Mom.

You are a dear for helping people like this, Buck. Steve says you're going to try to come in. It'll be good to see you. This is so awful. So far we know of several staffers who disappeared, several more we haven't heard from, including some in Chicago. Everybody from the senior staff is accounted for, now that we've heard from you. I hoped and prayed you'd be all right. Have you noticed it seems to have struck the innocents? Everyone we know who's gone is either a child or a very nice person. On the other hand, some truly wonderful people are still here. I'm glad you're one of them, and so is Steve. Call us.

No word whether she had been able to reach Buck's widowed father or married brother. Buck wondered if that was on purpose or if she simply had no news yet. His niece and nephew had to be gone if it was true that no children had survived. Buck gave up trying to reach the office directly but again successfully connected with his online service. He uploaded his files and a few hastily batted out messages of his whereabouts. That way, by the time the telephone system once again took on some semblance of normalcy, *Global Weekly* would have already gotten a head start on his stuff.

He hung up and disconnected to the grateful look of the next in line, then went looking for that doctor. No luck. Marge had referred to the innocents. The doctor assumed it was the Rapture. Steve had pooh-poohed space aliens. But how could you rule out anything at this point? His mind was already whirring with ideas for the story behind the disappearances. Talk about the assignment of a lifetime!

Buck got in line at the service desk, knowing his odds of getting to New York by conventional means were slim. While he waited he tried to remember what it was Chaim Rosenzweig, the Newsmaker of the Year, had told him about the young Nicolae Carpathia of Romania. Buck had told only Steve Plank about it, and Steve agreed it wasn't worth putting in the already tight story. Rosenzweig had been impressed with Carpathia, that was true. But why?

Buck sat on the floor in line and moved when he had to. He called up his archived files on the Rosenzweig interview and did a word search on Carpathia. He recalled having been embarrassed to admit to Rosenzweig that he had never heard of the man. As the taped interview transcripts scrolled past, he hit the pause button and read. When he noticed his low battery light flashing, he fished an extension cord out of his bag and plugged the computer into a socket along the wall. "Watch the cord," he called out occasionally as people passed. One of the women behind the counter hollered at him that he'd have to unplug.

He smiled at her. "And if I don't, are you going to have me thrown out? Arrested? Cut me some slack today, of all days!" Hardly anyone took note of the crazy man on the floor yelling at the counter woman. Such rarely happened in the Pan-Con Club, but nothing surprised anyone today.

+ + +

Rayford Steele disembarked on the helipad at Northwest Community Hospital in Arlington Heights, where the pilots had to get off and make room so a patient could be flown to Milwaukee. The other pilots hung around the entrance, hoping to share a cab, but Rayford had a better idea. He began walking.

He was about five miles from home, and he was betting he could hitch a ride easier than finding a cab. He hoped his captain's uniform and his clean-cut appearance would set someone's mind at ease about giving him a ride.

As he trudged along, his trenchcoat over his arm and his bag in his hand, he had an empty, despairing feeling. By now Hattie would be getting to her condo, checking her messages, trying to get calls through to her family. If he was right that Irene and Ray Jr. were gone, where would they have been when it happened?

Would he find evidence that they had disappeared rather than being killed in some related accident?

Rayford calculated that the disappearances would have taken place late evening, perhaps around 11 p.m. central time. Would anything have taken them away from home at that hour? He couldn't imagine what, and he doubted it.

A woman of about forty stopped for Rayford on Algonquin Road. When he thanked her and told her where he lived, she said she knew the area. "A friend of mine lives there. Well, lived there. Li Ng, the Asian girl on Channel 7 news?"

"I know her and her husband," Rayford said. "They still live on our street."

"Not anymore. They dedicated the noon newscast to her today. The whole family is gone."

Rayford exhaled loudly. "This is unbelievable. Have you lost people?"

"'Fraid so," she said, her voice quavery. "About a dozen nieces and nephews."

"Wow."

"You?"

"I don't know yet. I'm just getting back from a flight, and I haven't been able to reach anybody."

"Do you want me to wait for you?"

"No. I have a car. If I need to go anywhere, I'll be all right."

"O'Hare's closed, you know," she said.

"Really? Since when?"

"They just announced it on the radio. Runways are full of planes, terminals full of people, roads full of cars."

"Tell me about it."

As the woman drove, sniffling, into Mount Prospect, Rayford felt fatigue he had never endured before. Every few houses had driveways jammed with cars, people milling about. It appeared everyone everywhere had lost someone. He knew he would soon be counted among them.

"Can I offer you anything?" he asked the woman as she pulled into his driveway.

She shook her head. "I'm just glad to have been able to help. You could pray for me, if you think of it. I don't know if I can endure this."

"I'm not much for praying," Rayford admitted.

"You will be," she said. "I never was before either, but I am now."

"Then you can pray for me," he said.

"I will. Count on it."

Rayford stood in the driveway and waved to the woman till she was out of sight. The yard and the walk were spotless as usual, and the huge home, his trophy house, was sepulchral. He unlocked the front door. From the newspaper on the stoop to the closed drapes in the picture window to the bitter smell of burned coffee when he opened the door, everything pointed to what he dreaded.

Irene was a fastidious housekeeper. Her morning routine included the coffeepot on a timer kicking on at six, percolating her special blend of decaf with an egg. The radio was set to come on at 6:30, tuned to the local Christian station. The first thing Irene did when she came downstairs was open the drapes at the front and back of the house.

With a lump in his throat Rayford tossed the newspaper into the kitchen and took his time hanging up his coat and sliding his bag into the closet. He remembered the package Irene had mailed him at O'Hare and put it in his wide uniform pocket. He would carry it with him as he searched for evidence that she had disappeared. If she was gone, he sure hoped she had been right. He wanted above all else for her to have seen her dream realized, for her to have been taken away by Jesus in the twinkling of an eye—a thrilling, painless journey to his side in heaven, as she always loved to say. She deserved that if anybody did.

And Raymie. Where would he be? With her? Of course. He went with her to church, even when Rayford didn't go. He seemed to like it, to get into it. He even read his Bible and studied it.

Rayford unplugged the coffeepot that had been turning itself off and then back on for seven hours and had ruined the brew. He dumped the mess and left the pot in the sink. He flicked off the radio, which was piping the Christian station's network news hookup into the air, droning on about the tragedy and mayhem that had resulted from the disappearances.

He looked about the living room, dining room, and kitchen, expecting to see nothing but the usual neatness of Irene's home. His eyes filling with tears, he opened the drapes as she would have. Was it possible she had gone somewhere? Visited someone? Left him a message? But if she had and he did find her, what would that say about her own faith? Would that prove this was not the Rapture she believed in? Or would it mean she was lost, just like he was? For her sake, if this was the Rapture, he hoped she *was* gone. But the ache and the emptiness were already overwhelming.

He switched on the answering machine and heard all the same messages he had heard when he had gotten through from O'Hare, plus the message he had left. His own voice sounded strange to him. He detected in it a fatalism, as if he knew he was not leaving a message for his wife and son, but only pretending to.

He dreaded going upstairs. He moseyed through the family room to the garage exit. If only one of the cars was missing. And one was! Maybe she had gone somewhere! But as soon as he thought of it, Rayford slumped onto the step just inside the garage. It was his own BMW that was gone. The one he had driven to O'Hare the day before. It would be waiting for him when the traffic cleared.

The other two cars were there, Irene's and the one Chloe used when she was home. And all those memories of Raymie were there, too. His four-wheeler, his snowmobile, his bike. Rayford hated himself for his broken promises to spend more time with Raymie. He'd have plenty of time to regret that.

Rayford stood and heard the rattle of the envelope in his pocket. It was time to go upstairs.

+ + +

It was nearly Buck Williams's turn at the head of the line at the Pan-Con Club counter when he found the material he had been looking for on disk. At some point during their several days of taping, Buck had raised the issue of every other country trying to curry favor with Dr. Rosenzweig and hoping to gain access to his formula for its own gain.

"This has been an interesting aspect," Rosenzweig had allowed, his eyes twinkling. "I was most amused by a visit from the vice president of the United States himself. He wanted to honor me, to bring me to the president, to have a parade, to confer a degree, all that. He diplomatically said nothing about my owing him anything in return, but I would owe him everything, would I not? Much was said about what a friend of Israel the United States has been over the decades. And this has been true, no? How could I argue?

"But I pretended to see the awards and kindnesses as all for my own benefit, and I humbly turned them down. Because you see, young man, I am most humble, am I not?" The old man had laughed uproariously at himself and relayed several other stories of visiting dignitaries who worked at charming him.

"Was anyone sincere?" Buck had asked. "Did anyone impress you?"

"Yes!" Rosenzweig had said without hesitation. "From the most perplexing and surprising corner of the world—Romania. I do not know if he was sent or came on his own, but I suspect the latter because I believe he is the lowest-ranking official I entertained following the award. That is one of the reasons I wanted to see him. He asked for the audience himself. He did not go through typical political and protocol channels."

"And he was . . . ?"

"Nicolae Carpathia."

"Carpathia like the—?"

"Yes, like the Carpathian Mountains. A melodic name, you must admit. I found him most charming and humble. Not unlike myself!" Again he had laughed.

"I've not heard of him."

"You will! You will."

Buck had tried to lead the old man. "Because he's . . ."

"Impressive, that's all I can say."

"And he's some sort of a low-level diplomat at this point?"

"He is a member of the lower house of Romanian government."

"In the senate?"

"No, the senate is the upper house."

"Of course."

"Don't feel bad that you don't know, even though you are an international journalist. This is something only Romanians and amateur political scientists like me know. That is something I like to study."

"In your spare time."

"Precisely. But even I had not known of this man. I mean, I knew someone in the House of Deputies—that's what they call the lower house in Romania—was a peacemaker and leading a movement toward disarmament. But I did not know his name. I believe his goal is global disarmament, which we Israelis have come to distrust. But of course he must first bring about disarmament in his own country, which not even you will see in your lifetime. This man is about your age, by the way. Blond and blue-eyed, like the original Romanians, who came from Rome, before the Mongols affected their race."

"What did you like so much about him?"

"Let me count," Rosenzweig had said. "He knew my language as well as his own. And he speaks fluent English. Several others also, they tell me. Well educated but also widely self-taught. And I just like him as a person. Very bright. Very honest. Very open."

"What did he want from you?"

"That was what I liked the best. Because I found him so open and honest, I asked him outright that question. He insisted I call him Nicolae, and so I said, 'Nicolae' (this is after an hour of pleasantries), 'what do you want from me?' Do you know what he said, young man? He said, 'Dr. Rosenzweig, I seek only your goodwill.' What could I say? I said, 'Nicolae, you have it.' I am a bit of a pacifist myself, you know. Not unrealistically. I did not tell him this. I merely told him he had my goodwill. Which is something you also have."

"I suspect that is not something you bestow easily."

"That is why I like you and why you have it. One day you must meet Carpathia. You would like each other. His goals and dreams may never be realized even in his own country, but he is a man of high ideals. If he should emerge, you will hear of him. And as you are emerging in your own orbit, he will likely hear of you, or from you, am I right?"

"I hope you are."

Suddenly it was Buck's turn at the counter. He gathered up his extension cord and thanked the young woman for bearing with him. "Sorry about that," he said, pausing briefly for forgiveness that was not forthcoming. "It's just that today, of all days, well, you understand."

Apparently she did not understand. She'd had a rough day, too. She looked at him tolerantly and said, "What can I not do for you?"

"Oh, you mean because I did not do something you asked?"

"No," she said. "I'm saying that to everybody. It's my little joke because there's really nothing I can do for anybody. No flights are scheduled today. The airport is going to close any minute. Who knows how long it will take to clear all the wreckage and get any kind of traffic moving again? I mean, I'll take your request and everything, but I can't get your luggage, book you a flight, get you a phone, book you a hotel room, anything we love to do for our members. You are a member, aren't you?"

"Am I a member!"

"Gold or platinum?"

"Lady, I'm, like, a kryptonite member."

He flashed his card, showing that he was among the top 3 percent of air travelers in the world. If any flight had one seat in the cheapest section, it had to be given to him and upgraded to first class at no charge.

"Oh, my gosh," she said, "tell me you're not the Cameron Williams from that magazine."

"I am."

"*Time*? Honest?"

"Don't blaspheme. I'm from the competition."

"Oh, I knew that. The reason I know is that I wanted to get into journalism. I studied it in college. I just read about you, didn't I? Youngest award winner or most cover stories by someone under twelve?"

"Funny."

"Or something."

"I can't believe we're joking on a day like this," he said.

She suddenly clouded over. "I don't even want to think about it. So what could I do for you if I could do anything?"

"Here's the thing," Buck said. "I have to get to New York. Now don't give me that look. I know it's the worst place to try to get to right now. But you know people. You know pilots who fly on the side, charter stuff. You know what airports they would fly out of. Let's say I had unlimited resources and could pay whatever I needed to. Who would you send me to?"

She stared at him. "I can't believe you asked me that."

"Why?"

"Because I do know someone. He flies these little jets out of like Waukegan and Palwaukee airports. He's expensive and he's the type who would charge double during a crisis, especially if he knew who you were and how desperate."

"There won't be any hiding that. Give me the info."

\+ + +

Hearing it on the radio or seeing it on television was one thing. Encountering it for yourself was something else again. Rayford Steele had no idea how it would feel to find evidence that his own wife and son had vanished from the face of the earth.

At the top of the stairs he paused by the family photos. Irene, always one for order, had hung them chronologically, beginning with his and her great grandparents. Old, cracked black and whites of stern-faced, rawboned men and women of the Midwest. Then came the faded color shots of their grandparents on their fiftieth wedding anniversaries. Then their parents, their siblings, and themselves. How long had it been since he had studied their wedding photo, her with her flip hairstyle and him with his hair over his ears and muttonchops?

And those family pictures with Chloe eight years old, holding the baby! How grateful he was that Chloe was still here and that somehow he would connect with her! But what did this all say about the two of them? They were lost. He didn't know what to hope and pray for. That Irene and Raymie were still here and that this was not what it appeared?

He could wait no longer. Raymie's door was open a crack. His alarm was beeping. Rayford turned it off. On the bed was a book Raymie had been reading. Rayford slowly pulled the blankets back to reveal Raymie's Bulls pajama top, his underpants, and his socks. He sat on the bed and wept, nearly smiling at Irene's harping about Raymie's not wearing socks to bed.

He laid the clothes in a neat pile and noticed a picture of himself on the bed table. He stood smiling inside the terminal, his cap tucked under his arm, a 747 outside the window in the background. The picture was signed, "To Raymie with love, Dad." Under that he had written, "Rayford Steele, Captain, Pan-Continental Airlines, O'Hare." He shook his head. What kind of a dad autographs a picture for his own son?

Rayford's body felt like lead. It was all he could do to force himself to stand.

And then he was dizzy, realizing he hadn't eaten in hours. He slowly made his way out of Raymie's room without looking back, and he shut the door.

At the end of the hall he paused before the French doors that led to the master suite. What a beautiful, frilly place Irene had made it, decorated with needlepoint and country knickknacks. *Had* he ever told her he appreciated it? Had he ever appreciated it?

There was no alarm to turn off here. The smell of coffee had always roused Irene. Another picture of the two of them, him looking confidently at the camera, her gazing at him. He did not deserve her. He deserved this, he knew, to be mocked by his own self-centeredness and to be stripped of the most important person in his life.

He approached the bed, knowing what he would find. The indented pillow, the wrinkled covers. He could smell her, though he knew the bed would be cold. He carefully peeled back the blankets and sheet to reveal her locket, which carried a picture of him. Her flannel nightgown, the one he always kidded her about and which she wore only when he was not home, evidenced her now departed form.

His throat tight, his eyes full, he noticed her wedding ring near the pillow, where she always supported her cheek with her hand. It was too much to bear, and he broke down. He gathered the ring into his palm and sat on the edge of the bed, his body racked with fatigue and grief. He put the ring in his jacket pocket and noticed the package she had mailed. Tearing it open, he found two of his favorite homemade cookies with hearts drawn on the top in chocolate.

What a sweet, sweet woman! he thought. I never deserved her, never loved her enough! He set the cookies on the bedside table, their essence filling the air. With wooden fingers he removed his clothes and let them fall to the floor. He climbed into the bed and lay facedown, gathering Irene's nightgown in his arms so he could smell her and imagine her close to him.

And Rayford cried himself to sleep.

5

BUCK WILLIAMS ducked into a stall in the Pan-Con Club men's room to double-check his inventory. Tucked in a special pouch inside his jeans, he carried thousands of dollars' worth of traveler's checks, redeemable in dollars, marks, or yen. His one leather bag contained two changes of clothes, his laptop, cellular phone, tape recorder, accessories, toiletries, and some serious, insulated winter gear.

He had packed for a ten-day trip to Britain when he left New York three days before the apocalyptic disappearances. His practice overseas was to do his own laundry in the sink and let it dry a whole day while wearing one outfit and having one more in reserve. That way he was never burdened with lots of luggage.

Buck had gone out of his way to stop in Chicago first to mend fences with the *Global Weekly*'s bureau chief there, a fiftyish black woman named Lucinda Washington. He had gotten crossways with her—what else was new?—when he scooped her staff on, of all things, a sports story that was right under their noses. An aging Bears legend had finally found enough partners to help him buy a professional football team, and Buck had somehow sniffed it out, tracked him down, gotten the story, and run with it.

"I admire you, Cameron," Lucinda Washington had said, characteristically refusing to use his nickname. "I always have, as irritating as you can be. But the very least you should have done was let me know."

"And let you assign somebody who should have been on top of this anyway?"

"Sports isn't even your gig, Cameron. After doing the Newsmaker of the Year and covering the defeat of Russia by Israel, or I should say by God himself, how can you even get interested in penny-ante stuff like this? You Ivy League types aren't supposed to like anything but lacrosse and rugby, are you?"

"This was bigger than a sports story, Lucy, and—"

"Hey!"

"Sorry, *Lucinda*. And wasn't that just a bit of stereotyping? Lacrosse and rugby?"

They had shared a laugh.

"I'm not even saying you should have told me you were in town," she had said. "All I'm saying is, at least let me know before the piece runs in the *Weekly*. My people and I were embarrassed enough to get beat like that, especially by the legendary Cameron Williams, but for it to be a, well—"

"That's why you squealed on me?"

Lucinda had laughed again. "That's why I told Plank it would take a face-to-face to get you back in my good graces."

"And what made you think I'd care about that?"

"Because you love me," she had said. "You can't help yourself." Buck had smiled. "But, Cameron, if I catch you in my town again, on my beat without my knowledge, I'm gonna whip your tail."

"Well, I'll tell you what, Lucinda. Let me give you a lead I don't have time to follow up on. I happen to know the NFL franchise purchase is not going to go through after all. The money was shaky and the league's gonna reject the offer. Your local legend is going to be embarrassed."

Lucinda had begun scribbling furiously. "You're not serious," she had said, reaching for her phone.

"No, I'm not, but it was sure fun to see you swing into action."

"You creep," she had said. "Anybody else I'd be throwing out of here on his can."

"But you love me. You can't help yourself."

"That wasn't even Christian," she had said.

"Don't start with that again."

"Come on, Cameron. You know you got your mind right when you saw what God did for Israel."

"Granted, but don't start calling me a Christian. Deist is as much as I'll cop to."

"Stay in town long enough to come to my church, and God'll getcha."

"He's already got me, Lucinda. But Jesus is another thing. The Israelis hate Jesus, but look what God did for them."

"The Lord works in—"

"Mysterious ways, yeah, I know. Anyway, I'm going to London Monday. Working on a hot tip from a friend there."

"Yeah? What?"

"Not on your life. We don't know each other that well yet."

She had laughed, and they had parted with a friendly embrace. That had been three days ago.

Buck had boarded the ill-fated flight to London prepared for anything.

He was following a tip from a former Princeton classmate, a Welshman who had been working in the London financial district since graduate school. Dirk Burton had been a reliable source in the past, tipping off Buck about secret high-level meetings among international financiers. For years Buck had been slightly amused at Dirk's tendency to buy into conspiracy theories. "Let me get this straight," Buck had asked him once, "you think these guys are the real world leaders, right?"

"I wouldn't go that far, Cam," Dirk had said. "All I know is, they're big, they're private, and after they meet, major things happen."

"So you think they get world leaders elected, handpick dictators, that kind of a thing?"

"I don't belong to the conspiracy book club, if that's what you mean."

"Then where do you get this stuff, Dirk? Come on, you're a relatively sophisticated guy. Power brokers behind the scenes? Movers and shakers who control the money?"

"All I know is, the London exchange, the Tokyo exchange, the New York exchange—we all basically drift until these guys meet. Then things happen."

"You mean like when the New York Stock Exchange has a blip because of some presidential decision or some vote of Congress, it's really because of your secret group?"

"No, but that's a perfect example. If there's a blip in your market because of your president's health, imagine what it does to world markets when the real money people get together."

"But how does the market know they're meeting? I thought you were the only one who knew."

"Cam, be serious. OK, not a lot of people agree with me, but then I don't say this to just anyone. One of our muckety-mucks is part of this group. When they have a meeting, no, nothing happens right away. But a few days later, a week, changes occur."

"Like what?"

"You're going to call me crazy, but a friend of mine is related to a girl who works for the secretary of our guy in this group, and—"

"Whoa! Hold it! What's the trail here?"

"OK, maybe the connection is a little remote, but you know the old guy's secretary is not going to say anything. Anyway, the scuttlebutt is that this guy is real hot on getting the whole world onto one currency. You know half our time is spent on exchange rates and all that. Takes computers forever to constantly readjust every day, based on the whims of the markets."

Buck was not convinced. "One global currency? Never happen," he had said.

"How can you flatly say that?"

"Too bizarre. Too impractical. Look what happened in the States when they tried to bring in the metric system."

"Should have happened. You Yanks are such rubes."

"Metrics were only necessary for international trade. Not for how far it is to the outfield wall at Yankee Stadium or how many kilometers it is from Indianapolis to Atlanta."

"I know, Cam. Your people thought you'd be paving the way for the Communists to take over if you made maps and distance markers easy for them to read. And where are your Commies now?"

Buck had passed off most of Dirk Burton's ideas until a few years later when Dirk had called him in the middle of the night. "Cameron," he had said, unaware of the nickname bestowed by his friend's colleagues, "I can't talk long. You can pursue this or you can just watch it happen and wish it had been your story. But you remember that stuff I was saying about the one world currency?"

"Yeah. I'm still dubious."

"Fine, but I'm telling you the word here is that our guy pushed the idea at the last meeting of these secret financiers and something's brewing."

"What's brewing?"

"Well, there's going to be a major United Nations Monetary Conference, and the topic is going to be streamlining currency."

"Big deal."

"It *is* a big deal, Cameron. Our guy got shot down. He, of course, was pushing for world currency to become pounds sterling."

"What a surprise that that won't happen. Look at your economy."

"But listen, the big news, if you can believe any leak out of the secret meeting, is that they have it down to three currencies for the entire world, hoping to go to just one inside a decade."

"No way. Won't happen."

"Cameron, if my information is correct, the initial stage is a done deal. The U.N. conference is just window dressing."

"And the decision has already been made by your secret puppeteers."

"That's right."

"I don't know, Dirk. You're a buddy, but I think you would rather be doing what I'm doing."

"Who wouldn't?"

"Well, that's true. I sure wouldn't want to be doing what you're doing."

"But I'm not wrong, Cameron. Test my information."

"How?"

"I'll predict what's going to come out of the U.N. within two weeks, and if I'm right, you start treating me with a little deference, a little respect."

Buck realized that he and Dirk had been sparring the way everyone at Princeton had during weekend pizza and beer bashes in the dorms. "Dirk, listen. That sounds interesting, and I'm listening. But you do know, don't you, all kidding aside, that I wouldn't think any less of you even if you were way off base here?"

"Well, thanks, Cam. Really. That means a lot to me. And for that little tidbit, I'm going to give you a bonus. I'm not only going to tell you that the U.N. resolution is going to be for dollars, marks, and yen within five years, but I'm also going to tell you that the real power behind the power is an American."

"What do you mean, the power behind the power?"

"The mightiest of the secret group of international money men."

"This guy runs the group, in other words?"

"He's the one who shot down sterling as one of the currencies and has dollars in mind for the one world commodity in the end."

"I'm listening."

"Jonathan Stonagal."

Buck had hoped Dirk would name someone ludicrous so he could burst into laughter. But he had to admit, if only to himself, that if there was anything to this, Stonagal would be a logical choice. One of the richest men in the world and long known as an American power broker, Stonagal would have to be involved if serious global finance was being discussed. Though he was already in his eighties and appeared infirm in news photos, he not only owned the biggest banks and financial institutions in the United States, but he also owned or had huge interests in the same throughout the world.

Though Dirk was a friend, Buck had felt the need to play him along a bit, to keep him eager to provide information. "Dirk, I'm going back to bed. I appreciate all this and find it very interesting. I'm going to see what comes out of this U.N. deal, and I'm also going to see if I can trace the movements of Jonathan Stonagal. If it happens the way you think, you'll be my best informant. Meanwhile, see if you can find out for me how many are in this secret group and where they meet."

"That's easy," Dirk had said. "There are at least ten, though more than that sometimes come to the meetings, including some heads of state."

"U.S. presidents?"

"Occasionally, believe it or not."

"That's sort of one of the popular conspiracy theories here, Dirk."

"That doesn't mean it isn't true. And they usually meet in France. I don't know why. Some kind of private chalet or something there gives them a sense of security."

"But nothing escapes your friend of a friend of a relative of a subordinate of a secretary, or whatever."

"Laugh all you want, Cam. Our guy in the group, Joshua Todd-Cothran, may just not be quite as buttoned-down as the rest."

"Todd-Cothran? Doesn't he run the London Exchange?"

"That's the guy."

"Not buttoned-down? How could he have that position and not be? Plus, who ever heard of a Brit who was not buttoned-down?"

"It happens."

"Good night, Dirk."

Of course, it had all proven correct. The U.N. made its resolution. Buck discovered that Jonathan Stonagal had lived in the Plaza Hotel in New York during the ten days of the confab. Mr. Todd-Cothran of London had been one of the more eloquent speakers, expressing such eagerness to see the matter through that he volunteered to carry the torch back to the prime minister regarding Great Britain moving to the mark from the pound.

Many Third World countries fought the change, but within a few years the three currencies had swept the globe. Buck had told only Steve Plank of his tip on the U.N. meetings, but he didn't say where he'd gotten the information, and neither he nor Plank felt it worth a speculative article. "Too risky," Steve had said. Soon they both wished they had run with it in advance. "You'd have become even more of a legend, Buck."

Dirk and Buck had become closer than ever, and it wasn't unusual for Buck to visit London on short notice. If Dirk had a serious lead, Buck packed and went. His trips had often turned into excursions into countries and climates that surprised him, thus he had packed the emergency gear. Now, it appeared, it was superfluous. He was stuck in Chicago after the most electrifying phenomenon in world history, trying to get to New York.

Despite the incredible capabilities of his laptop, there was still no substitute for the pocket notebook. Buck scribbled a list of things to do before setting off again:

Call Ken Ritz, charter pilot
Call Dad and Jeff
Call Hattie Durham with news of family
Call Lucinda Washington about local hotel
Call Dirk Burton

+ + +

The phone awakened Rayford Steele. He had not moved for hours. It was early evening and beginning to get dark. "Hello?" he said, unable to mask the sleepy huskiness in his voice.

"Captain Steele?" It was the frantic voice of Hattie Durham.

"Yes, Hattie. Are you all right?"

"I've been trying to reach you for hours! My phone was dead for the longest time, then everything was busy. I thought I was getting a ring on your phone, but you never answered. I don't know anything about my mother or my sisters. What about you?"

Rayford sat up, dizzy and disoriented. "I got a message from Chloe," he said.

"I knew that," she said. "You told me at O'Hare. Are your wife and son all right?"

"No."

"No?"

Rayford was silent. What else was there to say?

"Do you know anything for sure?" Hattie asked.

"I'm afraid I do," he said. "Their bedclothes are here."

"Oh, no! Rayford, I'm sorry! Is there anything I can do?"

"No, thanks."

"Do you want some company?"

"No, thanks."

"I'm scared."

"So am I, Hattie."

"What are you going to do?"

"Keep trying to get Chloe. Hope she can come home or I can get to her."

"Where is she?"

"Stanford. Palo Alto."

"My people are in California, too," Hattie said. "They've got all kinds of trouble out there, even worse than here."

"I imagine it's because of the time difference," Rayford said. "More people on the roads, that sort of thing."

"I'm scared to death of what's become of my family."

"Let me know what you find out, Hattie, OK?"

"I will, but you were supposed to call me. 'Course my phone was dead, and then I couldn't get through to you."

"I wish I could say I tried to call you, Hattie, but I didn't. This is hard for me."

"Let me know if you need me, Rayford. You know, just someone to talk to or be with."

"I will. And you let me know what you find out about your family."

He almost wished he hadn't added that. Losing his wife and child made him realize what a vapid relationship he had been pursuing with a twenty-seven-year-old woman. He hardly knew her, and he certainly didn't much care what happened to her family any more than he cared when he heard about a remote tragedy on the news. He knew Hattie was not a bad person. In fact, she was nice and friendly. But that was not why he had been interested in her. It had merely been a physical attraction, something he had been smart enough or lucky enough or naive enough not to have acted upon. He felt guilty for having considered it, and now his own grief would obliterate all but the most common courtesy of simply caring for a coworker.

"There's my call waiting," she said. "Can you hold?"

"No, just go ahead and take it. I'll call you later."

"I'll call you back, Rayford."

"Well, OK."

* * *

Buck Williams had gotten back in line and gained access to a pay phone. This time he wasn't trying to hook up his computer to it. He simply wanted to see how many personal calls he could make. He reached Ken Ritz's answering machine first.

"This is Ritz's Charter Service. Here's the deal in light of the crisis: I've got Learjets at both Palwaukee and Waukegan, but I've lost my other flyer. I can get to either airport, but right now they're not lettin' anyone into any of the major strips. Can't get into Milwaukee, O'Hare, Kennedy, Logan, National, Dulles, Dallas, Atlanta. I can get into some of the smaller, outlying airports, but it's a seller's market. Sorry to be so opportunistic, but I'm asking two dollars a mile, cash up front. If I can find someone who wants to come back from where you're goin', I might be able to give you a little discount. I'm checkin' this tape tonight and will take off first thing in the morning. Longest trip with guaranteed cash gets me. If your stop is on the way, I'll try to squeeze you in. Leave me a message and I'll get back to you."

That was a laugh. How would Ken Ritz get hold of Buck? With his cellular phone unreliable, the only thing he could think of was to leave his New York voice-mail number. "Mr. Ritz, my name is Buck Williams, and I need to get as close to New York City as you can get me. I'll pay the full fare you're asking in traveler's checks, redeemable in whatever currency you want." Sometimes that was attractive to private contractors because they kept up with the differences in currency and could make a little margin on the exchange. "I'm at O'Hare and will try to find a place to stay in the suburbs. Just to save you time, let me just pick somewhere between here and Waukegan. If I get a new number in the meantime, I'll call it in. Meanwhile, you may leave a message for me at the following New York number."

Buck was still unable to get through to his office directly, but his voice-mail number worked. He retrieved his new messages, mostly from coworkers checking on him and lamenting the loss of mutual friends. Then there was the welcome message from Marge Potter, who was a genius to think of leaving it there for him. "Buck, if you get this, call your father in Tucson. He and your brother are together, and I hate to tell you here, but they're having trouble reaching Jeff's wife and the kids. They should have news by the time you call. Your father was most grateful to hear that you were all right."

Buck's voice mail also noted that he still had a saved message. That was the one from Dirk Burton that had spurred his trip in the first place. He would need to listen to it again when he had time. Meanwhile, he left a message for Marge that if she had time and an open line, she needed to let Dirk know Buck's flight never made it to Heathrow. Of course, Dirk would know that by now, but he needed to know Buck wasn't among the missing and that he would get there in due time.

Buck hung up and dialed his father. The line was busy, but it was not the same kind of a tone that tells you the lines are down or that the whole system is kaput. Neither was it that irritating recording he'd grown so used to. He knew it would be only a matter of time before he could get through. Jeff must be beside himself not knowing about his wife, Sharon, and the kids. They'd had their differences and had even been separated before the children came along, but for several years the marriage had been better. Jeff's wife had proven forgiving and conciliatory. Jeff himself admitted he was puzzled that she would take him back. "Call me undeserving, but grateful," he once told Buck. Their son and daughter, who both looked like Jeff, were precious.

Buck pulled out the number the beautiful blonde flight attendant had given him and chastised himself for not trying again to reach her earlier. It took a while for her to answer.

"Hattie Durham, this is Buck Williams."

"Who?"

"Cameron Williams, from the *Global*—"

"Oh yes! Any news?"

"Yes, ma'am, good news."

"Oh, thank God! Tell me."

"Someone from my office tells me they reached your mother and that she and your sisters are fine."

"Oh, thank you, thank you, thank you! I wonder why they haven't called here? Maybe they've tried. My phone has been haywire."

"There are other problems in California, ma'am. Lines down, that kind of a thing. It may be a while before you can talk to them."

"I know. I heard. Well, I sure appreciate this. How about you? Have you been able to reach your family?"

"I got word that my dad and brother are OK. We still don't know about my sister-in-law and the kids."

"Oh. How old are the kids?"

"Can't remember. Both under ten, but I don't know exactly."

"Oh." Hattie sounded sad, guarded.

"Why?" Buck asked.

"Oh, nothing. It's just that—"

"What?"

"You can't go by what I say."

"Tell me, Miss Durham."

"Well, you remember what I told you on the plane. And on the news it looks like all children are gone, even unborn ones."

"Yeah."

"I'm not saying that means your brother's children are—"

"I know."

"I'm sorry I brought that up."

"No, it's OK. This is too strange, isn't it?"

"Yeah. I just got off the phone with the captain who piloted the flight you were on. He lost his wife and son, but his daughter is OK. She's in California, too."

"How old is she?"

"About twenty, I guess. She's at Stanford."

"Oh."

"Mr. Williams, what did you call yourself?"

"Buck. It's a nickname."

"Well, Buck, I know better than to say what I said about your niece and nephew. I hope there are exceptions and that yours are OK." She began to cry.

"Miss Durham, it's OK. You have to admit, no one is thinking straight right now."

"You can call me Hattie."

That struck him as humorous under the circumstances. She had been apologizing for being inappropriate, yet she didn't want to be too formal. If he was Buck, she was Hattie.

"I suppose I shouldn't tie up this line," he said. "I just wanted to get the news to you. I thought maybe by now you already knew."

"No, and thanks again. Would you mind calling me again sometime, if you think of it? You seem like a nice person, and I appreciate what you did for me. It would be nice to hear from you again. This is kind of a scary, lonely time."

He couldn't argue with that understatement. Funny, her request had sounded like anything but a come-on. She seemed wholly sincere, and he was sure she was. A nice, scared, lonely woman whose world had been skewed, just like his and everyone's he knew.

When Buck got off the phone, he saw the young woman at the counter flagging him down. "Listen," she whispered, "they don't want me making an announcement that would start a stampede, but we just heard something interesting. The livery companies have gotten together and moved their communications center out to a median strip near the Mannheim Road interchange."

"Where's that?"

"Just outside the airport. There's no traffic coming into the terminals anyway. Total gridlock. But if you can walk as far as that interchange, supposedly you'll find all those guys with walkie-talkies trying to get limos in and out from there."

"I can imagine the prices."

"No, you probably can't."

"I can imagine the wait."

"Like standing in line for a rental car in Orlando," she said.

Buck had never done that, but he could imagine that, too. And she was right. After he had hiked, with a crowd, to the Mannheim interchange, he found a mob surrounding the dispatchers. Intermittent announcements got everyone's attention.

"We're filling every car. A hundred bucks a head to any suburb. Cash only. Nothing's going to Chicago."

"No cards?" someone shouted.

"I'll say it again," the dispatcher said. "Cash only. If you know you've got cash or a checkbook at home, you can plead with the driver to trust you till you get there." He called out a listing of which companies were heading which directions. Passengers ran to fill the cars as they lined up on the shoulder of the expressway.

Buck handed a hundred-dollar traveler's check to the dispatcher for the northern suburbs. An hour and a half later, he joined several others in a limo. After checking his cellular phone again to no avail, he offered the driver fifty dollars to use his phone. "No guarantees," the driver said. "Sometimes I get through, sometimes I don't."

Buck checked the phone log in his laptop for Lucinda Washington's home number and dialed. A teenage boy answered, "Washingtons."

"Cameron Williams of *Global Weekly* calling for Lucinda."

"My mom's not here," the young man said.

"Is she still at the office? I need a recommendation where to stay near Waukegan."

"She's nowhere," the boy said. "I'm the only one left. Mama, Daddy, everybody else is gone. Disappeared."

"Are you sure?"

"Their clothes are here, right where they were sitting. My daddy's contact lenses are still on top of his bathrobe."

"Oh, man! I'm sorry, son."

"That's all right. I know where they are, and I can't even say I'm surprised."

"You know where they are?"

"If you know my mama, you know where she is, too. She's in heaven."

"Yeah, well, are you all right? Is there someone to look after you?"

"My uncle's here. And a guy from our church. Probably the only one who's still around."

"You're all right then?"

"I'm all right."

Cameron folded the phone and handed it back to the driver. "Any idea where I should stay if I'm trying to fly out of Waukegan in the morning?"

"The chain hotels are probably full, but there's a couple of fleabags on Washington you might sneak into. You'd be close enough to the airport. You'd be my last drop-off."

"Fair enough. They got phones in those dives?"

"More likely a phone and a TV than running water."

6

IT HAD BEEN AGES since Rayford Steele had been drunk. Irene had never been much of a drinker, and she had become a teetotaler during the last few years. She insisted he hide any hard stuff if he had to have it in the house at all. She didn't want Raymie even knowing his daddy still drank.

"That's dishonest," Rayford had countered.

"It's prudent," she said. "He doesn't know everything, and he doesn't have to know everything."

"How does that jibe with your insistence that we be totally truthful?"

"Telling the whole truth doesn't always mean telling everything you know. You tell your crew you're taking a bathroom break, but you don't go into detail about what you're doing in there, do you?"

"Irene!"

"I'm just saying you don't have to make it obvious to your preteen son that you drink hard liquor."

He had found her point hard to argue, and he had kept his bourbon stashed high and out of sight. If ever there was a moment that called for a stiff drink, this was it. He reached behind the empty cake cover in the highest cabinet over the sink and pulled down a half-finished fifth of whiskey. His inclination, knowing no one he cared about would ever see, was to tip it straight up and guzzle. But even at a time like this there were conventions and manners. Guzzling booze from the bottle was simply not his style.

Rayford poured three inches into a wide crystal glass and threw it back like a veteran. That was about as out of character as he could find comfortable. The stuff hit the back of his throat and burned all the way down, giving him a chill that made him shudder and groan. *What an idiot!* he thought. *And on an empty stomach, too.*

He was already getting a buzz when he replaced the bottle, then thought better of it. He slipped it into the garbage under the sink. Would this be a nice memorial to Irene, giving up even the occasional hard drink? There would be no benefit to Raymie now, but he didn't feel right about drinking alone anyway. Did he have the capacity to become a closet drunk? *Who doesn't?* he wondered. Regardless, he wasn't going to cash in his maturity because of what had happened.

Rayford's sleep had been deep but not long enough. He had few immediate chores. First he had to connect with Chloe. Second he had to find out what Pan-Con wanted from him in the next week. Even normal regulations wouldn't have grounded him after an overly long flight and a diverted landing. But who knew what was going on now?

How many pilots had they lost? When would runways be cleared? Flights scheduled? If he knew anything about the airlines, it would all be about dollars. As soon as they could get those machines airborne, they could start being profitable again. Well, Pan-Con had been good to him. He would hang in there and do his part. But what was he supposed to do about this grief, this despair, this empty ache?

Finally he understood the bereaved who complained when their loved one was too mangled to see or whose body had been destroyed. They often complained that there was no sense of closure and that the grieving process was more difficult because they had a hard time imagining their loved one actually dead.

That had always seemed strange to him. Who would want to see a wife or child stretched out and made up for a funeral? Wouldn't you want to remember them alive and happy as they were? But he knew better now. He had no doubt that his wife and son were gone as surely as if they had died, as his own parents had years before. Irene and Ray would not be coming back, and he didn't know if he would ever see them again, because he didn't know if there were second chances on this heaven thing.

He longed to be able to see their bodies, at least—in bed, in a casket, anywhere. He would have given anything for one last glimpse. It wouldn't have made them any less dead to him, but maybe he wouldn't feel so abandoned, so empty.

Rayford knew there would not likely be phone connections between Illinois and California for hours, maybe days. Yet he had to try. He dialed Stanford, the main administration number, and didn't even get a busy signal or a recorded message. He dialed Chloe's room. Still nothing. Every half hour or so he hit the redial button. He refused to hope she would answer; if she did, it would be a wonderful surprise.

Rayford found himself ravenous and knew he'd better get something in his stomach before the few ounces of booze did a number on him. He mounted the stairs again, stopping in Raymie's room to pick up the little pile of clothes by which he would remember the boy. He put them in a cardboard gift box he found in Irene's closet, then placed her nightgown, locket, and ring in another.

He took the boxes downstairs, along with the two cookies she had mailed him. The rest of that batch of cookies had to be around somewhere. He found them in a Tupperware bowl in the cupboard. He was grateful that their smell and taste would remind him of her until they were gone.

Rayford added a couple to the two he had brought down, put them on a paper plate, and poured himself a glass of milk. He sat at the kitchen table next to the phone but couldn't force himself to eat. He felt paralyzed. To busy himself, he erased the calls on the answering machine and added a new outgoing message. He said, "This is Rayford Steele. If you must, please leave a very brief message. I am trying to leave this line open for my daughter. Chloe, if it's you, I'm either sleeping or close by, so give me a chance to pick up. If we don't connect for some reason, do whatever you have to, to get home. Any airline can charge it to me. I love you."

And with that he slowly ate his cookies, the smell and taste bringing images to him of Irene in the kitchen, and the milk making him long for his boy. This was going to be hard, so hard.

He was exhausted, and yet he couldn't bring himself to go upstairs again. He knew he would have to force himself to sleep in his own bedroom that night. For now he would stretch out on the couch in the living room and hope Chloe would get through. He idly pushed the redial button again, and this time he got the quick busy signal that told him something was happening. At the very least, lines were being worked on. That was progress. He knew she was thinking of him while he was thinking of her. But she had no idea what might have happened to her mother or her brother. Would he have to tell her by phone? He feared he would. She would surely ask.

He lumbered to the couch and lay down, a sob in his throat but no more tears to accompany it. If only Chloe would somehow get his message and get started home, he could at least tell her face-to-face.

Rayford lay there grieving, knowing the television would be full of scenes he didn't want to see, dedicated around the clock to the tragedy and mayhem all over the world. And then it hit him. He sat up, staring out the window in the darkness. He owed it to Chloe not to fail her. He loved her and she was all he had left. He had to find out how they had missed everything Irene had been trying to tell them, why it had been so hard to accept and believe. Above all, he had to study, to learn, to be prepared for whatever happened next.

If the disappearances were of God, if they had been his doing, was this the end of it? The Christians, the real believers, get taken away, and the rest are left to grieve and mourn and realize their error? Maybe so. Maybe that was the price. *But then what happens when we die?* he thought. *If heaven is real, if the Rapture was a fact, what does that say about hell and judgment? Is that our fate? We go through this hell of regret and remorse, and then we literally go to hell, too?*

Irene had always talked of a loving God, but even God's love and mercy had to have limits. Had everyone who denied the truth pushed God to his limit? Was there no more mercy, no second chance? Maybe there wasn't, and if that was so, that was so.

But if there were options, if there was still a way to find the truth and believe or accept or whatever it was Irene said one was supposed to do, Rayford was going to find it. Would it mean admitting that he didn't know everything? That he had relied on himself and that now he felt stupid and weak and worthless? He could admit that. After a lifetime of achieving, of excelling, of being better than most and the best in most circles, he had been as humbled as was possible in one stroke.

There was so much he didn't know, so much he didn't understand. But if the answers were still there, he would find them. He didn't know whom to ask or where to start, but this was something he and Chloe could do together. They'd always gotten along all right. She'd gone through the typical teenage independence, but she had never done anything stupid or irreparable as far as he knew. In fact, they had probably been too close; she was too much like him.

It wasn't simply Raymie's age and innocence that had allowed his mother's influence to affect him so. It was his spirit. He didn't have the killer instinct, the "me first" attitude Rayford thought he would need to succeed in the real world. He wasn't effeminate, but Rayford had worried that he might be a mama's boy—too compassionate, too sensitive, too caring. He was always looking out for someone else when Rayford thought he should be looking out for number one.

How grateful he was now that Raymie took after his mother more than he took after his father. And how he wished there had been some of that in Chloe. She was competitive, a driver, someone who had to be convinced and persuaded. She could be kind and generous when it suited her purpose, but she was like her dad. She took care of herself.

Good job, big shot, Rayford told himself. *The girl you were so proud of because she was so much like you is in your same predicament.*

That, he decided, would have to change. As soon as they reconnected, that *would* change. They would be on a mission, a quest for truth. If he was already too late, he would have to accept and deal with that. He'd always been one who went for a goal and accepted the consequences. Only these consequences were eternal. He hoped against all hope that there was another chance at truth and knowledge out there somewhere. The only problem was that the ones who knew were gone.

\+ \+ \+

The Midpoint Motel on Washington Street, a few miles from the tiny Waukegan Airport, was tacky enough that there wasn't a waiting list. Buck Williams was pleasantly surprised they had not even raised their rates for the crisis. When he saw the room, he knew why, and he wondered what two places in the world this dive was midpoint *between*. Whatever they were, either had to be better. There was a phone, however, and a shower, a bed, and a TV. Run-down as it was, it would suffice. First Buck called his voice mail in New York. Nothing from this Ritz character or anything else new, so he listened to his saved message from Dirk Burton, which reminded him why he had felt it so important to get to London. Buck tapped it into his laptop as he listened:

Cameron, you always tell me this message center is confidential, and I hope you're right. I'm not even going to identify myself, but you know who it is. Let me tell you something major and encourage you to come here as quickly as possible. The big man, your compatriot, the one I call the supreme power broker internationally, met here the other day with the one I call our mucke-ty-muck. You know who I mean. There was a third party at the meeting. All I know is that he's from Europe, probably Eastern Europe. I don't know what their plans are for him, but apparently something on a huge scale.

My sources say your man has met with each of his key people and this same European in different locations. He introduced him to people in China, the Vatican, Israel, France, Germany, here, and the States. Something is cooking, and I don't even want to suggest what it is other than in person. Visit me as soon as you can. In case that's not possible, let me just encourage this: Watch the news for the installation of a new leader in Europe. If you say, as I did, that no elections are scheduled and no changes of power are imminent, you'll get my drift. Come soon, friend.

Buck called Ken Ritz's machine to tell him where he was. Then he tried calling west once again and finally got through. Buck was surprised at what a relief it was to hear his father's voice, though he sounded tired, discouraged, and not a little panicky.

"Everybody OK out there, Dad?"

"Well, not everybody. Jeff was here with me, but he's taken the four-wheel drive to see if he can get to the accident site where Sharon was last seen."

"Accident?"

"She was pickin' up the kids at a retreat or something, something to do with her church. She doesn't go with us anymore, you know. Story is, she never got there. Car flipped over. No trace of her, 'cept her clothes, and you know what that means."

"She's gone?"

"Looks that way. Jeff can't accept it. He's takin' it hard. Wants to see for himself. Trouble is, the kids are gone, too, all of 'em. All their friends, everybody at that retreat thing in the mountains. State police found all the kids' clothes, about a hundred sets of them, and some kind of a late-night snack burning on the stove."

"Whew, boy! Tell Jeff I'm thinking of him. If he wants to talk, I'm here."

"I can't imagine he'll want to talk, Cameron, unless you have some answers."

"That's one thing I haven't got, Dad. I don't know who does. I have this feeling that whoever had the answers is gone."

"This is awful, Cam. I wish you were out here with us."

"Yeah, I'll bet."

"You bein' sarcastic?"

"Just expressing the truth, Dad. If you wanted me out there, it'd be the first time."

"Well, this is the kind of time when maybe we change our minds."

"About me? I doubt it."

"Cameron, let's not get into this, huh? For once, think of somebody other than yourself. You lost a sister-in-law and a niece and a nephew yesterday, and your brother'll probably never get over it."

Buck bit his tongue. Why did he always have to do this, and especially right now? His dad was right. If only Buck could admit that, maybe they could move on. He had been resented by the family ever since he'd gone on to college, following his academic prowess to the Ivy League. Where he came from, the kids were supposed to follow their parents into the business. His dad's was trucking fuel into the state, mostly from Oklahoma and Texas. It was a tough business with local people thinking the resources ought to all come from their own state. Jeff had worked his way up in the little business, starting in the office, then driving a truck, now running the day-to-day operations.

There had been a lot of bad blood, especially since Cameron was away at school when his mother fell ill. She had insisted he stay in school, but when he missed coming home for Christmas due to money problems, his dad and brother never really forgave him. His mother died while he was away, and he got the cold shoulder even at her funeral.

Some healing had occurred over the years, mostly because his family loved to claim him and brag about him once he became known as a journalistic prodigy. He had let bygones be bygones but resented that he was now welcome because he was somebody. And so he rarely went home. There was too much baggage to reconcile completely, but he was still angry with himself for opening old wounds when his family was suffering.

"If there's some kind of memorial service or something, I'll try to make it, Dad. All right?"

"You'll *try*?"

"That's all I can promise. You can imagine how busy things are at *Global* right now. Needless to say, this is the story of the century."

"Will you be writing the cover story?"

"I'll have a lot to do with the coverage, yeah."

"But the cover?"

Buck sighed, suddenly tired. It was no wonder. He'd been awake nearly twenty-four hours. "I don't know, Dad. I've already filed a lot of stuff. My guess is this next issue will be a huge special with lots of stuff from all over. It's unlikely my piece would be the sole cover article. It looks like I do have the assignment for a pretty major treatment two weeks from now."

He hoped that would satisfy his dad. He wanted to get off and get some sleep. But it didn't.

"What's that mean? What's the story?"

"Oh, I'll be pulling together several writers' pieces on the theories behind what's happened."

"That'll be a big job. Everybody I talk to has a different idea. You know your brother is afraid it was like the last judgment of God or something."

"He does?"

"Yeah. But I don't think so."

"Why not, Dad?" He didn't really want to get into a lengthy discussion, but this surprised him.

"Because I asked our pastor. He said if it was Jesus Christ taking people to heaven, he and I and you and Jeff would be gone, too. Makes sense."

"Does it? I've never claimed any devotion to the faith."

"The heck you haven't. You always get into this liberal, East Coast baloney. You know good and well we had you in church and Sunday school from the time you were a baby. You're as much a Christian as any one of us."

Cameron wanted to say, "Precisely my point." But he didn't. It was the lack of any connection between his family's church attendance and their daily lives that made him quit going to church altogether the day it became his choice.

"Yeah, well, tell Jeff I'm thinking about him, huh? And if I can work it out at all, I'll get back there for whatever he's going to do about Sharon and the kids."

Buck was grateful the Midpoint at least had plenty of hot water for a long shower. He had forgotten about the nagging throb at the back of his head until the water hit it and loosened the bandage. He didn't have anything to redress it, so he just let it bleed a while, then found some ice. In the morning he would find a bandage, just for looks. For now, he had had it. He was bone weary.

There was no remote control for the TV and no way he would get up once he stretched out. He turned CNN on low so it wouldn't interrupt his sleep, and he watched the world roundup before dozing off. Images from around the globe were almost more than he could take, but news was his business. He remembered the many earthquakes and wars of the last decade and the nightly coverage that was so moving. Now here was a thousand times more of the same, all on the same day. Never in history had more people been killed in one day than those who disappeared all at once. Had they been killed? Were they dead? Would they be back?

Buck couldn't take his eyes, heavy as they were, off the screen as image after image showed disappearances caught on home videotape. From some countries came professional tapes of live television shows in progress, a host's microphone landing atop his empty clothes, bouncing off his shoes, and making a racket as it rolled across the floor. The audience screamed. One of the cameras panned the crowd, which had been at capacity a moment before. Now several seats were empty, clothes draped across them.

Nothing could have been scripted like this, Buck thought, blinking slowly. If somebody tried to sell a screenplay about millions of people disappearing, leaving everything but their bodies behind, it would be laughed off.

Buck was not aware that he was asleep until the cheap phone jangled so loudly it sounded as if it would rattle itself off the table. He groped for it.

"Sorry to bother you, Mr. Williams, but I just noticed you was off the phone there. While you was talkin', you got a call. Guy name of Ritz. Says you can call him or you can just be waitin' for him outside at six in the mornin'."

"OK. Thanks."

"What're you gonna do? Call him or meet him?"

"Why do you need to know?"

"Oh, I ain't bein' nosy or nothin'. It's just that if you're leavin' here at six, I gotta get payment in advance. You got the long-distance call and all. And I don't get up till seven."

"I'll tell you what, uh, what was your name?"

"Mack."

"I'll tell you what, Mack. I left you my charge card number, so you know I'm not going to sneak out on you. But in the morning I'm going to leave a traveler's check in the room for you, covering the price of the room and a lot more than enough for the phone call. You get my meaning?"

"A tip?"

"Yes, sir."

"That would be nice."

"What I need for you to do for me is slip a bandage under my door."

"I got one. You need it right now? You all right?"

"I'm fine. Not now. When you turn in. Nice and quiet like. And turn off my phone, OK, just in case? If I have to get up that early, I've got to do some serious sleeping right now. Can you handle that for me, Mack?"

"I sure can. I'll turn it off right now. You want a wake-up call?"

"No, thanks," Buck said, and he smiled when he realized the phone was dead in his hand. Mack was as good as his word. If he found that bandage in the morning, he would leave Mack a good tip. Buck forced himself to get up and shut off the TV set and the light. He was the type who could look at his watch before retiring and wake up precisely when he told himself to. It was nearly midnight. He would be up at five-thirty.

By the time he hit the mattress, he was out. When he awoke five and a half hours later, he had not moved a muscle.

\+ + +

Rayford felt as if he were sleepwalking as he padded through the kitchen to head upstairs. He couldn't believe how tired he still was after his long nap and his fitful dozing on the couch. The newspaper was still rolled up and rubber-banded on a chair where he had tossed it. If he had any trouble sleeping upstairs, maybe he would glance at the paper. It should be interesting to read the meaningless news of a world that didn't realize it was going to suffer the worst trauma in its history just after the paper had been set in type.

Rayford punched the redial button on the phone and walked slowly toward the stairs, only half listening. What was that? The dial tone had been interrupted, and the phone in Chloe's dorm room was ringing. He hurried to the phone as a girl answered.

"Chloe?"

"No. Mr. Steele?"

"Yes!"

"This is Amy. Chloe's trying to find a way back there. She'll try to call you along the way, sometime tomorrow. If she can't get through, she'll call you when she gets there or she'll get a cab home."

"She's on her way?"

"Yeah. She didn't want to wait. She tried calling and calling, but—"

"Yeah, I know. Thanks, Amy. Are you all right?"

"Scared to death, like everybody else."

"I can imagine. Did you lose anyone?"

"No, and I feel kinda guilty about that. Seems like everyone I know lost somebody. I mean I lost a few friends, but nobody close, no family."

Rayford didn't know whether to express congratulations or remorse. If this was what he now believed it had been, this poor child hardly knew anyone who'd been taken to heaven.

"Well," he said, "I'm glad you're all right."

"How about you?" she said. "Chloe's mom and brother?"

"I'm afraid they're gone, Amy."

"Oh, no!"

"But I would appreciate your letting me tell Chloe, just in case she reaches you before she reaches me."

"Oh, don't worry. I don't think I could tell her even if you wanted me to."

Rayford lay in bed several minutes, then idly thumbed through the first section of the paper. Hmm. A surprise move in Romania.

> *Democratic elections became passé when, with the seeming unanimous consensus of the people and both the upper and lower houses of government, a popular young businessman/politician assumed the role of president of the country. Nicolae Carpathia, a 33-year-old born in Cluj, had in recent months taken the nation by storm with his popular, persuasive speaking, charming the populace, friend and foe alike. Reforms he proposed for the country saw him swept to prominence and power.*

Rayford glanced at the photo of the young Carpathia, a strikingly handsome blond who looked not unlike a young Robert Redford. *Wonder if he would've wanted the job had he known what was about to happen?* Rayford thought. *Whatever he has to offer won't amount to a hill of beans now.*

7

KEN RITZ roared up to the Midpoint precisely at six, rolled down his window, and said, "You Williams?"

"I'm your man," Buck said. He climbed into the late model four-wheel drive with his one bag. Fingering his freshly bandaged head, Buck smiled at the thought of Mack enjoying his extra twenty bucks.

Ritz was tall and lean with a weathered face and a shock of salt-and-pepper hair. "Let's get down to business," he said. "It's 740 miles from O'Hare to JFK and 746 from Milwaukee to JFK. I'm gonna get you as close to JFK as I can, and we're about equidistant between O'Hare and Milwaukee, so let's call it 743 air miles. Multiply that by two bucks, you're talkin' fourteen hundred and eighty-six. Round it off to fifteen hundred for the taxi service, and we got us a deal."

"Deal," Buck said, pulling out his checks and starting to sign. "Pretty expensive taxi."

Ritz laughed. "Especially for a guy coming out of the Midpoint."

"It was lovely."

Ritz parked in a metal Quonset hut at the Waukegan airport and chatted while running through preflight procedures. "No crashes here," he said. "There were two at Palwaukee. They lost a couple of staff people here though. Weirder than weird, wasn't it?"

Buck and Ritz shared stories of lost relatives, where they were when it happened, and exactly who they were. "Never flew a writer before," Ken said. "Charter, I mean. Must've flown a bunch of your types when I was commercial."

"Better money on your own?"

"Yeah, but I didn't know that when I switched. It wasn't my choice."

They were climbing into the Lear. Buck shot him a double take. "You were grounded?"

"Don't worry, partner," the pilot said. "I'll get you there."

"You owe it to me to tell me if you were grounded."

"I was fired. There's a difference."

"Depends on what you were fired for, doesn't it?"

"True enough. This ought to make you feel real good. I was fired for bein' too careful. Beat that."

"Talk to me," Buck said.

"You remember a lot of years ago when there was all that flak about puddle jumpers goin' down in icy weather?"

"Yeah, until they made some adjustments or something."

"Right. Well, you remember that one pilot refused to fly even after he was told to and the public was assured everything up to that point was explainable or a fluke?"

"Uh-huh."

"And you remember that there was another crash right after that, which proved the pilot right?"

"Vaguely."

"Well, I remember it plain as day, because you're lookin' at him."

"I do feel better."

"You know how many of those same model puddle jumpers are in the air today? Not a one. When you're right, you're right. But was I reinstated? No. Once a troublemaker, always a troublemaker. Lots of my colleagues were grateful though. And some pilots' widows were pretty angry that I got ignored and then canned, too late for their husbands."

"Ouch."

As the jet screamed east, Ritz wanted to know what Buck thought of the disappearances. "Funny you should ask," Buck said. "I've got to start working on that in earnest today. What's your read of it? And do you mind if I flip on a tape recorder?"

"Fine," Ritz said. "Dangedest thing I've ever seen. 'Course, that doesn't make me unique. I have to say, though, I've always believed in UFOs."

"You're kidding! A levelheaded, safety-conscious pilot?"

Ritz nodded. "I'm not talking about little green men or space aliens who kidnap people. I'm talking about some of the more documentable stuff, like some astronauts have seen, and some pilots."

"You ever see anything?"

"Nope. Well, a couple of unexplainable things. Some lights or mirages. Once I thought I was flying too close to a squad of helicopters. Not too far from here either. Glenview Naval Air Station. I radioed a warning, then lost sight of them. I suppose that's explainable. I could have been going faster than I realized and not been as close as I thought. But I never got an answer, no acknowledgment that they were even airborne. Glenview wouldn't confirm it. I shrugged it off, but a few weeks later, close to the same spot, my instruments went wacky on me. Dials spinning, meters sticking, that kind of thing."

"What did you make of that?"

"Magnetic field or some force like that. Could be explainable, too. You know there's no sense reporting strange occurrences or sightings near a military base, because they just reject 'em out of hand. They don't even take seriously anything strange within several miles of a commercial airport. That's why you never hear stories of UFOs near O'Hare. Not even considered."

"So, you don't buy the kidnapping space aliens, but you connect the disappearances with UFOs?"

"I'm just sayin' it's not like *E.T.*, with creatures and all that. I think our ideas of what space people would look like are way too simple and rudimentary. If there is intelligent life out there, and there has to be just because of the sheer odds—"

"What do you mean?"

"The vastness of space."

"Oh, so many stars and so much area that something has to be out there somewhere."

"Exactly. And I agree with people who think those beings are more intelligent than we are. Otherwise, they wouldn't have made it here, if they are here. And if they are, I'm thinking they're sophisticated and advanced enough that they can do things to us we've never dreamed of."

"Like making people disappear right out of their clothes."

"Sounded pretty silly until the other night, didn't it?"

Buck nodded.

"I've always laughed about people assuming these beings could read our thoughts or get into our heads and stuff," Ritz continued. "But look who's missing. Everybody I've read about or heard about or knew who's now gone was either under twelve years old or was an unusual personality."

"With all the people who disappeared, you think they had something in common?"

"Well, they've got something in common now, wouldn't you say?"

"But something set them apart, made them easier to snatch?" Buck asked.

"That's what I think."

"So we're still here because we were strong enough to resist, or maybe we weren't worth the trouble."

Ritz nodded. "Something like that. It's almost like some force or power was able to read the level of resistance or weakness, and once that force got sunk in, it was able to rip those people right off the earth. They disappeared in an instant, so they had to be dematerialized. The question is whether they were destroyed in the process or could be reassembled."

"What do you think, Mr. Ritz?"

"At first I would have said no. But a week ago I would have told you that millions of people all over the world disappearing into thin air sounds like a B movie. When I allow for the fact that it actually happened, I have to allow for the next logical step. Maybe they're somewhere specific in some form, and maybe they can return."

"That's a comforting thought," Buck said. "But is it more than wishful thinking?"

"Hardly. That idea and fifty cents would be worth half a dollar. I fly planes for money. I haven't got a clue. I'm still as much in shock as the next guy, and I don't mind tellin' you, I'm scared."

"Of?"

"That it might happen again. If it was anything like I think it was, maybe all this force needs to do now is crank up the power somehow and they can get older people, smarter people, people with more resistance that they ignored the first time around."

Buck shrugged and sat in silence for a few minutes. Finally he said, "There's a little hole in your argument. I know of some people who are missing who seem as strong as anyone."

"I wasn't talking physical strength."

"Neither was I." Buck thought about Lucinda Washington. "I lost a friend and coworker who was bright, healthy, happy, strong, and a forceful personality."

"Well, I'm not saying I know everything or even anything. You wanted my theory; there it is."

* * *

Rayford Steele lay on his back, staring at the ceiling. Sleep had come hard and intermittently, and he hated the logy feeling. He didn't want to watch the news. He didn't want to read the paper, even knowing a new one had flopped up onto the porch before dawn. All he wanted was for Chloe to get home so they could grieve together. There was nothing, he decided, more lonely than grief.

He and his daughter would have work to do, too. He wanted to investigate, to learn, to know, to act. He started by searching for a Bible, not the family Bible that had collected dust on his shelf for years, but Irene's. Hers would have notes in it, maybe something that would point him in the right direction.

It wasn't hard to find. It was usually within arm's reach of where she slept. He found it on the floor, next to the bed. Would there be some guide? An index?

Something that referred to the Rapture or the judgment or something? If not, maybe he'd start at the end. If *genesis* meant "beginning," maybe *revelation* had something to do with the end, even though it didn't mean that. The only Bible verse Rayford could quote by heart was Genesis 1:1: "In the beginning God created the heavens and the earth." He hoped there'd be some corresponding verse at the end of the Bible that said something like, "In the end God took all his people to heaven and gave everybody else one more chance."

But no such luck. The very last verse in the Bible meant nothing to him. It said, "The grace of the Lord Jesus be with you all. Amen." And it sounded like the religious mumbo jumbo he had heard in church. He backed up a verse and read, "He who testifies to these things says, 'Yes, I am coming quickly.' Amen. Come, Lord Jesus."

Now he was getting somewhere. Who was this who testified of these things, and what were these things? The quoted words were in red. What did that mean? He looked through the Bible and then noticed on the spine, "Words of Christ in red." So Jesus said he was coming quickly. Had he come? And if the Bible was as old as it seemed, what did "quickly" mean? It must not have meant soon, unless it was from the perspective of someone with a long view of history. Maybe Jesus meant that when he came, he would do it quickly. Was that what this was all about? Rayford glanced at the last chapter as a whole. Three other verses had red letters, and two of those repeated the business about coming quickly.

Rayford could make no sense of the text of the chapter. It seemed old and formal. But near the end of the chapter was a verse that ended with words that had a strange impact on him. Without a hint of their meaning, he read, "Let the one who is thirsty come; let the one who wishes take the water of life without cost."

Jesus wouldn't have been the one who was thirsty. He would not have been the one who wished to take the water of life. That, Rayford assumed, referred to the reader. It struck him that he was thirsty, soul thirsty. But what was the water of life? He had already paid a terrible cost for missing it. Whatever it was, it had been in this book for hundreds of years.

Rayford idly leafed through the Bible to other passages, none of which made sense to him. They discouraged him because they didn't seem to flow together, to refer to each other, to have a direction. Language and concepts foreign to him were not helping.

Here and there he saw notes in the margins in Irene's delicate handwriting. Sometimes she simply wrote, "Precious." He was determined to study and find someone who could explain those passages to him. He was tempted to write *precious* next to that verse in Revelation about taking the water of life without cost. It sounded precious to him, though he couldn't yet make it compute.

Worst of all, he feared he was reading the Bible too late. Clearly he was too late to have gone to heaven with his wife and son. But was he too late, period?

In the front flyleaf was last Sunday's church bulletin. What was this, Wednesday morning? Three days ago he had been where? In the garage. Raymie had begged him to go with them to church. He promised he would next Sunday. "That's what you said last week," Raymie had said.

"Do you want me to fix this four-wheeler for you or not? I don't have all the time in the world."

Raymie was not one for pushing a guilt trip. He just repeated, "Next Sunday?"

"For sure," Rayford had said. And now he wished next Sunday were here. He wished even more that Raymie were there to go with him because he *would* go. Or would he? Would he be off work that day? And would there be church? Was anyone left in that congregation? He pulled the bulletin from Irene's Bible and circled the phone number. Later that day, after he checked in with Pan-Continental, he would call the church office and see if anything was going on.

He was about to set the Bible on the bed table when he grew curious and opened the front flyleaf again. On the first white-papered page he saw the inscription. He had given this Bible to Irene on their first wedding anniversary. How could he have forgotten, and what had he been thinking? She was no more devout than he back then, but she talked about wanting to get serious about church attendance before the children came along. He had been angling for something or trying to impress her. Maybe he thought she would think him spiritual if he gave her a gift like that. Maybe he was hoping she would let him off the hook and go to church by herself if he proved his spiritual sensitivity with this gift.

For years he had tolerated church. They had gone to one that demanded little and offered a lot. They made many friends and had found their doctor, dentist, insurance man, and even country club entrée in that church. Rayford was revered, proudly introduced as a 747 captain to newcomers and guests, and even served on the church board for several years.

When Irene discovered the Christian radio station and what she called "real preaching and teaching," she grew disenchanted with their church and began searching for a new one. That gave Rayford the opportunity to quit going at all, telling her that when she found one she really liked, he would start going again. She found one, and he tried it occasionally, but it was a little too literal and personal and challenging for him. He was not revered. He felt like a project. And he pretty much stayed away.

Rayford noticed another bit of Irene's handwriting. It was labeled her prayer list, and he was at the top. She had written, "Rafe, for his salvation and that

I be a loving wife to him. Chloe, that she come to Christ and live in purity. Ray Jr., that he never stray from his strong, childlike faith." Then she had listed her pastor, political leaders, missionaries, world conflict, and several friends and other relatives.

"For his salvation," Rayford whispered. "Salvation." Another ten-dollar church word that had never really impressed him. He knew Irene's new church was interested in the salvation of souls, something he'd never heard in the previous church. But the closer he had gotten to the concept, the more he had been repelled. Didn't salvation have something to do with confirmation, baptism, testifying, getting religion, being holy? He hadn't wanted to deal with it, whatever it was. And now he was desperate to know exactly what it meant.

+ + +

Ken Ritz radioed ahead to airports in suburban New York, finally getting clearance to touch down at Easton, Pennsylvania. "You know," Ritz said, "these are the old stompin' grounds of Larry Holmes, once the heavyweight champion of the world."

"The guy that beat Ali?"

"One and the same. If he was still around, whoever was takin' people might've got a knock on the noggin from ol' Larry. You can bet on that."

The pilot asked personnel in Easton if they could arrange a ride to New York City for his passenger.

"You're joking, right, Lear?"

"Didn't mean to, over."

"We got a guy can get him to within a couple of miles of the subway. No cars in or out of the city yet, and even the trains have some kind of a complicated route that takes them around bad sites."

"Bad sites?" Buck repeated.

"Say again," Ritz radioed.

"Haven't you been watching the news? Some of the worst disasters in the city were the result of disappearing motormen and dispatchers. Six trains were involved in head-ons with lots of deaths. Several trains ran up the back of other ones. It'll be days before they clear all the tracks and replace cars. You sure your man wants to get into midtown?"

"Roger. Seems like the type who can handle it."

"Hope he's got good hiking boots, over."

It cost Buck another premium for a ride close enough to the train that he could walk the rest of the way. His driver had not even been a cabbie, nor the vehicle a cab. But it might as well have been. It was just as decrepit and unsafe.

A two-mile walk got him to the train platform at about noon, where he waited more than forty minutes with a mass of humanity, only to find himself among the last half who had to wait another half hour for the next train. The zigzag ride took two hours to get to Manhattan, and all during the trip Buck tapped at the keys on his laptop or stared out the window at the gridlock that went on for miles. He knew many of his locally based colleagues would have already filed similar reports, so his only hope of scoring with Steve Plank and having this see publication was if his were more powerfully or eloquently written. He was in such awe of the scene that he doubted he could pull it off. At the very least he was adding drama to his own memoirs. New York City was at a standstill, and the biggest surprise was that they were letting people in at all. No doubt many of these, like him, lived here and needed to get to their homes and apartments.

The train lurched to a stop, far short of where he had been told it would reach. The garbled announcement, the best he could make out, informed passengers that this was the new last stop. Their next jog would have put them in the middle of a crane site where cars were being lifted off the track. Buck calculated about a fifteen-mile walk to his office and another five to his apartment.

Fortunately, Buck was in great shape. He put everything into his bag and shortened the strap so he could carry it close to his body without it swinging. He set off at what he guessed was a four-mile-per-hour pace, and three hours later he was hurting. He was sure he had blisters, and his neck and shoulders were tired from the bag and strap. He was sweating through his clothes, and there was no way he was going to get to his apartment before stopping in at the office.

"Oh, God, help me," Buck breathed, more exasperated than praying. But if there was a God, he decided, God had a sense of humor. Leaning against a brick wall in an alley in plain sight was a yellow bicycle with a cardboard sign clipped to it. It read, "Borrow this bike. Take it where you like. Leave it for someone else in need. No charge."

Only in New York, he thought. *Nobody steals something that's free.*

He thought about breathing a prayer of thanks, but somehow the world he was looking at didn't show any other evidence of a benevolent Creator. He mounted the bike, realized how long it had been since he had been aboard one, and wobbled off till he found his balance. It wasn't long before he cruised into midtown between the snarl of wreckage and wreckers. Only a few other people were traveling as efficiently as he was—couriers on bikes, two others on yellow bikes just like his, and cops on horseback.

Security was tight at the *Global Weekly* building, which somehow didn't surprise him. After identifying himself to a new desk clerk, he rode to the twenty-seventh floor, stopped in the public washroom to freshen up, and finally entered the main suites of the magazine. The receptionist immediately buzzed Steve Plank's office, and both Steve and Marge Potter hurried out to embrace and welcome him.

Buck Williams was hit with a strange, new emotion. He nearly wept. He realized he, along with everyone else, was enduring a hideous trauma and that he had no doubt been running on adrenaline. But somehow, getting back to familiar territory—especially with the expense and effort it had taken—made him feel as if he had come home. He was with people who cared about him. This was his family. He was really, really glad to see them, and it appeared the feeling was mutual.

He bit his lip to keep from clouding up, and as he followed Steve and Marge down the hall past his tiny, cluttered office and into Steve's spacious office/conference room, he asked if they had heard about Lucinda Washington.

Marge stopped in the corridor, bringing her hands to her face. "Yes," she managed, "and I wasn't going to do this again. We've lost several. Where does the grieving start and end?"

With that, Buck lost it. He couldn't pretend any longer, though he was as surprised as anyone at his own sensitivity. Steve put an arm around his secretary and guided her and Buck into his office, where others from the senior staff waited.

They cheered when they saw Buck. These people, the ones he had worked with, fought with, feuded with, irritated, and scooped, now seemed genuinely glad to see him. They could have no idea how he felt. "Boy, it's good to be back here," he said, then sat and buried his head in his hands. His body began to shake, and he could fight the tears no longer. He began to sob, right there in front of his colleagues and competitors.

He tried to wipe the tears away and compose himself, but when he looked up, forcing an embarrassed smile, he noticed everyone else was emotional, too. "It's all right, Bucky," one said. "If this is your first cry, you'll discover it won't be your last. We're all just as scared and stunned and grief stricken as you are."

"Yeah," another said, "but his personal account will no doubt be more compelling." Which made everyone laugh and cry all the more.

* * *

Rayford talked himself into calling the Pan-Con Flight Center early in the afternoon. He learned that he was to report in for a Friday flight two days later. "Really?" he said.

"Don't count on actually flying it," he was told. "Not too many flights are expected to be lifting off by then. Certainly none till late tomorrow, and maybe not even then."

"There's a chance I'll get called off before I leave home?"

"More than a chance, but that's your assignment for now."

"What's the route?"

"ORD to BOS to JFK."

"Hmm. Chicago, Boston, New York. Home when?"

"Saturday night."

"Good."

"Why? Got a date?"

"Not funny."

"Oh, gosh, I'm sorry, Captain. I forgot who I was talking to."

"You know about my family?"

"Everybody here knows, sir. We're sorry. We heard it from the senior flight attendant on your aborted Heathrow run. You got the word on your first officer on that flight, didn't you?"

"I heard something but never got any official word."

"What'd you hear?"

"Suicide."

"Right. Awful."

"Can you check on something for me?"

"If it's in my power, Captain."

"My daughter is trying to get back this way from California."

"Unlikely."

"I know, but she's on her way. Trying anyway. She'll more than likely try to fly Pan. Can you check and see if she's on any of the manifests coming east?"

"Shouldn't be too hard. There are precious few, and you know none of them will be landing here."

"How about Milwaukee?"

"Don't think so." He was tapping computer keys. "Where would she originate?"

"Somewhere near Palo Alto."

"Not good."

"Why?"

"Hardly anything coming out of there. Let me check."

Rayford could hear the man talking to himself, trying things, suggesting options. "Air California to Utah. Hey! Found her! Name Chloe with your last name?"

"That's her!"

"She checked in at Palo Alto. Pan put her on a bus to some outlying strip. Flew her to Salt Lake City on Air California. First time out of the state for that plane, I'll bet. She got on a Pan-Con plane, oh, an oldie, and they took her to, um, oh brother. Enid, Oklahoma."

"Enid? That's never been on our routes."

"No kidding. They were overrun with Dallas's spillover, too. Anyway, she's flying Ozark to Springfield, Illinois."

"Ozark!"

"I just work here, Cap."

"Well, somebody's trying to make it work, aren't they?"

"Yeah, the good news is, we've got a turboprop or two down there that can get her up into the area, but it doesn't say where she might land. It might not even come up on this screen because they won't know till they get close."

"How will I know where to pick her up?"

"You may not. I'm sure she'll call you when she lands. Who knows? Maybe she'll just show up."

"That would be nice."

"Well, I'm sorry for what you're going through, sir, but you can be grateful your daughter didn't get on Pan-Con directly out of Palo Alto. The last one out of there went down last night. No survivors."

"And this was after the disappearances?"

"Just last night. Totally unrelated."

"Wouldn't that have been a kick in the teeth?" Rayford said.

"Indeed."

8

WHEN THE OTHER senior writers and editors drifted back to their offices, Steve Plank insisted Buck Williams go home and rest before coming back for an eight o'clock meeting that evening.

"I'd rather get done now and go home for the night."

"I know," the executive editor said, "but we've got a lot to do and I want you sharp."

Still, Buck was reluctant. "How soon can I get to London?"

"What have you got there?"

Buck filled Steve in on his tip about a major U.S. financier meeting with international colleagues and introducing a rising European politico. "Oh, man, Buck," Steve said, "we're all over that. You mean Carpathia."

Buck was stunned. "I do?"

"He was the guy Rosenzweig was so impressed with."

"Yeah, but you think he's the one my informant is—"

"Man, you *have* been out of touch," Steve said. "It's not that big a deal. The financier has to be Jonathan Stonagal, who seems to be sponsoring him. I told you Carpathia was coming to address the U.N., didn't I?"

"So he's the new Romanian ambassador to the U.N.?" Buck said.

"Hardly."

"What then?"

"President of the country."

"Didn't they just elect a leader, what, eighteen months ago?" Buck said, remembering Dirk's tip that a new leader would seem out of place and time.

"Big shake-up there," Steve said. "Better check it out."

"I will."

"I don't mean you. I really don't think there's much of a story. The guy is young and dashing and all that, charming and persuasive as I understand it. He had been a meteoric business star, making a killing when Romanian markets opened to the West years ago. But as of last week he wasn't even in their senate yet. He was only in the lower house."

"The House of Deputies," Buck said.

"How did you know that?"

Buck grinned. "Rosenzweig educated me."

"For a minute there I thought you really did know everything. That's what you get accused of around here, you know."

"What a crime."

"But you play it with such humility."

"That's me. So, Steve, why don't you think it's important that a guy like Carpathia comes from nowhere to unseat the president of Romania?"

"He didn't exactly come from nowhere. His businesses were built on Stonagal financing. And Carpathia has been a disarmament crusader, very popular with his colleagues and the people."

"But disarmament doesn't fit with Stonagal. Isn't he a closet hawk?"

Plank nodded.

"So there are mysteries."

"Some, but, Buck, what could be bigger than the story you're on? You haven't got time to fool with a guy who becomes president of a nonstrategic country."

"There's something there, though, Steve. My guy in London tips me off. Carpathia's tied in with the most influential nonpolitician in the world. He goes from lower house to president without a popular election."

"And—"

"There's more? Which side of this argument are you on? Did he have the sitting president killed or something?"

"Interesting you should say that, because the only wrinkle in Carpathia's history is some rumors that he was ruthless with his business competition years ago."

"How ruthless?"

"People took dirt naps."

"Ooh, Steve, you talk just like a mobster."

"And listen, the previous president stepped down for Carpathia. Insisted on his installation."

"And you say there's no story here?"

"This is like the old South American coups, Buck. A new one every week. Big deal. So Carpathia's beholden to Stonagal. All that means is that Stonagal will have free rein in the financial world of an Eastern European country that thinks the best thing that ever happened to it was the destruction of Russia."

"But, Steve, this is like a freshman congressman becoming president of the United States in an off-election year, no vote, president steps aside, and everybody's happy."

"No, no, no, big difference. We're talking Romania here, Buck. *Romania.*

Nonstrategic, scant gross national product, never invaded anybody, never anyone's strategically. There's nothing there but low-level internal politics."

"It still smells major to me," Buck said. "Rosenzweig was high on this guy, and he's an astute observer. Now Carpathia's coming to speak at the U.N. What next?"

"You forget he was coming to the U.N. *before* he became president of Romania."

"That's another puzzle. He was a nobody."

"He's a new name and face in disarmament. He gets his season in the sun, his fifteen minutes of fame. Trust me, you're not going to hear of him again."

"Stonagal had to be behind the U.N. gig, too," Buck said. "You know Diamond John is a personal friend of our ambassador."

"Stonagal is a personal friend of every elected official from the president to the mayors of most medium-sized cities, Buck. So what? He knows how to play the game. He reminds me of old Joe Kennedy or one of the Rockefellers, all right? What's your point?"

"Just that Carpathia is speaking at the U.N. on Stonagal's influence."

"Probably. So what?"

"He's up to something."

"Stonagal's always up to something, keeping the skids greased for one of his projects. OK, so he gets a businessman into Romanian politics, maybe even gets him installed as president. Who knows, maybe he even got him his little audience with Rosenzweig, which never amounted to anything. Now he gets Carpathia a little international exposure. That happens all the time because of guys like Stonagal. Would you rather chase this nonstory than tie together a cover piece that tries to make sense of the most monumental and tragic phenomenon in the history of the world?"

"Hmm, let me think about that," Buck said, smiling, as Plank punched him.

"Man, you can sure chase rabbit trails," the executive editor said.

"You used to like my instincts."

"I still do, but you're a little sleep-deprived right now."

"I'm definitely not going to London? Because I've got to tell my guy."

"Marge tried to reach the guy who was supposed to meet your plane. She can tell you how to get through and all that. But be back here by eight. I'm bringing in the department editors interested in the various international meetings coming here this month. You're going to be tying that coverage together, so—"

"So they can all hate me in the same meeting?" Buck said.

"They'll feel important."

"But *is* it important? You want me to ignore Carpathia, but you're going to complicate my life with, what was it, an ecumenical religious convention and a one-world-currency confab?"

"You *are* short on sleep, aren't you, Buck? This is why I'm still your boss. Don't you get it? Yes, I want coordination and I want a well-written piece. But think about it. This gives you automatic entrée to all these dignitaries. We're talking Jewish Nationalist leaders interested in one world government—"

"Unlikely and hardly compelling."

"—Orthodox Jews from all over the world looking at rebuilding the temple, or some such—"

"I'm being overrun by Jews."

"—international monetarists setting the stage for one world currency—"

"Also unlikely."

"But this will let you keep an eye on your favorite power broker—"

"Stonagal."

"Right, and heads of various religious groups looking to cooperate internationally."

"Bore me to death, why don't you? These people are discussing impossibilities. Since when have religious groups been able to get along?"

"You're still not getting it, Buck. You're going to have access to all these people—religious, monied, political—while trying to write a piece about what happened and why it happened. You can get the thinking of the greatest minds from the most diverse viewpoints."

Buck shrugged in surrender. "You've got a point. I still say our department editors are going to resent me."

"There's something to be said for consistency."

"I still want to try to get to Carpathia."

"That won't be hard. He's already a media darling in Europe. Eager to talk."

"And Stonagal."

"You know he never talks to the press, Buck."

"I like a challenge."

"Go home and take a load off. See you at eight."

Marge Potter was preparing to leave as Buck approached. "Oh yes," Marge said, setting down her stuff and flipping through her notebook. "I tried Dirk Burton several times. Got through once to his voice mail and left him your message. Received no confirmation. OK?"

"Thanks."

Buck wasn't sure he'd be able to rest at home with everything flying through his brain. He was pleasantly surprised when he reached street level to find that representatives of various cab companies were posted outside office buildings, directing people to cabs that could reach certain areas via circuitous routes. For premium fares, of course. For thirty dollars, in a shared cab, Buck was let off two blocks from his apartment. In three hours he would have to be back at the office, so he made arrangements with the cabbie to meet him at the same spot at seven forty-five. That, he decided, would be a miracle. With all the cabs in New York, he had never before had to make such an arrangement, and to his knowledge had never even seen the same cabbie twice.

* * *

Rayford was pacing, miserable. He came to the painful realization that this was the worst season of his life. He had never even come close before. His parents had been older than those of his peers. When they had died within two years of each other, it had been a relief. They were not well, not lucid. He loved them and they were no burden, but they had virtually died to him years before, due to strokes and other ailments. When they did pass, Rayford had grieved in a way, but mostly he was just sentimental about them. He had good memories, he appreciated the kindness and sympathy he received at their funerals, and he got on with his life. Whatever tears he shed were not from remorse or heartache. He felt primarily nostalgic and melancholy.

The rest of his life had been without complication or pain. Becoming a pilot was akin to rising to any other highly paid professional level. You had to be intelligent and disciplined, accomplished. He came through the ranks in the usual way—military-reserve duty, small planes, then bigger ones, then jets and fighters. Finally he had reached the pinnacle.

He had met Irene in Reserve Officer Training Corps in college. She had been an army brat who had never rebelled. Many of her chums had turned their backs on military life and didn't even want to own up to it. Her father had been killed in battle and her mother married another military man, so Irene had seen or lived on nearly every army base in the United States.

They were married when Rayford was a senior in college and Irene a sophomore. She dropped out when he went into the military, and everything had been on schedule since. They had Chloe during their first year of marriage but, due to complications, waited another eight years for Ray Jr. Rayford was thrilled with both children, but he had to admit he had longed for a namesake boy.

Unfortunately, Raymie came along during a bleak period for Rayford. He was thirty and feeling older, and he didn't enjoy having a pregnant wife. Many people thought, because of his premature but not unattractive gray hair, that he was older, and so he endured the jokes about being an old father. It was a particularly difficult pregnancy for Irene, and Raymie was a couple of weeks late. Chloe was a spirited eight-year-old, so Rayford disengaged as much as possible.

Irene, he believed, slipped into at least some mild depression during that time and was short tempered with him and weepy. At work Rayford was in charge, listened to, and admired. He had been rated for the biggest, latest, and most sophisticated planes in the Pan-Continental stable. His work life was going swimmingly; he didn't enjoy going home.

He had drunk more during that period than ever before or since, and the marriage had gone through its most trying time. He was frequently late getting home and at times even fibbed about his schedule so he could leave a day early or come back a day late. Irene accused him of all manner of affairs, and because she was wrong, he denied them with great vigor and, he felt, justified anger.

The truth was, he was hoping for and angling for just what she was charging. What frustrated him so was that, despite his looks and bearing, it just wasn't in him to pull it off. He didn't have the moves, the patter, the style. A flight attendant had once called him a hunk, but he felt like a geek, an egghead. Sure, he had access to any woman with a price, but that was beneath him. While he toyed with and hoped for an old-fashioned affair, he somehow couldn't bring himself to stoop to something as tawdry as paying for sex.

Had Irene known how hard he was trying to be unfaithful, she would have left him. As it was, he had indulged in that make-out session at the Christmas party before Raymie was born, but he was so inebriated he could hardly remember it.

The guilt and nearly spoiling his image straightened him up and made him cut down on his drinking. Seeing Raymie born sobered him even more. It was time to grow up and take as much responsibility as a husband and father as he did as a pilot.

But now, as Rayford ran all those memories through his throbbing head, he felt the deepest regret and remorse a man can feel. He felt like a failure. He was so unworthy of Irene. Somehow he knew now, though he had never allowed himself to consider it before, that she couldn't in any way have been as naive or stupid as he had hoped and imagined. She had to have known how vapid he was, how shallow, and yes, cheap. And yet she had stayed by him, loved him, fought to keep the marriage together.

He couldn't argue that she became a different person after she switched churches and got serious about her faith. She preached at him at first, sure. She was excited and wanted him to discover what she had found. He ran. Eventually she either gave up or resigned herself to the fact that he was not going to come around by her pleading or cajoling. Now he knew from seeing her list that she had never given up. She had simply taken to praying for him.

No wonder Rayford had never gotten that close to ultimately defiling his marriage with Hattie Durham. Hattie! How ashamed he was of that silly pursuit! For all he knew, Hattie was innocent. She had never bad-mouthed his wife or the fact that he was married. She had never suggested anything inappropriate, at least for her age. Young people were more touchy and flirtatious, and she claimed no moral or religious code. That Rayford had obsessed over the possibilities with Hattie, while she probably hardly knew it, made him feel all the more foolish.

Where was this guilt coming from? He had locked eyes with Hattie numerous times, and they had spent hours alone together over dinners in various cities. But she had never asked him to her room or tried to kiss him or even hold his hand. Maybe she would have responded had he been the aggressor, but maybe not. She might just as easily have been offended, insulted, disappointed.

Rayford shook his head. Not only was he guilty of lusting after a woman to whom he had no right, but he was still such a klutz he hadn't even known how to pursue her.

And now he faced the darkest hours of his soul. He was nervous about Chloe. He wanted her home and safe in the worst way, hoping that having his own flesh and blood in the house would somehow assuage his grief and pain. He knew he should be hungry again, but nothing appealed. Even the fragrant and tasty cookies he thought he would have to ration had become painful reminders of Irene. Maybe tomorrow.

Rayford switched on the television, not out of interest in seeing more mayhem, but with the hope of some news of order, traffic clearing, people connecting. After a minute or two of the same old same old, he turned it off again. He rejected the idea of calling O'Hare about the likelihood of getting in to get his car, because he didn't want to tie up the phone for even a minute in case Chloe was trying to get through. It had been hours since he'd heard she left Palo Alto. How long would it take to make all those crazy connections and finally get on an Ozark flight from Springfield to the Chicago area? He remembered the oldest joke in the airline industry: Ozark spelled backward is Krazo. Only it didn't amuse him just then.

He leaped when the phone rang, but it was not Chloe. "I'm sorry, Captain," Hattie said. "I promised to call you back, but I fell asleep after the call I took and have been out ever since."

"That's quite all right, Hattie. In fact, I need to—"

"I mean, I didn't want to bother you anyway at a time like this."

"No, that's OK, I just—"

"Have you talked to Chloe?"

"I'm waiting for her to call right now, so I really have to get off!"

Rayford had been more curt than he intended and Hattie was, at first, silent. "Well, all right then. I'm sorry."

"I'll call you, Hattie. OK?"

"OK."

She had sounded hurt. He was sorry about that, but not sorry that he had gotten rid of her for the time being. He knew she was only trying to help and be kind, but she hadn't been listening. She was alone and afraid just like he was, and no doubt by now she had found out about her family. Oh, no! He hadn't even asked about them! She would hate him, and why shouldn't she? *How selfish could I be?* he wondered.

Eager as he was to hear from Chloe, he had to risk a couple more minutes on the phone. He dialed Hattie, but her line was busy.

* * *

Buck tried calling Dirk Burton in London as soon as he got home, not wanting to wait longer with the time difference overseas. He got a puzzling response. Dirk's personal answering machine ran through its usual message, but as soon as the leave-a-message beep sounded, a longer tone indicated that the tape was full. Strange. Dirk was either sleeping through it all or—

Buck had not considered that Dirk could have disappeared. Besides leaving Buck with a million questions about Stonagal, Carpathia, Todd-Cothran, and the whole phenomenon, Dirk was one of his best friends from Princeton. *Oh, please let this be a coincidence,* he thought. *Let him be traveling.*

As soon as Buck hung up, his phone rang. Of all people, it was Hattie Durham. She was crying. "I'm sorry to bother you, Mr. Williams, and I had promised myself I would never use your home number—"

"That's all right, Hattie. What is it?"

"Well, it's silly really, but I just went through something, and I don't have anybody to talk to about it. I couldn't get through to my mother and sisters, and well, I just thought maybe you'd understand."

"Try me."

She told Buck about her call to Captain Steele and brought him up to date on who Steele was, that he had lost his wife and son, and that she had been late calling him back after hearing her good news from Buck. "And then he just brushed me off because he's waiting for a call from his daughter."

"I can understand that," Buck tried, rolling his eyes. How did he get into this lonely hearts club? Didn't she have any girlfriends to unload on?

"I can, too," she said. "That's just it. And I know he's grieving because it's like his wife and son are dead, but he knew I was on pins and needles about my family, and he never even asked."

"Well, I'm sure it is all just part of the tension of the moment, the grief, like you say, and—"

"Oh, I know it. I just wanted to talk to somebody, and I thought of you."

"Well, hey, anytime," Buck lied. *Oh, boy,* he thought. *My home number is definitely going to come off that next batch of business cards.* "Listen, I'd better let you go. I've got an evening meeting tonight myself, and—"

"Well, thanks for listening."

"I understand," he said, though he doubted he ever would. Maybe Hattie showed more depth and sense when she wasn't under stress. He hoped so.

+ + +

Rayford was glad Hattie's line was busy, because he could tell her he had tried to call her right back, but he didn't have to tie up his phone any longer. A minute later, his phone rang again.

"Captain, it's me again. I'm sorry, I won't keep you long, but I thought you might have tried to call me. I shut off the call waiting like I promised, but I've been on the phone, so—"

"As a matter of fact, I did, Hattie. What have you found out about your family?"

"They're fine." She was crying.

"Oh, thank God," he said.

Rayford wondered what had gotten into him. He said he was happy for her, but he had come to the conclusion that those who had not disappeared had missed out on the greatest event of cosmic history. But what was he supposed to say—"Oh, I'm sorry your family was left behind, too"?

When he hung up, Rayford sat next to the phone with a nagging feeling that he had for sure missed Chloe's call this time. It made him mad. His stomach was growling and he knew he should eat, but he had decided he would hold off as long as possible, hoping to eat with Chloe when she arrived. Knowing her, she wouldn't have eaten a thing.

9

BUCK'S SUBCONSCIOUS waking system failed him that evening, but by 8:45 p.m. he was back in Steve Plank's office, disheveled and apologetic. And he had been right. He felt the resentment from veteran department editors. Juan Ortiz, chief of the international politics section, was incensed that Buck should have anything to do with the summit conference Juan planned to cover in two weeks.

"The Jewish Nationalists are discussing an issue I have been following for years. Who would have believed they would consider warming to one world government? That they would even entertain the discussion is monumental. They're meeting here, rather than in Jerusalem or Tel Aviv, because their idea is so revolutionary. Most Israeli Nationalists think the Holy Land has gone too far with its bounty already. This is historic."

"Then what's your problem," Plank said, "with my adding our top guy to the coverage?"

"Because *I* am your top guy on this."

"I'm trying to make sense of all these meetings," Plank said.

Jimmy Borland, the religion editor, weighed in. "I understand Juan's objections, but I've got two meetings at the same time. I welcome the help."

"Now we're getting somewhere," Plank said.

"But I'll be frank, Buck," Borland added. "I want a say in the final piece."

"Of course," Plank said.

"Not so fast," Buck said. "I don't want to be treated like a pool reporter here. I'm going to have my own take on these meetings, and I'm not trying to horn in on your expert territories. I wouldn't want to do the coverages of the individual meetings themselves. I want to bring some coordination, find the meaning, the common denominators. Jimmy, your two groups—the religious Jews who want to rebuild the temple and the ecumenicalists who want some sort of one-world religious order—are they going to be at odds with each other? Will there be religious Jews—"

"Orthodox."

"OK, Orthodox Jews at the ecumenical meeting? Because that seems at cross purposes with rebuilding the temple."

"Well, at least you're thinking like a religion editor," Jimmy said. "That's encouraging."

"But what's your thought?"

"I don't know. That's what makes this so interesting. That they should meet at the same time in the same city is too good to be true."

Financial editor Barbara Donahue brought closure to the discussion. "I've dealt with you before on these kinds of efforts, Steve," she said. "And I appreciate the way you let everybody vent without threat. But we all know your mind is made up about Buck's involvement, so let's lick our wounds and get on with it. If we each get to put our own spin on the coverage in our departments and have some input on the overall piece that I assume goes in the main well, let's get on with it."

Even Ortiz nodded, though to Buck he seemed reluctant.

"Buck's the quarterback," Plank said, "so keep in touch with him. He'll report to me. You want to say anything, Buck?"

"Just thanks a lot," he said ruefully, causing everyone to chuckle. "Barbara, your monetarists are meeting right at the U.N., like they did when they went to the three-currency thing?"

She nodded. "Same place and pretty much the same people."

"How involved is Jonathan Stonagal?"

"Overtly, you mean?" she said.

"Well, everybody knows he's circumspect. But is there a Stonagal influence?"

"Does a duck have lips?"

Buck smiled and jotted a note. "I'll take that as a yes. I'd like to hang around that one, maybe try to get to Diamond John."

"Good luck. He probably won't show his face."

"But he'll be in town, won't he, Barbara? Wasn't he at the Plaza for the duration last time?"

"You do get around, don't you?" she said.

"Well, he only had each of the principals up to his suite every day."

Juan Ortiz raised a hand. "I'm going along with this, and I have nothing personal against you, Buck. But I don't believe there is a way to coordinate this story without inventing some tie-in. I mean, if you want to lead off a feature story by saying there were four important international meetings in town almost all at once, fine. But to make them interrelated would be stretching."

"If I find that they aren't interrelated, there won't be an overall story," Buck said. "Fair enough?"

\+ + +

Rayford Steele was nearly beside himself with worry, compounded by his grief. Where was Chloe? He had been inside all day, pacing, mourning, thinking. He felt stale and claustrophobic. He had called Pan-Continental and was told his car might be released by the time he got back from his weekend flight. The news on TV showed the amazing progress being made at clearing the roadways and getting mass transportation rolling again. But the landscape would appear tacky for months. Cranes and wreckers had run out of junkyards, so the twisted wreckages remained in hazardous piles at the sides of roads and expressways.

By the time Rayford got around to calling his wife's church, it was after hours, and he was grateful he wouldn't have to talk to anyone. As he hoped, a new message was on their answering machine, though it was communicated by a stunned-sounding male voice.

"You have reached New Hope Village Church. We are planning a weekly Bible study, but for the time being we will meet just once each Sunday at 10 a.m. While our entire staff, except me, and most of our congregation are gone, the few of us left are maintaining the building and distributing a videotape our senior pastor prepared for a time such as this. You may come by the church office anytime to pick up a free copy, and we look forward to seeing you Sunday morning."

Well, of course, Rayford thought, *that pastor had often spoken of the Rapture of the church.* That was why Irene was so enamored with it. What a creative idea, to tape a message for those who had been left behind! He and Chloe would have to get one the next day. He hoped she would be as interested as he was in discovering the truth.

Rayford gazed out the front window in the darkness, just in time to see Chloe, one big suitcase on the ground next to her, paying a cabdriver. He ran from the house in his stocking feet and gathered her into his arms. "Oh, Daddy!" she wailed. "How's everybody?"

He shook his head.

"I don't want to hear this," she said, pulling away from him and looking to the house as if expecting her mother or brother to appear in the doorway.

"It's just you and me, Chloe," Rayford said, and they stood together in the darkness, crying.

\+ + +

It was Friday before Buck Williams was able to track down Dirk Burton. He reached the supervisor in Dirk's area of the London Exchange. "You must tell me precisely who you are and your specific relationship to Mr. Burton before

I am allowed to inform you as to his disposition," Nigel Leonard said. "I am also constrained to inform you that this conversation shall be taped, beginning immediately."

"I'm sorry?"

"I'm taping our conversation, sir. If that is a problem for you, you may disconnect."

"I don't follow."

"What's to follow? You understand what a tape is, do you?"

"Of course, and I'm turning mine on now as well, if you don't mind."

"Well, I *do* mind, Mr. Williams. Why on earth would *you* be taping?"

"Why would *you*?"

"We are the ones with a most unfortunate situation, and we need to investigate all leads."

"What situation? Was Dirk among those who disappeared?"

"Nothing so tidy as that, I'm afraid."

"Tell me."

"First your reason for asking."

"I'm an old friend. We were college classmates."

"Where?"

"Princeton."

"Very well. When?"

Buck told him.

"Very well. The last time you spoke to him?"

"I don't recall, OK? We've been trading voice-mail messages."

"Your occupation?"

Buck hesitated. "Senior writer, *Global Weekly*, New York."

"Would your interest be journalistic in nature?"

"I won't preclude that," Buck said, trying not to let his anger seep through, "but I can't imagine that my friend, important as he is to me, is of interest to my readers."

"Mr. Williams," Nigel said carefully, "allow me to state categorically, on both our tapes apparently, that what I am about to say is strictly off the record. Do you understand?"

"I—"

"Because I am aware that both in your country and in the British Commonwealth, anything said following an assertion that we are off the record is protected."

"Granted," Buck said.

"Beg pardon?"

"You heard me. Granted. We're off the record. Now where is Dirk?"

"Mr. Burton's body was discovered in his flat this morning. He had suffered a bullet wound to the head. I'm sorry, as you were a friend, but suicide has been determined."

Buck was nearly speechless. "By whom?" he managed.

"The authorities."

"What authorities?"

"Scotland Yard and security personnel here at the exchange."

Scotland Yard? Buck thought. *We'll see about that.* "Why is the exchange involved?"

"We're protective of our information and our personnel, sir."

"Suicide is impossible, you know," Buck said.

"Do I?"

"If you are his supervisor, you know."

"There have been countless suicides since the disappearances, sir."

Buck was shaking his head as if Nigel could see him from across the Atlantic. "Dirk didn't kill himself, and you know it."

"Sir, I can appreciate your sentiments, but I don't know any more than you did what was in Mr. Burton's mind. I was partial to him, but I would not be in a position to question the conclusion of the medical examiner."

Buck slammed the phone down and marched into Steve Plank's office. He told Steve what he had heard.

"That's terrible," Steve said.

"I have a contact at Scotland Yard who knows Dirk, but I don't dare talk to him about it by phone. Can I have Marge book me on the next flight to London? I'll be back in time for all these summits, but I've got to go."

"If you can get a flight. I don't know that JFK is even open yet."

"How about La Guardia?"

"Ask Marge. You know Carpathia will be here tomorrow."

"You said yourself he was small potatoes. Maybe he'll still be here when I get back."

+ + +

Rayford Steele hadn't been able to talk his grieving daughter into leaving the house. Chloe had spent hours in her little brother's room, and then in her parents' bedroom, picking through their personal effects to add to the boxes of memories her father had put together. Rayford felt so bad for her. He had secretly hoped she would be of comfort to him. He knew she would be eventually. But for now she needed time to face her own loss. Once she had cried herself out, she was ready to talk. And after she had reminisced to the point where Rayford didn't know if his heart could take any more, she finally changed the subject to the phenomenon of the disappearances themselves.

"Daddy, in California they're actually buying into the space invasion theory."

"You're kidding."

"No. Maybe it's because you were always so practical and skeptical about all that tabloid newspaper stuff, but I just can't get into it. I mean, it has to be something supernatural or otherworldly, but—"

"But what?"

"It just seems that if some alien life force was capable of doing this, they would also be capable of communicating to us. Wouldn't they want to take over now or demand ransom or get us to do something for them?"

"Who? Martians?"

"Daddy! I'm not saying I believe it. I'm saying I don't. But doesn't my reasoning make sense?"

"You don't have to convince me. I admit I wouldn't have dreamed any of this even possible a week ago, but my logic has been stretched to the breaking point."

Rayford hoped Chloe would ask his theory. He didn't want to start right in on a religious theme. She had always been antagonistic about that, having stopped going to church in high school when both he and Irene gave up fighting with her over it. She was a good kid, never in trouble. She made grades good enough to get her a partial academic scholarship, and though she occasionally stayed out too late and went through a boy-crazy period in high school, they had never had to bail her out of jail and there was never any evidence of drug use. He didn't take that lightly.

Rayford and Irene knew Chloe had come home from more than one party drunk enough to spend the night vomiting. The first time, he and Irene chose to ignore it, to act as if it didn't happen. They believed she was levelheaded enough to know better the next time. When the next time came, Rayford had a chat with her.

"I know, I know, I know, OK, Dad? You don't need to start in on me."

"I'm not starting in on you. I want to make sure you know enough to not drive if you drink too much."

"Of course I do."

"And you know how stupid and dangerous it is to drink too much."

"I thought you weren't starting in on me."

"Just tell me you know."

"I think I already said that."

He had shaken his head and said nothing.

"Daddy, don't give up on me. Go ahead, give me both barrels. Prove you care."

"Don't make fun of me," he had said. "Someday you're going to have a child and you won't know what to say or do either. When you love somebody with all your heart and all you care about is her welfare—"

Rayford hadn't been able to continue. For the first time in his adult life, he had choked up. It had never happened during his arguments with Irene. He had always been too defensive, concerned too much about making his point to think about how much he cared for her. But with Chloe, he really wanted to say the right thing, to protect her from herself. He wanted her to know how much he loved her, and it was coming out all wrong. It was as if he were punishing, lecturing, reprimanding, condescending. That had caused him to break.

Though he hadn't planned it, that involuntary show of emotion got through to Chloe. For months she had been drifting from him, from both her parents. She had been sullen, cold, independent, sarcastic, challenging. He knew it was all part of growing up and becoming one's own person, but it was a painful, scary time.

As he bit his lip and breathed deeply, hoping to regain composure and not embarrass himself, Chloe had come to him and wrapped her arms around his neck, just as she had as a little girl. "Oh, Daddy, don't cry," she had said. "I know you love me. I know you care. Don't worry about me. I learned my lesson and I won't be stupid again, I promise."

He had dissolved into tears, and so had she. They had bonded as never before. He didn't recall ever having to discipline her again, and though she had not come back to church, he had started to drift by then himself. They had become buddies, and she was growing up to be just like him. Irene had kidded him that their children each had their own favorite parent.

Now, just days after Irene and Raymie had disappeared, Rayford hoped the relationship that had really begun with an emotional moment when Chloe was in high school would blossom so they could talk. What was more important than what had happened? He knew now what her crazy college friends and the typical Californian believed. What else was new? He always generalized that people on the West Coast afforded the tabloids the same weight Midwesterners gave the *Chicago Tribune* or even the *New York Times*.

Late in the day, Friday, Rayford and Chloe reluctantly agreed they should eat, and they worked together in the kitchen, rustling up a healthy mixture of fruits and vegetables. There was something calming and healing about working with her in silence. It was painful on the one hand, because anything domestic reminded him of Irene. And when they sat to eat, they automatically sat in their customary spots at either end of the table—which made the other two open spots that much more conspicuous.

Rayford noticed Chloe clouding up again, and he knew she was feeling what he was. It hadn't been that many years since they had enjoyed three or four meals a week together as a family. Irene had always sat on his left, Raymie on his right, and Chloe directly across. The emptiness and the silence were jarring.

Rayford was ravenous and finished a huge salad. Chloe stopped eating soon after she had begun and wept silently, her head down, tears falling in her lap. Her father took her hand, and she rose and sat in his lap, hiding her face and sobbing. His heart aching for her, Rayford rocked her until she was silent. "Where are they?" she whined at last.

"You want to know where I think they are?" he said. "Do you really want to know?"

"Of course!"

"I believe they are in heaven."

"Oh, Daddy! There were some religious nuts at school who were saying that, but if they knew so much about it, how come they didn't go?"

"Maybe they realized they had been wrong and had missed their opportunity."

"You think that's what we've done?" Chloe said, returning to her chair.

"I'm afraid so. Didn't your mother tell you she believed that Jesus could come back some day and take his people directly to heaven before they died?"

"Sure, but she was always more religious than the rest of us. I thought she was just getting a little carried away."

"Good choice of words."

"Hm?"

"She got carried away, Chloe. Raymie too."

"You don't really believe that, do you?"

"I do."

"That's about as crazy as the Martian invasion theory."

Rayford felt defensive. "So what's *your* theory?"

Chloe began to clear the table and spoke with her back to him. "I'm honest enough to admit I don't know."

"So now I'm not being honest?"

Chloe turned to face him, sympathy on her face. "Don't you see, Dad? You've gravitated to the least painful possibility. If we were voting, my first choice would be that my mom and my little brother are in heaven with God, sitting on clouds, playing their harps."

"So I'm deluding myself, is that what you're saying?"

"Daddy, I don't fault you. But you have to admit this is pretty far-fetched."

Now Rayford was angry. "What's more far-fetched than people disappearing right out of their clothes? Who else could have done that? Years ago we'd have blamed it on the Soviets, said they had developed some super new technology, some death ray that affected only human flesh and bone. But there's no Soviet threat anymore, and the Russians lost people, too. And how did this . . . this whatever it was—how did it choose who to take and who to leave?"

"You're saying the only logical explanation is God, that he took his own and left the rest of us?"

"That's what I'm saying."

"I don't want to hear this."

"Chloe, our own family is a perfect picture of what happened. If what I'm saying is right, the logical two people are gone and the logical two were left."

"You think I'm that much of a sinner?"

"Chloe, listen. Whatever you are, I am. I'm not judging you. If I'm right about this, we missed something. I always called myself a Christian, mostly because I was raised that way and I wasn't Jewish."

"Now you're saying you're not a Christian?"

"Chloe, I think the Christians are gone."

"So I'm not a Christian either?"

"You're my daughter and the only other member of my family still left; I love you more than anything on earth. But if the Christians are gone and everyone else is left, I don't think anyone is a Christian."

"Some kind of a super Christian, you mean."

"Yeah, a true Christian. Apparently those who were taken were recognized by God as truly his. How else can I say it?"

"Daddy, what does this make God? Some sick, sadistic dictator?"

"Careful, honey. You think I'm wrong, but what if I'm right?"

"Then God is spiteful, hateful, mean. Who wants to go to heaven with a God like that?"

"If that's where your mom and Raymie are, that's where I want to be."

"I want to be with them, too, Daddy! But tell me how this fits with a loving, merciful God. When I went to church, I got tired of hearing how loving God is. He never answered *my* prayers and I never felt like he knew me or cared about me. Now you're saying I was right. He didn't. I didn't qualify, so I got left behind? You'd better hope you're not right."

"But if I'm not right, who is right, Chloe? Where are they? Where is everybody?"

"See? You've latched onto this heaven thing because it makes you feel better. But it makes me feel worse. I don't buy it. I don't even want to consider it."

Rayford dropped the subject and went to watch television. Limited regular programming had resumed, but he was still able to find continuing news coverage. He was struck by the unusual name of the new Romanian president he had recently read about. Carpathia. He was scheduled to arrive at La Guardia in New York on Saturday and hold a press conference Monday morning before addressing the United Nations.

So La Guardia was open. That was where Rayford was supposed to fly later that evening with an oversold flight. He called Pan-Continental at O'Hare. "Glad you called," a supervisor said. "I was about to call you. Is your 777 rating up to date?"

"No. I used to fly them regularly, but I prefer the 747 and haven't kept my currency this year on the '77."

"That's all we're flying east this weekend. We'll have to get somebody else. And you need to get rated soon, just so we have flexibility."

"Duly noted. What's next for me?"

"You want a Monday run to Atlanta and back the same day?"

"On a . . . ?"

"'47."

"Sounds perfect. Can you tell me if there'll be room on that flight?"

"For?"

"A family member."

"Let me check." Rayford heard the computer keys and the distracted voice. "While I'm checking, ah, we got a request from a crew member to be assigned to your next flight, only I think she was thinking you'd be going on that run tonight, Logan to JFK and back."

"Who? Hattie Durham?"

"Let me see. Right."

"So is she assigned to Boston and New York?"

"Uh-huh."

"And I'm not, so that question is moot, right?"

"I guess so. You got any leanings one way or the other?"

"I'm sorry?"

"She's gonna ask again, is my guess. You have any objection to her being assigned to one of your upcoming flights?"

"Well, it won't be Atlanta, right? That's too soon."

"Right."

Rayford sighed. "No objections, I guess. No, wait. Let's just let it happen if it happens."

"I'm not following you, Captain."

"I'm just saying if she gets assigned in the normal course, I have no objection. But let's not go through any gymnastics to make it happen."

"Gotcha. And your flight to Atlanta looks like it could handle your freebie. Name?"

"Chloe Steele."

"I'll put her in first class, but if they sell out, you know I've got to bump her back."

When Rayford got off the phone, Chloe drifted into the room. "I'm not flying tonight," he said.

"Is that good news or bad news?"

"I'm relieved. I get to spend more time with you."

"After the way I talked to you? I figured you'd want me out of sight and out of mind."

"Chloe, we can talk frankly to each other. You're my family. I hate to think of being away from you at all. I've got a down-and-back flight to Atlanta Monday and have you booked in first class if you want to go."

"Sure."

"And I only wish you hadn't said one thing."

"Which?"

"That you don't even want to consider my theory. You've always liked my theories. I don't mind your saying you don't buy it. I don't know enough to articulate it in a way that makes any sense. But your mother talked about this. Once she even warned me that if I didn't know for sure I'd be going if Christ returned for his people, I shouldn't be flip about it."

"But you were?"

"I sure was. But never again."

"Well, Daddy, I'm not being flip about it. I just can't accept it, that's all."

"That's fair. But don't say you won't even consider it."

"Well, did you consider the space invaders theory?"

"As a matter of fact, I did."

"You're kidding."

"I considered everything. This was so far beyond human experience, what were we supposed to think?"

"OK, so if I take back that I won't even consider it, what does that mean? We become religious fanatics all of a sudden, start going to church, what? And who says it's not too late? If you're right, maybe we missed our chance forever."

"That's what we have to find out, don't you think? Let's check this out, see if there's anything to it. If there is, we should want nothing more than to know if there's still a chance we can be with Mom and Raymie again someday."

Chloe sat shaking her head. "Gee, Dad. I don't know."

"Listen, I called the church your mom was going to."

"Oh, brother."

He told her about the recording and the offer of the tape.

"Dad! A tape for those left behind? Please!"

"You're coming at this as a skeptic, so sure it sounds ridiculous to you. I see no other logical explanation, so I can't wait to hear the tape."

"You're desperate."

"Of course I am! Aren't you?"

"I'm miserable and scared, but I'm not so desperate that I'm going to lose my faculties. Oh, Daddy, I'm sorry. Don't look at me like that. I don't blame you for checking this out. Go ahead, and don't worry about me."

"Will you go with me?"

"I'd rather not. But if you want me to . . ."

"You can wait in the car."

"It's not that. I'm not afraid of meeting someone I disagree with."

"We'll go over there tomorrow," Rayford said, disappointed in her reaction but no less determined to follow through, for her sake as much as his. If he was right, he did not want to fail his own daughter.

10

CAMERON WILLIAMS convinced himself he should not call his and Dirk Burton's mutual friend at Scotland Yard before leaving New York. With communications as difficult as they had been for days and after the strange conversation with Dirk's supervisor, Buck didn't want to risk someone listening in. The last thing he wanted was to compromise his Scotland Yard contact's integrity.

Buck took both his real and his phony passport and visa—a customary safety precaution—caught a late flight to London out of La Guardia Friday night, and arrived at Heathrow Saturday morning. He checked into the Tavistock Hotel and slept until midafternoon. Then he set out to find the truth about Dirk's death.

He started by calling Scotland Yard and asking for his friend Alan Tompkins, a mid-level operative. They were almost the same age, and Tompkins was a thin, dark-haired, and slightly rumpled investigator Buck had interviewed for a story on British terrorism.

They had taken to each other and even enjoyed an evening at a pub with Dirk. Dirk, Alan, and Buck had become pals, and whenever Buck visited, the three got together. Now, by phone, he tried to communicate to Tompkins in such a way that Alan would catch on quickly and not give away that they were friends—in case the line was tapped.

"Mr. Tompkins, you don't know me, but my name is Cameron Williams of *Global Weekly*." Before Alan could laugh and greet his friend, Buck quickly continued, "I'm here in London to do a story preliminary to the international monetary conference at the United Nations."

Alan sounded suddenly serious. "How can I help you, sir? What does that have to do with Scotland Yard?"

"I'm having trouble locating my interview subject, and I suspect foul play."

"And your subject?"

"His name is Burton. Dirk Burton. He works at the exchange."

"Let me do some checking and call you back."

A few minutes later, Buck's phone rang.

"Yes, Tompkins from the Yard. I wonder if you would be so kind as to come in and see me."

* * *

Early on Saturday morning in Mount Prospect, Illinois, Rayford Steele phoned the New Hope Village Church again. This time a man answered the phone. Rayford introduced himself as the husband of a former parishioner. "I know you, sir," the man said. "We've met. I'm Bruce Barnes, the visitation pastor."

"Oh, yes, hi."

"By former parishioner, I assume you're telling me that Irene is no longer with us?"

"That's right, and our son."

"Ray Jr., wasn't it?"

"Right."

"You also had an older daughter, did you not, a nonattender?"

"Chloe."

"And she—?"

"Is here with me. I was wondering what you all make of this—how many people have disappeared, are you still meeting, that kind of thing. I know you have a service on Sundays and that you're offering this tape."

"Well, you know just about everything then, Mr. Steele. Nearly every member and regular attender of this church is gone. I am the only person on the staff who remains. I have asked a few women to help out in the office. I have no idea how many will show up Sunday, but it would be a privilege to see you again."

"I'm very interested in that tape."

"I'd be happy to give you one in advance. It's what I will be discussing Sunday morning."

"I don't know how to ask this, Mr. Barnes."

"Bruce."

"Bruce. You'll be teaching or preaching or what?"

"Discussing. I will be playing the tape for any who have not heard it, and then we will discuss it."

"But you . . . I mean, how do you account for the fact that you are still here?"

"Mr. Steele, there is only one explanation for that, and I would prefer to discuss it with you in person. If I know when you might come by for the tape, I'll be sure to be here."

Rayford told him he and perhaps Chloe would come by that afternoon.

* * *

Alan Tompkins waited just inside the vestibule at Scotland Yard. When Buck arrived, Alan formally shook his hand and led him to a rundown compact, which he drove quickly to a dark pub a few miles away. "Let's not talk till we get there," Alan said, continually checking his mirrors. "I need to concentrate." Buck had never seen his friend so agitated and, yes, scared.

The pair took pints of dark ale to a booth in a secluded corner, but Alan never touched his. Buck, who hadn't eaten since the flight, switched his empty mug for Alan's full one and downed it, too. When the waitress came for the mugs, Buck ordered a sandwich. Alan declined, and Buck, knowing his limit, ordered a soda.

"I know this will be like pouring petrol on a flame," Alan began, "but I need to tell you this is a nasty business and that you want to stay as far away from it as you can."

"Darn right you're fanning my flame," Buck said. "What's going on?"

"Well, they say it's suicide, but—"

"But you and I both know that's nonsense. What's the evidence? Have you been to the scene?"

"I have. Shot through the temple, gun in his hand. No note."

"Anything missing?"

"Didn't appear to be, but, Cameron, you know what this is about."

"I don't!"

"Come, come, man. Dirk was a conspiracy theorist, always sniffing around Todd-Cothran's involvement with international money men, his role in the three-currency conference, even his association with your Stonagal chap."

"Alan, there are books about this stuff. People make a hobby of ascribing all manner of evil to the Tri-Lateral Commission, the Illuminati, even the Freemasons, for goodness sake. Dirk thought Todd-Cothran and Stonagal were part of something he called the Council of Ten or the Council of Wise Men. So what? It's harmless."

"But when you have an employee, admittedly several levels removed from the head of the exchange, trying to connect his boss to conspiracy theories, he has a problem."

Buck sighed. "So he gets called on the carpet, maybe he gets fired. But tell me how he gets dead or pushed to suicide."

"I'm going to tell you something, Cameron," Alan said. "I know he was murdered."

"Well, I'm pretty sure he was, too, because I think I'd have had a clue if he was suicidal."

"They're trying to pin it on his remorse over losing people in the great disappearance, but it won't wash. He didn't lose anybody close as far as I know."

"But you *know* he was murdered? Pretty strong words for an investigator."

"I know because I knew him, not because I'm an investigator."

"That won't hold up," Buck said. "I can also say I knew him and that he couldn't have committed suicide, but I'm prejudiced."

"Cameron, this is so simple it would be a cliché if Dirk wasn't our friend. What did we always kid him about?"

"Lots of things. Why?"

"We kidded him about being such a klutz."

"Yeah. So?"

"If he was with us right now, where would he be sitting?"

It suddenly dawned on Buck what Alan was driving at. "He would be sitting to one of our lefts, and he was such a klutz because he was left-handed."

"He was shot through the right temple and the so-called suicide weapon was found in his right hand."

"So what did your bosses say when you told them he was left-handed and that this had to be murder?"

"You're the first person I've told."

"Alan! What are you saying?"

"I'm saying I love my family. My parents are still living and I have an older brother and sister. I have a former wife I'm still fond of. I wouldn't mind snuffing her myself, but I certainly wouldn't want anyone else harming her."

"What are you afraid of?"

"I'm afraid of whoever was behind Dirk's murder, of course."

"But you'd have all of Scotland Yard behind you, man! You call yourself a law-enforcement officer and you're going to let this slide?"

"Yes, and that's just what you're going to do!"

"I am not. I wouldn't be able to live with myself."

"Do something about this and you won't be alive at all."

Buck waved the barmaid over and asked for chips. She brought him a heaping, greasy mass. It was just what he wanted. The ale had worked on him and the sandwich had not been enough to counteract it. He felt light-headed, and he was afraid he might not be hungry again for a long time.

"I'm listening," he whispered. "What are you trying to tell me? Who's gotten to you?"

"If you believe me, you won't like it."

"I have no reason not to believe you and I already don't like it. Now spill."

"Dirk's death was ruled a suicide and that was that. Scene cleared, body cremated.

I asked about an autopsy and was laughed off. My superior officer, Captain Sullivan, asked what I thought an autopsy would show. I told him abrasions, scrapes, signs of a struggle. He asked if I thought it made sense that a bloke would wrestle with himself before shooting himself. I kept the personal knowledge to myself."

"Why?"

"I smelled something."

"What if I put a story in an international magazine that pointed out the discrepancies? Something would have to happen."

"I have been told to tell you to go home and forget you ever heard about this suicide."

Buck squinted in disbelief. "Nobody knew I was coming."

"I think that's true, but somebody assumed you might show up. I wasn't surprised you came."

"Why should you be? My friend is dead, ostensibly by his own hand. I wasn't going to ignore that."

"You're going to ignore it now."

"You think I'm going to turn coward just because you did?"

"Cameron, you know me better than that."

"I wonder if I know you at all! I thought we were kindred spirits. We were justice freaks, Alan. Seekers of truth. I'm a journalist; you're an investigator. We're skeptics. What is this running from the truth, especially when it concerns our friend?"

"Did you hear me? I said I was told to call you off, if and when you showed up."

"Then why did you let me come to the Yard?"

"I'd have been in trouble if I had tipped you off."

"With whom?"

"I thought you'd never ask. I was visited by what you in America call a goon."

"A heavy?"

"Precisely."

"He threatened you?"

"He did. He said if I didn't want what had happened to my friend to happen to me or to my family, I would do as he said. I was afraid he was the same guy who had murdered Dirk."

"And he probably was. So, why didn't you report the threat?"

"I was going to. I started by trying to handle it myself. I told him he didn't have to worry about me. The next day I went to the exchange and asked for a meeting with Mr. Todd-Cothran."

"The big man himself?"

"In the flesh. I don't have an appointment, of course, but I insist it's Scotland Yard business, and he allows me in. His very office is intimidating. All mahogany and dark green draperies. Well, I get right down to business. I tell him, 'Sir, I believe you've had an employee murdered.' And just as calm as you like, he says, 'Tell you what, governor'—which is a term cockneys use on each other, not something people of his station usually call people of mine. Anyway, he says, 'Tell you what, governor, the next time somebody visits your flat at ten o'clock at night, as a certain gentleman did last night, greet him for me, won't you?'"

"What did you say?"

"What could I say? I was stunned to silence! I just looked at him and nodded. 'And let me tell you something else,' he says. 'Tell your friend Williams to keep out of this.' I say, 'Williams?' like I don't know who he's talking about. He ignores that because, of course, he knows better."

"Somebody listened to Dirk's voice mail."

"No question. And he says, 'If he needs convincing, just tell him I'm as partial as he is to Dad and Jeff.' That your brother?"

Buck nodded. "So you caved?"

"What was I supposed to do? I tried playing Mr. Brave Boy. I said, 'I could be wired. I could be recording this conversation.' Cool as can be, he said, 'Metal detector would have picked it up.' 'I've got a good memory. I'll expose you,' I told him. He said, 'At your own risk, governor. Who's going to believe you over me? Marianne wouldn't even believe you—of course, she might not be healthy enough to understand.'"

"Marianne?"

"My sister. But that's not the half of it. As if he needs to drive the point home, he called my captain on his speakerphone. He said to him, 'Sullivan, if one of your men was to come to my office and harass me about anything, what should I do?' And Sullivan, one of my idols, sounded like a little baby. He said, 'Mr. Todd-Cothran, sir, you do whatever you need to do.' And Todd-Cothran said, 'What if I was to kill him where he sits?' And Sullivan said, 'Sir, I'm sure it would be justifiable homicide.' Now get this. Todd-Cothran said, right over the phone to Scotland Yard, where you know they tape every incoming call, and Todd-Cothran knows it just as well, 'What if his name happened to be Alan Tompkins?' Just like that, plain as day. And Sullivan said, 'I'd come over there and dispose of the body myself.' Well, I got the picture."

"So you have no one to turn to."

"Nobody I can think of."

"And I'm supposed to just turn tail and run."

Alan nodded. "I have to report back to Todd-Cothran that I've delivered the message. He'll expect you on the next plane out."

"And if I'm not?"

"No guarantees, but I wouldn't push it."

Buck shoved the plates aside and pushed his chair back. "Alan, you don't know me well, but you have to know I'm not the type of guy who takes this stuff sitting down."

"That's what I was afraid of. I'm not either, but where do I turn? What do I do? You'd think someone somewhere can be trusted, but what can anyone do? If this proves Dirk was right, that he got too close to some clandestine thing Todd-Cothran was into, where does it end? Does it include your man Stonagal? And how about the others on the international team of financiers they meet with? Have you considered that they may own everybody? I grew up reading the stories about your Chicago mobsters who had paid off cops and judges and even politicians. No one could touch them."

Buck nodded. "No one could touch them except the ones who couldn't be bought."

"The Untouchables?"

"Those were my heroes," Buck said.

"Mine too," Alan said. "That's why I'm an investigator. But if the Yard is dirty, who do I turn to?"

Buck rested his chin in his hand. "Do you think you're being watched? Followed?"

"I've been looking for that. So far, no."

"Nobody knows where we are now?"

"I tried to keep an eye out for a tail. In my professional opinion, we're here unnoticed. What are you going to do, Cameron?"

"There's precious little I can do here, apparently. Maybe I'll head back right away under a different name and make it look, to whoever cares, like I'm being obstinate and staying here."

"What's the use?"

"I may be scared, Alan, but I will look for my angle. And somehow I will find the person with the clout to help. I don't know your country well enough to know whom to trust. Of course I trust you, but you've been incapacitated."

"Am I weak, Cameron? Do you see that I have a choice?"

Buck shook his head. "I feel for you," he said. "I can't say what I'd do in your place."

The barmaid was making some sort of an announcement, asking people a question at every other table or so. As she neared them, Buck and Alan fell silent to hear. "Anyone drivin' a light green sedan? Fella says the inside light is on."

"That's mine," Alan said. "I don't remember even having the inside light on."

"Me either," Buck said, "but it was light out when we got here. Maybe we didn't notice."

"I'll get it. Probably won't hurt anything, but that old beater's battery can't take much."

"Careful," Buck said. "Be sure no one was tampering with it."

"Unlikely. We're right in front, remember."

Buck leaned out of his chair and followed Alan with his eyes as the investigator strolled out. Sure enough, the car's inside light could be seen from inside the pub. Alan went around to the driver's side and reached in to turn the light off. When he came back he said, "Gettin' daft in my old age. Next I'll be leavin' the headlights on."

Buck was sad, thinking of his friend's predicament. What a spot, working at something you'd wanted all your life to do and knowing that your superiors were beholden to what amounted to an international thug. "I'm going to call the airport and see if I can get a flight tonight."

"Nothin's going your way this time of the evening," Alan said.

"I'll take something to Frankfurt and head back from there in the morning. I don't think I should test my luck here."

"There's a phone up by the door. I'll pay the girl."

"I insist," Buck said, sliding a fifty-mark bill across the table.

Buck was on the phone to Heathrow while Alan counted the change from the barmaid. Buck got a seat on a flight to Frankfurt forty-five minutes later that would allow him to catch a Sunday morning flight to JFK.

"Oh, Kennedy's open, is it?" he said.

"Just an hour ago," the woman said. "Limited flights, but your Pan-Continental out of Germany goes there in the morning. How many passengers?"

"One."

"Name?"

Buck peeked in his wallet to remind himself of the name on his phony British passport. "Pardon?" he said, stalling, as Alan approached.

"Name, sir."

"Oh, sorry. Oreskovich. George Oreskovich."

Alan mouthed that he would be in the car. Buck nodded.

"All right, sir," the woman said. "You're all set with a flight to Frankfurt this evening, continuing to JFK in New York tomorrow. Can I do anything else for you?"

"No, thank you."

As Buck hung up, the door of the pub was blown into the room and a blinding flash and deafening crash sent patrons screaming to the floor. As people crept to the door to see what had happened, Buck stared in horror at the frame and melted tires of what had been Alan's Scotland Yard–issue sedan. Windows had been blown out all up and down the street and a siren was already sounding. A leg and part of a torso lay on the sidewalk—the remains of Alan Tompkins.

As the patrons surged out to get a look at the burning wreckage, Buck elbowed his way through them, pulling his real passport and identification from his wallet. In the confusion he flipped the documents near what was left of the car and hoped they wouldn't get burned beyond readability. Whoever wanted him dead could assume him dead. Then he slipped through the crowd into the now-empty pub and sprinted to the back. But there was no back door, only a window. He raised it and crawled through, finding himself in a two-foot alleyway between buildings. Scraping his clothes on both sides as he hurried to a side street, he ran two blocks and hailed a cab. "The Tavistock," he said.

A few minutes later, when the cabbie was within three blocks of his hotel, Buck saw squad cars in front of the place and blocking traffic. "Just run me out to Heathrow, please," he said. He realized he had left his laptop among his things, but he had no choice. He had transferred the best stuff electronically already, but who knew who would have access to his material now?

"You don't need anything at the hotel then?" the cabbie said.

"No. I was just going to see someone."

"Very good, sir."

More authorities seemed to be combing Heathrow. "You wouldn't know where a fellow could get a hat like yours, would you?" Buck asked the cabbie as he paid.

"This old thing? I might be persuaded to part with it. I've got more than one other just like it. A souvenir, eh?"

"Will this do?" Buck said, pressing a large bill into his hand.

"It'll more than do, sir, and thank you kindly." The driver removed his official London cabbie pin and handed over the cap.

Buck pressed the too-large fisherman's style hat down over his ears and hurried into the terminal. He paid cash for his tickets in the name of George Oreskovich, a naturalized Englishman from Poland on his way to a holiday in the States, via Frankfurt. He was in the air before the authorities knew he was gone.

11

RAYFORD WAS GLAD he could take Chloe out for a drive Saturday after having been cooped up with their grief. He was glad she had agreed to accompany him to the church.

Chloe had been sleepy and quiet all day. She had mentioned the idea of dropping out of the university for a semester and taking some classes locally. Rayford liked it. He was thinking of her. Then he realized she was thinking of him, and he was touched.

As they chatted on the short drive, he reminded her that after their day trip to Atlanta Monday they would have to drive home separately from O'Hare so he could get his car back. She smiled at him. "I think I can handle that, now that I'm twenty."

"I do treat you like a little girl sometimes, don't I?" he said.

"Not too much anymore," she said. "You can make up for it, though."

"I know what you're going to say."

"You don't either," she said. "Guess."

"You're going to say I can make up for treating you like a little girl by letting you have your own mind today, by not trying to talk you into anything."

"That goes without saying, I hope. But you're wrong, smart guy. I was going to say you could convince me you see me as a responsible adult by letting me drive *your* car back from the airport Monday."

"That's easy," Rayford said, suddenly switching to a babyish voice. "Would that make you feel like a big girl? OK, Daddy will do that."

She punched him and smiled, then quickly sobered. "It's amazing what amuses me these days," she said. "Good grief, I feel like an awful person."

Rayford let that comment hang in the air as he turned the corner and the tasteful little church came into view. "Don't make too much of what I just said," Chloe said. "I don't have to come in, do I?"

"No, but I'd appreciate it."

She pursed her lips and shook her head, but when he parked and got out, she followed.

Bruce Barnes was short and slightly pudgy, with curly hair and wire-rimmed glasses. He dressed casually but with class, and Rayford guessed him to be in his early thirties. He emerged from the sanctuary with a small vacuum in his hands. "Sorry," he said. "You must be the Steeles. I'm kind of the whole staff around here now, except for Loretta."

"Hello," an older woman said from behind Rayford and Chloe. She stood in the doorway of the church offices sunken-eyed and disheveled, as if she'd come through a war. After pleasantries she retreated to a desk in the outer office.

"She's putting together a little program for tomorrow," Barnes said. "Tough thing is, we have no idea how many to expect. Will you be here?"

"Not sure yet," Rayford said. "I probably will be."

They both looked at Chloe. She smiled politely. "I probably won't be," she said.

"Well, I've got the tape for you," Barnes said. "But I'd like to ask for a few more minutes of your time."

"I've got time," Rayford said.

"I'm with him," Chloe said resignedly.

Barnes led them to the senior pastor's office. "I don't sit at his desk or use his library," the younger man said, "but I do work in here at his conference table. I don't know what's going to happen to me or to the church, and I certainly don't want to be presumptuous. I can't imagine God would call me to take over this work, but if he does, I want to be ready."

"And how will he call you?" Chloe said, a smile playing at her mouth. "By phone?"

Barnes didn't respond in kind. "To tell you the truth, it wouldn't surprise me. I don't know about you, but he got my attention last week. A phone call from heaven would have been less traumatic."

Chloe raised her eyebrows, apparently in surrender to his point.

"Folks, Loretta there looks like I feel. We're shell-shocked and we're devastated, because we know exactly what happened."

"Or you think you do," Chloe said. Rayford tried to catch her eye to encourage her to back off, but she seemed unwilling to look at him. "There's every kind of theory you want on every TV show in the country."

"I know that," Barnes said.

"And each is self-serving," she added. "The tabloids say it was space invaders, which would prove the stupid stories they've been running for years. The government says it's some sort of enemy, so we can spend more on high-tech defense. You're going to say it was God so you can start rebuilding your church."

Bruce Barnes sat back and looked at Chloe, then at her father. "I'm going to ask you something," he said, turning to her again. "Could you let me tell you my story briefly, without interrupting or saying anything, unless there's something you don't understand?"

Chloe stared at him without responding.

"I don't want to be rude, but I don't want you to be either. I asked for a few moments of your time. If I still have it, I want to try to make use of it. Then I'll leave you alone. You can do anything you want with what I tell you. Tell me I'm crazy, tell me I'm self-serving. Leave and never come back. That's up to you. But can I have the floor for a few minutes?"

Rayford thought Barnes was brilliant. He had put Chloe in her place, leaving her no smart remark. She merely waved a hand of permission, for which Barnes thanked her, and he began.

"May I call you by your first names?"

Rayford nodded. Chloe didn't respond.

"Ray, is it? And Chloe? I sit here before you a broken man. And Loretta? If anyone has a right to feel as bad as I do, it's Loretta. She's the only person in her whole clan who is still here. She had six living brothers and sisters, I don't know how many aunts and uncles and cousins and nieces and nephews. They had a wedding here last year and she must have had a hundred relatives alone. They're all gone, every one of them."

"That's awful," Chloe said. "We lost my mom and my little brother, you know. Oh, I'm sorry. I wasn't going to say anything."

"It's all right," Barnes said. "My situation is almost as bad as Loretta's, only on a smaller scale. Of course it's not small for me. Let me tell you my story." As soon as he began with seemingly innocuous details, his voice grew thick and quiet. "I was in bed with my wife. She was sleeping. I was reading. Our children had been down for a couple of hours. They were five, three, and one. The oldest was a girl, the other two boys. That was normal for us—me reading while my wife slept. She worked so hard with the kids and a part-time job that she was always knocked out by nine or so.

"I was reading a sports magazine, trying to turn the pages quietly, and every once in a while she would sigh. Once she even asked how much longer I would be. I knew I should go in the other room or just turn the light off and try to sleep myself. But I told her, 'Not long,' hoping she'd fall asleep and I could just read the whole magazine. I can usually tell by her breathing if she's sleeping soundly enough that my light doesn't bother her. And after a while I heard that deep breathing.

"I was glad. My plan was to read till midnight. I was propped up on an elbow with my back to her, using a pillow to shield the light a little. I don't know how much longer I had been reading when I felt the bed move and sensed she had gotten up. I assumed she was going to the bathroom and only hoped she didn't wake up to the point where she'd bug me about still having the light on when she got back. She's a tiny little thing, and it didn't hit me that I didn't hear her walk to the bathroom. But, like I say, I was engrossed in my reading.

"After a few more minutes I called out, 'Hon, you OK?' And I didn't hear anything. I began wondering, was it just my imagination that she had gotten up? I reached behind me and she was not there, so I called out again. I thought maybe she was checking on the kids, but usually she's such a sound sleeper that unless she's heard one of them she doesn't do that.

"Well, probably another minute or two went by before I turned over and noticed that she was not only gone, but that it also appeared she had pulled the sheet and covers back up toward her pillow. Now you can imagine what I thought. I thought she was so frustrated at me for still reading that she had given up waiting for me to turn off the light and decided to go sleep on the couch. I'm a fairly decent husband, so I went out to apologize and bring her back to bed.

"You know what happened. She wasn't out on the couch. She wasn't in the bathroom. I poked my head into each of the kids' rooms and whispered for her, thinking maybe she was rocking one of them or sitting in there. Nothing. The lights were off all over the house, except for my bedside. I didn't want to wake the kids by yelling for her, so I just turned on the hall light and checked their rooms again.

"I'm ashamed to say I still didn't have a clue until I noticed my oldest two kids weren't in their beds. My first thought was that they had gone into the baby's room, like they do sometimes, to sleep on the floor. Then I thought my wife had taken one or both of them to the kitchen for something. Frankly I was just a little perturbed that I didn't know what was going on in the middle of the night.

"When the baby was not in his crib, I turned the light on, stuck my head out the door and called down the hall for my wife. No answer. Then I noticed the baby's footie pajamas in the crib, and I knew. I just knew. It hit me all of a sudden. I ran from room to room, pulling back the covers and finding the kids' pajamas. I didn't want to, but I tore the cover back from my wife's side of the bed and there was her nightgown, her rings, and even her hair clips on the pillow."

Rayford was fighting the tears, remembering his own similar experience. Barnes took a deep breath and exhaled, wiping his eyes. "Well, I started phoning around," he said. "I started with the pastor, but of course I got his answering machine. A couple of other places I got answering machines, too, so I grabbed the church directory and started looking up older folks, the people I thought might not like answering machines and wouldn't have one. I let their phones ring off the hook. No answers.

"Of course I knew it was unlikely I'd find anybody. For some reason I ran out and jumped in my car and raced over here to the church. There was Loretta, sitting in her car in her robe, hair up in curlers, crying her eyes out. We came into the foyer and sat by the potted plants, crying and holding each other, knowing exactly what had happened. Within about half an hour, a few others showed up. We basically commiserated and wondered aloud what we were supposed to do next. Then somebody remembered Pastor's Rapture tape."

"His what?" Chloe asked.

"Our senior pastor loved to preach about the coming of Christ to rapture his church, to take believers, dead and alive, to heaven before a period of tribulation on the earth. He was particularly inspired once a couple of years ago."

Rayford turned to Chloe. "You remember your mother talking about that. She was so enthusiastic about it."

"Oh yeah, I do."

"Well," Barnes said, "the pastor used that sermon and had himself videotaped in this office speaking directly to people who were left behind. He put it in the church library with instructions to get it out and play it if most everyone seemed to have disappeared. We all watched it a couple of times the other night. A few people wanted to argue with God, trying to tell us that they really had been believers and should have been taken with the others, but we all knew the truth. We had been phony. There wasn't a one of us who didn't know what it meant to be a true Christian. We knew we weren't and that we had been left behind."

Rayford had trouble speaking, but he had to ask. "Mr. Barnes, you were on the staff here."

"Right."

"How did you miss it?"

"I'm going to tell you, Ray, because I no longer have anything to hide. I'm ashamed of myself, and if I never really had the desire or the motivation to tell others about Christ before, I sure have it now. I just feel awful that it took the most cataclysmic event in history to reach me. I was raised in the church. My parents and brothers and sisters were all Christians.

"I loved church. It was my life, my culture. I thought I believed everything there was to believe in the Bible. The Bible says that if you believe in Christ you have eternal life, so I assumed I was covered.

"I especially liked the parts about God being forgiving. I was a sinner, and I never changed. I just kept getting forgiveness because I thought God was bound to do that. He had to. Verses that said if we confessed our sins he was faithful and just to forgive us and to cleanse us. I knew other verses said you had to believe *and* receive, to trust and to abide, but to me that was sort of theological mumbo jumbo. I wanted the bottom line, the easiest route, the simplest path. I knew other verses said that we are not to continue in sin just because God shows grace.

"I thought I had a great life. I even went to Bible college. In church and at school, I said the right things and prayed in public and even encouraged people in their Christian lives. But I was still a sinner. I even said that. I told people I wasn't perfect; I was forgiven."

"My wife said that," Rayford said.

"The difference is," Bruce said, "she was sincere. I lied. I told my wife that we tithed to the church, you know, that we gave ten percent of our income. I hardly ever gave any, except when the plate was passed I might drop in a few bills to make it look good. Every week I would confess that to God, promising to do better next time.

"I encouraged people to share their faith, to tell other people how to become Christians. But on my own I never did that. My job was to visit people in their homes and nursing homes and hospitals every day. I was good at it. I encouraged them, smiled at them, talked with them, prayed with them, even read Scripture to them. But I never did that on my own, privately.

"I was lazy. I cut corners. When people thought I was out calling, I might be at a movie in another town. I was also lustful. I read things I shouldn't have read, looked at magazines that fed my lusts."

Rayford winced. That hit too close to home.

"I had a real racket going," Barnes was saying, "and I bought into it. Down deep, way down deep, I knew better. I knew it was too good to be true. I knew that true Christians were known by what their lives produced and that I was producing nothing. But I comforted myself that there were worse people around who called themselves Christians.

"I wasn't a rapist or a child molester or an adulterer, though many times I felt unfaithful to my wife because of my lusts. But I could always pray and confess and feel as though I was clean. It should have been obvious to me. When people found out I was on the pastoral staff at New Hope, I would tell them about the cool pastor and the neat church, but I was shy about telling them about Christ. If they challenged me and asked if New Hope was one of those churches that said Jesus was the only way to God, I did everything but deny it. I wanted them to think I was OK, that I was with it. I may be a Christian and even a pastor, but don't lump me with the weirdos. Above all, don't do that.

"I see now, of course, that God *is* a sin-forgiving God, because we're human and we need that. But we are to receive his gift, abide in Christ, and allow him to live through us. I used what I thought was my security as a license to do what I wanted. I could basically live in sin and pretend to be devout. I had a great family and a nice work environment. And as miserable as I was privately most of the time, I really believed I would go to heaven when I died.

"I hardly ever read my Bible except when preparing a talk or lesson. I didn't have the 'mind of Christ.' *Christian*, I knew vaguely, means 'Christ one' or 'one like Christ.' That sure wasn't me, and I found out in the worst way possible.

"Let me just say to you both—this is your decision. These are your lives. But I know, and Loretta knows, and a few others who were playing around the edges here at this church know exactly what happened a few nights ago. Jesus Christ returned for his true family, and the rest of us were left behind."

Bruce looked Chloe in the eyes. "There is no doubt in my mind that we have witnessed the Rapture. My biggest fear, once I realized the truth, was that there was no more hope for me. I had missed it, I had been a phony, I had set up my own brand of Christianity that may have made for a life of freedom but had cost me my soul. I had heard people say that when the church was raptured, God's Spirit would be gone from the earth. The logic was that when Jesus went to heaven after his resurrection, the Holy Spirit that God gave to the church was embodied in believers. So when they were taken, the Spirit would be gone, and there would be no more hope for anyone left. You can't know the relief when Pastor's tape showed me otherwise.

"We realize how stupid we were, but those of us in this church—at least the ones who felt drawn to this building the night everyone else disappeared—are now as zealous as we can be. No one who comes here will leave without knowing exactly what we believe and what we think is necessary for them to have a relationship with God."

Chloe stood and paced, her arms folded across her chest. "That's a pretty interesting story," she said. "What was the deal with Loretta? How did she miss it if her whole extended family were true Christians?"

"You should have her tell you sometime," Bruce said. "But she tells me it was pride and embarrassment that kept her from Christ. She was a middle child in a very religious family, and she said she was in her late teens before she even thought seriously about her personal faith. She had just drifted along with the family to church and all the related activities. As she grew up, got married, became a mother and a grandmother, she just let everyone assume she was a spiritual giant. She was revered around here. Only she had never believed and received Christ for herself."

"So," Chloe said, "this believing and receiving stuff, this living for Christ or letting him live through you, that's what my mother meant when she talked about salvation, getting saved?"

Bruce nodded. "From sin and hell and judgment."

"Meantime, we're not saved from all that."

"That's right."

"You really believe this."

"I do."

"It's pretty freaky stuff, you have to admit."

"Not to me. Not anymore."

Rayford, always one for precision and order, asked, "So, what did you do? What did my wife do? What made her more of a Christian, or, ah . . . what, uh—"

"Saved her?" Bruce said.

"Yes," Rayford said. "That's exactly what I want to know. If you're right, and I've already told Chloe that I think I see this now, we need to know how it works. How it goes. How does a person get from one situation to the other? Obviously, we were not saved from being left, and we're here to face life without our loved ones who were true Christians. So, how do we become true Christians?"

"I'm going to walk you through that," Bruce said. "And I'm going to send you home with the tape. And I'm going to go through this all in detail tomorrow morning at ten for whoever shows up. I'll probably do the same lesson every Sunday morning for as long as people need to know. One thing I'm sure of, as important as all the other sermons and lessons are, nothing matters like this one."

While Chloe stood with her back to the wall, arms still folded, watching and listening, Bruce turned to Rayford. "It's really quite simple. God made it easy. That doesn't mean it's not a supernatural transaction or that we can pick and choose the good parts—as I tried to do. But if we see the truth and act on it, God won't withhold salvation from us.

"First, we have to see ourselves as God sees us. The Bible says all have sinned, that there is none righteous, no not one. It also says we can't save ourselves. Lots of people thought they could earn their way to God or to heaven by doing good things, but that's probably the biggest misconception ever. Ask anyone on the street what they think the Bible or the church says about getting to heaven, and nine of ten would say it has something to do with doing good and living right.

"We're to do that, of course, but not so we can earn our salvation. We're to do that in *response* to our salvation. The Bible says that it's not by works of righteousness that we have done, but by his mercy God saved us. It also says that we are saved by grace through Christ, not of ourselves, so we can't brag about our goodness.

"Jesus took our sins and paid the penalty for them so we wouldn't have to. The payment is death, and he died in our place because he loved us. When we tell Christ that we acknowledge ourselves as sinners and lost, and receive his gift of salvation, he saves us. A transaction takes place. We go from darkness to light, from lost to found; we're saved. The Bible says that to those who receive him, he gives the power to become sons of God. That's what Jesus is—the Son of God. When we become sons of God, we have what Jesus has: a relationship with God, eternal life, and because Jesus paid our penalty, we also have forgiveness for our sins."

Rayford sat stunned. He sneaked a peek at Chloe. She looked frozen, but she didn't appear antagonistic. Rayford felt he had found exactly what he was looking for. It was what he had suspected and had heard bits and pieces of over the years, but he had never put it all together. In spite of himself, he was still reserved enough to want to mull it over, to see and hear the tape, and to discuss it with Chloe.

"I have to ask you," Bruce said, "something I never wanted to ask people before. I want to know if you're ready to receive Christ right now. I would be happy to pray with you and lead you in how to talk to God about this."

"No," Chloe said quickly, looking at her dad as if afraid he was going to do something foolish.

"No?" Bruce was clearly surprised. "Need more time?"

"At least," Chloe said. "Surely this isn't something you rush into."

"Well, let me tell you," Bruce said. "It's something I wish I had rushed into. I believe God has forgiven me and that I have a job to do here. But I don't know what's going to happen now, with the true Christians all gone. I'd sure rather have come to this point years ago than now, when it was nearly too late. You can imagine that I would much rather be in heaven with my family right now."

"But then who would tell us about this?" Rayford asked.

"Oh, I'm grateful for that opportunity," Bruce said. "But it has cost me dearly."

"I understand." Rayford could feel Bruce's eyes burning into him as if the young man knew Rayford was nearly ready to make a commitment. But he had never rushed into anything in his life. And while he didn't put this on the same scale as dealing with a salesman, he needed time to think, a cooling-off period. He was analytical, and while this suddenly made a world of sense to him and he didn't doubt at all Bruce's theory of the disappearances, he would not act immediately. "I'd appreciate the tape, and I can guarantee you, I will be back tomorrow."

Bruce looked at Chloe. "No guarantees from me," she said, "but I appreciate your time and I will watch the tape."

"That's all I can ask," Bruce said. "But let me leave you with one little reminder of urgency. You may have heard this off and on your whole lives, the way I did. Maybe you haven't. But I need to tell you that you don't have any guarantees. It's too late for you to disappear like your loved ones did a few days ago. But people die every day in car accidents, plane crashes—oh, sorry, I'm sure you're a good pilot—all kinds of tragedies. I'm not going to push you into something you're not ready for, but just let me encourage you that if God impresses upon you that this is true, don't put it off. What would be worse than finally finding God and then dying without him because you waited too long?"

12

BUCK CHECKED INTO the Frankfurt Hilton at the airport under his phony name, knowing he had to call the States before his family and his colleagues heard he was dead. He started by finding a pay phone in the lobby and dialing his father's number in Arizona. With the time difference, it was shortly after noon on Saturday there.

"I'm really sorry about this, Dad, but you're going to hear I was killed in some sort of a car bombing, terrorist attack, that kind of thing."

"What the devil is going on, Cameron?"

"I can't get into it now, Dad. I just want you to know I'm all right. I'm calling from overseas, but I'd rather not say where. I'll be back tomorrow, but I'm going to have to lay low for a while."

"Your sister-in-law and niece and nephew's memorial services are tomorrow evening," Mr. Williams said.

"Oh, no. Dad, it would really be obvious if I showed up there. I'm sorry. Tell Jeff how really sorry I am."

"Well, do we have to play this charade out? I mean should we make it a memorial for you, too?"

"No, I'm not going to be able to play dead that long. Once the people at the *Global* find out I'm all right, the secret won't hold for long."

"Are you going to be in danger when whoever thinks they killed you finds out?"

"Probably, but Dad, I've got to get off now. Tell Jeff for me, huh?"

"I will. Be careful."

Buck switched to another phone and called the *Global*. Disguising his voice, he asked the receptionist to plug him into Steve Plank's after-hours voice mail. "Steve, you know who this is. No matter what you hear in the next twenty-four hours, I'm all right. I will call you tomorrow and we can meet. Let the others believe what they hear for now. I'm going to need to remain incognito until I can find someone who can really help. Talk to you soon, Steve."

* * *

Chloe was silent in the car. Rayford fought the urge to jabber. That was not his nature, but he felt the same urgency he had sensed in Bruce Barnes. He wanted to remain sensible, yes, analytical. He wanted to study, to pray, to be sure. But wasn't that just insurance? Could he be more sure?

What had he done in his raising of Chloe that could make her so cautious, so careful, that she might look down her nose at what was so obvious to him? He had found the truth, and Bruce was right. They needed to act on it before anything happened to them.

The news was full of crime, looting, people taking advantage of the chaos. People were being shot, maimed, raped, killed. The roadways were more dangerous than ever. Emergency units were understaffed, fewer air and ground traffic controllers manned the airports, fewer qualified pilots and crews flew the planes.

People checked the graves of loved ones to see if their corpses had disappeared, and unscrupulous types pretended to do the same while looking for valuables that might have been buried with the wealthy. It had become an ugly world overnight, and Rayford was worried about his and Chloe's safety. He didn't want to go much longer without watching the tape and making good on the decision he had already made.

"Can we watch it together?" he suggested.

"I'd really rather not, Dad. I can see where you're going with this, and I'm not comfortable with it yet. This is very personal. It isn't a group or family thing."

"I'm not so sure about that."

"Well, don't push me. You deal with it on your own, and I will later."

"You know I'm just worried about you and that I love you and care about you, don't you?"

"Of course."

"Will you watch it before the church meeting tomorrow?"

"Daddy, please. You're going to push me away if you keep bugging me about it. I'm not sure I even want to go to that. I heard his pitch today and he said himself it's going to be the same thing tomorrow."

"Well, what if I decide to become a Christian tomorrow? I'd kind of like you there."

Chloe looked at him. "I don't know, Dad. It's not like graduation or something."

"Maybe it is. I feel like your mother and your brother got promoted and I didn't."

"Gross."

"I'm serious. They qualified for heaven. I didn't."

"I don't want to talk about this now."

"OK, but let me just say one more thing. If you don't go tomorrow, I wish you'd watch the tape while I'm gone."

"Oh, I—"

"Because I'd really like to have you settle this thing before our flight Monday. Air travel is becoming more dangerous, and you never know what might happen."

"Daddy, come on! All my life all I've heard you do is set people straight about how safe flying is. Every time there's a crash, someone asks if you aren't afraid or if you've ever had a close call, and you rattle off all these statistics about how flying is so many times safer than riding in a car. So don't start with that."

Rayford gave up. He would deal with his own soul and pray for his daughter, but clearly there would be no badgering her into the faith.

Chloe went to bed early Saturday night while Rayford settled in front of the television and popped in the video. "Hello," came the pleasant voice of the pastor Rayford had met several times. As he spoke he sat on the edge of the desk in the very office Rayford had just visited. "My name is Vernon Billings, and I'm pastor of the New Hope Village Church of Mount Prospect, Illinois. As you watch this tape, I can only imagine the fear and despair you face, for this is being recorded for viewing only after the disappearance of God's people from the earth.

"That you are watching indicates you have been left behind. You are no doubt stunned, shocked, afraid, and remorseful. I would like you to consider what I have to say here as instructions for life following Christ's rapture of his church. That is what has happened. Anyone you know or knew of who had placed his or her trust in Christ alone for salvation has been taken to heaven by Christ.

"Let me show you from the Bible exactly what has happened. You won't need this proof by now, because you will have experienced the most shocking event of history. But as this tape was made beforehand and I am confident that I will be gone, ask yourself, how did he know? Here's how, from 1 Corinthians 15:51-57."

The screen began to scroll with the passage of Scripture. Rayford hit the pause button and ran to get Irene's Bible. It took him a while to find 1 Corinthians, and though it was slightly different in her translation, the meaning was the same.

The pastor said, "Let me read to you what the great missionary evangelist, the apostle Paul, wrote to the Christians at the church in the city of Corinth:

"Behold, I tell you a mystery: We shall not all sleep, but we shall all be changed—in a moment, in the twinkling of an eye, at the last trumpet. For the trumpet will sound, and the dead will be raised incorruptible, and we shall be changed. For this corruptible must put on incorruption, and this mortal must put on immortality. So when this corruptible has put on incorruption, and this mortal has put on immortality, then shall be brought to pass the saying that is written: 'Death is swallowed up in victory. O Death, where is your sting? O Hades, where is your victory?' The sting of death is sin, and the strength of sin is the law. But thanks be to God, who gives us the victory through our Lord Jesus Christ."

Rayford was confused. He could follow some of that, but the rest was like gibberish to him. He let the tape roll. Pastor Billings continued, "Let me paraphrase some of that so you'll understand it clearly. When Paul says we shall not all sleep, he means that we shall not all die. And he's saying that this corruptible being must put on an incorruptible body which is to last for all of eternity. When these things have happened, when the Christians who have already died and those that are still living receive their immortal bodies, the Rapture of the church will have taken place.

"Every person who believed in and accepted the sacrificial death, burial, and resurrection of Jesus Christ anticipated his coming again for them. As you see this tape, all those will have already seen the fulfillment of the promise of Christ when he said, 'I will come again and receive you unto Myself; that where I am, there you may be also.'

"I believe that all such people were literally taken from the earth, leaving everything material behind. If you have discovered that millions of people are missing and that babies and children have vanished, you know what I am saying is true. Up to a certain age, which is probably different for each individual, we believe God will not hold a child accountable for a decision that must be made with heart and mind, fully cognizant of the ramifications. You may also find that unborn children have disappeared from their mothers' wombs. I can only imagine the pain and heartache of a world without precious children, and the deep despair of parents who will miss them so.

"Paul's prophetic letter to the Corinthians said this would occur in the twinkling of an eye. You may have seen a loved one standing before you, and suddenly they were gone. I don't envy you that shock.

"The Bible says that men's hearts will fail them for fear. That means to me that there will be heart attacks due to shock, people will commit suicide in their despair, and you know better than I the chaos that will result from Christians disappearing from various modes of transportation, with the loss of firefighters and police officers and emergency workers of all sorts.

"Depending on when you're viewing this tape, you may have already found that martial law is in effect in many places, emergency measures trying to keep evil elements from looting and fighting over the spoils of what is left. Governments will tumble and there will be international disorder.

"You may wonder why this has happened. Some believe this is the judgment of God on an ungodly world. Actually, that is to come later. Strange as this may sound to you, this is God's final effort to get the attention of every person who has ignored or rejected him. He is allowing now a vast period of trial and tribulation to come to you who remain. He has removed his church from a corrupt world that seeks its own way, its own pleasures, its own ends.

"I believe God's purpose in this is to allow those who remain to take stock of themselves and leave their frantic search for pleasure and self-fulfillment, and turn to the Bible for truth and to Christ for salvation.

"Let me encourage you that your loved ones, your children and infants, your friends, and your acquaintances have not been snatched away by some evil force or some invasion from outer space. That will likely be a common explanation. What sounded ludicrous to you before might sound logical now, but it is not.

"Also, Scripture indicates that there will be a great lie, announced with the help of the media and perpetrated by a self-styled world leader. Jesus himself prophesied about such a person. He said, 'I have come in My Father's name, and you do not receive Me; if another comes in his own name, him you will receive.'

"Let me warn you personally to beware of such a leader of humanity who may emerge from Europe. He will turn out to be a great deceiver who will step forward with signs and wonders that will be so impressive that many will believe he is of God. He will gain a great following among those who are left, and many will believe he is a miracle worker.

"The deceiver will promise strength and peace and security, but the Bible says he will speak out against the Most High and will wear down the saints of the Most High. That's why I warn you to beware now of a new leader with great charisma trying to take over the world during this terrible time of chaos and confusion. This person is known in the Bible as Antichrist. He will make many promises, but he will not keep them. You must trust in the promises of God Almighty through his Son, Jesus Christ.

"I believe the Bible teaches that the Rapture of the church ushers in a seven-year period of trial and tribulation, during which terrible things will happen. If you have not received Christ as your Savior, your soul is in jeopardy. And because of the cataclysmic events that will take place during this period, your very life is in danger. If you turn to Christ, you may still have to die as a martyr."

Rayford paused the tape. He had been prepared for the salvation stuff. But tribulation and trial? Losing his loved ones, facing the pride and self-centeredness that had kept him out of heaven—wasn't that enough? There would be *more*?

And what of this "great deceiver" the pastor had talked about? Maybe he had taken this prophecy business too far. But this was no snake-oil salesman. This was a sincere, honest, trustworthy man—a man of God. If what the pastor said about the disappearances was true—and Rayford knew in his heart that it was—then the man deserved his attention, his respect.

It was time to move beyond being a critic, an analyst never satisfied with the evidence. The proof was before him: the empty chairs, the lonely bed, the hole in his heart. There was only one course of action. He punched the play button.

"It doesn't make any difference, at this point, why you're still on earth. You may have been too selfish or prideful or busy, or perhaps you simply didn't take the time to examine the claims of Christ for yourself. The point now is, you have another chance. Don't miss it.

"The disappearance of the saints and children, the chaos left behind, and the despairing of the heartbroken are evidence that what I'm saying is true. Pray that God will help you. Receive his salvation gift right now. And resist the lies and efforts of the Antichrist, who is sure to rise up soon. Remember, he will deceive many. Don't be counted among them.

"Nearly eight hundred years before Jesus came to earth the first time, Isaiah in the Old Testament prophesied that the kingdoms of nations will be in great conflict and their faces shall be as flames. To me, this portends World War III, a thermonuclear war that will wipe out millions.

"Bible prophecy is history written in advance. I urge you to find books on this subject or find people who may have been experts in this area but who for some reason did not receive Christ before and were left behind. Study so you'll know what is coming and you can be prepared.

"You'll find that government and religion will change, war and inflation will erupt, there will be widespread death and destruction, martyrdom of saints, and even a devastating earthquake. Be prepared.

"God wants to forgive you your sins and assure you of heaven. Listen to Ezekiel 33:11: 'I have no pleasure in the death of the wicked, but that the wicked turn from his way and live.'

"If you accept God's message of salvation, his Holy Spirit will come in unto you and make you spiritually born anew. You don't need to understand all this theologically. You can become a child of God by praying to him right now as I lead you—"

Rayford paused the tape again and saw the concern on the pastor's face, the compassion in his eyes. He knew friends and acquaintances would think him crazy, perhaps even his own daughter would. But this rang true with him. Rayford didn't understand about the seven years of tribulation and this new leader, the liar who was supposed to emerge. But he knew he needed Christ in his life. He needed forgiveness of sin and the assurance that one day he would join his wife and son in heaven.

Rayford sat with his head in his hands, his heart pounding. There was no sound from upstairs where Chloe rested. He was alone with his thoughts, alone with God, and he felt God's presence. Rayford slid to his knees on the carpet. He had never knelt in worship before, but he sensed the seriousness and the reverence of the moment. He pushed the play button and tossed the remote control aside. He set his hands palms down before him and rested his forehead on them, his face on the floor. The pastor said, "Pray after me," and Rayford did. "Dear God, I admit that I'm a sinner. I am sorry for my sins. Please forgive me and save me. I ask this in the name of Jesus, who died for me. I trust in him right now. I believe that the sinless blood of Jesus is sufficient to pay the price for my salvation. Thank you for hearing me and receiving me. Thank you for saving my soul."

As the pastor continued with words of assurance, quoting verses that promised that whoever called upon the name of the Lord would be saved and that God would not cast out anyone who sought him, Rayford stayed where he was. As the tape finished the pastor said, "If you were genuine, you are saved, born again, a child of God." Rayford wanted to talk to God more. He wanted to be specific about his sin. He knew he was forgiven, but in a childlike way, he wanted God to know that he knew what kind of a person he had been.

He confessed his pride. Pride in his intelligence. Pride in his looks. Pride in his abilities. He confessed his lusts, how he had neglected his wife, how he had sought his own pleasure. How he had worshiped money and things. When he was through, he felt clean. The tape had scared him, all that talk about the tough times ahead, but he knew he would rather face them as a true believer than in the state he had been.

His first prayer following that was for Chloe. He would worry about her and pray for her constantly until he was sure she had joined him in this new life.

\+ + +

Buck arrived at JFK and immediately called Steve Plank. "Stay right where you are, Buck, you renegade. Do you know who wants to talk with you?"

"I couldn't guess."

"Nicolae Carpathia himself."

"Yeah, right."

"I'm serious. He's here and he's got your old friend Chaim Rosenzweig with him. Apparently Chaim sang your praises, and with all the media after him, he's asking for you. So I'll come get you, you'll tell me what in the world you've gotten yourself into, we'll get you undead, and you can have that great interview you've been looking for."

Buck hung up and clapped. *This is too good to be true, he thought. If there's one guy who's above these international terrorists and bullies and even the dirt at the London Exchange and Scotland Yard, it will be this Carpathia. If Rosenzweig likes him, he's got to be all right.*

\+ + +

Rayford couldn't wait to go to New Hope the next morning. He began reading the New Testament, and he scrounged around the house for any books or study guides Irene had collected. Though much of it was still difficult to understand, he found himself so hungry and thirsty for the story of the life of Christ that he read through all four Gospels until it was late and he fell asleep.

All Rayford could think of throughout the reading was that he was now part of this family that included his wife and son. Though he was scared of what the pastor had predicted on the tape about all the bad things that would happen in the world now that the church had been raptured, he was also excited about his new faith. He knew he would one day be with God and Christ, and he wanted that for Chloe more than ever.

Rayford kept himself from bugging her. He determined not to tell her what he had done unless she asked. She didn't ask before he left for church in the morning, but she apologized for not going with him. "I will go with you sometime," she said. "I promise. I'm not being antagonistic. I'm just not ready."

Rayford fought the urge to warn her not to wait too long. He also wanted to plead with her to watch the tape, but she knew he had watched it and she asked him nothing about it. He had rewound it and left it in the VCR, hoping and praying she would watch it while he was gone.

Rayford got to the church just before ten o'clock and was shocked to have to park nearly three blocks away. The place was packed. Few were carrying Bibles, and hardly anyone was dressed up. These were scared, desperate people who filled every pew, including in the balcony. Rayford wound up standing in the back with nowhere to sit.

Right at ten o'clock, Bruce began, but he asked Loretta to stand by the door and make sure any latecomers were welcomed. Despite the crowd, he did not use the platform spotlights, nor did he stand in the pulpit. He had placed a single microphone stand in front of the first pew, and he simply talked to the people.

Bruce introduced himself and said, "I'm not in the pulpit because that is a place for people who are trained and called to it. I am in a place of leadership and teaching today by default. Normally we at this church would be thrilled to see a crowd like this," he said. "But I'm not about to tell you how great it is to see you here. I know you're here seeking to know what happened to your children and loved ones, and I believe I have the answer. Obviously, I didn't have it before, or I too would be gone. We'll not be singing or making any announcements, except to tell you we have a Bible study scheduled for Wednesday night at seven. We will not be taking any offering, though we will have to start doing that next week to meet our expenses. The church has some money in the bank, but we do have a mortgage and I have living expenses."

Bruce then told the same story he had told Rayford and Chloe the day before, and his voice was the only sound in the place. Many wept. He showed the videotape, and more than a hundred people prayed along with the pastor at the end. Bruce urged them to begin coming to New Hope.

He added, "I know many of you may still be skeptical. You may believe what happened was of God, but you still don't like it and you resent him for it. If you would like to come back and vent and ask questions this evening, I will be here. But I choose not to offer that opportunity this morning because so many here are brand-new in their faith and I don't want to confuse the issue. Rest assured we will be open to any honest question.

"I do want to open the floor to anyone who received Christ this morning and would like to confess it before us. The Bible tells us to do that, to make known our decision and our stand. Feel free to come to the microphone."

Rayford was the first to move, but as he came down the aisle he sensed many falling in behind him. Dozens waited to tell their stories, to say where they'd been on their spiritual journey. Most were just like he was, having been on the edges of the truth through a loved one or friend, but never fully accepting the truth about Christ.

Their stories were moving and hardly anyone left, even when the clock swept past noon and forty or fifty more still stood in line. All seemed to need to tell of the ones who had left them. At two o'clock, when everyone was hungry and tired, Bruce said, "I'm going to have to bring this to a close. One thing I wasn't going to do today was anything traditionally churchy, including singing. But I feel we need to praise the Lord for what has happened here today. Let me teach you a simple chorus of adoration."

Bruce sang a brief song from Scripture, honoring God the Father, Jesus his Son, and the Holy Spirit. When the people joined in, quietly and reverently and heartfelt, Rayford was too choked up to sing. One by one people stopped singing and mouthed the words or hummed, they were so overcome. Rayford believed it was the most moving moment of his life. How he longed to share it with Irene and Raymie and Chloe.

People seemed reluctant to leave, even after Bruce closed in prayer. Many stayed to get acquainted, and it became obvious a new congregation had begun. The name of the church was more appropriate than ever. New Hope. Bruce shook hands with people as they left, and no one ducked him or hurried past. When Rayford shook his hand, Bruce asked, "Are you busy this afternoon? Would you be able to join me for a bite?"

"I'd want to call my daughter first, but sure."

Rayford let Chloe know where he'd be. She didn't ask about the church meeting, except to say, "It went long, huh? Lot of people there?" And he simply told her yes on both counts. He was committed to not saying more unless she asked. He hoped and prayed her curiosity would get the best of her, and if he then could do justice to what had happened that day, maybe she would wish she'd been in on it. At the very least, she would have to recognize how it had affected him.

At a small restaurant in nearby Arlington Heights, Bruce looked exhausted but happy. He told Rayford he felt such a mix of emotions he hardly knew what to make of them. "My grief over the loss of my family is still so raw I can hardly function. I still feel shame over my phoniness. And yet since I repented of my sins and truly received Christ, in just a few days he has blessed me beyond anything I could have imagined. My house is lonely and cold and carries painful memories. And yet look what happened today. I've been given this new flock to shepherd, a reason for living."

Rayford merely nodded. He sensed Bruce simply needed someone to talk to.

"Ray," Bruce said, "churches are usually built by seminary-trained pastors and elders who have been Christians most of their lives. We don't have that luxury. I don't know what kind of leadership model we're going to have. It doesn't make sense to have elders when the interim pastor, which is all I can call myself, is himself a brand-new Christian and so is everybody else. But we're going to need a core of people who care about each other and are committed to the body. Loretta and a few of the people I met with the night of the Rapture are already part of that team, along with a couple of older men who were in the church for years but somehow missed the point as well.

"I know this is very new to you, but I feel as if I should ask you to join our little core group. We will be at the church for the Sunday morning meeting, the occasional Sunday evening meeting, the Wednesday night Bible study, and we will meet at my home one other evening every week. That's where we will pray for each other, keep each other accountable, and study a little deeper to stay ahead of the new congregation. Are you willing?"

Rayford sat back. "Wow," he said. "I don't know. I'm so new at this."

"We all are."

"Yeah, but you were raised in it, Bruce. You know this stuff."

"I only missed the most important point."

"Well, I'll tell you what appeals to me about it. I'm hungry for knowledge of the Bible. And I need a friend."

"So do I," Bruce said. "That's the risk. We could wind up grating on each other."

"I'm willing to take the risk if you are," Rayford said. "As long as I'm not expected to take any leadership role."

"Deal," Barnes said, thrusting out his hand. Rayford shook it. Neither smiled. Rayford had the feeling this was the beginning of a relationship born of tragedy and need. He just hoped it worked out. When Rayford finally arrived home, Chloe was eager to hear all about it. She was amazed at what her father told her and said she was embarrassed to say she had not watched the tape yet. "But I will now, Dad, before we go to Atlanta. You're really into this, aren't you? It sounds like something I want to check out, even if I don't do anything about it."

Rayford had been home about twenty minutes and had changed into his pajamas and robe to relax for the rest of the evening when Chloe called out to him. "Dad, almost forgot. A Hattie Durham called for you several times. She sounded pretty agitated. Said she works with you."

"Yeah," Rayford said. "She wanted to be assigned to my next flight and I ducked her. She probably found out and wants to know why."

"Why *did* you duck her?"

"It's a long story. I'll tell you sometime."

Rayford was reaching for the phone when it rang. It was Bruce. "I forgot to confirm," he said. "If you've agreed to be part of the core team, the first responsibility is tonight's meeting with the disenchanted and the skeptics."

"You *are* going to be a tough taskmaster, aren't you?"

"I'll understand if you weren't planning on it."

"Bruce," Rayford said, "except for heaven, there's no place I'd rather be. I wouldn't miss it. I might even be able to get Chloe to come to this one."

"What one?" Chloe asked when he hung up.

"In a minute," he said. "Let me call Hattie and calm the waters."

Rayford was surprised that Hattie said nothing about their flight assignments. "I just got some disconcerting news," she said. "You remember that writer from *Global Weekly* who was on our flight, the one who had his computer hooked up to the in-flight phone?"

"Vaguely."

"His name was Cameron Williams, and I talked to him by phone a couple of times since the flight. I tried calling him from the airport in New York last night but couldn't get through."

"Uh-huh."

"I just heard on the news that he was killed in England in a car bombing."

"You're kidding!"

"I'm not. Isn't that too bizarre? Rayford, sometimes I don't know how much of this I can take. I hardly knew this guy, but I was so shocked I just broke down when I heard. I'm sorry to bother you with it, but I thought you might remember him."

"No, that's all right, Hattie. And I know how overwhelming this is for you because it has been for me, too. I've got a lot to talk to you about, actually."

"You do?"

"Could we get together sometime soon?"

"I've put in to work one of your flights," she said. "Maybe if that works out."

"Maybe," he said. "And if it doesn't, maybe you could come over for dinner with Chloe and me."

"I'd like that, Rayford. I really would."

13

BUCK WILLIAMS sat near an exit at JFK Airport reading his own obituary. "Magazine Writer Assumed Dead," the headline read.

Cameron Williams, 30, the youngest senior writer on the staff of any weekly newsmagazine, is feared dead after a mysterious car bombing outside a London pub Saturday night that took the life of a Scotland Yard investigator.

Williams, a five-year employee of Global Weekly, *had won a Pulitzer as a reporter for the* Boston Globe *before joining the magazine as a staff reporter at 25. He quickly rose to the position of senior writer and has since written more than three dozen cover stories, four times assigned the* Weekly's *Newsmaker of the Year story.*

The journalist won the prestigious Ernest Hemingway Prize for war correspondence when he chronicled the destruction of the Russian air force over Israel 14 months ago. According to Steve Plank, executive editor of Global Weekly, *the administration of the magazine is refusing to confirm the report of Williams's death "until we see hard evidence."*

Williams's father and a married brother reside in Tucson, where Williams lost his sister-in-law, niece, and nephew in last week's disappearances.

Scotland Yard reports that the London bombing appeared to be the work of Northern Ireland terrorists and might have been a case of retribution. Captain Howard Sullivan called his 29-year-old subordinate, victim Alan Tompkins, "one of the finest men and brightest investigators it has been my privilege to work with."

Sullivan added that Williams and Tompkins had become friends after the writer had interviewed the investigator for an article on terrorism in England several years ago. The two had just emerged from the Armitage Arms Pub in London when a bomb exploded in Tompkins's Scotland Yard vehicle.

Tompkins's remains have been identified, though only items of personal identification of Williams were recovered from the scene.

\+ + +

Rayford Steele had a plan. He had decided to be honest with Chloe about his attraction to Hattie Durham and how guilty he felt about it. He knew it would disappoint Chloe, even if it didn't shock her. He intended to talk about his new desire to share his faith with Hattie, hoping he could make some progress with Chloe without her feeling threatened. Chloe had gone with him to the church meeting for skeptics the night before, as she promised. But she had left a little over halfway through. She also fulfilled her promise to watch the video the former pastor had taped. They had discussed neither the meeting nor the video.

They wouldn't have much time together once they arrived at O'Hare, so Rayford broached the subject in the car as they gaped at the wreckage and debris lining the roadways. Between their house and the airport, they saw more than a dozen homes that had been gutted by fire. Rayford's theory was that families had disappeared, leaving something on the stove.

"And you think this was God's doing?" Chloe said, not disrespectfully.

"I do."

"I thought he was supposed to be a God of love and order," she said.

"I believe he is. This was his plan."

"There were plenty of tragedies and senseless deaths before this."

"I don't understand all that either," Rayford said. "But like Bruce said last night, we live in a fallen world. God left control of it pretty much to Satan."

"Oh, brother," she said. "Do you wonder why I walked out?"

"I figured it was because the questions and answers were hitting a little too close to home."

"Maybe they were, but all this stuff about Satan and the Fall and sin and all that . . ." She stopped and shook her head.

"I don't claim to understand it any better than you do, honey," Rayford said. "But I know I'm a sinner and that this world is full of them."

"And you consider me one."

"If you're part of everybody, then, yes, I do. Don't you?"

"Not on purpose."

"You're never selfish, greedy, jealous, petty, spiteful?"

"I try not to be, at least not at anyone else's expense."

"But you think you're exempt from what the Bible says about everybody being a sinner, about there not being one righteous person anywhere, 'No not one'?"

"I don't know, Daddy. I just have no idea."

"You know what I'm worried about, of course."

"Yeah, I know. You think the time is short, that in this new dangerous world I'm going to wait too long to decide what I'm going to do, and then it'll be too late."

"I couldn't have said it better myself, Chloe. I just hope you know I'm thinking only of you, nothing else."

"You don't have to worry about that, Daddy."

"What did you think of the video? Did it make sense to you?"

"It made a lot of sense if you buy into all that. I mean, you have to start with that as a foundation. Then it all works neatly. But if you're not sure about God and the Bible and sin and heaven and hell, then you're still wondering what happened and why."

"And that's where you are?"

"I don't know where I am, Dad."

Rayford fought the urge to plead with her. If they had enough time over lunch in Atlanta, he would try the approach of telling her about Hattie. The plane was supposed to sit only about forty-five minutes before the return to O'Hare. Rayford wondered if it was fair to pray for a delay.

\+ + +

"Nice cap," Steve Plank said as he hurried into JFK and slapped Buck on the shoulder. "And what's this? Two day's growth?"

"I was never too much for disguises," Buck said.

"You're not famous enough to need to hide," Steve said. "You staying away from your apartment for a while?"

"Yeah, and probably yours. You sure you weren't followed?"

"You're being a little paranoid, aren't you, Buck?"

"I have a right," Buck said as they climbed into a cab. "Central Park," he informed the driver. Then he told Steve the entire story.

"What makes you think Carpathia is going to help?" Plank asked later as they walked through the park. "If the Yard and the exchange are behind this, and you think Carpathia is linked to Todd-Cothran and Stonagal, you might be asking Carpathia to turn against his own angels."

They strolled under a bridge to elude the hot spring sun. "I have a hunch about this guy," Buck said, his voice echoing off the cobblestone walls. "It wouldn't surprise me to discover that he met with Stonagal and Todd-Cothran in London the other day. But I have to believe he's a pawn."

Steve pointed to a bench and they sat. "Well, I met Carpathia this morning at his press conference," Steve said, "and all I can say is that I hope you're right."

"Rosenzweig was impressed with him, and that's one insightful old scientist."

"Carpathia's impressive," Steve conceded. "He's handsome as a young Robert Redford, and this morning he spoke in nine languages, so fluently you'd have thought each was his native tongue. The media is eating him up."

"You say that as if you're not the media," Buck said.

Steve shrugged. "I'm proving my own point. I've learned to be a skeptic, to let *People* and the tabloids chase the personalities. But here's a guy with substance, with a brain, with something to say. I liked him. I mean, I saw him only in a press conference setting, but he seems to have a plan. You'll like him, and you're a bigger skeptic than I am. Plus he wants to see you."

"Tell me about that."

"I told you. He's got a little entourage of nobodies, with one exception."

"Rosenzweig."

"Right."

"What's Chaim's connection?"

"Nobody's sure yet, but Carpathia seems to attract experts and consultants who keep him up to speed on technology, politics, finances, and all that. And you know, Buck, he's not that much older than you are. I think they said this morning he's thirty-three."

"Nine languages?"

Plank nodded.

"Do you remember which ones?"

"Why would you ask that?"

"Just thinking."

Steve pulled a reporter's notebook from his side pocket. "You want 'em in alphabetical order?"

"Sure."

"Arabic, Chinese, English, French, German, Hungarian, Romanian, Russian, and Spanish."

"One more time," Buck said, thinking.

Steve repeated them. "What's on your mind?"

"This guy's the consummate politician."

"He is not. Trust me, this was no trick. He knew these languages well and used them effectively."

"But don't you see which languages they are, Steve? Think about it."

"Spare me the effort."

"The six languages of the United Nations, plus the three languages of his own country."

"No kidding?"

Buck nodded. "So am I gonna get to meet him soon?"

\+ + +

The flight to Atlanta was full and busy, and Rayford had to change altitudes continually to avoid choppy air. He got to see Chloe for only a few seconds while his first officer was in the cockpit and the plane was on autopilot. Rayford made a hurried walk-through but had no time to chat.

He got his wish in Atlanta. Another 747 had to be flown back to Chicago in the middle of the afternoon, and the only other pilot available had to be back earlier. Chicago coordinated with Atlanta, switched the two assignments, and found a seat for Chloe, too. That gave Rayford and Chloe more than two hours for lunch, enough time to get away from the airport.

Their cab driver, a young woman with a beautiful lilt to her voice, asked if they wanted to see "a truly unbelievable sight."

"If it's not out of the way."

"It's just a couple of blocks from where y'all are going," she said.

She maneuvered around several detours and construction horses, then through two streets manned by traffic cops. "Over yonder," she said, pointing, and she pulled into a sandy parking lot rimmed by three-foot concrete-block walls. "Can you see that parking garage 'cross the way?"

"What in the world?" Chloe said.

"Strange, isn't it?" the cabbie said.

"What happened?" Rayford asked.

"This has been going on since the vanishings," she said.

They peered at a six-story garage with cars seemingly jammed into each other at all angles in a gridlock so tight and convoluted that cranes worked to lift them out through the open sides of the structure.

"They were all in there after a late ball game that night," she said. "The police say it was bad anyway, long lines of cars trying to get out, people taking turns merging and lots of 'em not taking turns at all. So some people who got tired of waiting just tried to edge in and make other people let 'em in, you know."

"Yeah."

"And then, poof, they say more than a third of the cars ain't got drivers, just like that. If they had room, they kept going till they hit other cars or the wall. If they didn't have room, they just pushed up against the car in front of 'em. The ones that were left couldn't go one way or the other. It was such a mess that people just left their cars and climbed over other cars and went looking for help. They started at dawn moving the cars on the ground levels with tow trucks, then they got them cranes in there by noon, and they been at it ever since."

Rayford and Chloe sat and watched, shaking their heads. Cranes normally used for hoisting beams up to new buildings were wrapping cables around cars, tugging, yanking, dragging them past each other and through openings in the concrete to clear the garage. It appeared it would take several more days.

"How about you?" Rayford asked the driver. "Did you lose people?"

"Yes, sir. My mama and my grandmama and two baby sisters. But I know where they are. They're in heaven, just like my mama always said."

"I believe you're right," Rayford said. "My wife and son are gone, too."

"Are you saved now?" the girl asked.

Rayford was shocked by her forthrightness, but he knew exactly what she meant. "I am," he said.

"I am, too. You got to be blind or somethin' to not see the light now."

Rayford wanted to peek at Chloe, but he did not. He tipped the young woman generously when they got to the restaurant. Over lunch he told Chloe of his history with Hattie, such as it was.

She was silent a long time, and when she spoke her voice was weak. "So you never actually acted on it?" she said.

"Thankfully, no. I never would have been able to live with myself."

"It would have broken Mom's heart, that's for sure."

He nodded miserably. "Sometimes I feel as bad as if I had been unfaithful to her. But I justified my considering it because your mom was so obsessed with her faith."

"I know. Funny thing, though. That kept me straighter at school than I might have been otherwise. I mean, I'm sure Mom would be disappointed to know a lot of the things I've said and done while I've been away—don't ask. But knowing how sincere and devout she was, and what high hopes and expectations she had for me, kept me from doing something really stupid. I knew she was praying for me. She told me every time she wrote."

"Did she also tell you about the end times, Chloe?"

"Sure. All the time."

"But you still don't buy it?"

"I want to, Dad. I really do. But I have to be intellectually honest with myself."

It was all Rayford could do to stay calm. Had he been this pseudosophisticated at that age? Of course he had. He had run everything through that maddening intellectual grid—until recently, when the supernatural came crashing through his academic pretense. But like the cabbie had said, you'd have to be blind not to see the light now, no matter how educated you thought you were.

"I'm going to invite Hattie to dinner with us this week," he said.

Chloe narrowed her eyes. "What, you feel like you're available now?"

Rayford was stunned at his own reaction. He had to keep himself from slapping his own daughter, something he had never done. He gritted his teeth. "How can you say that after all I've just told you?" he said. "That's insulting."

"So was what you were hoping for with this Hattie Durham, Dad. Do you think she was unaware of what was going on? How do you think she'll interpret this? She may come on like gangbusters."

"I'm going to make it clear what my intentions are, and they are totally honorable, more honorable than they ever could have been before, because I had nothing of worth to offer her."

"So, now you're going to switch from hitting on her to preaching at her."

He wanted to argue, but he couldn't. "I care about her as a person, and I want her to know the truth and be able to act on it."

"And what if she doesn't?"

"That's her choice. I can only do my part."

"Is that how you feel about me, too? If I don't act on it the way you want, you'll be satisfied that you've done your part?"

"I should, but obviously I care much more about you than I do Hattie."

"You should have thought of that before you risked everything to chase her."

Rayford was offended again, but he had brought this on himself and felt he deserved it. "Maybe that's why I never did anything about it," he said. "Ever think of that?"

"This is all news to me," she said. "I hope you restrained yourself because of your wife and kids."

"I almost didn't."

"So I gather. What if this strategy with Hattie just makes you all the more attractive to her? What's to keep you from being attracted to her, too? It's not like you're still married, if you're convinced Mom is in heaven."

Rayford ordered dessert and laid his napkin on the table. "Maybe I'm being naive, but your mother being in heaven is just like losing her to sudden death. The last thing on my mind is another woman, and certainly not Hattie. She's too young and immature, and I'm too disgusted with myself for having been tempted by her in the first place. I want to be up front with her and see what she says. It'll be instructive to know whether all this was just in my mind."

"You mean for future reference?"

"Chloe, I love you, but you're being bratty."

"I know. I'm sorry. That was uncalled for. But seriously, how will you know if she tells you the truth? If you tell her you were interested for the wrong reasons and that you aren't interested anymore, why should she be vulnerable enough to admit she thought you two had possibilities?"

Rayford shrugged. "You may be right. But I have to be honest with her even if she's not honest with me. I owe her that much. I want her to take me seriously when I tell her what I think she needs now."

"I don't know, Dad. I think it's a little too soon to be pushing her toward God."

"How soon is too soon, Chloe? There are no guarantees, not now."

+ + +

Steve pulled from his breast pocket two sets of press credentials, permitting the bearers to attend Nicolae Carpathia's speech to the General Assembly of the United Nations that very afternoon. Buck's credentials were in the name of George Oreskovich.

"Do I take care of you, or what?"

"Unbelievable," Buck said. "How much time do we have?"

"A little over an hour," Steve said, rising to hail a cab. "And like I said, he wants to meet you."

"He reads, doesn't he? He's got to think I'm dead."

"I suppose. But he'll remember me from this morning, and I'll be able to assure him it will be just as valuable for him to be interviewed by George Oreskovich as by the legendary Cameron Williams."

"Yeah, but Steve, if he's like the other politicians I know, he's hung up on image, on high-profile journalists. Like it or not, that's what I've become. How are you going to get him to settle for an unknown?"

"I don't know. Maybe I'll tell him it's really you. Then, while you're with him, I'll release the report that your obit was wrong and that right now you're doing a cover-story interview with Carpathia."

"A cover story? You've come a long way from calling him a low-level bureaucrat from a nonstrategic country."

"I was at the press conference, Buck. I met him. And I can at least gauge the competition. If we don't feature him prominently, we'll be the only national magazine that doesn't."

"Like I say, if he's like the typical politician—"

"You can put that out of your mind, Buck. You're going to find this guy the farthest thing you've ever seen from the typical politician. You're going to thank me for getting you the exclusive interview with him."

"I thought that was his idea because of my colossal name," Buck said, smiling.

"So? I could have turned him down."

"Yeah, and been the executive editor of the only national magazine that fails to cover the most exciting new face to visit the States."

"Believe me, Buck," Steve said during the ride to the U.N. building, "this is going to be a refreshing change from the doom and gloom we've been writing and reading for days."

The two used their press credentials to get in, but Buck hung back out of sight of his colleagues and the competition until all were seated in the General Assembly. Steve held a seat for him in the back, where he would not draw attention when he slipped in at the last minute. Meanwhile, Steve would use his cellular phone to call in the story of Buck's reappearance, so it would hit the news by the end of the day.

Carpathia entered the assembly in a dignified yet inauspicious manner, though he had an entourage of a half dozen, including Chaim Rosenzweig and a financial wizard from the French government. Carpathia appeared an inch or two over six feet tall, broad shouldered, thick chested, trim, athletic, tanned, and blond. His thick shock of hair was trimmed neatly around the ears, sideburns, and neck, and his navy-on-navy pinstripe suit and matching tie were exquisitely conservative.

Even from a distance, the man seemed to carry himself with a sense of humility and purpose. His presence dominated the room, and yet he did not seem preoccupied or impressed with himself. His jewelry was understated. His jaw and nose were Roman and strong, his piercing blue eyes set deep under thick brows.

Buck was struck that Carpathia carried no notebook, and he assumed the man must have his speech notes in his breast pocket. Either that or they were being carried by an aide. Buck was wrong on both counts.

Secretary-General Mwangati Ngumo of Botswana announced that the assembly was privileged to hear briefly from the new president of the nation of Romania and that the formal introduction of their guest would be made by the Honorable Dr. Chaim Rosenzweig, with whom they were all familiar.

Rosenzweig hurried to the podium with a vigor that belied his age, and he initially received a more enthusiastic response than did Carpathia. The popular Israeli statesman and scholar said simply that it gave him great pleasure to introduce "to this worthy and august body a young man I respect and admire as much as anyone I've ever met. Please welcome His Honor, President Nicolae Carpathia of Romania."

Carpathia rose, turned to the assembly, and nodded humbly, then shook hands warmly with Rosenzweig. With courtly manners he remained at the side of the lectern until the older man was seated, then stood relaxed and smiling before speaking extemporaneously. Not only did he not use notes, but he also never hesitated, misspoke, or took his eyes off his audience.

He spoke earnestly, with passion, with a frequent smile, and with occasional, appropriate humor. He mentioned respectfully that he was aware that it had not been a full week yet since the disappearance of millions all over the world, including many who would have been "in this very room." Carpathia spoke primarily in perfect English with only a hint of a Romanian accent. He used no contractions and enunciated every syllable of every word. Once again he employed all nine languages with which he was fluent, each time translating himself into English.

In one of the most touching scenes Buck had ever witnessed, Carpathia began by announcing that he was humbled and moved to visit "for the first time this historic site, where nation after nation has set its sights. One by one they have come from all over the globe on pilgrimages as sacred as any to the Holy Lands, exposing their faces to the heat of the rising sun. Here they have taken their stand for peace in a once-and-for-all, rock-solid commitment to putting behind them the insanity of war and bloodshed. These nations, great and small, have had their fill of the death and maiming of their most promising citizens in the prime of their youth.

"Our forebears were thinking globally long before I was born," Carpathia said. "In 1944, the year the International Monetary Fund and the World Bank were established, this great host nation, the United States of America, along with the British Commonwealth and the Union of Soviet Socialist Republics, met at the famous Dumbarton Oaks Conference to propose the birth of this body."

Displaying his grasp of history and his photographic memory of dates and places, Carpathia intoned, "From its official birth on October 24, 1945, and that first meeting of your General Assembly in London, January 10, 1946, to this day, tribes and nations have come together to pledge their wholehearted commitment to peace, brotherhood, and the global community."

He began in almost a whisper, "From lands distant and near they have come: from Afghanistan, Albania, Algeria . . ." He continued, his voice rising and falling dramatically with the careful pronunciation of the name of each member country of the United Nations. Buck sensed a passion, a love for these countries and the ideals of the U.N. Carpathia was clearly moved as he plunged on, listing country after country, not droning but neither in any hurry.

A minute into his list, representatives noticed that with each name, someone from that country rose in dignity and stood erect, as if voting anew for peace among nations. Carpathia smiled and nodded at each as they rose, and nearly every country was represented. Because of the cosmic trauma the world had endured, they had come looking for answers, for help, for support. Now they had been given the opportunity to take their stand once again.

Buck was tired and felt grimy, wearing two-day-old clothes. But his worries were a distant memory as Carpathia moved along. By the time he got into the *Ss* in his alphabetical listing, those standing had begun to quietly applaud each new country mentioned. It was a dignified, powerful thing, this show of respect and admiration, this re-welcome into the global village. The applause was not so loud that it kept anyone from hearing Carpathia, but it was so heartfelt and moving that Buck couldn't suppress the lump in his throat. Then he noticed something peculiar. The press representatives from various countries were standing with their ambassadors and delegations. Even the objectivity of the world press had temporarily vanished in what they might previously have written off as jingoism, superpatriotism, or sanctimony.

Buck found himself eager to stand as well, ruing the fact that his country was near the end of the alphabet, but feeling pride and anticipation welling up within him. As more and more countries were named and their people stood proudly, the applause grew louder, merely because of the increased numbers. Carpathia was up to the task, his voice growing more emotional and powerful with each new country name.

On and on he thundered as people stood and clapped. "Somalia! South Africa! Spain! Sri Lanka! Sudan! Suriname! Swaziland! Sweden! Syria!"

More than five minutes into the recitation, Carpathia had not missed a beat. He had never once hesitated, stammered, or mispronounced a syllable. Buck was on the edge of his seat as the speaker swept through the *Ts* and reached "Uganda! Ukraine! The United Arab Emirates! The United Kingdom! The United States of America!" And Buck leaped to his feet, Steve right with him, along with dozens of other members of the press.

Something had happened in the disappearances of loved ones all over the globe. Journalism might never be the same. Oh, there would be skeptics and those who worshiped objectivity. But what had happened to brotherly love? What had become of depending on one another? What had happened to the brotherhood of men and nations?

It was back. And while no one expected that the press might become the public-relations agency for a new political star, Carpathia certainly had them in his corner this afternoon. By the end of his litany of nearly two hundred nations, young Nicolae was at an emotional, fevered pitch. With such electricity and power in the simple naming of all the countries who had longed to be united with each other, Carpathia had brought the entire crowd to its feet in full voice and applause, press and representative alike. Even the cynical Steve Plank and Buck Williams continued to clap and cheer, never once appearing embarrassed at their loss of detached objectivity.

And there was more, as the Nicolae Carpathia juggernaut sailed on. Over the next half hour he displayed such an intimate knowledge of the United Nations that it was as if he had invented and developed the organization himself. For someone who had never before set foot on American soil, let alone visited the United Nations, he displayed amazing understanding of its inner workings.

During his speech he casually worked in the name of every secretary-general from Trygve Lie of Norway to Ngumo and mentioned their terms of office not just by year but also by specific day and date of their installation and conclusion. He displayed awareness and understanding of each of the six principal organs of the U.N., their functions, their current members, and their particular challenges.

Then he swept through the eighteen U.N. agencies, mentioning every one, its current director, and its headquarters city. This was an amazing display, and suddenly it was no wonder this man had risen so quickly in his own nation, no wonder the previous leader had stepped aside. No wonder New York had already embraced him.

After this, Buck knew, Nicolae Carpathia would be embraced by all of America. And then the world.

14

RAYFORD'S PLANE touched down in Chicago during rush hour late Monday afternoon. By the time he and Chloe got to their cars, they had not had the opportunity to continue their conversation. "Remember, you promised to let me drive your car home," Chloe said.

"Is it that important to you?" he asked.

"Not really. I just like it. May I?"

"Sure. Just let me get my phone out of it. I want to see when Hattie can join us for dinner. That's all right with you, isn't it?"

"As long as you don't expect me to cook or something sexist and domestic like that."

"I hadn't even thought of it. She loves Chinese. We'll order some."

"She loves Chinese?" Chloe repeated. "You are familiar with this woman, aren't you?"

Rayford shook his head. "It's not like that. I mean, yes, I probably know more about her than I should. But I can tell you the culinary preferences of a dozen crew members, and I hardly know anything else about them."

Rayford retrieved his phone from the BMW and turned the ignition switch far enough to read the gas gauge. "You picked the right car," he said. "It's almost full. You'll beat me home. Your mother's car is on empty. You going to be all right there by yourself for a few minutes? I think I'll pick up a few groceries while I'm out."

Chloe hesitated. "It's eerie in there when you're by yourself, isn't it?" she said.

"A little. But we've got to get used to it."

"You're right," she said quickly. "They're gone. And I don't believe in ghosts. I'll be fine. But don't be long."

* * *

At the post-U.N.-appearance press conference for Nicolae Carpathia of Romania, Buck briefly found himself the center of attention. Someone recognized him and expressed surprise and pleasure that he was alive. Buck tried to quiet everyone and tell them that it had all been a misunderstanding, but the furor continued as Chaim Rosenzweig saw him and hurried over, covering Buck's hand with both of his and pumping vigorously. "Oh, I am so glad to see you alive and well," he said. "I heard dreadful news about your demise. And President Carpathia was also disappointed to hear of it. He had so wanted to meet you and had agreed to an exclusive interview."

"Can we still do that?" Buck whispered, to the boos and catcalls of the competition.

"You'll do anything to get a scoop," someone groused. "Even have yourself blown up."

"It will probably not be possible until late tonight," Rosenzweig said. His hand swept the room, crowded with TV cameras, lights, microphones, and the press. "His schedule is full all day, and he has a photo shoot at *People* magazine early this evening. Perhaps following that. I'll speak to him."

"What's your connection?" Buck asked, but the old man put a finger to his lips and pulled away to return and sit near Carpathia as the press conference began.

The young Romanian was no less impressive and persuasive up close, beginning the session with his own statement before fielding questions. He conducted himself like an old pro, though Buck knew his press relations in Romania and the limited other areas of Europe he had visited would not have provided him this experience.

At one point or another, Buck noticed, Carpathia met the eyes of every person in the room, at least briefly. He never looked down, never looked away, never looked up. It was as if he had nothing to hide and nothing to fear. He was in command of himself and seemingly unaffected by the fuss and attention.

He seemed to have unusually good eyesight; it was clear he could see people's name tags from across the room. Anytime he spoke to members of the press, he referred to them by name as Mr. or Ms. so-and-so. He insisted that people call him by whatever name made them comfortable. "Even Nick," he said, smiling. But no one did. They followed his lead and called him "Mr. President" or "Mr. Carpathia."

Carpathia spoke in the same impassioned and articulate tones he had used in his speech. Buck wondered if this was always the same, in public or private. Whatever else he brought to the world scene, he had a mastery of spoken communication second to none.

"Let me begin by saying what an honor it is for me to be in this country and at this historic site. It has been a dream of mine since I was a small boy in Cluj to one day see this place."

The initial pleasantries over, Carpathia launched into another minispeech, again showing incredible knowledge and grasp of the U.N. and its mission. "You will recall," he said, "that in the previous century the U.N. seemed to be in decline. U.S. president Ronald Reagan escalated the East-West controversies, and the U.N. seemed a thing of the past with its emphasis on North-South conflicts. This organization was in trouble financially, with few members willing to pay their share. With the end of the Cold War in the 1990s, however, your next president, Mr. Bush, recognized what he called the 'new world order,' which resonated deep within my young heart. The original basis for the U.N. charter promised cooperation among the first fifty-one members, including the great powers."

Carpathia went on to discuss the various peacekeeping military actions the U.N. had taken since the Korean conflict of the 1950s. "As you know," he said, speaking again of things long before he was born, "the U.N. has its legacy in the League of Nations, which I believe was the first international peacekeeping body. It came about at the end of the First World War, but when it failed to prevent a second, it became anachronistic. Out of that failure came the United Nations, which must remain strong to prevent World War III, which would result in the end of life as we know it."

After Carpathia outlined his eagerness to support the U.N. in any way possible, someone interjected a question about the disappearances. He became suddenly serious and unsmiling, and spoke with compassion and warmth.

"Many people in my country lost loved ones to this horrible phenomenon. I know that many people all over the world have theories, and I wish not to denigrate any one of them, the people or their ideas. I have asked Dr. Chaim Rosenzweig of Israel to work with a team to try to make sense of this great tragedy and allow us to take steps toward preventing anything similar from ever happening again.

"When the time is appropriate I will allow Dr. Rosenzweig to speak for himself, but for now I can tell you that the theory that makes the most sense to me is briefly as follows: The world has been stockpiling nuclear weapons for innumerable years. Since the United States dropped atomic bombs on Japan in 1945 and the Soviet Union first detonated its own devices September 23, 1949, the world has been at risk of nuclear holocaust. Dr. Rosenzweig and his team of renowned scholars are close to the discovery of an atmospheric phenomenon that may have caused the vanishing of so many people instantaneously."

"What kind of a phenomenon?" Buck asked.

Carpathia glanced briefly at his name tag and then into his eyes. "I do not want to be premature, Mr. Oreskovich," he said. Several members of the press snickered, but Carpathia never lost pace. "Or I should say, 'Mr. Cameron Williams of *Global Weekly*.'" This elicited amused applause throughout the room. Buck was stunned.

"Dr. Rosenzweig believes that some confluence of electromagnetism in the atmosphere, combined with as yet unknown or unexplained atomic ionization from the nuclear power and weaponry throughout the world, could have been ignited or triggered—perhaps by a natural cause like lightning, or even by an intelligent life-form that discovered this possibility before we did—and caused this instant action throughout the world."

"Sort of like someone striking a match in a room full of gasoline vapors?" a journalist suggested.

Carpathia nodded thoughtfully.

"How is that different from the idea of aliens from outer space zapping everybody?"

"It is not wholly different," Carpathia conceded, "but I am more inclined to believe in the natural theory, that lightning reacted with some subatomic field."

"Why would the disappearances be so random? Why some people and not others?"

"I do not know," Carpathia said. "And Dr. Rosenzweig tells me they have come to no conclusions on that either. At this point they are postulating that certain people's levels of electricity made them more likely to be affected. That would account for all the children and babies and even fetal material that vanished. Their electromagnetism was not developed to the point where it could resist whatever happened."

"What do you say to people who believe this was the work of God, that he raptured his church?"

Carpathia smiled compassionately. "Let me be careful to say that I do not and will not criticize any sincere person's belief system. That is the basis for true harmony and brotherhood, peace and respect among peoples. I do not accept that theory because I know many, many more people who should be gone if the righteous were taken to heaven. If there is a God, I respectfully submit that this is not the capricious way in which he would operate. By the same token, you will not hear me express any disrespect for those who disagree."

Buck was then astonished to hear Carpathia say that he had been invited to speak at the upcoming ecumenical religious confab scheduled that month in New York. "There I will discuss my views of millenarianism, eschatology, the Last Judgment, and the second coming of Christ. Dr. Rosenzweig was kind enough to arrange that invitation, and until then I think it would be best if I did not attempt to speak on those subjects informally."

"How long will you be in New York?"

"If the people of Romania will permit me, I may be here an entire month. I hate to be away from my people, but they understand that I am concerned for the greater global good, and with technology as it is today and the wonderful people in positions of influence in Romania, I feel confident I can keep in contact and that my nation will not suffer for my brief absence."

By the time of the evening network news, a new international star had been born. He even had a nickname: Saint Nick. More than sound bites had been taken from the floor of the U.N. and the press conference. Carpathia enjoyed several minutes on each telecast, rousing the U.N. audience with the recitation of countries, urgently calling for a recommitment to world peace.

He had carefully avoided specific talk of global disarmament. His was a message of love and peace and understanding and brotherhood, and to quit fighting seemed to go without saying. No doubt he would be back to hammer home that point, but in the meantime, Carpathia was on the charmed ride of his life.

Broadcast commentators urged that he be named an adjunct adviser to the U.N. secretary-general and that he visit each headquarters of the various U.N. agencies around the world. By late that evening, he was invited to make appearances at each of the international meetings coming up within the next few weeks.

He was seen in the company of Jonathan Stonagal, no surprise to Buck. And immediately following the press conference he was whisked away to other appointments. Dr. Rosenzweig found Buck. "I was able to get a commitment from him for late this evening," the old man said. "He has several interviews, mostly with the television people, and then he will be live on ABC's *Nightline* with Wallace Theodore. Following that, he will return to his hotel and will be happy to give you an uninterrupted half hour."

Buck told Steve he wanted to hurry home to his apartment, get freshened up, get his messages, run to the office and educate himself as quickly as possible from the files, and be totally prepared for the interview. Steve agreed to accompany him.

"But I'm still paranoid," Buck admitted. "If Stonagal is related in any way to Todd-Cothran, and we know he is, who knows what he thinks about what happened in London?"

"That's a long shot," Steve said. "Even if that dirt goes into the exchange and Scotland Yard, that doesn't mean Stonagal would have any interest in it. I would think he'd want to stay as far from it as possible."

"But, Steve, you have to agree it's likely that Dirk Burton was murdered because he got too close to Todd-Cothran's secret connections with Stonagal's international group. If they wipe out people they see as their enemies—even friends of their enemies like Alan Tompkins and I were—where will they stop?"

"But you're assuming Stonagal was aware of what happened in London. He's bigger than that. Todd-Cothran or the guy at the Yard may have seen you as a threat, but Stonagal has probably never heard of you."

"You don't think he reads the *Weekly*?"

"Don't be hurt. You're like a gnat to him if he even knows your name."

"You know what a swat with a magazine can do to a gnat, Steve?"

"There's one big hole in your argument," Steve said later as they entered Buck's apartment. "If Stonagal *is* dangerous to you, what does that make Carpathia?"

"Like I said, Carpathia can be only a pawn."

"Buck! You just heard him. Did I overrate him?"

"No."

"Were you blown away?"

"Yes."

"Does he look like anybody's pawn?"

"No. So I can assume only that he knows nothing about this."

"You're pretty sure he met with Todd-Cothran and Stonagal in London before coming here?"

"That had to be business," Buck said. "Planning for the trip and his involvement with international advisers."

"You're taking a big risk," Steve said.

"I have no choice. Anyway, I'm willing. Until he proves otherwise, I'm going to trust Nicolae Carpathia."

"Hmph," Steve said.

"What?"

"It's just that usually you work the other way around. You distrust someone until they prove otherwise."

"Well, it's a new world, Steve. Nothing's the same as it was last week, is it?"

And Buck pushed the button on his answering machine while beginning to undress for his shower.

* * *

Rayford pulled into his driveway with a sack of groceries on the seat beside him. He had gotten a hold of Hattie Durham, who wanted to keep him on the phone talking until he begged off. She was delighted with the dinner invitation and said she could come three nights later, on Thursday.

Rayford guessed he was half an hour behind Chloe, and he was impressed that she had left the garage door open for him. When he found the door locked between the garage and the house, however, he was concerned. He knocked. No answer.

Rayford reopened the garage door to go around to the front, but just before shutting it on his way out, he stopped. Something was different in the garage. He flipped on the light to add to the single bulb of the door opener. All three cars were in their places, but—

Rayford walked around the Jeep at the end. Raymie's stuff was missing! His bike. His four-wheeler. What was this?

Rayford jogged to the front door. The window of the storm door was broken and the door hung on one hinge. The main door had been kicked in. No small feat, as the door was huge and heavy with a dead bolt. The entire frame had been obliterated and lay in pieces on the floor of the entryway. Rayford rushed in, calling for Chloe.

He ran from room to room, praying nothing had happened to the only family member he had left. Everything of immediate material value seemed to be gone. Radios, televisions, VCRs, jewelry, CD players, video games, the silver, even the china. To his relief there was no sign of blood or struggle.

Rayford was on the phone to the police when his call waiting clicked. "I hate to put you on hold," he said, "but that may be my daughter."

It was. "Oh, Daddy!" she said, crying. "Are you all right? I came in through the garage and saw all that stuff missing. I thought maybe they'd come back, so I locked the door to the garage and was going to lock the front, but I saw the glass and wood and everything, so I ran out the back. I'm three doors down."

"They're not coming back, hon," he said. "I'll come get you."

"Mr. Anderson said he would walk me home."

A few minutes later Chloe sat rocking on the couch, her arms folded across her stomach. She told the police officer what she had told her father; then he took Rayford's statement. "You folks don't use your burglar alarm?"

Rayford shook his head. "That's my fault. We used it for years when we didn't need it, and I got tired of being awakened in the middle of the night with the false alarms and the . . . the, uh—"

"Calls from us, I know," the cop said. "That's what everybody says. But this time it would have been worth it, huh?"

"Hindsight and all that," Rayford said. "Never really thought we needed the security in this neighborhood."

"This kind of crime is up two hundred percent here in the last week alone," the officer said. "The bad guys know we don't have the time or manpower to do a blessed thing about it."

"Well, will you put my daughter's mind at ease and tell her they aren't interested in hurting us and that they won't be back?"

"That's right, miss," he said. "Your dad should get this door boarded up till it can be fixed, and I would arm that security system. But I wouldn't expect a repeat visit, at least not by the same bunch. We talked to the people across the street. They saw some kind of a carpet-service minivan here for about half an hour this afternoon. They went in the front, came through, opened the garage door, backed into the empty space in there, and carted your stuff off almost under your noses."

"Nobody saw them break in the front?"

"Your neighbors don't have a clear view of your entrance. Nobody really does. Slick job."

"I'm just glad Chloe didn't walk in on them," Rayford said.

The cop nodded on his way out. "You can be grateful for that. I imagine your insurance will take care of a lot of this. I don't expect to be recovering any of it. We haven't had any luck with the other cases."

Rayford embraced Chloe, who was still shaking. "Can you do me a favor, Dad?" she said.

"Anything."

"I want another copy of that video, the one from the pastor."

"I'll call Bruce, and we'll pick one up tonight."

Suddenly Chloe laughed.

"Now this is funny?" Rayford said.

"I just had a thought," she said, smiling through her tears. "What if the burglars watch that tape?"

15

ONE OF THE FIRST messages on Buck's answering machine was from the flight attendant he had met the week before. "Mr. Williams, this is Hattie Durham," she said. "I'm in New York on another flight and thought I'd call to say hi and thanks again for helping me make contact with my family. I'll wait a second and keep jabbering here, in case you're screening your calls. It would be fun to get together for a drink or something, but don't feel obligated. Well, maybe another time."

"So who's that?" Steve called out as Buck hesitated near the bathroom door, waiting to hear all the messages before getting into the shower.

"Just a girl," he said.

"Nice?"

"Better than nice. Gorgeous."

"Better call her back."

"Don't worry."

Several other messages were unimportant. Then came two that had been left that very afternoon. The first was from Captain Howard Sullivan of Scotland Yard. "Ah yes, Mr. Williams. I hesitate to leave this message on your machine, but I would like to speak with you at your earliest convenience. As you know, two gentlemen with whom you were associated have met with untimely demises here in London. I would like to ask you a few questions. You may be hearing from other agencies, as you were seen with one of the victims just before his unfortunate end. Please call me." And he left the number.

The next message had come less than half an hour later and was from Georges Lafitte, an operative with Interpol, the international police organization headquartered in Lyons, France. "Mr. Williams," he said in a thick French accent, "as soon as you get this message, I would like you to call me from the nearest police station. They will know how to contact us directly, and they will have a printout of information on why we need to speak with you. For your own sake, I would urge you not to delay."

Buck leaned out to stare at Steve, who looked as puzzled as Buck was. "What are you now?" Steve asked. "A suspect?"

"I'd better not be. After what I heard from Alan about Sullivan and how he's in Todd-Cothran's pocket, there's no way I'm going to London and voluntarily put myself in their custody. These messages aren't binding, are they? I don't have to act on them just because I heard them, do I?"

Steve shrugged. "Nobody but me knows you heard them. Anyway, international agencies have no jurisdiction here."

"You think I might be extradited?"

"If they try to link you with either of those deaths."

\+ + +

Chloe didn't want to stay home alone that evening. She rode with her father to the church where Bruce Barnes met them and gave them another video. He shook his head when he heard about the break-in. "It's becoming epidemic," he said. "It's as if the inner city has moved to the suburbs. We're no safer here anymore."

It was all Rayford could do to keep from telling Bruce that replacing the stolen tape was Chloe's idea. He wanted to tell Bruce to keep praying, that she must still be thinking about things. Maybe the invasion of the house had made her feel vulnerable. Maybe she was getting the point that the world was much more dangerous now, that there were no guarantees, that her own time could be short. But Rayford also knew he could offend her, insult her, push her away if he used this situation to sic Bruce on her. She had enough information; he just had to let God work on her. Still, he was encouraged and wanted to let Bruce know what was going on. He supposed he would have to wait for a more opportune time.

While they were out, Rayford bought items that needed to be replaced right away, including a TV and VCR. He arranged to have the front door fixed and got the insurance paperwork started. Most important, he armed the security system. Still, he knew, neither he nor Chloe would sleep soundly that night.

They came home to a phone call from Hattie Durham. Rayford thought she sounded lonely. She didn't seem to have a real reason to call. She simply told him she was grateful for the dinner invitation and was looking forward to it. He told her what had happened at their home, and she sounded genuinely troubled.

"Things are getting so strange," she said. "You know I have a sister who works in a pregnancy clinic."

"Uh-huh," Rayford said. "You've mentioned it."

"They do family planning and counseling and referrals for terminating pregnancies."

"Right."

"And they're set up to do abortions right there."

Hattie seemed to be waiting for some signal of affirmation or acknowledgment that he was listening. Rayford grew impatient and remained silent.

"Anyway," she said, "I won't keep you. But my sister told me they have zero business."

"Well, that would make sense, given the disappearances of unborn babies."

"My sister didn't sound too happy about that."

"Hattie, I imagine everyone's horrified by that. Parents are grieving all over the world."

"But the women my sister and her people were counseling *wanted* abortions."

Rayford groped for a pertinent response. "Yes, so maybe those women are grateful they didn't have to go through the abortion itself."

"Maybe, but my sister and her bosses and the rest of the staff are out of work now until people start getting pregnant again."

"I get it. It's a money thing."

"They have to work. They have expenses and families."

"And aside from abortion counseling and abortions, they have nothing to do?"

"Nothing. Isn't that awful? I mean, whatever happened put my sister and a lot of people like her out of business, and nobody really knows yet whether anyone will be able to get pregnant again."

Rayford had to admit he had never found Hattie guilty of brilliance, but now he wished he could look into her eyes. "Hattie, um, I don't know how to ask this. But are you saying your sister is hoping women can get pregnant again so they'll need abortions and she can keep working?"

"Well, sure. What is she going to do otherwise? Counseling jobs in other fields are pretty hard to come by, you know."

He nodded, feeling stupid, knowing she couldn't see him. What kind of lunacy was this? He shouldn't waste his energy arguing with someone who clearly didn't have a clue, but he couldn't help himself.

"I guess I always thought clinics like the one where your sister works considered these unwanted pregnancies a nuisance. Shouldn't they be glad if such problems disappear, and even happier—except for the small complication that the human race will eventually cease to exist—if pregnancies never happen again?"

The irony was lost on her. "But, Rayford, that's her job. That's what the center is all about. It's sort of like owning a gas station and nobody needing gas or oil or tires anymore."

"Supply and demand."

"Exactly! See? They need unwanted pregnancies because that's their business."

"Sort of like doctors wanting people to be sick or injured so they have something to do?"

"Now you've got it, Rayford."

* * *

After Buck had shaved and showered, Steve told him, "I was paged a minute ago. New York City detectives are looking for you at the office. Unfortunately, someone told them you would be at the Plaza with Carpathia later."

"Brilliant!"

"I know. Maybe you ought to just face this."

"Not yet, Steve. Let me get the Carpathia interview and get that piece started. Then I can extricate myself from this mess."

"You're hoping Carpathia can help."

"Precisely."

"What if you can't get to him before somebody gets to you?"

"I've got to. I've still got my Oreskovich press credentials and identification. If the cops are waiting for me at the Plaza, maybe they won't recognize me at first."

"C'mon, Buck. You think they aren't on to your phony ID by now, after you slipped out of Europe with it? Let me switch with you. If they think I'm you trying to pass yourself off as Oreskovich, that may buy you enough time to get in to see Carpathia."

Buck shrugged. "Worth a try," he said. "I don't want to stay here, but I want to see Carpathia on *Nightline*."

"Want to come to my place?"

"They'll probably look for me there before long."

"Let me call Marge. She and her husband don't live far away."

"Don't use my phone."

Steve grimaced. "You act like you're in a spy movie." Steve used his own cellular phone. Marge insisted they come over right away. She said her husband liked to watch his *M*A*S*H* rerun at that time of night but that she could talk him into taping it tonight.

Buck and Steve saw two unmarked squad cars pull up in front of Buck's apartment building as they climbed into a cab. "It *is* like a spy movie," Buck said.

Marge's husband was none too pleased to be displaced from his favorite spot and his favorite show, but even he was intrigued when *Nightline* began. Carpathia was either a natural or well-coached. He looked directly into the camera whenever possible and appeared to be speaking to individual viewers.

"Your speech at the United Nations," Wallace Theodore began, "which was sandwiched between two press conferences today, seems to have electrified New

York, and because so much of it has been aired on both early evening and late night local newscasts, you've become a popular man in this country seemingly all at once."

Carpathia smiled. "Like anyone from Europe, particularly Eastern Europe, I am amazed at your technology. I—"

"But isn't it true, sir, that your roots are actually in Western Europe? Though you were born in Romania, are you not by heritage actually Italian?"

"That is true, as it is true of many native Romanians. Thus the name of our country. But as I was saying about your technology. It is amazing, but I confess I did not come to your country to become or to be made into a celebrity. I have a goal, a mission, a message, and it has nothing to do with my popularity or my personal—"

"But is it not true that you just came from a photo session with *People* magazine?"

"Yes, but I—"

"And is it not also true that they have already named you their newest Sexiest Man Alive?"

"I do not know what that means, really. I submitted to an interview that was mostly about my childhood and my business and political career, and I was under the impression that they do this sexy-man coverage in January each year, so it is too early for next year and too close to this year's."

"Yes, and I'm sure, Mr. Carpathia, that you were as thrilled as we were over the young singing star who was so named two months ago, but—"

"I regret to say I was not aware of the young man before I saw his photograph on the cover of the magazine."

"But, sir, are you saying you are not aware that *People* magazine is breaking tradition by, in effect, unseating their current sexiest man and installing you in his place with next week's issue?"

"I believe they tried to tell me that, but I do not understand. The young man did some damage to a hotel or some such thing, and so—"

"And so you were a convenient replacement for him."

"I know nothing about that, and to be perfectly honest, I might not have submitted to the interview under those circumstances. I do not consider myself sexy. I am on a crusade to see the peoples of the world come together. I do not seek a position of power or authority. I simply ask to be heard. I hope my message comes through in the article in the magazine as well."

"You already have a position of both power and authority, Mr. Carpathia."

"Well, our little country asked me to serve, and I was willing."

"How do you respond to those who say you skirted protocol and that your elevation to the presidency in Romania was partially effected by strong-arm tactics?"

"I would say that that is the perfect way to attack a pacifist, one who is committed to disarmament not only in Romania and the rest of Europe but also globally."

"So you deny having a business rival murdered seven years ago and using intimidation and powerful friends in America to usurp the president's authority in Romania?"

"The so-called murdered rival was one of my dearest friends, and I mourn him bitterly to this day. The few American friends I have may be influential here, but they could not have any bearing on Romanian politics. You must know that our former president asked me to replace him for personal reasons."

"But that completely ignores your constitution's procedure for succession to power."

"This was voted upon by the people and by the government and ratified with a huge majority."

"After the fact."

"In a way, yes. But in another way, had they not ratified it, both popularly and within the houses of government, I would have been the briefest reigning president in our nation's history."

Marge's husband growled, "This Roman kid is light on his feet."

"Romanian," Marge corrected.

"I heard him say he's a full-blood Eye-talian," her husband said. Marge winked at Steve and Buck.

Buck was amazed at Carpathia's thought processes and command of language. Theodore asked him, "Why the United Nations? Some would say you would have more impact and get more mileage out of an appearance before our Senate and House of Representatives."

"I would not even dream of such a privilege," Carpathia said. "But, you see, I was not looking for mileage. The U.N. was envisioned originally as a peacekeeping effort. It must return to that role."

"You hinted today, and I hear it in your voice even now, that you have a specific plan for the U.N. that would make it better and which would be of some help during this unusually horrific season in history."

"I do. I did not feel it was my place to suggest such changes when I was a guest; however, I have no hesitation in this context. I am a proponent of disarmament. That is no secret. While I am impressed with the wide-ranging capabilities, plans, and programs of the United Nations, I do believe, with a few minor adjustments and the cooperation of its members, it can be all it was meant to be. We can truly become a global community."

"Can you briefly outline that in a few seconds?"

Carpathia's laugh appeared deep and genuine. "That is always dangerous," he said, "but I will try. As you know, the Security Council of the United Nations has five permanent members: the United States, the Russian Federation, Britain, France, and China. There are also ten temporary members, two each from five different regions of the world, which serve for two-year terms.

"I respect the proprietary nature of the original five. I propose choosing another five, just one each from the five different regions of the world. Drop the temporary members. Then you would have ten permanent members of the Security Council, but the rest of my plan is revolutionary. Currently the five permanent members have veto power. Votes on procedure require a nine-vote majority; votes on substance require a majority, including all five permanent members. I propose a tougher system. I propose unanimity."

"I beg your pardon?"

"Select carefully the representative ten permanent members. They must get input and support from all the countries in their respective regions."

"It sounds like a nightmare."

"But it would work, and here is why. A nightmare is what happened to us last week. The time is right for the peoples of the world to rise up and insist that their governments disarm and destroy all but ten percent of their weapons. That ten percent would be, in effect, donated to the United Nations so it could return to its rightful place as a global peacekeeping body, with the authority and the power and the equipment to do the job."

Carpathia went on to educate the audience that it was in 1965 that the U.N. amended its original charter to increase the Security Council from 11 to 15. He said that the original veto power of the permanent members had hampered military peace efforts, such as in Korea and during the Cold War.

"Sir, where did you get your encyclopedic knowledge of the U.N. and world affairs?"

"We all find time to do what we really want to do. This is my passion."

"What is your personal goal? A leadership role in the European Common Market?"

"Romania is not even a member, as you know. But no, I have no personal goal of leadership, except as a voice. We must disarm, we must empower the United Nations, we must move to one currency, and we must become a global village."

\+ + +

Rayford and Chloe sat in silence before their new television, taken with the fresh face and encouraging ideas of Nicolae Carpathia. "What a guy!" Chloe said at last. "I haven't heard a politician with anything to say since I was a little girl, and I didn't understand half of it then."

"He is something," Rayford agreed. "It's especially nice to see somebody who doesn't seem to have a personal agenda."

Chloe smiled. "So you're not going to start comparing him with the liar the pastor's tape warned us of, somebody from Europe who tries to take over the world?"

"Hardly," Rayford said. "There's nothing evil or self-seeking about this guy. Something tells me the deceiver the pastor talked about would be a little more obvious."

"But," Chloe said, "if he's a deceiver, maybe he's a good one."

"Hey, which side of this argument are you on? Does this guy look like the Antichrist to you?"

She shook her head. "He looks like a breath of fresh air to me. If he starts trying to weasel his way into power, I might be suspicious, but a pacifist, content to be president of a small country? His only influence is his wisdom, and his only power is his sincerity and humility."

The phone rang. It was Hattie, eager to talk to Rayford. She was nearly manic with praise for Carpathia. "Did you see that guy? He's so handsome! I just have to meet him. Do you have any flights scheduled to New York?"

"Wednesday I have a late morning flight and come back the next morning. Then we're going to see you for dinner that night, right?"

"Yeah, and that's great, but Rayford, would you mind if I tried to work that flight? I heard on the news that the death report on that magazine writer was wrong and he's in New York. I'm going to see if I can meet with him and get him to introduce me to this Carpathia."

"You think he knows him?"

"Buck knows everybody. He does all these big international stories. He's got to. Even if he doesn't, I wouldn't mind seeing Buck."

That was a relief to Rayford. So Hattie wasn't afraid to talk about two younger guys she was clearly interested in seeing, or at least meeting. He was sure she wasn't just saying it to test his level of interest. Surely she knew he wasn't interested in anyone with his wife so recently gone. Rayford wondered whether he should follow through on his plan to be honest with her about his past feelings for her. Maybe he should just jump right into urging that she watch the pastor's videotape.

"Well, good luck with it," Rayford said lamely.

"But can I apply for your flight?"

"Why don't you just see if it comes up that way on the schedule?"

"Rayford!"

"What?"

"You don't want me on your flight! Why? Have I said or done something?"

"Why do you think that?"

"You think I don't know you squashed my last request?"

"I didn't exactly squash it. I just said—"

"You might as well have."

"I said what I just told you. I'm not opposed to your working my flights, but why don't you just let them come as they come?"

"You know the odds of that! If I wait, the odds are against me. If I push for certain ones, with my seniority I can usually get them. Now what's the deal, Rayford?"

"Can we talk about this when you come for dinner?"

"Let's talk about it now."

Rayford paused, groping for words. "Look what your special requests do to the schedules, Hattie. Everybody else has to slide to accommodate you."

"That's your reason? You're worried about everybody else?"

He didn't want to lie. "Partly," he said.

"That never bothered you before. You used to encourage me to request your flights and sometimes you checked with me to make sure I had done it."

"I know."

"So, what's changed?"

"Hattie, please. I don't want to discuss this by phone."

"Then meet me somewhere."

"I can't do that. I can't leave Chloe so soon after we've had a burglary."

"Then I'll come there."

"It's late."

"Rayford! Are you brushing me off?"

"If I was brushing you off, I wouldn't have invited you to dinner."

"With your daughter at your home? I think I'm getting set up for the royal brush."

"Hattie, what are you saying?"

"Only that you enjoyed running around with me in private, pretending like something was going on."

"I'll admit that."

"And I do feel bad about your wife, Rayford, I really do. You're probably feeling guilty, even though we never did anything to feel guilty about. But don't cast me aside before you have a chance to get over your loss and start living again."

"That's not it. Hattie, what's to cast aside? It's not like we had a relationship. If we did, why are you so interested in this magazine guy and the Romanian?"

"Everybody's interested in Carpathia," she said. "And Buck is the only way I know of to get to him. You can't think I have designs on him. Really! An international newsmaker? Come on, Rayford."

"I don't care if you do. I'm only saying, how does that jibe with whatever you thought we had going?"

"You want me to not go to New York and to forget about both of them?"

"Not at all. I'm hardly saying that."

"Because I will. If I had ever thought there was really a chance with you, I'd have pursued it, believe me."

Rayford was taken aback. His fears and assumptions were correct, but now he felt defensive. "You never thought there was a chance?"

"You hardly gave me any indication. For all I knew you thought I was a cute kid, way too young, fun to be with, but don't touch."

"There's some truth to that."

"But you never once wished it was something more, Rayford?"

"That's something I would like to talk with you about, Hattie."

"You can answer it right now."

Rayford sighed. "Yes, there were times I wished it was something more."

"Well, glory be. I missed my guess. I had given up, figured you were an untouchable."

"I am."

"Now, sure. I can understand that. You're in pain and probably worse because you were considering someone besides your wife for a while. But does that mean I can't even fly with you, talk to you, have a drink with you? We could go back to the way things used to be, and except for what's in your mind there still wouldn't be anything wrong with it."

"It doesn't mean you can't talk with me or work with me when our schedules coincide. If I didn't want to have anything to do with you, I wouldn't have invited you over."

"I can see what that's all about, Rayford. You can't tell me I wasn't going to get the 'let's be friends' routine."

"Maybe that and a little more."

"Like what?"

"Just something I want to tell you about."

"What if I told you I'm not interested in that kind of socializing? I don't expect you to run to me now that your wife is gone, but I didn't expect to be ignored either."

"How is having you over for dinner ignoring you?"

"Why did you never have me over before?"

Rayford was silent.

"Well?"

"It would have been inappropriate," he muttered.

"And now it's inappropriate to meet any other way?"

"Frankly, yes. But I do want to talk to you, and it isn't about brushing you off."

"Is my curiosity supposed to force me to come now, Rayford? Because, I'll tell you what, I have to decline. I'm going to be busy. Accept my regrets. Something came up, unavoidable, you understand."

"Please. Hattie. We really want you to come. I want you to."

"Rayford, don't bother. There are plenty of flights to New York. I won't go through any gymnastics to get on yours. In fact, I'll make sure I stay away from them."

"You don't have to do that."

"Of course I do. No hard feelings. I would have liked to have met Chloe, but you probably would have felt obligated to tell her you once nearly fell for me."

"Hattie, will you listen to me for a second? Please."

"No."

"I want you to come over Thursday night, and I really have something important to talk to you about."

"Tell me what it is."

"Not on the phone."

"Then I'm not coming."

"If I tell you generally, will you?"

"Depends."

"Well, I know what the disappearances were all about, all right? I know what they meant, and I want to help you find the truth."

Hattie was dead silent for a long moment. "You haven't become some kind of a fanatic, have you?"

Rayford had to think about that one. The answer was yes, he most certainly had, but he wasn't going to say that. "You know me better than that."

"I thought I did."

"Trust me, this is worth your time."

"Give me the basics, and I'll tell you if I want to hear it."

"Absolutely not," Rayford said, surprising himself with his resolve. "That I will not do, except in person."

"Then I'm not coming."

"Hattie!"

"Good-bye, Rayford."

"Hat—"

She hung up.

16

"I WOULDN'T DO this for just anybody," Steve Plank said after he and Buck had thanked Marge and headed to separate cabs. "I don't know how long I can hold them off and convince them I'm you pretending to be someone else, so don't be far behind."

"Don't worry."

Steve took the first cab, Buck's George Oreskovich press credentials on his chest. He was to go directly to the Plaza Hotel, where he would ask for his appointment with Carpathia. Buck's hope was that Steve would be immediately intercepted, arrested as Buck, and clear the way for Buck to get in. If Buck was accosted by authorities, he would show his identity as Steve Plank. Both knew the plan was flimsy, but Buck was willing to try anything to keep from being extradited and framed for Alan Tompkins's murder, and possibly even Dirk Burton's.

Buck asked his cabbie to wait about a minute after Steve had left for the Plaza. He arrived at the hotel in the midst of flashing police lights, a paddy wagon, and several unmarked cars. As he threaded his way through onlookers, the police hustled Steve, hands cuffed behind his back, out the door and down the steps.

"I'm telling you," Steve said. "The name's Oreskovich!"

"We know who you are, Williams. Save your breath."

"That's not Cam Williams!" another reporter said, pointing and laughing. "You idiots! That's Steve Plank."

"Yeah, that's it," Plank joined in. "I'm Williams's boss from the *Weekly*!"

"Sure you are," a plainclothesman said, stuffing him into an unmarked car.

Buck ducked the reporter who had recognized Plank, but when he got inside and picked up a courtesy phone to call Rosenzweig's room, another press colleague, Eric Miller, whirled around and covered his own phone, whispering, "Williams, what's going on? The cops just shuttled your boss out of here, claiming he was you!"

"Do me a favor," Buck said. "Sit on this for at least half an hour. You owe me that."

"I owe you nothing, Williams," Miller said. "But you look scared enough. Give me your word you'll tell me first what's going on."

"All right. You'll be the first press guy I tell anyway. Can't promise I won't tell someone else."

"Who?"

"Nice try."

"If you're trying to call Carpathia, Cameron, you can forget it. We've been trying all night. He's not giving any more interviews tonight."

"Is he back?"

"He's back, but he's incommunicado."

Rosenzweig answered Buck's call. "Chaim, it's Cameron Williams. May I come up?"

Eric Miller slammed his phone down and moved close.

"Cameron!" Rosenzweig said. "I can't keep up with you. First you're dead, then you're alive. We just got a call that you had been arrested in the lobby and would be questioned about a murder in London."

Buck didn't want Miller to detect anything. "Chaim, I have to move quickly. I'll be using the name Plank, all right?"

"I'll arrange it with Nicolae and get him to my room somehow. You come." He told Buck the number.

Buck put a finger to his lips so Miller wouldn't ask, but he couldn't shake him. He jogged to the elevator, but Eric stepped on with him. A couple tried to join them. "I'm sorry, folks," Buck said. "This car is malfunctioning." The couple left but Miller stayed. Buck didn't want him to see what floor he was going to, so he waited till the doors shut, then turned the car off. He grabbed Miller's shirt at the neck and pressed him against the wall.

"Listen, Eric, I told you I'd call you first with what's shakin' here, but if you try to horn in on this or follow me, I'm gonna leave you dry."

Miller shook loose and straightened his clothes. "All right, Williams! Geez! Lighten up!"

"Yeah, I lighten up and you come snooping around."

"That's my job, man. Don't forget that."

"Mine too, Eric, but I don't follow other people's leads. I make my own."

"You interviewing Carpathia? Just tell me that."

"No, I'm risking my life to see if a movie star's in the house."

"So it's Carpathia then, really?"

"I didn't say that."

"C'mon, man, let me in on it! I'll give you anything!"

"You said Carpathia wasn't giving any more interviews tonight," Buck said.

"And he's not giving any more to anybody except the networks and national outlets, so I'll never get to him."

"That's your problem."

"Williams!"

Buck reached for Miller's throat again. "I'm going!" Eric said.

When Buck emerged at the VIP floor, he was astounded to see that Miller had somehow beat him there and was hurriedly introducing himself to a uniformed guard as Steve Plank. "Mr. Rosenzweig is waiting for you, sir," the guard said.

"Wait a minute!" Buck shouted, showing Steve's press credentials. "I'm Plank. Run this impostor off."

The guard put a hand on each man. "You'll both have to wait here while I call the house detective."

Buck said, "Just call Rosenzweig and have him come out here."

The guard shrugged and punched in the room number on a portable phone. Miller leaned in, saw the number, and sprinted toward the room. Buck took off after him, the unarmed guard yelling and still trying to reach someone on the phone.

Buck, younger and in better shape, overtook Miller and tackled him in the hallway, causing doors up and down the corridor to open. "Take your brawl somewhere else," a woman shouted.

Buck yanked Miller to his feet and put him in a headlock. "You are a clown, Eric. You really think Rosenzweig would let a stranger into his room?"

"I can sweet-talk my way into anywhere, Buck, and you know you would do the same thing."

"Problem is, I already did. Now beat it."

The guard caught up with them. "Dr. Rosenzweig will be out in a minute."

"I have just one question for him," Miller said.

"No, you don't," Buck said. He turned to the guard. "He doesn't."

"Let the old man decide," the guard said, then just as suddenly stepped aside, pulling Buck and Miller with him to clear the hall. There, sweeping past them, were four men in dark suits, surrounding the unmistakable Nicolae Carpathia.

"Excuse me, gentlemen," Carpathia said. "Pardon me."

"Oh, Mr. Carpathia, sir. I mean President Carpathia," Miller called out.

"Sir?" Carpathia said, turning to face him. The bodyguards glowered. "Oh, hello, Mr. Williams," Carpathia said, noticing Buck. "Or should I say Mr. Oreskovich? Or should I say Mr. Plank?"

The interloper stepped forward. "Eric Miller from *Seaboard Monthly*."

"I know it well, Mr. Miller," Carpathia said, "but I am late for an appointment. If you will call me tomorrow, I will talk to you by phone. Fair enough?"

Miller looked overwhelmed. He nodded and backed away. "I thought you said your name was Plank!" the guard said, causing everyone but Miller to smile.

"Come on in, Buck," Carpathia said, motioning him to follow. Buck was silent. "That is what they call you, is it not?"

"Yes, sir," Buck said, certain that not even Rosenzweig knew that.

* * *

Rayford felt terrible about Hattie Durham. Things couldn't have gone worse. Why hadn't he just let her work his flight? She'd have been none the wiser and he could have eased into his real reason for inviting her to dinner Thursday night. Now he had spoiled everything.

How would he get to Chloe now? His real motive, even for talking with Hattie, was to communicate to Chloe. Hadn't she seen enough yet? Shouldn't he be more encouraged by her insistence on replacing the stolen videotape? He asked if she wanted to go to New York with him for the overnight trip. She said she'd rather stay home and start looking into taking classes locally. He wanted to push, but he didn't dare.

After she had gone to bed, he called Bruce Barnes and told him his frustrations.

"You're trying too hard, Rayford," the younger man said. "I should think telling other people about our faith would be easier than ever now, but I've run into the same kind of resistance."

"It's really hard when it's your own daughter."

"I can imagine," Bruce said.

"No, you can't," Rayford said. "But it's all right."

* * *

Chaim Rosenzweig was in a beautiful suite of rooms. The bodyguards were posted out front, while Carpathia invited Rosenzweig and Buck into a private parlor for a meeting of just the three of them. Carpathia shed his coat and laid it carefully across the back of a couch. "Make yourselves comfortable, gentlemen," he said.

"I do not need to be here, Nicolae," Rosenzweig whispered.

"Oh, nonsense, Doctor!" Carpathia said. "You do not mind, do you, Buck?"

"Not at all."

"You do not mind my calling you Buck, do you?"

"No, sir, but usually it's just people at—"

"Your magazine, yes, I know. They call you that because you buck the traditions and the trends and the conventions, am I right?"

"Yes, but how—"

"Buck, this has been the most incredible day of my life. I have felt so welcome here. And the people have seemed so receptive to my proposals. I am overwhelmed. I shall go back to my country a happy and satisfied man. But not soon. I have been asked to stay longer. Did you know that?"

"I heard."

"It is amazing, is it not, that all those different international meetings right here in New York over the next few weeks are all about the worldwide cooperation in which I am interested?"

"It is," Buck said. "And I've been assigned to cover them."

"Then we will be getting to know each other better."

"I look forward to that, sir. I was most moved at the U.N. today."

"Thank you."

"And Dr. Rosenzweig has told me so much about you."

"As he has told me much about you."

There was a knock at the door. Carpathia looked pained. "I had hoped we would not be disturbed." Rosenzweig rose slowly and shuffled to the door and a subdued conversation.

He slipped back to Buck. "We'll have to give him a couple of minutes, Cameron," he whispered, "for an important phone call."

"Oh, no," Carpathia said. "I will take it later. This meeting is a priority for me—"

"Sir," Rosenzweig said, "begging your pardon . . . it is the president."

"The president?"

"Of the United States."

Buck rose quickly to leave with Rosenzweig, but Carpathia insisted they stay. "I am not such a dignitary that I would not share this honor with my old friend and my new friend. Sit down!"

They sat and he pushed the speaker button on the phone. "This is Nicolae Carpathia speaking."

"Mr. Carpathia, this is Fitz. Gerald Fitzhugh."

"Mr. President, I am honored to hear from you."

"Well, hey, it's good to have you here!"

"I appreciated your note of congratulations on my presidency, sir, and your immediate recognition of my administration."

"Boy, that was a heckuva thing, how you took over there. I wasn't sure what had happened at first, but I don't suppose you were either."

"That is exactly right. I am still getting used to it."

"Well, take it from a guy who's been in the saddle for six years. You don't ever get used to it. You just develop calluses in the right places, if you know what I mean."

"Yes, sir."

"Listen, the reason I called is this. I know you're gonna be here a little longer than you expected, so I want you to spend a night or two here with me and Wilma. Can you do that?"

"In Washington?"

"Right here at the White House."

"That would be such a privilege."

"We'll have somebody talk to your people about the right time, but it's got to be soon 'cause Congress is in session, and I know they'll want to hear from you."

Carpathia shook his head and Buck thought he seemed overcome emotionally. "I would be more than honored, sir."

"Speaking of something that was a heckuva thing, your speech today and your interview tonight—well, that was something. Look forward to meetin' ya."

"The feeling is mutual, sir."

Buck was only a little less overcome than Carpathia and Rosenzweig. He had long since lost his awe of U.S. presidents, especially this one, who insisted on being called Fitz. He had done a Newsmaker of the Year piece on Fitzhugh—Buck's first, Fitz's second. On the other hand, it wasn't every day that the president called the room in which you sat.

The glow of the call seemed to stay with Carpathia, but he quickly changed the subject. "Buck, I want to answer all your questions and give you whatever you need. You have been so good to Chaim, and I am prepared to give you a bit of a secret—you would call it a scoop. But first, you are in deep trouble, my friend. And I want to help you if I can."

Buck had no idea how Carpathia knew he was in trouble. So he wouldn't even have to bring him up to speed and ask for his help? This was too good to be true. The question was, what did Carpathia know, and what did he need to know?

The Romanian sat forward and looked directly into Buck's eyes. That gave Buck such a feeling of peace and security that he felt free to tell him everything. Everything. Even that his friend Dirk had tipped him off about someone meeting with Stonagal and Todd-Cothran, and Buck's assuming it was Carpathia.

"It *was* I," Carpathia said. "But let me make this very clear. I know nothing of any conspiracy. I have never even heard of such a thing. Mr. Stonagal felt it would be good for me to meet some of his colleagues and men of international influence. I formed no opinions about any of them, neither am I beholden to any of them.

"I will tell you something, Mr. Williams. I believe your story. I do not know you except by your work and your reputation with people I respect, such as Dr. Rosenzweig. But your account has the ring of truth. I have been told that you are wanted in London for the murder of the Scotland Yard agent and that they have several witnesses who will swear they saw you distract Tompkins, plant the device, and activate it from within the pub."

"That's crazy."

"Well, of course it is if you were mourning the mysterious death of your mutual friend."

"That's exactly what we were doing, Mr. Carpathia. That and trying to get to the bottom of it."

Rosenzweig was called to the door again; then he whispered in Carpathia's ear. "Buck, come here," Carpathia said, rising and leading Buck toward a window, away from Rosenzweig. "Your plan to get in here while being pursued was most ingenious, but your boss has been identified and now they know you are here. They would like to take you into custody and extradite you to England."

"If that happens and Tompkins's theory is right," Buck said, "I'm a dead man."

"You believe they will kill you?"

"They killed Burton and they killed Tompkins. I'm much more dangerous to them with my potential readership."

"If this plot is as you and your friends say it is, Cameron, writing about these people, exposing them, will not protect you."

"I know. Maybe I should do it anyway. I don't see any way out."

"I can make this go away for you."

Buck's mind was suddenly reeling. This was what he had wanted, but he had feared Carpathia could do nothing quickly enough to keep him from getting into Todd-Cothran's and Sullivan's hands. Was it possible Carpathia was in deeper with these people than he had let on?

"Sir, I need your help. But I am a journalist first. I can't be bought or bargained with."

"Oh, of course not. I would never ask such a thing. Let me tell you what I can do for you. I will arrange to have the London tragedies revisited and reevaluated, exonerating you."

"How will you do that?"

"Does it matter, if it is the truth?"

Buck thought a moment. "It *is* the truth."

"Of course."

"But how will you do that? You have maintained this innocence, Mr. Carpathia, this man-from-nowhere persona. How can you affect what has happened in London?"

Carpathia sighed. "Buck, I told you your friend Dirk was wrong about a conspiracy. That is true. I am not in bed with Todd-Cothran or Stonagal or any of the other international leaders I have been honored to meet recently. However, there are important decisions and actions coming up that will affect them, and it is my privilege to have a say in those developments."

Buck asked Carpathia if he minded if they sat down again. Carpathia signaled to Rosenzweig to leave them for a few minutes. "Look," Buck said when they were seated, "I'm a young man, but I've been around the block. It feels to me as if I'm about to find out just how deep into this—well, if it's not a conspiracy, it's something organized—how deep into this thing you are. I can play along and save my life, or I can refuse and you let me take my chances in London."

Carpathia held up a hand and shook his head. "Buck, let me reiterate that we are talking politics and diplomacy, not skullduggery or crime."

"I'm listening."

"First," Carpathia said, "a little background. I believe in the power of money. Do you?"

"No."

"You will. I was a better-than-average businessman in Romania while still in secondary school. I studied at night, many languages, the ones I needed to succeed. During the day I ran my own import-and-export businesses and made myself wealthy. But what I thought was wealth was paltry compared to what was possible. I needed to learn that. I learned it the hard way. I borrowed millions from a European bank, then found that someone in that bank informed my major competitor what I was doing. I was defeated at my own game, defaulted on my loan, and was struggling. Then that same bank bailed me out and ruined my rival. I didn't mean to or want to hurt the rival. He was used by the bank to lock me into a relationship."

"Was that bank owned by an influential American?"

Carpathia ignored the question. "What I had to learn, in just over a decade, is how much money is out there."

"Out there?"

"In the banks of the world."

"Especially those owned by Jonathan Stonagal," Buck suggested.

Carpathia still wasn't biting. "That kind of capital is power."

"This is the kind of thing I write against."

"It is about to save your life."

"I'm still listening."

"That kind of money gets a man's attention. He becomes willing to make concessions for it. He begins to see the wisdom of letting someone else, a younger man, someone with more enthusiasm and vigor and fresh vision take over."

"That's what happened in Romania?"

"Buck, do not insult me. The former president of Romania asked me of his own free will to replace him, and the support for that move was unanimous within the government and almost totally favorable among the masses. Everyone is better off."

"The former president is out of power."

"He lives in luxury."

Buck could not breathe. What was Carpathia implying? Buck stared at him, unable to move, unable to respond. Carpathia continued. "Secretary-General Ngumo presides over a country that is starving. The world is ripe for my plan of ten members of the Security Council. These things will work together. The secretary-general must devote his time to the problems within Botswana. With the right incentive, he will do that. He will be a happy, prosperous man, with a happy and prosperous people. But first he will endorse my plan for the Security Council. The representatives from each of the ten will be an interesting mix, some current ambassadors, but mostly new people with good financial backgrounds and progressive ideas."

"Are you telling me you will become secretary-general of the U.N.?"

"I would never seek such a position, but how could I refuse such an honor? Who could turn his back on such an enormous responsibility?"

"How much say will you have about who represents each of the ten permanent members of the Security Council?"

"I will merely be there to provide servant leadership. Are you aware of that concept? One leads by serving, not by dictating."

"Let me take a wild guess," Buck said. "Todd-Cothran is in line for a role on your new Security Council."

Carpathia sat back, as if learning something. "Would that not be interesting?" he said. "A nonpolitician, a brilliant financial mind, one who was wise enough and kind enough and globally minded enough to allow the world to go to a three-currency system that did not include his own pounds sterling? He brings no baggage to such a role. The world would have a certain level of comfort with him, would they not?"

"I suppose they would," Buck said, his mind black with depression as if he were losing his soul before his very eyes. "Unless, that is, Todd-Cothran were in the middle of a mysterious suicide, a car bombing, that sort of a thing."

Carpathia smiled. "I should think a man in a position of international potential like that would want a very clean house just now."

"And you could effect that?"

"Buck, you overestimate me. I am just saying that if you are right, I might try to stop what is clearly an unethical and illegal action against an innocent man—you. I cannot see how there is anything wrong with that."

* * *

Rayford Steele could not sleep. For some reason he was overcome anew with grief and remorse over the loss of his wife and son. He slid out of bed and onto his knees, burying his face in the sheet on the side where his wife used to sleep. He had been so tired, so tense, so worried about Chloe that he had pushed from his heart and mind and soul his terrible loss. He believed totally that his wife and son were in heaven, and he knew they were better off than they had ever been.

Rayford knew he had been forgiven for mocking his wife, for never really listening, for having ignored God for so many years. He was grateful he had been given a second chance and that he now had new friends and a place to learn the Bible. But that didn't stop the aching emptiness in his heart, the longing to hold his wife and son, to kiss them and tell them how much he loved them. He prayed for the grief to lessen, but part of him wanted it, needed it, to remain.

In a way he felt he deserved this pain, though he knew better. He was beginning to understand the forgiveness of God, and Bruce had told him that he needn't continue to feel shame over sin that had been dealt with.

As Rayford knelt praying and weeping, a new anguish flooded over him. He felt hopeless about Chloe. Everything he had tried had failed. He knew it had been only days since the disappearance of her mother and brother, and even less time since his own conversion. What more could he say or do? Bruce had encouraged him just to pray, but he was not made that way. He would pray, of course, but he had always been a man of action.

Now, every action seemed to push her farther away. He felt that if he said or did anything more, he would be responsible for her deciding against Christ once and for all. Rayford had never felt more powerless and desperate. How he longed to have Irene and Raymie with him right then. And how he despaired over Chloe.

He had been praying silently, but the torment welled up within him, and despite himself he heard his own muffled cries, "Chloe! Oh, Chloe! Chloe!"

He wept bitterly in the darkness, suddenly jarred by a creak and footsteps.

He turned quickly to see Chloe, the dim light from her room silhouetting her robed form in the doorway. He didn't know what she had heard.

"Are you all right, Dad?" she asked quietly.

"Yeah."

"Nightmare?"

"No. I'm sorry to disturb you."

"I miss them, too," she said, her voice quavery. Rayford turned and sat with his back to the bed. He held his arms open to her. She came and sat next to him, letting him hold her.

"I believe I'll see them again someday," he said.

"I know you do," she said, no disrespect in her voice. "I know you do."

17

AFTER A FEW MINUTES, Chloe gave Rayford evidence that she had heard his cry. "Don't worry about me, Daddy, OK? I'm getting there."

Getting where? Did she mean that her decision was just a matter of time or simply that she was getting over her grief? He wanted so badly to tell her he was worried, but she knew that. Her very presence brought him comfort, but when she padded back to her room he felt desperately alone again.

He could not sleep. He tiptoed downstairs and turned on the new TV, tuning in CNN. From Israel came the strangest report. The screen showed a mob in front of the famous Wailing Wall, surrounding two men who seemed to be shouting.

"No one knows the two men," said the CNN reporter on the scene, "who refer to each other as Eli and Moishe. They have stood here before the Wailing Wall since just before dawn, preaching in a style frankly reminiscent of the old American evangelists. Of course the Orthodox Jews here are in an uproar, charging the two with desecrating this holy place by proclaiming that Jesus Christ of the New Testament is the fulfillment of the Torah's prophecy of a messiah.

"Thus far there has been no violence, though tempers are flaring, and authorities keep a watchful eye. Israeli police and military personnel have always been loath to enter this area, leaving religious zealots here to handle their own problems. This is the most explosive situation in the Holy Land since the destruction of the Russian air force, and this newly prosperous nation has been concerned almost primarily with outside threats.

"For CNN, this is Dan Bennett in Jerusalem."

Had it not been so late, Rayford would have called Bruce Barnes. He sat there, feeling a part of the family of believers to which the two men in Jerusalem apparently belonged. This was exactly what he had been learning, that Jesus was the Messiah of the Old Testament. Bruce had told him and the rest of the core group at New Hope that there would soon spring up 144,000 Jews who would believe in Christ and begin to evangelize around the world. Were these the first two?

The CNN anchorwoman turned to national news. "New York is still abuzz following several appearances today by new Romanian president Nicolae Carpathia. The thirty-three-year-old leader wowed the media at a small press conference this morning, followed by a masterful speech to the United Nations General Assembly in which he had the entire crowd standing and cheering, including the press. He reportedly sat for a cover photo session with *People* magazine and will be their first ever Sexiest Man Alive to appear less than a year after the previous designate.

"Associates of Carpathia have announced that he has already extended his schedule to include addresses to several international meetings in New York over the next two weeks and that he has been invited by President Fitzhugh to speak to a joint session of Congress and spend a night at the White House.

"At a press conference this afternoon the president voiced support for the new leader."

The president's image filled the screen. "At this difficult hour in world history, it's crucial that lovers of peace and unity step forward to remind us that we're part of a global community. Any friend of peace is a friend of the United States, and Mr. Carpathia is a friend of peace."

CNN broadcast a question asked of the president. "Sir, what do you think of Carpathia's ideas for the U.N.?"

"Let me just say this: I don't believe I've ever heard anybody, inside or outside the U.N., show such a total grasp of the history and organization and direction of the place. He's done his homework, and he has a plan. I was listening. I hope the respective ambassadors and Secretary-General Ngumo were, too. No one should see a fresh vision as a threat. I'm sure every leader in the world shares my view that we need all the help we can get at this hour."

The anchorwoman continued: "Out of New York late this evening comes a report that a *Global Weekly* writer has been cleared of all charges and suspicion in the death of a Scotland Yard investigator. Cameron Williams, award-winning senior writer at the *Weekly*, had been feared dead in a car bombing that took the life of the investigator Alan Tompkins, who was also an acquaintance of Williams.

"Tompkins's remains had been identified and Williams's passport and ID were found among the rubble after the explosion. Williams's assumed death was reported in newspapers across the country, but he reappeared in New York late this afternoon and was seen at the United Nations press conference following Nicolae Carpathia's speech.

"Earlier this evening, Williams was considered an international fugitive, wanted by both Scotland Yard and Interpol for questioning in connection with the bombing death. Both agencies have since announced he has been cleared of all charges and is considered lucky to have escaped unharmed.

"In sports news, Major League Baseball teams in spring training face the daunting task of replacing the dozens of players lost in the cosmic disappearances. . . ."

Rayford still was not sleepy. He made himself coffee, then phoned the twenty-four-hour line that kept track of flight and crew assignments. He had an idea. "Can you tell me whether I can still get Hattie Durham assigned to my JFK run Wednesday?" he asked.

"I'll see what I can do," came the response. "Whoops, no. I guess you can't. She's going to New York already. Yours is the 10 a.m. flight. Hers is the 8 a.m."

+ + +

Buck Williams had returned to his apartment after midnight, assured by Nicolae Carpathia that his worries were over. Carpathia had phoned Jonathan Stonagal, put him on speakerphone, and Stonagal had done the same as he made the middle-of-the-night phone call to London that cleared Williams. Buck heard Todd-Cothran's husky-voiced agreement to call off the Yard and Interpol. "But my package is secure?" Todd-Cothran asked.

"Guaranteed," Stonagal had said.

Most alarming to Buck was that Stonagal did his own dirty work, at least in this instance. Buck had looked accusingly at Carpathia, despite his relief and gratitude.

"Mr. Williams," Carpathia said, "I was confident Jonathan could handle this, but I am just as ignorant of the details as you are."

"But this just proves Dirk was right! Stonagal *is* conspiring with Todd-Cothran, and you knew it! And Stonagal promised him his package was secure, whatever that means."

"I assure you I knew nothing until you told me, Buck. I had no prior knowledge."

"But now you know. Can you still in good conscience allow Stonagal to help promote you in international politics?"

"Trust me, I will deal with them both."

"But there have to be many more! What about all the other so-called dignitaries you met?"

"Buck, just be assured there is no place around me for insincerity or injustice. I will deal with them in due time."

"And meanwhile?"

"What would you advise? It seems to me that I am in no position to do anything right now. They seem intent on elevating me, but until they do I can do nothing but what your media calls whistle-blowing. How far would I get with that, before I know how far their tentacles reach? Before recently, would you not have thought Scotland Yard would be a trustworthy place to start?"

Buck nodded miserably. "I know what you mean, but I hate this. They know that you know."

"That may work to my advantage. They may think I am with them, that this makes me even more dependent upon them."

"Doesn't it?"

"Only temporarily. You have my word. I *will* deal with this. For now I am glad to have extricated you from a most delicate situation."

"I'm glad, too, Mr. Carpathia. Is there anything I can do for you?"

The Romanian smiled. "Well, I need a press secretary."

"I was afraid you were going to say that. I'm not your man."

"Of course not. I would not have dreamed of asking."

As a joke, Buck suggested, "What about the man you met in the hall?"

Carpathia displayed his prodigious memory once more. "That Eric Miller fellow?"

"He's the one. You'd love him."

"And I already told him to call me tomorrow. May I say you recommended him?"

Buck shook his head. "I was kidding." He told Carpathia what had happened in the lobby, on the elevator, and in the hall before Miller introduced himself. Nicolae was not amused. "I'll rack my brain and see if I can think of another candidate for you," Buck said. "Now you promised me a scoop tonight, too."

"True. It is new information, but it must not be announced until I have the ability to effect it."

"I'm listening."

"Israel is particularly vulnerable, as they were before Russia tried to invade them. They were lucky that time, but the rest of the world resents their prosperity. They need protection. The U.N. can give it to them. In exchange for the chemical formula that makes the desert bloom, the world will be content to grant them peace. If the other nations disarm and surrender a tenth of their weapons to the U.N., only the U.N. will have to sign a peace accord with Israel. Their prime minister has given Dr. Rosenzweig the freedom to negotiate such an agreement because he is the true owner of the formula. They are, of course, insisting on guarantees of protection for no less than seven years."

Buck sat shaking his head. "You're going to get the Nobel Peace prize, *Time*'s Man of the Year, and our Newsmaker of the Year."

"Those certainly are not my goals."

Buck left Carpathia believing that as deeply as he had ever believed anything. Here was a man unaffected by the money that could buy lesser men.

At his apartment Buck discovered yet another phone message from Hattie Durham. He had to call that girl.

+ + +

Bruce Barnes called the core group together for an emergency meeting at New Hope Village Church Tuesday afternoon. Rayford drove over, hoping it would be worth his time and that Chloe wouldn't mind being home alone for a while. They had both been edgy since the break-in.

Bruce gathered everyone around his desk in the office. He began by praying that he would be lucid and instructive in spite of his excitement and then had everyone turn to the book of Revelation.

Bruce's eyes were bright and his voice carried the same passion and emotion as when he had called. Rayford wondered what had him so excited. He had asked Bruce on the phone, but Bruce insisted on telling everyone in person.

"I don't want to keep you long," he said, "but I'm onto something deep here and wanted to share it. In a way, I want you all to be wary, to be wise as serpents and harmless as doves, as the Bible says.

"As you know, I've been studying Revelation and several commentaries about end-times events. Well, today in the pastor's files I ran across one of his sermons on the subject. I've been reading the Bible and the books on the subject, and here's what I've found."

Bruce pulled up the first blank sheet on a flip chart and showed a time line he had drawn. "I'll take the time to carefully teach you this over the next several weeks, but it looks to me, and to many of the experts who came before us, that this period of history we're in right now will last for seven years. The first twenty-one months encompass what the Bible calls the seven Seal Judgments, or the Judgments of the Seven-Sealed Scroll. Then comes another twenty-one-month period in which we will see the seven Trumpet Judgments. In the last forty-two months of this seven years of tribulation, if we have survived, we will endure the most severe tests, the seven Vial Judgments. That last half of the seven years is called the Great Tribulation, and if we are alive at the end of it, we will be rewarded by seeing the Glorious Appearing of Christ."

Loretta raised her hand. "Why do you keep saying 'if we survive'? What are these judgments?"

"They get progressively worse, and if I'm reading this right, they will be harder and harder to survive. If we die, we will be in heaven with Christ and our loved ones. But we may suffer horrible deaths. If we somehow make it through the seven terrible years, especially the last half, the Glorious Appearing will be all that more glorious. Christ will come back to set up his thousand-year reign on earth."

"The Millennium."

"Exactly. Now, that's a long time off, and of course we may be only days from the beginning of the first twenty-one-month period. Again, if I'm reading it right, the Antichrist will soon come to power, promising peace and trying to unite the world."

"What's wrong with uniting the world?" someone asked. "At a time like this it seems we need to come together."

"There might be nothing wrong with that, except that the Antichrist will be a great deceiver, and when his true goals are revealed, he will be opposed. This will result in a great war, probably World War III."

"How soon?"

"I fear it will be very soon. We need to watch for the new world leader."

"What about the young man from Europe who is so popular with the United Nations?"

"I'm impressed with him," Bruce said. "I will have to be careful and study what he says and does. He seems too humble and self-effacing to fit the description of this one who would take over the world."

"But we're ripe for someone to do just that," one of the older men said. "I found myself wishing that guy was our president." Several others agreed.

"We need to keep an eye on him," Bruce said. "But for now, let me just briefly outline the Seven-Sealed Scroll from Revelation five, and then I'll let you go. On the one hand, I don't want to give you a spirit of fear, but we all know we're still here because we neglected salvation before the Rapture. I know we're all grateful for the second chance, but we cannot expect to escape the trials that are coming."

Bruce explained that the first four seals in the scroll were described as men on four horses: a white horse, a red horse, a black horse, and a pale horse. "The white horseman apparently is the Antichrist, who ushers in one to three months of diplomacy while getting organized and promising peace.

"The red horse signifies war. The Antichrist will be opposed by three rulers from the south, and millions will be killed."

"In World War III?"

"That's my assumption."

"That would mean within the next six months."

"I'm afraid so. And immediately following that, which will take only three to six months because of the nuclear weaponry available, the Bible predicts inflation and famine—the black horse. As the rich get richer, the poor starve to death. More millions will die that way."

"So if we survive the war, we need to stockpile food?"

Bruce nodded. "I would."

"We should work together."

"Good idea, because it gets worse. That killer famine could be as short as two or three months before the arrival of the fourth Seal Judgment, the fourth horseman on the pale horse—the symbol of death. Besides the postwar famine, a plague will sweep the entire world. Before the fifth Seal Judgment, a quarter of the world's current population will be dead."

"What's the fifth Seal Judgment?"

"Well," Bruce said, "you're going to recognize this one because we've talked about it before. Remember my telling you about the 144,000 Jewish witnesses who try to evangelize the world for Christ? Many of their converts, perhaps millions, will be martyred by the world leader and the harlot, which is the name for the one world religion that denies Christ."

Rayford was furiously taking notes. He wondered what he would have thought about such crazy talk just three weeks earlier. How could he have missed this? God had tried to warn his people by putting his Word in written form centuries before. For all Rayford's education and intelligence, he felt he had been a fool. Now he couldn't get enough of this information, though it was becoming clear that the odds were against a person living until the Glorious Appearing of Christ.

"The sixth Seal Judgment," Bruce continued, "is God pouring out his wrath against the killing of his saints. This will come in the form of a worldwide earthquake so devastating that no instruments would be able to measure it. It will be so bad that people will cry out for rocks to fall on them and put them out of their misery." Several in the room began to weep. "The seventh seal introduces the seven Trumpet Judgments, which will take place in the second quarter of this seven-year period."

"The second twenty-one months," Rayford clarified.

"Right. I don't want to get into those tonight, but I warn you they are progressively worse. I want to leave you with a little encouragement. You remember we talked briefly about the two witnesses, and I said I would study that more carefully? Revelation 11:3-14 makes it clear that God's two special witnesses, with supernatural power to work miracles, will prophesy one thousand two hundred and sixty days, clothed in sackcloth. Anyone who tries to harm them will be devoured. No rain will fall during the time that they prophesy. They will be able to turn water to blood and to strike the earth with plagues whenever they want.

"Satan will kill them at the end of three and a half years, and their bodies will lie in the street of the city where Christ was crucified. The people they have tormented will celebrate their deaths, not allowing their bodies to be buried. But after three and a half days, they will rise from the dead and ascend to heaven in a cloud while their enemies watch. God will send another great earthquake, a tenth of the city will fall, and seven thousand people will die. The rest will be terrified and give glory to God."

Rayford glanced around the office as people murmured among themselves. They had all seen it, the report of the two crazy men preaching about Jesus at the Wailing Wall in Jerusalem.

"Is that them?" someone asked.

"Who else could it be?" Bruce said. "It has not rained in Jerusalem since the disappearances. These men came out of nowhere. They have the miraculous power of saints like Elijah and Moses, and they call each other Eli and Moishe. At this moment, the men are still preaching."

"The witnesses."

"Yes, the witnesses. If any one of us still harbored any doubts or fears, not sure what has been going on, these witnesses should allay them all. I believe these witnesses will see hundreds of thousands of converts, the 144,000, who will preach Christ to the world. We're on their side. We have to do our parts."

+ + +

Buck reached Hattie Durham at her home number Tuesday night. "So, you're coming through New York?" he said.

"Yes," she said, "and I'd love to see you and maybe get to meet a VIP."

"You mean other than me?"

"Cute," she said. "Have you met Nicolae Carpathia yet?"

"Of course."

"I knew it! I was just telling someone the other day that I'd love to meet that man."

"No promises, but I'll see what I can do. Where should we meet?"

"My flight gets in there about eleven and I have a one o'clock appointment in the Pan-Con Club. But if we don't get back in time for that, it's OK. I don't fly out till morning, and I didn't even tell the guy I would meet him at one."

"Another guy?" Buck said. "You've got some weekend planned."

"It's nothing like that," she said. "It's a pilot who wants to talk to me about something, and I'm not sure I even want to listen. If I'm back and have time, fine. But I haven't committed to it. Why don't we meet at the club and see where we want to go from there?"

"I'll try to arrange the meeting with Mr. Carpathia, probably at his hotel."

* * *

It was late Tuesday night when Chloe changed her mind and agreed to go to New York with her father. "I can see you're not ready to be out without me," she said, embracing him and smiling. "It's nice to be needed."

"To tell you the truth," he said, "I'm going to insist on a meeting with Hattie, and I want you there."

"For her protection or yours?"

"Not funny. I've left her a message insisting that she see me in the Pan-Con Club at JFK at one in the afternoon. Whether she will or not, I don't know. Either way, you and I will get some time together."

"Daddy, time together is all we've had. I'd think you'd be tired of me by now."

"That'll never happen, Chloe."

* * *

Early Wednesday morning Buck was summoned to the office of Stanton Bailey, publisher of *Global Weekly*. In all his years of award-winning work, he had been in there only twice, once to celebrate his Hemingway war correspondence award and once on a Christmas tour of what the employees enviously called Mahogany Row.

Buck ducked in to see Steve first, only to be told by Marge that he was in with the publisher already. Her eyes were red and puffy. "What's happening?" he said.

"You know I can't say anything," she said. "Just get in there."

Buck's imagination ran wild as he entered the suite of offices inhabited by the brass. He hadn't known Plank had been summoned, too. What could it mean? Were they in trouble for the shenanigans they had pulled Monday night? Had Mr. Bailey somehow found out the details of the London business and how Buck had escaped? And he certainly hoped this meeting would be over in time for his appointment with Hattie Durham.

Bailey's receptionist pointed him to the publisher's outer office, where his secretary raised one brow and waved him in. "You're not going to announce me?" he joked. She smirked and returned to her work.

Buck knocked quietly and carefully pushed open the door. Plank sat with his back to Buck and didn't turn. Bailey didn't rise but beckoned him in. "Sit right there next to your boss," Bailey said, which Buck thought an interesting choice of words. Of course, it was true, but that was not how Steve was usually addressed.

Buck sat and said, "Steve."

Steve nodded but kept looking at Bailey.

"Couple of things, Williams," Bailey began, "before I get down to business. You're cleared of everything overseas, right?"

Buck nodded. "Yes, sir. There should never have been any doubt."

"Well, 'course there shouldn't, but you were lucky. I guess it was smart to make it look like whoever was after you got you, but you made us think that for a while too, you know."

"Sorry. I'm afraid that was unavoidable."

"And you wound up giving them ammunition to use against you if they wanted to bust you for some reason."

"I know. That surprised me."

"But you got it taken care of."

"Right."

"How?"

"Sir?"

"What part of 'how' don't you understand? How did you extricate yourself? We got word there were witnesses who say you did it."

"There must have been enough others who knew the truth. Tompkins was a friend of mine. I had no reason to kill him, and I sure didn't have the means. I wouldn't have the slightest idea how to make a bomb or transport it or detonate it."

"You could have paid to have it done."

"But I didn't. I don't run in those circles, and if I did, I wouldn't have had Alan killed."

"Well, the news coverage is all vague enough that none of us look bad. Just looks like a misunderstanding."

"Which it was."

"Of course it was. Cameron, I asked to see you this morning because I have just accepted one of the least welcome resignations I have ever received."

Buck sat silent, his head spinning.

"Steve here tells me this will be news to you, so let me just drop it on you. He is resigning immediately to accept the position of international press secretary to Nicolae Carpathia. He's received an offer we can't come close to, and while I don't think it's wise or a good fit, he does, and it's his life. What do you think about that?"

Buck couldn't contain himself. "I think it stinks. Steve, what are you thinking of? You're going to move to Romania?"

"I'll be headquartered here, Buck. At the Plaza."

"Nice."

"I'll say."

"Steve, this isn't you. You're not a PR guy."

"Carpathia is no ordinary political leader. Tell me you weren't on your feet cheering Monday."

"I was, but—"

"But nothing. This is the opportunity of a lifetime. Nothing else would have lured me from this job."

Buck shook his head. "I can't believe it. I knew Carpathia was looking for somebody, but—"

Steve laughed. "Tell the truth, Buck. He offered it to you first, didn't he?"

"No."

"He as much as told me he did."

"Well, he didn't. Matter of fact, I recommended Miller from *Seaboard*."

Plank recoiled and shot a glance at Bailey. "Really?"

"Yeah, why not? He's more the type."

"Buck," Steve said, "Eric Miller's body washed up on Staten Island last night. He fell off the ferry and drowned."

"Well," Bailey said summarily, "enough of that ugly business. Steve has recommended you to replace him."

Buck was still reeling from the news about Miller, but he heard the offer. "Oh, please," he said, "you're not serious."

"You wouldn't want the job?" Bailey asked. "Shape the magazine, determine the coverage, still write the top stories yourself? Sure you would. By policy it would almost double your salary, and if that's what it took to get you to agree, I'd guarantee it."

"That's not it," Buck said. "I'm too young for the job I've got now."

"You don't believe that or you wouldn't be as good at it as you are."

"Yeah, but that's the sentiment of the staff."

"What else is new?" Bailey roared. "They think I'm too old. They thought Steve was too laid-back. Others thought he was too pushy. They'd complain if we brought in the pope himself."

"I thought he was missing."

"You know what I mean. Now how about it?"

"I could never replace Steve, sir. I'm sorry. People may have complained, but they knew he was fair and in their corner."

"And so would you be."

"But they'd never give me the benefit of the doubt. They'd be in here undermining me and complaining from day one."

"I wouldn't allow it. Now, Buck, this offer isn't going to sit on the table indefinitely. I want you to take it, and I want to be able to announce it immediately."

Buck shrugged and looked at the floor. "Can I have a day to think about it?"

"Twenty-four hours. Meantime, don't say a word to anybody. Plank, anybody else know about you?"

"Only Marge."

"We can trust her. She'll never tell a soul. I had a three-year affair with her and never worried about anybody finding out."

Steve and Buck flinched.

"Well," Bailey said, "you never knew, did you?"

"No," they said in unison.

"See how tight-lipped she is?" He waited a beat. "I'm kidding, boys. I'm kidding!"

He was still laughing as they left the office.

18

BUCK FOLLOWED Steve to his office. "Did you hear about those kooks at the Wailing Wall?" Steve said.

"Like I'm interested in that right now," Buck said. "Yeah, I saw them, and no, I don't want to cover that story. Now what is this?"

"This will be your office, Buck. Marge will be your secretary."

"You can't possibly think I would want your job. First off, we can't afford to lose you. You're the only sane person here."

"Including you?"

"Especially including me. You must have really run interference for me with Bailey if he thinks I would be anything but a powder keg in your job."

"*Your* job."

"You think I should take it."

"You bet I do. I suggested no one else and Bailey had no other candidates."

"He'd have all the candidates he wanted if he just announced the opening. Who wouldn't want this job, besides me?"

"If it's such a plum, why *don't* you want it?"

"I'd feel as if I were sitting in your chair."

"So order your own chair."

"You know what I mean, Steve. It won't be the same without you. This job isn't me."

"Look at it this way, Buck. If you don't take it, you have no say in who becomes your new boss. Anybody on this staff you want to work for?"

"Yeah, you."

"Too late. I'm gone tomorrow. Now seriously, you want to work for Juan?"

"You wouldn't recommend him."

"I'm not going to recommend anybody but you. You don't take it, you're on your own. You take your chances you'll wind up working for a colleague who already resents you. How many hot assignments you think you'll get then?"

"If I got dumped on, I'd threaten to go to *Time* or somewhere. Bailey wouldn't let that happen."

"You turn down a promotion, he might make it happen. Rejecting advancement is not a good career move."

"I just want to write."

"Tell me you haven't thought you could run this editorial department better than I do at times."

"A lot of times."

"Here's your chance."

"Bailey would never stand for my assigning myself all the best stuff."

"Make that a condition of your acceptance. If he doesn't like it, it's his decision, not yours."

For the first time, Buck allowed a sliver of light to enter his head about the possibility of taking the executive editor job. "I still can't believe you'd leave to become a press secretary, Steve. Even for Nicolae Carpathia."

"Do you know what's in store for him, Buck?"

"A little."

"There's a sea of power and influence and money behind him that will propel him to world prominence so quick it'll make everyone's head spin."

"Listen to yourself. You're supposed to be a journalist."

"I hear myself, Buck. I wouldn't feel this way about anybody else. No U.S. president could turn my head like this, no U.N. secretary-general."

"You think he'll be bigger than that."

"The world is ready for Carpathia, Buck. You were there Monday. You saw it. You heard it. Have you ever met anyone like him?"

"No."

"You never will again, either. If you ask me, Romania is too small for him. Europe is too small for him. The U.N. is too small for him."

"What's he gonna be, Steve, king of the world?"

Steve laughed. "That won't be the title, but don't put it past him. The best part is, he's not even aware of his own presence. He doesn't seek these roles. They are thrust upon him because of his intellect, his power, his passion."

"You know, of course, that Stonagal is behind him."

"Of course. But he'll soon supersede Stonagal in influence because of his charisma. Stonagal can't be too visible, and so he will never have the masses behind him. When Nicolae comes to power, he'll in essence have jurisdiction over Stonagal."

"Wouldn't that be something?"

"I say it'll happen sooner than any of us can imagine, Buck."

"Except you, of course."

"That's exactly how I feel. You know I've always had good instincts. I'm sure

I'm sitting on one of the greatest rises to power of anyone in history. Maybe *the* greatest. And I'll be right there helping it happen."

"What do you think of *my* instincts, Steve?"

Steve pressed his lips together. "Other than your writing and reporting, your instincts are the things I most envy."

"Then rest easy. My gut feeling is the same as yours. And except that I could never be anybody's press secretary, I almost envy you. You *are* uniquely positioned to enjoy the ride of your life."

Steve smiled. "We'll keep in touch. You'll always have access, to me and to Nicolae."

"I can't ask for more than that."

Marge interrupted on the intercom without signaling first. "Hit your TV, Steve, or whoever's TV it is now."

Steve smiled at Buck and switched it on. CNN was broadcasting live from Jerusalem, where two men had tried to attack the preachers at the Wailing Wall. Dan Bennett was on the scene for CNN.

"It was an ugly and dangerous confrontation for what many here are calling the two heretical prophets, known only as Moishe and Eli," Bennett said. "We know these names only because they have referred to each other thus, but we have been unable to locate anyone who knows any more about them. We know of no last names, no cities of origin, no families or friends. They have been taking turns speaking—preaching, if you will—for hours and continuing to claim that Jesus Christ is the Messiah. They have proclaimed over and over that the great worldwide disappearances last week, including many here in Israel, evidenced Christ's rapture of his church.

"A heckler asked why they had not disappeared, if they knew so much. The one called Moishe answered, and I quote, 'Where we come from and where we go, you cannot know.' His companion, Eli, was quoted, 'In my Father's house are many mansions,' apparently a New Testament quotation attributed to Christ."

Steve and Buck exchanged glances.

"Surrounded by zealots most of the day, the preachers were finally attacked just moments ago by two men in their midtwenties. Watch the tape as our cameras caught the action. You can see the two at the back of the crowd, working their way to the front. Both are wearing long, hooded robes and are bearded. You can see that they produce weapons as they emerge from the crowd.

"One has an Uzi automatic weapon and the other a bayonet-type knife that appears to have come from an Israeli-issue military rifle. The one wielding the knife surges forward first, displaying his weapon to Moishe, who had been speaking. Eli, behind him, immediately falls to his knees, his face toward the sky. Moishe stops speaking and merely looks at the man, who appears to trip. He sprawls while the man with the Uzi points the weapon at the preachers and appears to pull the trigger.

"There is no sound of gunfire as the Uzi apparently jams, and the attacker seems to trip over his partner and both wind up on the ground. The group of onlookers has backed away and run for cover, but watch again closely as we rerun this. The one with the gun seems to fall of his own accord.

"As we speak, both attackers lie at the feet of the preachers, who continue to preach. Angry onlookers demand help for the attackers, and Moishe is speaking in Hebrew. Let's listen and we'll translate as we go.

"He's saying, 'Men of Zion, pick up your dead! Remove from before us these jackals who have no power over us!'

"A few from the crowd approach tentatively while Israeli soldiers gather at the entrance to the Wall. The zealots are waving them off. Eli is speaking.

"'You who aid the fallen are not in danger unless you come against the anointed ones of the Most High,' apparently referring to himself and his partner. The fallen attackers are being rolled onto their backs, and those attending them are weeping and shouting and backing away. 'Dead! Both dead!' they are saying, and now the crowd seems to want the soldiers to enter. They are clearing the way. The soldiers are, of course, heavily armed. Whether they will try to arrest the strangers, we don't know, but from what we saw, the two preachers neither attacked nor defended themselves against the men now on the ground.

"Moishe is speaking again: 'Carry off your dead, but do not come nigh to us, says the Lord God of Hosts!' This he has said with such volume and authority that the soldiers quickly have checked pulses and carried off the men. We will report any word we receive on the two who attempted to attack the preachers here at the Wailing Wall in Jerusalem. At this moment, the preachers have continued their shouting, proclaiming, 'Jesus of Nazareth, born in Bethlehem, King of the Jews, the chosen one, ruler of all nations.'

"In Israel, Dan Bennett for CNN."

Marge and a few others on the staff had drifted into Steve's office during the telecast. "If that doesn't beat all," one said. "What a couple of kooks."

"Which two?" Buck said. "You can't say the preachers, whoever they are, didn't warn 'em."

"What's going on over there?" someone else asked.

"All I know," Buck said, "is that things happen there that no one can explain."

Steve raised his eyebrows. "If you believe in the Virgin Birth, that's been true for centuries."

Buck rose. "I've got to get to JFK," he said.

"What are you gonna do about the job?"

"I've got twenty-four hours, remember?"

"Don't use them all. Answer too quick, you look eager; too slow, you look indecisive."

Buck knew Steve was right. He was going to have to accept the promotion just to protect himself from other pretenders. He didn't want to be obsessed with it all day. Buck was glad for the diversion of seeing Hattie Durham. His only question now was whether he would recognize her. They had met under most traumatic circumstances.

* * *

Rayford and Chloe arrived in New York just after noon on Wednesday and went directly to the Pan-Con Club to wait for Hattie Durham. "I'm guessing she won't show," Chloe said.

"Why?"

"Because I wouldn't if I were her."

"You're not her, thank God."

"Oh, don't put her down, Dad. What makes you any better?"

Rayford felt awful. Chloe was right. Why should he think less of Hattie just because she seemed dim at times? That hadn't bothered him when he had seen her only as a physical diversion. And now, just because she had been nasty with him on the phone and never acknowledged his last invitation to meet today, he had categorized her as less desirable or less deserving.

"I *am* no better," he conceded. "But why wouldn't you show up if you were her?"

"Because I'd have an idea of what you'd have in mind. You're going to tell her you no longer have feelings for her, but that now you care about her eternal soul."

"You make that sound cheap."

"Why should it impress her that you care about her soul when she thinks you used to be interested in her as a person?"

"That's just it, Chloe. I wasn't ever interested in her as a person."

"She doesn't know that. Because you were so circumspect and so careful, she thought you were better than most men, who would just come right out and hit on her. I'm sure she feels bad about Mom, and she probably understands that you're not in any state of mind to start a new relationship. But it can't make her day to be sent away like it was just as much her fault."

"It *was*, though."

"No, it wasn't, Dad. She was available. You shouldn't have been, but you were giving signals like you were. In this day and age, that made you fair game."

He shook his head. "Maybe that was why I was never good at that game."

"I'm glad, for Mom's sake, that you weren't."

"So, you think I shouldn't what, let her down easy or tell her about God?"

"You've already let her down, Daddy. She guessed what you were going to say and you confirmed it. That's why I say she won't come. She's still hurt. Probably mad."

"Oh, she was mad, all right."

"Then what makes you think she's going to be receptive to your heaven pitch?"

"It's not a pitch! Anyway, doesn't it prove I care about her in a genuine way now?"

Chloe went and got a soft drink. When she returned and sat next to her father, she put a hand on his shoulder. "I don't want to sound like a know-it-all," she said. "I know you're more than twice my age, but let me give you an idea how a woman thinks, especially someone like Hattie. OK?"

"I'm all ears."

"Does she have any religious background?"

"I don't think so."

"You never asked? She never said?"

"Neither of us ever gave it much thought."

"You never complained to her about Mom's obsession, like you sometimes did with me?"

"Come to think of it, I did. Of course, I was trying to use that to prove that your mother and I were not communicating."

"But Hattie didn't say anything about her own thoughts about God?"

Rayford tried to remember. "You know, I think she did say something supportive, or maybe sympathetic, about your mom."

"That makes sense. Even if she had wanted to come between you, she might have wanted to be sure you were the one putting the wedge between yourself and Mom, not her."

"I'm not following."

"That's not my point anyway. What I'm getting at is that you can't expect someone who is not even a church person to give a rip about heaven and God and all that. I'm having trouble dealing with it, and I love you and know it's become the most important thing in your life. You can't assume she has any interest, especially if it comes to her as a sort of a consolation prize."

"For?"

"For losing your attention."

"But my attention is purer now, more genuine!"

"To you, maybe. To her this is going to be much less attractive than the possibility of having someone who might love her and be there for her."

"That's what God will do for her."

"Which sounds real good to you. I'm just telling you, Dad, it's not going to be something she wants to hear right now."

"So, what if she does show up? Should I not talk to her about it?"

"I don't know. If she shows, that might mean she's still hoping there's a chance with you. Is there?"

"No!"

"Then you owe it to her to make that clear. But don't be so emphatic, and don't choose that time to try to sell her on—"

"Stop talking about my faith as something I'm trying to sell or pitch."

"Sorry. I'm just trying to reflect how it's going to sound to her."

Rayford had no idea what to say or do about Hattie now. He feared his daughter was right, and that gave him a glimpse of where her mind was, too. Bruce Barnes had told him that most people are blind and deaf to the truth until they find it; then it makes all the sense in the world. How could he argue? That's what had happened to him.

+ + +

Hattie had rushed up to Buck when he arrived at the club around eleven. His anticipation of any possibilities dissipated when the first thing out of her mouth was, "So, am I gonna get to meet Nicolae Carpathia?"

When Buck had originally promised to try to introduce her to Nicolae, he hadn't thought it through. Now, after hearing Steve rhapsodize about the prominence of Carpathia, he felt trivial calling to ask if he could introduce a friend, a fan. He called Dr. Rosenzweig. "Doc, I feel kinda stupid about this, and maybe you should just say no, that he's too busy. I know he's got a lot on his plate and this girl is no one he needs to meet."

"It's a girl?"

"Well, a young woman. She's a flight attendant."

"You want him to meet a flight attendant?"

Buck didn't know what to say. That reaction was exactly what he had feared. When he hesitated, he heard Rosenzweig cover the phone and call out for Carpathia. "Doc, no! Don't ask him!"

But he did. Rosenzweig came back on and said, "Nicolae says that any friend of yours is a friend of his. He has a few moments, but only a few moments, right now."

Buck and Hattie rushed to the Plaza in a cab. Buck realized immediately how awkward he felt and how much worse he was about to feel. Whatever reputation he enjoyed with Rosenzweig and Carpathia as an international journalist would forever be marred. He would be known as the hanger-on who dragged a groupie up to shake hands with Nicolae.

Buck couldn't hide his discomfort, and on the elevator he blurted, "He really has only a second, so we shouldn't stay long."

Hattie stared at him. "I know how to treat VIPs, you know," she said. "I often serve them on flights."

"Of course you do."

"I mean, if you're embarrassed by me or—"

"It's not that at all, Hattie."

"If you think I won't know how to act—"

"I'm sorry. I'm just thinking of his schedule."

"Well, right now we're on his schedule, aren't we?"

He sighed. "I guess we are."

Why, oh, why, do I get myself into these things?

In the hallway Hattie stopped by a mirror and checked her face. A bodyguard opened the door, nodded at Buck, and looked Hattie over from head to toe. She ignored him, craning her neck to find Carpathia. Dr. Rosenzweig emerged from the parlor. "Cameron," he said, "a moment please."

Buck excused himself from Hattie, who looked none too pleased. Rosenzweig pulled him aside and whispered, "He wonders if you could join him alone first?"

Here it comes, Buck thought, flashing Hattie an apologetic look and holding up a finger to indicate he would not be long. *Carpathia's gonna have my neck for wasting his time.*

He found Nicolae standing a few feet in front of the TV, watching CNN. His arms were crossed, his chin in his hand. He glanced Buck's way and waved him in. Buck shut the door behind him, feeling as if he had been sent to the principal's office. But Nicolae did not mention Hattie.

"Have you seen this business in Jerusalem?" he said. Buck said he had. "Strangest thing I have ever seen."

"Not me," Buck said.

"No?"

"I was near Tel Aviv when Russia attacked."

Carpathia kept his eyes on the screen as CNN played over and over the attack on the preachers and the collapsing of the would-be assassins. "Yes," he mumbled. "That would have been something akin to this. Something unexplainable. Heart attacks, they say."

"Pardon?"

"The attackers are dead of heart attacks."

"I hadn't heard that."

"Yes. And the Uzi did not jam. It is in perfect working order."

Nicolae seemed transfixed by the images. He continued to watch as he talked. "I wondered what you thought of my choice for press secretary."

"I was stunned."

"I thought you might be. Look at this. The preachers never touched either of them. What are the odds? Were they scared to death, was that it?"

The question was rhetorical. Buck didn't answer.

"Hm, hm, hm," Carpathia exclaimed, the least articulate Buck had ever heard him. "Strange indeed. There is no question Plank can do the job though, do you agree?"

"Of course. I hope you know you've crippled the *Weekly*."

"Ah! I have strengthened it. What better way to have the person I want at the top?"

Buck shuddered, relieved when Carpathia looked away from the TV at last. "This makes me feel just like Jonathan Stonagal, maneuvering people into positions." He laughed, and Buck was pleased to see that he was kidding.

"Did you hear what happened to Eric Miller?" Buck asked.

"Your friend from *Seaboard Monthly*? No. What?"

"Drowned last night."

Carpathia looked shocked. "You do not say! Dreadful!"

"Listen, Mr. Carpathia—"

"Buck, please! Call me Nicolae."

"I'm not sure I'll be comfortable doing that. I just wanted to apologize for bringing this girl up to meet you. She's just a flight attendant, and—"

"Nobody is just anything," he said, taking Buck's arm. "Everyone is of equal value, regardless of their station."

Carpathia led Buck to the door, insisting he be introduced. Hattie was appropriate and reserved, though she giggled when Carpathia kissed her on each cheek. He asked her about herself, her family, her job. Buck wondered if he had ever taken a Carnegie course on how to win friends and influence people.

"Cameron," Dr. Rosenzweig whispered. "Telephone."

Buck took it in the other room. It was Marge. "I hoped you'd be there," she said. "You just got a call from Carolyn Miller, Eric's wife. She's pretty shook up and really wants to talk to you."

"I can't call her from here, Marge."

"Well, get back to her as soon as you get a minute."

"What's it about?"

"I have no idea, but she sounded desperate. Here's her number."

When Buck reemerged, Carpathia was shaking hands with Hattie and then kissed her hand. "I am charmed," he said. "Thank you, Mr. Williams. And Miss Durham, it shall be my pleasure should our paths cross again."

Buck ushered her out and found her nearly overcome. "Some guy, huh?" he said.

"He gave me his number!" she said, nearly squealing.

"His number?"

Hattie showed Buck the business card Nicolae had handed her. It showed his title as president of the Republic of Romania, but his address was not Bucharest as one would expect. It was the Plaza Hotel, his suite number, phone number, and all. Buck was speechless. Carpathia had penciled in another phone number, not at the Plaza, but also in New York. Buck memorized it.

"We can eat at the Pan-Con Club," Hattie said. "I don't really want to see this pilot at one, but I think I will, just to brag about meeting Nicolae."

"Oh, now it's Nicolae, is it?" Buck managed, still shaken by Carpathia's business card. "Trying to make someone jealous?"

"Something like that," she said.

"Would you excuse me a second?" he said. "I need to make a call before we head back."

Hattie waited in the lobby while Buck ducked around the corner and dialed Carolyn Miller. She sounded horrible, as if she had been crying for hours and hadn't slept, which was no doubt true.

"Oh, Mr. Williams, I appreciate your calling."

"Of course, ma'am, and I am so sorry about your loss. I—"

"You remember that we've met?"

"I'm sorry, Mrs. Miller. Refresh me."

"On the presidential yacht two summers ago."

"Certainly! Forgive me."

"I just didn't want you to think we'd never met. Mr. Williams, my husband called me last night before heading for the ferry. He said he was tracking a big story at the Plaza and had run into you."

"True."

"He told me a crazy story about how you two had a wrestling match or something over an interview with this Romanian guy who spoke at—"

"Also true. It wasn't anything serious, ma'am. Just a disagreement. No hard feelings."

"That's how I took it. But that was the last conversation I'll ever have with him, and it's driving me crazy. Do you know how cold it was last night?"

"Nippy, as I recall," Buck said, puzzled at her abrupt change of subject.

"Cold, sir. Too cold to be standing outside on the ferry, wouldn't you say?"

"Yes, ma'am."

"And even if he was, he's a good swimmer. He was a champion in high school."

"All due respect, ma'am, but that had to be—what, thirty years ago?"

"But he's still a strong swimmer. Trust me. I know."

"What are you saying, Mrs. Miller?"

"I don't know!" she shouted, crying. "I just wondered if you could shed any light. I mean, he fell off the ferry and drowned? It doesn't make any sense!"

"It doesn't to me either, ma'am, and I wish I could help. But I can't."

"I know," she said. "I was just hoping."

"Ma'am, is someone with you, watching out for you?"

"Yes, I'm OK. I have family here."

"I'll be thinking of you."

"Thank you."

Buck could see Hattie in a reflection. She seemed patient enough. He called a friend at the telephone company. "Alex! Do me a favor. Can you still tell me who's listed if I give you a number?"

"Long as you don't tell anybody I'm doin' it."

"You know me, man."

"Go ahead."

Buck recited the number he had memorized from the card Carpathia had given Hattie. Alex was back to him in seconds, reading off the information as it scrolled onto his computer screen. "New York, U.N., administrative offices, secretary-general's office, unlisted private line, bypasses switchboard, bypasses secretary. OK?"

"OK, Alex. I owe you."

Buck was lost. He couldn't make any of this compute. He jogged out to Hattie. "I'm gonna be another minute," he said. "Do you mind?"

"No. As long as we can get back by one. No telling how long that pilot will wait. He's got his daughter with him."

Buck turned back to the phones, glad he had no interest in competing with Carpathia or this pilot for Hattie Durham's affection. He called Steve. Marge answered and he was short with her. "Hey, it's me. I need Plank right away."

"Well, have a nice day yourself," she said and rang him through.

"Steve," he said quickly, "your boy just made his first mistake."

"What're you talking about, Buck?"

"Is your first job going to be announcing Carpathia as the new secretary-general?"

Silence.

"Steve? What's next?"

"You're a good reporter, Buck. The best. How did this get out?"

Buck told him about the business card.

"Whew! That doesn't sound like Nicolae. I can't imagine it was an oversight. Must have been on purpose."

"Maybe he's assuming this Durham woman is too ditzy to figure it out," Buck said, "or that she wouldn't show me. But how does he know she won't call the number too soon and ask for him there?"

"As long as she waits until tomorrow, Buck, he'll be all right."

"Tomorrow?"

"You can't use this, all right? Are we off the record?"

"Steve! Who do you think you're talking to? Are you working for Carpathia already? You're still my boss. You don't want me to run with something, you just tell me. Remember?"

"Well, I'm telling you. The Kalahari Desert makes up much of Botswana where Secretary-General Ngumo is from. He returns there tomorrow a hero, having become the first leader to gain access to the Israeli fertilizer formula."

"And how did he do that?"

"By his stellar diplomacy, of course."

"And he cannot be expected to handle the duties of both the U.N. and Botswana during this strategic moment in Botswana history, right, Steve?"

"And why should he, when someone is so perfectly suited to step right in? We were there Monday, Buck. Who's going to oppose this?"

"Don't you?"

"I think it's brilliant."

"You're going to be a perfect press secretary, Steve. And I've decided to accept your old job."

"Good for you! Now you'll sit on this till tomorrow, you got it?"

"Promise. But will you tell me one more thing?"

"If I can, Buck."

"What did Eric Miller get too close to? What lead was he tracking?"

Steve's voice became hollow, his tone flat. "All I know about Eric Miller," he said, "is that he got too close to the railing on the Staten Island Ferry."

19

RAYFORD WATCHED Chloe as she wandered around the Pan-Con Club, then stared out the window. He felt like a wimp. For days he had told himself not to push, not to badger her. He knew her. She was like him. She would run the other way if he pushed too hard. She had even talked him into backing off of Hattie Durham, should Hattie show up.

What was the matter with him? Nothing was as it was before or would ever be again. If Bruce Barnes was right, the disappearance of God's people was only the beginning of the most cataclysmic period in the history of the world. *And here I am,* Rayford thought, *worried about offending people. I'm liable to "not offend" my own daughter right into hell.*

Rayford also felt bad about his approach to Hattie. He had dealt with his own wrong in having pursued her, and he regretted having led her on. But he could no longer treat her with kid gloves, either. What scared him most was that it seemed, from what Bruce was teaching, that many people would be deceived during these days. Whoever came forward with proclamations of peace and unity had to be suspect. There would be no peace. There would be no unity. This was the beginning of the end, and all would be chaos from now on.

The chaos would make peacemakers and smooth talkers only more attractive. And to people who didn't want to admit that God had been behind the disappearances, any other explanation would salve their consciences. There was no more time for polite conversation, for gentle persuasion. Rayford had to direct people to the Bible, to the prophetic portions. He felt so limited in his understanding. He had always been an erudite reader, but this stuff from Revelation and Daniel and Ezekiel was new and strange to him. Frighteningly, it made sense. He had begun taking Irene's Bible with him everywhere he went, reading it whenever possible. While the first officer read magazines during his downtime, Rayford would pull out the Bible.

"What in the world?" he was asked more than once.

Unashamed, he said he was finding answers and direction he had never seen before. But with his own daughter and his friend? He had been too polite.

Rayford looked at his watch. Still a few minutes before one o'clock. He caught Chloe's eye and signaled that he was going to make a phone call. He dialed Bruce Barnes and told him what he had been thinking.

"You're right, Rayford. I went through a few days of that, worried what people would think of me, not wanting to turn anybody off. It just doesn't make sense anymore, does it?"

"No, it doesn't. Bruce, I need support. I'm going to start becoming obnoxious, I'm afraid. If Chloe wants to laugh or run the other way, I'm going to force her to make a decision. She'll have to know exactly what she's doing. She'll have to face what we've found in the Bible and deal with it. I mean, the two preachers in Israel alone are enough to give me the confidence that things are happening exactly the way the Bible said they would."

"Have you been watching this morning?"

"From a distance here in the terminal. They keep rerunning the attack."

"Rayford, get to a TV right now."

"What?"

"I'm hanging up, Ray. See what happened to the attackers and see if that doesn't confirm everything we read about the two witnesses."

"Bruce—"

"Go, Rayford. And start witnessing yourself, with total confidence."

Bruce hung up on him. Rayford knew him well enough, despite their brief relationship, to be more intrigued than offended. He hurried to a TV monitor where he was stunned to hear the report of the deaths of the attackers. He dug out Irene's Bible and read the passage from Revelation Bruce had spoken from. The men in Jerusalem were the two witnesses, preaching Christ. They had been attacked, and they didn't even have to respond. The attackers had fallen dead and no harm had been done to the witnesses.

Now, on CNN, Rayford watched as crowds surged into the area in front of the Wailing Wall to listen to the witnesses. People knelt, weeping, some with their faces on the ground. These were people who had felt the preachers were desecrating the holy place. Now it appeared they were believing what the witnesses said. Or was it merely fear?

Rayford knew better. He knew that the first of the 144,000 Jewish evangelists were being converted to Christ before his eyes. Without taking his gaze from the screen, he prayed silently, *God, fill me with courage, with power, with whatever I need to be a witness. I don't want to be afraid anymore. I don't want to wait any longer. I don't want to worry about offending. Give me a persuasiveness rooted in the truth of your Word. I know it is your Spirit that draws people, but use me. I want to reach Chloe. I want to reach Hattie. Please, Lord. Help me.*

* * *

Buck Williams felt naked without his equipment bag. He would feel ready to work only when he had his cellular phone, his tape recorder, and his new laptop. He asked the cabbie to stop by the *Global Weekly* office so he could pick up the bag. Hattie waited in the cab, but she told him she was not going to be happy if she missed her appointment. Buck stood by the window of the cab. "I'll just be a minute," he said. "I thought you weren't sure whether you wanted to see this guy."

"Well, now I do, OK? Call it revenge or rubbing it in or whatever you want, but it's not often you get to tell a captain you've met someone he hasn't."

"You talking about Nicolae Carpathia or me?"

"Very funny. Anyway, he has met you."

"This is the captain from that flight where you and I met?"

"Yes—now hurry!"

"I might want to meet him."

"Go!"

Buck called Marge from the lobby. "Could you meet me at the elevator with my equipment bag? I've got a cab waiting here."

"I would," she said, "but both Steve and the old man are asking for you."

What now? he wondered. Buck checked his watch, wishing the elevator was faster. Such was life in the skyscrapers.

He grabbed his bag from Marge, breezed into Steve's office, and said, "What's up? I'm on the run."

"Boss wants to see us."

"What's it about?" Buck said as they headed down the hall.

"Eric Miller, I think. Maybe more. You know Bailey wasn't thrilled at my short notice. He only agreed to it thinking that you'd jump at the promotion, because you know where everything is and what's planned for the next couple of weeks."

In Bailey's office the boss got right to the point. "I'm gonna ask you two some pointed questions, and I want some quick and straight answers. A whole bunch of stuff is coming down right now, and we're gonna be on top of every bit of it. First off, Plank, rumors are flying that Mwangati Ngumo is calling a press conference for late this afternoon, and everybody thinks he's stepping down as secretary-general."

"Really?" Plank said.

"Don't play dumb with me," Bailey growled. "It doesn't take a genius to figure what's happening here. If he's stepping down, your guy knows about it. You forget I was in charge of the African bureau when Botswana became an associate member of the European Common Market. Jonathan Stonagal had his fingers all over that, and everybody knows he's one of this Carpathia guy's angels. What's the connection?"

Buck saw Steve pale. Bailey knew more than either of them expected. For the first time in years, Steve sounded nervous, almost panicky. "I'll tell you what I know," he said, but Buck guessed there was more he didn't say. "My first assignment tomorrow morning is to deny Carpathia's interest in the job. He's going to say he has too many revolutionary ideas and that he would insist on almost unanimous approval on the parts of the current members. They would have to agree to his ideas for reorganization, a change of emphasis, and a few other things."

"Like what?"

"I'm not at liberty to—"

Bailey rose, his face red. "Let me tell you something, Plank. I like you. You've been a superstar for me. I sold you to the rest of the brass when nobody else recognized you had what it takes. You sold me on this punk here, and he's made us all look good. But I paid you six figures long before you deserved it because I knew someday it would pay off. And it did. Now, I'm telling you that nothing you say here is gonna go past these walls, so I don't want you holdin' out on me.

"You brats think that because I'm two or three years from the pasture, I don't still have contacts, don't have my ear to the ground. Well, let me tell you, my phone's been ringing off the hook since you left here this morning, and I've got a gut feeling something big is coming down. Now what is it?"

"Who's been calling you, sir?" Plank said.

"Well, first off, I get a call from a guy who knows the vice president of Romania. Word over there is the guy has been asked to be prepared to run the day-to-day stuff indefinitely. He's not going to become the new president because they just got one, but that tells me Carpathia expects to be here a while.

"Then, people I know in Africa tell me Ngumo has some inside track on the Israeli formula but that he's quietly not happy about the deal requiring him to step down from the U.N. He's going to do it, but there's going to be trouble if everything doesn't go as promised.

"Then, of all things, I get a call from the publisher at *Seaboard Monthly* wanting to talk to me about how you, Cameron, and his guy that drowned last night were working the same angle on Carpathia, and whether I think you're going to mysteriously get dead, too. I told him that as far as I knew, you were working on a general cover story about the guy and that we were going to be positive. He said his guy had intended to take a slightly different approach—you know, zig when everybody else is zagging. Miller was doing a story on the meaning behind the disappearances, which I know you were planning for an issue or two from now. How that ties in with Carpathia, and why it might paint him in a dark light, I don't know. Do you?"

Buck shook his head. "I see them as two totally different pieces. I asked Carpathia what he made of what happened, and everybody has heard that answer. I didn't know that's what Miller was working on, and I sure wouldn't have thought he would somehow link Carpathia with the disappearances."

Bailey sat back down. "To tell you the truth, when I first took the call from the guy at *Seaboard*, I thought he was calling for a reference on you, Cameron. I was thinking, if I lose both these turkeys the same week, I'm taking early retirement. Can we get that stuff out of the way, before I make Plank tell me what else he knows?"

"What stuff?" Buck said.

"You looking to leave?"

"I'm not."

"You taking the promotion?"

"I am."

"Good! Now, Steve. What else is Carpathia gonna push for before he accepts the U.N. job?" Plank hesitated and looked as if he were considering whether he should tell what he knew. "I'm telling you, you owe me," Bailey said. "Now I don't intend to use this. I just want to know. Cameron and I have to decide which story we're going to push first. I want to get him onto the one that interests me most, the one about what was behind the disappearances. Sometimes I think we get too snooty as a newsmagazine and we forget that everyday people out there are scared to death, wanting to make some sense of all this. Now, Steve, you can trust me. I already told you I won't tell anyone or compromise you. Just run it down for me. What does Carpathia want, and is he going to take this job?"

Steve pursed his lips and began reluctantly. "He wants a new Security Council setup, which will include some of his own ideas for ambassadors."

"Like Todd-Cothran from England?" Buck said.

"Probably temporarily. He's not entirely pleased with that relationship, as you may know."

Buck suddenly realized that Steve knew everything.

"And?" Bailey pressed.

"He wants Ngumo personally to insist on him as his replacement, a large majority vote of the representatives, and two other things that, frankly, I don't think he'll get. Militarily, he wants a commitment to disarmament from member nations, the destruction of ninety percent of their weapons, and the donation of the other ten percent to the U.N."

"For peacekeeping purposes," Bailey said. "Naive, but logical sounding. You're right, he probably won't get that. What else?"

"Probably the most controversial and least likely. The logistics alone are incredible, the cost, the . . . everything."

"What?"

"He wants to move the U.N."

"Move it?"

Steve nodded.

"Where?"

"It sounds stupid."

"Everything sounds stupid these days," Bailey said.

"He wants to move it to Babylon."

"You're not serious."

"*He* is."

"I hear they've been renovating that city for years. Millions of dollars invested in making it, what, New Babylon?"

"Billions."

"Think anyone will agree to that?"

"Depends how bad they want him." Steve chuckled. "He's on *The Tonight Show* tonight."

"He'll be more popular than ever!"

"He's meeting right now with the heads of all these international groups that are in town for unity meetings."

"What does he want with them?"

"We're still confidential here, right?" Steve asked.

"Of course."

"He's asking for resolutions supporting some of the things he wants to do. The seven-year peace treaty with Israel, in exchange for his ability to broker the desert-fertilizer formula. The move to New Babylon. The establishment of one religion for the world, probably headquartered in Italy."

"He's not going to get far with the Jews on that one."

"They're an exception. He's going to help them rebuild their temple during the years of the peace treaty. He believes they deserve special treatment."

"And they do," Bailey said. "The man is brilliant. Not only have I never seen someone with such revolutionary ideas, but I've also never seen anyone who moves so quickly."

"Aren't either of you the least bit shaky about this guy?" Buck said. "It looks to me like people who get too close wind up eliminated."

"Shaky?" Bailey said. "Well, I think he's a little naive, and I'll be very surprised if he gets everything he's asking for. But then he's a politician. He won't couch these as ultimatums, and he can still accept the position even if he doesn't get them. It sounds like he may have run roughshod over Ngumo, but I think he had Botswana's best interest in mind. Carpathia will be a better U.N. chief. And he's right. If what happened in Israel happens in Botswana, Ngumo needs to stay close to home and manage the prosperity. Shaky? No. I'm as impressed with the guy as you two are. He's what we need right now. Nothing wrong with unity and togetherness at a time of crisis."

"What about Eric Miller?"

"I think people are making too much of that. We don't know that his death wasn't just what it appeared and was only coincidental with his run-in with you and Carpathia. Anyway, Carpathia didn't know what Miller was after, did he?"

"Not that I know of," Buck said, but he noticed that Steve said nothing.

Marge buzzed in on the intercom. "Cameron has an urgent message from a Hattie Durham. Says she can't wait any longer."

"Oh, no," Buck said. "Marge, apologize all over the place for me. Tell her it was unavoidable and that I'll either call her or catch up with her later."

Bailey looked disgusted. "Is this what I can expect from you on work time, Cameron?"

"Actually, I introduced her to Carpathia this morning, and I want her to introduce me to an airline captain in town today for part of that story on what people think happened last week."

"I'll make no bones about it, Cameron," Bailey said. "Let's do the big Carpathia story next issue, then follow up with the theories behind the vanishings after that. If you ask me, that could be the most talked about story we've ever done. I thought we beat *Time* and everybody else on our coverage of the event itself. I liked your stuff, by the way. I don't know that we'll have anything terribly fresh or different about Carpathia, but we have to give it all we've got. Frankly, I love the idea of you running the point on this coverage of all the theories. You must have one of your own."

"I wish I did," Buck said. "I'm as in the dark as anybody. What I'm finding, though, is that the people who have a theory believe in it totally."

"Well, I've got mine," Bailey said. "And it's almost eerie how close it matches Carpathia's, or Rosenzweig's, or whoever. I've got relatives who believe the space alien stuff. I've got an uncle who thinks it was Jesus, but he also thinks Jesus forgot *him*. Ha! I think it was natural, some kind of a phenomenon where all our high-tech stuff interacted with the forces of nature and we really did a number on ourselves. Now come on, Cameron. Where are you on this?"

"I'm in the perfect position for my assignment," he said. "I haven't the foggiest."

"What are people saying?"

"The usual. A doctor at O'Hare told me he was sure it was the Rapture. Other people have said the same. You know our Chicago bureau chief—"

"Lucinda Washington? It's going to be your job to find a replacement for her, you know. You'll have to go there, get the lay of the land, get acquainted. But you were saying?"

"Her son believes she and the rest of the family were taken to heaven."

"So, how'd *he* get left behind?"

"I'm not sure what the deal is on that," Buck said. "Some Christians are better than others or something. That's one thing I'm going to find out before I finish this piece. This flight attendant who just called, I'm not sure what she thinks, but she said the captain she's meeting today thinks he has an idea."

"An airline captain," Bailey repeated. "That would be interesting. Unless his idea is the same as the other scientific types. Well, carry on. Steve, we're gonna announce this today. Good luck, and don't worry about anything you've said here finding its way into the magazine, unless we get it through other sources. We're agreed on that, aren't we, Williams?"

"Yes, sir," Buck said.

Steve didn't look so sure.

Buck ran to the elevator and called information for the number of the Pan-Con Club. He asked them to page Hattie, but when they couldn't locate her, he assumed she hadn't arrived yet or had gone out with her pilot friend. He left a message to have her call him on his cellular phone, then headed that way in a cab just in case.

His mind was whirring. He agreed with Stanton Bailey that the big story was what had been behind the disappearances, but he was also becoming suspicious of Nicolae Carpathia. Maybe he shouldn't be. Maybe he should focus on Jonathan Stonagal. Carpathia should be smart enough to see that his elevation could help Stonagal in ways that would be unfair to his competitors. But Carpathia had pledged that he would "deal with" both Stonagal and Todd-Cothran, knowing full well they were behind illegal deeds.

Did that make Carpathia innocent? Buck certainly hoped so. He had never in his life wanted to believe more in a person. In the days since the disappearances, he'd hardly had a second to think for himself. The loss of his sister-in-law and niece and nephew tugged at his heart almost constantly, and something made him wonder if there wasn't something to this Rapture thing. If anybody in his orbit would be taken to heaven, it would have been them.

But he knew better than that, didn't he? He was Ivy League educated. He had left the church when he left the claustrophobic family situation that threatened to drive him crazy as a young man. He had never considered himself religious, despite a prayer for help and deliverance once in a while. He had built his life around achievement, excitement, and—he couldn't deny it—attention. He loved the status that came with having his byline, his writing, his thinking in a national magazine. And yet there was a certain loneliness in his existence, especially now with Steve moving on. Buck had dated and had considered escalating a couple of serious relationships, but he had always been considered too mobile for a woman who wanted stability.

Since the clearly supernatural event he had witnessed in Israel with the destruction of the Russian air force, he had known the world was changing. Things would never again be as they had been. He wasn't buying the space alien theory of the disappearances, and while it very well could be attributed to some incredible cosmic energy reaction, who or what was behind that? The incident at the Wailing Wall was another unexplainable bit of the supernatural.

Buck found himself more intrigued by the "whys and wherefores" story, as he liked to think of it, than even the rise of Nicolae Carpathia. As taken as he was with the man, Buck hoped against hope that he wasn't just another slick politician. He was the best Buck had ever seen, but was it possible that Dirk's death, Alan's death, Eric's death, and Buck's predicament were totally independent of Carpathia?

He hoped so. He wanted to believe a person could come along once in a generation who could capture the imagination of the world. Could Carpathia be another Lincoln, a Roosevelt, or the embodiment of Camelot that Kennedy had appeared to some?

On impulse, as the cab crawled into the impossible traffic at JFK, Buck plugged his laptop modem into his cellular phone and brought up a news service on his screen. He quickly called up Eric Miller's major pieces for the last two years and was stunned to find he had written about the rebuilding and improvement in Babylon. The title of Miller's series was "New Babylon, Stonagal's Latest Dream." A quick scan of the article showed that the bulk of the financing came from Stonagal banks throughout the world. And of course there was a quote attributed to Stonagal: "Just coincidence. I have no idea the particulars of the financing undertaken by our various institutions."

Buck knew that the bottom line with Nicolae Carpathia would have nothing to do with Mwangati Ngumo or Israel or even the new Security Council. To Buck, the litmus test for Carpathia was what he did about Jonathan Stonagal once Carpathia was installed as secretary-general of the United Nations.

Because if the rest of the U.N. went along with Nicolae's conditions, he would become the most powerful leader in the world overnight. He would have the ability to enforce his wishes militarily if every member were disarmed and U.N. might were increased. The world would have to be desperate for a leader they trusted implicitly to agree to such an arrangement. And the only leader worth the mantle would be one with zero tolerance for a murderous, behind-the-scenes schemer like Jonathan Stonagal.

20

RAYFORD AND CHLOE Steele waited until one-thirty in the afternoon, then decided to head for their hotel. On their way out of the Pan-Con Club, Rayford stopped to leave a message for Hattie, in case she came in. "We just got another message for her," the girl at the counter said. "A secretary for a Cameron Williams said Mr. Williams would catch up with her here if she would call him when she got in."

"When did that message come?" Rayford asked.

"Just after one."

"Maybe we'll wait a few more minutes."

Rayford and Chloe were sitting near the entrance when Hattie rushed in. Rayford smiled at her, but she immediately seemed to slow, as if she had just happened to run into them. "Oh, hi," she said, showing her identification at the counter and taking her message. Rayford let her play her game. He deserved it.

"I really shouldn't have come to see you," she said, after being introduced to Chloe. "And now that I'm here, I should return this call. It's from the writer I told you about. He introduced me to Nicolae Carpathia this morning."

"You don't say."

Hattie nodded, smiling. "And Mr. Carpathia gave me his card. Did you know he's going to be named *People* magazine's Sexiest Man Alive?"

"I had heard that, yes. Well, I'm impressed. Quite a morning for you, wasn't it? And how is Mr. Williams?"

"Very nice, but very busy. I'd better call him. Excuse me."

\+ \+ \+

Buck was on an escalator inside the terminal when his phone rang. "Well, hello yourself," Hattie said.

"I am so sorry, Miss Durham."

"Oh, please," she said. "Anybody who leaves me in midtown Manhattan in an expensive cab can call me by my first name. I insist."

"And I insist on paying for that cab."

"I'm just kidding, Buck. I'm going to meet with this captain and his daughter, so don't feel obligated to come over."

"Well, I'm already here," he said.

"Oh."

"But that's all right. I've got plenty to do. It was good to see you again, and next time you come through New York—"

"Buck, I don't want you to feel obligated to entertain me."

"I don't."

"Sure you do. You're a nice guy, but it's obvious we're not kindred spirits. Thanks for seeing me and especially for introducing me to Mr. Carpathia."

"Hattie, I could use a favor. Would it be possible to introduce me to this captain? I'd like to interview him. Is he staying overnight?"

"I'll ask him. You should meet his daughter anyway. She's a doll."

"Maybe I'll interview her, too."

"Yeah, good approach."

"Just ask him, Hattie, please."

+ + +

Rayford wondered if Hattie had a date with Buck Williams that evening. The right thing to do would be to invite her to dinner at his and Chloe's hotel. Now she was waving him over to the pay phone.

"Rayford, Buck Williams wants to meet you. He's doing a story and wants to interview you."

"Really? Me?" he said. "About what?"

"I don't know. I didn't ask. I suppose about flying or the disappearances. You *were* in the air when it happened."

"Tell him sure, I'll see him. In fact, why don't you ask him to join the three of us for dinner tonight, if you're free." Hattie stared at Rayford as if she had been tricked into something. "Come on, Hattie. You and I will talk this afternoon, then we'll all get together for dinner at six at the Carlisle."

She turned back to the phone and told Buck. "Where are you now?" she asked. She paused. "You're not!" Hattie peeked around the corner, laughed, and waved. Covering the mouthpiece, she turned to Rayford. "That's him, right there on the portable phone!"

"Well, why don't you both hang up and you can make the introductions," Rayford said. Hattie and Buck hung up, and Buck tucked his phone away as he entered.

"He's with us," Rayford told the woman at the desk. He shook Buck's hand. "So you're the writer for *Global Weekly* who was on my plane."

"That's me," Buck said.

"What do you want to interview me about?"

"Your take on the disappearances. I'm doing a cover story on the theories behind what happened, and it would be good to get your perspective as a professional and as someone who was right in the middle of the turmoil when it happened."

What an opportunity! Rayford thought. "Happy to," he said. "You can join us for dinner then?"

"You bet," Buck said. "And this is your daughter?"

* * *

Buck was stunned. He loved Chloe's name, her eyes, her smile. She looked directly at him and gave a firm handshake, something he liked in a woman. So many women felt it was feminine to offer a limp hand. *What a beautiful girl!* he thought. He had been tempted to tell Captain Steele that, as of the next day, he would no longer be just a writer but would become executive editor. But he feared that would sound like bragging, not complaining, so he had said nothing.

"Look," Hattie said, "the captain and I need a few minutes, so why don't you two get acquainted and we'll all get back together later. Do you have time, Buck?"

I do now, he thought. "Sure," he said, looking at Chloe and her father. "Is that all right with you two?"

The captain seemed to hesitate, but his daughter looked at him expectantly. She was clearly old enough to make her own decisions, but apparently she didn't want to make things awkward for her dad.

"It's OK," Captain Steele said hesitantly. "We'll be in here."

"I'll stash my bag, and we'll just take a walk in the terminal," Buck said. "If you want to, Chloe."

She smiled and nodded.

It had been a long time since Buck had felt awkward and shy around a girl. As he and Chloe strolled and talked, he didn't know where to look and was self-conscious about where to put his hands. Should he keep them in his pockets or let them hang free? Let them swing? Would she rather sit down or people watch or window-shop?

He asked her about herself and where she went to college, what she was interested in. She told him about her mother and her brother, and he sympathized. Buck was impressed at how smart and articulate and mature she seemed. This was a girl he could be interested in, but she had to be at least ten years younger than he was.

She wanted to know about his life and career. He told her anything she asked but little more. Only when she asked if he had lost anybody in the vanishings did he tell her about his family in Tucson and his friends in England. Naturally, he said nothing about the Stonagal or Todd-Cothran connections.

When the conversation lulled, Chloe caught him gazing at her, and he looked away. When he looked back, she was looking at him. They smiled shyly. *This is crazy,* he thought. He was dying to know if she had a boyfriend, but he wasn't about to ask.

Her questions were more along the lines of a young person asking a veteran professional about his career. She envied his travel and experience. He pooh-poohed it, assuring her she would tire of that kind of a life.

"Ever been married?" she asked.

He was glad she had asked. He was happy to tell her no, that he had never really been serious enough with anyone to be engaged. "How about you?" he asked, feeling the discussion was now fair game. "How many times have you been married?"

She laughed. "Only had one steady. When I was a freshman in college, he was a senior. I thought it was love, but when he graduated, I never heard from him again."

"Literally?"

"He went on some kind of an overseas trip, sent me a cheap souvenir, and that was the end of it. He's married now."

"His loss."

"Thank you."

Buck felt bolder. "What was he, blind?" She didn't respond. Buck mentally kicked himself and tried to recover. "I mean, some guys don't know what they have."

She was still silent, and he felt like an idiot. *How can I be so successful at some things and such a klutz at others?* he wondered.

She stopped in front of a gourmet bakery shop. "You feel like a cookie?" she asked.

"Why? Do I look like one?"

"How did I know that was coming?" she said. "Buy me a cookie and I'll let that groaner die a natural death."

"Of old age, you mean," he said.

"Now *that* was funny."

+ + +

Rayford was as earnest, honest, and forthright with Hattie as he had ever been. They sat across from each other in overstuffed chairs in the corner of a large, noisy room where they could not be heard by anyone else.

"Hattie," he said, "I'm not here to argue with you or even to have a conversation. There are things I must tell you, and I want you just to listen."

"I don't get to say anything? Because there may be things I'll want you to know, too."

"Of course I'll let you tell me anything you want, but this first part, my part, I don't want to be a dialogue. I have to get some things off my chest, and I want you to get the whole picture before you respond, OK?"

She shrugged. "I don't see how I have a choice."

"You had a choice, Hattie. You didn't have to come."

"I didn't really want to come. I told you that and you left that guilt-trip message, begging me to meet you here."

Rayford was frustrated. "You see what I didn't want to get into?" he said. "How can I apologize when all you want to do is argue about why you're here?"

"You want to apologize, Rayford? I would never stand in the way of that."

She was being sarcastic, but he had gotten her attention. "Yes, I do. Now will you let me?" She nodded. "Because I want to get through this, to set the record straight, to take all the blame I should, and then I want to tell you what I hinted at on the phone the other night."

"About how you've discovered what the vanishings are all about."

He held up a hand. "Don't get ahead of me."

"Sorry," she said, putting her hand over her mouth. "But why don't you just let me hear it when you answer Buck's questions tonight?" Rayford rolled his eyes. "I was just wondering," she said. "Just a suggestion so you don't have to repeat yourself."

"Thank you," he said, "but I'll tell you why. This is so important and so personal that I need to tell you privately. And I don't mind telling it over and over, and if my guess is right, you won't mind hearing it again and again."

Hattie raised her eyebrows as if to say she would be surprised, but she said, "You have the floor. I won't interrupt again."

Rayford leaned forward and rested his elbows on his knees, gesturing as he spoke. "Hattie, I owe you a huge apology, and I want your forgiveness. We were friends. We enjoyed each other's company. I loved being with you and spending time with you. I found you beautiful and exciting, and I think you know I was interested in a relationship with you."

She looked surprised, but Rayford assumed that, had it not been for her pledge of silence, she would have told him he had a pretty laid-back way of showing interest. He continued.

"Probably the only reason I never pursued anything further with you was because I didn't have any experience in such things. But it was only a matter of time. If I had found you willing, I'd have eventually done something wrong." She furrowed her brow and looked offended.

"Yes," he said, "it would have been wrong. I was married, not happily and not successfully, but that was my fault. Still, I had made a vow, a commitment, and no matter how I justified my interest in you, it would have been wrong."

He could tell from her look that she disagreed. "Anyway, I led you on. I wasn't totally honest. But now I have to tell you how grateful I am that I didn't do something—well, stupid. It would not have been right for you either. I know I'm not your judge and jury, and your morals are your own decision. But there would have been no future for us.

"It isn't just that we're so far apart in age, but the fact is that the only real interest I had in you was physical. You have a right to hate me for that, and I'm not proud of it. I did not love you. You have to agree, that would have been no kind of a life for you."

She nodded, appearing to cloud up. He smiled. "I'll let you break your silence temporarily," he said. "I need to know that you at least forgive me."

"Sometimes I wonder if honesty is always the best policy," she said. "I might have been able to accept this if you had just said your wife's disappearance made you feel guilty about what we had going. I know we didn't really have anything going yet, but that would have been a kinder way to put it."

"Kinder but dishonest. Hattie, I'm through being dishonest. Everything in me would rather be kind and gentle and keep you from resenting me, but I just can't be phony anymore. I was not genuine for years."

"And now you are?"

"To the point where it's unattractive to you," he said. She nodded again. "Why would I want to do that? Everybody likes to be liked. I could have blamed this on something else, on my wife, whatever. But I want to be able to live with myself. I want to be able to convince you, when I talk about even more important things, that I have no ulterior motives."

Hattie's lips quivered. She pressed them together and looked down, a tear rolling down her cheek. It was all Rayford could do to keep from embracing her. There would be nothing sensual about it, but he couldn't afford to give a wrong signal. "Hattie," he said. "I'm so sorry. Forgive me."

She nodded, unable to speak. She tried to say something but couldn't regain her composure.

"Now, after all that," Rayford said, "I somehow have to convince you that I do care for you as a friend and as a person."

Hattie held up both hands, fighting not to cry. She shook her head, as if not ready for this. "Don't," she managed. "Not right now."

"Hattie, I've got to."

"Please, give me a minute."

"Take your time, but don't run from me now," he said. "I would be no friend if I didn't tell you what I've found, what I've learned, what I'm discovering more of each day."

Hattie buried her face in her hands and cried. "I wasn't going to do this," she said. "I wasn't going to give you the satisfaction."

Rayford spoke as tenderly as he could. "Now you're going to offend *me*," he said. "If you take nothing else from this conversation, you must know that your tears give me no satisfaction. Every one of them is a dagger to me. I'm responsible. I was wrong."

"Give me a minute," she said, hurrying off.

Rayford dug out Irene's Bible and quickly scanned some passages. He had decided not to sit talking to Hattie with the Bible open. He didn't want to embarrass or intimidate her, despite his newfound courage and determination.

* * *

"You're gonna find my dad's theory of the disappearings very interesting," Chloe said.

"Am I?" Buck said. She nodded and he noticed a dab of chocolate at the corner of her mouth. He said, "May I?" extending his hand. She raised her chin and he transferred the chocolate to his thumb. Now what should he do? Wipe it on a napkin? Impulsively he put his thumb to his lips.

"Gross!" she said. "How embarrassing! What if I have the creeping crud or something?"

"Then now we've both got it," he said, and they laughed. Buck realized he was blushing, something he hadn't done for years, and so he changed the subject. "You say your dad's theory, as if maybe it's not yours, too. Do you two disagree?"

"He thinks we do, because I argue with him and give him a hard time about it. I just don't want to be too easy to convince, but if I had to be honest, I'd have to say we're pretty close. See, he thinks that—"

Buck held up a hand. "Oh, I'm sorry, don't tell me. I want to get it fresh from him, on tape."

"Oh. Excuse me."

"No, it's OK. I didn't mean to embarrass you, but that's just how I like to work. I'd love to hear your theory, too. We're going to get some college kids' ideas, but it would be unlikely we would use two people from the same family. Of course, you just told me that you pretty much agree with your father, so I'd better wait and hear them both at the same time."

She had fallen silent and looked serious. "I'm sorry, Chloe, I didn't mean to imply I'm not interested in *your* theory."

"It's not that," she said. "But you just kind of categorized me there."

"Categorized you?"

"As a college kid."

"Ooh, I did, didn't I? My fault. I know better. Collegians aren't kids. I don't see you as a kid, although you are a lot younger than I am."

"Collegians? I haven't heard that term in a while."

"I *am* showing my age, aren't I?"

"How old *are* you, Buck?"

"Thirty and a half, going on thirty-one," he said with a twinkle.

"I say, how old are you?" she shouted, as if talking to a deaf old man. Buck roared.

"I'd buy you another cookie, little girl, but I don't want to spoil your appetite."

"You'd better not. My dad loves good food, and he's buying tonight. Save room."

"I will, Chloe."

"Can I tell you something, without you thinking I'm weird?" she said.

"Too late," he said.

She frowned and punched him. "I was just going to say that I like the way you say my name."

"I didn't know there was any other way to say it," he said.

"Oh, there is. Even my friends slip into making it one syllable, like Cloy."

"Chloe," he repeated.

"Yeah," she said. "Like that. Two syllables, long *O*, long *E*."

"I like your name." He slipped into an old man's husky voice. "It's a young person's name. How old are you, kid?"

"Twenty and a half, going on twenty-one."

"Oh, my goodness," he said, still in character, "I'm consortin' with a minor!"

As they headed back toward the Pan-Con Club, Chloe said, "If you promise not to make a big deal of my youth, I won't make a big deal of your age."

"Deal," he said, a smile playing at his lips. "You play a lot older."

"I'll take that as a compliment," she said, smiling self-consciously as if she wasn't sure he was serious.

"Oh, do," he said. "Few people your age are as well-read and articulate as you are."

"That was definitely a compliment," she said.

"You catch on quick."

"Did you really interview Nicolae Carpathia?"

He nodded. "We're almost buddies."

"No kidding?"

"Well, not really. But we hit it off."

"Tell me about him."

And so Buck did.

* * *

Hattie returned slightly refreshed but still puffy-eyed and sat again as if ready for more punishment. Rayford reiterated that he was sincere about his apology, and she said, "Let's just put that behind us, shall we?"

"I need to know you forgive me," he said.

"You seem really hung up on that, Rayford. Would that let you off the hook, ease your conscience?"

"I guess maybe it would," he said. "Mostly it would tell me you believe I'm sincere."

"I believe it," she said. "It doesn't make it any more pleasant or easier to take, but if it makes you feel better, I do believe you mean it. And I don't hold grudges, so I guess that's forgiveness."

"I'll take what I can get," he said. "Now I want to be very honest with you."

"Uh-oh, there's more? Or is this where you educate me about what happened last week?"

"Yeah, this is it, but I need to tell you that Chloe advised against getting into this right now."

"In the same conversation as the, uh, other, you mean."

"Right."

"Smart girl," she said. "We must understand each other."

"Well, you're not that far apart in age."

"Wrong thing to say, Rayford. If you were going to use that you're-young-enough-to-be-my-daughter approach, you should have brought it up earlier."

"Not unless I fathered you when I was fifteen," Rayford said. "Anyway, Chloe is convinced you're not going to be in the mood for this just now."

"Why? Does this require some reaction? Do I have to buy into your idea or something?"

"That's my hope, but no. If it's something you can't handle right now, I'll understand. But I think you'll see the urgency of it."

Rayford felt much like Bruce Barnes had sounded the day they met. He was full of passion and persuasion, and he felt his prayers for courage and coherence were answered as he spoke. He told Hattie of his history with God, having been raised in a churchgoing home and how he and Irene had attended various churches throughout their marriage. He even told her that Irene's preoccupation with end-time events had been one thing that made him consider looking elsewhere for companionship.

Rayford could tell by Hattie's look that she knew where he was going, that he had now come to agree with Irene and had bought the whole package. Hattie sat motionless as he told the story of knowing what he would find at home that morning after they had landed at O'Hare.

He told her of calling the church, meeting Bruce, Bruce's story, the videotape, their studies, the prophecies from the Bible, the preachers in Israel that clearly paralleled the two witnesses spoken of in Revelation.

Rayford told her how he had prayed the prayer with the pastor as the videotape rolled and how he now felt so responsible for Chloe and wanted her to find God, too. Hattie stared at him. Nothing in her body language or expression encouraged him, but he kept going. He didn't ask her to pray with him. He simply told her he would no longer apologize for what he believed.

"You can see, at least, how if a person truly accepts this, he must tell other people. He would be no friend if he didn't." Hattie wouldn't even give him the satisfaction of a nod to concede that point.

After nearly half an hour, he exhausted his new knowledge, and he concluded, "Hattie, I want you to think about it, consider it, watch the tape, talk to Bruce if you want to. I can't make you believe. All I can do is make you aware of what I have come to accept as the truth. I care about you and wouldn't want you to miss out simply because no one ever told you."

Finally, Hattie sat back and sighed. "Well, that's sweet, Rayford. It really is. I appreciate your telling me all that. It hits me real strange and different, because I never knew that stuff was in the Bible. My family went to church when I was a kid, mostly on holidays or if we got invited, but I never heard anything like that. I *will* think about it. I sort of have to. Once you hear something like this, it's hard to put it out of your mind for a while. Is this what you're going to tell Buck Williams at dinner?"

"Word for word."

She chuckled. "Wonder if any of it will find its way into his magazine."

"Probably along with space aliens, germ gas, and death rays," Rayford said.

21

WHEN BUCK AND CHLOE reconnected with Hattie and Chloe's father, it was clear Hattie had been crying. Buck didn't feel close enough to ask what was wrong, and she never offered.

Buck was glad for the opportunity to interview Rayford Steele, but his emotions were mixed. The reactions of the captain who had piloted the plane on which he had been a passenger when the disappearances occurred would add drama to his story. But even more, he wanted to spend time with Chloe. Buck would run back to the office, then home to change, and meet them later at the Carlisle. At the office he took a call from Stanton Bailey, asking how soon he could go to Chicago to get Lucinda Washington replaced. "Soon, but I don't want to miss developments at the U.N."

"Everything happening there tomorrow morning you already know about from Plank," Bailey said. "Word I get is it's already starting to come down. Plank assumes his new position in the morning, denies Carpathia's interest, reiterates what it would take, and we all wait and see if anybody bites. I don't think they will."

"I wish they would," Buck said, still hoping he could trust Carpathia and eager to see what the man would do about Stonagal and Todd-Cothran.

"I do, too," Bailey said, "but what are the odds? He's a man for this time, but his global disarmament and his reorganization plans are too ambitious. It'll never happen."

"I know, but if you were deciding, wouldn't you go along with it?"

"Yeah," Bailey said, sighing. "I probably would. I'm so tired of war and violence. I'd probably even go for moving the place to this New Babylon."

"Maybe the U.N. delegates will be smart enough to know the world is ready for Carpathia," Buck said.

"Wouldn't that be too good to be true?" Bailey said. "Don't bet the farm or hold your breath or whatever it is you're not supposed to do when the odds are against you."

Buck told his new boss he would fly to Chicago the next morning and get back to New York by Sunday night. "I'll get the lay of the land, find out who's solid in Chicago and whether we need to look at outside applicants."

"I'd prefer staying inside," Bailey said. "But it's my style to let you make those decisions."

Buck phoned Pan-Con Airlines, knowing Rayford Steele's flight left at eight the next morning. He told the reservation clerk his traveling companion was Chloe Steele. "Yes," she said, "Ms. Steele is flying complimentary in first class. There is a seat open next to her. Will you be a guest of the crew as well?"

"No."

He booked a cheap seat and charged it to the magazine, then upgraded to the seat next to Chloe. He would say nothing that night about going to Chicago.

It had been ages since Buck had worn a tie, but this was, after all, the Carlisle Hotel dining room. He wouldn't have gotten in without one. Fortunately they were directed to a private table in a little alcove where he could stash his bag without appearing gauche. His tablemates assumed he needed the bag for his equipment, not aware he had packed a change of clothes, too.

Chloe was radiant, looking five years older in a classy evening dress. It was clear she and Hattie had spent the late afternoon in a beauty salon.

* * *

Rayford thought his daughter looked stunning that evening, and he wondered what the magazine writer thought of her. Clearly this Williams guy was too old for her.

Rayford had spent his free hours before dinner napping and then praying that he would have the same courage and clarity he'd had with Hattie. He had no idea what she thought except that he was "sweet" for telling her everything. He wasn't sure whether that was sarcasm or condescension. He could only hope he had gotten through. That she had spent time alone with Chloe might have been good. Rayford hoped Chloe wasn't so antagonistic and closed-minded that she had become an ally against him with Hattie.

At the restaurant Williams seemed to gaze at Chloe and ignore Hattie. Rayford considered this insensitive, but it didn't seem to bother Hattie. Maybe Hattie was matchmaking behind his back. Rayford himself had said nothing about Hattie's new look for the evening, but that was by design. She was striking and always had been, but he was not going down that path again.

During dinner Rayford kept the conversation light. Buck said to let him know when he was ready to be interviewed. After dessert Rayford spoke to the waiter privately. "We'd like to spend another hour or so here, if it's all right."

"Sir, we do have an extensive reservation list—"

"I wouldn't want this table to be less than profitable for you," Rayford said, pressing a large bill into the waiter's palm, "so boot us out whenever it becomes necessary."

The waiter peeked at the bill and slipped it into his pocket. "I'm sure you will not be disturbed," he said. And the water glasses were always full.

Rayford enjoyed answering Williams's initial questions about his job, his training, his background and upbringing, but he was eager to get on with his new mission in life. And finally the question came.

\+ + +

Buck tried to concentrate on the captain's answers but felt himself trying to impress Chloe, too. Everyone in the business knew he was one of the best in the world at interviewing. That and his ability to quickly sift through the stuff and make a readable, engaging article of it had made him who he was.

Buck had breezed through the preliminaries, and he liked this guy. Steele seemed honest and sincere, smart and articulate. He realized he had seen a lot of Rayford in Chloe. "I'm ready," he said, "to ask your idea of what happened on that fateful flight to London. Do you have a theory?"

The captain hesitated and smiled as if gathering himself. "I have more than a theory," he said. "You may think this sounds crazy coming from a technically-minded person like me, but I believe I have found the truth and know exactly what happened."

Buck knew this would play well in the magazine. "Gotta appreciate a man who knows his mind," he said. "Here's your chance to tell the world."

Chloe chose that moment to gently touch Buck's arm and ask if he minded if she excused herself for a moment.

"I'll join you," Hattie said.

Buck smiled, watching them go. "What was that?" he said. "A conspiracy? Were they supposed to leave me alone with you, or have they heard this before and don't want to rehash it?"

\+ + +

Rayford was privately frustrated, almost to the point of anger. That was the second time in a few hours that Chloe had somehow been spirited away at a crucial time. "I assure you that is not the case," he said, forcing himself to smile. He couldn't slow down and wait for their return. The question had been asked, he felt ready, and so he stepped off the edge of a social cliff, saying things he knew could get him categorized as a kook. As he had done with Hattie, he outlined his own spotty spiritual history and brought Williams up to the present in a little over half an hour, covering every detail he felt was relevant. At some point the women returned.

* * *

Buck sat without interrupting as this most lucid and earnest professional calmly propounded a theory that only three weeks before Buck would have found absurd. It sounded like things he had heard in church and from friends, but this guy had chapter and verse from the Bible to back it up. And this business of the two preachers in Jerusalem representing two witnesses predicted in the book of Revelation? Buck was aghast. He finally broke in.

"That's interesting," he said. "Have you heard the latest?" Buck told him what he had seen on CNN during his few brief minutes at his apartment. "Apparently thousands are making some sort of a pilgrimage to the Wailing Wall. They're lined up for miles, trying to get in and hear the preaching. Many are converting and going out themselves to preach. The authorities seem powerless to keep them out, despite the opposition of the Orthodox Jews. Anyone who comes against the preachers is struck dumb or paralyzed, and many of the old orthodox guard are joining forces with the preachers."

"Amazing," the pilot responded. "But even more amazing, it was all predicted in the Bible."

Buck was desperate to maintain his composure. He wasn't sure what he was hearing, but Steele was impressive. Maybe the man was reaching to link Bible prophecy with what was happening in Israel, but no one else had an explanation. What Steele had read to Buck from Revelation appeared clear. Maybe it was wrong. Maybe it was mumbo jumbo. But it was the only theory that tied the incidents so closely to any sort of explanation. What else would give Buck this constant case of the chills?

Buck focused on Captain Steele, his pulse racing, looking neither right nor left. He could not move. He was certain the women could hear his crashing heart. Was all this possible? Could it be true? Had he been exposed to a clear work of God in the destruction of the Russian air corps just to set him up for a moment like this? Could he shake his head and make it all go away? Could he sleep on it and come to his senses in the morning? Would a conversation with Bailey or Plank set him straight, snap him out of this silliness?

He sensed not. Something about this demanded attention. He wanted to believe something that tied everything together and made it make sense. But Buck also wanted to believe in Nicolae Carpathia. Maybe Buck was going through a scary time where he was vulnerable to impressive people. That wasn't like him, but then, who *was* himself these days? Who could be expected to be himself during times like these?

Buck didn't want to rationalize this away, to talk himself out of it. He wanted to ask Rayford Steele about his own sister-in-law and niece and nephew. But that would be personal, that would not relate to the story he was working on. This had not begun as a personal quest, a search for truth. This was merely a fact-finding mission, an element in a bigger story.

In no way did Buck even begin to think he was going to pick a favorite theory and espouse it as *Global Weekly*'s position. He was supposed to round up all the theories, from the plausible to the bizarre. Readers would add their own in the Letters column, or they would make a decision based on the credibility of the sources. This airline pilot, unless Buck made him look like a lunatic, would come off profound and convincing.

For the first time in his memory Buck Williams was speechless.

* * *

Rayford was certain he was not getting through. He only hoped this writer was astute enough to understand, to quote him correctly, and to represent his views in such a way that readers might look into Christianity. It was clear that Williams wasn't buying it personally. If Rayford had to guess, he'd say Williams was trying to hide a smirk—or else he was so amused, or amazed, that he couldn't frame a response.

Rayford had to remind himself that his purpose was to get through to Chloe first and then maybe to influence the reading public, if the thing found its way into print. If Cameron Williams thought Rayford was totally out to lunch, he might just leave him out, along with all his cockamamie views.

* * *

Buck did not trust himself to respond with coherence. He still had chills, yet he felt sticky with sweat. What was happening to him? He managed a whisper. "I want to thank you for your time, and for dinner," he said. "I will get back to you before using any of your quotes." That was nonsense, of course. He had said it only to give himself a reason to reconnect with the pilot. He might have a lot of personal questions about this, but he never allowed people he interviewed to see their quotes in advance. He trusted his tape recorder and his memory, and he had never been accused of misquoting.

Buck looked back up at the captain and saw a strange look cross his face. He looked—what? Disappointed? Yes, then resigned.

Suddenly Buck remembered who he was dealing with. This was an intelligent, educated man. Surely he knew that reporters never checked back with their sources. He probably thought he was getting a journalistic brush-off.

A rookie mistake, Buck, he reprimanded himself. *You just underestimated your own source.*

Buck was putting his equipment away when he noticed Chloe was crying, tears streaming down her face. What was it with these women? Hattie Durham had been weeping when she and the captain had finished talking that afternoon. Now Chloe.

Buck could identify, at least with Chloe. If she was crying because she had been moved by her father's sincerity and earnestness, it was no surprise. Buck had a lump in his throat, and for the first time since he had lain face-down in fear in Israel during the Russian attack, he wished he had a private place to cry.

"Could I ask you one more thing, off the record?" he said. "May I ask what you and Hattie were talking about this afternoon in the club?"

"Buck!" Hattie scolded. "That's none of your—"

"If you don't want to say, I'll understand," Buck said. "I was just curious."

"Well, much of it was personal," the captain said.

"Fair enough."

"But, Hattie, I don't see any harm in telling him that the rest of it was what we just went over. Do you?"

She shrugged.

"Still off the record, Hattie," Buck said, "do you mind if I ask your reaction to all this?"

"Why off the record?" Hattie snapped. "The opinions of a pilot are important but the opinions of a flight attendant aren't?"

"I'll put you on the machine if you want," he said. "I didn't know you wanted to be on the record."

"I don't," she said. "I just wanted to be asked. It's too late now."

"And you don't care to say what you think—"

"No, I'll tell you. I think Rayford is sincere and thoughtful. Whether he's right, I have no idea. That's all beyond me and very foreign. But I am convinced he believes it. Whether he should or not, with his background and all that, I don't know. Maybe he's susceptible to it because of losing his family."

Buck nodded, realizing he was closer to buying Rayford's theory than Hattie was. He glanced at Chloe, hoping she had composed herself and that he could draw her out. She still had a tissue pressed under her eyes.

"Please don't ask me right now," she said.

* * *

Rayford was not surprised at Hattie's response, but he was profoundly disappointed with Chloe's. He was convinced she didn't want to embarrass him by saying how off the wall he sounded. He should have been grateful, he guessed. At least she was still sensitive to his feelings. Maybe he should have been more sensitive to hers, but he had decided he couldn't let those gentilities remain priorities anymore. He was going to contend for the faith with her until she made a decision. For tonight, however, it was clear she had heard enough. He wouldn't be pushing her anymore. He only hoped he could sleep despite his remorse over her condition. He loved her so much.

"Mr. Williams," he said, standing and thrusting out his hand, "it's been a pleasure. The pastor I told you about in Illinois really has a handle on this stuff and knows much more than I do about the Antichrist and all. It might be worth a call if you want to know any more. Bruce Barnes, New Hope Village Church, Mount Prospect."

"I'll keep that in mind," Buck said.

Rayford was convinced Williams was merely being polite.

* * *

Talking to this Barnes was a great idea, Buck thought. Maybe he'd find the time the next day in Chicago. That way he could pursue this for himself and not confuse the professional angle with his own interest.

The foursome moseyed to the lobby. "I'm going to say my good-nights," Hattie said. "I've got the earlier flight tomorrow." She thanked Rayford for dinner, whispered something to Chloe—which seemed to get no response—and thanked Buck for his hospitality that morning. "I may just call Mr. Carpathia one of these days," she said. Buck resisted the urge to tell her what he knew about Carpathia's immediate future. He doubted the man would have time for her.

Chloe looked as if she wanted to follow Hattie to the elevators and yet wanted to say something to Buck as well. He was shocked when she said, "Give us a minute, will you, Daddy? I'll be right up."

Buck found himself flattered that Chloe had hung back to say good-bye personally, but she was still emotional. Her voice was quavery as she formally told him what a good time she had had that day. He tried to prolong the conversation.

"Your dad is a pretty impressive guy," he said.

"I know," she said. "Especially lately."

"I can see why you might agree with him on a lot of that stuff."

"You can?"

"Sure! I have a lot of thinking to do myself. You give him a hard time about it though, huh?"

"I used to. Not anymore."

"Why not?"

"You can see how much it means to him."

Buck nodded. She seemed on the edge emotionally again. He reached to take her hand. "It's been wonderful spending time with you," he said.

She chuckled, as if embarrassed about what she was thinking.

"What?" he pressed.

"Oh, nothing. It's silly."

"C'mon, what? We've both been silly today."

"Well, I feel stupid," she said. "I just met you and I'm really gonna miss you. If you get through Chicago, you have to call."

"It's a promise," Buck said. "I can't say when, but let's just say sooner than you think."

22

BUCK DID NOT SLEEP WELL. Partly he was excited about his morning surprise. He could only hope Chloe would be happy about it. The larger part of his mind reeled with wonder. If this was true, all that Rayford Steele had postulated—and Buck knew instinctively that if any of it was true, all of it was true—why had it taken Buck a lifetime to come to it? Could he have been searching for this all the time, hardly knowing he was looking?

Yet even Captain Steele—an organized, analytical airline pilot—had missed it, and Steele claimed to have had a proponent, a devotee, almost a fanatic living under his own roof. Buck was so restless he had to leave his bed and pace. Strangely, somehow, he was not upset, not miserable. He was simply overwhelmed. None of this would have made a bit of sense to him just days before, and now, for the first time since Israel, he was unable to separate himself from his story.

The Holy Land attack had been a watershed event in his life. He had stared his own mortality in the face and had to acknowledge that something otherworldly—yes, supernatural, something directly from God almighty—had been thrust upon those dusty hills in the form of a fire in the sky. And he had known beyond a doubt for the first time in his life that unexplainable things out there could not be dissected and evaluated scientifically from a detached Ivy League perspective.

Buck had always prided himself on standing apart from the pack, for including the human, the everyday, the everyman element in his stories when others resisted such vulnerability. This skill allowed readers to identify with him, to taste and feel and smell those things most important to them. But he had still been able, even after his closest brush with death, to let the reader live it without revealing Buck's own deep angst about the very existence of God. Now, that separation seemed impossible. How could he cover this most important story of his life, one that had already probed closest to his soul, without subconsciously revealing his private turmoil?

He was, he knew by the wee hours, leaning over the line. He wasn't ready to pray yet, to try to talk to a God he had ignored for so long. He hadn't even prayed when he became convinced of God's existence that night in Israel. What had been the matter with him? Everyone in the world, at least those intellectually honest with themselves, had to admit there was a God after that night. Amazing coincidences had occurred before, but that had defied all logic.

To win against the mighty Russians was an upset, of course. But Israel's history was replete with such legends. Yet to not defend yourself and suffer no casualties? That was beyond all comprehension—apart from the direct intervention of God.

Why, Buck wondered, hadn't that made more of an impact on his own introspective inventory? In the lonely darkness he came to the painful realization that he had long ago compartmentalized this most basic of human needs and had rendered it a nonissue. What did it say about him, what despicable kind of a subhuman creature had he become, that even the stark evidence of the Israel miracle—for it could be called nothing less—had not thawed his spirit's receptiveness to God?

Not that many months later came the great disappearance of millions around the world. Dozens had vanished from the plane in which he was a passenger. What more did he need? It already seemed as if he were living in a science fiction thriller. Without question he had lived through the most cataclysmic event in history. Buck realized he'd not had a second to think in the last two weeks. Had it not been for the personal tragedies he had witnessed, he might have been more private in his approach to what appeared to be a universe out of control.

He wanted to meet this Bruce Barnes, not even pretending to be interviewing him for an article. Buck was on a personal quest now, looking to satisfy deep needs. For so many years he had rejected the idea of a personal God or that he had need of God—if there was one. The idea would take some getting used to. Captain Steele had talked about everyone being a sinner. Buck was not unrealistic about that. He knew his life would never stand up to the standards of a Sunday school teacher. But he had always hoped that if he faced God someday, his good would outweigh his bad and that relatively speaking, he was as good or better than the next guy. That would have to do.

Now, if Rayford Steele and all his Bible verses could be believed, it didn't make any difference how good Buck was or where he stood in relation to anybody else. One archaic phrase had struck him and rolled around in his head. *There is none righteous, no, not one.* Well, he had never considered himself righteous. Could he go to the next level and admit his need for God, for forgiveness, for Christ?

Was it possible? Could he be on the cusp of becoming a born-again Christian?

He had been almost relieved when Rayford Steele had used that term. Buck had read and even written about "those kinds" of people, but even at his level of worldly wisdom he had never quite understood the phrase. He had always considered the "born-again" label akin to "ultraright-winger" or "fundamentalist." Now, if he chose to take a step he had never dreamed of taking, if he could not somehow talk himself out of this truth he could no longer intellectually ignore, he would also take upon himself a task: educating the world on what that confusing little term really meant.

Buck finally dozed on the couch in his living room, despite a lamp shining close to his face. He slept soundly for a couple of hours but awoke in time to get to the airport. The prospect of surprising Chloe and traveling with her gave him a rush that helped overcome his fatigue. But even more exciting was the possibility that another answer man awaited him in Chicago, a man he trusted simply on the recommendation of a pilot who had seemed to speak the truth with authority. It would be fun someday to tell Rayford Steele how much that otherwise innocuous interview had meant to him. But Buck assumed Steele had already figured that out. That was probably why Steele had seemed so passionate.

+ + +

If this signaled the soon beginning of the tribulation period predicted in the Bible, and Rayford had no doubt that it did, he wondered if there would be any joy in it. Bruce didn't seem to think there would be, aside from the few converts they might be privileged to win. So far Rayford felt he was a failure. While he was certain God had given him the words and the courage to say them, he felt he had done something wrong in communicating to Hattie. Maybe she was right. Maybe he had been self-serving. It had to appear to her that he was merely getting out from under his own load of guilt. But he knew better. Before God he believed his motives pure. Yet clearly he had not persuaded Hattie of more than that he was sincere and that he believed. What good was that? If he believed and she didn't, she had to assume he believed something bogus, or she would have to admit she was ignoring the truth. What he had told her carried no other option.

And his performance during the interview with Cameron Williams! At the time, Rayford had felt good about it, articulate, calm, rational. He knew he was discussing revolutionary, jarring stuff, but he felt God had enabled him to be lucid. Yet if he couldn't get any more reaction out of the reporter than polite deference, what kind of a witness could he be? From the depths of his soul Rayford wanted to be more productive. He believed he had wasted his life before this, and he had only a short period to make up for lost time. He was eternally grateful for his own salvation, but now he wanted to share it, to bring more people to Christ. The magazine interview had been an incredible opportunity, but in his gut he felt it had not come off well. Was it even worth the effort to pray for another chance? Rayford believed he had seen the last of Cameron Williams. He wouldn't be calling Bruce Barnes, and Rayford's quotes would never see the pages of *Global Weekly*.

As Rayford shaved and showered and dressed, he heard Chloe packing. She had obviously been embarrassed by him last night, probably even apologized to Mr. Williams for her father's absurd ramblings. At least she had tapped on his door and said good night when she came in. That was *something*, wasn't it?

Every time Rayford thought of Chloe, he felt a tightness in his chest, a great emptiness and grief. He could live with his other failures if he must, but his knees nearly buckled as he prayed silently for Chloe. *I cannot lose her,* he thought, and he believed he would trade his own salvation for hers if that was what it took.

With that commitment, he sensed God speaking to him, impressing upon him that that was precisely the burden required for winning people, for leading them to Christ. That was the attitude of Jesus himself, being willing to take on himself the punishment of men and women so they could live.

Rayford was emboldened anew as he prayed for Chloe, still fighting the nagging fear of failure. "God, I need encouragement," he breathed. "I need to know I haven't turned her off forever." She had said good night, but he had also heard her crying in bed.

He emerged in uniform and smiled at her as she stood by the door, dressed casually for travel. "Ready, sweetie?" he said tentatively.

She nodded and seemed to work up a smile, then embraced him tight and long, pressing her cheek against his chest. *Thank you,* he prayed silently, wondering if he should say anything. Was this the time? Dare he press now?

Again he felt deeply impressed of God, as if the Lord were speaking directly to his spirit, *Patience. Let her be. Let her be.* Keeping silent seemed as hard as anything he had ever done. Chloe said nothing either. They grabbed a light breakfast and headed to JFK.

Chloe was the first passenger on the plane. "I'll try to get back and see you," Rayford told her before heading to the cockpit.

"Don't worry if you can't," she said. "I'll understand."

* * *

Buck waited until everyone else had boarded. As he approached his seat next to Chloe, her body was turned toward the window, arms crossed, chin in her hand.

Whether she even had her eyes open, Buck couldn't tell. He assumed she would turn to glance as he sat next to her, and he couldn't suppress a smile, anticipating her reaction and only slightly worried that she would be less positive than he hoped.

He sat and waited, but she did not turn. Was she sleeping? Staring? Meditating? Praying? Was it possible she was crying? Buck hoped not. He already cared for her enough to be bothered when she seemed in pain.

And now he had a problem. As he warily watched for the change in position that would allow Chloe to see him in her peripheral vision, he was suddenly awash in fatigue. His muscles and joints ached, his eyes burned. His head felt like lead. No way was he going to fall asleep and have her discover him dozing next to her.

Buck gestured to get the attendant's attention. "Coke, please," he whispered. The temporary caffeine rush would allow him to stay awake a little longer.

When Chloe didn't move even to watch the safety instructions, Buck grew impatient. Still, he didn't want to reveal himself. He wanted to be discovered. And so he waited.

She must have grown weary of her position, because she stretched and used her feet to push her carry-on bag under the seat in front of her. She took a last sip of her juice and set it on the small tray between them. She stared at Buck's glove-leather boots, the ones he had worn the day before. Chloe's eyes traveled up to his smiling, expectant face.

Her reaction was more than worth the wait. She folded her hands and drew them to her mouth, her eyes filling. Then she took his hand in both of hers. "Oh, Buck," she whispered. "Oh, Buck."

"It's nice to see you, too," he said.

Chloe quickly let go of his hand as if catching herself. "I don't mean to act like a schoolgirl," she said, "but have you ever received a direct answer to prayer?"

Buck shot her a double take. "I thought your dad was the praying member of your family."

"He is," she said. "But I just tried out my first one in years, and God answered it."

"You prayed I would sit next to you?"

"Oh, no, I never would have dreamed of anything that impossible. How did you do it, Buck?"

He told her. "It wasn't hard once I knew your flight time, and I said I was traveling with you to get next to you."

"But why? Where are you going?"

"You don't know where this plane's going? San José, I hope."

She laughed.

"But come on now, Chloe. Finish your story. I've never been an answer to prayer before."

"It's kind of a long story."

"I think we've got time."

She took his hand again. "Buck, this is too special. This is the nicest thing anyone's done for me in a long time."

"You said you were going to miss me, but I didn't do it only for you. I've got business in Chicago."

She giggled and let go again. "I wasn't talking about you, Buck, though this is sweet. I was talking about God doing the nice thing for me."

Buck couldn't hide his embarrassment. "I knew that," he said.

And she told him her story. "You might have noticed I was pretty upset last night. I was so moved by my dad's story. I mean, I had heard it before. But all of a sudden he seemed so loving, so interested in people. Could you tell how important it was to him and how serious he was about it?"

"Who couldn't?"

"If I didn't know better, Buck, I would have thought he was trying to convince you personally rather than just answering your questions."

"I'm not so sure he wasn't."

"Did it offend you?"

"Not at all, Chloe. To tell you the truth, he was getting to me."

Chloe fell silent and shook her head. When she finally spoke she was nearly whispering, and Buck had to lean toward her to hear. He loved the sound of her voice. "Buck," she said, "he was getting to me, too, and I don't mean my dad."

"Too bizarre," he said. "I was up half the night thinking about this."

"It won't be long for either of us, will it?" she said. Buck didn't respond, but he knew what she meant.

"When do I get to be the answer to prayer?" he prodded.

"Oh, right. I was sitting there at dinner with my dad pouring his guts out to you, and I suddenly realized why he wanted me to be there when he said the same things to Hattie. I gave him such a hard time at first that he backed off on me, and now that he had the knowledge and the real need to convince me, he was afraid to come right at me. He wanted me to get it indirectly. And I did. I didn't hear how he started because Hattie and I were in the ladies' room, but I had probably heard that before. When I got back, I was transfixed.

"It wasn't that I was hearing anything new. It was new to me when I heard it from Bruce Barnes and saw that videotape, but my dad showed such urgency and confidence. Buck, there's no other explanation for those two guys in Jerusalem, is there, except that they have to be the two witnesses talked about in the Bible?"

Buck nodded.

"So, Dad and God were getting to me, but I wasn't ready yet. I was crying because I love him so much and because it's true. It's all true, Buck, do you know that?"

"I think I do, Chloe."

"But still I couldn't talk to my dad about it. I didn't know what was in my way. I've always been so blasted independent. I knew he was frustrated with me, maybe disappointed, and all I could do was cry. I had to think, to try to pray, to sort it out. Hattie was no help. She doesn't get it and maybe never will. All she cared about was trivial stuff, like trying to matchmake you and me."

Buck smiled and tried to look insulted. "That's trivial?"

"Well, compared to what we're talking about right now, I'd have to say so."

"Gotta give you that one," Buck said.

She laughed. "So I knew something was wrong with Dad because I talked to you for only, what, three minutes or so before I went up?"

"Less than that, probably."

"By the time I got to our suite, he was already in bed. So I told him good night, just to make sure he was still talking to me. He was. And then I tossed and turned, not ready to take the last step, crying about my dad's worrying so much about me and loving me so much."

"That's while I was up, probably," Buck said.

"But," Chloe said, "this is so out of character for me. Even though I'm there, I mean, I'm right there. You follow me?"

Buck nodded. "I've been going through the same thing."

"I've been convinced," she said, "but I'm still fighting. I'm supposed to be an intellectual. I have critical friends to answer to. Who's going to believe this? Who's going to think I haven't lost my mind?"

"Believe me, I understand," Buck said, amazed at the similarities between their journeys.

"So, I was stuck," she said. "I wasn't getting anywhere. I tried to encourage my dad by not being so distant, but I could tell he saw me suffering, but I don't think he had any idea how close I was. I got on this plane, desperate for some closure, pardon the psychobabble, and I started wondering if God answers your prayers before you're . . . um, you know, before you're actually a . . ."

"Born-again Christian," Buck offered.

"Exactly. I don't know why that's so hard for me to say. Maybe somebody who knows better can tell me for sure, but I prayed and I think God answered.

Tell me this, Buck, just with your cognitive-reasoning skills. If there is a God and if this is all true, wouldn't he want us to know? I mean, God wouldn't make it hard to learn and he wouldn't, or I should say he *couldn't*, ignore a desperate prayer, could he?"

"I don't see how he could, no."

"Well, that's what I think. So I think it was a good test, a reasonable one, and that I wasn't out of line. I'm convinced God answered."

"And I was the answer."

"And you were the answer."

"Chloe, what exactly did you pray for?"

"Oh, well, the prayer itself wasn't that big of a deal, until it was answered. I just told God I needed a little more. I felt bad that all the stuff I'd heard and all that I knew from my dad wasn't enough. I just prayed really sincerely and said I would appreciate it if God could show me personally that he cared, that he knew what I was going through, and that he wanted me to know he was there."

Buck felt a strange emotion—that if he tried to speak, his voice would be husky and he might be unable to finish a sentence. He pressed his hand over his mouth to compose himself. Chloe stared at him. "And you feel I was the answer to that prayer?" he said at last.

"No doubt in my mind. See, like I said, I wouldn't even have conceived of praying that you would wind up next to me on the biggest day of my life. I wasn't even sure I'd ever see you again. But it's as if God knew better than I did that there was no one I would rather see today than you."

Buck was touched, moved beyond expression. He had wanted to see her, too. Otherwise, he could have flown on Hattie's flight or any one of a dozen that would have gotten him to Chicago that morning. Buck just looked at her. "So, what are you going to do now, Chloe? It seems to me that God has called your bluff. It wasn't a bluff, exactly, but you asked and he delivered. Sounds like you're obligated."

"I have no choice," she agreed. "Not that I want one. From what I've gathered from Bruce Barnes and the tape and Dad, you don't have to have somebody lead you through this, and you don't have to be in a church or anything. Just like I prayed for a clearer sign, I can pray about this."

"Your dad made that clear last night."

"You want to join me?" she asked.

Buck hesitated. "Don't take this personally, Chloe, but I'm not ready."

"What more do you need? . . . Oh, I'm sorry, Buck. I'm doing just what my dad did the day he became a Christian. He could hardly help himself, and I was so awful to him. But if you're not ready, you're not ready."

"I won't need to be forced," Buck said. "Like you, I feel like I'm right on the doorstep. But I'm pretty careful, and I want to talk to this Barnes guy today. I have to tell you, though, my remaining doubts can hardly stand up to what's happening to you."

"You know, Buck," Chloe said, "I promise this will be the last thing I say about it, but I'm thinking the same way my dad did. I have this urge to tell you not to wait too long because you never know what might happen."

"I hear you," he said. "I'm going to have to take my chances this plane won't go down because I still feel I need to talk to Barnes, but you have a point."

Chloe turned and looked over her shoulder. "There are two vacant seats right there," she said. She stopped a passing attendant. "Can I give you a message for my dad?"

"Sure. Is he captain or first officer?"

"Captain. Please just tell him his daughter has extremely good news for him."

"Extremely good news," the attendant repeated.

\+ + +

Rayford was manually flying the plane as a diversion when his senior flight attendant gave him the message. He had no idea what it meant, but it was so unlike Chloe to initiate communication lately, he was intrigued.

He asked his first officer to take over. Rayford unstrapped himself and made his way out, surprised to see Cameron Williams. He hoped Williams wasn't the extent of Chloe's good news. Pleasant as it was to think the man might already be making good on his promise to look up Bruce Barnes, Rayford also hoped that Chloe wasn't about to announce some ill-advised whirlwind romance in the bud.

He shook hands with the writer and expressed his pleasant, but wary, surprise. Chloe reached for his neck with both hands and gently pulled him down to where she could whisper to him. "Daddy, could you and I sit back there for a couple of minutes so I can talk to you?"

\+ + +

Buck sensed disappointment in Captain Steele's eyes at first. He looked forward to telling the pilot why he was glad to be flying to Chicago. Sitting next to Chloe had been only a bonus. He peeked back at Steele with his daughter, engaged in intense conversation and then praying together. Buck wondered if there was any airline regulation against that. He knew Rayford couldn't fraternize for long.

In a few minutes Chloe stepped into the aisle, and Rayford stood and embraced her. They both appeared overcome with emotion. A middle-aged couple across the aisle leaned out and stared, brows raised. The captain noticed, straightened, and headed toward the cockpit. "My daughter," he said awkwardly, pointing at Chloe who smiled through her tears. "She's my daughter."

The couple looked at each other and the woman spoke. "Right. And I'm the queen of England," she said, and Buck laughed out loud.

23

BUCK CALLED New Hope Village Church to set up an early evening meeting with Bruce Barnes, then spent most of the afternoon at the Chicago bureau of *Global Weekly*. News of his becoming their boss had swept the place, and he was greeted with coolness by Lucinda Washington's former assistant, a young woman in sensible shoes. She told him in no uncertain terms, "Plank did nothing about replacing Lucinda, so I assumed I would move into her slot."

Her attitude and presumption alone made Buck say, "That's unlikely, but you'll be the first to know. I wouldn't be moving offices just yet."

The rest of the staff still grieved over Lucinda's disappearance and seemed grateful for Buck's visit. Steve Plank had hardly ever come to Chicago and had not been there since Lucinda had vanished.

Buck camped out in Lucinda's old office, interviewing key people at twenty-minute intervals. He also told each about his writing assignment and asked their personal theories of what had happened. His final question to each was, "Where do you think Lucinda Washington is right now?" More than half said they didn't want to be quoted but expressed variations of, "If there's a heaven, that's where she is."

Near the end of the day, Buck was told that CNN was live at the U.N. with big news. He invited the staff into the office and they watched together. "In the most dramatic and far-reaching overhaul of an international organization anyone can remember," came the report, "Romanian president Nicolae Carpathia was catapulted into reluctant leadership of the United Nations by a nearly unanimous vote. Carpathia, who insisted on sweeping changes in direction and jurisdiction of the United Nations, in what appeared an effort to gracefully decline the position, became secretary-general here just moments ago.

"As late as this morning his press secretary and spokesman, Steven Plank, former executive editor of the *Global Weekly*, had denied Carpathia's interest in the job and outlined myriad demands the Romanian would insist upon before even considering the position. Plank said the request for Carpathia's elevation came from outgoing Secretary-General Mwangati Ngumo of Botswana. We asked Ngumo why he was stepping down."

Ngumo's face filled the screen, eyes downcast, his expression carefully masked. "I have long been aware that divided loyalties between my country and the United Nations have made me less effective in each role. I had to choose, and I am first and foremost a Motswana. We have the opportunity now to become prosperous, due to the generosity of our friends in Israel. The time is right, and the new man is more than right. I will cooperate with him to the fullest."

"Would you, sir, have stepped down had Mr. Carpathia declined the position?"

Ngumo hesitated. "Yes," he said, "I would have. Perhaps not today, and not with as much confidence in the future of the United Nations, but yes, eventually."

The CNN reporter continued, "In only a matter of hours, every request Carpathia had outlined in an early morning press conference was moved as official business, voted upon, and ratified by the body. Within a year the United Nations headquarters will move to New Babylon. The makeup of the Security Council will change to ten permanent members within the month, and a press conference is expected Monday morning in which Carpathia will introduce several of his personal choices for delegates to that body.

"There is no guarantee, of course, that even member nations will unanimously go along with the move to destroy ninety percent of their military strength and turn over the remaining ten percent to the U.N. But several ambassadors expressed their confidence 'in equipping and arming an international peacekeeping body with a thoroughgoing pacifist and committed disarmament activist as its head.' Carpathia himself was quoted as saying, 'The U.N. will not need its military might if no one else has any, and I look forward to the day when even the U.N. disarms.'

"Also coming out of today's meetings was the announcement of a seven-year pact between U.N. members and Israel, guaranteeing its borders and promising peace. In exchange, Israel will allow the U.N. to selectively franchise the use of the fertilizer formula, developed by Nobel prizewinner Dr. Chaim Rosenzweig, which makes desert sands tillable and has made Israel a top exporter."

Buck stared as CNN broadcast Rosenzweig's excitement and unequivocal endorsement of Carpathia. The news also carried a report that Carpathia had asked several international groups already in New York for upcoming meetings to get together this weekend to hammer out proposals, resolutions, and accords. "I urge them to move quickly toward anything that contributes to world peace and a sense of global unity."

A reporter asked Carpathia if that included plans for one world religion and eventually one world government. His response: "I can think of little more encouraging than the religions of the world finally cooperating. Some of the worst examples of discord and infighting have been between groups whose overall mission is love among people. Every devotee of pure religion should welcome this potential. The day of hatred is past. Lovers of humankind are uniting."

The CNN anchor continued, "Among other developments today, there are rumors of the organization of groups espousing one world government. Carpathia was asked if he aspired to a position of leadership in such an organization."

Carpathia looked directly into the network pool camera and with moist eyes and thick voice said, "I am overwhelmed to have been asked to serve as secretary-general of the United Nations. I aspire to nothing else. While the idea of one world government resonates deep within me, I can say only that there are many more qualified candidates to lead such a venture. It would be my privilege to serve in any way I am asked, and while I do not see myself in the leadership role, I will commit the resources of the United Nations to such an effort, if asked."

Smooth, Buck thought, his mind reeling. As commentators and world leaders endorsed one world currency, one language, and even the largesse of Carpathia expressing his support for the rebuilding of the temple in Israel, the staff of *Global Weekly*'s Chicago bureau seemed in a mood to party. "This is the first time in years I've felt optimistic about society," one reporter said.

Another added, "This has to be the first time I've smiled since the disappearances. We're supposed to be objective and cynical, but how can you not like this? It'll take years to effect all this stuff, but someday, somewhere down the line, we're going to see world peace. No more weapons, no more wars, no more border disputes or bigotry based on language or religion. Whew! Who'd have believed it would come to this?"

Buck took a call from Steve Plank. "You been watching what's going on?" Plank said.

"Who hasn't?"

"Pretty exciting, isn't it?"

"Mind-boggling."

"Listen, Carpathia wants you here Monday morning."

"What for?"

"He likes you, man. Don't knock it. Before the press conference he's going to have a meeting with his top people and the ten delegates to the permanent Security Council."

"And he wants me there?"

"Yup. And you can guess who some of his top people are."

"Tell me."

"Well, one's obvious."

"Stonagal."

"Of course."

"And Todd-Cothran. I assume he'll move in as new ambassador from the U.K."

"Maybe not," Steve said. "Another Brit is there. I don't know his name, but he's also with this international finance group Stonagal runs."

"You think Carpathia told Stonagal to have someone else in the wings, in case Carpathia wants to squeeze Todd-Cothran out?"

"Could be, but nobody tells Stonagal anything."

"Not even Carpathia?"

"Especially not Carpathia. He knows who made him. But he's honest and sincere, Buck. Nicolae will not do anything illegal or underhanded or even too political. He's pure, man. Pure as the driven snow. So, can you make it?"

"Guess I'd better. How many press will be there?"

"You ready for this? Only you."

"You're kidding."

"I'm serious. He likes you, Buck."

"What's the catch?"

"No catch. He didn't ask for a thing, not even favorable coverage. He knows you have to be objective and fair. The media will get the whole scoop at the press conference afterward."

"Obviously I can't pass this up," Buck said, aware his voice sounded flat.

"What's the matter, Buck? This is history! This is the world the way we've always wanted it and hoped it would be."

"I hope you're right."

"I'm right. There's something else Carpathia wants."

"So there *is* a catch."

"No, nothing hinges on this. If you can't do it, you can't do it. You're still welcome Monday morning. But he wants to see that stewardess friend of yours again."

"Steve, no one calls them stews anymore. They're flight attendants."

"Whatever. Bring her with you if you can."

"Why doesn't he ask her himself? What am I now, a pimp?"

"C'mon, Buck. It's not like that. Lonely guy in a position like this? He can't be out hustling up dates. You introduced them, remember? He trusts you."

He must, Buck thought, *if he's inviting me to his big pre-press-conference meeting.* "I'll ask her," he said. "No promises."

"Don't let me down, buddy."

* * *

Rayford Steele was as happy as he had been since his own decision to receive Christ. To see Chloe smiling, to see her hungry to read Irene's Bible, to be able to pray with her and talk about everything together was more than he had dreamed of. "One thing we need to do," he said, "is to get you your own Bible. You're going to wear that one out."

"I want to join that core group of yours," she said. "I want to get all the stuff from Bruce firsthand. The only part that bothers me is that it sounds like things are going to get worse."

Late in the afternoon they dropped in on Bruce, who confirmed Chloe's view. "I'm thrilled to welcome you into the family," he said, "but you're right. God's people are in for dark days. Everybody is. I've been thinking and praying about what we're supposed to do as a church between now and the Glorious Appearing."

Chloe wanted to know all about that, so Bruce showed her from the Bible why he believed Christ would appear in seven years, at the end of the Tribulation. "Most Christians will be martyred or die from war, famine, plagues, or earthquakes," he said.

Chloe smiled. "This isn't funny," she said, "but maybe I should have thought of that before I signed on. You're going to have trouble convincing people to join the cause with that in your sign-up brochure."

Bruce grimaced. "Yes, but the alternative is worse. We all missed out the first time around. We could be in heaven right now if we'd listened to our loved ones. Dying a horrible death during this period is not my preference, but I'd sure rather do it this way than while I was still lost. Everyone else is in danger of death, too. The only difference is, we have one more way to die than they do."

"As martyrs."

"Right."

Rayford sat listening, aware how his world had changed in such a short time. It had not been that long ago that he had been a respected pilot at the top of his profession, living a phony life, a shell of a man. Now here he was, talking secretly in the office of a local church with his daughter and a young pastor, trying to determine how they would survive seven years of tribulation following the Rapture of the church.

"We have our core group," Bruce said, "and Chloe, you're welcome to join us if you're serious about total commitment."

"What's the option?" she said. "If what you're saying is true, there's no room for dabbling."

"You're right. But I've also been thinking about a smaller group within the core. I'm looking for people of unusual intelligence and courage. I don't mean to disparage the sincerity of others in the church, especially those on the leadership team. But some of them are timid, some old, many infirm. I've been praying about sort of an inner circle of people who want to do more than just survive."

"What are you getting at?" Rayford asked. "Going on the offensive?"

"Something like that. It's one thing to hide in here, studying, figuring out what's going on so we can keep from being deceived. It's great to pray for the witnesses springing up out of Israel, and it's nice to know there are other pockets of believers all over the world. But doesn't part of you want to jump into the battle?"

Rayford was intrigued but not sure. Chloe was more eager. "A cause," she said. "Something not just to die for but to live for."

"Yes!"

"A group, a team, a force," Chloe said.

"You've got it. A force."

Chloe's eyes were bright with interest. Rayford loved her youth and her eagerness to commit to a cause that to her was only hours old. "And what is it you call this period?" she asked.

"The Tribulation," Bruce said.

"So your little group inside the group, a sort of Green Berets, would be your Tribulation force."

"Tribulation Force," Bruce said, looking at Rayford and rising to scribble it on his flip chart. "I like it. Make no mistake, it won't be fun. It would be the most dangerous cause a person could ever join. We would study, prepare, and speak out. When it becomes obvious who the Antichrist is, the false prophet, the evil, counterfeit religion, we'll have to oppose them, speak out against them. We would be targeted. Christians content to hide in basements with their Bibles might escape everything but earthquakes and wars, but we will be vulnerable to everything.

"There will come a time, Chloe, that followers of Antichrist will be required to bear the sign of the beast. There are all kinds of theories on what form that might take, from a tattoo to a stamp on the forehead that might be detected only under infrared light. But obviously we would refuse to bear that mark. That very act of defiance will be a mark in itself. We will be the naked ones, the ones devoid of the protection of belonging to the majority. You still want to be part of the Tribulation Force?"

Rayford nodded and smiled at his daughter's firm reply. "I wouldn't miss it."

\+ + +

Two hours after the Steeles had left, Buck Williams parked his rental car in front of New Hope Village Church in Mount Prospect, Illinois. He had a sense of destiny tinged with fear. Who would this Bruce Barnes be? What would he look like? And would he be able to detect a non-Christian at a glance?

Buck sat in the car, his head in his hands. He was too analytical, he knew, to make a rash decision. Even his leaving home years before to pursue an education and become a journalist had been plotted for years. To his family it came like a thunderbolt, but to young Cameron Williams it was a logical next step, a part of his long-range plan.

Where Buck sat now was not part of any plan. Nothing that had happened since that ill-fated flight to Heathrow had fit into any predefined pattern for him. He had always liked the serendipity of life, but he processed it through a grid of logic, attacked it from a perspective of order. The firestorm of Israel had jarred him, but even then he had been acting from a standpoint of order. He had a career, a position, a role. He had been in Israel on assignment, and though he hadn't expected to become a war correspondent overnight, he had been prepared by the way he had ordered his life.

But nothing had prepared him for the disappearances or for the violent deaths of his friends. While he should have been prepared for this promotion, that hadn't been part of his plan, either. Now his theory article was bringing him close to flames he had never known were burning in his soul. He felt alone, exposed, vulnerable, and yet this meeting with Bruce Barnes had been his idea. Sure, the airline pilot had suggested it, but Buck could have ignored him without remorse. This trip had not been about getting in a few extra hours with the beautiful Chloe, and the Chicago bureau could have waited. He was here, he knew, for this meeting. Buck felt a bone weariness as he headed for the church.

It was a pleasant surprise to find that Bruce Barnes was someone near Buck's own age. He seemed bright and earnest, having that same authority and passion Rayford Steele exhibited. It had been a long time since Buck had been in a church. This one seemed innocuous enough, fairly new and modern, neat and efficient. He and the young pastor met in a modest office.

"Your friends, the Steeles, told me you might call," Barnes said.

Buck was struck by his honesty. In the world in which Buck moved, he might have kept that information to himself, that edge. But he realized that the pastor had no interest in an edge. There was nothing to hide here. In essence, Buck was looking for information and Bruce was interested in providing it.

"I want to tell you right off," Bruce said, "that I am aware of your work and respect your talent. But to be frank, I no longer have time for the pleasantries and small talk that used to characterize my work. We live in perilous times. I have a message and an answer for people genuinely seeking. I tell everyone in advance that I have quit apologizing for what I'm going to say. If that's a ground rule you can live with, I have all the time you need."

"Well, sir," Buck said, nearly staggered by the emotion and humility he heard in his own voice, "I appreciate that. I don't know how long I'll need, because I'm not here on business. It might have made sense to get a pastor's view for my story, but people can guess what pastors think, especially based on the other people I'm quoting."

"Like Captain Steele."

Buck nodded. "I'm here for myself, and I have to tell you frankly, I don't know where I am on this. Not that long ago I would never have set foot in a place like this or dreamed anything intellectually worthwhile could come out of here. I know that wasn't exactly journalistically fair of me, but as long as you're being honest, I will be, too.

"I was impressed with Captain Steele. That's one smart guy, a good thinker, and he's into this. You seem like a bright person, and—I don't know. I'm listening, that's all I'll say."

Bruce began by telling Buck his life story, being raised in a Christian home, going to Bible college, marrying a Christian, becoming a pastor, the whole thing. He clarified that he knew the story of Christ and the way of forgiveness and a relationship with God. "I thought I had the best of both worlds. But the Scripture is clear that you can't serve two masters. You can't have it both ways. I discovered that truth in the severest way." And he told of losing his family and friends, everyone dear to him. He wept as he spoke. "The pain is every bit as great today as it was when it happened," he said.

Then Bruce outlined, as Rayford had done, the plan of salvation from beginning to end. Buck grew nervous, anxious. He wanted a break. He interrupted and asked if Bruce wanted to know a little more about him. "Sure," Bruce said.

Buck told of his own history, concentrating most on the Russia/Israel conflict and the roughly fourteen months since. "I can see," Bruce said at last, "that God is trying to get your attention."

"Well, he's got it," Buck said. "I just have to warn you, I'm not an easy sell. All this is interesting and sounds more plausible than ever, but it's just not me to jump into something."

"Nobody can force you or badger you into this, Mr. Williams, but I must also say again that we live in perilous times. We don't know how much pondering time we have."

"You sound like Chloe Steele."

"And she sounds like her father," Bruce said, smiling.

"And he, I guess, sounds like you. I can see why you all consider this so urgent, but like I say—"

"I understand," Bruce said. "If you have the time right now, let me take a different tack. I know you're a bright guy, so you might as well have all the information you need before you leave here."

Buck breathed easier. He had feared Bruce was about to pop the question, pushing him to pray the prayer both Rayford Steele and Chloe had talked about. He accepted that that would be part of it, that it would signal the transaction and start his relationship with God—someone he had never before really spoken to. But he wasn't ready. At least he didn't think he was. And he would not be pushed.

"I don't have to be back in New York until Monday morning," he said, "so I'll take as much time tonight as you'll give me."

"I don't mean to be morbid, Mr. Williams, but I have no family responsibilities anymore. I have a core group meeting tomorrow and church Sunday. You're welcome to attend. But I have enough energy to go to midnight if you do."

"I'm all yours."

Bruce spent the next several hours giving Buck a crash course in prophecy and the end times. Buck had heard much of the information about the Rapture and the two witnesses, and he had picked up snippets about the Antichrist. But when Bruce got to the parts about the great one-world religion that would spring up, the lying, so-called peacemaker who would bring bloodshed through war, the Antichrist who would divide the world into ten kingdoms, Buck's blood ran cold. He fell silent, no longer peppering Bruce with questions or comments. He scribbled notes as fast as he could.

Did he dare tell this unpretentious man that he believed Nicolae Carpathia could be the very man the Scriptures talked about? Could all this be coincidental? His fingers began to shake when Bruce told of the prediction of a seven-year pact between Antichrist and Israel, of the rebuilding of the temple, and even of Babylon becoming headquarters for a new world order.

Finally, as midnight came, Buck was overcome. He felt a terrible fear deep in his gut. Bruce Barnes could have had no knowledge whatever of the plans of Nicolae Carpathia before they had been announced on the news that afternoon. At one point he thought of accusing Bruce of having based everything he was saying on the CNN report he had heard and seen, but even if he had, here it was in black and white in the Bible.

"Did you see the news today?" Buck asked.

"Not today," Bruce said. "I've been in meetings since noon and grabbed a bite just before you got here."

Buck told him what had happened at the U.N. Bruce paled. "That's why we've been hearing all those clicking sounds on my answering machine," Bruce said. "I turned the ringer off on the phone, so the only way you can tell when a call comes in is by the clicking on the answering machine. People are calling to let me know. They do that a lot. We talk about what the Bible says may happen, and when it does, people check in."

"You think Carpathia is this Antichrist?"

"I don't see how I could come to any other conclusion."

"But I really believed in the guy."

"Why not? Most of us did. Self-effacing, interested in the welfare of the people, humble, not looking for power or leadership. But the Antichrist is a deceiver. And he has the power to control men's minds. He can make people see lies as truth."

Buck told Bruce of his invitation to the pre-press-conference meeting.

"You must not go," Bruce said.

"I can't *not* go," Buck said. "This is the opportunity of a lifetime."

"I'm sorry," Bruce said. "I have no authority over you, but let me plead with you, warn you, about what happens next. The Antichrist will solidify his power with a show of strength."

"He already has."

"Yes, but it appears that all these long-range agreements he has been conceded will take months or years to effect. Now he has to show some potency. What might he do to entrench himself so solidly that no one can oppose him?"

"I don't know."

"He undoubtedly has ulterior motives for wanting you there."

"I'm no good to him."

"You would be if he controlled you."

"But he doesn't."

"If he is the evil one the Bible speaks of, there is little he does not have the power to do. I warn you not to go there without protection."

"A bodyguard?"

"At least. But if Carpathia is the Antichrist, do you want to face him without God?"

Buck was taken aback. This conversation was bizarre enough without wondering if Bruce was using any means necessary to get him to convert. No doubt it had been a sincere and logical question, yet Buck felt pressured. "I see what you mean," he said slowly, "but I don't think I'm going to get hypnotized or anything."

"Mr. Williams, you have to do what you have to do, but I'm pleading with you. If you go into that meeting without God in your life, you will be in mortal and spiritual danger."

He told Buck about his conversation with the Steeles and how they had collectively come up with the idea of a Tribulation Force. "It's a band of serious-minded people who will boldly oppose the Antichrist. I just didn't expect that his identity would become so obvious so soon."

The Tribulation Force stirred something deep within Buck. It took him back to his earliest days as a writer, when he believed he had the power to change the world. He would stay up all hours of the night, plotting with his colleagues how they would have the courage and the audacity to stand up to oppression, to big government, to bigotry. He had lost that fire and verve over the years as he won accolades for his writing. He still wanted to do the right things, but he had lost the passion of the all-for-one and one-for-all philosophy as his talent and celebrity began to outstrip those same colleagues.

The idealist, the maverick in him, gravitated toward such ideas, but he caught himself before he talked himself into becoming a believer in Christ just because of an exciting little club he could join.

"Do you think I could sit in on your core group meeting tomorrow?" he asked.

"I'm afraid not," Bruce said. "I think you'd find it interesting and I personally believe it would help convince you, but it is limited to our leadership team. Truth is, I'll be going over with them tomorrow what you and I are talking about tonight, so it would be a rerun for you anyway."

"And church Sunday?"

"You're very welcome, but I must say, it's going to be the same theme I use every Sunday. You've heard it from Ray Steele and you've heard it from me. If hearing it one more time would help, then come on out and see how many seekers and finders there are. If it's anything like the last two Sundays, it will be standing room only."

Buck stood and stretched. He had kept Bruce long past midnight, and he apologized.

"No need," Bruce said. "This is what I do."

"Do you know where I can get a Bible?"

"I've got one you can have," Bruce said.

* * *

The next day the core group enthusiastically and emotionally welcomed its newest member, Chloe Steele. They spent much of the day studying the news and trying to determine the likelihood of Nicolae Carpathia's being the Antichrist. No one could argue otherwise.

Bruce told the story of Buck Williams, without using his name or mentioning his connection with Rayford and Chloe. Chloe cried silently as the group prayed for his safety and for his soul.

24

BUCK SPENT SATURDAY holed up in the otherwise empty Chicago bureau office, getting a head start on his article on the theory behind the disappearances. His mind continually swirled, forcing him to think about Carpathia and what he would say in that piece about how the man seemed to be a perfect parallel to biblical prophecy. Fortunately, he could wait on writing that until after the big day Monday.

Around lunchtime, Buck reached Steve Plank at the Plaza Hotel in New York. "I'll be there Monday morning," he said, "but I'm not inviting Hattie Durham."

"Why not? It's a small request, friend to friend."

"You to me?"

"Nick to you."

"So now it's Nick, is it? Well, he and I are not close enough for that familiarity, and I don't provide female companionship even to my friends."

"Not even for me?"

"If I knew you would treat her with respect, Steve, I'd set you up with Hattie."

"You're really not going to do this for Carpathia?"

"No. Am I uninvited?"

"I'm not going to tell him."

"How are you going to explain it when she doesn't show?"

"I'll ask her myself, Buck, you prude."

Buck didn't say he would warn Hattie not to go. He asked Steve if he could get one more exclusive with Carpathia before starting his cover story on him.

"I'll see what I can do, but you can't even do a small favor and you want another break?"

"He likes me, you said. You know I'm going to do the complete piece on the guy. He needs this."

"If you watched TV yesterday, you know he doesn't need anything. We need him."

"Do we? Have you run into any schools of thought that link him to end-times events in the Bible?"

Steve Plank did not respond.

"Steve?"

"I'm here."

"Well, have you? Anybody that thinks he might fill the bill for one of the villains of the book of Revelation?"

Steve said nothing.

"Hello, Steve."

"I'm still here."

"C'mon, old buddy. You're the press secretary. You know all. How's he going to respond if I hit him with that?"

Steve was still silent.

"Don't do this to me, Steve. I'm not saying that's where I am or that anybody who knows anything or who matters thinks that way. I'm doing the piece on what was behind the disappearances, and you know that takes me into all kinds of religious realms. Nobody anywhere has drawn any parallels here?"

This time when Steve said nothing, Buck merely looked at his watch, determined to wait him out. About twenty seconds after a loud silence, Steve spoke softly. "Buck, I have a two-word answer for you. Are you ready?"

"I'm ready."

"Staten Island."

"Are you tellin' me that—?"

"Don't say the name, Buck! You never know who's listening."

"So you're threatening me with—"

"I'm not threatening. I'm warning. Let me say I'm cautioning you."

"And let me remind you, Steve, that I don't warn well. You remember that, don't you, from ages ago when we worked together and you thought I was the toughest bird dog you'd ever sent on a story?"

"Just don't go sniffing the wrong brier patch, Buck."

"Let me ask you this then, Steve."

"Careful, please."

"You want to talk to me on another line?"

"No, Buck, I just want you to be careful what you say so I can be, too."

Buck began scribbling furiously on a yellow pad. "Fair enough," he said, writing, *Carpathia or Stonagal resp. for Eric Miller?* "What I want to know is this: If you think I should stay off the ferry, is it because of the guy behind the wheel, or because of the guy who supplies his fuel?"

"The latter," Steve said without hesitation.

Buck circled *Stonagal.* "Then you don't think the guy behind the wheel is even aware of what the fuel distributor does in his behalf."

"Correct."

"So if someone got too close to the pilot, the pilot might be protected and not even know it."

"Correct."

"But if he found out about it?"

"He'd deal with it."

"That's what I expect to see soon."

"I can't comment on that."

"Can you tell me who you really work for?"

"I work for who it appears to you I work for."

What in the world did that mean? Carpathia or Stonagal? How could he get Steve to say on a phone from within the Plaza that might be bugged?

"You work for the Romanian businessman?"

"Of course."

Buck nearly kicked himself. That could be either Carpathia or Stonagal. "You do?" he said, hoping for more.

"My boss moves mountains, doesn't he?" Steve said.

"He sure does," Buck said, circling *Carpathia* this time. "You must be pleased with everything going on these days."

"I am."

Buck scribbled, *Carpathia. End times. Antichrist?* "And you're telling me straight up that the other issue I raised is dangerous but also hogwash."

"Total roll in the muck."

"And I shouldn't even broach the subject with him, in spite of the fact that I'm a writer who covers all the bases and asks the tough questions?"

"If I thought you would consider mentioning it, I could not encourage the interview or the story."

"Boy, it didn't take long for you to become a company man."

+ + +

After the core-group meeting, Rayford Steele talked privately with Bruce Barnes and was updated on the meeting with Buck. "I can't discuss the private matters," Bruce said, "but only one thing stands in the way of my being convinced that this Carpathia guy is the Antichrist. I can't make it compute geographically. Almost every end-times writer I respect believes the Antichrist will come out of Western Europe, maybe Greece or Italy or Turkey."

Rayford didn't know what to make of that. "You notice Carpathia doesn't look Romanian. Aren't they mostly dark?"

"Yeah. Let me call Mr. Williams. He gave me a number. I wonder how much more he knows about Carpathia." Bruce dialed and put Buck on the speakerphone. "Ray Steele is with me."

"Hey, Captain," Buck said.

"We're just doing some studying here," Bruce said, "and we've hit a snag." He told Buck what they had found and asked for more information.

"Well, he comes from a town, one of the larger university towns, called Cluj, and—"

"Oh, he does? I guess I thought he was from a mountainous region, you know, because of his name."

"His name?" Buck repeated, doodling it on his legal pad.

"You know, being named after the Carpathian Mountains and all. Or does that name mean something else over there?"

Buck sat up straight and it hit him! Steve had been trying to tell him he worked for Stonagal and *not* Carpathia. And of course all the new U.N. delegates would feel beholden to Stonagal because he had introduced them to Carpathia. Maybe *Stonagal* was the Antichrist! Where had *his* lineage begun?

"Well," Buck said, trying to concentrate, "maybe he was named after the mountains, but he was born in Cluj and his ancestry, way back, is Roman. That accounts for the blond hair and blue eyes."

Bruce thanked him and asked if he would see Buck in church the next day. Rayford thought Buck sounded distracted and noncommittal. "I haven't ruled it out," Buck said.

\+ + +

Yes, Buck thought, hanging up. *I'll be there all right.* He wanted every last bit of input before he went to New York to write a story that could cost him his career and maybe his life. He didn't know the truth, but he had never backed off from looking for it, and he wouldn't begin now. He phoned Hattie Durham.

"Hattie," he said, "you're going to get a call inviting you to New York."

"I already did."

"They wanted me to ask you, but I told them to do it themselves."

"They did."

"They want you to see Carpathia again, provide him some companionship next week if you're free."

"I know and I am and I will."

"I'm advising you not to do it."

She laughed. "Right, I'm going to turn down a date with the most powerful man in the world? I don't think so."

"That would be my advice."

"Whatever for?"

"Because you don't strike me as that kind of girl."

"First, I'm not a girl. I'm almost as old as you are, and I don't need a parent or legal guardian."

"I'm talking as a friend."

"You're not my friend, Buck. It was obvious you didn't even like me. I tried to shove you off onto Rayford Steele's little girl, and I'm not sure you even had the brains to pick up on that."

"Hattie, maybe I don't know you. But you don't seem the type who would allow herself to be taken advantage of by a stranger."

"You're pretty much a stranger, and you're trying to tell me what to do."

"Well, *are* you that kind of a person? By not passing along the invitation, was I protecting you from something you might enjoy?"

"You'd better believe it."

"I can't talk you out of it?"

"You can't even try," she said, and she hung up.

Buck shook his head and leaned back in his chair, holding the yellow pad in front of him. *My boss moves mountains, Steve had said. Carpathia is a mountain. Stonagal is the mover and shaker behind him. Steve thinks he's really wired in deep. He's not only press secretary to the man Hattie Durham correctly called the most powerful man on earth, but Steve is also actually in league with the man behind the man.*

Buck wondered what Rayford or Chloe would do if they knew Hattie had been invited to New York to be Carpathia's companion for a few days. In the end, he decided it was none of his, or their, business.

+ + +

Rayford and Chloe watched for Buck until the last minute the next morning, but they could no longer save a seat for him when the sanctuary and the balcony filled. When Bruce began his message, Chloe nudged her father and pointed out the window, down onto the walk before the front door. There, in a small crowd listening to an external speaker, was Buck. Rayford raised a celebratory fist and whispered to Chloe, "Wonder what you're going to pray for this morning?"

Bruce played the former pastor's videotape, told his own story again, talked briefly about prophecy, invited people to receive Christ, and then opened the microphone for personal accounts. As had happened the previous two weeks, people streamed forward and stood in line until well after one in the afternoon, eager to tell how they had now, finally, trusted Christ.

Chloe told her father she had wanted to be first, as he had been, but by the time she made her way down from the last row of the balcony, she was one of the last. She told her story, including the sign she believed God had given her in the form of a friend who sat beside her on the flight home. Rayford knew she could not see Buck over the crowd, and Rayford couldn't either.

When the meeting was over, Rayford and Chloe went outside to find Buck, but he was gone. They went for lunch with Bruce, and when they got home, Chloe found a note from Buck on the front door.

It isn't that I didn't want to say good-bye. But I don't. I'll be back for bureau business and maybe just to see you, if you'll allow it. I've got a lot to think about right now, as you know, and frankly, I don't want my attraction to you to get in the way of that thinking. And it would. You are a lovely person, Chloe, and I was moved to tears by your story. You had told me before, but to hear it in that place and in that circumstance this morning was beautiful. Would you do something I have never asked anyone to do for me ever before? Would you pray for me? I will call you or see you soon. I promise. Buck.

* * *

Buck felt more alone than ever on the flight home. He was in coach on a full plane, but he knew no one. He read several sections from the Bible Bruce had given him and had marked for him, prompting the woman next to him to ask questions. He answered in such a way that she could tell he was not in the mood for conversation. He didn't want to be rude, but neither did he want to mislead anyone with his limited knowledge.

Sleep was no easier for him that night, though he refused to allow himself to pace. He was going into a meeting in the morning that he had been warned to stay away from. Bruce Barnes had sounded convinced that if Nicolae Carpathia were the Antichrist, Buck ran the danger of being mentally overcome, brainwashed, hypnotized, or worse.

As he wearily showered and dressed in the morning, Buck concluded he had come a long way from thinking that the religious angle was on the fringe. He had gone from bemused puzzlement at people thinking their loved ones had flown to heaven to believing that much of what was happening had been foretold in the Bible. He was no longer wondering or doubting, he told himself. There was no other explanation for the two witnesses in Jerusalem. Nor for the disappearances.

And the furthest stretch of all, this business of an Antichrist who deceives so many . . . well, in Buck's mind it was no longer an issue of whether it was literal or true. He was long past that. He had already progressed to trying to decide who the Antichrist was: Carpathia or Stonagal. Buck still leaned toward Stonagal.

He slung his bag over his shoulder, tempted to take the gun from his bedside table but knowing he would never get it through the metal detectors. Anyway, he sensed, that was not the kind of protection he needed. What he needed was safekeeping for his mind and for his spirit.

All the way to the United Nations he agonized. *Do I pray?* he asked himself. *Do I "pray the prayer" as so many of those people said yesterday morning? Would I be doing it just to protect myself from the voodoo or the heebie-jeebies?* He decided that becoming a believer could not be for the purpose of having a good luck charm. That would cheapen it. Surely God didn't work that way. And if Bruce Barnes could be believed, there was no more protection for believers now, during this period, than there was for anyone else. Huge numbers of people were going to die in the next seven years, Christian or not. The question was, *then* where would they be?

There was only one reason to make the transaction, he decided—if he truly believed he could be forgiven and become one of God's people. God had become more than a force of nature or even a miracle worker to Buck, as God had been in the skies of Israel that night. It only made sense that if God made people, he would want to communicate with them, to connect with them.

Buck entered the U.N. through hordes of reporters already setting up for the press conference. Limousines disgorged VIPs and crowds waited behind police barriers. Buck saw Stanton Bailey in a crowd near the door. "What are you doing here?" Buck said, realizing that in five years at *Global* he had never seen Bailey outside the building.

"Just taking advantage of my position so I can be at this press conference. Proud you're going to be in the preliminary meeting. Be sure to remember everything. Thanks for transmitting your first draft of the theory piece. I know you've got a lot to do yet, but it's a terrific start. Gonna be a winner."

"Thanks," Buck said, and Bailey gave him a thumbs-up. Buck realized that if that had happened a month before, he would have had to stifle a laugh at the corny old guy and would have told his colleagues what an idiot he worked for. Now he was strangely grateful for the encouragement. Bailey could have no hint what Buck was going through.

\+ + +

Chloe Steele told her father of her plans to finally look into local college classes that Monday. "And I was thinking," she said, "about trying to get together with Hattie for lunch."

"I thought you didn't care for her," Rayford said.

"I don't, but that's no excuse. She doesn't even know what's happened to me. She's not answering her phone. Any idea what her schedule is?"

"No, but I have to check my own. I'll see if she's flying today."

Rayford was told that not only was Hattie not scheduled that day but also that she had requested a thirty-day leave of absence. "That's odd," he told Chloe. "Maybe she's got family troubles out West."

"Maybe she's just taking some time off," Chloe said. "I'll call her later when I'm out. What are you doing today?"

"I promised Bruce I'd come over and watch that Carpathia press conference later this morning."

"What time's that?"

"Ten our time, I think."

"Well, if Hattie's not around for lunch, maybe I'll come by there."

"Call us either way, hon, and we'll wait for you."

\+ \+ \+

Buck's credentials were waiting for him at an information desk in the U.N. lobby. He was directed up to a private conference room off the suite of offices into which Nicolae Carpathia had already moved. Buck was at least twenty minutes early, but as he emerged from the elevator he felt alone in a crowd. He saw no one he recognized as he began the long walk down a corridor of glass and steel leading to the room where he was to join Steve, the ten designated ambassadors representing the permanent members of the new Security Council, several aides and advisers to the new secretary-general (including Rosenzweig, Stonagal, and various other members of his international brotherhood of financial wizards), and of course, Carpathia himself.

Buck had always been energetic and confident. Others had noticed his purposeful stride on assignment. Now his gait was slow and unsure, and with every step his dread increased. The lights seemed to grow dimmer, the walls close in. His pulse increased and he had a sense of foreboding.

The gripping fear reminded him of Israel, when he believed he was going to die. Was he about to die? He couldn't imagine physical danger, yet clearly people who got in Carpathia's way, or in the way of Stonagal's plans for Carpathia, were now dead. Would he be just another in a line that stretched from Carpathia's business rival in Romania years before, through Dirk Burton and Alan Tompkins, to Eric Miller?

No, what he feared, he knew, was not mortal danger. At least not now, not here. The closer he got to the conference room, the more he was repelled by a sense of evil, as if personified in that place. Almost without thinking, Buck found himself silently praying, *God, be with me. Protect me.*

He felt no sense of relief. If anything, his thoughts of God made his recognition of evil more intense. He stopped ten feet from the open door, and though he heard laughter and banter, he was nearly paralyzed by the atmosphere of blackness. He wanted to be anywhere but there, and yet he knew he could not retreat. This was the room in which the new leaders of the world congregated, and any sane person would have given anything to be there.

Buck realized that what he really wanted was to have been there. He wished it were over, that he had seen this welcoming of new people, this brief speech of commitment or whatever it was to be, and was already writing about it.

He tried to force himself toward the door, his thoughts deafening. Again he cried out to God, and he felt a coward—just like everyone else, praying in the foxhole. He had ignored God for most of his life, and now when he felt the darkest anguish of his soul, he was figuratively on his knees.

Yet he did not belong to God. Not yet. He knew that. God had answered Chloe's prayer for a sign before she had actually made the spiritual transaction. Why couldn't he have answered Buck's plea for calm and peace?

Buck could not move until Steve Plank noticed him. "Buck! We're almost ready to begin. Come on in."

But Buck felt terrible, panicky. "Steve, I need to run to the washroom. Do I have a minute?"

Steve glanced at his watch. "You've got five," he said. "And when you get back, you'll be right over there."

Steve pointed to a chair at one corner of a square block of tables. The journalist in Buck liked it. The perfect vantage point. His eyes darted to the nameplates in front of each spot. He would face the main table, where Carpathia had placed himself directly next to Stonagal . . . or had Stonagal been in charge of the seating? Next to Carpathia on the other side was a hastily hand-lettered nameplate with "Personal Assistant" written on it. "Is that you?" Buck said.

"Nope." Steve pointed at the corner opposite Buck's chair.

"Is Todd-Cothran here?" Buck said.

"Of course. Right there in the light gray."

The Brit looked insignificant enough. But just beyond him were both Stonagal—in charcoal—and Carpathia, looking perfect in a black suit, white shirt, electric-blue tie, and a gold stickpin. Buck shuddered at the sight of him, but Carpathia flashed a smile and waved him over. Buck signaled that he would be a minute. "Now you've got only four minutes," Steve said. "Get going."

Buck put his bag in a corner next to a heavyset, white-haired security guard, waved at his old friend Chaim Rosenzweig, and jogged to the washroom. He placed a janitor's bucket outside and locked the door. Buck backed up against the door, thrust his hands deep into his pockets, and dropped his chin to his chest, remembering Bruce's advice that he could talk to God the same way he talked to a friend. "God," he said, "I need you, and not just for this meeting."

And as he prayed he believed. This was no experiment, no halfhearted attempt. He wasn't just hoping or trying something out. Buck knew he was talking to God himself. He admitted he needed God, that he knew he was as lost and as sinful as anyone. He didn't specifically pray the prayer he had heard others talk about, but when he finished he had covered the same territory and the deal was done. Buck was not the type to go into anything lightly. As well as he knew anything, he knew there would be no turning back.

Buck headed to the conference room, more quickly this time but strangely with no more confidence. He hadn't prayed for courage or peace this time. This prayer had been for his own soul. He hadn't known what he would feel, but he didn't expect this continued sense of dread.

He didn't hesitate, however. When he walked in, everyone was in place—Carpathia, Stonagal, Todd-Cothran, Rosenzweig, Steve, and the financial powers and ambassadors. And one person Buck never expected—Hattie Durham. He stared, dumbfounded, as she took her place as Nicolae Carpathia's personal assistant. She winked at him, but he did not acknowledge her. He hurried to his bag, nodded his thanks to the armed guard, and took only a notebook to his seat.

While no special feeling had come with Buck's decision, he had a heightened sensitivity that something was happening here. There wasn't a doubt in his mind that the Antichrist of the Bible was in this room. And despite all he knew about Stonagal and what the man had engineered in England and despite the ill feeling that came over him as he observed his smugness, Buck sensed the truest, deepest, darkest spirit of evil as he watched Carpathia take his place. Nicolae waited till everyone was seated, then rose with pseudodignity.

"Gentlemen . . . and lady," he began, "this is an important moment. In a few minutes we will greet the press and introduce those of you who shall be entrusted to lead the new world order into a golden era. The global village has become united, and we face the greatest task and the greatest opportunity ever bestowed upon humankind."

25

NICOLAE CARPATHIA stepped out from his place at the table and went to each person individually. He greeted each by name, asking him to stand, shaking his hand, and kissing him on both cheeks. He skipped Hattie and started with the new British ambassador.

"Mr. Todd-Cothran," he said, "you shall be introduced as the ambassador of the Great States of Britain, which now include much of Western and Eastern Europe. I welcome you to the team and confer upon you all the rights and privileges that go with your new station. May you display to me and to those in your charge the consistency and wisdom that have brought you to this position."

"Thank you, sir," Todd-Cothran said, and sat down as Carpathia moved on. Todd-Cothran appeared shocked, as did several others, when Nicolae repeated the same sentiment, including precisely the same title—ambassador of the Great States of Britain—to the British financier next to him. Todd-Cothran smiled tolerantly. Obviously, Carpathia had merely misspoken and should have referred to the man as one of his financial advisers. Yet Buck had never seen Carpathia make such a slip.

All around the four-sided table configuration Carpathia went, one by one, saying exactly the same words to every ambassador, but customizing the litany to include the appropriate name and title. The recitation changed only slightly for his personal aides and advisers.

When Carpathia got to Buck he seemed to hesitate. Buck was slow on the draw, as if he wasn't sure he was to be included in this. Carpathia's warm smile welcomed him to stand. Buck was slightly off balance, trying to hold pen and notebook while shaking hands with the dramatic Carpathia. Nicolae's grip was firm and strong, and he maintained it throughout his recitation. He looked directly into Buck's eyes and spoke with quiet authority.

"Mr. Williams," he said, "I welcome you to the team and confer upon you all the rights and privileges that go with your station. . . ."

What was this? It was not what Buck expected, but it was so affirming, so flattering. He was not part of any team, and no rights or privileges should be conferred upon him! He shook his head slightly to signal that Carpathia was again confused, that he had apparently mistaken Buck for someone else. But Nicolae nodded slightly and smiled all the more, looking more deeply into Buck's eyes. He knew what he was doing.

"May you display to me and to those in your charge the consistency and wisdom that have brought you to this position."

Buck wanted to stand taller, to thank his mentor, his leader, the bestower of this honor. But no! It wasn't right! He didn't work for Carpathia. He was an independent journalist, not a supporter, not a follower, and certainly not an employee. His spirit resisted the temptation to say, "Thank you, sir," as everyone else had. He sensed and read the evil of the man and it was all he could do to keep from pointing at him and calling him the Antichrist. He could almost hear himself screaming it at Carpathia.

Nicolae still stared, still smiled, still gripped his hand. After an awkward silence, Buck heard chuckles, and Carpathia said, "You are most welcome, my slightly overcome and tongue-tied friend." The others laughed and applauded as Carpathia kissed him, but Buck did not smile. Neither did he thank the secretary-general. Bile rose in his throat.

As Carpathia moved on, Buck realized what he had endured. Had he not belonged to God he would have been swept into the web of this man of deceit. He could see it in the others' faces. They were honored beyond measure to be elevated to this tier of power and confidence, even Chaim Rosenzweig. Hattie seemed to melt in Carpathia's presence.

Bruce Barnes had pleaded with Buck not to attend this meeting, and now Buck knew why. Had he come in unprepared, had he not been prayed for by Bruce and Chloe and probably Captain Steele, who knows whether he would have made his decision and his commitment to Christ in time to have the power to resist the lure of acceptance and power?

Carpathia went through the ceremony with Steve, who gushed with pride. Nicolae eventually covered everyone in the room except the security guard, Hattie, and Jonathan Stonagal. He returned to his place and turned first to Hattie.

"Ms. Durham," he said, taking both her hands in his, "you shall be introduced as my personal assistant, having turned your back on a stellar career in the aviation industry. I welcome you to the team and confer upon you all the rights and privileges that go with your new station. May you display to me and to those in your charge the consistency and wisdom that have brought you to this position."

Buck tried to catch Hattie's eye and shake his head, but she was zeroed in on her new boss. Was this Buck's fault? He had introduced her to Carpathia in the first place. Was she still reachable? Would he have access? He glanced around the room. Everyone stared with beatific smiles as Hattie breathed her heartfelt thanks and sat down again.

Carpathia dramatically turned to Jonathan Stonagal. The latter smiled a knowing smile and stood regally. "Where do I begin, Jonathan, my friend?" Carpathia said. Stonagal dropped his head gratefully and others murmured their agreement that this indeed was the man among men in the room. Carpathia took Stonagal's hand and began formally, "Mr. Stonagal, you have meant more to me than anyone on earth." Stonagal looked up and smiled, locking eyes with Carpathia.

"I welcome you to the team," Carpathia said, "and confer upon you all the rights and privileges that go with your new station."

Stonagal flinched, clearly not interested in being considered a part of the team, to be welcomed by the very man he had maneuvered into the presidency of Romania and now the secretary-generalship of the United Nations. His smile froze, then disappeared as Carpathia continued, "May you display to me and to those in your charge the consistency and wisdom that have brought you to this position."

Rather than thanking Carpathia, Stonagal wrenched his hand away and glared at the younger man. Carpathia continued to gaze directly at him and spoke in quieter, warmer tones, "Mr. Stonagal, you may be seated."

"I will not!" Stonagal said.

"Sir, I have been having a bit of sport at your expense because I knew you would understand."

Stonagal reddened, clearly chagrined that he had overreacted. "I beg your pardon, Nicolae," Stonagal said, forcing a smile but obviously insulted at having been pushed into this shocking display.

"Please, my friend," Carpathia said. "Please be seated. Gentlemen, and lady, we have only a few minutes before we meet the media."

Buck's eyes were still on Stonagal, who was seething.

"I would like to present to you all just a bit of an object lesson in leadership, followership, and may I say, chain of command. Mr. Scott M. Otterness, would you approach me, please?" The guard in the corner jerked in surprise and hurried to Carpathia. "One of my leadership techniques is my power of observation, combined with a prodigious memory," Carpathia said.

Buck couldn't take his eyes off Stonagal, who appeared to be considering revenge for having been embarrassed. He seemed ready to stand at any second and put Carpathia in his place.

"Mr. Otterness here was surprised because we had not been introduced, had we, sir?"

"No, sir, Mr. Carpathia, sir, we had not."

"And yet I knew your name."

The aging guard smiled and nodded.

"I can also tell you the make and model and caliber of the weapon you carry on your hip. I will not look as you remove it and display it to this group."

Buck watched in horror as Mr. Otterness unsnapped the leather strap holding the huge gun in his holster. He fumbled for it and held it with two hands so everyone but Carpathia, who had averted his eyes, could see it. Stonagal, still red-faced, appeared to be hyperventilating.

"I observed, sir, that you were issued a thirty-eight-caliber police special with a four-inch barrel, loaded with high-velocity hollow-point shells."

"You are correct," Otterness said gleefully.

"May I hold it, please?"

"Certainly, sir."

"Thank you. You may return to your post, guarding Mr. Williams's bag, which contains a tape recorder, a cellular phone, and a computer. Am I correct, Cameron?"

Buck stared at him, refusing to answer. He heard Stonagal grumble about "some sort of a parlor trick." Carpathia continued to look at Buck. Neither spoke. "What is this?" Stonagal whispered. "You're acting like a child."

"I would like to tell you all what you are about to see," Carpathia said, and Buck felt anew the wash of evil in the room. He wanted more than anything to rub the gooseflesh from his arms and run for his life. But he was frozen where he sat. The others seemed transfixed but not troubled, as he and Stonagal were.

"I am going to ask Mr. Stonagal to rise once more," Carpathia said, the large ugly weapon safely at his side. "Jonathan, if you please."

Stonagal sat staring at him. Carpathia smiled. "Jonathan, you know you can trust me. I love you for all you have meant to me, and I humbly ask you to assist me in this demonstration. I see part of my role as a teacher. You have said that yourself, and you have been my teacher for years."

Stonagal stood, wary and rigid.

"And now I am going to ask that we switch places."

Stonagal swore. "What is this?" he demanded.

"It will become clear quickly, and I will not need your help anymore."

To the others, Buck knew, it sounded as if Carpathia meant he would no longer need Stonagal's help for whatever this demonstration was. Just as he had sent the guard back to the corner unarmed, they had to assume he would thank Stonagal and let him return to his seat.

Stonagal, with a disgusted frown, stepped out and traded places with Carpathia. That put Carpathia to Stonagal's right. On Stonagal's left sat Hattie, and beyond her, Mr. Todd-Cothran.

"And now I am going to ask you to kneel, Jonathan," Carpathia said, his smile and his light tone having disappeared. To Buck it seemed as if everyone in the room sucked in a breath and held it.

"That I will not do," Stonagal said.

"Yes, you will," Carpathia said quietly. "Do it now."

"No, sir, I will not," Stonagal said. "Have you lost your mind? I will not be humiliated. If you think you have risen to a position over me, you are mistaken."

Carpathia raised the .38, cocked it, and stuck the barrel into Stonagal's right ear. The older man at first jerked away, but Carpathia said, "Move again and you are dead."

Several others stood, including Rosenzweig, who cried plaintively, "Nicolae!"

"Everyone be seated, please," Carpathia said, calm again. "Jonathan, on your knees."

Painfully, the old man crouched, using Hattie's chair for support. He did not face Carpathia or look at him. The gun was still in his ear. Hattie sat pale and frozen.

"My dear," Carpathia said, leaning toward her over Stonagal's head, "you will want to slide your chair back about three feet so as not to soil your outfit."

She did not move.

Stonagal began to whimper. "Nicolae, why are you doing this? I am your friend! I am no threat!"

"Begging does not become you, Jonathan. Please be quiet. Hattie," he continued, looking directly into her eyes now, "stand and move your chair back and be seated. Hair, skin, skull tissue, and brain matter will mostly be absorbed by Mr. Todd-Cothran and the others next to him. I do not want anything to get on you."

Hattie moved her chair back, her fingers trembling.

Stonagal whined, "No, Nicolae, no!"

Carpathia was in no hurry. "I am going to kill Mr. Stonagal with a painless hollow-point round to the brain which he will neither hear nor feel. The rest of us will experience some ringing in our ears. This will be instructive for you all. You will understand cognitively that I am in charge, that I fear no man, and that no one can oppose me."

Mr. Otterness reached for his forehead, as if dizzy, and slumped to one knee. Buck considered a suicidal dive across the table for the gun, but he knew that others might die for his effort. He looked to Steve, who sat motionless as the others. Mr. Todd-Cothran shut his eyes and grimaced, as if expecting the report any second.

"When Mr. Stonagal is dead, I will tell you what you will remember. And lest anyone feel I have not been fair, let me not neglect to add that more than gore will wind up on Mr. Todd-Cothran's suit. A high-velocity bullet at this range will also kill him, which, as you know, Mr. Williams, is something I promised you I would deal with in due time."

Todd-Cothran opened his eyes at that news, and Buck heard himself shouting, "No!" as Carpathia pulled the trigger. The blast rattled the windows and even the door. Stonagal's head crashed into the toppling Todd-Cothran, and both were plainly dead before their entwined bodies reached the floor.

Several chairs rolled back from the table as their occupants covered their heads in fear. Buck stared, mouth open, as Carpathia calmly placed the gun in Stonagal's limp right hand and twisted his finger around the trigger.

Hattie shivered in her seat and appeared to try to emit a scream that would not come. Carpathia took the floor again.

"What we have just witnessed here," he said kindly, as if speaking to children, "was a horrible, tragic end to two otherwise extravagantly productive lives. These men were two I respected and admired more than any others in the world. What compelled Mr. Stonagal to rush the guard, disarm him, take his own life and that of his British colleague, I do not know and may never fully understand."

Buck fought within himself to keep his sanity, to maintain a clear mind, to—as his boss had told him on the way in—"remember everything."

Carpathia continued, his eyes moist. "All I can tell you is that Jonathan Stonagal told me as recently as at breakfast this morning that he felt personally responsible for two recent violent deaths in England and that he could no longer live with the guilt. Honestly, I thought he was going to turn himself in to international authorities later today. And if he had not, I would have had to. How he conspired with Mr. Todd-Cothran, which led to the deaths in England, I do not know. But if he was responsible, then in a sad way, perhaps justice was meted out here today.

"We are all horrified and traumatized by having witnessed this. Who would not be? My first act as secretary-general will be to close the U.N. for the remainder of the day and to pronounce my regrettable benedictory obituary on the lives of two old friends. I trust you will all be able to deal with this unfortunate occurrence and that it will not forever hamper your ability to serve in your strategic roles.

"Thank you, gentlemen. While Ms. Durham phones security, I will be polling you for your version of what happened here."

Hattie ran to the phone and could barely make herself understood in her hysteria. "Come quick! There's been a suicide and two men are dead! It was awful! Hurry!"

"Mr. Plank?" Carpathia said.

"That was unbelievable," Steve said, and Buck knew he was dead serious. "When Mr. Stonagal grabbed the gun, I thought he was going to kill us all!"

Carpathia called on the United States ambassador.

"Why, I've known Jonathan for years," he said. "Who would have thought he could do something like this?"

"I'm just glad you're all right, Mr. Secretary-General," Chaim Rosenzweig said.

"Well, I am not all right," Carpathia said. "And I will not be all right for a long time. These were my friends."

And that's how it went, all around the room. Buck's body felt like lead, knowing Carpathia would eventually get to him and that he was the only one in the room not under Nicolae's hypnotic power. But what if Buck said so? Would he be killed next? Of course he would! He had to be. Could he lie? Should he?

He prayed desperately as Carpathia moved from man to man, making certain they had all seen what he wanted them to see and that they were sincerely convinced of it.

Silence, God seemed to impress upon Buck's heart. *Not a word!*

Buck was so grateful to feel the presence of God in the midst of this evil and mayhem that he was moved to tears. When Carpathia got to him Buck's cheeks were wet and he could not speak. He shook his head and held up a hand. "Awful, was it not, Cameron? The suicide that took Mr. Todd-Cothran with it?"

Buck could not speak and wouldn't have if he could. "You cared for and respected them both, Cameron, because you were unaware that they tried to have you killed in London." And Carpathia moved on to the guard.

"Why could you not keep him from taking your gun, Scott?"

The old man had risen. "It happened so fast! I knew who he was, an important rich man, and when he hurried over to me I didn't know what he wanted. He ripped that gun right out of my holster, and before I could react he had shot himself."

"Yes, yes," Carpathia said as security rushed into the room. Everyone talked at once as Carpathia retreated to a corner, sobbing over the loss of his friends.

A plainclothesman asked questions. Buck headed him off. "You have enough eyewitnesses here. Let me leave you my card and you can call if you need me, hmm?" The cop traded cards with him and Buck was permitted to leave.

Buck grabbed his bag and sprinted for a cab, rushing back to the office. He shut and locked his office door and began furiously banging out every detail of the story. He had produced several pages when he received a call from Stanton Bailey. The old man could hardly catch his breath between his demanding questions, not allowing Buck to answer.

"Where have you been? Why weren't you at the press conference? Were you in there when Stonagal offed himself and took the Brit with him? You should have been here. There's prestige for us having you in there. How are you going to convince anybody you were in there when you didn't show up for the press conference? Cameron, what's the deal?"

"I hurried back here to get the story into the system."

"Don't you have an exclusive with Carpathia now?"

Buck had forgotten that, and Plank hadn't reconfirmed it. What was he supposed to do about that? He prayed but sensed no leading. How he needed to talk to Bruce or Chloe or even Captain Steele! "I'll call Steve and see," he said.

Buck knew he couldn't wait long to make the call, but he was desperate to know what to do. Should he allow himself to be in a room alone with Carpathia? And if he did, should he pretend to be under his mind control as everyone else seemed to be? If he hadn't seen this for himself, he wouldn't have believed it. Would he always be able to resist the influence with God's help? He didn't know.

He dialed Steve's pager and the call was returned a couple of minutes later. "Really busy here, Buck. What's up?"

"I was wondering if I've still got that exclusive with Carpathia."

"You're kidding, right? You heard what happened here and you want an exclusive?"

"Heard? I was there, Steve."

"Well, if you were here, then you probably know what happened before the press conference."

"Steve! I saw it with my own eyes."

"You're not following me, Buck. I'm saying if you were here for the press conference, you heard about the Stonagal suicide in the preliminary meeting, the one you were supposed to come to."

Buck didn't know what to say. "You saw me there, Steve."

"I didn't even see you at the press conference."

"I wasn't *at* the press conference, Steve, but I was in the room when Stonagal and Todd-Cothran died."

"I don't have time for this, Buck. It's not funny. You were supposed to be there, you weren't there. I resent it, Carpathia is offended, and no, no exclusive."

"I have credentials! I got them downstairs!"

"Then why didn't you use them?"

"I did!"

Steve hung up on him. Marge buzzed and said the boss was on the line again. "What's the deal with you not even going to that meeting?" Bailey said.

"I was there! You saw me go in!"

"Yeah, I saw you. You were that close. What did you do, find something more important to do? You got some fast talking to do, Cameron!"

"I'm telling you I was there! I'll show you my credentials."

"I just checked the credential list, and you're not on it."

"Of course I'm on it. I'll show 'em to you."

"Your name's there, I'm saying, but it's not checked off."

"Mr. Bailey, I'm looking at my credentials right now. They're in my hand."

"Your credentials don't mean dirt if you didn't use 'em, Cameron. Now where were you?"

"Read my story," Buck said. "You'll know exactly where I was."

"I just talked to three, four people who *were* there, including a U.N. guard and Carpathia's personal assistant, not to mention Plank. None of them saw you; you weren't there."

"A cop saw me! We traded cards!"

"I'm coming back to the office, Williams. If you're not there when I get there, you're fired."

"I'll be here."

Buck dug out the cop's card and called the number. "Precinct station," a voice said.

Buck read off the card, "Detective Sergeant Billy Cenni, please."

"What's the name again?"

"Cenni, or maybe it's a hard *C*? Kenny?"

"Don't recognize it. You got the right precinct?"

Buck repeated the number from the card.

"That's our number, but that ain't our guy."

"How would I locate him?"

"I'm busy here, pal. Call midtown."

"It's important. Do you have a department directory?"

"Listen, we got thousands of cops."

"Just look up C-E-N-N-I for me, will ya?"

"Just a minute." Soon he was back on. "Nothing, OK?"

"Could he be new?"

"He could be your sister for all I know."

"Where do I call?"

He gave Buck the number for police headquarters. Buck ran through the whole conversation again, but this time he had reached a pleasant young woman. "Let me check one more thing for you," she said. "I'll get personnel on the line because they won't tell you anything unless you're a uniformed officer anyway."

He listened as she spelled the name for personnel. "Uh-huh, uh-huh," she said. "Thank you. I'll tell him." And she came back to Buck. "Sir? Personnel says there is nobody in the New York Police Department named Cenni, and there never has been. If somebody's got a phony police business card dolled up, they'd like to see it."

All Buck could do now was try to convince Stanton Bailey.

* * *

Rayford Steele, Chloe, and Bruce Barnes watched the U.N. press conference, straining to see Buck. "Where is he?" Chloe said. "He has to be there somewhere. Everybody else from that meeting is there. Who's the girl?"

Rayford stood when he saw her and silently pointed at the screen. "Dad!" Chloe said. "You're not thinking what I'm thinking?"

"It sure looks like her," Rayford said.

"Shh," Bruce said, "he's introducing everybody."

"And my new personal assistant, having given up a career in the aviation industry . . ."

Rayford flopped into a chair. "I hope Buck wasn't behind that."

"Me, too," Bruce said. "That would mean he could have been sucked in, too."

The news of the Stonagal suicide and Todd-Cothran's accidental death stunned them. "Maybe Buck took my advice and didn't go," Bruce said. "I sure hope so."

"That doesn't sound like him," Chloe said.

"No, it doesn't," Rayford said.

"I know," Bruce said. "But I can hope. I don't want to find out that he's met with foul play. Who knows what happened in there, and him going in with only our prayers?"

"I'd like to think that would be enough," Chloe said.

"No," Bruce said. "He needed the covering of God himself."

* * *

By the time Stanton Bailey stormed into Buck's office an hour later, Buck realized he was up against a force with which he could not compete. The record of his having been at that meeting had been erased, including from the minds of everyone in the room. He knew Steve wasn't faking it. He honestly believed Buck had not been there. The power Carpathia held over those people knew no limits. If Buck had needed any proof that his own faith was real and that God was now in his life, he had it. Had he not received Christ before entering that room, he was convinced he would be just another of Carpathia's puppets.

Bailey was not in a discussing mood, so Buck let the old man talk, not trying to defend himself. "I don't want any more of this nonsense about your having been there. I know you were in the building and I see your credentials, but you know and I know and everybody who *was* in there knows that you weren't. I don't know what you thought was more important, but you were wrong. This is unacceptable and unforgivable, Cameron. I can't have you as my executive editor."

"I'll gladly go back to senior writer," Buck said.

"Can't go along with that either, pal. I want you out of New York. I'm going to put you in the Chicago bureau."

"I'll be happy to run that for you."

Bailey shook his head. "You don't get it, do you, Cameron? I don't trust you. I should fire you. But I know you'd just wind up with somebody else."

"I don't want to be with anybody else."

"Good, because if you tried to jump to the competition, I'd have to tell them about this stunt. You're going to be a staff writer out of Chicago, working for the woman who was Lucinda's assistant there. I'm calling her today to give her the news. It'll mean a whopping cut in pay, especially considering what you would've gotten with the promotion. You take a few days off, get your things in order here, get that apartment sublet, and find yourself a place in Chicago. Someday I want you to come clean with me, son. That was the sorriest excuse for news gathering I've ever seen, and by one of the best in the business."

Mr. Bailey slammed the door.

Buck couldn't wait to talk to his friends in Illinois, but he didn't want to call from his office or his apartment, and he didn't know for sure whether his cellular phone was safe. He packed his stuff and took a cab to the airport, asking the cabbie to stop at a pay phone a mile outside the terminal.

Not getting an answer at the Steeles', he dialed the church. Bruce answered and told him Chloe and Rayford were there. "Put them on the speakerphone," he said. "I'm taking the three o'clock American flight to O'Hare. But let me tell you this: Carpathia is your man, no question. He fills the bill to the last detail. I felt your prayers in the meeting. God protected me. I'm moving to Chicago, and I want to be a member of, what did you call it, Bruce?"

"The Tribulation Force?"

"That's it!"

"Does this mean—?" Chloe began.

"You know exactly what it means," Buck said. "Count me in."

"What happened, Buck?" Chloe asked.

"I'd rather tell you about it in person," he said. "But have I got a story for you! And you're the only people I know who are going to believe it."

When his plane finally touched down, Buck hurried up the jet way and through the gate where he was joyously greeted by Chloe, Bruce, and Rayford Steele. They all embraced him, even the staid captain. As they huddled in a corner, Bruce prayed, thanking God for their new brother and for protecting him.

They moved through the terminal toward the parking garage, striding four abreast, arms around each other's shoulders, knit with a common purpose. Rayford Steele, Chloe Steele, Buck Williams, and Bruce Barnes faced the gravest dangers anyone could face, and they knew their mission.

The task of the Tribulation Force was clear and their goal nothing less than to stand and fight the enemies of God during the seven most chaotic years the planet would ever see.

TRIBULATION FORCE

✠ ✠ ✠

To those readers of Left Behind
who wrote to tell us of its impact

1

IT WAS RAYFORD STEELE'S turn for a break. He pulled the headphones down onto his neck and dug into his flight bag for his wife's Bible, marveling at how quickly his life had changed. How many hours had he wasted during idle moments like this, poring over newspapers and magazines that had nothing to say? After all that had happened, only one book could hold his interest.

The Boeing 747 was on auto from Baltimore to a four o'clock Friday afternoon landing at Chicago O'Hare, but Rayford's new first officer, Nick, sat staring ahead anyway, as if piloting the plane. *Doesn't want to talk to me anymore,* Rayford thought. *Knew what was coming and shut me down before I opened my mouth.*

"Is it going to offend you if I sit reading this for a while?" Rayford asked.

The younger man turned and pulled the left phone away from his own ear. "Say again?"

Rayford repeated himself, pointing to the Bible. It had belonged to the wife he hadn't seen for more than two weeks and probably would not see for another seven years.

"As long as you don't expect me to listen."

"I got that loud and clear, Nick. You understand I don't care what you think of me, don't you?"

"Sir?"

Rayford leaned close and spoke louder. "What you think of me would have been hugely important a few weeks ago," he said. "But—"

"Yeah, I know, OK? I got it, Steele, all right? You and lots of other people think the whole thing was Jesus. Not buying. Delude yourself, but leave me out of it."

Rayford raised his brows and shrugged. "You wouldn't respect me if I hadn't tried."

"Don't be too sure."

But when Rayford turned back to his reading, it was the *Chicago Tribune* sticking out of his bag that grabbed his attention.

The *Tribune*, like every other paper in the world, carried the front-page story: During a private meeting at the United Nations, just before a Nicolae Carpathia press conference, a horrifying murder/suicide had occurred. New U.N. Secretary-General Nicolae Carpathia had just installed the ten new members of the expanded Security Council, seeming to err by inaugurating two men to the same position of U.N. ambassador from the Great States of Britain.

According to the witnesses, billionaire Jonathan Stonagal, Carpathia's friend and financial backer, suddenly overpowered a guard, stole his handgun, and shot himself in the head, the bullet passing through and killing one of the new ambassadors from Britain.

The United Nations had been closed for the day, and Carpathia was despondent over the tragic loss of his two dear friends and trusted advisers.

Bizarre as it might seem, Rayford Steele was one of only four people on the planet who knew the truth about Nicolae Carpathia—that he was a liar, a hypnotic brainwasher, the Antichrist himself. Others might suspect Carpathia of being other than he seemed, but only Rayford, his daughter, his pastor, and his new friend, journalist Buck Williams, knew for sure.

Buck had been one of the seventeen in that United Nations meeting room. And he had witnessed something entirely different—not a murder/suicide, but a double murder. Carpathia himself, according to Buck, had methodically borrowed the guard's gun, forced his old friend Jonathan Stonagal to kneel, then killed Stonagal and the British ambassador with one shot.

Carpathia had choreographed the murders, and then, while the witnesses sat in horror, Carpathia quietly told them what they had seen—the same story the newspapers now carried. Every witness in that room but one corroborated it. Most chilling, they believed it. Even Steve Plank, Buck's former boss, now Carpathia's press agent. Even Hattie Durham, Rayford's onetime flight attendant, who had become Carpathia's personal assistant. Everyone except Buck Williams.

Rayford had been dubious when Buck told his version in Bruce Barnes's office two nights ago. "You're the only person in the room who saw it your way?" he had challenged the writer.

"Captain Steele," Buck had said, "we all saw it the same way. But then Carpathia calmly described what he wanted us to think we had seen, and everybody but me immediately accepted it as truth. I want to know how he explains that he had the dead man's successor already there and sworn in when the murder took place. But now there's no evidence I was even there. It's as if Carpathia washed me from their memories. People I know now swear I wasn't there, and they aren't joking."

Chloe and Bruce Barnes had looked at each other and then back at Buck.

Buck had finally become a believer, just before entering the meeting at the U.N. "I'm absolutely convinced that if I had gone into that room without God," Buck said, "I would have been reprogrammed too."

"But now if you just tell the world the truth—"

"Sir, I've been reassigned to Chicago because my boss believes I missed that meeting. Steve Plank asked why I had not accepted his invitation. I haven't talked to Hattie yet, but you know she won't remember I was there."

"The biggest question," Bruce Barnes said, "is what Carpathia thinks is in your head. Does he think he's erased the truth from *your* mind? If he knows you know, you're in grave danger."

Now, as Rayford read the bizarre story in the paper, he noticed Nick switching from autopilot to manual. "Initial descent," Nick said. "You want to bring her in?"

"Of course," Rayford said. Nick could have landed the plane, but Rayford felt responsible. He was the captain. He would answer for these people. And even though the plane could land itself, he had not lost the thrill of handling it. Few things reminded him of life as it had been just weeks before, but landing a 747 was one of them.

* * *

Buck Williams had spent the day buying a car—something he hadn't needed in Manhattan—and hunting for an apartment. He found a beautiful condo, at a place that advertised already-installed phones, midway between the *Global Weekly* Chicago bureau office and New Hope Village Church in Mount Prospect. He tried to convince himself it was the church that would keep drawing him west of the city, not Rayford Steele's daughter, Chloe. She was ten years his junior, and whatever attraction he might feel for her, he was certain she saw him as some sort of a wizened mentor.

Buck had put off going to the office. He wasn't expected there until the following Monday anyway, and he didn't relish facing Verna Zee. When it had been his assignment to find a replacement for veteran Lucinda Washington, the Chicago bureau chief who had disappeared, he had told the militant Verna she had jumped the gun by moving into her former boss's office. Now Buck had been demoted and Verna elevated. Suddenly, she was *his* boss.

But he didn't want to spend all weekend dreading the meeting, and neither did he want to appear too eager to see Chloe Steele again right away, so Buck drove to the office just before closing. Would Verna make him pay for his years of celebrity as an award-winning cover-story writer? Or would she make it even worse by killing him with kindness?

Buck felt the stares and smiles of the underlings as he moved through the outer office. By now, of course, everyone knew what had happened. They felt sorry for him, were stunned by his lapse of judgment. How could Buck Williams miss a meeting that would certainly be one of the most momentous in news history, even if it hadn't resulted in the double death? But they were also aware of Buck's credentials. Many, no doubt, would still consider it a privilege to work with him.

No surprise, Verna had already moved back into the big office. Buck winked at Alice, Verna's spike-haired young secretary, and peered in. It looked as if Verna had been there for years. She had already rearranged the furniture and hung her own pictures and plaques. Clearly, she was ensconced and loving every minute of it.

A pile of papers littered Verna's desk, and her computer screen was lit, but she seemed to be idly gazing out the window. Buck poked his head in and cleared his throat. He noticed a flash of recognition and then a quick recomposing. "Cameron," she said flatly, still seated. "I didn't expect you till Monday."

"Just checking in," he said. "You can call me Buck."

"I'll call you Cameron, if you don't mind, and—"

"I do mind. Please call—"

"Then I'll call you Cameron even if you *do* mind. Did you let anyone know you were coming?"

"I'm sorry?"

"Do you have an appointment?"

"An appointment?"

"With me. I have a schedule, you know."

"And there's no room for me on it?"

"You're asking for an appointment then?"

"If it's not inconvenient. I'd like to know where I'm going to land and what kind of assignments you have in mind for me, that kind of—"

"Those sound like things we can talk about when we meet," Verna said. "Alice! See if I have a slot in twenty minutes, please!"

"You do," Alice called out. "And I would be happy to show Mr. Williams his cubicle while he's waiting, if you—"

"I prefer to do that myself, Alice. Thank you. And could you shut my door?"

Alice looked apologetic as she rose and moved past Buck to shut the door. He thought she even rolled her eyes. "*You* can call me Buck," he whispered.

"Thanks," she said shyly, pointing to a chair beside her desk.

"I have to wait here, like seeing the principal?"

She nodded. "Someone called here for you earlier. Didn't leave her name. I told her you weren't expected till Monday."

"No message?"

"Sorry."

"So, where *is* my cubicle?"

Alice glanced at the closed door, as if fearing Verna could see her. She stood and pointed over the tops of several partitions toward a windowless corner in the back.

"That's where the coffeepot was last time I was here," Buck said.

"It still is," Alice said with a giggle. Her intercom buzzed. "Yes, ma'am?"

"Would you two mind whispering if you must talk while I'm working?"

"Sorry!" This time Alice did roll her eyes.

"I'm gonna go take a peek," Buck whispered, rising.

"Please don't," she said. "You'll get me in trouble with you-know-who."

Buck shook his head and sat back down. He thought of where he had been, whom he had met, the dangers he had faced in his career. And now he was whispering with a secretary he had to keep out of trouble from a wannabe boss who had never been able to write her way out of a paper bag.

Buck sighed. At least he was in Chicago with the only people he knew who really cared about him.

* * *

Despite his and Chloe's new faith, Rayford Steele found himself subject to deep mood swings. As he strode through O'Hare, passed brusquely and silently by Nick, he suddenly felt sad. How he missed Irene and Raymie! He knew beyond doubt they were in heaven, and that, if anything, they should be feeling sorry for him. But the world had changed so dramatically since the disappearances that hardly anyone he knew had recaptured any sense of equilibrium. He was grateful to have Bruce to teach him and Chloe and now Buck to stand with him in their mission, but sometimes the prospect of facing the future was overwhelming.

That's why it was such sweet relief to see Chloe's smiling face waiting at the end of the corridor. In two decades of flying, he had gotten used to passing passengers who were being greeted at the terminal. Most pilots were accustomed to simply disembarking and driving home alone.

Chloe and Rayford understood each other better than ever. They were fast becoming friends and confidants, and while they didn't agree on everything, they were knit in their grief and loss, tied in their new faith, and teammates on what they called the Tribulation Force.

Rayford embraced his daughter. "Anything wrong?"

"No, but Bruce has been trying to get you. He's called an emergency meeting of the core group for early this evening. I don't know what's up, but he'd like us to try to get hold of Buck."

"How'd you get here?"

"Cab. I knew your car was here."

"Where would Buck be?"

"He was going to look for a car and an apartment today. He could be anywhere."

"Did you call the *Weekly* office?"

"I talked to Alice, the secretary there, early this afternoon. He wasn't expected until Monday, but we can try again from the car. I mean, you can. You should call him, don't you think? Rather than me?"

Rayford suppressed a smile.

\+ + +

Alice sat at her desk leaning forward, her head cocked, gazing at Buck and trying not to laugh aloud as he regaled her with whispered wisecracks. All the while he wondered how much of the stuff from his palatial Manhattan office would fit into the cubicle he was to share with the communal coffeepot. The phone rang, and Buck could hear both ends of the conversation from the speakerphone. From just down the hall came the voice of the receptionist. "Alice, is Buck Williams still back there?"

"Right here."

"Call for him."

It was Rayford Steele, calling from his car. "At seven-thirty tonight?" Buck said. "Sure, I'll be there. What's up? Hm? Well, tell her I said hi, too, and I'll see you both at the church tonight."

He was hanging up as Verna came to the door and frowned at him. "A problem?" he said.

"You'll have your own phone soon enough," she said. "Come on in."

As soon as he was seated Verna sweetly informed him that he would no longer be the world-traveling, cover-story-writing, star headliner of *Global Weekly*. "We here in Chicago have an important but limited role in the magazine," she said. "We interpret national and international news from a local and regional perspective and submit our stories to New York."

Buck sat stiffly. "So I'm going to be assigned to the Chicago livestock markets?"

"You don't amuse me, Cameron. You never have. You will be assigned to whatever we need covered each week. Your work will pass through a senior editor and through me, and I will decide whether it is of enough significance and quality to pass along to New York."

Buck sighed. "I didn't ask the big boss what I was supposed to do with my works in progress. I don't suppose you know."

"Your contact with Stanton Bailey will now funnel through me as well. Is that understood?"

"Are you asking whether I understand, or whether I agree?"

"Neither," she said. "I'm asking whether you will comply."

"It's unlikely," Buck said, feeling his neck redden and his pulse surge. He didn't want to get into a shouting match with Verna. But neither was he going to sit for long under the thumb of someone who didn't belong in journalism, let alone in Lucinda Washington's old chair and supervising him.

"I will discuss this with Mr. Bailey," she said. "As you might imagine, I have all sorts of recourse at my disposal for insubordinate employees."

"I can imagine. Why don't you get him on the phone right now?"

"For what?"

"To find out what I'm supposed to do. I've accepted my demotion and my relocation. You know as well as I do that relegating me to regional stuff is a waste of my contacts and my experience."

"And your talent, I assume you're implying."

"Infer what you want. But before you put me on the bowling beat, I have dozens of hours invested in my cover story on the theory of the disappearances—ah, why am I talking to you about it?"

"Because I'm your boss, and because it's not likely a Chicago bureau staff writer will land a cover story."

"Not even a writer who has already done several? I dare you to call Bailey. The last time he said anything about my piece, he said he was sure it would be a winner."

"Yeah? The last time I talked to him, he told me about the last time he talked to you."

"It was a misunderstanding."

"It was a lie. You said you were someplace and everybody who was there says you weren't. I'd have fired you."

"If you'd had the power to fire me, I'd have quit."

"You want to quit?"

"I'll tell you what I want, Verna. I want—"

"I expect all my subordinates to call me Ms. Zee."

"You have no subordinates in this office," Buck said. "And aren't you—"

"You're dangerously close to the line, Cameron."

"Aren't you afraid *Ms. Zee* sounds too much like *Missy*?"

She stood. "Follow me." She bristled past him, stomping out of her office and down the long hallway in her sensible shoes.

Buck stopped at Alice's desk. "Thanks for everything, Alice," he said quickly. "I've got a bunch of stuff that's being shipped here that I might need to have you forward to my new apartment."

Alice was nodding but her smile froze when Verna hollered down the hall. "*Now*, Cameron!"

Buck slowly turned. "I'll get back to you, Alice." Buck moved deliberately enough to drive Verna crazy, and he noticed people in their cubicles pretending not to notice but fighting smiles.

Verna marched to the corner that served as the coffee room and pointed to a small desk with a phone and a file cabinet. Buck snorted.

"You'll have a computer in a week or so," she said.

"Have it delivered to my apartment."

"I'm afraid that's out of the question."

"No, Verna, what's out of the question is you trying to vent all your frustration from who knows where in one breath. You know as well as I do that no one with an ounce of self-respect would put up with this. If I have to work out of the Chicago area, I'm going to work at home with a computer and modem and fax machine. And if you expect to see me in this office again for any reason, you'll get Stanton Bailey on the phone right now."

Verna looked prepared to stand her ground right there, so Buck headed back to her office with her trailing him. He passed Alice, who looked stricken, and waited at Verna's desk until she caught up. "Are you dialing, or am I?" he demanded.

+ + +

Rayford and Chloe ate on the way home and arrived to an urgent phone message from Rayford's chief pilot. "Call me as soon as you get in."

With his cap under his arm and still wearing his uniform trench coat, Rayford punched the familiar numbers. "What's up, Earl?"

"Thanks for getting back to me right away, Ray. You and I go back a long way."

"Long enough that you should get to the point, Earl. What'd I do now?"

"This is not an official call, OK? Not a reprimand or a warning or anything. This is just friend to friend."

"So, friend to friend, Earl, should I sit down?"

"No, but let me tell you, buddy, you've got to knock off the proselytizing."

"The—?"

"Talking about God on the job, man."

"Earl, I back off when anyone says anything, and you know I don't let it get in the way of the job. Anyway, what do *you* think the disappearances were all about?"

"We've been through all that, Ray. I'm just telling you, Nicky Edwards is gonna write you up, and I want to be able to say you and I have already talked about it and you've agreed to back off."

"Write me up? Did I break a rule, violate procedure, commit a crime?"

"I don't know what he's going to call it, but you've been warned, all right?"

"I thought you said this wasn't official yet."

"It's not, Ray. Do you want it to be? Do I have to call you back tomorrow and drag you in here for a meeting and a memo for your file and all that, or can I just smooth everybody's feathers, tell 'em it was a misunderstanding, you're cool now, and it won't happen again?"

Rayford didn't respond at first.

"C'mon, Ray, this is a no-brainer. I don't like you having to think about this one."

"Well, I *will* have to think about it, Earl. I appreciate your tipping me off, but I'm not ready to concede anything just yet."

"Don't do this to me, Ray."

"I'm not doing it to you, Earl. I'm doing it to myself."

"Yeah, and I'm the one who has to find a replacement pilot certified for the 'forty-seven and the 'seventy-seven."

"You mean it's that serious! I could lose my job over this?"

"You bet you could."

"I'll still have to think about it."

"You've got it bad, Ray. Listen, in case you come to your senses and we can make this go away, you need to recertify on the 'seventy-seven soon. They're adding a half dozen more within a month or so, and they're going to be running them out of here. You want to be on that list. More money, you know."

"Not that big a deal to me anymore, Earl."

"I know."

"But the idea of flying the 777 *is* attractive. I'll get back to you."

"Don't make me wait, Ray."

+ + +

"I will get Mr. Bailey on the phone if I can," Verna said. "But you realize it's late in New York."

"He's always there, you know that. Use his direct, after-hours number."

"I don't have that."

"I'll write it down for you. He's probably interviewing a replacement for me."

"I'll call him, Cameron, and I will even let you have your say, but I am going to speak to him first, and I reserve the right to tell him how insubordinate and disrespectful you've been. Please wait outside."

Alice was gathering up her stuff as if about ready to leave when Buck emerged with a mischievous look. Others were streaming from the office to the parking lot and the train. "Did you hear all that?" Buck whispered.

"I hear everything," she mouthed. "And you know those new speakerphones, the ones that don't make you wait till the other person is done talking?"

He nodded.

"Well, they don't make it obvious you're listening in, either. You just shut off the transmit button, like this, and then if something happens to hit the speakerphone button, oops, then you can hear a conversation without being heard. Is that cool, or what?"

From the speakerphone on her desk came the sound of the phone ringing in New York.

"Stanton. Who's this?"

"Um, sir, sorry to bother you at this hour—"

"You got the number; you must have something important. Now who is this?"

"Verna Zee in Chicago."

"Yeah, Verna, what's happening?"

"I've got a situation here. Cameron Williams."

"Yeah, I was going to tell you to just stay out of his hair. He's working on a couple of big pieces for me. You got a nice spot there he can work in, or should we just let him work out of his apartment?"

"We have a place for him here, sir, but he was rude and insubordinate to me today and—"

"Listen, Verna, I don't want you to have to worry about Williams. He's been put out to pasture for something I can't figure out, but let's face it, he's still our star here and he's going to be doing pretty much the same thing he's been doing. He gets less money and a less prestigious title, and he doesn't get to work in New York, but he's going to get his assignments from here. You just don't worry yourself about him, all right? In fact, I think it would be better for you and for him if he *didn't* work out of that office."

"But, sir—"

"Something else, Verna?"

"Well, I wish you had let me know this in advance. I need you to back me on this. He was inappropriate with me, and—"

"What do you mean? He came on to you, made a pass at you, what?"

Buck and Alice pressed their hands over their mouths to keep from bursting with laughter. "No, sir, but he made it clear he is not going to be subordinate to me."

"Well, I'm sorry about that, Verna, but he's not, OK? I'm not going to waste Cameron Williams on regional stuff, not that we don't appreciate every inch of copy that comes out of your shop, understand."

"But, sir—"

"I'm sorry, Verna, is there more? Am I not being clear, or what's the problem? Just tell him to order his equipment, charge it to the Chicago account, and work directly for us here. Got that?"

"But shouldn't he apolog—"

"Verna, do you really need me to mediate some personality conflict from a thousand miles away? If you can't handle that job there . . ."

"I can, sir, and I will. Thank you, sir. Sorry to trouble you."

The intercom buzzed. "Alice, send him in."

"Yes, ma'am, and then may I—"

"Yes, you may go."

Buck sensed Alice taking her time gathering her belongings, however, staying within earshot. He strode into the office as if he expected to talk on the phone with Stanton Bailey.

"He doesn't need to talk with you. He made it clear that I'm not expected to put up with your shenanigans. I'm assigning you to work from your apartment."

Buck wanted to say that he was going to find it hard to pass up the digs she had prepared for him, but he was already feeling guilty about having eavesdropped on her conversation. This was something new. Guilt.

"I'll try to stay out of your way," he said.

"I'd appreciate that."

When he reached the parking lot, Alice was waiting. "That was great," she said.

"You ought to be ashamed of yourself." He smiled broadly.

"You listened too."

"That I did. See ya."

"I'm going to miss the six-thirty train," she said. "But it was worth it."

"How about if I drop you off? Show me where it is."

Alice waited while he unlocked the car door. "Nice car."

"Brand-new," he answered. And that was just how he felt.

* * *

Rayford and Chloe arrived at New Hope early. Bruce was there, finishing a sandwich he had ordered. He looked older than his early thirties. After greeting them, he pushed his wire rims up into his curly locks and tilted back in his squeaky chair. "You get hold of Buck?" he asked.

"Said he'd be here," Rayford said. "What's the emergency?"

"You hear the news today?"

"Thought I did. Something significant?"

"I think so. Let's wait for Buck."

"Then let me tell you in the meantime how I got in trouble today," Rayford said.

When he finished, Bruce was smiling. "Bet that's never been in your personnel file before."

Rayford shook his head and changed the subject. "It seems so strange to have Buck as part of the inner core, especially when he's so new to this."

"We're all new to it, aren't we?" Chloe said.

"True enough."

Bruce looked up and smiled. Rayford and Chloe turned to see Buck in the doorway.

2

BUCK DIDN'T KNOW how to respond when Rayford Steele greeted him warmly. He appreciated the warmth and openness of his three new friends, but something nagged at him and he held back a little. He still wasn't quite comfortable with this kind of affection. And what was this meeting about? The Tribulation Force was scheduled to meet regularly, so a specially called meeting had to mean something.

Chloe looked at him expectantly when she greeted him, yet she did not hug him, as Steele and Bruce Barnes had done. Her reticence was his fault, of course. They barely knew each other, but clearly there had been chemistry. They had given each other enough signals to begin a relationship, and in a note to Chloe, Buck had even admitted he was attracted to her. But he had to be careful. Both were brand-new in their faith, and they were only now learning what the future held. Only a fool would begin a relationship at a time like this.

And yet wasn't that exactly what he was—a fool? How could it have taken him so long to learn anything about Christ when he had been a stellar student, an international journalist, a so-called intellectual?

And what was happening to him now? He felt guilty about listening in on the phone while his bosses discussed him. He would never have given eavesdropping a second thought in the past. The tricks and schemes and outright lies he had told just to get a story would have filled a book. Would he be as good a journalist now with God in his life, seeming to prick his conscience over even little things?

\+ + +

Rayford sensed Buck's uneasiness and Chloe's hesitancy. But mostly he was struck by the nearly instantaneous change in Bruce's countenance. Bruce had smiled at Rayford's story of getting into trouble on the job, and he had smiled when Buck arrived. Suddenly, however, Bruce's face had clouded over. His smile had vanished, and he was having trouble composing himself.

Rayford was new to this kind of sensitivity. Before his wife and son had disappeared, he had not wept in years. He had always considered emotion weak and unmanly. But since the disappearances, he had seen many men weep. He was convinced that the global vanishings had been Christ rapturing his church, but for those who remained behind, the event had been catastrophic.

Even for him and for Chloe, who had become believers because of it, the horror of losing the rest of their family was excruciating. There were days when Rayford had been so grief-stricken and lonely for his wife and son that he wondered if he could go on. How could he have been so blind? What a failure he had been as a husband and father!

But Bruce had been a wise counselor. He too had lost a wife and children, and he, of all people, should have been prepared for the coming of Christ. With Bruce's support and the help of the other two in this room, Rayford knew he could go on. But there was more on Rayford's mind than just surviving. He was beginning to believe that he—and all of them—would have to take action, perhaps at the risk of their very lives.

If there had been a moment's doubt or hesitation about that, it was dispelled when Bruce Barnes finally found his voice. The young pastor pressed his lips together to keep them from quivering. His eyes were filling.

"I, uh, need to talk to you all," he began, leaning forward and pausing to compose himself. "With all the news coming out of New York by the minute these days, I've taken it upon myself to keep CNN on all the time. Rayford, you said you hadn't heard the latest. Chloe?" She shook her head. "Buck, I assume you have access to every Carpathia announcement as it breaks."

"Not today," Buck said. "I didn't get into the office until the end of the day, and I didn't hear a thing."

Bruce seemed to cloud up again; then he gave an apologetic smile. "It isn't that the news is so devastating," he said. "It's just that I feel such a tremendous responsibility for you all. You know I'm trying to run this church, but that seems so insignificant compared to my study of prophecy. I'm spending most of my days and evenings poring over the Bible and commentaries, and I feel the press of God on me."

"The press of God?" Rayford repeated. But Bruce broke into tears. Chloe reached across the desk and covered one of his hands with hers. Rayford and Buck also reached to touch Bruce.

"It's so hard," Bruce said, fighting to make himself understood. "And I know it's not just me. It's you guys and everybody who comes to this church. We're all hurting, we've all lost people, we all missed the truth."

"But now we've found it," Chloe said, "and God used you in that."

"I know. I just feel so full of conflicting emotions that I wonder what's next,"

Bruce said. "My house is so big and so cold and so lonely without my family that sometimes I don't even go home at night. Sometimes I just study until I fall asleep, and I go home in the morning only to shower and change and get back here."

Uncomfortable, Rayford looked away. Had he been the one trying to communicate with his friends, he would have wanted someone to change the subject, to get him back to what the meeting was about. But Bruce was a different kind of a guy. He had always communicated in his own way and in his own time.

Bruce reached for a tissue, and the other three sat back. When Bruce spoke again, his voice was still husky. "I feel an enormous weight on me," he said. "One of the things I had never been good at was reading the Bible every day. I pretended to be a believer, a so-called full-time Christian worker, but I didn't care about the Bible. Now I can't get enough of it."

+ + +

Buck could identify. He wanted to know everything God had been trying to communicate to him for years. That was one reason, besides Chloe, that he didn't mind relocating to Chicago. He wanted to come to this church and hear Bruce explain the Bible every time the doors were opened. He wanted to immerse himself in Bruce's insight and teaching as a member of this little core group.

He still had a job and he was writing important stuff, but learning to know God and listening to him seemed his primary occupation. The rest was just a means to an end.

Bruce looked up. "Now I know what people meant when they said they feasted on the Word. Sometimes I sit drinking it in for hours, losing track of time, forgetting to eat, weeping, and praying. Sometimes I just slip from my chair and fall to my knees, calling out to God to make it clear to me. Most frightening of all, he's doing just that."

Buck noticed Rayford and Chloe nodding. He was newer at this than they were, but he felt that same hunger and thirst for the Bible. But what was Bruce getting at? Was he saying that God had revealed something to him?

Bruce took a deep breath and stood. He stepped to the corner of the desk and sat on it, towering over the other three. "I need your prayers," he said. "God is showing me things, impressing truths on me that I can barely contain. And yet if I say them publicly, I will be ridiculed and maybe put myself in danger."

"Of course we'll pray," Rayford said. "But what does this have to do with today's news?"

"It has everything to do with the news, Rayford." Bruce shook his head. "Don't you see? We know Nicolae Carpathia is the Antichrist. Let's assume for the sake of argument that Buck's story of Carpathia's supernatural hypnotic power and the murder of those two men is ridiculous. Even so, there's plenty of evidence that Carpathia fits the prophetic descriptions. He's deceptive. He's charming. People are flocking to support him. He has been thrust to power, seemingly against his own wishes. He's pushing a one-world government, a one-world currency, a treaty with Israel, moving the U.N. to Babylon. That alone proves it. What are the odds that one man would promote all those things and *not* be the Antichrist?"

"We knew this was coming," Buck said. "But has he gone public with all that?"

"All today."

Buck let out a low whistle. "What did Carpathia say?"

"He announced it through his media guy, your former boss, what's his name?"

"Plank."

"Right. Steve Plank. They held a press conference so he could inform the media that Carpathia would be unavailable for several days while he conducted strategic high-level meetings."

"And he said what the meetings were about?"

"He said that Carpathia, while not seeking the position of leadership, felt an obligation to move quickly to unite the world in a move toward peace. He has assigned task forces to implement the disarming of the nations of the world and to confirm that it has been done. He is having the 10 percent of the weaponry that is not destroyed from each nation shipped to Babylon, which he has renamed New Babylon. The international financial community, whose representatives were already in New York for meetings, has been charged with the responsibility of settling on one currency."

"I never would have believed it." Buck frowned. "A friend tried to tell me about this a long time ago."

"That's not all," Bruce went on. "Do you think it was coincidental that leaders of the major religions were in New York when Carpathia arrived last week? How could this be anything but the fulfillment of prophecy? Carpathia is urging them to come together, to agree on some all-inclusive effort at tolerance that would respect their shared beliefs."

"Shared beliefs?" Chloe said. "Some of those religions are so far apart they would never agree."

"But they *are* agreeing," Bruce said. "Carpathia is apparently making deals. I don't know what he's offering, but an announcement is expected by the end of the week from the religious leaders. I'm guessing we'll see a one-world religion."

"Who'd fall for that?"

"Scripture indicates that many will."

* * *

Rayford's mind was reeling. It had been hard for him to concentrate on anything since the day of the disappearances. At times he still wondered if this was all a crazy nightmare, something he would wake up from and then change his ways. Was he Scrooge, who needed such a dream to see how wrong he'd been? Or was he George Bailey, Jimmy Stewart's character from *It's a Wonderful Life*, who got his wish and then wished he hadn't?

Rayford actually knew two people—Buck and Hattie—who had personally met the Antichrist! How bizarre was that? When he allowed himself to dwell on it, it sent a dark shiver of terror deep inside him. The cosmic battle between God and Satan had crashed into his own life, and in an instant he had gone from skeptical cynic, neglectful father, and lustful husband with a roving eye, to fanatical believer in Christ.

"Why has the news today set you off so much, Bruce?" Rayford asked. "I don't think any of us doubted Buck's story or had any lingering question about whether Carpathia was the Antichrist."

"I don't know, Rayford." Bruce returned to his chair. "All I know is that the closer I get to God, the deeper I get into the Bible, the heavier the burden seems on my shoulders. The world needs to know it is being deceived. I feel an urgency to preach Christ everywhere, not just here. This church is full of frightened people, and they're hungry for God. We're trying to meet that need, but more trouble is coming.

"The news that really got to me today was the announcement that the next major order of business for Carpathia is what he calls 'an understanding' between the global community and Israel, as well as what he calls 'a special arrangement' between the U.N. and the United States."

Buck sat up straighter. "What do you make of that?"

"I don't know what the U.S. thing is, because as much as I study I don't see America playing a role during this period of history. But we all know what the 'understanding' with Israel will be. I don't know what form it will take or what the benefit will be to the Holy Land, but clearly this is the seven-year treaty."

Chloe looked up. "And that actually signals the beginning of the seven-year period of tribulation."

"Exactly." Bruce looked at the group. "If that announcement says anything about a promise from Carpathia that Israel will be protected over the next seven years, it officially ushers in the Tribulation."

Buck was taking notes. "So the disappearances, the Rapture, didn't start the seven-year period?"

"No," Bruce said. "Part of me hoped that something would delay the treaty with Israel. Nothing in Scripture says it has to happen right away. But once it does, the clock starts ticking."

"But it starts ticking toward Christ setting up his kingdom on earth, right?" Buck asked. Rayford was impressed that Buck had learned so much so quickly.

Bruce nodded. "That's right. And that's the reason for this meeting. I need to tell you all something. I am going to have a two-hour meeting, right here in this office, every weeknight from eight to ten. Just for us."

"I'll be traveling a lot," Buck said.

"Me too," Rayford added.

Bruce held up a hand. "I can't force you to come, but I urge you. Anytime you're in town, be here. In our studies we're going to outline what God has revealed in the Scriptures. Some of it you've already heard me talk about. But if the treaty with Israel comes within the next few days, we have no time to waste. We need to be starting new churches, new cell groups of believers. I want to go to Israel and hear the two witnesses at the Wailing Wall. The Bible talks about 144,000 Jews springing up and traveling throughout the world. There is to be a great soul harvest, maybe a billion or more people, coming to Christ."

"That sounds fantastic," Chloe said. "We should be thrilled."

"I *am* thrilled," Bruce said. "But there will be little time to rejoice or to rest. Remember the seven Seal Judgments Revelation talks about?" She nodded. "Those will begin immediately, if I'm right. There will be an eighteen-month period of peace, but in the three months following that, the rest of the Seal Judgments will fall on the earth. One fourth of the world's population will be wiped out. I don't want to be maudlin, but will you look around this room and tell me what that means to you?"

Rayford didn't have to look around the room. He sat with the three people closest to him in the world. Was it possible that in less than two years, he could lose yet another loved one?

+ + +

Buck closed his notebook. He was not going to record the fact that someone in that room might be dead soon. He recalled that during his first day at college he had been asked to look to his right and to his left. The professor had said, "One of the three of you will not be here in a year." That was almost funny compared to this.

"We don't want to simply survive, though," Buck said. "We want to take action."

"I know," Bruce said. "I guess I'm just grieving in advance. This is going to be a long, hard road. We're all going to be busy and overworked, but we must plan ahead."

"I was thinking about going back to college," Chloe mused. "Not to Stanford, of course, but somewhere around here. Now I wonder, what's the point?"

"You can go to college right here," Bruce said. "Every night at eight. And there's something else."

"I thought there might be," Buck said.

"I think we need a shelter."

"A shelter?" Chloe said.

"Underground," Bruce said. "During the period of peace we can build it without suspicion. When the judgments come, we wouldn't be able to get away with anything like that."

"What are you talking about?" Buck asked.

"I'm talking about getting an earthmover in here and digging out a place we can escape to. War is coming—famine, plagues, and death."

Rayford held up a hand. "But I thought we weren't going to turn tail and run."

"We're not," Bruce said. "But if we don't plan ahead, if we don't have a place to retreat to, to regroup, to evade radiation and disease, we'll die trying to prove we're brave."

Buck was impressed that Bruce had a plan, a real plan. Bruce said he would order a huge water tank and have it delivered. It would sit at the edge of the parking lot for weeks, and people would assume it was just some sort of a storage tank. Then he would have an excavator dig out a crater big enough to house it.

Meanwhile, the four of them would stud up walls, run power and water lines into the hole, and generally get it prepared as a hideout. At some point Bruce would have the water tank taken away. People who saw that would assume it was the wrong size or defective. People who didn't see it taken away would assume it had been installed in the ground.

The Tribulation Force would attach the underground shelter to the church through a hidden passageway, but they would not use it until they had to. All their meetings would be in Bruce's office.

The meeting that night ended with prayer, the three newest believers praying for Bruce and his weight of leadership.

Buck urged Bruce to go home and get some sleep. On his way out, Buck turned to Chloe. "I'd show you my new car, but it doesn't seem like that big a deal anymore."

"I know what you mean." She smiled. "It looks nice, though. You want to join us for some dinner?"

"I'm not really hungry. Anyway, I've got to get started moving into my new place."

"Do you have furniture yet?" she asked. "You could stay with us until you get some. We've got plenty of room."

He thought about the irony of that. "Thanks," he said. "It's furnished."

Rayford came up from behind. "Where'd you land anyway, Buck?"

Buck described the condo, halfway between church and the *Weekly.*

"That's not far."

"No," Buck said. "I'll have everybody over once I get settled."

Rayford had opened his car door, and Chloe waited at the passenger door. The three of them stood silent and awkward in the dim light from the streetlamps. "Well," Buck said, "I'd better get going." Rayford slid into the car. Chloe still stood there. "See ya."

Chloe gave a little wave, and Buck turned away. He felt like an idiot. What was he going to do about her? He knew she was waiting, hoping for some sign that he was still interested. And he was. He was just having trouble showing it. He didn't know if it was because her father was there or because too much was happening in their lives right now.

Buck thought about Chloe's comment that there wasn't much use in going to college. That applied to romance as well, he thought. Sure, he was lonely. Sure, they had a lot in common. Sure, he was attracted to her, and it was clear she felt the same about him. But wasn't getting interested in a woman right now a little trivial, considering all Bruce had just talked about?

Buck had already fallen in love with God. That had to be his passion until Christ returned again. Would it be right, let alone prudent, to focus his attention on Chloe Steele at the same time? He tried to push her from his mind.

Fat chance.

+ + +

"You like him, don't you?" Rayford said as he pulled the car out of the parking lot.

"He's all right."

"I'm talking about Buck."

"I know who you're talking about. He's all right, but he hardly knows I exist anymore."

"There's a lot on his mind."

"I get more attention from Bruce, and he's got more on his mind than any of us."

"Let Buck get settled in and he'll come calling."

"He'll come calling?" Chloe said. "You sound like Pa on *Little House on the Prairie.*"

"Sorry."

"Anyway, I think Buck Williams is through calling."

Buck's apartment was antiseptic without his own stuff in it. He kicked off his shoes and called his voice mail in New York. He wanted to leave a message with Marge Potter, his former secretary there, asking when he could expect his boxes from the office. She beat him to the punch. The first of his three messages was from Marge. "I didn't know where to ship your stuff, so I overnighted it to the Chicago bureau office. Should be there Monday morning."

The second message was from the big boss, Stanton Bailey. "Give me a call sometime Monday, Cameron. I want to get your story by the end of next week, and we need to talk."

The third was from his old executive editor, Steve Plank, now Nicolae Carpathia's spokesman. "Buck, call me as soon as you can. Carpathia wants to talk to you."

Buck sniffed and chuckled and erased his messages. He recorded a thanks to Marge and an I-got-your-message-and-will-call-you to Bailey. He merely made a note with Steve's phone number and decided to wait to call him. *Carpathia wants to talk to you.* What a casual way to say, *The enemy of God is after you.* Buck could only wonder whether Carpathia knew he had not been brainwashed. What would the man do, or try to do, if he knew Buck's memory had not been altered? If he realized Buck knew he was a murderer, a liar, a beast?

\+ \+ \+

Rayford sat watching the television news, hearing commentators pontificate on the meaning of the announcements coming out of the United Nations. Most considered the scheduled move of the U.N. to the ruins of Babylon, south of Baghdad, a good thing. One said, "If Carpathia is sincere about disarming the world and stockpiling the remaining 10 percent of the hardware, I'd rather he store it in the Middle East, in the shadow of Tehran, than on an island off New York City. Besides, we can use the soon-to-be-abandoned U.N. building as a museum, honoring the most atrocious architecture this country has ever produced."

Pundits predicted frustration and failure in the proposed outcomes of the meetings between both the religious leaders and the financial experts. One said, "No single religion, as attractive as that sounds, and no one-world currency, as streamlined as that would be. These will be Carpathia's first major setbacks, and perhaps then the masses will become more realistic about him. The honeymoon will soon be over."

"Want some tea, Dad?" Chloe called from the kitchen. He declined, and she came out a minute later with her own. She sat on the other end of the couch from him, her slippered feet tucked up under her robe. Her freshly washed hair was wrapped in a towel.

"Got a date this weekend?" Rayford asked when the news broke for a commercial.

"Not funny," she said.

"It wasn't meant to be. Would that be so strange, someone asking you out?"

"The only person I want to ask me out has apparently changed his mind about me."

"Nonsense," Rayford said. "I can't imagine all that must be on Buck's mind."

"I thought *I* was on his mind, Dad. Now I sit here like a schoolgirl, wondering and hoping. It's all so stupid. Why should I care? I just met him. I hardly know him. I just admire him, that's all."

"You admire him?"

"Sure! Who wouldn't? He's smart, articulate, accomplished."

"Famous."

"Yeah, a little. But I'm not going to throw myself at him. I just thought he was interested, that's all. His note said he was attracted to me."

"How did you respond to that?"

"To him, you mean?"

Rayford nodded.

"I didn't. What was I supposed to do? I was attracted to him, too, but I didn't want to scare him off."

"Maybe he thinks he's scared you off. Maybe he thinks he came on too strong too soon. But you didn't feel that way?"

"In a way I did, but down deep it was right. I thought just being open to him and staying friendly would make the point."

Dad shrugged. "Maybe he needs more encouragement."

"He's not going to get it from me. Not my style. You know that."

"I know, hon," Rayford said, "but a lot has changed about you recently."

"Yeah, but my style hasn't." That made even her laugh. "Daddy, what am I going to do? I'm not ready to give up on him, but couldn't you see it wasn't the same? He should have asked me out for something to eat, but he didn't even accept our invitation."

"*Our* invitation? *I* was in on that?"

"Well, it wouldn't have been appropriate for me to ask him out by myself."

"I know. But maybe he didn't want to go out with me around."

"If he felt about me the way I thought he did, he would have. In fact, he would have asked me first and left you out of it. I mean . . . I didn't mean it that way, Dad."

"I know what you meant. I think you're being a little too gloomy too soon about this. Give him a day. See what a difference a night's sleep makes."

The news came back on, and Chloe sipped her tea. Rayford felt privileged that she would talk to him about things like this. He didn't remember that she had even talked to Irene much about guys. He knew he was her only port in a storm, but still he enjoyed her confidence. "I don't have to watch this if you want to talk some more," he told her. "There's nothing new here since what Bruce told us."

"No," she said, standing. "Frankly, I'm sick of myself. Sitting here talking about my love life, or lack of it, seems pretty juvenile at this point in history, don't you think? It's not like there's nothing to fill my time even if I don't go back to school. I want to memorize Ezekiel, Daniel, and Revelation for starters."

Rayford laughed. "You're kidding!"

"Of course! But you know what I mean, Dad? I never would have dreamed the Bible would even interest me, but now I'm reading it like there's no tomorrow."

Rayford fell silent, and he could tell Chloe was struck by her own unintentional irony. "I am too," he said. "I already know more about end-times prophecy than I ever knew existed. We're living it, right here, right now. There aren't many tomorrows left, are there?"

"Certainly not enough to waste pining away over a guy."

"He's a pretty impressive guy, Chlo'."

"You're a big help. Let me forget him, will you?"

Rayford smiled. "If I don't mention him, you'll forget him? Should we get him kicked out of the Tribulation Force?"

Chloe shook her head. "And anyway, how long has it been since you called me *Chlo*?"

"You used to like that."

"Yeah. When I was nine. 'Night, Dad."

"'Night, sweetheart. I love you."

Chloe had been heading toward the kitchen, but she stopped and turned and hurried back, bending to embrace him, careful not to spill her tea. "I love you too, Dad. More than ever and with all my heart."

* * *

Buck Williams lay on his stomach in his new bed for the first time. It felt strange. His was a nice place in a good building, but suburban Chicago was not

New York. It was too quiet. He had brought home a bag of fresh fruit, ignored it, watched the news, and turned on soft music. He decided to read the New Testament until he fell asleep.

Buck had been soaking up whatever he could from Bruce Barnes about what was to come next, but he found himself turning to the Gospels rather than the Old Testament or the Revelation prophecies. What a revolutionary Jesus turned out to be. Buck was fascinated with the character, the personality, the mission of the man. The Jesus he had always imagined or thought he knew about was an impostor. The Jesus of the Bible was a radical, a man of paradoxes.

Buck set the Bible on the nightstand and rolled onto his back, shielding his eyes from the light. *If you want to be rich, give your money away,* he told himself. *That's the gist of it. If you want to be exalted, humble yourself. Revenge sounds logical, but it's wrong. Love your enemies, pray for those who put you down. Bizarre.*

His mind wandered to Chloe. What was he doing? She wasn't blind. She was young, but she was not stupid. He couldn't lead her on and then change his mind, not without being up front. But *was* he changing his mind? Did he really want to just forget about her? Of course not. She was a wonderful person, fun to talk to. She was a fellow believer and compatriot. She would be a good friend, regardless.

So it had already come to that? He would give her the let's-be-friends line? Was that what he wanted?

God, what am I supposed to do? he prayed silently. *To tell you the truth, I'd love to be in love. I'd love to start a relationship with Chloe. But is she too young? Is this the wrong time to even be thinking about such a thing? I know you have a lot for us to do. What if we did fall in love? Should we get married? What would we do about children, if you're coming back in seven years? If there was ever a time to wonder about bringing children into this world, it's now.*

Buck pulled his arm away from his eyes and squinted at the light. Now what? Was God supposed to answer him aloud? He knew better than that. He swung his legs over the side and sat on the bed, his head in his hands.

What had gotten into him? All he wanted to know was whether he should keep pursuing Chloe. He started praying about it, and all of a sudden he was thinking about marriage and children. Craziness. *Maybe that's how God works,* he thought. *He leads you to logical, or illogical, conclusions.*

Based on that, he thought he had better not encourage Chloe anymore. She was interested, he could see that. If he showed the same interest, it would lead only one direction. In the new chaotic world they lived in, they would eventually grow desperate for each other. Should he allow that?

It didn't make sense. How could he let anything compete with his devotion to God? And yet he couldn't just ignore her, start treating her like a sister. No, he would do the right thing. He would talk to her about it. She was worth it, that was for sure. He would set an informal date, and they would have a chat. He would tell her straight out that, left to his own wishes, he would want to get to know her better. That would make her feel good, wouldn't it? But would he have the courage to follow through and tell her what he really thought—that neither of them should pursue a romantic relationship now?

He didn't know. But he was sure of one thing: if he didn't set it up right now, he probably never would. He looked at his watch. A little after ten-thirty. Would she still be up? He dialed the Steeles.

+ + +

Rayford heard the phone on his way up the stairs. He heard Chloe stir, but her light was off. "I'll get it, hon," he said. He hurried to his bed table and answered.

"Mr. Steele, it's Buck."

"Hey, Buck, you've got to quit calling me *Mister*. You're making me feel old."

"Aren't you old?" Buck said.

"Cute. Call me Ray. What can I do for you?"

"I was wondering if Chloe was still up."

"You know, I don't think she is, but I can check and see if she's still awake."

"No, that's all right," Buck said. "Just have her call me at her convenience, would you?" He gave Rayford his new number.

"Dad!" Chloe said a few minutes later. "You knew I was awake!"

"You didn't answer when I said I'd get it," he said. "I wasn't sure. Don't you think this is for the best? Let him wait till morning?"

"Oh, Dad!" she said. "I don't know. What do you think he wanted?"

"I have no idea."

"Ooh, I hate this!"

"I love it."

"You would."

3

SATURDAY MORNING Buck drove to New Hope Village Church, hoping to catch Bruce Barnes in his office. The secretary told him Bruce was finishing up his sermon preparation, but that she also knew he would want to see Buck. "You're part of Bruce's inner circle, aren't you?" she said.

Buck nodded. He guessed he was. Should it have been an honor? He felt so new, like such a baby, as a follower of Christ. Who would ever have predicted this for him? And yet who would have dreamed the Rapture would take place? He shook his head. *Only the millions who were ready,* he decided.

With the announcement that Buck was waiting, Bruce immediately swung open his door and embraced him. That was something new for Buck, too, all this hugging, especially among men. Bruce looked haggard. "Another long night?" Buck asked.

Bruce nodded. "But another long feast on the Word. I'm making up for lost time, you know. I've had these resources on hand for years and never took advantage of them. I'm trying to decide how to tell the congregation, probably within the next month, that I feel called to travel. People here are going to have to step up and help lead."

"You're afraid they'll feel abandoned?"

"Exactly. But I'm not leaving the church. I'll be here as much as I can. As I told you and the Steeles yesterday, this is a weight I feel God has put on me. There's joy in it—I'm learning so much. But it's scary, too, and I know I'm not up to it, apart from the Spirit's power. I think it's just another price I have to pay for having missed the truth the first time. But you didn't come to hear me complain."

"I just have two quick things, and then I'll let you get back to your study. First, and I've been pushing this from my mind the last few days, but I feel terrible about Hattie Durham. Remember her? Rayford's flight attendant—"

"The woman you introduced to Carpathia? Sure. The one Rayford almost had a fling with."

"Yeah, I suppose he feels bad about her too."

"I can't speak for him, Buck, but as I recall, you tried to warn her about Carpathia."

"I told her she might wind up being his plaything, yes, but at the time I had no idea who he really was."

"She went to New York on her own. It was her choice."

"But, Bruce, if I hadn't introduced them, he wouldn't have asked to see her again."

Bruce sat back and folded his arms. "You want to rescue her from Carpathia, is that it?"

"Of course."

"I don't see how you could do it without putting yourself in danger. She's no doubt enamored with her new life already. She's gone from being a flight attendant to being the personal assistant to the most powerful man in the world."

"Personal assistant and who knows what else."

Bruce nodded. "Probably so. I don't imagine he chose her for her clerical skills. Still, what do you do? Call her and tell her her new boss is the Antichrist and that she should leave him?"

Buck said, "That's why I'm here. I don't know what to do."

"And you think I do."

"I was hoping."

Bruce smiled wearily. "Now I know what my former senior pastor, Vern Billings, meant when he said people think their pastor should know everything."

"No advice then?"

"This is going to sound trite, Buck, but you have to do what you have to do."

"Meaning?"

"Meaning if you've prayed about it and feel a real leading from God to talk with Hattie, then do it. But you can imagine the consequences. The next person to know about it will be Carpathia. Look what he's done to you already."

"That's the issue," Buck said. "Somehow I have to find out how much Carpathia knows. Does he think he wiped from my memory that I was at that meeting, the way he wiped it from everyone else's? Or does he know I know what went on and that's why he got me in trouble, demoted, relocated, and all that?"

"And you wonder why I'm weary?" Bruce said. "My gut feeling is that if Carpathia knew you were a believer now and that you had been protected from his brainwashing, he'd have you killed. If he thinks he still has power over you, as he does over people without Christ in their lives, he'll try to use you."

Buck sat back and stared at the ceiling. "Interesting you should say that," he said. "That leads me to the second thing I wanted to talk with you about."

* * *

Rayford spent the morning on the phone finalizing arrangements for his recertification on the Boeing 777. Monday morning he was to fly as a passenger from O'Hare to Dallas, where he would practice takeoffs and landings on military runways a few miles from the Dallas–Fort Worth airport.

"I'm sorry, Chloe," he said when he was finally off the phone. "I forgot you wanted to call Buck back this morning."

"Correction," she said. "I wanted to call him back last night. In fact, I wanted to talk to him when he called."

Rayford held up both hands in surrender. "My mistake," he said. "Guilty. The phone is yours."

"No thanks."

Rayford raised his brows at his daughter. "What? Now you're going to punish Buck because of me? Call him!"

"No, the truth is I think this worked out for the best. I wanted to talk to him last night, but you were probably right. I would have seemed too eager, too forward. And he said I should call him back at my convenience. Well, first thing in the morning wouldn't be that convenient. In fact, I'll see him in church tomorrow, right?"

Rayford shook his head. "Now you're going to play games with him? You were worried about obsessing over him like a schoolgirl, and now you're acting like one."

Chloe looked hurt. "Oh, thanks, Dad. Just remember, letting him wait was your idea."

"That was just overnight. Don't involve me in this if it's going to get silly."

* * *

"Well, Buck, here's your chance to check in on Hattie," Bruce Barnes said. "What do *you* think Carpathia wants?"

Buck shook his head. "No idea."

"Do you trust this Steve Plank?"

"Yeah, I trust him. I worked for Steve for years. The scary thing is, he welcomed me to Carpathia's pre-press-conference meeting, told me where to sit, told me who the various people were. Then later he asked why I hadn't shown up. Told me Carpathia was a little put out that I wasn't there."

"And you know him well enough to know whether he's being straight with you."

"Frankly, Bruce, he's the main reason I believe that Carpathia is the fulfillment of these prophecies we're studying. Steve is a hard-nosed journalist from the old school. That he could be talked into leaving legitimate news coverage to be spokesman for a world politician shows Carpathia's power of persuasion. Even I turned down that job. But to sit through that carnage and then forget that I was even there, that's just . . ."

"Unnatural."

"Exactly. I'll tell you what was weird, though. Something in me wanted to believe Carpathia when he explained what had happened. Pictures began forming in my mind of Stonagal shooting himself and killing Todd-Cothran in the process."

Bruce shook his head. "I confess that when you first told us that story, I thought you had gone mad."

"I would have agreed with you, except for one thing."

"What's that?"

"Well, all those other people saw it happen and remembered it one way. I remembered it entirely differently. If Steve had just told me I hadn't seen it right, maybe I would have thought I was going crazy and had myself committed. But instead he told me I wasn't even there! Bruce, *no one* remembers I was there! Well, tell me I'm in denial, but that's hogwash. I was back in my office recording every detail into my computer by the time the news media got Carpathia's version. If I wasn't there, how did I know that Stonagal and Todd-Cothran would be carried out of there in body bags?"

"You don't have to persuade me, Buck," Bruce said. "I'm on your side. The question now is, what does Carpathia want? Do you think if he talks to you in private he'll reveal his true self? or threaten you? or let you know he's aware that you know the truth?"

"For what purpose?"

"To intimidate you. To use you."

"Maybe. Maybe all he wants to do is try to read me, try to determine whether he succeeded in brainwashing me, too."

"It's pretty dangerous business, that's all I've got to say."

"I hope that's *not* all you've got to say, Bruce. I was hoping for a little more counsel."

"I'll pray about it," Bruce said. "But right now I don't know what to tell you."

"Well, at least I have to call Steve back. I don't know whether Carpathia wants to talk by phone or in person."

"Can you wait until Monday?"

"Sure. I can tell him I assumed he wanted me to call him back during business hours, but I can't guarantee he won't call me in the meantime."

"He has your new number?"

"No. Steve calls my voice mail in New York."

"Easy enough to ignore."

Buck shrugged and nodded. "If that's what you think I should do."

"Since when have I become your adviser?"

"Since you became my pastor."

+ + +

When Rayford returned from running errands that morning, he realized from her body language and terse comments that he had offended Chloe. "Let's talk," he said.

"About what?"

"About how you have to cut me some slack. I was never very good at this parenting thing, and now I'm having trouble treating you like the adult that you are. I'm sorry I called you a schoolgirl. You handle Buck any way you think is right, and ignore me, all right?"

Chloe smiled. "I was ignoring you already. I don't need your permission for that."

"Then you forgive me?"

"Don't worry about me, Dad. I can't stay mad at you for long anymore. Seems to me we need each other. I called Buck, by the way."

"Really?"

She nodded. "No answer. I guess he wasn't waiting by the phone."

"Did you leave a message?"

"No machine yet, I guess. I'll see him at church tomorrow."

"Will you tell him you called?"

Chloe smiled mischievously. "Probably not."

+ + +

Buck spent the rest of the day tweaking his cover story for *Global Weekly* on the theories behind the disappearances. He felt good about it, deciding it might be the best work he had ever done. It included everything from the tabloid-like attack by Hitler's ghost, UFOs, and aliens, to the belief that this was some sort of cosmic evolutionary cleansing, a survival-of-the-fittest adjustment in the world's population.

In the middle of the piece, Buck had included what he believed was the truth, of course, but he did not editorialize. It was, as usual, a third-person, straight news-analysis article. No one but his new friends would know that he agreed with the airline pilot and the pastor and several others he interviewed—that the disappearances had been a result of Christ's rapture of his church.

Most interesting to Buck was the interpretation of the event on the part of other churchmen. A lot of Catholics were confused, because while many remained, some had disappeared—including the new pope, who had been installed just a few months before the vanishings. He had stirred up controversy in the church with a new doctrine that seemed to coincide more with the "heresy" of Martin Luther than with the historic orthodoxy they were used to. When the pope had disappeared, some Catholic scholars had concluded that this was indeed an act of God. "Those who opposed the orthodox teaching of the Mother Church were winnowed out from among us," Peter Cardinal Mathews of Cincinnati, a leading archbishop, had told Buck. "The Scripture says that in the last days it will be as in the days of Noah. And you'll recall that in the days of Noah, the good people remained and the evil ones were washed away."

"So," Buck concluded, "the fact that we're still here proves we're the good guys?"

"I wouldn't put it so crassly," Archbishop Mathews had said, "but, yes, that's my position."

"What does that say about all the wonderful people who vanished?"

"That perhaps they were not so wonderful."

"And the children and babies?"

The bishop had shifted uncomfortably. "That I leave to God," he said. "I have to believe that perhaps he was protecting the innocents."

"From what?"

"I'm not sure. I don't take the Apocrypha literally, but there are dire predictions of what might be yet to come."

"So you would not relegate the vanished young ones to the winnowing of the evil?"

"No. Many of the little ones who disappeared I baptized myself, so I know they are in Christ and with God."

"And yet they are gone."

"They are gone."

"And we remain."

"We should take great solace in that."

"Few people take solace in it, Excellency."

"I understand that. This is a very difficult time. I myself am grieving the loss of a sister and an aunt. But they had left the church."

"They had?"

"They opposed the teaching. Wonderful women, most kind. Most earnest, I must add. But I fear they have been separated as chaff from wheat. Yet those of us who remain should be confident in our standing with God as never before."

Buck had been bold enough to ask the archbishop to comment on certain passages of Scripture, primarily Ephesians 2:8-9: "For by grace you have been saved through faith, and that not of yourselves; it is the gift of God, not of works, lest anyone should boast."

"Now you see," the archbishop said, "this is precisely my point. People have been taking verses like that out of context for centuries and trying to build doctrine on them."

"But there are other passages just like those," Buck said.

"I understand that, but, listen, you're not Catholic, are you?"

"No, sir."

"Well, see, you don't understand the broad sweep of the historical church."

"Excuse me, but explain to me why so many non-Catholics are still here, if your hypothesis is right."

"God knows," Archbishop Mathews had said. "He knows hearts. He knows more than we do."

"That's for sure," Buck said.

Of course Buck left his personal comments and opinions out of the article, but he was able to work in the Scripture and the archbishop's attempt to explain away the doctrine of grace. Buck planned to transmit the finished article to the *Global Weekly* offices in New York on Monday.

As he worked, Buck kept an ear open for the phone. Very few people had his new number. Only the Steeles, Bruce, and Alice, Verna Zee's secretary. He expected his answering machine, his desktop computer, fax machine, and other office equipment, along with files from the office, to arrive at the Chicago bureau Monday. Then he would feel more at home and equipped to work out of the second bedroom.

Buck had half expected to hear from Chloe. He thought he had left it with Rayford that she would call at her convenience. Maybe she was the type who didn't call men, even when she had missed their call. On the other hand, she was not quite twenty-one yet, and he admitted he had no idea about the customs and mores of her generation. Maybe she saw him as a big brother or even a father figure and was repulsed by the idea that he might be interested in her. That didn't jibe with her look and her body language from the night before, but he hadn't been encouraging then, either.

He simply wanted to do the right thing, to talk with her—to clarify that the timing was bad for them, and that they should become close friends and compatriots in the common cause. But then he felt foolish. What if she had not even considered anything more than that? He would be explaining away something that wasn't even there.

But maybe she had phoned when he was with Bruce that morning. He would just call her. Invite her to see his new place when she had time, and then they would have their talk. He would play it by ear, trying to determine what her expectations had been, and then either let her down easy or ignore a subject that didn't need to be raised.

Rayford answered the phone. "Chloe!" he called out. "Buck Williams for you!"

He could hear her voice in the background. "Could you tell him I'll call him back? Better yet, I'll see him in church tomorrow."

"I heard that," Buck said. "Fair enough. See you then."

Apparently she's not wasting any energy worrying about us, Buck decided. He dialed his voice mail in New York. The only message was from Steve Plank.

"Buck, what's the deal? How long does it take to get settled? Do I have to call the Chicago bureau? I've left messages there, but old man Bailey told me you'd be working out of your own place.

"Did you get my message that Carpathia wants to talk to you? People don't make a habit of making him wait, my friend. I'm stalling him, telling him you're in transit, relocating, and all that. But he had sort of hoped to see you this weekend. I honestly don't know what he wants, except that he's still high on you. He's not holding a grudge over your standing him up on his invitation to that meeting, if you're worried about that.

"Tell you the truth, Buck, the newsman in you would have wanted to be there and should have been there. But you'd have been as rattled by it as I have been. A violent suicide before your eyes is no easy thing to forget.

"Listen, call me so I can get you two together. Bailey tells me you're putting the finishing touches on the theory article. If you can get with Carpathia soon enough, you can include his ideas. He's made no secret of them, but an exclusive quote or two wouldn't hurt either, right? You know where to reach me any time of the day or night."

Buck stored the message. What was he supposed to do? It sounded as if Carpathia wanted a private face-to-face. Not many days before, Buck would have jumped at the chance. To interview the leading personality in the world on the eve of the delivery of your most important cover story? Still, Buck was a new believer, convinced that Carpathia was the Antichrist himself. He had seen the man's power. And Buck was just getting started in his faith. He didn't know much about the Antichrist. Was the man omniscient like God? Could he read Buck's mind?

Carpathia obviously could manipulate people and brainwash minds. But did that mean he knew what people were thinking, too? Was Buck able to resist Carpathia only because he had the Spirit of Christ within him? He wished there was something in the Bible that specifically outlined the powers of the Antichrist. Then he would know what he was dealing with.

At the very least, Carpathia had to be curious about Buck. He must have wondered, when Buck slipped away from the conference room where the murders had been committed, whether there had been some glitch in his own mind-control powers. Otherwise, why erase from everyone else's mind not only the murders, replacing them with a picture of a bizarre suicide, but also the memory that Buck had been there at all?

Clearly, Nicolae had tried to cover himself by making everyone else forget Buck was there. If such a move was supposed to make Buck doubt his own sanity, it hadn't worked. God had been with Buck that day. He saw what he saw, and nothing could shake that. There was no second-guessing, no twinge of wondering if he was merely in denial. One thing was sure, he would not tell Carpathia what he knew. If Carpathia was certain Buck had not been tricked, he would have no recourse but to have him eliminated. If Buck could keep Carpathia thinking he had succeeded, it would give them one small advantage in the war against the forces of evil. What Buck or the Tribulation Force might do with that advantage, he could not fathom.

But he did know one thing. He would not return Steve Plank's call until Monday.

\+ \+ \+

Rayford was glad he and Chloe had decided to go early to church. The place was jammed every week. Rayford smiled at his daughter. Chloe looked the best he had seen her since coming home from college. He wanted to tease her, to ask her if she was dressing for Buck Williams or for God, but he let it go.

He took one of the last spots in the parking lot and saw cars lined up around the block, looking for places on the street to park. People were grieving. They were terror-stricken. They were looking for hope, for answers, for God. They were finding him here, and the word was spreading.

Few people who sat under the earnest and emotional teaching of Bruce Barnes could come away doubting that the vanishings had been the work of God. The church had been snatched away, and they had all been left behind. Bruce's message was that Jesus was coming again in what the Bible called the Glorious Appearing seven years after the beginning of the Tribulation. By then, he said, three-fourths of the world's remaining population would be wiped out, and probably a larger percentage of believers in Christ. Bruce's exhortation was not a call to the timid. It was a challenge to the convinced, to those who had been persuaded by God's most dramatic invasion of human life since the incarnation of Jesus Christ as a mortal baby.

Bruce had already told the Steeles and Buck that a quarter of the earth's population would die during the second, third, and fourth judgments from the Seven-Sealed Scroll of Revelation. He cited Revelation 6:8, where the apostle John had written, "So I looked, and behold, a pale horse. And the name of him who sat on it was Death, and Hades followed with him. And power was given to them over a fourth of the earth, to kill with sword, with hunger, with death, and by the beasts of the earth."

But what was to come after that was even worse.

A minute or two after they had settled in their seats, Rayford felt a tap on the shoulder. He turned just as Chloe did. Buck Williams sat directly behind them in the fourth row and had touched them simultaneously. "Hey, strangers," he said. Rayford stood and embraced Buck. That alone told him how much had changed in him in just a matter of weeks. Chloe was cordial, shaking Buck's hand.

After they were seated again, Buck leaned forward and whispered, "Chloe, the reason I was calling was that I wondered—"

But the music had begun.

* * *

Buck stood to sing with everyone else. Many seemed to know the songs and the words. He had to follow as the words were projected on the wall and try to pick up the melodies. The choruses were simple and catchy, but they were new to him. Many of these people, he decided, had had plenty of exposure to church—more than he had. How had they missed the truth?

After a couple of choruses, a disheveled Bruce Barnes hurried to the pulpit—not the large one on the platform, but a small lectern at floor level. He carried his Bible, two large books, and a sheaf of papers he was having trouble controlling. He smiled sheepishly.

"Good morning," he began. "I realize a word of explanation is in order. Usually we sing more, but we don't have time for that today. Usually my tie is straighter, my shirt fully tucked in, my suit coat buttoned. That seems a little less crucial this morning. Usually we take up an offering. Be assured we still need it, but please find the baskets on your way out at noon, if indeed I let you out that early.

"I want to take the extra time this morning because I feel an urgency greater even than the last few weeks. I don't want you to worry about me. I haven't become a wild-eyed madman, a cultist, or anything other than what I have been since I realized I had missed the Rapture.

"I have told my closest advisers that God has weighed heavily upon me this week, and they are praying with me that I will be wise and discerning, that I will not go off half-cocked and shooting at some new and strange doctrine. I have read more, prayed more, and studied more this week than ever, and I am eager to tell you what God has told me.

"Does God speak to me audibly? No. I wish he would. I wish he had. If he had, I probably would not be here today. But he wanted me to accept him by faith, not by his proving himself in some more dramatic way than simply sending his Son to die for me. He has left us his Word, and it gives us all we need to know."

Buck felt a lump in his throat as he watched his new friend beg and plead and cajole his listeners to hear, to understand, to make themselves available to God for the instruction God wanted them to have. Bruce told his own story yet again, how he had lived a phony life of pietism and churchianity for years, and how when God came to call, he had been found wanting and had been left behind, without his wife and precious children. Buck had heard the story more than once, yet it never failed to move him. Some sobbed aloud. Those hearing it for the first time got Bruce's abbreviated version. "I never want to stop telling what Christ has done for me," he said. "Tell your stories. People can identify with your grief and your loss and your loneliness. I will never again be ashamed of the gospel of Christ. The Bible says that the Cross offends. If you are offended, I am doing my job. If you are attracted to Christ, the Spirit is doing his work.

"We've already missed the Rapture, and now we live in what will soon become the most perilous period of history. Evangelists used to warn parishioners that they could be struck by a car or die in a fire and thus they should not put off coming to Christ. I'm telling you that should you be struck by a car or caught in a fire, it may be the most merciful way you can die. Be ready this time. Be ready. I will tell you how to get ready.

"My sermon title today is 'The Four Horsemen of the Apocalypse,' and I want to concentrate on the first, the rider of the white horse. If you've always thought the Four Horsemen of the Apocalypse was a Notre Dame football backfield, God has a lesson for you today."

Buck had never seen Bruce so earnest, so inspired. As he spoke he referred to his notes, to the reference books, to the Bible. He began to perspire and often wiped sweat from his brow with his pocket handkerchief, which he took time to admit he knew was a faux pas. It seemed to Buck that the congregants, as one, merely chuckled with him as encouragement to keep on. Most were taking notes. Nearly everyone followed along in a Bible, their own or one provided in the pews.

Bruce explained that the book of Revelation, John's account of what God had revealed to him about the last days, spoke of what was to come after Christ had raptured his church. "Does anyone here doubt we're in the last days right now?" he thundered. "Millions disappear, and then what? Then what?"

Bruce explained that the Bible predicts first a treaty between a world leader and Israel. "Some believe the seven-year tribulation period has already begun and that it began with the Rapture. We feel the trials and tribulations already from the disappearance of millions, including our friends and loved ones, don't we? But that is nothing compared to the tribulation to come.

"During these seven years, God will pour out three consecutive sets of judgments—seven seals in a scroll, which we call the Seal Judgments; seven trumpets; and seven bowls. These judgments, I believe, are handed down for the purposes of shaking us loose from whatever shred of security we might have left. If the Rapture didn't get your attention, the judgments will. And if the judgments don't, you're going to die apart from God. Horrible as these judgments will be, I urge you to see them as final warnings from a loving God who is not willing that any should perish.

"As the scroll is opened and the seals are broken, revealing the judgments, the first four are represented by horsemen—the Four Horsemen of the Apocalypse. If you have ever been exposed to such imagery and language before, you probably considered it only symbolic, as I did. Is there anyone here who still considers the prophetic teaching of Scripture mere symbolism?"

Bruce waited a dramatic moment. "I thought not. Heed this teaching. The Seal Judgments will take us about twenty-one months from the signing of the treaty with Israel. In the coming weeks I will teach about the fourteen remaining judgments that will carry us through the end of the seven-year period, but for now, let's concentrate on the first four of the seven seals."

As Bruce plunged ahead, Buck was struck that the last speaker he had heard who was so captivating was Nicolae Carpathia. But Carpathia's impression had been choreographed, manipulated. Bruce wasn't trying to impress anyone with anything but the truth of the Word of God. Would he tell this body that he believed he knew who the Antichrist was? In a way Buck hoped he would. But that might be considered slander, to publicly finger someone as the archenemy of almighty God.

Or would Bruce simply tell what the Bible said and let the people come to their own conclusions? The news was already full of rumors about some impending agreement between Carpathia—or at least the Carpathia-led U.N.—and Israel. If Bruce predicted a pact that was borne out over the next few days, who could doubt him?

* * *

Rayford was more than fascinated. He was stunned. In many ways, Bruce was reading his mind. Not long ago he would have scoffed at such teaching, at such a literal take on so clearly a poetic and metaphoric passage. But what Bruce said made sense. The young man hadn't been preaching more than a few weeks. That had not been his calling or his training. But this wasn't preaching as much as teaching, and Bruce's passion, the immersion of his soul into the subject, made it all the more compelling.

"I don't have time to get into the second and third and fourth horsemen this morning," Bruce said, "except to say that the rider on the red horse signifies war, the black horse famine, and the pale horse death. Just a little something to look forward to," he added wryly, and some chuckled nervously. "But I warned you this is not for the faint of heart."

He sped toward his point and his conclusion by reading from Revelation 6:1-2: "Now I saw when the Lamb opened one of the seals; and I heard one of the four living creatures saying with a voice like thunder, 'Come and see.' And I looked, and behold, a white horse. He who sat on it had a bow; and a crown was given to him, and he went out conquering and to conquer."

Bruce dramatically moved back a step and began clearing off the small lectern. "Don't worry," he said, "I'm not finished." To Rayford's surprise, people began to applaud. Bruce said, "Are you clapping because you want me to finish, or because you want me to go on all afternoon?"

And the people clapped all the more. Rayford wondered what was happening. He applauded too, and Chloe and Buck were doing the same. They were drinking this in, and they wanted more and more. Clearly Bruce had been in tune with what God was showing him. He had said over and over that this was not new truth, that the commentaries he cited were decades old, and that the doctrine of the end times was much, much older than that. But those who had relegated this kind of teaching to the literalists, the fundamentalists, the closed-minded evangelicals, had been left behind. All of a sudden it was all right to take Scripture at its word! If nothing else convinced people, losing so many to the Rapture finally reached them.

Bruce stood before the bare lectern now with only his Bible in his hand. "I want to tell you now what I believe the Bible is saying about the rider of the white horse, the first horseman of the Apocalypse. I will not give my opinion. I will not draw any conclusion. I will simply leave it to God to help you draw any parallels that need to be drawn. I will tell you only this in advance: This millenniums-old account reads as fresh to me as tomorrow's newspaper."

4

BUCK SAT IN THE PEW behind Rayford and Chloe Steele and glanced at his watch. More than an hour had flown by since he had last checked. His stomach told him he was hungry, or at least that he could eat. His mind told him he could sit there all day, listening to Bruce Barnes explain from the Bible what was happening today and what would happen tomorrow. His heart told him he was on a precipice. He knew where Bruce was going with this teaching, with this imagery from the book of Revelation. Not only did he know who the rider of the white horse was, Buck knew the rider personally. He had experienced the power of the Antichrist.

Buck had spent enough time with Bruce and the Steeles, poring over the passages, to know beyond doubt that Nicolae Carpathia embodied the enemy of God. And yet he could not jump to his feet and corroborate Bruce's message with his own account. Neither could Bruce reveal that he knew precisely who the Antichrist was, or that someone in this very church had met him.

For years Buck had been an inveterate name-dropper. He had run in high circles for so long that it was not uncommon for him to be able to say, "Met him," "Interviewed her," "Know him," "Was with her in Paris," "Stayed in their home."

But that self-centeredness had been swept away by the disappearances and his experiences on the front lines of supernatural events. The old Buck Williams would have welcomed the prospect of letting on that he was a personal acquaintance of not only the leading personality in the world, but also the very Antichrist foretold in Scripture. Now he simply sat riveted as his friend preached on.

"Let me clarify," Bruce was saying, "that I don't believe it is God's intent to convey individual personality through the imagery of these horsemen, but rather world conditions. They don't all refer to specific people, because, for instance, the fourth horseman is called Death.

"Ah, but the first horseman! Notice that it is the Lamb who opens the first seal and reveals that horseman. The Lamb is Jesus Christ, the Son of God, who died for our sins, was resurrected, and recently raptured his church.

"In Scripture the first in a succession is always important—the firstborn, the first day of the week, the first commandment. The first rider, the first of the four horses of the first seven judgments, is important! He sets the tone. He is the key to understanding the rest of the horsemen, the rest of the Seal Judgments, indeed, the rest of all of the judgments.

"Who is this first horseman? Clearly he represents the Antichrist and his kingdom. His purpose is 'conquering and to conquer.' He has a bow in his hand, a symbol of aggressive warfare, and yet there is no mention of an arrow. So how will he conquer? Other passages indicate that he is a 'willful king' and that he will triumph through diplomacy. He will usher in a false peace, promising world unity. Will he be victorious? Yes! He has a crown."

\+ + +

In one way, this was all new to Rayford, and he knew it was to Chloe as well. But they had been so immersed in this teaching with Bruce since they had come to faith in Christ that Rayford anticipated every detail. It seemed he was becoming an instant expert, and he could not recall having ever picked up on a subject so quickly. He had always been a good student, especially in science and math. He had been a quick study in aviation. But this was cosmic. This was life. This was the real world. It explained what had happened to his wife and son, what he and his daughter would endure, and what would happen tomorrow and for the next several years.

Rayford admired Bruce. The young man had instantly realized that his phony brand of Christianity had failed him at the most pivotal point in human history. He had immediately repented and dedicated himself to the task of rescuing everyone possible. Bruce Barnes had surrendered himself to the cause.

Under other circumstances, Rayford might have worried about Bruce, fearing he was wearing himself out, stretching himself too thin. But Bruce seemed energized, fulfilled. He would need more sleep, sure, but for now he was brimming with the truth and eager to share it. And if the others were like Rayford, they could think of nothing they would rather do than sit here under that instruction.

"We'll talk next week and following about the next three horsemen of the Apocalypse," Bruce was saying, "but let me just leave you with something to watch for. The rider of the white horse is the Antichrist, who comes as a deceiver promising peace and uniting the world. The Old Testament book of Daniel—chapter 9, verses 24 through 27—says he will sign a treaty with Israel.

"He will appear to be their friend and protector, but in the end he will be their conqueror and destroyer. I must close for this week, but we'll talk more about why this happens and what will come of it. Let me close by telling you how you can be sure *I* am not the Antichrist."

That got people's attention, including Rayford's. There was embarrassed laughter.

"I'm not implying that you suspect me," Bruce said, to more laughs. "But we may get to the point where every leader is suspect. Remember, however, that you will never hear peace promised from this pulpit. The Bible is clear that we will have perhaps a year and a half of peace following the pact with Israel. But in the long run, I predict the opposite of peace. The other three horsemen are coming, and they bring war, famine, plagues, and death. That is not a popular message, not a warm fuzzy you can cling to this week. Our only hope is in Christ, and even in him we will likely suffer. See you next week."

Rayford sensed a restlessness in the crowd as Bruce closed in prayer, as if others felt the same way he did. He wanted to hear more, and he had a million questions. Usually the organist began playing near the end of Bruce's prayer and Bruce immediately headed to the back of the church where he shook hands with people as they left. But today Bruce didn't get as far as the aisle before he was stopped by people who embraced him, thanked him, and began asking questions.

Rayford and Chloe were in one of the rows closest to the front, and though Rayford was aware that Buck was talking to Chloe, he also heard what people were asking Bruce.

"Are you saying that Nicolae Carpathia is the Antichrist?" one asked.

"Did you hear me say that?" Bruce said.

"No, but it was pretty clear. They're already talking on the news about his plans and some sort of deal with Israel."

"Keep reading and studying," Bruce said.

"But it can't be Carpathia, can it? Does he strike you as a liar?"

"How does he strike you?" Bruce said.

"As a savior."

"Almost like a messiah?" Bruce pressed.

"Yeah!"

"There is only one Savior, one Messiah."

"I know, spiritually, but politically I mean. Don't tell me Carpathia's not what he seems to be."

"I'll tell you only what Scripture says," Bruce said, "and I will urge you to listen carefully to the news. We must be wise as serpents and gentle as doves."

"That's how I would have described Carpathia," a woman said.

"Be careful," Bruce said, "about ascribing Christlike attributes to anyone who doesn't align himself with Christ."

\+ + +

As the service ended, Buck took Chloe's arm, but she seemed less responsive than he might have hoped. She turned slowly to see what he wanted, and her expression bore no sign of that expectant look she'd had Friday night. Clearly, he had somehow wounded her. "I'm sure you're wondering what I was calling about," he began.

"I figured you'd tell me eventually."

"I just wondered if you wanted to see my new place." He told her where it was. "Maybe you could drop over late tomorrow morning and see it, and then we could get some lunch."

"I don't know," Chloe said. "I don't think I can do lunch, but if I'm over that way maybe I'll stop by."

"OK." Buck was deflated. Apparently it wasn't going to be difficult to let her down gently. It certainly wasn't going to break her heart.

\+ + +

As Chloe slipped into the crowd, Rayford reached to shake Buck's hand. "So how are you, my friend?"

"I'm doing all right," Buck said. "Getting settled in."

A question gnawed at Rayford. He looked at the ceiling and then back at Buck. In his peripheral vision he saw hundreds of people milling about, wanting their individual moments with Bruce Barnes. "Buck, let me ask you something. Do you ever regret introducing Hattie Durham to Carpathia?"

Buck pressed his lips together and shut his eyes, rubbing his forehead with his fingers. "Every day," he whispered. "I was just talking to Bruce about that."

Rayford nodded and knelt on the pew seat, facing Buck. Buck sat. "I wondered," Rayford said. "I have a lot of regrets about her. We were friends, you know. Coworkers, but friends, too."

"I gathered," Buck said.

"We never had a relationship or anything like that," Rayford assured him. "But I find myself caring about what happens to her."

"I hear she's taken a thirty-day leave of absence from Pan-Con."

"Yeah," Rayford said, "but that's just window dressing. You know Carpathia's going to want to keep her around, and he'll find the money to pay her more than she's making with us."

"No doubt."

"She's got to be enamored of the job, not to mention him. And who knows where that relationship might go?"

"Like Bruce says, I don't think he hired her for her brain," Buck said.

Rayford nodded. So they agreed. Hattie Durham was going to become one of Carpathia's diversions. If there had ever been hope for her soul, it would be remote as long as she was in his orbit every day.

"I worry about her," Rayford continued, "and yet because of our friendship I don't feel I'm in a position to warn her. She was one of the first people I tried to tell about Christ. She was not receptive. Before that I had implied more of an interest in her than I had a right to have, and naturally she's not real positive about me just now."

Buck leaned forward. "Maybe I'll get a chance to talk to Hattie sometime soon."

"But what will you say?" Rayford asked. "For all we know they may already be intimate. She'll tell him everything she knows. If she tells him you've become a believer and that you're trying to rescue her, he'll know he had no impact on your mind when he was brainwashing everyone else."

Buck nodded. "I've thought about that. But I feel responsible for her being there. I *am* responsible for her being there. We can pray for her, but I'm going to feel pretty useless if I can't do something concrete to get her out of there. We've got to get her back here where she can learn the truth."

"I wonder if she's already moved to New York," Rayford said. "Maybe we'll find a reason for Chloe to call her apartment in Des Plaines."

As they separated and made their way out of the church, Rayford began wondering how much he should encourage the relationship between Chloe and Buck. He liked Buck a lot, what little he knew of him. He believed him, trusted him, considered him a brother. He was bright and insightful for a young guy. But the idea that his daughter might date or even fall in love with a man on speaking terms with the Antichrist . . . it was too much to fathom. He would have to be frank with them both about it, if it appeared their relationship was going anywhere.

But once he joined Chloe in the car he realized that was not something he needed to fret about just yet.

"Don't tell me you've invited Buck to join us for lunch," she said.

"Didn't even think of it. Why?"

"He's treating me like a sister, and yet he wants me to drop in and see his place tomorrow."

Rayford wanted to say "So what?" and ask her if she didn't think she was reading too much into the words and actions of a man she barely knew. For all she knew, Buck could be madly in love with her and not know how to broach it. Rayford said nothing.

"You're right," she said. "I'm obsessing."

"I didn't say a word."

"I can read your mind," she said. "Anyway, I'm mad at myself. I come away from a message like that one, and all I can think about is a guy I've somehow let slip away. It's not important. Who cares?"

"You do, apparently."

"But I shouldn't. Old things are passed away and all things have become new," she said. "Worrying about guys should definitely be an old thing. There's no time for trivia now."

"Suit yourself."

"That's just what I don't want to do. If I suited myself I'd see Buck this afternoon and find out where we stand."

"But you're not going to?"

She shook her head.

"Then would you do me a favor? Would you try to reach Hattie Durham for me?"

"Why?"

"Actually, I'm just curious to know whether she's already moved to New York."

"Why wouldn't she have? Carpathia's hired her, hasn't he?"

"I don't know. She's on a thirty-day leave. Just call her apartment. If she's got a machine running, then she's not made up her mind yet."

"Why don't *you* call her?"

"I think I've intruded enough in her life."

* * *

Buck stopped for Chinese carryout on the way home and sat eating alone, staring out the window. He turned on a ball game but ignored it, keeping the sound low. His mind was full of conflict. His story was ready to be transmitted to New York, and he would be eager for a reaction from Stanton Bailey. He also looked forward to getting his office machines and files, which should arrive at the Chicago bureau office in the morning. It would be good to pick those up and get organized.

He couldn't shake Bruce's message, either. It wasn't so much the content as Bruce's passion. He needed to get to know Bruce better. Maybe that would be a cure for his loneliness—and Bruce's. If Buck himself were this lonely, it had to be much worse for a man who had had a wife and children. Buck was used to a solitary life, but he'd had a network of friends in New York. Here, unless he heard from the office or someone else in the Tribulation Force, the phone was not going to ring.

He certainly wasn't handling the Chloe situation well. When he had been demoted, Buck had considered the relocation from New York to Chicago a positive turn—he would get to see more of her, he'd be in a good church, get good training, have a core of friends. But he also felt he had been on the right track when he began to slow his pursuit of her. The timing was bad. Who pursues a relationship during the end of the world?

Buck knew—or at least believed—that Chloe was not toying with him. She wasn't playing hard to get just to keep him interested. But whether she was doing it on purpose or not, it was working, and he felt foolish to be dwelling on it.

Whatever had happened, however she was acting, and for whatever reason, he owed it to her to have it out. He might regret the let's-be-friends routine, but he didn't see that he had any other choice. He owed it to her and to himself to just pursue the friendship and see what came of it. For all he knew, she wouldn't be interested in more than that anyway.

He reached for the phone, but when he put it to his ear, he heard a strange tone, and then a recorded voice. "You have a message. Please push star two to hear it."

A message? I never ordered voice mail. He pushed the buttons. It was Steve Plank.

"Buck, where the devil are you, man? If you're not going to answer your voice mail, I'm going to quit leaving messages there. I know you're unlisted there, but if you think Nicolae Carpathia is someone to trifle with, ask yourself how I got your phone number. You'll wish you had these resources as a journalist. Now, Buck, friend to friend, I know you check your messages often, and you know Carpathia wants to talk to you. Why didn't you call me? You're making me look bad. I told him I'd track you down and that you'd come and see him. I told him I didn't understand your not accepting his invitation to the installation meeting, but that I know you like a brother and you wouldn't stand him up again.

"Now he wants to see you. I don't know what it's all about or even whether I'll sit in on it. I don't know if it's on the record, but you can certainly ask him for a few quotes for your article. Just get here. You can hand deliver your article to the *Weekly*, say hi to your old friend Miss Durham, and find out what Nicolae wants. There's a first-class ticket waiting for you at O'Hare under the name of McGillicuddy for a nine o'clock flight tomorrow morning. A limo will meet your plane, and you'll have lunch with Carpathia. Just do it, Buck. Maybe he wants to thank you for introducing him to Hattie. They seem to be hitting it off.

"Now, Buck, if I don't hear from you, I'm going to assume you'll be here. Don't disappoint me."

* * *

"What's the scoop?" Rayford asked.

Chloe imitated the recorded voice. "'The number you have dialed has been disconnected. The new number is . . .'"

"Is what?"

She handed him a scrap of paper. The area code was for New York City. Rayford sighed. "Do you have Buck's new number?"

"It's on the wall by the phone."

* * *

Buck called Bruce Barnes. "I hate to ask you this, Bruce," he said. "But could we get together tonight?"

"I'm about to take a nap," Bruce said.

"You should sleep through. We can do it another time."

"No, I'm not going to sleep through. You want the four of us to meet, or just you and me?"

"Just us."

"How about I come to your place then? I'm getting tired of the office and the empty house."

They agreed on seven o'clock, and Buck decided he would take his phone off the hook after one more call. He didn't want to risk talking to Plank, or worse, Carpathia, until he had talked over and prayed about his plans with Bruce. Steve had said he would assume Buck was coming unless he heard back, but it would be just like Steve to check in with him again. And Carpathia was totally unpredictable.

Buck called Alice, the Chicago bureau secretary. "I need a favor," he said.

"Anything," she said.

He told her he might be flying to New York in the morning but he didn't want Verna Zee knowing about it. "I also don't want to wait any longer for my stuff, so I'd like to bring you my extra key before I head for the airport. If you wouldn't mind bringing that stuff over here for me and locking back up, I'd really appreciate it."

"No problem. I have to be going that way late morning anyway. I'm picking up my fiancé at the airport. Verna doesn't have to know I'm delivering your stuff on the way."

* * *

"You want to go to Dallas with me tomorrow morning, Chlo'?" Rayford asked.

"I don't think so. You're going to be in 777s all day anyway, right?"

Rayford nodded.

"I'll stay around here. Maybe I'll take Buck up on his offer to see his place."

Rayford shook his head. "I can't keep up with you," he said. "Now you *want* to go over there and see the guy who treats you like a sister?"

"I wouldn't be going to see him," she said. "I'd be going to see his place."

"Ah," Rayford said. "My mistake."

* * *

"You hungry?" Buck asked before Bruce had even gotten in the door that evening.

"I could eat," Bruce said.

"Let's go out," Buck suggested. "You can see the place when we get back."

They settled into a booth in a dark corner of a noisy pizza place, and Buck filled Bruce in on the latest from Steve Plank.

"You thinking about going?" Bruce asked.

"I don't know what to think, and if you knew me better, you'd know that's pretty bizarre for me. My instincts as a journalist say yes, of course—go, no question. Who wouldn't? But I know who this guy is, and the last time I saw him he put a bullet through two men."

"I'd sure like to get Rayford's and Chloe's input on this."

"I thought you might," Buck said. "But I'd like to ask you to hold off on that. If I go, I'd rather they not know."

"Buck, if you go, you're going to want all the prayer support you can get."

"Well, you can tell them after I'm gone or something. I should be having lunch with Carpathia around noon or a little after, New York time. You can just tell them I'm on an important trip."

"If that's what you want. But you have to realize, this is not how I see the core group."

"I know, and I agree. But they both might see this as pretty reckless, and maybe it is. If I do it, I don't want to disappoint them until I've had a chance to debrief them and explain myself."

"Why not do that in advance?"

Buck cocked his head and shrugged. "Because I haven't sorted it out myself yet."

"It sounds to me like you've already made up your mind to go."

"I suppose I have."

"Do you want me to talk you out of it?"

"Not really. Do you want to?"

"I'm as much at a loss as you are, Buck. I can't see anything positive coming from it. He's a dangerous man and a murderer. He could wipe you out and get away with it. He did it before with a roomful of witnesses. On the other hand, how long can you dodge him? He gets access to your unlisted phone number two days after you move in. He can find you, and if you avoid him you'll certainly make him mad."

"I know. This way I can just tell him I was busy moving in and getting settled—"

"Which you were."

"—Which I was, and then I'm there on time, on his ticket, wondering what he wants."

"He'll be trying to read you, to find out how much you remember about what he did."

"I don't know what I'll say. I didn't know what I'd do at the installation meeting either. I sensed the evil in that room, but I also knew God was with me. I didn't know what to say or how to react, but as I look back on it, God led me perfectly just to be silent and let Carpathia come to whatever conclusion he wanted to."

"You can depend on God this time, too, Buck. But you should have some sort of plan, go over in your mind what you might say or not say, that sort of thing."

"In other words, instead of sleeping tonight?"

Bruce smiled. "I don't suppose there's much prospect of that."

"I don't suppose."

By the time Buck gave Bruce the quick tour of his place, Buck had decided to go to New York in the morning.

"Why don't you just call your friend . . . ," Bruce began.

"Plank?"

"Yeah, Plank, and tell him you're coming. Then you can quit dreading his call and leave your phone open for me or whoever else might want to talk to you."

Buck nodded. "Good idea."

But after leaving a message for Steve, Buck got no more calls that night. He thought about calling Chloe to tell her not to come by the next morning, but he didn't want to have to tell her why or make up something, and he was convinced she wasn't coming anyway. She certainly hadn't sounded interested that morning.

Buck slept fitfully. Fortunately, the next morning he didn't see Verna until after he had dropped off his key to Alice and was driving out of the lot. Verna was driving in, and she did not see him.

Buck had no identification with the name *McGillicuddy* on it. At O'Hare he picked up an envelope under the phony name and realized that not even the young woman at the counter would have known a ticket was inside.

At the gate he checked in about half an hour before boarding was to begin. "Mr. McGillicuddy," the middle-aged man at the counter said, "you are free to preboard if you wish."

"Thanks," Buck said.

He knew that first-class passengers, frequent flyers, the elderly, and people with small children boarded first. But as Buck went to sit in the waiting area, the man asked, "You don't wish to board right away?"

"I'm sorry?" Buck said. "Now?"

"Yes, sir."

Buck looked around, wondering if he had missed something. Few people were even in line yet, let alone preboarding.

"You have the exclusive privilege of boarding at your leisure, but of course it's not required. Your choice."

Buck shrugged. "Sure, I'll board now."

Only one flight attendant was on the plane. The coach section was still being cleaned. Nevertheless, the flight attendant offered him champagne, juice, or a soft drink and allowed him to look at a breakfast menu.

Buck had never been a drinker, so he declined the champagne, and he was too keyed up to eat. The flight attendant said, "Are you sure? An entire bottle has been set aside for you." She looked at her clipboard. "'Compliments of N. C.'"

"Thanks anyway." Buck shook his head. Was there no end to what Carpathia could—or would—do?

"You don't want to take it with you?"

"No, ma'am. Thanks. Would you like it?"

The attendant gave him a stunned look. "Are you kidding? It's Dom Pérignon!"

"Feel free."

"Really?"

"Sure."

"Well, would you sign that you accepted it so I don't get in trouble for taking it?" Buck signed the clipboard. What next?

"Um, sir?" the attendant said. "What is your name?"

"I'm sorry," Buck said. "I wasn't thinking." He took the clipboard, crossed out his own name, and signed "B. McGillicuddy."

Normally coach passengers would steal glances at those in first class, but now even the other first-class passengers checked Buck out. He had tried not to be showy, but clearly he was getting preferential treatment. He was waiting on board when they arrived, and during the flight the attendants hovered felicitously around him, topping off his drink and asking if he wanted anything else. Whom had Carpathia paid for this treatment, and how much?

At Kennedy International, Buck did not have to look for someone holding a placard with his name on it. A uniformed driver strode directly to him as he appeared at the end of the jetway, reached for his carry-on, and asked if he had checked any bags.

"No."

"Very good, sir. Follow me to the car, please."

Buck was a world traveler and had been treated like both a king and a pauper over the years. Yet even he found this routine unsettling. He followed the driver meekly through the airport to a black stretch limo at the curb. The driver opened the door, and Buck stepped from the sun into the dark interior.

He had not told the driver his name and had not been asked. He assumed this was all part of Carpathia's hospitality. But what if he had been mistaken for someone else? What if this was just a colossal blunder?

As his eyes adjusted to the low light and the tinted windows, Buck noticed a man in a dark suit sitting with his back to the driver, staring at him. "You with the U.N.," Buck asked, "or do you work directly for Mr. Carpathia?"

The man did not respond. Nor did he move. Buck leaned forward. "Excuse me!" he said. "Do you—"

The man put a finger to his lips. *Fair enough,* Buck thought. *I don't need to know.* He was curious, though, whether he was meeting Carpathia at the U.N. or at a restaurant. And it would have been nice to know whether Steve Plank would be there.

"You mind if I talk to the driver?" Buck said. No reaction. "Excuse me, driver?"

But there was Plexiglas between the front seat and the rest of the chassis. The man who looked like a bodyguard still sat staring, and Buck wondered if this would be his last ride. Strangely, he didn't experience the dread that had overwhelmed him that last time. He didn't know if this was from God, or if he was just naive. For all he knew, he could be on his way to his own execution. The only record of his trip was a mistaken signature on the flight attendant's clipboard, and he had crossed that out.

\+ \+ \+

Rayford Steele sat in the cockpit of a Boeing 777 on the military runway in the shadow of Dallas–Fort Worth. A certifying examiner in the first officer's seat had already clarified that he was there only to take notes. Rayford was to run through the proper preflight checklist, communicate to the tower, wait for clearance, take off, follow tower instructions for the proper flight path, enter a holding pattern, and land. He was not told how many times he might have to repeat that entire sequence, or whether anything else would be required.

"Remember," the examiner said, "I'm not here to teach you a thing or to bail you out. I answer no questions, and I touch no controls."

The preflight check went off without a hitch. Taxiing the 777 was different from the huge, bulky feel of the 747, but Rayford managed. When he received clearance, he throttled up and felt the unusually responsive thrust from the aerodynamic wonder. As the plane hurtled down the runway like a racehorse eager to run, Rayford said to the examiner, "This is like the Porsche of airplanes, isn't it?"

The examiner didn't even look at him, let alone answer.

The takeoff was powerful and true, and Rayford was reminded of flying the powerful but much smaller fighter planes from his military days. "More like a Jaguar?" he asked the examiner, and that at least elicited a tiny smile and a slight nod.

Rayford's landing was picture-perfect. The examiner waited until he had taxied back into position and shut down the engines. Then he said, "Let's do that two more times and get you on your way."

* * *

Buck Williams' limo was soon stuck in traffic. Buck wished he'd brought something to read. Why did this have to be so mysterious? He didn't understand the point of his treatment on both ends of the plane ride. The only other time someone had suggested he use an alias was when a competing magazine was making an offer they hoped he couldn't refuse, and they didn't want *Global Weekly* to get wind he was even considering it.

Buck could see the United Nations headquarters in the distance, but he still didn't know whether that was his destination until the driver swept past the appropriate exit. He hoped they were headed somewhere nice for lunch. Besides the fact that he had skipped breakfast, he also liked the prospect of eating more than that of dying.

* * *

As Rayford was escorted to the Pan-Con courtesy van for his ride to DFW airport, his examiner handed him a business-size envelope. "So did I pass?" Rayford said lightly.

"You won't know that for about a week," the man said.

Then what's this? Rayford wondered, entering the van and tearing open the envelope. Inside was a single sheet of United Nations stationery, already embossed with *Hattie Durham, Personal Assistant to the Secretary-General.* The handwritten message read simply:

Captain Steele,
I assume you know that the brand-new Air Force One is a 777.
Your friend,
Hattie Durham

5

BUCK BEGAN TO FEEL more confident that he wasn't in mortal danger. Too many people had been involved in getting him from Chicago to New York and now to midtown. On the other hand, if Nicolae Carpathia could get away with murder in front of more than a dozen eyewitnesses, he could certainly eliminate one magazine writer.

The limo eventually wound its way to the docks, where it stopped on the circle drive in front of the exclusive Manhattan Harbor Yacht Club. As the doorman approached, the chauffeur lowered the front passenger window and waved a finger at him, as if warning him to stay away from the car. Then the bodyguard got out, holding the car door, and Buck stepped into the sunshine. "Follow, please," the bodyguard said.

Buck would have felt right at home in the Yacht Club except that he was walking with a suited man who conspicuously guided him past a long line of patrons waiting for tables. The maître d' glanced up and nodded as Buck followed his escort to the edge of the dining room. There the man stopped and whispered, "You will dine with the gentleman in the booth by the window."

Buck looked. Someone waved vigorously at him, drawing stares. Because the sun was to the man's back, Buck saw only the silhouette of a smallish, stooped man with wild wisps of hair. "I will be back for you at one-thirty sharp," the bodyguard said. "Don't leave the dining room without me."

"But—"

The bodyguard slipped away, and Buck glanced at the maître d', who ignored him. Still self-conscious, Buck made his way through the crowd of tables to the booth by the window, where he was exuberantly greeted by his old friend Chaim Rosenzweig. The man knew enough to whisper in public, but his enthusiasm was boundless.

"Cameron!" the Israeli exulted in his thick accent. "How good to see you! Sit down, sit down! This a lovely place, no? Only the best for friends of the secretary-general."

"Will he be joining us, sir?"

Rosenzweig looked surprised. "No, no! Much too busy. Hardly ever able to get away. Entertaining heads of state, ambassadors, everyone wants a piece of him. I hardly see him more than five minutes a day myself!"

"How long will you be in town?" Buck asked, accepting a menu and allowing the waiter to drape a linen napkin on his lap.

"Not much longer. By the end of this week Nicolae and I are to finish preparations for his visit to Israel. What a glorious day it will be!"

"Tell me about it, Doctor."

"I will! I will! But first we must catch up!" The old man suddenly grew serious and spoke in a somber voice. He reached across the table and covered Buck's hand with both of his. "Cameron, I am your friend. You must tell me straight out. How could you have missed such an important meeting? I am a scientist, yes, but I also consider myself somewhat of a diplomat. I worked hard behind the scenes with Nicolae and with your friend, Mr. Plank, to be sure you were invited. I don't understand."

"I don't understand either," Buck said. What else could he say? Rosenzweig, creator of a formula that made the Israeli deserts bloom like a greenhouse, had been his friend ever since Buck profiled him as *Global Weekly*'s Newsmaker of the Year more than a year before. Rosenzweig was the one who had first mentioned the name Nicolae Carpathia to Buck. Carpathia had been a low-level politico from Romania who had asked for a private audience with Rosenzweig after the formula had become famous.

Heads of state from all over the world had tried to curry favor with Israel to get access to the formula. Many countries sent diplomats to sweet-talk Rosenzweig himself when they got nowhere with the Israeli prime minister. Oddly, Carpathia was the one who most impressed Rosenzweig. He had arranged the visit himself and come on his own, and at the time he seemed to have no power to make any deals, even if Rosenzweig had been open to one. All Carpathia had sought from Rosenzweig was his good will. And he got it. Now, Buck realized, it was paying off.

"Where were you?" Dr. Rosenzweig asked.

"That's the question of the ages," Buck said. "Where are any of us?"

Rosenzweig's eyes twinkled, though Buck felt like a fool. He was talking gibberish, but he didn't know what else to say. He couldn't tell the man, *I was there! I saw the same thing you saw, but you were brainwashed by Carpathia because he's the Antichrist!*

Rosenzweig was a bright, quick man with a love for intrigue. "So, you don't want to tell me. All right. Not being there was your loss. Of course, you were spared the horror it turned into, but what a historic meeting nonetheless. Get the salmon. You'll love it."

Buck had always, *always* made it a habit to ignore recommendations in restaurants. It probably was one of the reasons for his nickname. He realized how rattled he was when he ordered what Rosenzweig suggested. And he loved it.

"Let me ask *you* something now, Dr. Rosenzweig."

"Please! Please, *Chaim*."

"I can't call you Chaim, sir. A Nobel Prize winner?"

"Please, you will honor me. Please!"

"All right, Chaim," Buck said, barely able to get the name out. "Why am I here? What is this all about?"

The old man pulled the napkin from his lap, wiped his whole bearded face with it, balled it up, and plopped it onto his plate. He pushed the plate aside, sat back, and crossed his legs. Buck had seen people warm to a subject before, but never with as much relish as Chaim Rosenzweig.

"So, the journalist in you comes out, eh? Let me begin by telling you that this is your lucky day. Nicolae has in mind for you an honor that is such a privilege I cannot tell you."

"But you will tell me, won't you, sir?"

"I will tell you what I have been instructed to tell you, and no more. The rest will come from Nicolae himself." Rosenzweig glanced at his watch, a plastic-banded twenty-dollar toy that seemed incongruous with his international status. "Good. We have time. He has allotted thirty minutes for your visit, so please keep that in mind. I know you are friends and you may want to apologize for missing his meeting, but just remember that he has a lot to offer you and not much time to do it. He flies to Washington late this afternoon for a meeting with the president. By the way, the president offered to meet in New York, if you can imagine, but Nicolae, humble as he is, would hear nothing of it."

"You find Carpathia humble?"

"Probably as humble as any leader I have ever met, Cameron. Of course, I know many public servants and private people who are humble and have a right to be! But most politicians, heads of state, world leaders, they are full of themselves. Many of them have much to be proud of and in many ways it is their egos that allow them to accomplish what they accomplish. But never have I seen a man like this."

"He's pretty impressive," Buck admitted.

"That's not the half of it," Dr. Rosenzweig insisted. "Think about it, Cameron. He has not sought these positions. He rose from a low position in the Romanian government to become president of that nation when an election was not even scheduled. He resisted it!"

I'll bet, Buck thought.

"And when he was invited to speak at the United Nations not a month ago, he was so intimidated and felt so unworthy, he almost declined. But you were there! You heard the speech. I would have nominated him for prime minister of Israel if I thought he would have taken it! Almost immediately the secretary-general stepped down and insisted Nicolae replace him. And he was elected unanimously, enthusiastically, and he has been endorsed by nearly every head of state around the world.

"Cameron, he has ideas upon ideas! He is the consummate diplomat. He speaks so many languages that he hardly ever needs an interpreter, even for the chiefs of some of the remote tribes in South America and Africa! The other day he shared a few phrases understood only by an Australian Aborigine!"

"Let me just stop you for a second, Chaim," Buck said. "You know, of course, that in exchange for stepping down from the secretary-generalship of the U.N., Mwangati Ngumo was promised access to your formula for use in Botswana. It wasn't quite so selfless and altruistic as it seemed, and—"

"Of course, Nicolae has told me all about that. But it was not part of any agreement. It was a gesture of his personal gratitude for what President Ngumo has done for the United Nations over the years."

"But how can he show his personal gratitude by giving away *your* formula, sir? No one else anywhere has access to it, and—"

"I was more than happy to offer it."

"You were?" Buck's mind reeled. Was there no limit to Carpathia's persuasive power?

The old man uncrossed his legs and leaned forward, his elbows on the table. "Cameron, it all ties together. This is part of why you're here. The agreement with the former secretary-general was an experiment, a model."

"I'm listening, Doctor."

"It's too early to tell, of course, but if the formula works as well as it has in Israel, Botswana will immediately become one of the most fertile countries in all of Africa, if not the world. Already President Ngumo has seen his stature rise within his own nation. Everyone agrees he was distracted from his duties at the U.N. and that the world is better now for the new leadership."

Buck shrugged, but apparently Rosenzweig didn't notice. "And so Carpathia plans to do more of this, brokering your formula for favors?"

"No, no! You're missing the point. Yes, I have persuaded the Israeli government to license use of the formula to the secretary-general of the United Nations."

"Oh, Chaim! For what? Billions of dollars that Israel no longer needs? It makes no sense! Having the formula made you the richest nation on earth for its size and solved myriad problems, but it was the exclusivity that made it work! Why do you think the Russians attacked you? They don't need your land! There's no oil to be found! They wanted the formula! Imagine if all the vast reaches of that nation were fertile!"

Dr. Rosenzweig held up a hand. "I understand that, Cameron. But money has nothing to do with this. I need no money. Israel needs no money."

"Then what could Carpathia offer that is worthy of the trade?"

"What has Israel prayed for since the beginning of her existence, Cameron? And I am not talking about her rebirth in 1948. From the beginning of time as the chosen people of God, what have we prayed for?"

Buck's blood ran cold, and he could only sit there and nod resignedly. Rosenzweig answered his own question. "*Shalom.* Peace. 'Pray for the peace of Israel.' We are a fragile, vulnerable land. We know God Almighty supernaturally protected us from the onslaught of the Russians. Do you know that there was so much death among their troops that the bodies had to be buried in a common grave, a crater gouged from our precious soil by one of their bombs, which God rendered harmless? We had to burn some of their bodies and bones. And the debris from their weapons of destruction was so massive that we have used it as a raw resource and are refabricating it into marketable goods. Cameron," he added ominously, "so many of their planes crashed—well, all of them, of course. They still had burnable fuel, enough that we estimate we will be able to use it for five to eight more years. Can you see why peace is so attractive to us?"

"Chaim, you said yourself that God Almighty protected you. There could be no other explanation for what happened the night of that invasion. With God on your side, why do you need to barter with Carpathia for protection?"

"Cameron, Cameron," Rosenzweig said wearily, "history has shown our God to be capricious when it comes to our welfare. From the children of Israel wandering forty years in the desert to the Six-Day War to the Russian invasion to now, we do not understand him. He lends us his favor when it suits his eternal plan, which we cannot comprehend. We pray, we seek him, we try to curry his favor. But in the meantime we believe that God helps those who help themselves. You know, of course, that this is why you are here."

"I know nothing," Buck said.

"Well, it's part of why you're here. You understand that such an agreement takes a lot of homework—"

"What agreement are we talking about?"

"I'm sorry, Cameron, I thought you were following. You do not think it was easy even for me, despite my stature within my own country, to persuade the powers to release a license to the formula even to a man as attractive as Nicolae."

"Of course not."

"And you are right. Some of the meetings went long into the night, and every time I felt I had convinced someone, another was brought in. Every new ear had to be convinced. Many times I nearly gave up in despair. But finally, finally, with many conditions, I was empowered to hammer out an arrangement with the United Nations."

"With Carpathia, you mean."

"Of course. Make no mistake. He is the United Nations now."

"You got that right," Buck said.

"Part of the agreement is that I become part of his senior staff, an adviser. I will cochair the committee that decides where the formula will be licensed."

"And no money changes hands?"

"None."

"And Israel gets protection from her neighbors from the United Nations?"

"Oh, it is much more complex than that, Cameron. You see, the formula is now tied into Nicolae's global disarmament policy. Any nation even suspected of resisting the destruction of 90 percent of its weapons and the surrender of the remaining 10 percent to Nicolae—or I should say to the U.N. —will never be allowed to even be considered as an applicant for a license. Nicolae has pledged that he—and I will be there to ensure this, of course—will be more than judicious in licensing our nearest neighbors and most dangerous enemies."

"There has to be more than that."

"Oh, there is, but the crux of it is this, Cameron. Once the world has been disarmed, Israel should not have to worry about protecting her borders."

"That's naive."

"Not as naive as it might appear, because if there is one thing Nicolae Carpathia is not, it is naive. Knowing full well that some nations may hoard or hide weapons or produce new ones, the full agreement between the sovereign state of Israel and Security Council of the United Nations—with the personal signature of Nicolae Carpathia—makes a solemn promise. Any nation that threatens Israel will suffer immediate extinction, using the full complement of weaponry available to the U.N. With every country donating 10 percent, you can imagine the firepower."

"What I cannot imagine, Chaim, is an avowed pacifist, a rabid global-disarmament proponent for his entire political career, threatening to blow countries off the face of the earth."

"It's only semantics, Cameron," Rosenzweig said. "Nicolae is a pragmatist. There is a good bit of the idealist in him, of course, but he knows that the best way to keep the peace is to have the wherewithal to enforce it."

"And this agreement lasts for—?"

"As long as we want it. We offered ten years, but Nicolae said he would not require the freedom to license the formula for that long. He said he would ask for only seven years, and then the full rights to the formula return to us. Most generous. And if we want to renew the agreement every seven years, we are free to do that, too."

You won't have any need for a peace treaty in seven years, Buck thought. "So, what does this have to do with me?" he asked.

"That's the best part," Rosenzweig said. "At least for me, because it honors you. It is no secret that Nicolae is aware of your status as the most accomplished journalist in the world. And to prove that he bears no ill will for your snub of his last invitation, he is going to ask you to come to Israel for the signing of the treaty."

Buck shook his head.

"I know it is overwhelming," Rosenzweig said.

\+ \+ \+

Rayford's plane hit the ground at O'Hare at one o'clock Chicago time. He called home and got the answering machine. "Yeah, Chloe," he said, "I'm back earlier than I thought. Just wanted you to know I'll be there within the hour and—"

Chloe grabbed the phone. She sounded awful. "Hi, Dad," she mumbled.

"You under the weather?"

"No. Just upset. Dad, did you know that Buck Williams is living with someone?"

"What!?"

"It's true. And they're engaged! I saw her. She was carrying boxes into his condo. A skinny little spike-haired girl in a short skirt."

"Maybe you had the wrong place."

"It was the right place."

"You're jumping to conclusions."

"Dad, listen to me. I was so mad I just drove around a while, then sat in a parking lot and cried. Then around noon I went to see him at the *Global Weekly* office, and there she was, getting out of her car. I said, 'Do you work here?' and she said, 'Yes, may I help you?' and I said, 'I think I saw you earlier today,' and she said, 'You might have. I was with my fiancé. Is there someone here you need to see?' I just turned and left, Dad."

"You didn't talk to Buck then?"

"Are you kidding? I may never talk to him again. Just a minute. Someone's at the door."

A minute later Chloe came back on. "I can't believe it. If he thinks this makes any difference . . ."

"What?"

"Flowers! And of course they're anonymous. He had to have seen me driving by and knew how I'd feel. Unless you want these, you'll find them in the trash when you get home."

\+ + +

At a few minutes after two in New York, Buck waited with Chaim Rosenzweig in the opulent waiting room outside the office of the secretary-general of the United Nations. Chaim was merrily going on about something, and Buck pretended to pay attention. He was praying silently, not knowing if his foreboding sense of evil was psychological because he knew Nicolae Carpathia was nearby, or if the man truly emitted some sort of demonic aura detectable to followers of Christ. Buck was warmed by the knowledge that Bruce was praying for him right then, and he was having second thoughts about not informing Rayford and Chloe of his trip. His return ticket was for the 5 p.m. flight, so he knew he'd be back in time for the first of the 8 p.m. study sessions Bruce had planned. Buck looked forward to it already. He might even see if Chloe wanted to have a late dinner, just the two of them, before the meeting.

"So what do you think about that?" Dr. Rosenzweig said.

"I'm so sorry, Doctor," Buck said. "My mind was elsewhere."

"Cameron, don't be nervous. Nicolae was upset, yes, but he has only good things in store for you."

Buck shrugged and nodded.

"Anyway, I was saying. My dear friend Rabbi Tsion Ben-Judah has finished his three-year study, and it wouldn't surprise me if he wins a Nobel Prize for it."

"His three-year study?"

"You weren't listening at all, were you, my friend?"

"I'm sorry."

"You must do better when you are with Nicolae, promise me."

"I will. Forgive me."

"It's all right. But listen, Rabbi Ben-Judah was commissioned by the Hebrew Institute of Biblical Research to do a three-year study."

"A study of what?"

"Something about the prophecies relating to Messiah so we Jews will recognize him when he comes."

Buck was stunned. The Messiah had come, and the Jews left behind had missed him. When he had come the first time most did not recognize him. What should Buck say to his friend? If he declared himself a "Tribulation saint," as Bruce liked to refer to new believers since the Rapture, what might he be doing to himself? Rosenzweig was a confidant of Carpathia's. Buck wanted to say that a legitimate study of messianic prophecies could lead only to Jesus. But he said only, "What *are* the major prophecies pointing to the Messiah?"

"To tell you the truth," Dr. Rosenzweig said, "I don't know. I was not a religious Jew until God destroyed the Russian Air Force, and I can't say I'm devout now. I always took the messianic prophecies the way I took the rest of the Torah. Symbolic. The rabbi at the temple I attended occasionally in Tel Aviv said himself that it was not important whether we believed that God was a literal being or just a concept. That fit with my humanist view of the world. Religious people, Jewish or otherwise, seldom impressed me any more than the atheist with a good heart.

"Dr. Ben-Judah was a student of mine twenty-five years ago. He was always an unabashed religious Jew, Orthodox but short of a fundamentalist. Of course he became a rabbi, but certainly not because of anything I taught him. I liked him and always have. He recently told me he had finished the study and that it was the most fulfilling and rewarding work he has ever done." Rosenzweig paused. "I suppose you are wondering why I tell you this."

"Frankly, yes."

"I'm lobbying for Rabbi Ben-Judah's inclusion on Nicolae Carpathia's staff."

"As?"

"Spiritual adviser."

"He's looking for one?"

"Not that he knows of!" Rosenzweig said, roaring with laughter and slapping his knee. "But so far he has trusted my judgment. That's why you're here."

Buck lifted an eyebrow. "I thought it was because Carpathia thinks I'm the best journalist in the world."

Dr. Rosenzweig leaned forward and whispered conspiratorially, "And why do you think he believes that?"

✣ ✣ ✣

Rayford had had trouble reaching Chloe from his car phone, but he finally got through. "Wondered if you wanted to go out with your old man tonight," he suggested, thinking she needed to be cheered up.

"I don't know," she said. "I appreciate it, Dad, but we're going to Bruce's eight o'clock meeting, aren't we?"

"I'd like to," Rayford said.

"Let's stay in. I'm all right. I was just on the phone with Bruce. I wanted to know if he knew whether Buck was coming tonight."

"And?"

"He wasn't entirely sure. He hoped so. I hope not."

"Chloe!"

"I'm just afraid of what I'll say, Dad. No wonder he's been cool toward me with that, that, whatever-you-call-her in his life. But the flowers! What was that all about?"

"You don't even know they were from him."

"Oh, Dad! Unless they were from you, they were from Buck."

Rayford laughed. "I wish I'd thought of it."

"So do I."

* * *

Hattie Durham approached Buck and Chaim Rosenzweig, and they both stood. "Mr. Williams!" she said, embracing him. "I haven't seen you since I took this job."

Yes, you have, Buck thought. *You just don't remember.*

"The secretary-general and Mr. Plank will see you now," she told Buck. She turned to Dr. Rosenzweig. "Doctor, the secretary-general asks that you be prepared to join the meeting in about twenty-five minutes."

"Certainly," the old man said. He winked at Buck and squeezed his shoulder.

Buck followed Hattie past several desks and down a mahogany-appointed hallway, and he realized he had never seen her out of uniform. Today she wore a tailored suit that made her look like a classy, wealthy, sophisticated woman. The look only enhanced her stunning beauty. Even her speech seemed more cultured than he remembered. Her exposure to Nicolae Carpathia seemed to have improved her presence.

Hattie tapped lightly on the office door and poked her head in. "Mr. Secretary-General and Mr. Plank, Cameron Williams of *Global Weekly*." Hattie pushed the door open and slipped away as Nicolae Carpathia advanced, reaching for Buck's hand with both of his. Buck seemed strangely calmed by the man and his smile. "Buck!" he said. "May I call you Buck?"

"You always have," Buck said.

"Come! Come! Sit! You and Steve know each other, of course."

Buck was more struck with Steve's appearance than with Carpathia's. Nicolae had always dressed formally, with perfectly coordinated accessories, suit coat buttoned, everything in place. But Steve, despite his position as executive editor of one of the most prestigious magazines in the world, had not always dressed the way you might expect a journalist to dress. He had always worn the obligatory suspenders and long-sleeved shirts, of course, but he was usually seen with his tie loosened and his sleeves rolled up, looking like a middle-aged yuppie or an Ivy League student.

Today, however, Steve looked like a clone of Carpathia. He carried a thin, black-leather portfolio and from head to toe looked as if he had come off the cover of a Fortune 500 edition of *GQ*. Even his hairstyle had a European flair—razor cut, blow-dried, styled, and moussed. He wore new, designer-frame glasses, a charcoal suit just this side of pitch-black, a white shirt with a collar pin and tie that probably cost what he used to pay for a sports coat. The shoes were soft leather and looked Italian, and if Buck wasn't mistaken, there was a new diamond ring on Steve's right hand.

Carpathia pulled an extra chair from his conference table, added it to the two before his desk, and sat with Buck and Steve. *Right out of a management book,* Buck thought. *Break down the barrier between the superior and the subordinate.*

Yet despite the attempt at an equal playing field, it was clear the intent of the meeting was to impress Buck. And he was impressed. Hattie and Steve had already changed enough to be nearly unrecognizable. And every time Buck looked at Carpathia's strong, angular features and quick, seemingly genuine disarming smile, he wished with everything in him that the man was who he appeared to be and not who Buck knew him to be.

He never forgot, never lost sight of the fact that he was in the presence of the slickest, most conniving personality in history. He only wished he knew someone as charming as Carpathia who was real.

Buck felt for Steve, and yet he had not been consulted before Steve had left *Global Weekly* for Carpathia's staff. Now, much as Buck wanted to tell him about his newfound faith, he could trust no one. Unless Carpathia had the supernatural ability to know everything, Buck hoped and prayed he would not detect that Buck was an enemy agent within his camp. "Let me begin with a humorous idiom," Carpathia said, "and then we will excuse Steve and have a heart-to-heart, just you and me, hmm?"

Buck nodded.

"Something I have heard only since coming to this country is the phrase 'the elephant in the room.' Have you heard that phrase, Buck?"

"You mean about people who get together and don't talk about the obvious, like the fact that one of them has just been diagnosed with a terminal illness?"

"Exactly. So, let us talk about the elephant in the room and be done with it, and then we can move on. All right?"

Buck nodded again, his pulse increasing.

"I confess I was confused and a little hurt that you did not attend the private meeting where I installed the new ambassadors. However, as it turned out, it would have been as traumatic for you as it was for the rest of us."

It was all Buck could do to keep from being sarcastic. One thing he could not and would not do was apologize. How could he say he was sorry for missing a meeting he had not missed?

"I wanted to be there and wouldn't have missed it for anything," Buck said. Carpathia seemed to look right through him and sat as if waiting for the rest of the thought. "Frankly," Buck added, "that whole day seems a blur to me now." A blur with vivid details he would never forget.

Carpathia seemed to loosen up. His formal pose melted and he leaned forward, elbows on his knees, and looked from Buck to Steve and back. He looked peeved. "So, all right," he said, "apparently there is no excuse, no apology, no explanation."

Buck glanced at Steve, who seemed to be trying to communicate with his eyes and a slight nod, as if to say, *Say something, Buck! Apologize! Explain!*

"What can I say?" Buck said. "I feel badly about that day." That was as close as he would come to saying what they wanted him to say. Buck knew Steve was innocent. Steve truly believed Buck had not been there. Carpathia, of course, had masterminded and choreographed the whole charade. Acting upset that he wasn't getting an apology or an explanation was the perfect move, Buck thought. Clearly, Carpathia was fishing for some evidence that Buck knew what had happened. All Buck could do was play dumb and be evasive and pray that God would somehow blind Carpathia to the truth that Buck was a believer and that he had been protected from susceptibility to Carpathia's power.

"All right," Carpathia said, sitting back and composing himself again. "We all feel bad, do we not? I grieve the loss of two compatriots, one a dear friend for many years." Buck felt his stomach turn. "Now, Buck, I want to talk to you as a journalist, and we will excuse our friend Mr. Plank."

Steve stood and patted Buck on the shoulder, leaving quietly. Buck became painfully aware that now it was just him and God sitting knee-to-knee with Nicolae Carpathia.

But it wasn't knee-to-knee for long. Nicolae suddenly rose and went back around his desk to the executive chair behind it. Just before he sat, he touched the intercom button, and Buck heard the door open behind him.

Hattie Durham whispered, "Excuse me," took the extra chair from in front of the desk, and put it back at the conference table. As she was leaving, she adjusted and straightened the chair Steve had used. Just as quietly, she slipped out. Buck thought that very strange, this seemingly scripted arrangement of the entire meeting, from the formal announcement of his presence, to the staging of who would be there and where they would sit. With the office now back to the way it was when Buck entered and Carpathia ensconced behind his massive desk, all pretense of equalizing the power base was gone.

Yet Carpathia still had the charm turned all the way up. He intertwined his fingers and stared at Buck, smiling. "Cameron Williams," he said slowly. "How does it feel to be the most celebrated journalist of your time?"

What kind of a question was that? It was precisely because Buck didn't ask such questions that he *was* a respected journalist. "Right now I'm just a demoted hack," he said.

"And humble besides," Carpathia said, grinning. "In a moment I am going to make clear to you that even though your stock may have fallen at *Global Weekly*, it has not fallen in the eyes of the rest of the world, and certainly not with me. I should have been more upset by your missing my meeting than your publisher was, and yet he overreacted. We can put these things behind us and move on. One mistake does not negate a lifetime of achievement."

Carpathia paused as if he expected Buck to respond. Buck was becoming more and more fond of silence. It seemed to be the right choice with Carpathia, and it certainly was the way God had led him during the murderous meeting when Carpathia had polled everyone to assess what they had seen. Buck believed silence had saved his life.

"By the way," Carpathia said when it was clear Buck had nothing to say, "do you have with you your cover story on the theories behind the vanishings?"

Buck couldn't hide his surprise. "As a matter of fact, I do."

Carpathia shrugged. "Steve told me about it. I would love to see it."

"I'm afraid I wouldn't be able to show it to anyone until the *Weekly* gets the final draft."

"Surely they have seen your working copy."

"Of course."

"Steve said you might want a quote or two from me."

"Frankly, unless you have something new, I think your views have already been so widely broadcast that they would be old to our readers."

Carpathia looked hurt.

"I mean," Buck said, "you still hold to the nuclear reaction with natural forces idea, right? That lightning may have triggered some spontaneous interaction between all the stockpiled nuclear weapons, and—"

"You know your friend Dr. Rosenzweig also subscribes to that theory."

"I understand that, yes sir."

"But it will not be represented in your article?"

"Sure it will. I thought the question was whether I needed a fresh quote from you. Unless your view has changed, I do not."

Carpathia looked at his watch. "As you know, I am on a tight schedule. Your trip was all right? Accommodations acceptable? A good lunch? Dr. Rosenzweig filled you in some?"

Buck nodded to every question.

"Assuming he told you about the U.N. treaty with Israel and that the signing will be a week from today in Jerusalem, let me extend a personal invitation to you to be there."

"I doubt the *Weekly* would send a Chicago staff writer to an international event of that magnitude."

"I am not asking that you join the press corps of thousands from around the world who will be seeking credentials as soon as the announcement is made. I am inviting you to be part of my delegation, to sit at the table with me. It will be a privilege no other media person in the world will have."

"*Global Weekly* has a policy that its journalists are not to accept any favors that might—"

"Buck, Buck," Carpathia said. "I am sorry to interrupt, but I will be very surprised if you are still an employee of *Global Weekly* a week from today. Very surprised."

Buck raised his eyebrows and looked skeptically at Carpathia. "Do you know something I don't know?" And as soon as it was out of his mouth, Buck realized he had unintentionally asked the core question of this meeting.

Carpathia laughed. "I know of no plans to fire you, no. I think the punishment for your blown assignment has already been meted out. And though you turned down an offer of employment from me before, I truly believe I have an opportunity for you that will change your mind."

Don't count on it, Buck thought. But he said, "I'm listening."

6

"BEFORE I GET INTO THAT," Carpathia said, stalling, a maddening trait of his that never failed to annoy Buck, "let me just reflect on something. Do you remember when I assured you that I could make a problem go away for you?"

Did Buck remember? Up to the day of the murders, it had been his most chilling look at Carpathia. An informant of Buck's, a Welshman with whom he had gone to college, had turned up dead after getting too close to an international banking scheme involving his own boss, Joshua Todd-Cothran, head of the London Exchange.

Buck had flown to England to investigate with a Scotland Yard friend, only to be nearly killed himself when the Yard agent died in a car bombing. Buck determined that what had been ruled the suicide of his Welsh friend had actually been a homicide, and Buck had had to escape Britain under a phony name. When he got back to New York, none other than Nicolae Carpathia promised him that if Todd-Cothran had been involved in anything underhanded, Carpathia himself would take care of it. Not long after, Todd-Cothran died before Buck's eyes at Carpathia's hand in a double murder that only Buck seemed to recall.

"I remember," Buck said flatly, the understatement of his life.

"I made clear that I would not tolerate insincerity or deviousness in my administration of the U.N. And the Todd-Cothran situation took care of itself, did it not?"

Took care of itself? Buck remained silent.

"Do you believe in luck, Mr. Williams?"

"No."

"You do not believe that luck comes to those who do the right things?"

"No."

"I do. I always have. Oh, the occasional bumbler or even criminal gets lucky once in a while. But usually the better someone does his job, the luckier he seems to be. You follow?"

"No."

"Let me simplify. You were in dire danger. People around you were dying.

I told you I would take care of that, and yet obviously I could have nothing personally to do with it. I confess that when I so boldly assured you that I could make your problems go away, I was not sure how I would effect that. Not being a religious person, I have to say that in this case, good karma was with me. Would you not agree?"

"To be perfectly honest with you, sir, I have no idea what you're saying."

"And you wonder why I like you so much?" Carpathia smiled broadly. "You are a person I need! What I am saying is that you and I both had a problem. You were on someone's hit list, and I had two people in my trust who were involved in serious crimes. By committing suicide and killing Todd-Cothran in the process, my old friend Jonathan Stonagal took care of the problems we both had. That is good karma, if I understand my Eastern friends."

"So while you say you're grieving over the deaths of your friends, in reality you're glad they're both dead."

Carpathia sat back, looking impressed. "Precisely. Glad for your sake. I grieve their loss. They were old friends and once trusted advisers, even mentors. But when they went bad, I was going to have to do something about it. And make no mistake, I would have. But Jonathan did it for me."

"Imagine that," Buck said. Carpathia's eyes bored into him as he seemed to examine Buck's mind.

"I never cease to be amazed," Nicolae continued, "at how quickly things change."

"I can't argue with that."

"Not a month ago I served in the Romanian senate. The next minute I was president of the country, and an hour later I became secretary-general of the United Nations."

Buck smiled at Carpathia's attempt at hyperbole, and yet his ascent to power had seemed almost that fast. Buck's smile faded when Carpathia added, "It is almost enough to make an atheist believe in God."

"But you ascribe it to good karma," Buck said.

"Frankly," Carpathia said, "it merely humbles me. In many ways it does seem this has been my destiny, but I never would have dreamed it or imagined it, let alone planned it. I have sought no office since I ran for the Romanian senate, and yet this has been thrust upon me. I can do nothing less than give it my all and hope I act in a manner worthy of the trust that has been placed in me."

A month earlier, Buck would have cursed the man to his face. He wondered if his sentiment showed. Apparently it did not.

"Buck," Carpathia continued, "I need you. And this time I am not going to take no for an answer."

* * *

Rayford hung up his car phone after talking with Bruce Barnes. Rayford had asked if he could come a few minutes early that night to show Bruce something, but he did not tell him what it was. He pulled the note from Hattie from his breast pocket and spread it across the steering wheel. What in the world did it mean, and how did she, or obviously her boss, know where to find him?

His car phone rang. He pushed a button and spoke into the speaker embedded in the visor in front of him. "Ray Steele," he said.

"Daddy, have you been on the phone?"

"Yeah, why?"

"Earl's been trying to reach you."

"What's up?"

"I don't know. Sounds serious though. I told him you were on the way home and he was surprised. He said something about nobody ever keeping him informed about anything. He thought you were coming back from Dallas later and—"

"So did I."

"Anyway, he had been hoping to catch you at O'Hare before you left."

"I'll call him. See you tonight. I'm going to go a little early to talk with Bruce. You can come with me and wait in the outer office, or we can take two cars."

"Yeah, right, Dad. I'm so sure I'll wait in the outer office and have to face Buck alone. I don't think so. You go ahead. I'll be a few minutes late."

"Oh, Chloe."

"Don't start, Dad."

* * *

Buck felt bold. Curious, but bold. Certainly he wanted to hear what Carpathia had in mind, but it seemed the man was most impressed when Buck spoke his mind. Buck wasn't ready to tell him all that he knew and what he really thought, and he probably never would, but he felt he owed it to himself to speak up now.

"I probably shouldn't have come without knowing what you wanted," Buck said. "I almost didn't. I took my time getting back to Steve."

"Oh, let us be frank and serious," Carpathia said. "I am a diplomat, and I am sincere. You must know me well enough by now to know that." He paused as if waiting for Buck to assure him it was true. Buck did not even nod. "But, come, come. You do not apologize or explain why you ignored my last invitation, and yet I hold no grudge. You could not have afforded to snub me again."

"I couldn't? What would have happened to me?"

"Perhaps it would have gotten back to Stanton Bailey again, and you would have been demoted even further. Or fired. Disgraced either way. I am not naive, Buck. I know the origin of your nickname, and it is part of what I admire so much about you. But you cannot keep bucking me. It is not that I consider myself anything special, but the world and the news media do. People ignore me at their peril."

"So I should be afraid of you, and that's why I should look favorably on whatever role you're about to offer me?"

"Oh, no! Afraid of ignoring me, yes, but only for the obvious, practical reasons I just outlined. But that fear should motivate you only to come when I ask and provide your way. It should never be the basis on which you decide to work with me. It will not take fear to persuade you on that score." Buck wanted to ask what it would take, but it was clear that was what Nicolae wanted him to ask, so he again said nothing.

"What is that old phrase from the movies you Americans are so fond of? 'An offer you cannot refuse'? That is what I have for you."

\+ \+ \+

"Rayford, I hate to do this to you, but we've got to talk face-to-face, and this afternoon."

"Earl, I'm almost home."

"I'm sorry. I wouldn't ask you if it wasn't important."

"What's up?"

"If I could tell you over the phone, I wouldn't be apologizing about insisting on the face-to-face, would I?"

"You want me to head back there right now?"

"Yes, and I'm sorry."

\+ \+ \+

"There are laws and there are rules," Carpathia was saying. "Laws I obey. Rules I do not mind ignoring if I can justify it. For instance, in your country you are not allowed to bring your own food into a sporting arena. Something about wanting to keep all the concession money for management. Fine. I can see why they would have such a rule, and if I were the owner, I would probably try to enforce the same. But I would not consider it a criminal act to smuggle in my own snack. You follow me?"

"I guess."

"There is a rule that pertains to heads of state and official bodies, like the United Nations. It is understood that only in a repressive dictatorship would the ruler have any ownership or financial interest in a major news media outlet."

"Absolutely."

"But is it a law?"

"In the United States it is."

"But internationally?"

"Not uniformly."

"There you go."

Carpathia clearly wanted Buck to ask where he was going, but Buck would not. "You are fond of the term *bottom line*," Nicolae said. "I have heard you use it. I know what it means. The bottom line here is that I am going to purchase major media, and I want you to be part of it."

"Part of what?"

"Part of the management team. I will become sole owner of the great newspapers of the world, the television networks, the wire services. You may run for me any one of those you wish."

"The secretary-general of the U.N. owning major media? How could you ever possibly justify that?"

"If laws need to be changed, they will change. If ever the time was right to have a positive influence on the media, Buck, it is now. Do you not agree?"

"I do not."

"Millions have vanished. People are scared. They are tired of war, tired of bloodshed, tired of chaos. They need to know that peace is within our grasp. The response to my plan to disarm the world has been met with almost unanimous favor."

"Not by the American militia movement."

"Bless them," Carpathia said, smiling. "If we accomplish what I have proposed, do you really think a bunch of zealots running around in the woods wearing fatigues and shooting off popguns will be a threat to the global community? Buck, I am merely responding to the heartfelt wishes of the decent citizens of the world. Of course there will still be bad apples, and I would never forbid the news media to give them fair coverage, but I do this with the purest of motives. I do not need money. I have a sea of money."

"The U.N. is that flush?"

"Buck, let me tell you something that few others know, and because I trust you, I know you will keep my confidence. Jonathan Stonagal named me the sole beneficiary of his estate."

Buck could not hide his surprise. That Carpathia might be named in the multibillionaire's will would have shocked no one, but sole beneficiary? That meant Carpathia now owned the major banks and financial institutions in the world.

"But, but, his family . . . ," Buck managed.

"I have already settled out of court with them. They pledge to keep silence and never again contest the will, and they get 100 million dollars each."

"That would silence me," Buck said. "But how much did they sacrifice by not getting their fair share?"

Carpathia smiled. "And you wonder why I admire you? You know that Jonathan was the wealthiest man in history. To him money was simply a commodity. He did not even carry a wallet. In his own charming way, he was frugal. He would let a lesser man pick up a dinner check, and in the next breath buy a company for hundreds of millions. It was just numbers to him."

"And what will it be for you?"

"Buck, I say this from the bottom of my heart. What this tremendous resource gives me is the opportunity to achieve my lifelong dream. I want peace. I want global disarmament. I want the peoples of the world to live as one. The world should have seen itself as one village as soon as air travel and satellite communications brought us all together decades ago. But it took the vanishings—which may have been the best thing that ever happened to this planet—to finally bring us together. When I speak, I am heard and seen nearly all over the world.

"I am not interested in personal wealth," Nicolae continued. "My history proves that. I know the value of money. I do not mind using it as a form of persuasion, if it is what motivates a person. But all I care about is mankind." Buck was sick to his stomach, and his mind was flooded with images. Carpathia staged Stonagal's "suicide" and manufactured more witnesses than any court would ever need. Now was the man trying to impress him with his altruism, his largesse?

Buck's mind flew to Chicago, and he suddenly missed Chloe. What was this? Something in him longed to simply talk with her. Of all the times for it to become crystal clear that he did not want to be "just friends," this was the worst. Was it merely Carpathia's shocking admission that made him long for something or someone comfortable and safe? There was a purity, a freshness about Chloe. How had he mistaken his feelings for her as mere fascination with a younger woman?

Carpathia stared at him. "Buck, you will never tell a living soul what I have told you today. No one must ever know. You will work for me, and you will enjoy privileges and opportunities beyond your imagination. You will think about it, but you will say yes in the end."

Buck fought to keep his mind on Chloe. He admired her father, and he was developing a deep bond with Bruce Barnes, a person with whom he would never have had anything in common before becoming a follower of Christ. But Chloe was the object of his attention, and he realized that God had planted these thoughts to help him resist the hypnotic, persuasive power of Nicolae Carpathia.

Did he love Chloe Steele? He couldn't say. He hardly knew her. Was he attracted to her? Of course. Did he want to date her, to begin a relationship with her? Absolutely.

"Buck, if you could live anywhere in the world, where would it be?"

Buck heard the question and stalled, pursing his lips to appear to be thinking about it. All he could think of was Chloe. What would she think if she knew this? Here he sat as the most-talked-about man in the world offered him a blank check, and all he could think about was a twenty-year-old college dropout from Chicago.

"Where, Buck?"

"I'm living there now," Buck said.

"Chicago?"

"Chicago."

In truth, he suddenly couldn't imagine living apart from Chloe. Her body language and responses the last couple of days told him he had alienated her somehow, but he had to believe it was not too late to turn that around. When he showed interest, she had too. When he gave an unclear signal, so did she. He would clarify his interest and hope for the best. There were still serious questions to consider, but for now all he knew was that he missed her terribly.

"Why would anyone want to live in Chicago?" Carpathia asked. "I know the airport is central, but what else does it offer? I am asking you to expand your horizons, Buck. Think Washington, London, Paris, Rome, New Babylon. You have lived here for years, and you know it is the capital of the world—at least until we relocate our headquarters."

"You asked me where I would like to live if I could live anywhere," Buck said. "Frankly, I *could* live anywhere. With the Internet and fax machines, I can file a story from the North Pole. I did not choose Chicago, but now I would not want to leave there."

"What if I offered you millions to relocate?"

Buck shrugged and chuckled. "You have a corner on the wealth of the world, and you say you are not motivated by money. Well, I have very little, and I am truly not motivated by it."

"What motivates you?"

Buck prayed quickly and silently. God, Christ, salvation, the Tribulation, love, friends, lost souls, the Bible, learning, preparing for the Glorious Appearing, New Hope Village Church, Chloe. Those were the things that motivated him, but could he say that? Should he? *God, give me the words!*

"I am motivated by truth and justice," Buck said flatly.

"Ah, and the American way!" Carpathia said. "Just like Superman!"

"More like Clark Kent," Buck said. "I'm just a reporter for a great metropolitan weekly."

"All right, you want to live in Chicago. What would you like to do, if you could do anything you wanted?"

Suddenly Buck snapped back to reality. He wished he could retreat to his private thoughts of Chloe, but he felt the pressure of the clock. This trip, strange as it had been, had been worth the grief just for that morsel about Carpathia's inheritance from Stonagal. He didn't like sparring with Nicolae, and he worried about the minefield represented by this latest question.

"Anything I wanted? I suppose I used to see myself one day in a publisher's role, you know, when I'm a little long in the tooth to be running all over the world chasing down stories. It would have been fun to have a great team of talented people and assign them, coach them, and put together a publication that showcased their abilities. I'd miss the legwork though, the research, the interviewing, and the writing."

"What if you could do both? Have the authority and the staff and the publication, and also give yourself some of the best assignments?"

"I suppose that would have been the ultimate."

"Buck, before I tell you how I can make that happen, tell me why you talk about your dreams in the past tense, as if you no longer have them."

Buck had not been careful. When he had relied on God for an answer, he had been given one. When he ventured out on his own, he had slipped. He knew the world had only seven more years, once the treaty was signed between Carpathia and Israel.

"I guess I just wonder how long this old world has," Buck said. "We're still digging out from the devastation of the disappearances, and—"

"Buck! You insult me! We are closer to world peace now than we have been in a hundred years! My humble proposals have found such receptive ears that I believe we are about to usher in an almost utopian global society! Trust me! Stay with me! Join me! You can fulfill all your dreams! You are not motivated by money? Good! Neither am I. Let me offer you resources that will allow you to never think or worry about money again.

"I can offer you a position, a publication, a staff, a headquarters, and even a retreat, that will allow you to do all you have ever wanted to do and even live in Chicago."

Carpathia paused, as he always did, waiting for Buck to bite. And Buck bit.

"This I've got to hear," he said.

"Excuse me one moment, Buck," Carpathia said, and he buzzed Hattie. Apparently he signaled her in a different way than usual, because rather than answering on the intercom, she appeared at the door behind Buck. He turned to acknowledge her, and she winked at him.

"Ms. Durham," Carpathia said, "would you inform Dr. Rosenzweig, Mr. Plank, and President Fitzhugh that I am running a bit behind schedule. I am estimating ten more minutes here, another ten with Chaim and Steve, and then we will be in Washington by five."

"Very good, sir."

\+ + +

Rayford parked at O'Hare and hurried through the terminal to the underground control center and Earl Halliday's office. Earl had been his chief pilot for years, and Rayford had grown from being one of his best young pilots to one of his veteran stars. Rayford felt fortunate to be at a place now where he and Earl could speak in shorthand, cutting through the bureaucratic red tape and getting to the heart of matters.

Earl was waiting outside his office door and looking at his watch when Rayford approached. "Good," Earl said. "C'mon in."

"Nice to see you, too," Rayford said, tucking his cap under his arm as he sat.

Earl sat in the only other chair in his cluttered office, the one behind his desk. "We've got a problem," he began.

"Thanks for easing into it," Rayford said. "Did Edwards write me up for, what did you call it, proselytizing?"

"That's only one part of the problem. If it wasn't for that, I'd be sitting here giving you some incredible news."

"Such as?"

"First tell me if I misunderstood you. When I first came down on you about talking about God on the job, you said you had to think about it. I said if you'd just assure me you'd back off, I'd make the write-up by Edwards go away. Right?"

"Right."

"Now, when you agreed to go to Dallas today to recertify, shouldn't I have been able to assume that meant you were going to play ball?"

"Not entirely. And I suppose you're wondering how my recert went."

"I already know how it went, Ray!" Earl snapped. "Now answer my question! Are you saying you went down there to get your papers on the 'seven-seven and all the while you had no intention of backing off from sounding so religious on the job?"

"I didn't say that."

"Say what you mean, then, Ray! You've never played games with me, and I'm too old for this. You hit *me* with all that church and Rapture stuff, and *I* was polite, wasn't I?"

"A little too polite."

"But I took it as a friend, just like you listen to me when I brag about my kids, right?"

"I wasn't bragging about anything."

"No, but you were excited about it. You found something that gave you comfort and helped explain your losses, and I say, great, whatever makes your boat float. You started pressing me about coming to church and reading my Bible and all that, and I told you, kindly I hope, that I considered that personal and that I would appreciate it if you'd lay off."

"And I did. Though I still pray for you."

"Well, hey, thanks. I also told you to watch it on the job, but no, you were still too new to it, still flush with the novelty of it, high as a guy who's just found the latest get-rich-quick scheme. So what do you do? You start pushing Nick Edwards, of all people. He's a comer, Ray, and people in high places here like him."

"I like him, too. That's why I care about him and his future."

"Yeah, all right, but he made it pretty clear he didn't want to hear any more, just like I did. You let up on me, so why couldn't you let up on him?"

"I thought I did."

"You thought you did." Earl pulled a file from his drawer and fingered his way to a certain page. "Then you deny telling him, and I quote, 'I don't care what you think of me'?"

"That's a little out of context, but, no, I wouldn't deny the spirit of that. All I was saying was that—"

"I know what you were saying, Ray, all right, because you said it to me, too! I told you I didn't want to see you become one of these wild-eyed fanatics who thinks he's better than everybody else and tries to get 'em saved. You said you just cared about me, which I appreciate, but I said you were getting close to losing my respect."

"And I said I didn't care."

"Well, can't you see how insulting that is?"

"Earl, how can I insult you when I care enough about your eternal soul to risk our friendship? I told Nick the same thing I told you, that what people feel about me isn't that important anymore. Part of me still cares, sure. Nobody wants to be seen as a fool. But if I don't tell you about Christ just because I'm worried about what you'll think of me, what kind of friend would I be?"

Earl sighed and shook his head, staring at the file again. "So, you contend that Nick took you out of context, but everything you just said is right here in this report."

"It is?"

"It is."

Rayford cocked his head. "What do you know about that? He heard me. He got the point."

"He certainly must not have agreed with the point. Otherwise, why this?" Earl shut the folder and slapped it.

"Earl, I was right where you and Nick are the night before the disappearances. I—"

"I've heard all this," Earl said.

"I'm just saying I understand your position. I was almost estranged from my wife because I thought she had become a fanatic."

"You told me."

"But my point now is that she *had* become a fanatic. She was right! She was proven right!"

"Rayford, if you want to preach, why don't you get out of aviation and into the ministry?"

"Are you firing me?"

"I hope I don't have to."

"Do you want me to apologize to Nicky, tell him I realized I pushed him too far but that my intentions were good?"

"I wish it was that easy."

"Isn't that what you offered the other day?"

"Yes! And I upheld my end of the bargain. I have not copied this file to Personnel or to my superiors, and I told Nicky I wouldn't. I said I would keep it, that it would become a permanent part of my personal file on you as my subordinate—"

"Which means nothing."

"Of course, you and I know that, and Nick is no dummy either. But it seemed to satisfy him. I assumed that your going to Dallas for recert was your way of telling me you heard what I was saying and that we were helping each other out."

Rayford nodded. "I had planned to be more judicious and try to be sure I didn't get you into trouble defending me for my actions."

"I didn't mind doing this, Ray. You're worth it. But you turned around and pulled the same stunt this morning. What were you thinking?"

Rayford flinched and sat back. He set his hat on the desk and held out both hands, palms up. "This morning? What are you talking about? I thought it went well, perfect in fact. Didn't I pass?"

Earl leaned across the desk and scowled. "You didn't pull the same thing with your examiner this morning that you've pulled with me and Nick and every other first officer you've worked with for the past few weeks?"

"Talk to him about God, you mean?"

"Yes!"

"No! In fact, I felt a little guilty about it. I said hardly anything to him. He was pretty severe, giving me the usual prattle about what he was and wasn't there for."

"You didn't preach at him?"

Rayford shook his head, trying to remember if he had done or said anything that could be misconstrued. "No. I didn't hide my Bible. Usually it's in my flight bag, but I had it out when I first met him, because I'd been reading it in the van. Hey, are you sure this complaint didn't come from the van driver? He saw me reading and asked about it, and we discussed what had happened."

"Your usual."

Rayford nodded. "But I didn't get any negative reaction from him."

"Neither did I. This complaint comes from your examiner."

"I don't understand it," Rayford said. "You believe me, don't you, Earl?"

"I wish I did," Earl said. "Now don't give me that look. I know we've been friends a long time, and I never once thought you lied to me. Remember that time you voluntarily grounded yourself because you didn't think your flight was going out and you'd had a few drinks?"

"I even offered to pay for another pilot."

"I know. But what am I supposed to think now, Ray? You say you didn't hassle this guy. I want to believe you. But you've done it to me and to Nick and to others. I gotta think you did _it_ this morning, too."

"Well, I'm going to have to talk with this guy," Rayford said.

"No, you're not."

"What, I can't confront my accuser? Earl, I didn't say a word to the man about God. I wish I had, especially if I'm going to have to take grief for it. I want to know why he said that. It had to be a misunderstanding, some secondhand complaint from the van driver, but like I say, I didn't sense any resistance from him. He must have said something to the examiner, though. Otherwise, where would the examiner even get the idea that I've done this before, unless the Bible just set him off?"

"I can't imagine the van driver having any contact with the examiner. Why would he, Ray?"

"I'm at a loss, Earl. I'm not sure I would have apologized if I had legitimately been in trouble for this, so I sure can't apologize for something I didn't do."

\+ + +

Buck recalled Rosenzweig telling him how the president had offered to come to New York to meet with Carpathia, but out of his vast humility, Nicolae had insisted on going to Washington. Now Carpathia casually has his personal assistant send word that he'll be late? Had he planned this? Was he systematically letting everyone know where they stood with him?

A few minutes later Hattie knocked and entered.

"Mr. Secretary-General," she said, "President Fitzhugh is sending *Air Force One* for you."

"Oh, tell him that will not be necessary," Carpathia said.

"Sir, he said it's already in the air and that you should come at your leisure. The pilot will let the White House know when you're on your way."

"Thank you Ms. Durham," Carpathia said. And to Buck, "What a nice man! You have met him?"

Buck nodded. "My first Newsmaker of the Year subject."

"His first or second time winning?"

"His second." Buck marveled anew at the encyclopedic memory of the man. Was there any doubt who the subject of this year's Newsmaker would be? It was an assignment Buck did not relish.

\+ + +

Earl shifted nervously. "Well, let me tell you, this comes at the worst possible time. The new *Air Force One*, which is scheduled to go into service next week, is a seven-seven-seven."

Rayford was nonplussed. The note from Hattie Durham, saying the same thing, was still in his pocket.

7

RAYFORD SHIFTED in his chair and watched his chief pilot's face. "I had heard that, yes," he hedged. "Is there anyone in America who hasn't heard about the new plane? I wouldn't mind seeing it, with everything they say is in it."

"It's top of the line, for sure," Earl said. "Absolute latest in technology, communications, security, and accommodations."

"You're the second person who's reminded me about that plane today. What's the point?"

"The point is, the White House has contacted our brass. Seems they think it's time their current pilot be put out to pasture. They want us to recommend a new guy. The people in Dallas narrowed a list to a half dozen senior pilots, and it came to me because your name is on it."

"Not interested."

"Not so fast! How can you say that? Who wouldn't want to fly one of the most advanced planes in the world, one outfitted like that, for the most powerful man on earth? Or I guess I should say the *second* most powerful, now that we've got this Carpathia guy at the U.N."

"Simple. I'd have to move to Washington."

"What's keeping you here? Is Chloe going back to school?"

"No."

"Then she's mobile too. Or does she have a job?"

"She's looking for one."

"Then let her find one in Washington. The job pays twice what you're making now, and you're already in the top 5 percent at Pan-Con."

"Money doesn't mean that much to me," Rayford said.

"Get off it!" Earl snapped. "Who calls me first when new numbers are in the air?"

"It's just not true of me anymore, Earl. And you know why."

"Yeah, spare me the sermon. But, Ray, the financial freedom to get a bigger, nicer place, run in different circles—"

"It's the circle I'm running in that's keeping me in Chicago. My church."

"Ray, the salary—"

"I don't care about the money. It's just Chloe and me now, remember?"

"Sorry."

"If anything, we ought to be downsizing. We've got more house than we need, and I've certainly got more money than I can spend."

"Then do it for the challenge! No regular route, a staff of first officers and navigators. You'll fly all over the world, a different place every time. It's an accomplishment, Ray."

"You said there were five other names."

"There are, and they're all good men. But if I lobby for you, you've got it. The problem is, I can't lobby for you with this Nick Edwards thing in the file."

"You said it was only in your file."

"It is, but with this morning's snafu, I can't risk hiding it. What if I get you the White House assignment and that examiner squawks? As soon as that gets out, Edwards sees it and corroborates the story. No assignment for you, and I look like an idiot for burying the complaint and championing you. End of story."

"It's the end of the story anyway," Rayford said. "I can't move."

Earl stood. "Rayford," he said slowly, "calm down and listen to me. Open your mind a little. Let me tell you what I'm hearing, and then just give me one chance to persuade you."

Rayford started to protest, but Earl cut him off.

"Please! I can't make your decision for you, and I won't try. But you have to let me finish. Even though I don't agree with your take on the disappearances, I'm happy for you that you've found some comfort in religion."

"It's not—"

"Ray, I know. I know. I've listened to you and I've heard you. To you it's not religion, it's Jesus Christ. Did I listen well, or what? I admire that you've given yourself to this. You're devout. I don't doubt you. But you don't just thumb your nose at an assignment that a thousand pilots would die for. Frankly, I'm not entirely sure you'd have to relocate. How often do you see a president of the United States traveling on a Sunday? Surely not more than you fly Sundays now."

"Because of seniority, I hardly ever fly Sundays."

"You can assign someone else to fly Sundays for you. You'll be the captain, the senior guy, in charge, the boss. You won't have me to answer to anymore."

"I'll do it!" Rayford said, smiling. "I'm kidding."

"Of course, it would make more sense for you to live in Washington, but I'll bet if your only condition is living in Chicago, they'd do it."

"No possible way."

"Why?"

"Because my church is not just about Sundays. We meet frequently. I'm close to the pastor. We meet almost every day."

"And you can't see living without that."

"I can't."

"Ray, what if this is a phase? What if you eventually lose your zeal? I'm not saying you're a phony or that you're going to turn your back on what you've found. I'm just saying the novelty might wear off, and you might be able to work somewhere else if you can get back to Chicago on the weekends."

"Why is this so important to you, Earl?"

"You don't know?"

"I don't."

"Because it's something I've dreamed of all my life," Earl said. "I kept up on all the latest certifications all my years in this position, and I've applied for the pilot's job with every new president."

"I never knew that."

"Of course you didn't. Who would admit that and let the world know he got his guts ripped out every four or eight years, seeing other guys get the job? Your getting it would be the next best thing. I could enjoy it vicariously."

"For that reason alone I wish I was free to take it."

Earl sat back down. "Well, thanks for that table scrap."

"I didn't mean it that way, Earl. I'm serious."

"I know you are. Truth is, I know a couple of the other yokels on the list, and I wouldn't let them drive my car."

"I thought you said they were good men."

"I'm just trying to tell you that if you don't take this, someone else will."

"Earl, I really don't think—"

Earl held up a hand. "Ray, do me a favor, will you? Will you not decide right now? I mean, I know you've pretty much already decided, but would you hold off telling me officially until you've slept on it?"

"I'll pray about it," Rayford conceded.

"I thought you might."

"Are you forbidding me from calling that examiner?"

"Absolutely. You want to file a grievance, do it on paper, through channels, the right way."

"You sure you want to recommend a guy you don't believe for a job like this?"

"If you tell me you didn't pressure the guy, I have to believe you."

"I didn't even broach the subject, Earl."

"This is crazy." Earl shook his head.

"Who did the complaint go to?"

"My secretary."

"From?"

"From his secretary, I guess."

"Can I see it?"

"I shouldn't."

"Let me see it, Earl. What do you think, I'm going to turn you in?"

Earl buzzed his secretary. "Francine, bring me your notes on the complaint you got from Dallas this morning." She brought him a single typed sheet. Earl read it and slid it across the desk to Rayford. It read:

Took a call at 11:37 a.m. from a woman who identified herself as Jean Garfield, secretary to Pan-Con Certification Examiner Jim Long of Dallas. Asked how to go about lodging a complaint of religious harassment against Rayford Steele due to his pressuring Long during his recert this a.m. Told her I would get back to her. She did not leave a number, but said she would call back later.

Rayford held up the paper. "Earl, you're a better detective than this."

"What do you mean?"

"This smells."

"You don't think it's legit?"

"First of all, my guy had a two-syllable last name on his ID badge. And when was the last time you remember an examiner having a secretary?"

Earl made a face. "Good call."

"Speaking of calls," Rayford said, "I'd like to know where that call came from. How hard would that be to determine?"

"Not hard. Francine! Call security for me, please."

"Would you mind asking her to check something else for me?" Rayford said. "Ask her to call Personnel and see if we have a Jim Long or a Jean Garfield working for Pan-Con."

* * *

"If you do not mind," Carpathia said, "I would now like to ask your friends to join us."

Now, already? Buck wondered. *Just in time for the big news, whatever it is?*

"This is your show," Buck said, surprised at Carpathia's pained expression. "Your meeting, I mean. Sure, invite them in."

Buck didn't know whether it was just his imagination, but it seemed both Steve Plank and Chaim Rosenzweig had bemused, knowing looks when they entered, trailed by Hattie. She set a chair from the conference table on the other side of Buck, and the men sat. Hattie left again. "Mr. Williams has a prerequisite," Carpathia announced, to the low murmur from Plank and Rosenzweig. "He must be headquartered in Chicago."

"That just helps narrow it down," Dr. Rosenzweig said. "Does it not?"

"It does indeed," Carpathia said. Buck glanced at Plank, who was nodding. The secretary-general turned toward Buck. "Here is my offer: You become president and publisher of the *Chicago Tribune*, which I shall acquire from the Wrigley family within the next two months. I will rename it *The Midwest Tribune* and publish it under the auspices of Global Community Enterprises. The headquarters will remain Tribune Tower in Chicago. Along with your job comes a limousine with driver, a personal valet, whatever staff you deem necessary, a home on the North Shore with domestic help, and a retreat home on Lake Geneva in southern Wisconsin. Beyond naming the publication and the publishing company, I will not intrude on your decision making. You will have complete freedom to run the paper any way you wish." His voice took a tone of sarcasm. "With your twin towers of truth and justice undergirding every word."

Buck wanted to laugh aloud. It didn't surprise him that Carpathia could afford such a purchase, but there was no way a man so visible could hide behind a publishing company name and break every rule of journalistic ethics by owning a major media outlet while serving as secretary-general of the United Nations.

"You'll never get away with it," Buck said. He kept silent about the real issue: that Carpathia would never give anyone in his charge complete freedom unless he believed he had total control of their mind.

"That will be *my* problem," Carpathia said.

"But with complete freedom," Buck said, "I would be your problem too. I am devoted to the tenet that the public has a right to know. So the first investigative piece I assign, or write myself, would be about ownership of the publication."

"I would welcome the publicity," Carpathia said. "What would be wrong with the United Nations owning a paper dedicated to news of the global community?"

"You wouldn't own it personally?"

"That is semantics. If it would be more appropriate for the U.N. to own it than for me, I would donate the money, or buy it and donate the company to the U.N."

"But then the *Tribune* becomes a house organ, an in-house sheet promoting the interests of the U.N."

"Which makes it legal."

"But which also makes it impotent as an independent news voice."

"That will be up to you."

"Are you serious? You would allow your own publication to criticize you? To take issue with the United Nations?"

"I welcome the accountability. My motives are pure, my goals are peaceful, and my audience is global."

Buck turned in frustration to Steve Plank, knowing full well that Steve was one who had already proven susceptible to Carpathia's power. "Steve, you're his media adviser! Tell him there's no credibility in such a venture! It would not be taken seriously."

"It wouldn't be taken seriously at first by other news media, Buck," Steve acknowledged. "But it won't be long before Global Community Publishing owns those media services too."

"So by monopolizing the publishing industry, you eliminate the competition and the public doesn't know the difference?"

Carpathia nodded. "That is one way to phrase it. And if my motives were anything but ideal, I would have a problem with it too. But what is wrong with controlling global news when we are headed toward peace and harmony and unity?"

"Where is the power to think for oneself?" Buck asked. "Where is the forum for diverse ideas? What happens to the court of public opinion?"

"The court of public opinion," Steve said, "is calling for more of what the secretary-general has to offer."

Buck was defeated, and he knew it. He couldn't expect Chaim Rosenzweig to understand the ethics of journalism, but when a veteran like Steve Plank could support a puff sheet for a benevolent dictator, what hope was there?

"I can't imagine being involved in such a venture," Buck said.

"I love this man!" Carpathia exulted, and Plank and Rosenzweig smiled and nodded. "Think about it. Mull it over. Somehow I will make it legal enough to be acceptable even to you, and then I will not take no for an answer. I want the paper, and I am going to get it. I want you to run it, and I am going to get you. Freedom, Buck Williams. Total freedom. The day you believe I am intruding, you may quit with full pay."

* * *

Having thanked Earl Halliday for his confidence and promising not to declare himself just yet—though Rayford could not imagine taking the job—he stood in the terminal at an otherwise deserted bank of pay phones. Francine, Earl's secretary, had confirmed that there was no Jean Garfield working for Pan-Con.

And while there were no fewer than six James Longs, four of them were baggage handlers and the other two were midlevel bureaucrats. None worked in Dallas, none was an examiner, and none had a secretary.

"Who's out to get you?" Earl had asked.

"I can't imagine."

Francine reported that the call she took that morning had been traced to New York. "It'll take them a few hours to get an exact phone number," she said, but Rayford knew in a flash who it was. He couldn't be sure *why* she would do it, but only Hattie Durham would pull a stunt like that. Only she would have access to Pan-Con people who would know where he was and what he was doing that morning. And what was that business about *Air Force One*?

He called information and got the number for the United Nations. After reaching the switchboard and then the administrative offices, he finally got Hattie, the fourth person to pick up the phone.

"Rayford Steele here," he said flatly.

"Oh, hi, Captain Steele!" The brightness in her voice made him cringe.

"I give up," Rayford said. "Whatever you're doing, you win."

"I don't follow."

"C'mon, Hattie, don't play dumb."

"Oh! My note! I just thought it was funny, because I was talking to a friend in Pan-Con traffic the other day, and she mentioned that my old friend was recerting on the 777 this morning in Dallas. Wasn't it funny that I had mail waiting for you? Wasn't that just the funniest?"

"Yeah, hilarious. What does it mean?"

"The message? Oh, nothing. Surely you knew that, right? Everybody knows the new *Air Force One* is going to be a 'seventy-seven, don't they?"

"Yeah, so why remind me?"

"It was a joke, Rayford. I was kidding you about recertifying as if you were going to be the president's new pilot. Don't you get it?"

Was it possible? Could she be that naive and innocent? Could she have done something that vapid and have been so coincidentally lucky? He wanted to ask how she knew he would be offered the job, but if she didn't know it, he certainly did not want to tell her.

"I get it. Very funny. So what was the phony complaint all about?"

"The phony complaint?"

"Don't waste my time, Hattie. You're the only person who knew where I was and what I was doing, and I come back to some bogus charge about religious harassment."

"Oh, that!" she laughed. "That was just a wild guess. You had an examiner, didn't you?"

"Yes, but I didn't—"

"And you had to give him the big pitch, didn't you?"

"No."

"Come now, Rayford. You gave it to me, to your own daughter, to Cameron Williams, to Earl Halliday, to just about everybody you've worked with since. Really? You didn't preach to the examiner?"

"As a matter of fact, I didn't."

"Well, OK, so I guessed wrong. But it's still funny, don't you think? And the odds were with me. What would you have thought if you *had* come on strong with him and then came back to a complaint? You would have apologized to him, and he would have denied it. I love practical jokes! C'mon, give me some credit."

"Hattie, if you're trying to get back at me for how I treated you, I suppose I deserve it."

"No, Rayford, it's not that! I'm over it. I'm over you. If we'd had a relationship, I would never be where I am today, and believe me, I never want to be anywhere else. But this wasn't revenge. It was just supposed to be funny. If it doesn't amuse you, I'm sorry."

"It got me into trouble."

"Oh, come on! How long would it take to check out a story like that?"

"All right, you win. Any more surprises for me?"

"Don't think so, but stay on your toes."

Rayford didn't buy a word of it. Carpathia had to know about the White House offer. Hattie's note and that offer, and what her little joke almost did to scotch the deal, were too coincidental to be her lame attempt at a practical joke. Rayford was not in a good mood when he returned to the parking garage. He only hoped Chloe was not still upset. If she was, maybe both of them could cool down before the meeting that night.

+ + +

Chaim Rosenzweig put a gnarled hand on Buck's knee. "I urge you to accept this most prestigious position. If you do not accept it, someone else will, and it will not be as good a paper."

Buck was not about to argue with Chaim. "Thank you," he said. "I have a lot to think about." But accepting the offer was not something he was going to consider. How he longed to talk about this, first to Chloe and then to Bruce and Rayford.

When Hattie Durham interrupted apologetically and moved to the desk to speak quietly with Carpathia, Steve began to whisper something to Buck. But Buck was blessed with the ability to discern what was worth listening to and what was worthy of ignoring. Right now he decided it would be more profitable to eavesdrop on Hattie and Nicolae than to pay attention to Steve. He leaned toward Steve, pretending to listen.

Buck knew Steve would be trying to sell him on the job, to assure him that it was Steve himself who lobbied for it, to admit that as a journalist it sounded crazy at first, but that this was a new world, blah, blah, blah. And so Buck nodded and maintained some eye contact, but he was listening to Hattie Durham and Carpathia.

"I just took a call from the target," she said.

"Yes? And?"

"It didn't take him long to figure it out."

"And *Air Force One*?"

"I don't think he has a clue."

"Good work. And the other?"

"No response yet."

"Thank you, dear."

The target. That didn't sound good. The rest of it he assumed had something to do with Carpathia's ride that afternoon on the president's plane.

Carpathia turned his attention back to his guest. "At the very least, Buck, talk this over with the people who care about you. And if you think of more specific dreams you would accomplish if resources were no object, remember that you are in the driver's seat right now. You are in a seller's market. I am the buyer, and I will get the man I want."

"You make me want to turn you down, just to show I cannot be bought."

"And as I have said so many times, that is the very reason you are the man for the job. Do not make the mistake of passing up the opportunity of a lifetime just to prove a small point."

Buck felt caught. On one side of him was a man he had admired and worked with for years, a journalist with principle. On the other was a man he loved like a father, a brilliant scientist who was in many ways naive enough to be the perfect foil, one of the pawns in an end-of-the-world chess game. Outside the door was an acquaintance he had met on an airplane when God had invaded the world. He had introduced her to Nicolae Carpathia just to show off, and look where they were now.

Directly in front of him, smiling that handsome, disarming smile, was Carpathia himself. Of the four people Buck was dealing with that afternoon,

Carpathia was the one he understood the most. He also understood that Carpathia was the one with whom he had the least influence. Was it too late to plead with Steve, to warn him of what he had gotten into? Too late to rescue Hattie from the stupidity of his introduction? Was Chaim too enamored with the geopolitical possibilities to listen to reason and truth?

And if he did confide in any of them, would that be the end of any hope that he could keep the truth from Carpathia—that Buck himself was protected from his power by God?

Buck couldn't wait to get back to Chicago. His condo was brand-new and didn't seem familiar. His friends were new too, but there was no one in the world he trusted more. Bruce would listen and study and pray and offer counsel. Rayford, with that scientific, analytical, pragmatic mind, would make suggestions, never forcing opinions.

But it was Chloe he missed the most. Was this of God? Had God impressed her upon Buck's mind at his most vulnerable moment with Carpathia? Buck hardly knew the woman. Woman? She was barely more than a girl, but she seemed . . . what? Mature? More than mature. Magnetic. When she listened to him, her eyes seemed to drink him in. She understood, empathized. She could give advice and feedback without saying a word.

There was a comfort zone with her, a feeling of safety. He had barely touched her twice. Once to wipe from her mouth a dab of chocolate from a cookie, and in church the morning before, just to get her attention. And yet now, a two-hour plane ride from her, he felt an overwhelming need to embrace her.

He couldn't do that, of course. He scarcely knew her and didn't want to scare her away. And yet in his mind he looked forward to the day when they felt comfortable enough to hold hands or draw close to each other. He imagined them sitting somewhere, just enjoying each other's company, her head on his chest, his arm around her.

And he realized how desperately lonely he had become.

\+ + +

Rayford found Chloe miserable. He had decided not to tell her yet of the events of his day. It had been too weird, and she had apparently had a doozy of a day herself. He held her and she wept. Rayford noticed a huge bouquet of flowers sticking out of a wastebasket.

"Those made it worse, Dad. At least my reaction showed me something—how much I cared for Buck."

"That sounds pretty analytical for you," Rayford said, regretting it as soon as it was out of his mouth.

"I can't be analytical because I'm a woman, is that it?"

"Sorry! I shouldn't have said it."

"I'm sitting here crying, so my whole response to this is emotional, right? Don't forget, Dad, five semesters on the dean's list. That's not emotional; that's analytical. I'm more like you than like Mom, remember?"

"Don't I know it. And because we are the way we are, we're still here."

"Well, I'm glad we've got each other. At least I was until you accused me of being a typical woman."

"I never said that."

"It's what you were thinking."

"Now you're a mind reader, too?"

"Yeah, I'm an emotional fortune-teller."

"I surrender," Rayford said.

"Oh, come on, Dad. Don't give up so soon. Nobody likes an easy loser."

* * *

On the plane, again coddled in first class, Buck had trouble not chuckling aloud. Publisher of the *Tribune*! In twenty years, maybe, if it wasn't owned by Carpathia and Christ wasn't returning first. Buck felt as if he had won the lottery in a society where money was useless.

After dinner he settled back and gazed at the setting sun. It had been many, many years since he had been drawn to a city because of a person. Would he be back in time to see her before tonight's meeting? If the traffic wasn't too bad, he might have enough time to talk the way he really wanted to.

Buck didn't want to scare Chloe off by being too specific, but he wanted to apologize for his waffling. He didn't want to push anything. Who knew? Maybe she had no interest. He was certain only that he did not want to be the one to close the door on any possibility. Maybe he should call her from the plane.

* * *

"Bruce offered me a job today," Chloe said.

"You're kidding," Rayford said. "What?"

"Something right up my alley. Study, research, preparation, teaching."

"Where? What?"

"At the church. He wants to 'multiply his ministry.'"

"A paid position?"

"Yep. Full time. I could work at home or at the church. He would give me assignments, help me develop curriculum, all that. He wants to go slow on the teaching part, since I'm so new at this. A lot of the people I'd be teaching have spent their lives in church and Sunday school."

"What would you teach?"

"The same things he's teaching. My research would help in his lesson preparation, too. I would eventually teach Sunday school classes and small groups. He's going to ask you and Buck to do the same, but of course he doesn't know yet what Buck's up to with his little fiancée."

"And you were prudent enough not to tell him."

"For now," Chloe said. "If Buck doesn't realize it's wrong—and maybe he doesn't—somebody needs to tell him."

"And you're signing up for the job."

"I will if no one else will. I'm the only one who knows firsthand right now."

"But don't you have just a little conflict of interest?"

"Dad, I had no idea how much I hoped that something would develop with Buck. Now I wouldn't want him if he threw himself at me."

The phone rang. Rayford answered it, then covered the mouthpiece. "Here's your chance to prove that," he said. "Buck calling from an airplane."

Chloe squinted as if trying to decide whether to be available. "Give me that," she said.

* * *

Buck was certain Rayford Steele would have told his daughter who was calling. But her hello sounded flat, and did not include his name, so he felt obligated to identify himself.

"Chloe, it's Buck! How are you?"

"I've been better."

"What's up? You sick?"

"I'm fine. Did you want something?"

"Um, yeah, I kind of wanted to see you tonight."

"Kind of?"

"Well, yeah, I mean I do. Can I?"

"I'll be seeing you at the meeting at eight, right?" she said.

"Yeah, but I was wondering if you'd have a little time before that."

"I don't know. What did you want?"

"Just to talk with you."

"I'm listening."

"Chloe, is something wrong? Am I missing something? You seem upset."

"The flowers are in the trash, if that's any hint," she said.

The flowers are in the trash, he repeated in his mind. That was an expression he hadn't heard. It must mean something to someone from her generation. He might be a famous writer, but he had sure missed that one.

"I'm sorry?" he said.

"It's a little too late for that," she said.

"I mean, I'm sorry—I missed what you were saying."

"You didn't hear me?"

"I heard you, but I don't get your meaning."

"What about 'the flowers are in the trash' do you not understand?"

Buck had been a little distant from her Friday night, but what was this? Well, she was worth the work. "Let's start with the flowers," he said.

"Yes, let's," she said.

"What flowers are we talking about?"

+ + +

Rayford motioned with both hands for Chloe to take it easy. He was afraid she was going to blow, and whatever was going on, she sure wasn't giving Buck an inch. If there was any truth to what Chloe was alleging, she wasn't going to help restore him this way. Maybe Buck *hadn't* thrown off all the trappings of his former life. Maybe there *were* some areas that would have to be dealt with forthrightly. But wasn't that true of all four of them in the Tribulation Force?

"I'll see you tonight, OK?" Chloe concluded. "No, not before the meeting. I don't know if I'll have time afterward or not. . . . Well, it depends on what time we get out, I guess. . . . Yes, he said eight to ten, but, Buck, do you get it that I don't really want to talk to you right now? And I don't know if I'll want to talk later. . . . Yes, see you then."

She hung up. "Ooh, that man is persistent! I'm seeing a side of him I never imagined."

"Still wish something would develop?" Rayford said.

She shook her head. "Whatever was there has been snuffed out now."

"But it still hurts."

"It sure does. I just didn't realize how much I was getting my hopes up."

"I'm sorry, honey."

She sank to the couch and rested her face in her hands. "Dad, I know we didn't owe each other anything, but don't you think he and I talked enough and connected enough that I should have known if there was someone in his life?"

"Seems like it, yes."

"Did I just totally misread him? Does he think it's OK to say he's attracted to me without telling me he's unavailable?"

"I can't imagine."

Rayford didn't know what else to say. If there was anything to what Chloe was saying, he was beginning to lose respect for Buck too. He seemed like such a good guy. Rayford only hoped they could help him.

* * *

Buck was wounded. He still longed to see Chloe, but it was not the idealistic dream he had imagined. He had done something or not done something, and it was going to take more than a little apology over mixed signals to get to the bottom of it.

The flowers are in the trash, he thought. Whatever in the world that meant.

8

BUCK'S CONDO DOOR nudged a stack of boxes when he entered. He'd have to send Alice a thank-you note. He only wished he had time to start arranging his home office, but he had to get going if he hoped to catch Chloe before the meeting.

He arrived at New Hope about half an hour early and saw Rayford's car parked next to Bruce's. *Good,* he thought, *everybody's here.* He glanced at his watch. Had he forgotten the time change? Was he late? He hurried into the office and knocked on Bruce's door as he stepped in. Bruce and Rayford looked up awkwardly. It was just the two of them.

"I'm sorry, I guess I'm a little early."

"Yeah, Buck," Bruce said. "We'll be a little while and we'll see you at eight, all right?"

"Sure. I'll just talk with Chloe. She here?"

"She'll be along a little later," Rayford said.

"OK, I'll just wait for her out here."

+ + +

"Well, first of all," Bruce told Rayford, "congratulations. Regardless of what you decide to do, that is a fantastic honor and an accomplishment. I can't imagine many pilots turning down that offer."

Rayford sat back. "Truthfully, I haven't spent much time thinking of it that way. I guess I should be grateful."

Bruce nodded. "I guess you should. Did you want advice, or just an ear? Obviously, I'll pray with you about it."

"I'm open to advice."

"Well, I feel so inadequate, Rayford. I appreciate that you want to stay here in Chicago, but you also have to consider whether this opportunity is from God. I want to stay around here too, but I feel him leading me to travel, to start more small groups, to visit Israel. I know you're not staying here just for me, but—"

"That's part of it, Bruce."

"And I appreciate that, but who knows how long I'll be here?"

"We need you, Bruce. I think it's clear God has you here for a reason."

"I suppose Chloe told you that I'm looking for more teachers."

"She did. And she's excited about it. And I'm willing to learn."

"Normally a church wouldn't put brand-new believers in the positions of leaders or teachers, but there's no alternative now. I'm virtually a new believer myself. I know you'd make a good teacher, Rayford. The problem is, I can't shake the thought that this opportunity with the president is a unique one you should seriously consider. Imagine the impact you might have on the president of the United States."

"Oh, I don't think the president and his pilot interact much, if at all."

"He doesn't interview a new pilot?"

"I doubt it."

"You'd think he'd want to get to know the man who has his life in his hands every time that plane leaves the ground."

"I'm sure he trusts the people who make that decision."

"But surely there will be occasions when you might interact."

Rayford shrugged. "Maybe."

"President Fitzhugh, strong and independent as he is, must be as personally frightened and searching as any private citizen. Think of the privilege of telling the leader of the free world about Christ."

"And losing my job over it," Rayford said.

"You'd have to pick your spots, of course. But the president lost several relatives in the Rapture. What was it he said when asked what he made of it? Something about being sure it wasn't God's doing, because he had always believed in God."

"You're talking about this as if I'm naturally going to take the job."

"Rayford, I can't make your decisions for you, but I need you to remember: Your loyalty now is not to this church or to the Tribulation Force or to me. Your loyalty is to Christ. If you decide not to pursue this opportunity, you had better be dead sure it's not of God."

It was just like Bruce, Rayford thought, *to put a whole new spin on this.* "Do you think I should say anything to Chloe or Buck?"

"We're all in this together," Bruce said.

"Meanwhile," Rayford said, "let me bounce something else off you. How do you feel about romance during this point of history?"

Bruce suddenly looked uncomfortable. "Good question," he said. "Frankly, I know why you're asking." Rayford doubted that. "I know the loneliness you must feel. At least you have Chloe for companionship, but you must have that same aching emptiness that I feel after losing my wife. I've thought about whether I'm to go on alone through the next seven or so years. I don't like the prospect, but I know I'll be busy. To be very transparent with you, I suppose I harbor some hope that God might bring someone into my life. Right now is too soon, of course. I'll grieve and mourn my wife for a long time, as if she were dead. I know she's in heaven, but she's dead to me. There are days when I feel so alone I can hardly breathe."

This was as self-revelatory as Bruce had been since telling his own story of having missed the Rapture, and Rayford was stunned that he had been the one to instigate it. He had merely been asking for Chloe's sake. She had become enamored of Buck, and if that wasn't going to work out, should she put herself in a situation where someone else might come along, or was that inappropriate, given the few years left before Christ's return again?

"I'm just curious about the logistics," Rayford explained. "If two people fell in love, what should they do about it? Does the Bible say anything about marriage during this period?"

"Not specifically," Bruce said, "as far as I can tell. But it doesn't prohibit it, either."

"And kids? Would it be prudent for a couple to bring children in this world now?"

"I haven't thought about that," Bruce said. "Would you want another child at your age?"

"Bruce! *I'm* not looking to marry again. I'm thinking of Chloe. I'm not saying she has any prospects, but if she did . . ."

Bruce squeaked back in his chair. "Imagine having a baby now," he said. "You wouldn't have to think about junior high school, let alone high school or college. You would be raising that child, preparing him or her for the return of Christ in just a few years."

"You'd also be guaranteeing a child a life of fear and danger and a 75 percent chance of dying during the judgments to come."

Bruce rested his chin in his hand, elbow on the desk. "True enough," he said. "I'd have to advise a lot of caution, prayer, and soul-searching before considering that."

+ + +

Buck had never been good at waiting. He browsed the shelves of the sitting area outside Bruce's office. Apparently this was where the former pastor had stored his less frequently used reference works. There appeared to be dozens of books on esoteric Old Testament themes. Buck leafed through a few of them, finding them dry.

Then he came across a church photo directory dated two years earlier. There, under the B's, was a picture of a younger, longer-haired Bruce Barnes. He looked a bit fuller in the face, wore a pasted-on smile, and surrounding him were his wife and children. What a treasure Bruce had lost! His wife was pleasant looking and plump, with a weary but genuine smile.

On the next page was Dr. Vernon Billings, the now-departed senior pastor. He looked at least in his mid-sixties and was shown with his petite wife and three children and their respective spouses. Bruce had already said that the entire family had been raptured. Pastor Billings had a Henry Fonda-ish quality, with deep crow's feet and a crinkly smile. He looked like a man Buck would have enjoyed knowing.

Buck flipped to the other end of the directory and found the Steeles. There was Rayford in his pilot's uniform, looking pretty much the same as he did today with perhaps slightly less gray in the hair and a little more definition in his face. And Irene. It was the first picture of her he had seen. She looked bright and cheery, and if you could believe the faddish study of photo-psychology, she appeared more devoted to her husband than he did to her. Her body leaned toward him. He sat rigid, straight up.

Also in the picture was Rayford Junior, identified in the caption as "Raymie, 10." He and his mother had asterisks by their names. Rayford did not. And neither did Chloe, who was listed as "18, Freshman, Stanford University, Palo Alto, California (not pictured)."

Buck flipped to the legend, which explained that an asterisk indicated a church member. The rest, he assumed, were mere attenders.

Buck looked at his watch. Ten to eight. He peered out the window to the parking lot. The Steeles' second car was there, next to Rayford's and Buck's and Bruce's. He put his hand on the glass to cut the glare and could make out Chloe behind the wheel. Ten minutes was hardly enough time to talk, but he could at least greet her and walk her inside.

As soon as Buck stepped out the door, Chloe emerged from the car and hurried toward the church. "Hey!" he said.

"Hello, Buck," she said, clearly without enthusiasm.

"Flowers still in the trash?" he tried, hoping for some clue to what was up with her.

"As a matter of fact they are," she said, brushing past him and opening the door herself. He followed her up the stairs, through the foyer, and into the offices.

"I don't think they're ready for us yet," he said, as she went directly to Bruce's door and knocked.

Apparently Bruce told her the same thing, and she backed out with an apology. Obviously Chloe would rather be anywhere but there and looking at anything but him. She had been crying, and her face was red and blotchy. He ached to reconnect with her. Something told him this was not just a mood, a part of her personality he would have to get used to. Something specific was plainly wrong, and Buck was in the middle of it. There was nothing he would rather do right then than get to the bottom of it. But that would have to wait.

Chloe sat with her arms and legs crossed, her top leg swinging.

"Look what I found," Buck said, thrusting the old church directory under her nose. She didn't even reach for it.

"Um-hm," she said.

Buck opened it to the *B*s and showed her Bruce's and Dr. Billings's families. Suddenly she softened, took the directory, and studied it. "Bruce's wife," she said softly. "And look at those children!"

"Your family is in there too," Buck said.

Chloe took her time getting to the *S*s, studying page after page of pictures as if looking for anyone else she recognized. "Went to high school with him," she said idly. "She and I were in the same fourth grade. Mrs. Schultz was my freshman P.E. teacher."

When she finally got to her own family she was overcome. Her face contorted and she stared, the tears coming. "Raymie when he was ten," she managed. Buck instinctively put a hand on her shoulder, and she stiffened. "Please don't do that."

"Sorry," he said, and the office door opened.

\+ + +

"Ready," Rayford said. He noticed that Buck looked sheepish and Chloe looked terrible. He hoped she hadn't started in on him already.

"Daddy, look," she said, standing and handing him the directory.

Rayford's throat tightened and he sucked in a huge breath when he saw the photo. He sighed painfully. It was almost too much to take.

He closed the directory and handed it to Buck, but at the same time he heard Bruce's chair squeak. "What're you guys looking at?"

\+ + +

"Just this," Buck said, showing him the cover and trying to replace it in the bookshelf. But Bruce reached for it. "It's a couple of years old," Buck added.

"About a month after we started coming here," Rayford said.

Bruce flipped right to the picture of his family, stood studying it for several seconds, and said, "You're in here, Rayford?"

"Yes," Rayford said simply, and Buck noticed him trying to get Chloe to move into the office.

Bruce turned to the Steele picture and nodded, smiling. He brought the directory back into the office with him, tucked it under his Bible and notebook, and opened the meeting in prayer.

Bruce started a little emotionally, but he soon warmed to his topic. He was flipping from Revelation to Ezekiel and Daniel and back again, comparing the prophetic passages to what was happening in New York and the rest of the world.

"Any of you hear the news about the two witnesses in Jerusalem today?"

Buck shook his head, and Rayford did the same. Chloe did not respond. She was not taking notes either or asking any questions. "A reporter said that a little band of a half dozen thugs tried to charge the two, but they all wound up burned to death."

"Burned?" Buck said.

"No one knew where the fire came from," Bruce said. "But we know, don't we?"

"Do we?"

"Look at Revelation 11. The angel tells the apostle John, '"And I will give power to my two witnesses, and they will prophesy one thousand two hundred and sixty days, clothed in sackcloth." These are the two olive trees and the two lampstands standing before the God of the earth. And if anyone wants to harm them, fire proceeds from their mouth and devours their enemies. And if anyone wants to harm them, he must be killed in this manner.'"

"They breathed fire on them like dragons?"

"It's right here in the book," Bruce said.

"I'd like to see that on CNN," Buck said.

"Keep watching," Bruce said. "We'll see more than that."

* * *

Rayford wondered if he would ever get used to the things God was revealing to him. He could hardly fathom how far he'd come, how much he had accepted in less than a month. There was something about the dramatic invasion of God into humankind and into himself specifically that had changed the way he thought. From being a man who had to have everything documented, he suddenly found himself believing without question the most ludicrous news accounts, as long as they were corroborated by Scripture. And the opposite was also true: He believed everything in the Bible. Sooner or later the news would carry the same story.

Bruce turned to Buck. "How did your day go?" To Rayford, it seemed like an inside question.

"More to talk about than I can get into here," Buck said.

"No kidding," Chloe snapped. It was the first thing she had said.

Buck glanced at her and said, "I'll debrief you tomorrow, Bruce, and then we can talk about it here tomorrow night."

"Oh, let's talk about it now," Chloe said. "We're all friends here."

Rayford wished he could shush his own daughter, but she was an adult. If she wanted to press an issue, regardless of how she came across, that was her prerogative.

"You don't even know where I was today," Buck told her, clearly puzzled.

"But I know who you were with."

Rayford saw the glance Buck shot at Bruce, but he didn't understand it. Obviously, something had transpired between the two of them that wasn't public knowledge yet. Could he have told Chloe that Buck met with Carpathia?

"Did you—?" Bruce shook his head.

"I don't think you know, Chloe," Buck said. "Let me discuss it with Bruce tomorrow, and I'll bring it up for prayer in our meeting tomorrow night."

"Yeah, sure," Chloe said. "But I have a question and a prayer request for tonight."

Bruce looked at his watch. "OK, shoot."

"I'm wondering what you think about dating relationships during this time."

"You're the second person who's asked me that today," Bruce said. "We must be lonely people." Chloe snorted, then scowled at Buck.

She must assume it was Buck who asked Bruce that earlier, Rayford thought.

"Let me make that a topic for one of our sessions," Bruce said.

"How about the next one?" Chloe pressed.

"All right. We can discuss it tomorrow night."

"And can you add to it what the rules are for morality for new believers?" Chloe said.

"Excuse me?"

"Talk about how we're supposed to live, now that we call ourselves followers of Christ. You know, like morals and sex and all of that."

* * *

Buck winced. Chloe didn't sound like herself. "All right," Bruce said. "We can cover that. But I don't think it'll come as any great shock to you to know that the rules that applied before the Rapture still apply. I mean, this could be a short lesson. We're called to purity, and I'm sure it won't surprise you—"

"It might not be so obvious to all of us," Chloe said.

"We'll deal with it tomorrow night then," Bruce said. "Anything else for right now?"

Before anyone said anything or even offered closing prayer requests, Chloe said, "Nope. See you tomorrow night then." And she left.

The three men prayed, and the meeting ended awkwardly, none of them wanting to talk, as Nicolae Carpathia had put it, about the elephant in the room.

Buck arrived home frustrated. He was not used to being unable to fix something, and most maddening, he didn't even know what was wrong. He changed out of his traveling clothes and into hiking boots, khakis, denim shirt, and leather jacket. He phoned the Steeles. Rayford answered but after a few minutes came back to the phone to say that Chloe was unavailable. Buck was only guessing, but it sounded as if Rayford was as frustrated with her as he was.

"Rayford, is she standing right there?"

"That's correct."

"Do you have any idea what her problem is?"

"Not totally."

"I want to get to the bottom of it," Buck said.

"I concur with that."

"I mean tonight."

"Affirmative. Absolutely. You can try her again tomorrow."

"Rayford, are you telling me it's all right for me to come there right now?"

"Yes, you're right. I can't promise she'll be here, but try again tomorrow."

"So if I came there right now, I would not be offending you."

"Not at all. We'll expect your call tomorrow then."

"I'm on my way."

"OK, Buck. Talk to you then."

* * *

Rayford didn't like deceiving Chloe. It was almost like lying. But he had enjoyed the coded banter with Buck. He remembered a little tiff he'd had when dating Irene years before. She was very upset with him over something and told him she didn't want him to call her until he heard from her, and she stormed off.

He hadn't known what to do, but his mother gave him some advice. "You go to her right now, find her, and put the ball in her court. She can walk away from you once, but if she sends you away when you're coming after her, then you'll know she's serious. She may not know her own mind, but down deep, if I know women, I know she'd rather you pursue her than let her run."

And so, in a way, he had encouraged Buck's instinct to do the same with Chloe. He knew they weren't an item yet, but he thought they both wanted it that way. He had no idea what this other woman in Buck's life was all about, but he was sure that if Buck forced the issue, Chloe would confront him about her and find out. If Buck was living with someone, that was a problem for Rayford and Bruce as well as for Chloe. But Chloe's evidence seemed thin at best.

"So he's going to try to call me tomorrow?" Chloe said.

"That's what I told him."

"How did he react?"

"He was just clarifying."

"You sounded pretty clear."

"I tried to be."

"I'm going to bed," she said.

"Why don't we talk awhile first?"

"I'm tired, Dad. And I'm talked out." She moved toward the stairs.

Rayford stalled her. "So, will you take his call tomorrow, you think?"

"I doubt it. I want to see how he reacts to Bruce's teaching tomorrow night."

"How do you think he'll react?"

"Dad! How would I know? All I know is what I saw this morning. Now let me go to bed."

"I just want to hear you out on this, hon. Talk to me."

"I'll talk to you tomorrow."

"Well, would you stay up and talk to me if I talked about me and my job situation instead of you and Buck?"

"Don't put me and Buck in the same sentence, Dad. And no, unless you're getting fired or switching jobs or something, I'd really rather do it another time."

Rayford knew he could snag her attention with what had happened to him that day, from the note from Hattie to the bogus harassment charge to the meeting with Earl Halliday. But he was more in a mood to talk about all that than she was. "Want to help me tidy up the kitchen?"

"Daddy, the kitchen is spotless. Anything you need done around here I'll do tomorrow, all right?"

"Coffee timer set for the morning?"

"Programmed since the beginning of time, Dad. What's with you?"

"I'm just feeling a little lonely. Not ready to turn in yet."

"If you need me to stay up with you I will, Dad. But why don't you just watch some TV and relax?"

Rayford couldn't delay her any longer. "I'll do that," he said. "I'll be right down here in the living room with the TV on, OK?"

She gave him a funny look and matched his tone. "And I'll be right up in my room at the top of the stairs with my light off, OK?"

He nodded.

She shook her head. "Now that we have both reported in and we know where the other will be and what we'll be doing, am I excused?"

"You're excused."

Rayford waited until Chloe started up the stairs to turn on the front porch light. Buck knew the address and the general area, as he had been there once before.

The news was ending and only talk shows coming on, but Rayford didn't care. He was sitting there only as a diversion anyway. He glanced through the curtains, looking for Buck's car. "Dad?" Chloe called down. "Could you turn that down a little? Or watch in your room?"

"I'll turn it down," he said, as headlights briefly flooded the living room and came up the drive. Before he adjusted the volume, he hurried to the door and intercepted Buck before he rang the bell. "I'm going upstairs to bed," he whispered. "Give me a second and then ring the bell. I'll be in the shower, and she'll have to answer it."

Rayford shut and deadbolted the door. He turned the television off and went upstairs.

As he passed Chloe's room he heard, "Daddy, you didn't have to turn it off. Just down."

"It's all right," he said. "I'm going to take a shower and get to bed."

"'Night, Dad."

"'Night, Chlo'."

Rayford stood in the shower with the water off and the master bath door open. As soon as he heard the doorbell, he turned on the water. He heard Chloe call, "Dad! Someone's at the door!"

"I'm in the shower!"

"Oh, Dad!"

* * *

This was a great idea! Buck thought, impressed that Rayford Steele trusted him enough to let him talk to his daughter when she obviously had something against him.

He waited a moment and rang the bell again. From inside he heard, "Just a minute, I'm coming!"

Chloe's face appeared in the tiny window in the middle of the ornate door. She rolled her eyes. "Buck!" she called through the closed door. "Call me tomorrow, will you? I was already in bed!"

"I need to talk to you!" Buck said.

"Not tonight."

"Yes, tonight," he said. "I'm not leaving till you talk to me."

"You're not?" she said.

"No, I'm not."

Chloe called his bluff. The porch light went out, and he heard her trotting up the stairs. He couldn't believe it. She was tougher than he thought. But he had said he wasn't leaving, and so he could not. If nothing else, Buck was a man of his word. Stubborn was more like it. But that had made him the journalist he was.

He still hadn't shaken the longing for Chloe that had come over him that afternoon in New York. He'd wait her out, he decided. He'd be on her stoop in the morning when she got up, if that's what it took.

Buck moved to the step at the edge of the porch and sat with his back to the front door, leaning on one of the stately pillars. He knew she would be able to see him if she came back to check. She'd probably be listening for his car, and she wouldn't hear a thing.

\+ + +

"Daddy!" Chloe called from Rayford's bedroom door. "Are you about done?"

"Not really! What's up?"

"Buck Williams is at the door, and he won't leave!"

"What do you want me to do about it?"

"Get rid of him!"

"You get rid of him! He's your problem!"

"You're my dad! It's your duty!"

"Did he harm you? Has he threatened you?"

"No! Now, Dad!"

"*I* don't want him to leave, Chloe! If *you* do, *you* send him away."

"I'm going to bed!" she said.

"So am I!"

Rayford turned off the shower and heard Chloe slam his bedroom door. Then hers. Would she really go to bed and leave Buck on the porch? Would Buck stay? Rayford tiptoed to his door and opened it far enough to be able to keep tabs on Chloe. Her door was still shut. Rayford slipped into bed and didn't move, listening. It was all he could do to keep from chuckling aloud. He had been put on the short list of candidates to be the new pilot for the president of the United States, and here he was, eavesdropping on his own daughter. It was the most fun he'd had in weeks.

\+ + +

Buck hadn't realized how chilly the night was until he had sat next to that cold pillar for a few minutes. His jacket squeaked when he moved, and he raised the fur-lined collar around his neck. The smell reminded him of the many places in the world he had dragged this old bomber jacket. More than once he had thought he'd die in the thing.

Buck stretched his legs in front of him and crossed them at the ankles, suddenly realizing how tired he was. If he had to sleep on this porch, he would.

Then, in the stillness, he heard the faint creaking of the steps inside. Chloe was creeping down to see if he was still there. If it had been Rayford, the steps would have been louder and more sure. Rayford would probably have told him to give it up and go home, that they would try to deal with the problem later. Buck heard the floor near the door creak. Just for effect, he tilted his head toward the pillar and rearranged his posture as if settling in for a snooze.

The footsteps back up the stairs were not so muffled. What now?

+ + +

Rayford had heard Chloe open her door and make her way down the stairs in the darkness. Now she was on her way back up. She whipped her door open and slapped at the light switch. Rayford leaned so he could see her emerge, which she did a moment later just before she turned out the light. Her hair was pinned atop her head, and she wore her floor-length terry cloth robe. She turned on the light at the top of the stairs and descended with a purpose. If Rayford had to guess, he didn't think she was running the man off.

+ + +

Buck saw his shadow on the lawn and knew a light was on behind him, but he didn't want to appear either overconfident or too eager. He stayed right where he was, as if already asleep. The door was unlocked and opened, but he heard nothing else. He sneaked a peek. That, apparently, was her invitation to come in. *I've come this far,* Buck thought. *That's not good enough.* He resumed his position, his back to the door.

Half a minute later he heard Chloe stomping to the door again. She swung open the storm door and said, "What do you want, an engraved invitation?"

"Wha—?" Buck said, pretending to be startled and turning around. "Is it morning already?"

"Very funny. Get in here. You've got ten minutes."

He stood to go in, but Chloe let the storm door slap shut as she went to sit on one end of the couch in the living room. Buck let himself in. "That's all right," he said, "I'll keep my coat."

"This visit was your idea, not mine," she said. "Forgive me if I don't treat you as if you were invited."

Chloe sat with her feet tucked under her, arms crossed, as if granting him an extremely reluctant audience. Buck draped his jacket across an easy chair and slid the footstool in front of Chloe. He sat there, staring at her, as if trying to think of where to begin.

"I'm hardly dressed for visitors," she said.

"You look great no matter what you're wearing."

"Spare me," she said. "What do you want?"

"Actually, I wanted to bring you flowers," he said. "Seeing as how yours are in the trash."

"Did you think I was kidding?" she said, pointing past him. He turned and looked. Sure enough, a huge bouquet of flowers was jammed in a wastebasket.

"I didn't think you were kidding," Buck said. "I just thought you were being figurative, and I hadn't heard the expression."

"What are you talking about?"

"When you told me the flowers were in the trash, I thought it was some sort of phrase I'd never heard. It had the flavor of 'the cat is out of the bag' or 'the water is under the bridge.'"

"I said the flowers were in the trash, and that's what I meant. I mean what *I* say, Buck."

Buck was at a loss. They seemed to be on different pages, and he wasn't even sure it was the same script. "Um, could you tell me why the flowers are in the trash? Maybe that would help clarify things for me."

"Because I didn't want them."

"Oh, silly me. Makes sense. And you didn't want them because . . ." He stopped and shook his head, as if she should fill in the blank.

"They insult me because of where they came from."

"And where did they come from?"

"OK, then because of *who* they came from."

"And they came from whom?"

"Oh, Buck, really! I don't have time for this and I'm not in the mood."

Chloe moved to stand and suddenly Buck was angry. "Chloe, wait just a minute." She sat back down and folded up again, looking perturbed. "You owe me an explanation."

"No, you owe *me* an explanation."

Buck sighed. "I'll explain anything you want, Chloe, but no more games. It was clear we were attracted to each other, and I know I gave off some less-than-interested signals Friday night, but today I realized—"

"This morning," she interrupted, obviously fighting tears, "I discovered why you seemed to have lost interest all of a sudden. You were feeling guilty about not telling me everything, and if you think those flowers fixed anything—"

"Chloe! Let's talk about real problems! I had nothing to do with those flowers."

For once, Chloe was silent.

9

CHLOE SAT LOOKING skeptically at Buck. "You didn't?" she managed finally.

He shook his head. "Apparently you have another admirer."

"Yeah, right," she said. "Another? As if that makes two?"

Buck spread his hands before him. "Chloe, there's obviously been a lack of communication here."

"Obviously."

"Call me presumptuous, but I was under the impression that we sort of hit it off from the moment we met." He paused and waited for a response.

She nodded. "Nothing serious," she said. "But yes, I thought we liked each other."

"And I was with you on the plane when you prayed with your dad," he said.

She nodded slightly.

"That was a special time," he continued.

"OK," she agreed.

"Then I went through my ordeal and couldn't wait to get back here to tell all of you about it."

Chloe's lip quivered. "That was the most incredible story I had ever heard, Buck, and I didn't doubt you for a second. I knew you were going through a lot, but I thought we had connected."

"I didn't know what to call it," Buck said, "but as I told you in my note that Sunday, I was attracted to you."

"Not only to me, apparently."

Buck was speechless. "Not only to you?" he repeated.

"Just go on with your speech."

Speech? She thinks this is a speech? And she thinks there's someone else? There hasn't been anyone else in years! Buck was deflated and thought of giving up, but he decided she was worth it. Misguided, jumping to strange conclusions for some reason, but worth it.

"Between Sunday and Friday night I did a lot of thinking about us."

"Here it comes," she said, tearing up again. What did she think? That he was prepared to sleep on her porch just to dump her for someone else when she finally let him in?

"I realize that Friday night I was giving you mixed signals," he said. "Well, maybe not so mixed. I was pulling away."

"There wasn't much to pull away from."

"But we were getting there, weren't we?" Buck said. "Didn't you think we were going to progress?"

"Sure. Until Friday night."

"I'm a little embarrassed to admit this—" he said hesitantly.

"You should be," she said.

"—but I realized I was being pretty premature, given how recently we had met, and your age, and—"

"So, there it is. It's not your age that's the problem, is it? It's my age."

"Chloe, I'm sorry. The issue was not your age or my age. The issue was the *difference* in our ages. Then I realized that with only about seven more years ahead of us, that becomes a nonissue. But I was all mixed up. I was thinking about our future, you know, what might come of our relationship, and we don't even have a relationship yet."

"And we're not going to, Buck. I'm not going to share you. If there was a future for us, it would be an exclusive relationship, and—oh, never mind. Here I go talking about stuff neither of us even considered before."

"Apparently we did," Buck said. "I just said I did, and it sounds like you've been looking ahead a little, too."

"Not any more, not since this morning."

"Chloe, I'm going to have to ask you something, and I don't want you to take it the wrong way. This may sound a little condescending, even parental, and I don't mean it to be." She sat stiffly, as if expecting a reprimand. "I'm going to ask you not to say anything for a minute, all right?"

"Pardon me?" she said. "I'm not allowed to speak?"

"That's not what I'm saying."

"It's what you just said."

Buck came just short of raising his voice. He knew his look and tone were stern, but he had to do something. "Chloe, you're not listening to me. You're not letting me finish a thought. There's some subtext here I know nothing about, and I can't defend myself against mysteries and fantasies. You keep talking about not sharing me—is there something you need to ask me or accuse me of before I can go on here?"

* * *

Rayford, who had been lying still and nearly holding his breath trying to listen, had heard very little of the conversation until Buck raised his voice. Rayford heard that and silently cheered. Chloe increased her volume, too. "I want to know about anybody else in your life before I even think—oh, Buck, what are we talking about? Aren't there a lot more important things to be thinking about right now?"

Rayford couldn't hear Buck's whispered response, and he was tired of trying. He moved to the doorway and called down to them. "Could you two either speak up or just whisper? If I can't hear, I'm going to sleep!"

"Go to sleep, Dad!" Chloe said.

* * *

Buck smiled. Chloe was also suppressing a grin.

"Chloe, all weekend I've been thinking about all the 'more important things' we have to think about. I almost had myself talked into giving you the let's-be-friends routine . . . until I was sitting in that office this afternoon and you came over me."

"*I* came over you? You saw me at the *Global Weekly* office?"

"The *Global Weekly* office? What are you talking about?"

Chloe hesitated. "Well, what office were you talking about?"

Buck grimaced. He hadn't planned to talk about his meeting with Carpathia. "Can we save that until we're back on even ground here? I was saying I was suddenly overwhelmed with the need to see you, to talk to you, to get back to you."

"Back from where? Or back from whom, I should ask."

"Well, I'd rather not get into that until I think you're ready to hear it."

"I'm ready, Buck, because I already know."

"How do you know?"

"Because I was there!"

"Chloe, if you were at the Chicago bureau office, then you know I wasn't there today, I mean, except for early this morning."

"So you *were* there."

"I was just dropping off some keys to Alice."

"Alice? That's her name?"

Buck nodded, lost.

"What's her last name, Buck?"

"Her last name? I don't know. I've always just called her Alice. She's new. She replaced Lucinda's secretary, who disappeared."

"You want me to believe you really don't know her last name?"

"Why should I lie about that? Do you know her?"

Chloe's eyes bored into him. Buck knew they were finally getting somewhere. He just didn't know where. "I can't say I know her, exactly," Chloe said. "I just talked to her, that's all."

"You talked to Alice," he repeated, trying to make it compute.

"She told me you and she were engaged."

"Oh, she did not!" Buck shouted, then quieted, peeking up the stairs. "What are you talking about?"

"We're talking about the same Alice, aren't we?" Chloe said. "Skinny, spiky dark hair, short skirt, works at *Global Weekly*?"

"That's her." Buck nodded. "But don't you think I'd know her last name if we were engaged? Plus, that would be mighty big news to her fiancé."

"So she's engaged, but not to you?" Chloe said, sounding doubtful.

"She told me something about picking up her fiancé today," he said. Chloe looked stricken. "Do you mind if I ask how you happened to be at the *Weekly* and talking to her? Were you looking for me?"

"As a matter of fact, I was," Chloe said. "I had seen her earlier, and I was surprised to see her there."

"Like I said, Chloe, I wasn't there today."

"Where were you?"

"I asked you first. Where had you seen Alice?"

Chloe spoke so softly Buck had to lean forward to hear. "At your condo."

Buck sat back, everything coming into focus. He wanted to laugh, but poor Chloe! He fought to stay serious. "It's my fault," he said. "I invited you, my plans changed, and I never told you."

"She had your keys," Chloe whispered.

Buck shook his head sympathetically. "I gave them to her so she could deliver some equipment I was expecting at the office. I had to be in New York today."

Buck's frustration with Chloe melted into sympathy. She couldn't maintain eye contact, and she was clearly on the verge of tears. "So you really didn't send the flowers," she whispered.

"If I'd known I needed to, I would have."

Chloe uncrossed her arms and buried her face in her hands. "Buck, I'm so embarrassed," she moaned, and the tears came. "I have no excuse. I was worried after Friday night, and then I just made a big thing out of nothing."

"I didn't know you cared that much," Buck said.

"Of course I cared. But I can't expect you to understand or to forgive me after I've been such a, such a—oh, if you don't even want to see me again, I'd understand." She was still hiding her face. "You'd better go," she added. "I wasn't presentable when you got here, and I'm certainly not now."

"Is it all right if I sleep on your porch? 'Cause I'd like to be here when you are presentable."

She peeked at him through her hands and smiled through her tears. "You don't have to do this, Buck."

"Chloe, I'm just sorry I contributed to this by not telling you about my trip."

"No, Buck. It was all my fault, and I'm so sorry."

"OK," he said. "You're sorry, and I forgive you. Can that be the end of it?"

"That's just going to make me cry more."

"What'd I do now?"

"You're just being too sweet about this!"

"I can't win!"

"Give me a minute, will you?" Chloe sprang from the couch and hurried up the stairs.

\+ \+ \+

Ever since asking them to either speak up or quiet down, Rayford had been sitting just out of sight at the top of the stairs. He tried to get up and sneak back into the master bedroom, but he was just rising when Chloe nearly ran into him.

"Dad!" she whispered. "What are you doing?!"

"Eavesdropping. What does it look like?"

"You're awful!"

"*I'm* awful? Look what you did to Buck! Way to hang a guy before he's tried."

"Dad, I was such a fool."

"It was just a comedy of errors, hon, and like Buck said, it only shows how much you cared."

"Did you know he was coming?"

Rayford nodded.

"Tonight? You knew he was coming tonight?"

"Guilty."

"And you made me answer the door."

"So shoot me."

"I ought to."

"No, you ought to thank me."

"That's for sure. You can go to bed now. I'm going to change and see if Buck wants to take a walk."

"So you're saying I can't come along? Or even follow from a distance?"

\+ + +

Buck heard whispering upstairs, then water running and drawers opening and shutting. Chloe came back down in jeans and a sweatshirt, a jacket, a cap, and tennis shoes. "Do you have to go?" she said. "Or do you want to take a walk?"

"You're not kicking me out after all?"

"We need to talk somewhere else so Dad can get to sleep."

"We were keeping him up?"

"Sort of."

\+ + +

Rayford heard the front door shut, then knelt by his bed. He prayed Chloe and Buck would be good for each other, regardless of what the future held for them. Even if they became only good friends, he would be grateful for that. He crawled into bed, falling into a light, fitful sleep, listening for Chloe's return and praying about the opportunity that had been presented him that day.

\+ + +

The night was nippy but clear as midnight approached. "Buck," Chloe said as they turned a corner to wend their way through the fashionable Arlington Heights subdivision, "I just want to say again how—"

Buck stopped and snagged Chloe's jacket sleeve. "Chloe, don't. We've got only seven years. We can't live in the past. We've both stumbled this weekend, and we've apologized, so let's be done with it."

"Really?"

"Absolutely." They continued walking. "'Course, I'm gonna need to find out who's sending you flowers."

"I've been thinking about that, and I have a suspicion."

"Who?"

"It's kind of embarrassing, because that might have been my fault too."

"Your old boyfriend?"

"No! I told you when we first met, we dated when I was a freshman and he was a senior. He graduated and I never heard from him again. He's married."

"Then it had better not be him. Any other guys at Stanford who wish you would come back?"

"Nobody with the style to send flowers."

"Your dad?"

"He already denied it."

"Who does that leave?"

"Think about it," Chloe said.

Buck squinted and thought. "Bruce!? Oh, no, you don't think . . . ?"

"Who else is there?"

"How would you have encouraged him?"

"I don't know. I like him a lot. I admire him. His honesty moves me, and he's so passionate and sincere."

"I know, and he has to be lonely. But it's only been a few weeks since he lost his family. I can't imagine it would be him."

"I tell him I enjoy his messages," Chloe said. "Maybe I'm being more friendly than I need to be. It's just that I never thought of him that way, you know?"

"Could you? He's a sharp young guy."

"Buck! He's older than you!"

"Not much."

"Yeah, but you're on the very end of the age spectrum I'd even consider."

"Well, thank you so much! How soon before you have to have me back to the home?"

"Oh, Buck, it's so embarrassing! I need Bruce as a friend and as a teacher!"

"You're sure you wouldn't consider more?"

She shook her head. "I just can't see it. It's not that he's unattractive, but I can't imagine ever thinking of him that way. You know, he asked me to work for him, full-time. I never even thought there might be an ulterior motive."

"Now don't jump to conclusions, Chloe."

"I'm good at that, aren't I?"

"You're asking the wrong person."

"What am I going to do, Buck? I don't want to hurt him. I can't tell him I don't think of him in that way. You know this all has to just be a reaction to his loss. Like he's on the rebound."

"I can't imagine what it would be like to lose a wife," Buck said.

"And kids."

"Yeah."

"You told me once that you were never serious about anyone."

"Right. Well, a couple of times I thought I was, but I had jumped the gun. One girl, a year ahead of me in grad school, dumped me because I was too slow to make a move on her."

"No!"

"Guess I'm a little old-fashioned that way."

"That's encouraging."

"I lost whatever feeling I had for her real quick."

"I can imagine. So you weren't the typical college guy?"

"You want the truth?"

"I don't know. Do I?"

"Depends. Would you rather hear that I have all kinds of experience because I'm such a cool guy, or that I'm a virgin?"

"You're going to tell me whatever I want to hear?"

"I'm going to tell you the truth. I just wouldn't mind knowing in advance which you'd want to hear."

"Experienced or a virgin," Chloe repeated. "That's a no-brainer. Definitely the latter."

"Bingo," Buck said softly, more from embarrassment than from braggadocio.

"Wow," Chloe said. "That's something to be proud of these days."

"I have to say I'm more grateful than proud. My reasons were not as pure as they would be today. I mean, I know it would have been wrong to sleep around, but I didn't abstain out of any sense of morality. When I had opportunities, I wasn't interested. And I was so focused on my studies and my future, I didn't have that many opportunities. Truth is, people always assumed I got around because I ran in pretty fast circles. But I was backward when it came to stuff like that. Kind of conservative."

"You're apologizing."

"Maybe. I don't mean to be. It's kind of embarrassing to be my age and totally inexperienced. I've always been sort of ahead of my generation in other ways."

"That's an understatement," Chloe said. "You think God was protecting you, even before you were aware of him?"

"I never thought of it that way, but it very well could be. I've never had to worry about disease and all the emotional stuff that goes with intimate relationships."

Buck self-consciously rubbed the back of his neck.

"This is embarrassing you, isn't it?" Chloe said.

"Yeah, a little."

"So I suppose you'd rather not hear about my sexual experience or lack of it."

Buck grimaced. "If you don't mind. See, I'm only thirty and I feel like an old-timer when you even use the word . . . *sex*. So maybe you should spare me."

"But Buck, what if something comes of our relationship? Aren't you going to be curious?"

"Maybe I'll ask you then."

"But what if by then you're already madly in love with me, and you find out something you can't live with?"

Buck was ashamed of himself. It was one thing to admit to a woman that you're a virgin when it seemed to put you in one of the smaller minorities in the world. But she was so straightforward, so direct. He didn't want to talk about this, to hear about it, to know, especially if she was more "experienced" than he. And yet she had a point. She seemed more comfortable talking about their future than he did, but he was the one who had decided to pursue a relationship. Rather than respond to her question, he just shrugged.

"I'll spare you the mystery," Chloe said. "My boyfriends in high school, and my boyfriend my freshman year at Stanford and I were not models of, what did my mother call it, propriety? But I'm happy to say we never had sex. That's probably the reason I never lasted with any of them."

"Um, Chloe, that's good news, but could we talk about something else?"

"You *are* an old codger, aren't you?"

"I guess." Buck blushed. "I can interview heads of state, but this kind of frankness is new to me."

"C'mon, Buck, you hear this and a lot worse on talk shows every day."

"But I don't put you in the category of a talk-show guest."

"Am I too blunt?"

"I'm just not used to it and not good at it."

Chloe chuckled. "What are the odds that two unmarried people are taking a walk at midnight in America and both of them are virgins?"

"Especially after all the Christians were taken away."

"Amazing," she said. "But you want to talk about something else."

"Do I!"

"Tell me why you had to go to New York."

* * *

It was after one o'clock when Rayford stirred at the sound of the front door. It opened but did not close. He heard Chloe and Buck chatting from just inside the door. "I've really got to get going," Buck said. "I'm expecting a response from New York on my article tomorrow morning, and I want to be awake enough to interact."

After Buck left, Rayford heard Chloe close the door. Her footsteps on the stairs seemed lighter than they had earlier in the evening. He heard her tiptoe to his door and peek in. "I'm awake, hon," he said. "Everything all right?"

"Better than all right," she said, coming to sit on the edge of the bed. "Thanks, Dad," she said in the darkness.

"You have a good talk?"

"Yeah. Buck is incredible."

"He kiss you?"

"No! Dad!"

"Hold hands?"

"No! Now stop it! We just talked. You wouldn't believe the offer he got today."

"Offer?"

"I don't have time to get into it tonight. You flying tomorrow?"

"No."

"We'll talk about it in the morning."

"I want to tell you about an offer I got today, too," Rayford said.

"What was it?"

"Too involved for tonight. I'm not going to take it anyway. We can talk about it in the morning."

"Dad, tell me one more time you didn't send those flowers just to cheer me up. I'll feel awful if you did and I trashed them."

"I didn't, Chlo'."

"That's good, I guess. But it wasn't Buck, either."

"You're sure?"

"Positive this time."

"Uh-oh."

"You thinking what I'm thinking, Dad?"

"I've been wondering about Bruce ever since I heard Buck tell you it wasn't him."

"What am I going to do, Dad?"

"If you're going to work with the man, you'll have to have a talk with him."

"Why is it my responsibility? I didn't start this! I didn't encourage it—at least I didn't mean to."

"Well, you could ignore it. I mean, he sent them anonymously. How were you supposed to know who they were from?"

"Yeah! I don't really know, do I?"

"Of course not."

"I'm supposed to see him tomorrow afternoon," she said, "to talk about this job."

"Then talk about the job."

"And ignore the flowers?"

"You sort of already did that, didn't you?"

Chloe laughed. "If he's got the guts to own up to sending them, then we can talk about what it all means."

"Sounds good."

"But, Dad, if Buck and I keep seeing each other, it's going to become obvious."

"You don't want people to know?"

"I don't want to shove it in Bruce's face, knowing how he feels about me."

"But you *don't* know."

"That's right, isn't it? If he doesn't tell me, I don't know."

"G'night, Chloe."

"But it's going to be awkward working for him or with him, won't it, Dad?"

"'Night, Chloe."

"I just don't want to—"

"Chloe! It's tomorrow already!"

"'Night, Dad."

* * *

Buck was awakened midmorning Tuesday by a call from Stanton Bailey. "Cameron!" he shouted. "You awake?"

"Yes, sir."

"You don't sound like it!"

"Wide-awake, sir."

"Late night?"

"Yes, but I'm awake now, Mr. —"

"You always were honest to a fault there, Cam. That's why I still don't understand your insisting you were at that meeting when—ah, that's behind us. You're exiled; I'm wishing you were replacing Plank here, but hey, what's done is done, huh?"

"Yes, sir."

"Well, you've still got it."

"Sir?"

"Still got the touch. How does it feel to write another award-winner?"

"Well, I'm glad you like it, Mr. Bailey, but I didn't write it for an award."

"We never do, do we? Ever craft one just to make it fit a category in some contest? Me neither. I've seen guys try it, though. Never works. They could take a lesson from you. Thorough, long but tight, all the quotes, all the angles, fair to every opinion. I thought it was real good of you not to make the alien kooks and the religious wackos look stupid. Everybody's got a right to his own opinion, right? And these represent the heartland of America, whether they believe it was something green from Mars or Jesus on a horse."

"Sir?"

"Or whatever imagery that is. You know what I mean. Anyway, this thing's a masterpiece, and I appreciate your usual great job and not letting this other business get you down. You keep up the good work, stay there in Chicago for an appropriate amount of time so it still looks like I've got some control over my star guy, and you'll be back in New York before you know it. When's your lease up?"

"A year, but actually I like it here, and—"

"Very funny. Just talk to me when they start pushing you on that lease, Cameron, and we'll get you back here. I don't know about executive editor, because we've got to fill that before then and it probably wouldn't make much sense, you going from the wilderness to the saddle. But we'll at least get your salary back up where it belongs, and you'll be back here doing what you do best."

"Well, thanks."

"Hey, take the day off! This thing'll hit the stands a week from yesterday and you'll be the talk of the town for a few days."

"I just might take you up on that."

"And listen, Cameron, stay out of that little gal's hair there. What's her name?"

"Verna Zee?"

"Yeah, Verna. She'll do all right, but just leave her alone. You don't even have to be over there unless you need to be for some reason. What's next on your plate?"

"Steve's trying to get me to go to Israel next week for the signing of the treaty between Israel and the U.N."

"We've got a slew of people going, Cameron. I was going to put the religion editor on the cover story."

"Jimmy Borland?"

"Problem?"

"Well, first, I don't see it as a religious story, especially with the one-world religion meeting going on in New York at the same time, the Jews talking about rebuilding the temple, and the Catholics voting on a new pope. And this is going to sound self-serving, but do you really think Jimmy can handle a cover story?"

"Probably not. It just seemed like a good fit. He's been over there so many times on his beat, and just about anything Israel does can be considered religious, right?"

"Not necessarily."

"I've always liked that you talk to me straight, Cameron. Too many yes people around here. So you don't think this is a religious thing just because it's happening in the so-called Holy Land."

"Anything Carpathia is involved in is geopolitical, even if it has some religious ramifications. A great religious angle over there, besides the temple thing, is those two preachers at the Wailing Wall."

"Yeah, what's with those crazies? Those two said it wasn't going to rain in Israel for three and a half years, and so far it hasn't! That's a dry land as it is, but if they go that long without rain, everything's gonna dry up and blow away. How dependent is that scientist guy's—uh, Rosenzweig's—formula on rain?"

"I'm not sure, sir. I know it requires less rain than if you tried to grow without it, but I think there still has to be water from somewhere to make it work."

"I'd like to see Jimmy get an exclusive with those two," Bailey said, "but they're dangerous, aren't they?"

"Sir?"

"Well, two guys tried to kill them and wound up dropping dead on the spot, and what was this thing the other day? A bunch of guys got burned up. People said those two called down fire from heaven!"

"Others were saying they breathed fire on them."

"I heard that too!" Bailey said. "That's some kind of halitosis problem, eh?"

Bailey was laughing, but Buck couldn't fake it. He believed the fire-breathing story because it was right out of Scripture, and neither did he put people who believed the Rapture in the same category as the UFO wackos.

"Anyway," Bailey continued, "I haven't told Borland he's got the cover, but I think rumor has it that he's in line for it. I could put you on it, and I'd rather, but somebody else would have to get bumped from the trip, because we're maxed out budgetwise. Maybe I could send one less photographer."

Buck was eager for a photographer to get some supernatural evidence on film. "No, don't do that," he said. "Plank is offering to let me fly over there as part of the U.N. contingency." There was a long silence. "Sir?"

"I don't know about that, Cameron. I'm impressed that they've apparently forgiven you for stiffing them last time, but how do you maintain objectivity when you're on their dime?"

"You have to trust me, sir. I have never traded favors."

"I know you haven't, and Plank knows you haven't. But does Carpathia understand journalism?"

"I'm not sure he does."

"Neither am I. You know what I'm afraid of."

"What's that?"

"That he'll try stealing you away."

"Not much chance of my going anywhere," Buck said.

"Still, I would have thought he'd be more upset at you than I was, and now he wants you to ride along on this deal-signing thing?"

"He actually wants me to sit in on the signing as part of his delegation."

"That would be totally inappropriate."

"I know."

"Unless you could make it clear that you're not part of the delegation. What a great spot! The only media person at the table!"

"Yeah, but how would I do that?"

"It could be something simple. Maybe you wear a patch on your jacket that makes it obvious you're with *Weekly*."

"I could do that."

"You could carry it with you and slap it on once everyone's in place."

"That sounds a little underhanded."

"Oh, don't kid yourself, son. Carpathia's a politician's politician, and he has all kinds of reasons for wanting you there with him. Not the least of which would be greasing the skids so you could slide out of *Global Weekly*."

"I have no such plans, sir."

"Well, I know you don't. Listen, do you think you could still get in on the signing, I mean be right there when it happens, with the involved parties instead of the press corps, even if you didn't ride with the U.N. delegation?"

"I don't know. I could ask."

"Well, ask. Because I'll spring for an extra ticket on a commercial flight before I'll see you go over there at U.N. expense. I don't want you owing Carpathia any favors, but there's not much I wouldn't do to see you peeking over his shoulder when he signs that treaty."

10

BUCK LIKED THE IDEA of taking the day off, not that he had anything ambitious planned anyway. He puttered around in the spare bedroom, setting up his office. Once everything was plugged in and tested, he checked his e-mail and found one long message from James Borland, religion editor of *Global Weekly*.

Uh-oh, he thought.

I'd get on the phone and have it out with you voice to voice. But I think better on paper and want to vent a little here before I get your usual excuses. You knew full well that I was in line for the treaty signing cover story. The thing's happening in the religious capital of the world, Cameron. Who did you think would handle it?

Just because I'm not your typical cover-story writer and haven't done one before doesn't mean I couldn't handle it. I might have come to you for advice on it anyway, but you probably would have wanted to share the byline, your name first.

The old man tells me that your writing it was his idea, but don't think I can't envision you talking your way into this one and me out of it. Well, I'm going to be in Israel, too. I'll stay out of your hair if you'll stay out of mine.

Buck immediately phoned Borland. "Jimmy," he said, "it's Buck."

"You got my e-mail?"

"I did."

"I have nothing more to say."

"I imagine not," Buck said. "You were pretty clear."

"Then what do you want?"

"Just to set the record straight."

"Yeah, you're going to convince me that your story lines up with Bailey's, that you didn't even ask for the assignment."

"To tell you the truth, Jim, I did tell Bailey I saw it as more of a political than a religious story, and I even wondered aloud whether you were up to it."

"And you don't think that constitutes running me off the story so you can write it?"

"I may have, Jim, but it wasn't intentional. I'm sorry, and if it means that much to you, I'll insist that you do it."

"Right. What's the catch?"

"That I get your stories, and one new one."

"You want my beat?"

"Just for a few weeks. In my mind, you've got the most enviable job on the *Weekly*."

"Why don't I trust you, Buck? You sound like Tom Sawyer trying to get me to paint your fence."

"I'm dead serious, Jim. You let me cover the one-world religion story, the rebuilding of the temple story, the two preachers at the Wailing Wall story, the vote for a new pope story, and another one in your bailiwick I haven't told anyone about yet, and I'll see to it you get to do the cover story on the treaty."

"I'll bite. What's the big scoop on my beat that I've missed?"

"You didn't miss it. I just have a friend who was in the right place at the right time."

"Who? What?"

"I won't reveal my source, but I happen to know that Rabbi Tsion Ben-Judah—"

"I know him."

"You do?"

"Well, I know of him. Everybody does. Pretty impressive guy."

"Have you heard what he's up to?"

"Some research project, isn't it? Something typically musty?"

"So that's another one you don't want. It sounds like I'm asking for Baltic and Mediterranean and offering Boardwalk and Park Place."

"That's exactly what it sounds like, Buck. You think I'm stupid?"

"I sure don't, Jimmy. That's one thing you don't understand. I'm not your enemy."

"Just my competitor, keeping the cover stories for yourself."

"I just offered you one!"

"Something doesn't wash, Buck. The one-world religion meeting is dry as dust, and the thing will never work anyway. Nothing's going to stand in the way of the Jews rebuilding their temple because no one but the Jews care. I'll grant you that those two guys at the Wailing Wall would be a great story, but more than a half-dozen people who've tried to get near them wound up dead. I have to think every journalist in the world has asked for an exclusive, but no one's had the guts to go in there. Everybody knows who the new pope's gonna be. And who in the world cares about the rabbi's research?"

"Whoa, back up a second there, Jim," Buck said. "Now, see, you've got a leg up on me on the pope thing because I have no idea who the new one will be."

"Oh, come on, Buck. Where have you been? All the smart money is on Archbishop Mathews out of—"

"Cincinnati? Really? I interviewed him for the—"

"I know, Buck. I saw it. Everybody around here has seen your next Pulitzer."

Buck was silent. Did the depths of jealousy know no bounds?

Borland must have sensed he'd gone too far. "Truthfully, Buck, I've got to hand it to you. That's going to be one good read. But you got no hint that he's got the inside track on the papacy?"

"None."

"He's a pretty crafty guy. He's got support coming out his ears, and I think he's a shoo-in. So do a lot of other people."

"So, since I know him and I think he trusts me, you won't mind that story being part of the trade?"

"Oh, you just assume we're making this trade now, is that it?" Jimmy said.

"Why not? How bad do you want the cover?"

"Buck, you think I don't know you're going to be part of the U.N. contingent at the signing and that you're going to be wearing a *Global Weekly* blazer or hat or something to get us a little play?"

"So make it part of your cover story. 'Substitute Religion Editor Gets to Stand Next to Secretary-General.'"

"Not funny. No way Plank gives you that plum and then settles for someone else writing the piece."

"I'm telling you, Jim, I'll insist on it."

"You weren't supposed to have any more bargaining power after missing that Carpathia meeting before. What makes you think Bailey will listen to you? You're just a Chicago bureau writer now."

Buck felt his old ego kick in, and the words were out before he could measure them. "Yeah, just a Chicago bureau writer who wrote next week's cover story and has been assigned the following week's too."

"Touché!"

"I'm sorry, Jim. That was out of line. But I'm serious about this. I'm not just bluffing to make you think your beat is a bigger deal than a cover story.

I'm convinced things are breaking religiously that make much more interesting stories than the treaty signing."

"Wait a minute, Buck. You're not one of the suckers buying into the prophetic, apocalyptic, all-this-has-been-foretold-in-the-Bible theories, are you?"

That's exactly what I am, Buck thought, but he couldn't afford to go public yet. "How widespread is that view?" Buck asked.

"You ought to know. You wrote the cover story."

"My story gives voice to all the opinions."

"Yeah, but you ran into the Rapture nuts. They'd love to see some spin on all these stories you want to do that shoehorns them into God's plan."

"You're the religion editor, Jim. Do they have a point?"

"Doesn't sound to me like something God would have done."

"You're allowing that there is a God."

"In a manner of speaking."

"What manner?"

"God is in all of us, Buck. You know my view."

"Your view hasn't changed since the disappearances?"

"Nope."

"Was God in the people who disappeared?"

"Sure."

"So now part of God is gone?"

"You're way too literal for me, Buck. Next you're going to tell me the treaty proves Carpathia's the Antichrist."

How I'd love to convince you, Buck thought. *And someday I'll try.* "I know the treaty is a big deal," he said. "Probably bigger than most people realize, but the signing is just the show. The fact that there's an agreement was the story, and that story has been told."

"The signing may just be show, but it's worth a cover, Buck. Why wouldn't you think I could handle it?"

"Tell me I can have the other stuff, and I'll see that you get it."

"Deal."

"You're serious?"

"'Course I'm serious. I'm sure you think you've pulled one over on me, but I'm no kid anymore, Buck. I don't care where this cover ranks with all the ones you've done. I'd like to have it for my scrapbook, my grandkids, all that."

"I understand."

"Yeah, you understand. You've got your whole life ahead of you, and you'll do twice as many covers as you've already done."

* * *

"Chloe! Come down here!"

Rayford stood in the living room, too stunned to even sit. He had just flipped on the TV and heard the special news bulletin.

Chloe came hurrying down the stairs. "I've got to get to the church," she said. "What's up?"

Rayford shushed her and they watched and listened. A CNN White House correspondent spoke. "Apparently this unusual gesture came as a result of a meeting early last evening between U.N. Secretary-General Nicolae Carpathia and President Gerald Fitzhugh. Fitzhugh has already led the way among heads of state in his unwavering support of the administration of the new secretary-general, but this lending of the new presidential aircraft sets a whole new standard.

"The White House sent the current *Air Force One* to New York late yesterday afternoon to collect Carpathia, and today comes this announcement that the maiden flight of the new *Air Force One* will carry Carpathia and not the president himself."

"What?" Chloe asked.

"The treaty signing in Israel," Rayford said.

"But the president is going, isn't he?"

"Yes, but on the old plane."

"I don't get it."

"Neither do I."

The CNN reporter continued, "Skeptics suspect a behind-the-scenes deal, but the president himself made this statement from the White House just moments ago."

CNN ran a tape. President Fitzhugh looked perturbed. "Naysayers and wholly political animals can have a field day with this gesture," the president said, "but peace-loving Americans and everyone tired of politics-as-usual will celebrate it. The new plane is beautiful. I've seen it. I'm proud of it. There's plenty of room on it for the entire United States and United Nations delegations, but I have decided it is only right that the U.N. contingency have the plane to themselves for this maiden voyage.

"Until our current *Air Force One* becomes *Air Force Two*, we will christen the new 777 '*Global Community One*' and offer it to Secretary-General Carpathia with our best wishes. It's time the world rallies round this lover of peace, and I am proud to lead the way by this small gesture.

"I also call upon my colleagues around the globe to seriously study the Carpathia disarmament proposal. Strong defense has been a sacred cow in our country for generations, but I'm sure we all agree that the time for a true, weaponless peace is long past due. I hope to have an announcement soon on our decisions in this regard."

"Dad, does this mean you would—?"

But Rayford silenced Chloe again with a gesture as CNN cut to New York for a live response from Carpathia.

Nicolae gazed directly into the camera, appearing to look right into the eyes of each viewer. His voice was quiet and emotional. "I would like to thank President Fitzhugh for this most generous gesture. We at the United Nations are deeply moved, grateful, and humbled. We look forward to a wonderful ceremony in Jerusalem next Monday."

"Man, is he slick." Rayford shook his head.

"That's the job you told me about. You'd be flying that plane?"

"I don't know. I suppose. I didn't realize the old *Air Force One* was going to become *Air Force Two*, the vice president's plane. I wonder if they're really retiring the current pilot. It's like musical chairs. If the current pilot stays with the 747 when it becomes *AF2,* what happens to the current *AF2* pilot?"

Chloe shrugged. "You're sure you don't want the job flying the new plane?"

"Surer now than ever. I don't want to have anything to do with Carpathia."

* * *

Buck took a call from Alice at the Chicago office. "You'd better get two lines into there," she said, "if you're going to keep working from home."

"I've got two lines," Buck said. "But one of 'em's for my computer."

"Well, Mr. Bailey's been trying to reach you, and he's been getting a busy signal."

"What did he call there for? He has to know I'm here."

"He didn't call here. Marge Potter was on with Verna about something else and told her."

"Bet Verna loved that."

"She sure did. She all but danced. She thinks you're in trouble with the big boss again."

"I doubt it."

"Know what she's guessing?"

"I can't wait."

"That Bailey didn't like your cover story and he's firing you."

Buck laughed.

"Not true?" Alice said.

"Quite the opposite," Buck said. "But do me a favor and don't tell Verna."

Buck thanked her for the deliveries the day before, spared her the story about Chloe having thought Alice was his fiancée, and got off so he could call Bailey. He got to Marge Potter first.

"Buck, I miss you already," she said. "What in the world happened?"

"Someday I'll lay it all out for you," he said. "I hear the boss has been trying to reach me."

"Well, I've been trying for him. Right now he's got Jim Borland in there, and I hear raised voices. Don't think I've ever heard Jim raise his voice before."

"You've heard Bailey raise his?"

Marge laughed. "Not more than twice a day," she said. "Anyway, I'll have him call you."

"You might want to interrupt them, Marge. Their meeting may be the reason he was trying to reach me."

Almost immediately Stanton Bailey was on the line. "Williams, you've got a lot of nerve acting like the executive editor you're not."

"Sir?"

"It's not your place to be assigning cover stories, telling Borland I originally had him in mind for the treaty piece, then kissing up to him by offering to take his garbage stories and letting him have your cover article."

"I didn't do that!"

"He didn't do that!" Borland hollered.

"I can't keep up with you two," Bailey said. "Now, what's the deal?"

+ + +

With Chloe gone to see about her new job at the church, Rayford thought about calling his chief pilot. Earl Halliday wanted to hear from him as soon as possible and would likely call him if Rayford didn't get back to Earl soon.

Today's news was the very kind of development that would seal Rayford's decision. He couldn't deny the prestige that would accompany being the president's pilot. And being Carpathia's might be even noisier. But Rayford's motives and dreams had swung 180 degrees. Being known as the pilot of *Air Force One*—or even *Global Community One*—for seven years was simply not on his wish list.

The size of his own house had sometimes embarrassed Rayford, even when four people were living there. At other times he had been proud of it. It evidenced his status, his station in life, the level of his achievement. Now it was a lonely place. He was so grateful to have Chloe home. Though he would not have said a word if she had returned to college, he didn't know what he would have done with himself during his off-hours. It was one thing to busy your mind with all that is necessary to transport hundreds of people safely by air. But to have virtually nothing to do at home but eat and sleep would have made the place unbearable.

Every room, every knickknack, every feminine touch reminded him of Irene. Occasionally something would jump out and flood his mind with Raymie, too. He found a piece of Raymie's favorite candy under a cushion on the couch. A couple of his books. A toy was hiding behind a potted plant.

Rayford was growing emotional, but he didn't mind as much any more. His grief was more melancholic than painful now. The closer he grew to God, the more he looked forward to being with him and with Irene and Raymie after the Glorious Appearing.

He allowed his memories to bring his loved ones closer in his mind and heart. Now that he shared their faith, he understood them and loved them all the more. When regret crept in, when he felt ashamed of the husband and father he had been, he merely prayed for forgiveness for having been so blind.

Rayford decided to cook for Chloe that night. He would prepare one of her favorite dishes—shrimp scampi with pasta and all the trimmings. He smiled. In spite of him and all the negative traits she had inherited, she had grown to be a wonderful person. If there was one clear example of how Christ could change a person, she was it. He wanted to tell her that, and dinner would be one expression. It was easy to buy things for her and take her out. He wanted to do something himself.

Rayford spent an hour at the grocery store and another hour and a half in the kitchen before he had everything cooking in anticipation of her arrival. He found himself identifying with Irene, remembering the hopeful expression on her face almost every night. He had said his thank-yous and complimented her enough, he supposed. But it wasn't until now that he realized she must have been doing that work for him out of the same love and devotion he felt for Chloe.

He had never grasped that, and his paltry attempts at compliments must have been seen as perfunctory as they were. Now there was no way to make it up to Irene, except to show up in the kingdom himself, with Chloe alongside.

+ + +

Buck hung up from the call with Stanton Bailey and Jim Borland wondering why he didn't just accept Carpathia's offer to manage the *Chicago Tribune* and be done with it. He had convinced them both that he was sincere and finally got the old man's gruff approval, but he wondered if it was worth being in the doghouse again. His goal was to tie the religious stories together so neatly that Borland would get an idea how his job should be done and Bailey would get a picture of what he needed in an executive editor.

Buck didn't want that job any more than he had when Steve Plank left and Buck had been talked into it. But he sure hoped Bailey found someone who would make it fun to work there again.

He banged out some notes on his computer, in essence outlining the assignments he had acquired in the trade with Jimmy Borland. He had made the same initial assumptions Borland did about all the breaking stories. But that was before he had studied prophecy, before he knew where Nicolae Carpathia fit into the sweep of history.

Now he was hoping all these things would break at essentially the same time. It was possible he was sitting on the direct fulfillment of centuries-old prophecies. Cover stories or not, these developments would have as much impact on the short remaining history of mankind as the treaty with Israel.

Buck called Steve Plank. "Any word yet?" Steve said. "Anything I can tell the secretary-general?"

"Is that what you call him?" Buck said, astonished. "Not even you can call him by name?"

"I choose not to. It's a matter of respect, Buck. Even Hattie calls him 'Mr. Secretary-General,' and if I'm not mistaken, they spend almost as much time together off the job as on the job."

"Don't rub it in. I know well enough that I introduced them."

"You regret it? You provided a world leader with someone he adores, and you changed Hattie's life forever."

"That's what I'm afraid of," Buck said, realizing he was dangerously close to showing his true colors to a Carpathia confidant.

"She was a nobody from nowhere, Buck, and now she's on the front page of history." That was not what Buck wanted to hear, but then he wasn't planning to tell Steve what he wanted to hear either. "So, what's the story, Buck?"

"I'm no closer to a decision today," Buck said. "You know where I stand."

"I don't understand you, Buck. Where's the glitch? What's going to make this not work? It's everything you've ever wanted."

"I'm a journalist, Steve, not a public relations guy."

"Is that what you're calling me?"

"That's what you are, Steve. I don't fault you for it, but don't pretend to be something you're not."

Clearly, Buck had offended his old friend. "Yeah, well, whatever," Steve said. "You called me, so what did you want?"

Buck told him of the deal he had made with Borland.

"Big mistake," Steve said, still clearly steamed. "You'll recall I never assigned him a cover story."

"This shouldn't be a cover story. The other pieces, the ones he's letting me handle, are the big stories."

Steve's voice rose. "This would have been the biggest cover story you've ever had! This will be the most widely covered event in history."

"You say that and tell me you're not a PR guy now?"

"Why? What?"

"The U.N. signs a peace treaty with Israel and you think it's bigger than the disappearances of billions all over the globe?"

"Well, yeah, that. Of course."

"'Well, yeah, that. Of course,'" Buck mimicked. "Good grief, Steve. The story is the treaty, not the ceremony. You know that."

"So you're not coming?"

"Of course I'm coming, but I'm not riding along with you guys."

"You don't want to be on the new *Air Force One*?"

"What?"

"C'mon, Mister International Journalist. Keep the news on, man."

\+ + +

Rayford looked forward to Chloe's arrival, but he also looked forward to the meeting of the core group that night. Chloe had told him Buck had been as much against accepting a job with Carpathia as Rayford was against accepting a job with the White House. But you never knew what Bruce would say. Sometimes he had a different view of things, and he often made a lot of sense. Rayford couldn't imagine how such changes could figure in to their new lives, but he was eager to talk about it and pray about it. He looked at his watch. His dinner should be done in half an hour. And that was when Chloe had said she'd be home.

\+ + +

"No," Buck said, "I wouldn't want to go over there on the new or the old *Air Force One*. I appreciate the invitation to be part of the delegation, and I'll still take you up on being at the table for the signing, but even Bailey agrees that *Global Weekly* ought to send me."

"You *told* Bailey about our offer?!"

"Not the job offer, of course. But about riding along, sure."

"Why do you think the trip to New York was so clandestine, Buck? You think we wanted the *Weekly* to know about this?"

"I figured you didn't want them to know I was being offered a job, which they don't know. But how was I supposed to explain showing up in Israel and being in on the signing?"

"We hoped it wouldn't make any difference to your former employer by then."

"Just don't make any assumptions, Steve," Buck said.

"You, either."

"Meaning?"

"Don't expect the offer of a lifetime to stay on the table if you're going to thumb your nose at an invitation like you did last time."

"So the job is tied to playing ball on the PR trip."

"If you want to put it that way."

"You're not making me feel any better about the idea, Steve."

"You know, Buck, I'm not sure you're cut out for politics and journalism at this level."

"I agree it's sunk to a new low."

"That's not what I meant. Anyway, remember your big-shot predictions about a new one-world currency? That it would never happen? Watch the news tomorrow, pal. And remember that it was all Nicolae Carpathia's doing, diplomacy behind the scenes."

Buck had seen Carpathia's so-called diplomacy. It was likely the same way he got the president of the United States to hand over a brand-new 777, not to mention how he got eyewitnesses to a murder to believe they'd seen a suicide.

It was time to tell Bruce about his trip.

* * *

"Rayford, can you come in?"

"When, Earl?"

"Right now. Big doings with the new *Air Force One*. Have you heard?"

"Yes, it's all over the news."

"You say the word, and you'll be flying that plane to Israel with Nicolae Carpathia on board."

"Not ready to decide yet."

"Ray, I need you in here. Can you come or not?"

"Not today, Earl. I'm in the middle of something here, and I'll have to see you tomorrow."

"What's so important?"

"It's personal."

"What, you've got another deal cooking?"

"I'm cooking, but not another deal. I happen to be preparing dinner for my daughter."

Rayford heard nothing for a moment. Finally: "Rayford, I'm all for family priorities. Heaven knows we've got enough pilots with bad marriages and messed-up kids. But your daughter—"

"Chloe."

"Right, she's college age, right? She'd understand, wouldn't she? Couldn't she put off dinner with Dad for a couple hours, knowing he might get the best flying job in the world?"

"I'll see you tomorrow, Earl. I've got that Baltimore run late morning, back late afternoon. I can see you before that."

"Nine o'clock?"

"Fine."

"Rayford, let me just warn you: If the other guys on the short list ever wanted this job, they're going to be drooling over it now. You can bet they're calling in all their chips, lining up their endorsements, trying to find out who knows who, all that."

"Good. Maybe one of them will get it and I won't have to worry about it anymore."

Earl Halliday sounded agitated. "Now, Rayford—," he began, but Rayford cut him off.

"Earl, after tomorrow morning let's agree not to waste any more of each other's time. You know my answer, and the only reason I haven't made it final yet is because you asked me not to for the sake of our friendship. I'm thinking about it, I'm praying about it, and I'm talking about it with people who care for me. I'm not going to be badgered or shamed into it. If I turn down a job that everyone else wants, and later I regret it, that'll be my problem."

\+ \+ \+

Buck was pulling into the parking lot at New Hope Village Church just as Chloe was pulling out. They drew up even with each other and rolled down their windows. "Hey, little girl," Buck said, "you know anything about this church?"

Chloe smiled. "Just that it's crowded every Sunday."

"Good. I'll try it. So, are you taking the job?"

"I could ask you the same question."

"I've already got a job."

"Looks like I have one, too," she said. "I learned more today than I learned in college last year."

"How'd it go with Bruce? I mean, did you tell him you knew he sent the flowers?"

Chloe looked over her shoulder, as if afraid Bruce might hear. "I'll have to tell you all about it," she said. "When we have time."

"After the meeting tonight?"

She shook her head. "I was up too late last night. Some guy, you know."

"Really?"

"Yeah. Couldn't get rid of him. Happens to me all the time."

"Later, Chloe."

Buck couldn't blame Bruce for whatever level of interest he had in Chloe. It just felt strange, competing with your new friend and pastor for a woman.

* * *

"Is that what it smells like?" Chloe exulted as she came in from the garage. "Shrimp scampi?" She entered the kitchen and gave her dad a kiss. "My favorite! Who's coming over?"

"The guest of honor just arrived," he said. "Would you rather eat in the dining room? We could move in there easily."

"No, this will be perfect. What's the occasion?"

"Your new job. Tell me all about it."

"Dad! What possessed you?"

"I just got in touch with my feminine side," he said.

"Oh, please!" she groaned. "Anything but that!"

During dinner she told him of Bruce's assignments and all the research and study she had done already.

"So, you're going to do this?"

"Learn and study and get paid for it? I think that's an easy call, Dad."

"And what about Bruce?"

She nodded. "What *about* Bruce?"

11

BY THE TIME RAYFORD and Chloe were doing the dishes, Rayford had heard all about her awkward encounter with Bruce. "So he never owned up to sending the flowers?" Rayford said.

"It was so strange, Dad," she said. "I kept trying to get the subject back onto loneliness and how much we all meant to each other, all four of us, and he seemed not to pick up on it. He would agree we all had needs, and then he would shift back to the subject of study or some other thing he wanted me to look up. I finally said I was just curious about romantic relationships during this period of history, and he said he might talk about it tonight. He said others had raised the same subject with him recently and that he had some questions too, so he had been studying it."

"Maybe he'll come clean tonight."

"It isn't a matter of coming clean, Dad. I don't expect him to tell me in front of you and Buck that he sent me the flowers. But maybe we'll be able to read between the lines and find out why he did it."

+ + +

Buck was still in Bruce's office when Rayford and Chloe arrived. Bruce began the nightly meeting of the Tribulation Force by getting everyone's permission to put on the table everything that was happening in each life. Everyone nodded.

After outlining the offers that Buck and Rayford had received, Bruce said he felt the need to confess his own sense of inadequacy for the role of pastor of a church of new believers. "I still deal with shame every day. I know I have been forgiven and restored, but living a lie for more than thirty years wears on a person, and even though God says our sins are separated as far as the east is from the west, it's hard for me to forget." He also admitted his loneliness and fatigue. "Especially," he said, "as I think about this pull toward traveling and trying to unite the little pockets of what the Bible calls 'tribulation saints.'"

Buck wanted to come right out and ask why he hadn't simply signed a card on Chloe's flowers, but he knew it wasn't his place. Bruce moved on to both

Rayford's and Buck's new job opportunities. "This may shock all of you, because I have not expressed an opinion yet, but Buck and Rayford, I think both of you should seriously consider accepting these jobs."

That threw the meeting into an uproar. It was the first time the four of them had spoken so forcefully on such personal subjects. Buck maintained that he would never be able to live with himself if he sold out his journalistic principles and allowed himself to manipulate the news and be manipulated by Nicolae Carpathia. He was impressed that Rayford did not seem to have his head turned by such a choice job offer, but he found himself agreeing with Bruce that Rayford should consider it.

"Sir," Buck said, "the very fact that you're not angling for it is a good sign. If you wanted it, knowing what you know now, we would all be worried about you. But think of the opportunity to be near the corridors of power."

"What's the advantage?" Rayford said.

"Maybe little to you personally," Buck said, "except for the income. But don't you think it would be of great benefit to us to have that kind of access to the president?"

Rayford told Buck he thought they all had a mistaken notion that the pilot of the president's plane would have more real knowledge than anyone who read the daily papers.

"That might be true now," Buck said. "But if Carpathia really buys up the major media outlets, someone next to the president would be one of the few who knows what's really going on."

"All the more reason for *you* to work for Carpathia," Rayford said.

"Maybe I should take your job and you should take mine," Buck said, and finally they were able to laugh.

"You see what's happening here," Bruce said. "We all see each other's situations more clearly and with more level heads than we see our own."

Rayford chuckled. "So you're saying we're both in denial."

Bruce smiled. "Maybe I am. It's possible God has sent these things your way just to test your motives and your loyalties, but they seem too huge to ignore."

Buck wondered if Rayford was wavering as much as he was now. Buck had been dead sure he would never consider such an offer from Carpathia. Now he didn't know what he thought.

Chloe broke the logjam. "I think you should both take the jobs."

Buck found it strange that Chloe would wait until a meeting of the four of them to make such an announcement, and it was clear her father felt the same.

"You said I should at least keep an open mind, Chlo'," Rayford said. "But you seriously think I should take this?"

Chloe nodded. "This isn't about the president. It's about Carpathia. If he is who we think he is, and we all know that he is, he'll quickly become more powerful than the president of the United States. One or both of you should get as close to him as possible."

"I *was* close to him once," Buck said. "And that's more than enough."

"If all you care about is your own sanity and safety," Chloe pressed. "I'm not discounting the horror you went through, Buck. But without someone on the inside, Carpathia is going to deceive everyone."

"But as soon as I tell what's really happening," Buck said, "he'll eliminate me."

"Maybe. But maybe God will protect you too. Maybe all you'll be able to do is tell us what's happening so we can tell the believers."

"I'd have to sell out every journalistic principle I have."

"And those are more sacred than your responsibilities to your brothers and sisters in Christ?"

Buck didn't know how to respond. This was one of the things he liked so much about Chloe. But independence and integrity had been so ingrained in him since the beginning of his journalism career that he could hardly get a mental handle on pretending to be something he was not. The idea of posing as a publisher while actually on Carpathia's payroll was too much to imagine.

Bruce jumped in and focused on Rayford. Buck was glad to have the spotlight off himself, but he could understand how Rayford must have felt. "I think yours is actually the easier decision, Rayford," Bruce said. "You put some major conditions on it, like being allowed to live here if it's that important to you, and see how serious they are."

\+ + +

Rayford was shaken. He looked at Buck. "If we were voting, would you make it three-to-one?"

"I could ask you the same," Buck said. "Apparently we're the only ones who don't think we should take these jobs."

"Maybe you should," Rayford said, only half kidding.

Buck laughed. "I'm open to considering that I've been blind, or at least shortsighted."

Rayford didn't know what he was open to considering, and he said so. Bruce suggested they pray on their knees—something each had done privately, but not as a group. Bruce brought his chair to the other side of the desk, and the four of them turned and knelt. Hearing the others pray always moved Rayford deeply.

He wished God would just tell him audibly what to do, but when he prayed, he simply asked that God would make it plain to all of them.

As Rayford knelt there, he realized he needed to surrender his will to God—again. Apparently this would be a daily thing, giving up the logical, the personal, the tightfisted, closely held stuff.

Rayford felt so small, so inadequate before God, that he could not seem to get low enough. He crouched, he squatted, he tucked his chin to his chest, and yet he still felt proud, exposed. Bruce had been praying aloud, but he suddenly stopped, and Rayford heard him weeping quietly. A lump formed in his own throat. He missed his family, but he was deeply grateful for Chloe, for his salvation, for these friends.

Rayford knelt there in front of his chair, his hands covering his face, praying silently. Whatever God wanted was what he wanted, even if it made no sense from a human standpoint. The overwhelming sense of unworthiness seemed to crush him, and he slipped to the floor and lay prostrate on the carpet. A fleeting thought of how ridiculous he must look assailed him, but he quickly pushed it aside. No one was watching, no one cared. And anyone who thought the sophisticated airplane pilot had taken leave of his senses would have been right.

Rayford stretched his long frame flat on the floor, the backs of his hands on the gritty carpet, his face buried in his palms. Occasionally one of the others would pray aloud briefly, and Rayford realized that all of them were now facedown on the floor.

Rayford lost track of the time, knowing only vaguely that minutes passed with no one saying anything. He had never felt so vividly the presence of God. So this was the feeling of dwelling on holy ground, what Moses must have felt when God told him to remove his shoes. Rayford wished he could sink lower into the carpet, could cut a hole in the floor and hide from the purity and infinite power of God.

He was not sure how long he lay there, praying, listening. After a while he heard Bruce get up and take his seat, humming a hymn. Soon they all sang quietly and returned to their chairs. All were teary-eyed. Finally Bruce spoke.

"We have experienced something unusual," he said. "I think we need to seal this with a recommitment to God and to each other. If there is anything between any of us that needs to be confessed or forgiven, let's not leave here without doing that. Chloe, last night you left us with some implications that were strong but unclear."

Rayford glanced at Chloe. "I apologize," she said. "It was a misunderstanding. Cleared up now."

"We don't need a session on sexual purity during the Tribulation?"

She smiled. "No, I think we're all pretty clear on that subject. There is something I would like clarified though, and I'm sorry to ask you this in front of the others—"

"That's all right," Bruce said. "Anything."

"Well, I received some flowers anonymously, and I want to know if they came from anyone in this room."

Bruce glanced away. "Buck?"

"Not me." Buck grimaced. "I've already suffered for being suspected."

When Bruce looked at him, Rayford just smiled and shook his head.

"That leaves me then," Bruce said.

"You?" Chloe said.

"Well, doesn't it? Didn't you just limit your suspects to those in this room?"

Chloe nodded.

"I guess you'll have to widen your search." Bruce said, blushing. "It wasn't me, but I'm flattered to be suspected. I only wish I'd thought of it."

Rayford's and Chloe's surprise must have showed, because Bruce immediately launched into an explanation. "Oh, I didn't mean what you think I mean," Bruce said. "It's just that . . . well, I think flowers are a wonderful gesture, and I hope they encouraged you, whoever they were from."

Bruce seemed relieved to change the subject and return to his teaching. He let Chloe tell some of what she had researched that day. At ten o'clock, when they were getting ready to leave, Buck turned to Rayford. "As wonderful as that prayer time was, I didn't get any direct leading about what to do."

"Me either."

"You must be the only two." Bruce glanced at Chloe, and she nodded. "It's pretty clear to us what you should do. And it's clear to each of you what the other should do. But no one can make these decisions for you."

+ + +

Buck walked Chloe out of the church.

"That was amazing," she said.

He nodded. "I don't know where I'd be without you people."

"Us people?" She smiled. "You couldn't have left the last word off that sentence, could you?"

"How could I say that to someone who has a secret admirer?"

She winked at him. "Maybe you'd better."

"Seriously, who do you think it is?"

"I don't even know where to begin."

"That many possibilities?"

"That few. In fact, none."

\+ + +

Rayford was beginning to wonder whether Hattie Durham had had anything to do with Chloe's flowers, but he wasn't going to suggest that to his daughter. What kind of crazy idea would have gone through Hattie's mind to spur such an act? Another example of her idea of a practical joke?

Wednesday morning in Earl Halliday's office at O'Hare, Rayford was surprised to find the president of Pan-Con himself, Leonard Gustafson. He had met Gustafson twice before. Rayford should have known something was up when he got off the elevator on the lower level. The place looked different. Desks were neater, neckties were tied, people looked busier, clutter and mess had been swept out of sight. People raised their eyebrows knowingly at Rayford as he strode toward Earl's office.

Gustafson, former military, was shorter than Rayford and thinner than Earl, but his mere presence was too big for Earl's little office. Another chair had been dragged in, but as Rayford entered, Gustafson leaped to his feet, his trench coat still draped over one arm, and pumped Rayford's hand.

"Steele, man, how are you?" he said, pointing to a chair as if this were his office. "I had to come through Chicago today on another matter, and when I found out you were coming to see Earl, well, I just wanted to be here and congratulate you and release you and wish you the best."

"Release me?"

"Well, not fire you, of course, but to set your mind at ease. You can rest assured there'll be no hard feelings here. You've had a remarkable, no, a stellar career with Pan-Con, and we'll miss you, but we're proud of you."

"Is the news release already written?" Rayford said.

Gustafson laughed a little too loudly. "That can be done right away, and of course we'll want to make the announcement. This will be a feather in your cap, just like it is in ours. You're our guy, and now you'll be his guy. You can't beat that, huh?"

"The other candidates have dropped out?"

"No, but suffice it to say we have inside information that the job is yours if you want it."

"How does that work? Somebody owed some favors?"

"No, Rayford, that's the crazy thing. You must have friends in high places."

"Not really. I've had no contact with the president, and I don't know anyone on his staff."

"Apparently you were recommended by the Carpathia administration. You know him?"

"Never met him."

"Know anyone who knows him?"

"As a matter of fact I do," Rayford muttered.

"Well, you played that card at the right time," Gustafson said. He clapped Rayford on the shoulder. "You're perfect for the job, Steele. We'll be thinking good thoughts about you."

"So I couldn't turn this down if I wanted to?"

Gustafson sat, leaning forward, elbows on his knees. "Earl told me you had some misgivings. Don't make the biggest mistake of your life, Rayford. You want this. You know you want this. It's here for the taking. Take it. I'd take it. Earl would take it. Anyone else on the list would die for it."

"It's too late to make the biggest mistake of my life," Rayford said.

"What's that?" Gustafson said, but Rayford saw Earl touch his arm, as if reminding him he was dealing with a religious fanatic who believed he had missed a chance to be in heaven. "Oh, yeah, that. Well, I mean since then," Gustafson added.

"Mr. Gustafson, how does Nicolae Carpathia tell the president of the United States who should pilot his plane?"

"I don't know! Who cares? Politics is politics, whether it's the Dems and the Repubs in this country or Labor and the Bolsheviks somewhere else."

Rayford thought the analogy a little sloppy, but he couldn't argue the logic. "So somebody's trading something for something, and I'm just the hired hand."

"Isn't that the truth with all of us?" Gustafson said. "But everybody loves Carpathia. He seems above all the politics. If I had to guess, I'd say the president is letting him use the new 'seven-seven just because he likes him."

Yeah, Rayford thought, *and I'm the Easter bunny.*

"So will you take the job?"

"I've never been pushed out of a job before."

"You're not being pushed, Rayford. We love you here. We just wouldn't be able to justify not having one of our top guys get the best job in the world in his profession."

"What about my record? A complaint has been lodged against me."

Gustafson smiled knowingly. "A complaint? I know nothing of a complaint? Do you, Earl?"

"Nothing's come across my desk, sir," he said. "And if it did, I'm sure it could be expedited beyond danger in a very short time."

"By the way, Rayford," Gustafson said, "are you familiar with a Nicholas Edwards?"

Rayford nodded.

"Friend of yours?"

"First officer a couple of times. I'd like to think we're friends, yes."

"Did you hear he had been promoted to captain?"

Rayford shook his head. *Politics,* he thought glumly.

"Nice, huh?" Gustafson said.

"Real nice," Rayford said, his head spinning.

"Anything else standing in your way?" Gustafson said.

Rayford could see his choices disappearing. "At the very least, and I'm still not saying I'll take it, I would have to be headquartered in Chicago."

Gustafson grimaced and shook his head. "Earl told me that. I don't get it. I would think you'd want to be out of here, away from the memories of your wife and other daughter."

"Son."

"Yeah, the college boy."

Rayford didn't correct him, but he saw Earl wince.

"Anyway," Gustafson said, "you could get your daughter away from whoever might be stalking her, and—"

"Sir?"

"—and you could get yourself a nice place outside D.C."

"Stalking her?"

"Well, maybe it's not that obvious yet, Rayford, but I sure as blazes wouldn't want my daughter to be hearing from somebody anonymously. I don't care what they were sending."

"But how did you—?"

"I mean, Rayford, you'd never forgive yourself if something happened to that little girl and you had a chance to get her away from whoever is threatening her."

"My daughter is not being stalked or threatened! What are you talking about?"

"I'm talking about the roses, or whatever the bouquet was. What was the deal with that?"

"That's what I'd like to know. As far as I know, only three people, besides whoever sent those, even know she got them. How did *you* find out?"

"I don't remember. Somebody just mentioned that sometimes a person has a reason to leave just as much as he has a reason to like the new opportunity."

"But if you're not pushing me out, I have no reason to leave."

"Not even if your daughter is getting hassled by someone?"

"Anyone who wanted to hassle her could find her in Washington just as easily as here," Rayford said.

"But still . . ."

"I don't like the idea that you know all this."

"Well, don't turn down the job of a lifetime over an insignificant mystery."

"It's not insignificant to me."

Gustafson stood. "I'm not accustomed to begging people to do what I ask."

"So if I don't take this, I'm history with Pan-Con?"

"You ought to be, but I suppose we'd have a tough time with a suit from you after we encouraged you to take the job of piloting the president."

Rayford had no intention of filing a suit, but he said nothing.

Gustafson sat again. "Do me a favor," he said. "Go to Washington. Talk to the people, probably the chiefs of staff. Tell them you'll make the run to Israel for the peace-treaty signing. Then decide what you want to do. Would you do that for me?"

Rayford knew Gustafson would never tell him where he'd heard about Chloe's flowers, and he figured his best bet was to pry it out of Hattie. "Yes," Rayford said at last. "I'll do that."

"Good!" Gustafson said, shaking hands with both Rayford and Earl. "I think we're halfway home. And Earl, make this run to Baltimore today Rayford's last before the trip to Israel. In fact, he's going to be so close to Washington, let's get somebody else to fly his plane back so he can meet with people at the White House today. Can we arrange that?"

"It's already done, sir."

"Earl," Gustafson said, "if you were ten years younger, you'd be the man for the job."

Rayford noticed the pain on Earl's face. Gustafson couldn't know how badly Halliday had wanted that very job. On the way to his plane, Rayford checked his mail slot. There, among the packages and interoffice memos, was a note. It read simply, "Thanks for your endorsement on my early promotion. I really appreciate it. And good luck to you. Signed, Captain Nicholas Edwards."

Several hours later Rayford left the cockpit of his 747 in Baltimore and was met by a Pan-Con operative who presented him with credentials that would get him into the White House. Upon his arrival, he was quickly whisked through the gate. A guard welcomed him by name and wished him luck. When he finally got to the office of an assistant to the chief of staff, Rayford made clear that he was agreeing only to fill in as pilot for the trip to Israel the following Monday.

"Very good," he was told. "We have already begun the character and reference check, the FBI probe, and the Secret Service interviewing. It will take a bit longer to complete anyway, so you'll be in a position to impress us and the president without being responsible for him until you've passed all checkpoints."

"You can authorize me to fly the U.N. secretary-general with less clearance on me than you'd need for the president?"

"Precisely. Anyway, you've already been approved by the U.N."

"I have?"

"You have."

"By whom?"

"By the secretary-general himself."

* * *

Buck was on the phone to Marge Potter at *Global Weekly* headquarters in New York when he heard the news. The entire world would go to dollars for currency within one year, the plan to be initiated and governed by the United Nations, funded by a one-tenth of one percent tax to the U.N. on every dollar.

"That doesn't sound unreasonable, does it?" Marge asked.

"Ask the financial editor, Marge," Buck said. "It'll be gazillions a year."

"And just how much is a gazillion?"

"More than either of us can count." Buck sighed. "You were going to do some checking, Marge, about finding someone to help arrange these religion interviews."

He could hear her shuffling papers. "You can catch your one-world religion guys here in New York," she said. "They're heading out Friday, but very few of them will be in Israel. Your temple guys will be in Jerusalem next week. We'll try to get in touch with those two kooks you want at the Wailing Wall, but the smart money here says not to count on it."

"I'll take my chances."

"And where would you like us to send your remains?"

"I'll survive."

"No one else has."

"But I'm not threatening them, Marge. I'm helping them broadcast their message."

"Whatever that is."

"You see why we need a story on them?"

"It's your life, Buck."

"Thank you."

"And you'd better get to this Cardinal Mathews on your way here. He's shuttling back and forth between the one-faith meetings in New York and the

Cincinnati archdiocese, and he's heading to the Vatican for the papal vote right after the treaty signing next Monday."

"But he *will* be in Jerusalem?"

"Oh, yes. There's some rumor floating around that in case he's the next pope he's making contacts in Jerusalem for some major shrine or something. But the Catholics would never leave the Vatican, would they?"

"You never know, Marge."

"Well, that's for sure. I hardly get time to think about these things, being gofer for you and everyone else around here who can't do his own legwork."

"You're the best, Marge."

"Flattery will get you, Buck."

"Get me what?"

"It'll just get you."

"What about my rabbi?"

"Your rabbi says he's refusing all news contacts until after he presents his findings."

"And when is that?"

"Word just came today that CNN is giving him an hour of uninterrupted time on their international satellite. Jews will be able to see it all over the world at the same time, but of course it will be in the middle of the night for some of them."

"And when is this?"

"Monday afternoon, after the signing of the treaty. Signing is at 10 a.m. Jerusalem time. Rabbi Ben-Judah goes on the air for an hour at two in the afternoon."

"Pretty shrewd, going on while the world's press elite is crowding Jerusalem."

"All these religious types are shrewd, Buck. The guy who'll probably be the next pope will be at the treaty signing, schmoozing the Israelis. This rabbi thinks he's so all-fired important that the treaty signing will be upstaged by the reading of his research paper. Be sure I'm right on my TV schedule there, Buck. I want to be absolutely certain I miss that one."

"Aw, c'mon, Marge. He's going to tell you how to spot the Messiah."

"I'm not even Jewish."

"Neither am I, but I'd sure want to be able to recognize the Messiah. Wouldn't you?"

"You want me to get serious and tell you the truth one time here, Buck? I think I've seen the Messiah. I think I recognize him. If there's really supposed to be somebody sent from God to save the world, I think he's the new secretary-general of the United Nations."

Buck shivered.

* * *

Rayford was priority listed as a first-class passenger for the next flight to Chicago out of Baltimore. He called Chloe from the airport to let her know why he would be later than expected.

"Hattie Durham's been trying to reach you."

"What does she want?"

"She's trying to set up a meeting with you and Carpathia before you become his pilot."

"I'm going to fly him round-trip to Tel Aviv. Why do I have to meet him?"

"More likely he feels he has to meet you. Hattie told him you were a Christian."

"Oh, great! He'll never trust me."

"Probably wants to keep an eye on you."

"I want to talk to Hattie in person, anyway. When does he want to see me?"

"Tomorrow."

"My life's getting too busy all of a sudden. What's new with you?"

"Something more from my secret admirer today," she said. "Candy this time."

"Candy!" Rayford said, spooked by the fears Leonard Gustafson had planted. "You didn't eat any of it, did you?"

"Not yet. Why?"

"Just don't touch that stuff till you know who it's from."

"Oh, Dad!"

"You never know, hon. Please, just don't take any chances."

"All right, but these are my favorites! They look so good."

"Don't even open them until we know, OK?"

"All right, but you're going to want some too. They're the same ones you always bring me from New York, from that one little department-store chain."

"Windmill Mints from Holman Meadows?"

"Those are the ones."

That was the height of insult. How many times had Rayford mentioned to Hattie that he had to get those mints from that store during layovers in New York. She had even accompanied him more than once. So Hattie wasn't even trying to hide that she was sending the mysterious gifts. What was the point? It didn't seem to fit as vengeance for the cavalier way he had treated her. What did it have to do with Chloe? And was Carpathia aware of—or even behind—something so pedestrian?

Rayford would find out, that was sure.

* * *

Buck felt alive again. His life had been in such turmoil since the disappearances, he had wondered if it would ever settle back into the hectic norm he so enjoyed. His spiritual journey had been one thing, his demotion and relocation another. But now he seemed back in the good graces of the brass at *Global Weekly*, and he had used his instincts to trade for what he considered the top-breaking stories in the world.

He sat in his new makeshift home office, faxing, e-mailing, phoning, working with Marge and with reporters at *Weekly*, and making contacts for himself as well. He had a lot of people to interview in a short time, and all the developments seemed to be breaking at once.

Though part of him was horrified at what had happened, Buck enjoyed the rush of it. He desperately wanted to convince his own family of the truth. His father and brother would hear none of it, however, and if he had not been busy with challenging, exciting work, that fact alone would have driven him crazy.

Buck had just a few days to get his work done before and after the treaty signing. It seemed his whole life was on fast-forward now, trying to cram as much into seven years as he could. He didn't know what heaven on earth would be like, though Bruce was trying to teach him and Rayford and Chloe. He longed for the Glorious Appearing and the thousand-year reign of Christ on the earth. But in his mind, until he learned and knew more, anything normal he wanted to accomplish—like investigative reporting and writing, falling in love, getting married, maybe having a child—all had to be done soon.

Chloe was the best part of this new life. But did he have the time to do justice to a relationship that promised to be more than anything he had ever experienced? She was different from any woman he had known, and yet he couldn't put a finger on that difference. Her faith had enriched her and made her a new person, and yet he had been attracted to her before either of them had received Christ.

The idea that their meeting might have been part of some divine plan boggled his mind. How he wished they had met years before and had been ready together for the Rapture! If he was going to get any time with her before starting his trip to Israel, it would have to be that very day.

Buck looked at his watch. He had time for one more call, then he would reach Chloe.

* * *

Rayford dozed with his earphones on in first class. Images from the news filled the screen in front of him, but he had lost interest in reports of record crime waves throughout the United States. The name Carpathia finally roused him.

The United Nations Security Council had been meeting several hours every day, finalizing plans for the one-world currency and the massive disarmament plan the secretary-general had instituted. Originally, the idea was to destroy 90 percent of weapons and donate the remaining 10 percent to the U.N. Now each contributing country would also invest its own soldiers in the U.N. peacekeeping forces.

Carpathia had asked the president of the United States to head up the verification committee, a highly controversial move. Enemies of the U.S. claimed Fitzhugh would be biased and untrustworthy, making certain they destroyed their weapons while the U.S. hoarded its own.

Carpathia himself addressed these issues in his customarily direct and sympathetic way. Rayford shuddered as he listened. Undoubtedly, he would have trusted and supported this man if Rayford hadn't been a Christian.

"The United States has long been a keeper of the peace," Carpathia said. "They will lead the way, destroying their weapons of destruction and shipping to New Babylon the remaining 10 percent. Peoples of the world will be free to come and inspect the work of the U.S., assuring themselves of full compliance and then following in like manner.

"Let me just add this," the secretary-general said. "This is a massive, major undertaking that could take years. Every country could justify month after month of procedural protocol, but we must not let this occur. The United States of America will set the example, and no other country will take longer than they do to destroy their weapons and donate the rest. By the time the new United Nations headquarters is completed in New Babylon, the weapons will be in place.

"The era of peace is at hand, and the world is finally, at long last, on the threshold of becoming one global community."

Carpathia's pronouncement was met with thunderous applause, even from the press.

Later, on the same newscast, Rayford saw a brief special on the new *Air Force One*, a 777 which would be delivered to Washington's Dulles Airport and then flown to New York to await its official maiden voyage under the control of "a new captain to be announced shortly. The new man has been culled from a list of top pilots from the major airlines."

In other news, Carpathia was quoted as saying that he and the ecumenical council of the meeting of religious leaders from around the world would have an exciting announcement by the next afternoon.

+ + +

Buck reached the assistant to Archbishop Peter Cardinal Mathews in Cincinnati. "Yes, he's here, but resting. He leaves tomorrow morning for New York for the final meeting of the ecumenical council, and then he'll be on to Israel and the Vatican."

"I would come anywhere, anytime, at his convenience," Buck said.

"I'll get back to you with an answer, one way or the other, within thirty minutes."

Buck phoned Chloe. "I've got only a few minutes right now," he said, "but can we get together, just the two of us, before the meeting tonight?"

"Sure, what's happening?"

"Nothing specific," he said. "It's just that I'd like to spend some time with you, now that you know I'm available."

"Available? That's what you are?"

"Yes, ma'am! And you?"

"I guess I'm available too. That means we've got something in common."

"Did you have plans this evening?"

"Nope. Dad's going to be a little late. He was interviewed at the White House today."

"He's taking the job then?"

"He's going to make the maiden voyage and then decide."

"I could have been on that flight."

"I know."

"Pick you up at six?" Buck said.

"I'd love it."

12

AS PROMISED, Cardinal Mathews's assistant called Buck back, and the news was good. The cardinal had been so impressed with Buck's interview of him for the soon-to-appear cover story that he said Buck could ride with him to New York the following morning.

Buck booked the last flight out of O'Hare to Cincinnati that evening. He surprised Chloe by showing up at six with Chinese food. He told her of his plans for the evening trip and added, "I didn't want to waste talking time trying to find a place to eat."

"My dad's going to be jealous when he gets home," she said. "He loves Chinese."

Buck reached deep into the big sack, pulled out an extra order, and grinned. "Gotta keep the dad happy."

Buck and Chloe sat in the kitchen, eating and talking for more than an hour. They talked about everything—their respective childhoods, families, major events of their lives, hopes, fears, and dreams. Buck loved to hear Chloe talk, not just what she said, but even her voice. He didn't know whether she was the best conversationalist he had ever met, or if he was simply falling for her. *Probably both,* he decided.

* * *

Rayford arrived to find Buck and Chloe at Raymie's computer, which had not been turned on since the week of the disappearances. Within a few minutes, Buck had Chloe connected to the Internet and set up with an e-mail address. "Now you can reach me anywhere in the world," he said.

Rayford left Buck and Chloe at the computer and examined the mints from Holman Meadows. The candies were still shrink-wrapped and had been delivered by a reputable company. They had been addressed to Chloe, but with no message. Rayford decided they had not been tampered with, and even if they had come from Hattie Durham for some inexplicable reason, there was no sense in not enjoying them.

"Whoever's in love with your daughter sure has good taste," Buck said.

"Thank you," Chloe said.

"I mean good taste in chocolate mints."

Chloe blushed. "I know what you meant," she said.

+ + +

At Rayford's insistence, Buck had agreed to leave his car in the Steele's garage during his trip. Buck and Chloe left the Tribulation Force meeting early to get to the airport. Traffic was lighter than he expected, and they arrived more than an hour before his flight. "We could have stayed longer at the church," he said.

"Better to be safe, though, don't you think?" she said. "I hate always running on the edge of lateness."

"Me too," he said, "but I usually do. You can just drop me at the curb."

"I don't mind waiting with you if you don't mind paying for the parking."

"You going to be all right going back to the car this time of night?"

"I've done it lots of times," she said. "There are a lot of security guards."

She parked and they strolled through the massive terminal. He lugged his leather over-the-shoulder case with his whole world in it. Chloe seemed awkward, but Buck had nothing for her to carry, and they weren't at the hand-holding stage yet, so they just kept moving. Every time he turned so she could hear him, his bag shifted and the strap slipped off his shoulder, so they eventually settled into a silent trek to the gate.

Buck checked in and found that it was going to be a nearly empty flight. "Wish you could come with me," he said lightly.

"I wish—," she began, but apparently thought better of saying it.

"What?"

She shook her head.

"You wish you could come with me too?"

She nodded. "But I can't and I won't, so let's not start with any of that."

"What would I do with you?" he said. "Put you in my bag?"

She laughed.

They stood at the windows, watching baggage handlers and ground traffic controllers in the night. Buck pretended to look out the window as he stared at Chloe's reflection a few inches from his own. A couple of times he sensed her focus had shifted from the tarmac to the glass as well, and he imagined he was holding her gaze. *Wishful thinking,* he decided.

"We're going to be delayed twenty minutes," the woman at the counter announced.

"Don't feel obligated to stay, Chloe," Buck said. "You want me to walk you back to the car?"

She laughed again. "You're really paranoid about that big old parking garage, aren't you? No, see, the deal is that I bring you here, wait with you at your gate so you won't feel lonely, and then I stay until you're safely on the plane. I wave as it takes off, pretend to be rooted to the spot, and only when the jet trail fades out of sight do I venture out to the car."

"What, do you make this stuff up as you go along?"

"Of course. Now sit down and relax and pretend you're a frequent worldwide traveler."

"I wish for once I could pretend I'm not."

"And then you'd be nervous about the flight and need me here?"

"I need you here anyway."

She looked away. *Slow down,* he told himself. This was the fun part, the parrying stage, but it was also maddeningly uncertain. He didn't want to say things to her just because he would be gone for a few days that he wouldn't say otherwise.

"I need you here too," she said lightly, "but you're leaving me."

"That is something I would never do."

"What, leave me?"

"Absolutely." He kept a humorous tone in an effort not to scare her off.

"Well, that's encouraging. Can't have any of this leaving stuff."

* * *

Rayford kept an ear out for Chloe while packing for his quick trip to New York the next afternoon. Earl had called, wanting to know if Carpathia's office had reached him.

"And is that the same Hattie Durham who used to work for us?" Earl asked.

"One and the same."

"She's Carpathia's secretary?"

"Something like that."

"Small world."

* * *

"I guess it would be silly to tell you to be careful in Cincinnati and New York and Israel, considering all you've been through," Chloe said.

Buck smiled. "Don't start your good-byes until you're ready to leave."

"I'm not leaving till your plane is out of sight," she said. "I told you that."

"We have time for a cookie," he said, pointing at a vendor in the corridor.

"We already had dessert," she said. "Chocolates and a cookie."

"Fortune cookies don't count," he said. "Come on. Don't you remember our first cookie?"

The day they had met, Chloe had eaten a cookie and he had dabbed a tiny piece of chocolate from the corner of her mouth with his thumb. Not knowing what to do with it, he had licked it off.

"I remember I was a slob," she said. "And you tried a very old joke."

"You feel like a cookie?" he said, setting her up the way she had him in New York that first day.

"Why, do I look like one?"

Buck laughed, not because the joke was any funnier than the first time, he decided, but because it was theirs and it was stupid.

"I'm really not hungry," she said as they peered through the glass as a bored teenager waited for their order.

"Me either," Buck said. "These are for later."

"Tonight later or tomorrow later?" she asked.

"Whenever we synchronize our watches."

"We're going to eat them together? I mean, at the same time?"

"Doesn't that sound exciting?"

"Your creativity never ceases."

Buck ordered two cookies in two bags.

"Can't do that," the teenager said.

"Then I want one cookie," he said, handing over the money and slipping some to Chloe.

"And I want one cookie," she said, money in hand.

The teenager made a face, bagged the cookies for each of them, and made change.

"More than one way to skin a cat," Buck said.

They moseyed back to the gate. A few more passengers had gathered, and the woman at the counter announced that their plane had finally arrived. Buck and Chloe sat watching as the arriving passengers filed past, looking tired.

Buck carefully folded his cookie sack and laid it in his carry-on bag. "I'll be on a plane to New York at eight tomorrow morning," he said. "I'll have this with coffee and think of you."

"That'll be seven o'clock my time," Chloe said. "I'll still be in bed, anticipating my cookie and dreaming of you."

We're still playing around the edges, Buck thought. *Neither of us will say anything serious.*

"I'll wait till you're up, then," he said. "Tell me when you're going to eat your cookie."

Chloe studied the ceiling. "Hmm," she mused. "When will you be in your most important, most formal meeting?"

"Probably sometime late morning at a big hotel in New York. Carpathia is coming for some joint announcement with Cardinal Mathews and other religious leaders."

"Whenever that is, I'll eat my cookie," Chloe said. "And I dare you to eat yours then, too."

"You'll learn not to dare me." Buck smiled, but he was only half kidding. "I know no fear."

"Ha!" she said. "You're afraid of the parking garage here, and you're not even the one walking through it alone!"

Buck reached for her cookie sack.

"What're you doing?" she said. "We're not hungry, remember?"

"Just smell this," he said. "Fragrance is such a memory enhancer."

He opened her cookie sack and held it up to his face. "Mmm," he said. "Cookie dough, chocolate, nuts, butter, you name it."

He tilted it toward her, and she leaned to sniff it. "I do love that smell," she said.

Buck reached with his other hand and cupped her cheek in his palm. She didn't pull away but held his look. "Remember this moment," he said. "I'll be thinking of you while I'm gone."

"Me too," she said. "Now close that bag. That cookie has to stay fresh so the smell will remind me."

* * *

Rayford awoke earlier than Chloe and padded down to the kitchen. He lifted the small cookie bag from the counter. *One left,* he thought, and was tempted. Instead he wrote Chloe a note. "Hope you don't mind. I couldn't resist." On the back he wrote, "Just kidding," and laid the note atop the bag. He had coffee and juice, then changed into his workout clothes and went for a run.

* * *

Buck sat in first class with Cardinal Mathews on the Cincy to New York morning flight. Mathews was in his late fifties, a beefy, jowly man with close-cropped black hair that appeared to be his own natural color. Only his collar evidenced his station. He carried an expensive briefcase and laptop computer, and Buck noticed from his ticket sleeve that he had checked four bags.

Mathews traveled with an aide, who merely deflected other people and said little. The aide moved to a seat in front of them so Buck could sit next to the archbishop. "Why didn't you tell me you were a candidate for the papacy?" Buck began.

"So, we're just going to jump right into it, are we?" Mathews said. "Don't you like a little champagne in the morning?"

"No thanks."

"Well, you won't mind if I have a little pick-me-up."

"Suit yourself. Tell me when you're available to chat."

Mathews's aide heard the conversation and signaled the flight attendant, who immediately brought the cardinal a glass of champagne. "The usual?" she said.

"Thank you, Caryn," he said, as if to an old friend. Apparently she was. When she was gone he whispered, "The Litewski family, from my first parish. Baptized her myself. She's worked this flight for years. Now where were we?"

Buck did not respond. He knew the cardinal had heard and remembered the question. If he wanted it repeated for his own ego, he could repeat it himself.

"Oh, yes, you were wondering why I didn't mention the papacy. I guess I thought everyone knew. Carpathia knew."

I'll bet he did, Buck thought. *Probably engineered it.* "Is Carpathia hoping you'll get it?"

"Off the record," Mathews whispered, "there is no hoping anymore. We have the votes."

"We?"

"That's the editorial *we*. We, us, me, I have the votes. Understand?"

"How can you be so sure?"

"I've been a member of the college of cardinals for more than ten years. I have never yet been surprised by a papal vote. You know what Nicolae calls me? He calls me P. M."

Buck shrugged. "He calls you by your initials? Is there some significance?"

Mathews's aide peeked back between the seats and shook his head. *So, I should know,* Buck surmised. But he had never been afraid of asking a dumb question.

"Pontifex Maximus," Mathews beamed. "Supreme Pope."

"Congratulations," Buck said.

"Thank you, but I trust you know that Nicolae has much more in mind for my papacy than merely leadership of the Holy Roman Catholic Mother Church."

"Tell me."

"It'll be announced later this morning, and if you do not quote me directly, I'll give you the first shot at it."

"Why would you do that?"

"Because I like you."

"You hardly know me."

"But I know Nicolae."

Buck sank in his seat. "And Nicolae likes me."

"Exactly."

"So this little ride-along was not really entirely the result of my legwork."

"Ah, no," Mathews said. "Carpathia endorsed you. He wants me to tell you everything. Just don't make me look bad or self-serving for what I tell you."

"Will the announcement make you appear that way?"

"No, because Carpathia himself will make that announcement."

"I'm listening."

* * *

"Secretary-General Carpathia's office, Ms. Durham speaking."

"Rayford Steele here."

"Rayford! How are—"

"Let me get to the point, Hattie. I want to come early this afternoon so I can speak with you privately for a few minutes."

"That would be wonderful, Captain Steele. I should tell you in advance, however, that I am seeing someone."

"That's not funny."

"I didn't intend it to be."

"Will you have time?"

"Certainly. Secretary-General Carpathia can see you at four. Shall I look for you at three-thirty?"

Rayford hung up the phone as Chloe came into the kitchen, dressed for work at the church. She saw his note. "Oh, Dad! You didn't!" she said, and he thought she was on the verge of tears. She grabbed the bag and shook it. A relieved look came over her as she turned the note over and laughed. "Grow up, Dad. For once in your life, act your age."

He was getting ready to head to the airport and she for work when CNN broadcast a press conference live from the meeting of international religious leaders in New York. "Watch this, Dad," she said. "Buck is there."

Rayford set his carry-on bag on the floor and went to stand next to Chloe, who held a mug of coffee in both hands. The CNN correspondent intoned an explanation of what was to come. "We're expecting a joint statement from the coalition of religious leaders and the United Nations, represented by new Secretary-General Nicolae Carpathia. He seems the man of the hour here, having helped hammer out propositions and pulling together representatives of widely varying systems of belief. Since he has been in office, not a day has passed without some major development.

"Speculation here is that the religions of the world are going to make some fresh attempt at addressing global issues in a more cohesive and tolerant way than ever before. Ecumenism has failed in the past, but we'll soon see if this time around there is some new wrinkle that can finally make it work. Stepping to the podium is Archbishop Peter Cardinal Mathews, prelate of the Cincinnati archdiocese of the Roman Catholic Church and widely seen as a potential successor to Pope John XXIV who served only a controversial five months before being listed among the missing in the disappearances just weeks ago."

The camera panned to the press conference platform, where more than two dozen religious leaders from around the world, all dressed in their native garb, jockeyed for position. As Archbishop Mathews worked his way through to the bank of microphones, Rayford heard Chloe squeal.

"There's Buck, Dad! Look! Right there!"

She pointed to a reporter who was not in the crowd with the rest of the journalists but seemed to teeter on the back edge of the raised platform. Buck appeared to be trying to keep his balance. Twice he stepped down only to step back up again.

As Mathews droned on about international cooperation, Rayford and Chloe stared at Buck in the back corner. No one else would have even noticed him. "What's he got?" Rayford said. "Is that some sort of a notebook or tape recorder?"

Chloe looked close and gasped. She ran to the kitchen and returned with her cookie sack. "It's his cookie!" she said. "We're going to eat our cookies at the same time!"

Rayford was lost, but he was sure glad he hadn't eaten that cookie. "What—?" he began, but Chloe shushed him.

"It smells just like last night!" she said.

Rayford snorted. "Just what did last night smell like?" he said.

"Shhh!"

And sure enough, as they watched, Buck quickly and quietly reached into his little sack, surreptitiously and almost invisibly slid out the cookie, put it to his mouth, and took a bite. Chloe matched him gesture for gesture, and Rayford noticed she was smiling and crying at the same time.

"You've got it bad," he said, and he left for the airport.

\+ + +

Buck had no idea whether his little antic had been seen by anyone, let alone Chloe Steele. What was this girl doing to him? He had somehow gone from international star journalist to love-struck romantic doing silly things for attention.

But, he hoped, not too much attention. Few people ever noticed anyone on the edge of a TV shot. For all he knew, Chloe could have been watching and not have seen him at all.

More important than his efforts was the major story that broke from what might otherwise have been labeled a typical international confab. Somehow Nicolae Carpathia, either by promising support for Mathews's papacy or by his uncanny ability to charm anyone, had gotten these religious leaders to produce a proposition of incredible significance.

They were announcing not only an effort to cooperate and be more tolerant of each other but also the formation of an entirely new religion, one that would incorporate the tenets of all.

"And lest that sound impossible to the devout members of each of our sects," Mathews said, "we are all, every one of us, in total unanimity. Our religions themselves have caused as much division and bloodshed around the world as any government, army, or weapon. From this day forward we will unite under the banner of the Global Community Faith. Our logo will contain sacred symbols from religions that represent all, and from here on will encompass all. Whether we believe God is a real person or merely a concept, God is in all and above all and around all. God is in us. God is us. We are God."

When the floor was opened to questions, many astute religion editors zeroed in. "What happens to the leadership of, say, Roman Catholicism? Will there be the need for a pope?"

"We will elect a pope," Mathews said. "And we expect that other major religions will continue to appoint leaders in their usual cycles. But these leaders will serve the Global Community Faith and be expected to maintain the loyalty and devotion of their parishioners to the larger cause."

"Is there one major tenet you all agree on?"

This was met with laughter by the participants. Mathews called on a Rastafarian to answer. Through an interpreter he said, "We believe two things concretely. First, in the basic goodness of humankind. Second, that the disappearances were a religious cleansing. Some religions saw many disappear. Others saw very few. Many saw none. But the fact that many were left from each proves that none was better than the other. We will be tolerant of all, believing that the best of us remain."

Buck moved around to the front and raised his hand. "Cameron Williams, *Global Weekly*," he said. "Follow-up question for the gentleman at the microphone or Mathews or whomever. How does this tenet of the basic goodness of humankind jibe with the idea that the bad people have been winnowed out? How did they miss possessing this basic goodness?"

No one moved to answer. The Rastafarian looked to Mathews, who stared blankly at Buck, clearly not wishing to act upset but also wanting to communicate that he felt ambushed.

Mathews finally took the microphone. "We are not here to debate theology," he said. "I happen to be one of those who believes that the disappearances constituted a cleansing, and that the basic goodness of humankind is the common denominator of those who remain. And this basic goodness is found in greater measure in no one other than United Nations Secretary-General Nicolae Carpathia. Welcome him, please!"

The platform erupted with religious leaders cheering. Some of the press clapped, and for the first time Buck became aware of a huge public contingent behind the press. Due to the spotlights, he had not seen them from the platform, and he had not heard them until Carpathia appeared.

Carpathia was his typical masterful self, giving all the credit to the leadership of the ecumenical body and endorsing this "historic, perfect idea, whose time is long overdue."

He took a few questions, including what would happen to the rebuilding of the Jewish temple in Jerusalem. "That, I am happy to say, will proceed. As many of you know, much money has been donated to this cause for decades, and some prefabrication of the temple in other sites has been underway for years. Once the reconstruction begins, completion should be without delay."

"But what happens to the Islamic Dome of the Rock?"

"I am so glad you asked that question," Carpathia said, and Buck wondered if he hadn't planted it. "Our Muslim brothers have agreed to move not only the shrine but also the sacred section of the rock to New Babylon, freeing the Jews to rebuild their temple on what they believe is the original site.

"And now, if you will indulge me for a moment longer, I would like to say that we clearly are at the most momentous juncture in world history. With the consolidation to one form of currency, with the cooperation and toleration of many religions into one, with worldwide disarmament and commitment to peace, the world is truly becoming one.

"Many of you have heard me use the term Global Community. This is a worthy name for our new cause. We can communicate with one another, worship with one another, trade with one another. With communications and travel advancements, we are no longer a conglomeration of countries and nations, but one complete global community, a village made up of equal citizens. I thank the leaders here who have assembled this piece of the beautiful mosaic, and I would like to make an announcement in their honor.

"With the move of the United Nations headquarters to New Babylon will come a new name for our great organization. We will become known as the Global Community!" When applause finally subsided, Carpathia concluded, "Thus the name of the new one-world religion, Global Community Faith, is precisely appropriate."

Carpathia was being whisked away as camera and sound crews began tearing down the press conference site. Nicolae saw Buck and broke stride, telling his bodyguards he wanted to talk with someone. They formed a human wall around him as Carpathia embraced Buck. It was all Buck could do to not recoil. "Be careful of what you're doing to my journalistic independence," he whispered in Carpathia's ear.

"Any good news for me yet?" Carpathia asked, holding Buck at arm's length and looking into his eyes.

"Not yet, sir."

"I will see you in Jerusalem?"

"Of course."

"You will keep in touch with Steve?"

"I will."

"You tell him what it will take, and we will do it. That is a promise."

Buck sidled over to a small group where Peter Mathews was holding court. Buck waited until the archbishop noticed him; then he leaned forward and whispered, "What'd I miss?"

"What do you mean? You were there."

"You said Carpathia would make some announcement about an expanded role for the next pope, something bigger and more important even than the Catholic Church."

Mathews stood shaking his head. "Perhaps I had you overrated, friend. I am not the pope yet, but couldn't you tell from the secretary-general's statement that there will be need for a head of the new religion? What better place to headquarter it than the Vatican? And who better to lead it than the new pope?"

"So you'll be the pope of popes."

Mathews smiled and nodded. "P. M.," he said.

\+ \+ \+

Two hours later, Rayford Steele arrived at the United Nations. He had been praying silently since he phoned Bruce Barnes just before he boarded his flight. "I feel like I'm going to meet the devil," Rayford said. "Not much in this life scares me, Bruce. I've always taken pride in that. But I've got to tell you, this is awful."

"First, Rayford, only if you were encountering the Antichrist in the second half of the Tribulation would you actually be dealing with the person who was possessed by Satan himself."

"So what is Carpathia? Some second-rate demon?"

"No, you need prayer support. You know what happened in Buck's presence."

"Buck is ten years younger, and in better shape," Rayford said. "I feel as if I'll fall apart in there."

"You won't. Stay strong. God knows where you are, and he has perfect timing. I'll be praying, and you know Chloe and Buck will be too."

That was of great comfort to Rayford, and it was particularly encouraging to know that Buck was in town. Just knowing he was in close proximity made Rayford feel less alone. Yet in his anxiety over meeting Carpathia face-to-face, he did not want to look past the ordeal of confronting Hattie Durham.

Hattie was waiting when he stepped off the elevator. He had hoped to have a moment to get the lay of the land, to freshen up, to take a deep breath. But there she stood in all her youthful beauty, more stunning than ever because of a tan and expensively tailored clothes on a frame that needed no help. He did not expect what he saw, and he sensed evil in the place when a flash of longing for her briefly invaded his mind.

Rayford's old nature immediately reminded him why she had distracted him during a wintry season of his marriage. He prayed silently, thanking God for sparing him from having done something he would have regretted forever. And as soon as Hattie opened her mouth, he was brought back to reality. Her diction and articulation were more refined, but this was still a woman without a clue, and he could hear it in her tone.

"Captain Steele," she gushed. "How wonderful to see you again! How is everyone else?"

"Everyone else?"

"You know, Chloe and Buck and everybody."

Chloe and Buck are *everybody,* he thought, but he didn't say so.

"Everybody's fine."

"Oh, that's wonderful."

"Is there a private place we can talk?"

She led him to her work area, which was disconcertingly open. No one was around to overhear them, but the ceilings were at least twenty feet high. Her desk and tables and file cabinets were set in a cavernous area, much like a railway station, with no confining walls. Footsteps echoed, and Rayford had the distinct impression that they were a long way from the offices of the secretary-general.

"So, what's new with you since I saw you last, Captain Steele?"

"Hattie, I don't want to be unkind, but you can stop with the 'Captain Steele' and the pretending to not know what's new. What's new is that you and your new boss have invaded my job and my family, and I seem powerless to do anything about it."

13

STANTON BAILEY gripped the armrests of his big chair and rocked back, studying Buck Williams.

"Cameron," he said, "I have never been able to figure you. What was that sack lunch business all about?"

"It was just a cookie. I was hungry."

"I'm always hungry," Bailey roared, "but I don't eat on TV!"

"I wasn't sure I could be seen."

"Well, now you know. And if Carpathia and Plank still let you at the signing table in Jerusalem, no sack lunches."

"It was a cookie."

"No cookies either!"

* * *

After years as Hattie Durham's captain, Rayford now felt like her subordinate, sitting across from her impressive desk. Apparently his coming straight to the point had sobered her.

"Rayford, listen," she said, "I still like you in spite of how you dumped me, all right? I would never do anything to hurt you."

"Trying to get a complaint about me into my personnel file is not going to hurt me?"

"That was just a joke. You saw right through it."

"It brought me a lot of grief. And the note waiting for me in Dallas about the new *Air Force One* being a 777."

"Same thing, I told you. A joke."

"Not funny. Too coincidental."

"Well, Rayford, if you can't take a little teasing, then fine, I won't bother. I just thought, friend to friend, a little fun wouldn't hurt."

"Come on, Hattie. You think I'm buying this? This is not your style. You don't pull practical jokes on your friends. It's just not you."

"OK, I'm sorry."

"That's not good enough."

"Well, excuse me, but I don't answer to you anymore."

Somehow Hattie Durham had the capacity to rattle Rayford more than anyone else did. He took a deep breath and fought for composure. "Hattie, I want you to tell me about the flowers and candy."

Hattie was the worst bluffer in the world. "Flowers and candy?" she repeated after a guilty pause.

"Stop with the games," Rayford said. "Just accept that I know it was you and tell me why."

"I only do what I'm told, Rayford."

"See? This is beyond me. I should be asking the most powerful man in the world why he sent my daughter, someone he has never met, flowers and candy? Is he pursuing her? And if he is, why doesn't he sign his name?"

"He's not pursuing her, Rayford! He's seeing someone."

"What does that mean?"

"He has a relationship."

"Anybody we know?" Rayford gave her a disgusted look.

Hattie seemed to be fighting a grin. "It's safe to say we're an item, but the press doesn't know, so we'd appreciate it—"

"I'll make a deal with you. You quit with the anonymous gifts to Chloe, tell me what the point was, and I'll keep your little secret—how's that?"

Hattie leaned forward conspiratorially. "OK," she said, "here's what I think, all right? I mean, I don't know. Like I said, I just do what I'm told. But that's one brilliant mind in there."

Rayford didn't doubt that. He just wondered why Nicolae Carpathia was spending time on such trivia.

"Go on."

"He really wants you as his pilot."

"OK," Rayford said tentatively.

"You'll do it?"

"Do what? I'm just saying I follow you, though I'm not sure I really do. He wants me as his pilot, and so . . . ?"

"But he knows you're happy where you are."

"Still with you, I think."

"He wants to provide not just a job that might lure you away, but also something on your end that might push you from where you are."

"My daughter being pursued by him would push me toward him?"

"No, silly. You weren't supposed to find out who it was!"

"I see. I would be worried that it was someone from Chicago, so I would be inclined to move and take another job."

"There you go."

"I've got lots of questions, Hattie."

"Shoot."

"Why would someone pursuing my daughter make me want to run? She's almost twenty-one. It's time she was pursued."

"But we did it anonymously. That should have seemed a little dangerous, a little upsetting."

"It was."

"Then we did our job."

"Hattie, did you think I wouldn't put two and two together when you sent Chloe's favorite mints, available only at Holman Meadows in New York?"

"Hmph," she said, "maybe that wasn't too swift."

"OK, let's say it worked. I think my daughter's being stalked or pursued by someone who seems sinister. As close as Carpathia is to the president, doesn't he know they're after me to pilot *Air Force One*?"

"Rayford! Duh! *That's* the job he wants you to take."

Rayford slumped and sighed. "Hattie, for the love of all things sacred, just tell me what's going on. I get hints from the White House and Pan-Con that it's Carpathia who wants me in there. I'm approved sight unseen to fly the U.N. delegation to Israel. Carpathia wants me as his pilot but first he wants me to be the captain of *Air Force One*?"

Maddeningly, Hattie turned a tolerant and condescending smile on him. "Rayford Steele," she said in a schoolmarmish tone, "you just don't get it yet, do you? You don't really know who Nicolae Carpathia is."

Rayford was stunned for a second. He knew better than she did who Nicolae Carpathia really was. The question was whether *she* had any inkling. "Tell me," he said. "Help me understand."

Hattie looked behind her, as if expecting Carpathia at any moment. Rayford knew no one could sneak up on them in this echoing, marble-floored edifice. "Nicolae is not going to give back the plane."

"Excuse me?"

"You heard me. It's already been flown to New York. You're going to see it today. It's being painted."

"Painted?"

"You'll see."

Rayford's mind reeled. The plane would have been painted in Seattle before being flown to D.C. Why would it be painted again?

"How's he going to get away with not returning it?"

"He's going to thank the president for the gift, and—"

"He already did that the other day. I heard him."

"But this time he will make it obvious he's thanking the president for a *gift*, not for a *loan*. You get hired by the White House first, and you come with the plane, on the president's salary budget. What can the president do, look betrayed? Say Nicolae is lying? He'll just have to find a way to look as generous as Nicolae makes him out to be. Is that brilliant?"

"It's boorish. It's thievery. Why would I want to work for a man like that? Why would *you*?"

"I'll work with and for Nicolae for as long as he'll let me, Rayford. I have never learned so much in so short a time. This is not thievery at all. Nicolae says the United States is looking for ways to support the U.N. now, and here is a way. You know the world is coming together, and someone is going to lead the new one-world government. Getting this plane is one way to show that President Fitzhugh defers to Secretary-General Carpathia."

Hattie sounded like a parrot. Carpathia had taught her well, if not to understand, at least to believe.

"OK," Rayford summarized, "Carpathia somehow gets Pan-Con and the White House to put me at the top of the list of pilots for *Air Force One*. He has you agitate me at home so I'll want to move. I take the job, he gets the plane and never gives it back. I'm the pilot, but I'm paid by the U.S. government. And this all ties in with Carpathia eventually becoming the leader of the world."

Hattie rested her chin in her entwined fingers, elbows on the desk. She cocked her head. "That wasn't so complicated, was it?"

"I don't get why I'm so important to him."

"He asked who was the best pilot I ever worked for and why."

"And I won," Rayford said.

"You won."

"Did you tell him we almost had a fling?"

"Did we?"

"Never mind."

"Of course I didn't tell him that, and neither will you if you want to keep a good job."

"But you told him I was a Christian."

"Sure, why not? You tell everyone else. I think *he's* a Christian, anyway."

"Nicolae Carpathia?"

"Of course! At least he lives by Christian principles. He's always concerned for the greater good. That's one of his favorite phrases. Like this airplane deal.

He knows the U.S. wants to do this, even if they didn't think of it. They might feel a little put out for a while, but since it is for the greater good of the world, they'll eventually see that and be glad they did it. They'll look like generous heroes, and he's doing that for them. That's Christian, isn't it?"

* * *

Buck was scribbling furiously. He had left his tape recorder in his bag at the hotel, expecting to get it when he returned from the *Global Weekly* office to interview Rabbi Marc Feinberg, one of the key proponents of rebuilding the Jewish temple. But when Buck had entered the hotel lobby, he had nearly run into Feinberg, who was pulling a large trunk on wheels. "I'm sorry, my friend. I was able to get an earlier flight, and I'm going. Walk with me."

Buck had dug his notebook from one pocket and pen from the other. "How do you feel about the pronouncements?" Buck asked.

"Let me say this: Today I have become a bit of a politician. Do I believe God is a concept? No! I believe God is a person! Do I believe that all the religions of the world can work together and become one? No, probably not. My God is a jealous God and will share his glory with no other. However, can we tolerate each other? Certainly.

"But, you may ask, why do I say I have become a politician? Because I will compromise for the sake of rebuilding the temple. As long as I do not have to sacrifice my belief in the one true God of Abraham, Isaac, and Jacob, I will tolerate and cooperate with anyone with a good heart. I do not agree with them or with their methods, many of them, but if they want to get along, I want to get along. Above all, I want the temple rebuilt on its original site. This was virtually done as of today. I predict the temple will be constructed within the year."

The rabbi burst through the front doors and asked the doorman to hail him a cab. "But, sir," Buck said, "if the head of the new one-world religion considers himself a Christian—"

Feinberg waved Buck off. "Ach! We all know it will be Mathews, and that he will likely be the next pope, too! *Considers* himself a Christian? He *is* a Christian through and through! He believes Jesus was Messiah. I'd sooner believe Carpathia is Messiah."

"You're serious?"

"Believe me, I have considered it. Messiah is to bring justice and lasting peace. Look what Carpathia has done in just weeks! Does he fit all the criteria? We'll find out Monday. Are you aware that my colleague Rabbi Tsion Ben-Judah is—"

"Yes, I'll be watching." There were plenty of other sources Buck could talk to about Carpathia, and he wanted to speak with Ben-Judah personally. What he wanted from Feinberg was the temple story. He redirected the subject. "What is so important about the rebuilding of the temple?"

Rabbi Feinberg stepped and spun, watching the line of cabs, obviously worried about the time. But though he did not maintain eye contact with Buck, he continued to expound. He gave Buck the short course, as if teaching a class of Gentiles interested in Jewish history.

"King David wanted to build a temple for the Lord," he said. "But God felt David had shed too much blood as a man of war, so he let David's son Solomon build it. It was magnificent. Jerusalem was the city where God would place his name and where his people would come to worship. The glory of God appeared in the temple, and it became a symbol of the hand of God protecting the nation. The people felt so secure that even when they turned from God, they believed Jerusalem was impregnable, as long as the temple stood."

A cab pulled up and the doorman loaded the large valise into the trunk. "Pay the man and ride with me," Feinberg said. Buck had to smile as he pulled a bill from his pocket and pressed it into the doorman's hand. Even if he had to pay for the cab ride, it would be a cheap interview.

"Kennedy," Feinberg told the driver.

"Do you have a phone?" Buck asked the driver.

The driver handed him a cellular phone. "Credit-card calls only."

Buck asked to see Feinberg's bill so he could get the number of the hotel. He called the concierge and told her he would need his bag stored longer than he had expected. "Sir, someone took that bag for you."

"Someone what?"

"Took that bag for you. Said he was your friend and would see that you got it."

Buck was stunned. "You let my bag be taken by a stranger who claimed to be a friend of mine?"

"Sir, it's not as bleak as all that. I think the man could easily be located if necessary. He's on the news every night."

"Mr. Carpathia?"

"Yes, sir. One of his people, a Mr. Plank, promised he would deliver it to you."

Feinberg seemed pleased when Buck finally got off the phone. "Back to the temple!" he shouted, and the driver pulled his foot off the gas. "Not you!" Feinberg said. "Us!"

Buck wondered what a man with such unbounded energy and enthusiasm might do in another profession. "You'd have been a killer racquetball player," he said.

"I *am* a killer racquetball player!" Feinberg said. "I'm an A-minus. What are you?"

"Retired."

"And so young!"

"Too busy."

"Never too busy for physical exercise," the rabbi said, smacking himself on his flat, hard stomach. "Ah, the temple," he said. The cab was soon stuck in traffic, and Buck kept scribbling.

\+ + +

When Hattie excused herself to answer the phone on her desk, Rayford slipped his New Testament and Psalms from his pocket. He had been memorizing verses from the Psalms, and as his anxiety over meeting Carpathia grew, he turned to those favorites and ran them over in his mind.

He found Psalm 91 and read verses he had underlined: "He who dwells in the secret place of the Most High shall abide under the shadow of the Almighty. I will say of the Lord, 'He is my refuge and my fortress; My God, in Him I will trust.' A thousand may fall at your side, and ten thousand at your right hand; but it shall not come near you. No evil shall befall you, nor shall any plague come near your dwelling; for He shall give His angels charge over you, to keep you in all your ways."

When he looked up, Hattie was off the phone and looking at him expectantly. "Sorry," he said, closing the Bible.

"That's all right," she said. "The secretary-general is ready for you."

\+ + +

With the cabby's assurance that the rabbi was not going to miss his plane, Feinberg warmed to his subject. "The temple and the city of Jerusalem were destroyed by King Nebuchadnezzar. Seventy years later a decree was given to rebuild the city and eventually the temple. The new temple, under the direction of Zerubbabel and Joshua, the high priest, was so inferior to the temple of Solomon that some of the elders wept when they saw the foundation.

"Still, that temple served Israel until it was desecrated by Antiochus Epiphanes, a Greco-Roman ruler. About 40 BC, Herod the Great had the temple destroyed piece by piece and rebuilt. That became known as Herod's Temple. And you know what became of that."

"I'm sorry, I don't."

"You're a religion writer and you don't know what happened to Herod's Temple?"

"I'm actually a pinch hitter for the religion writer on this story."

"A pinch hitter?"

Buck smiled. "You're an A-minus racquetball player and you don't know what a pinch hitter is?"

"It's not a racquetball term, I know that," Rabbi Feinberg said. "And other than football, which you call soccer, I don't care about other sports. Let me tell you what happened to Herod's Temple. Titus, a Roman general, laid siege to Jerusalem, and even though he gave orders that the temple not be destroyed, the Jews did not trust him. They burned it rather than allow it to fall into pagan hands. Today the Temple Mount, the site of the old Jewish temple, is occupied by the Mohammedans and houses the Muslim mosque called the Dome of the Rock."

Buck was curious. "How were the Muslims persuaded to move the Dome of the Rock?"

"That proves the magnificence of Carpathia," Feinberg said. "Who but Messiah could ask devout Muslims to move the shrine that in their religion is second in importance only to Mecca, the birthplace of Mohammed? But you see, the Temple Mount, the Dome of the Rock, is built right over Mount Moriah, where we believe Abraham expressed his willingness to God to sacrifice his son Isaac. Of course we do not believe Mohammed to be divine, so as long as a Muslim mosque occupies the Temple Mount, we believe our holy place is being defiled."

"So this is a great day for Israel."

"A great day! Since the birth of our nation, we have collected millions from around the world for the rebuilding of the temple. Work has begun. Many prefabricated walls are finished and will be shipped in. I will live to see the reconstruction of the temple, and it will be even more spectacular than in the days of Solomon!"

+ + +

"At last we meet," Nicolae Carpathia said, rising and coming around his desk to shake hands with Rayford Steele. "Thank you, Ms. Durham. We will sit right here."

Hattie left and shut the door. Nicolae pointed to a chair and sat down across from Rayford. "And so our little circle is connected."

Rayford felt strangely calmed. He was being prayed for, and his mind was full of the promises from the Psalms. "Sir?"

"It is interesting to me how small the world is. Perhaps that is why I believe so strongly that we are becoming truly a global community. Would you believe I met you through an Israeli botanist named Chaim Rosenzweig?"

"I know the name, of course, but we have never met."

"Indeed you have not. But you will. If not while you are here, then Saturday on the plane to Israel. He introduced me to a young journalist who had written about him. That journalist met your flight attendant, Ms. Durham, while on your plane, and eventually introduced her to me. She is now my assistant, and she introduced you to me. A small world."

Earl Halliday had said the same thing when he'd heard that Hattie Durham, a former Pan-Con employee, was working for the man who wanted Rayford as pilot of *Air Force One*. Rayford did not respond to Carpathia. He didn't believe they had met coincidentally. It was not such a small world. It was possible all had been where God had wanted them to be so Rayford could be sitting where he was today. This wasn't something he wanted or had sought, but he was finally open to it.

"So, you want to be the pilot of *Air Force One*."

"No, sir, that was not my desire. I am willing to fly her to Jerusalem with your delegation, at the request of the White House, and then decide about the request to become the pilot."

"You did not seek the position?"

"No, sir."

"But you are willing."

"To give it a try."

"Mr. Steele, I want to make a prediction. I want to presume that you will see this plane, experience the latest technology, and want never to fly anything less."

"That may very well be." *But not for that reason,* Rayford thought. *Only if it's what God wants.*

"I also want to let you in on a little secret, something that has not been announced yet. Ms. Durham has assured me that you are a man who can be trusted, a man of your word, and as of recently also a religious man."

Rayford nodded, unwilling to say anything.

"Then I will trust you to keep my confidence until this is announced. *Air Force One* is being lent to the United Nations as a gesture of support by the president of the United States."

"That's been on the news, sir."

"Of course, but what has not been announced is that the plane will then be given to us, along with the crew, for our exclusive use."

"How nice of President Fitzhugh to offer that."

"How nice indeed," Carpathia said. "And how generous."

Rayford understood how people could be charmed by Carpathia, but sitting across from him and knowing he was lying made it easier to resist his charm.

"When do you fly back?" Carpathia said.

"I left it open. I'm at your disposal. I do need to be home before we leave Saturday, however."

"I like your style," Carpathia said. "You are at my disposal. That is nice. You realize, of course, that should you get this job—and you will—that this is not a platform for proselytizing."

"Meaning?"

"Meaning that the United Nations, which shall become known as Global Community, and I in particular, are proactively nonsectarian."

"I am a believer in Christ," Rayford said. "I attend church. I read my Bible. I tell people what I believe."

"But not on the job."

"If you become my superior and that becomes a directive, I will be obligated to obey."

"I will and it will and you will," Carpathia said. "Just so we understand each other."

"Clearly."

"I like you, and I believe we can work together."

"I don't know you, sir, but I believe I can work with anybody." Where had that come from? Rayford almost smiled. If he could work with the Antichrist, who couldn't he work with?

+ + +

As the cab pulled up to the curb at Kennedy International, Rabbi Marc Feinberg said, "I'm sure you won't mind including my trip in your total, as you did interview me."

"Certainly," Buck said. "*Global Weekly* is more than happy to provide you a trip to the airport, provided we don't have to fly you to Israel."

"Now that you mention it—," the rabbi said with a twinkle, but he did not finish the thought. He merely waved, retrieved his valise from the cabby, and hurried into the terminal.

+ + +

Nicolae Carpathia pressed the intercom button. "Ms. Durham, have you arranged for a car to the hangar?"

"Yes, sir. Rear entrance."

"We are ready."

"I'll buzz you when security arrives."

"Thank you." Nicolae turned to Rayford. "I want you to see the plane."

"Certainly," Rayford said, though he would rather have started toward home. Why on earth had he said he was at Carpathia's disposal?

* * *

"Back to the hotel, sir?"

"No," Buck said. "The U.N. building, please. And let me use your cell phone again, would you?"

"Credit—"

"Card calls only, I know." He phoned Steve Plank at the U.N. "What's the idea of absconding with my bag?"

"Just trying to do you a favor, old buddy. You at the Plaza? I'll bring it to you."

"That's where I'm staying, but let me come to you. That's what you intended anyway, wasn't it?"

"Yup."

"Be there in an hour."

"Carpathia may not be here."

"I'm not coming to see him. I'm coming to see you."

* * *

When Hattie buzzed, Carpathia stood and his door opened. Two security guards flanked Nicolae and Rayford as they made their way through the corridors to a freight elevator, down to the first floor below ground level, and into a parking dock, where a limousine waited. The driver leaped out to open the door for Carpathia. Rayford was walked around to the other side, where his door was opened.

Rayford found it strange that though he had been offered no refreshment at the office, Carpathia now insisted on showing him everything available in the limo, from whiskey to wine, to beer and soft drinks. Rayford accepted a Coke.

"Are you not a drinker?"

"Not anymore."

"Used to be?"

"Never a hard drinker, but occasionally unwise. I haven't touched a drop since I lost my family."

"I was sorry to hear of that."

"Thank you, but I have come to terms with it. I miss them terribly—"

"Of course."

"But I have peace about it."

"Your religion believes that Jesus Christ has taken his own to heaven, is that it?"

"That's it."

"I will not pretend that I share that belief, but I respect any comfort the thought may bring you."

Rayford wanted to argue, but he wondered at the advisability of doing what Bruce Barnes would call 'witnessing' to the Antichrist.

"I am not a drinker either," Carpathia said, sipping seltzer water.

\+ + +

"So why didn't you let me come to you?" Steve Plank said. "I would have."

"I need a favor."

"We can trade favors, Buck. Say yes to Carpathia's offer and you'll never have to ask for anything again as long as you live."

"To tell you the truth, Steve, I have too many good stories in the hopper right now to even think about jumping."

"Write them for us."

"No can do. But help me if you can. I want to get in to see those two guys at the Wailing Wall."

"Nicolae hates those two. Thinks they're crazy. Obviously they are."

"Then he shouldn't have a problem with my trying to interview them."

"I'll see what I can do. He's with a pilot candidate today."

"You don't say."

\+ + +

Carpathia and Rayford stepped from the limo outside a huge hangar at Kennedy. Carpathia said to the driver, "Tell Frederick we would like the usual drama."

When the hangar doors opened, the plane was illuminated with brilliant spotlights. On the side facing Rayford were the words *Air Force One* and the seal of the president of the United States. As they walked around to the other side, however, Rayford saw the team of painters high on scaffolding. The seal and the name had been eliminated. In its place was the old logo of the United Nations but with the words *Global Community* in place of the current name. And in place of the name of the aircraft, painters were putting the finishing touches on *Global Community One*.

"How long until both sides are finished?" Carpathia called out to a foreman.

"It'll be dry on both sides by midnight!" came the answer. "This side took about six hours. Other side will go quicker. Airworthy by Saturday easily!"

Carpathia flashed a thumbs-up sign, and the workers in the hangar applauded. "We would like to board," Carpathia whispered, and within minutes a lift had been jury-rigged that allowed them to enter from the rear of the sparkling new plane. Rayford had toured countless new aircraft and was usually impressed, but he had never seen anything like this.

Every detail was richly appointed, expensive, functional, and beautiful. In the rear were full bathrooms with showers. Then came the press area, large enough for parties. Every seat had its own phone, modem jack, VCR, and TV. A restaurant was midship, fully stocked and with room to move and breathe.

Closer to the front came the presidential living quarters and conference room. One room contained high-tech security and surveillance equipment, backup communications, and technology allowing the plane to communicate with anyone anywhere in the world.

Directly behind the cockpit were the crew living quarters, including a private apartment for the pilot. "You will not want to stay on the plane when we land somewhere for a few days," Nicolae said. "But you would be hard-pressed to find better accommodations anywhere."

\+ + +

Buck was in Steve's office when Hattie Durham dropped in to inform Steve that Nicolae was out for a while. "Oh, Mr. Williams!" she said. "I can't thank you enough for introducing me to Mr. Carpathia."

Buck didn't know what to say. He didn't want to tell her she was welcome. In truth he felt awful about it. He just nodded.

"You know who was in today?" she said.

He knew, but he didn't let on. "Who?"

Buck realized he would have to stay on his toes with her and with Steve, and especially with Carpathia. They must not know how close he was to Rayford, and if he could keep from them any knowledge of his developing relationship with Chloe, so much the better.

"Rayford Steele. He was the pilot the day I met you on the plane."

"I remember," he said.

"Did you know he was up for pilot of *Air Force One*?"

"That would be quite an honor, wouldn't it?"

"He deserves it. He's the best pilot I ever worked for."

Buck felt awkward, talking about his new friend and brother in Christ as if he barely knew him. "What makes a good pilot?" Buck asked.

"A smooth takeoff and landing. Lots of communication with the passengers. And treating the crew like peers rather than slaves."

"Impressive," Buck said.

"You want to see the plane?" Steve said.

"May I?"

"It's in an auxiliary hangar at Kennedy."

"I was just out there."

"Want to go back?"

Buck shrugged. "Someone else has already been assigned the story of the new plane and pilot and all that, but sure, I'd love to see it."

"You can still fly on it to Israel."

"No, I can't," Buck said. "My boss was crystal clear on that point."

* * *

When Rayford arrived home that evening, he knew Chloe would be able to tell he was pensive. "Bruce canceled the meeting for tonight," she said.

"Good," Rayford said. "I'm exhausted."

"So tell me about Carpathia."

Rayford tried. What was there to say? The man was friendly, charming, smooth, and except for the lying might have made even Rayford wonder if they had misjudged him. "But there's no longer any doubt about his identity, is there?" he concluded.

"Not in my mind," Chloe said. "But I haven't met him."

"Knowing you, he wouldn't fool you for a second."

"I hope so," she said. "But Buck admits he's amazing."

"Have you heard from Buck?"

"He's supposed to call at midnight his time."

"Do I need to stay up to make sure you're awake?"

"Hardly. He doesn't even know we ate our cookies at the same time. I wouldn't miss telling him that for anything."

14

BUCK WILLIAMS was cashing in all his journalistic chips. After trying to sleep off jet lag in the King David Hotel on Saturday, he had left messages for Chaim Rosenzweig, Marc Feinberg, and even Peter Mathews. According to Steve Plank, Nicolae Carpathia had turned down flat Buck's request for help in getting near the two preachers at the Wailing Wall.

"I told you," Steve said. "He thinks those guys are nuts, and he's disappointed you think they're worth a story."

"So he doesn't know anybody who can get me in there?"

"It's a restricted area."

"Precisely my point. Have we finally found something Nicolae the Great can't do?"

Steve had been angry. "You know as well as I do that he could buy the Wailing Wall," he spat. "But you're not going to get close to the place with his help. He doesn't want you there, Buck. For once in your life, get a clue and stay away."

"Yeah, that sounds like me."

"Buck, let me ask you something. If you defy Carpathia and then either turn down his offer or make him so irritated that he withdraws it, where are you going to work?"

"I'll work."

"Where? Can't you see that his influence reaches everywhere? People love him! They'll do anything for him. People come away from meetings with him doing things they never would have dreamed they'd do."

Tell me about it, Buck thought.

"I've got work to do," Buck said. "Thanks anyway."

"*Right now* you've got work to do. But nothing is permanent."

Steve had never spoken truer words, though he didn't know it.

Buck's second strikeout was with Peter Mathews. He was ensconced in a penthouse suite in a five-star hotel in Tel Aviv, and though he did take Buck's call, he was dismissive. "I admire you, Williams," he said, "but I think I've given you all the best stuff I know, on and off the record. I don't have any connection with the guys at the Wall, but I'll give you a quote, if that's what you want."

"What I want is to find someone who can get me close enough so I can talk to these two men myself. If they want to kill me or burn me up or ignore me, that'll be their prerogative."

"I am allowed close to the Wailing Wall because of my position, but I'm not interested in helping you get there. I'm sorry. On the record, I think these are two elderly Torah students who are pretending to be Moses and Elijah reincarnated. Their costumes are bad, their preaching is worse. Why people have died trying to hurt them, I have no idea. Maybe these two old coots have compatriots hidden among the masses who pick people off who look like threats. Now, I've got to go. You'll be at the signing Monday?"

"That's why I'm here, sir."

"I'll see you there. Do yourself a favor and don't tarnish your reputation by making a story out of those two. If you want a story, you ought to tag along with me this afternoon as I tour possible sites for Vatican involvement in Jerusalem."

"But, sir, what do you make of the fact that it hasn't rained in Jerusalem since those two began preaching?"

"I don't make anything of it, except maybe that not even the clouds want to hear what they have to say. It hardly ever rains here anyway."

\+ + +

Rayford had met the crew of *Global Community One* just a couple of hours before takeoff. Not one had ever worked for Pan-Continental. In a brief pep talk he had emphasized that safety was paramount. "That is why every one of us is here. Proper procedure and protocol come next. We do everything by the book, and we keep our logs and checklists as we go. We look sharp, we stay in the background, we serve our hosts and passengers. While we are deferential to the dignitaries and serve them, their safety is our primary concern. The best airplane crew is an invisible one. People feel comfort and security when they see uniforms and service, not individuals."

Rayford's first officer was older than Rayford and probably had wanted the pilot's position. But he was friendly and efficient. The navigator was a young man Rayford would not have chosen, but he did his job. The cabin crew had worked together on *Air Force One* and seemed overly impressed with the new plane, but Rayford couldn't fault them for that. It was a technological marvel, but they would soon get used to it and take it for granted.

Flying the 777 was, as Rayford had commented to the certifying examiner in

Dallas, like sitting behind the wheel of a Jaguar. But the excitement wore off as the flight stretched on. After a while he left the plane in the control of his first officer and slipped into his own living quarters. He stretched out on the bed and was suddenly struck by how utterly lonely he was. How proud Irene would have been of this moment, when he had the top job in the flying world. But to him it meant little, though he felt in his spirit that he was doing what God had led him to do. Why, he had no idea. But deep inside Rayford felt sure he had flown his last route for Pan-Con.

He phoned Chloe and woke her. "Sorry, Chlo'," he said.

"That's all right, Dad. Is it exciting?"

"Oh, yeah, I can't deny that."

They had discussed that the plane-to-ground communications were likely under surveillance, so there would be no disparaging talk about Carpathia or anyone else in his orbit. And they would not mention Buck by name.

"Who do you know there?"

"Only Hattie really. I'm kind of lonely."

"Me too. I haven't heard from anyone else yet. I'm supposed to get a call early Monday morning, your time. When will you be in Jerusalem?"

"In about three hours we land in Tel Aviv and are transported by luxury motor coaches to Jerusalem."

"You aren't flying into Jerusalem?"

"No. A 777 can't land near there. Tel Aviv is only thirty-five miles from Jerusalem."

"When will you be home?"

"Well, we were scheduled to leave Tel Aviv Tuesday morning, but now they tell us that we'll be flying on to Baghdad Monday afternoon and we'll leave from there Tuesday morning. It adds six hundred air miles, about another hour, to the total trip."

"What's in Baghdad?"

"The only airport near Babylon that will take a plane this size. Carpathia wants to tour Babylon and show his people the plans."

"Will you go along?"

"I imagine I will. It's about fifty miles south of Baghdad by bus. If I take this job I imagine I'll be seeing a lot of the Middle East over the next few years."

"I miss you already. I wish I could be there."

"I know who you miss, Chloe."

"I miss you too, Dad."

"Ah, I'll be chopped liver to you within a month. I can see where you and what's-his-name are going."

"Bruce phoned. He said he got a strange call from some woman named Amanda White, claiming to have known Mom. She told Bruce she met Mom at one of the church's home Bible study groups and only just remembered her name. She said it came to her because she knew it sounded like iron and steel."

"Hmm," Rayford said. "Irene Steele. Guess I never thought of it that way. What'd she want?"

"She said she finally became a Christian, mostly because of remembering things Mom said at that Bible study, and now she's looking for a church. She wondered if New Hope was still up and running."

"Where's she been?"

"Grieving her husband and two grown daughters. She lost them in the Rapture."

"Your mom was that instrumental in her life, and yet she didn't remember her name?"

"Go figure," Chloe said.

* * *

Buck napped for about an hour and a half before taking a call from Chaim Rosenzweig, who had just gotten in. "Even I will need to adjust to the time difference, Cameron," Dr. Rosenzweig said. "No matter how many times I make the trip, the jet lag attacks. How long have you been in the country?"

"I arrived yesterday morning. I need your help." Buck told Rosenzweig he needed to get closer to the Wailing Wall. "I tried," he said, "but I probably didn't get within a hundred yards. The two men were preaching, and the crowds were much bigger than I ever saw on CNN."

"Oh, there are bigger crowds now as we get closer to the signing of the covenant. Perhaps in light of the signing, the pair have stepped up their activities. More and more people are coming to hear them, and apparently they are even seeing Orthodox Jews converting to Christianity. Very strange. Nicolae asked about them on the way over and watched some of the coverage on the television. He was as angry as I have ever seen him."

"What did he say?"

"That was just it. He said nothing. I thought he looked flushed, and his jaw was set. I know him just a little, you understand, but I can tell when he is agitated."

"Chaim, I need your help."

"Cameron, I am not Orthodox. I do not go to the Wall, and even if I could, I would probably not risk the danger. I don't recommend that you do either. The bigger story here is the covenant signing Monday morning. Nicolae and the Israeli delegation and I finalized everything in New York Friday. Nicolae was brilliant. He is amazing, Cameron. I long for the day when we both are working for him."

"Chaim, please. I know every journalist in the world would love to have an exclusive with the two preachers, but I am the one who will not give up until I get it or die trying."

"That's just what you might do."

"Doctor, I've never asked you for anything but your time, and you've always been most generous."

"I don't know what I can do for you, Cameron. I would take you there myself if I thought I could get in. But you will not be able to get in anyway."

"But you must know someone with access."

"Of course I do! I know many Orthodox Jews, many rabbis. But—"

"What about Ben-Judah?"

"Oh, Cameron! He is so busy. His live report on the research project will be broadcast Monday afternoon. He must be cramming like a schoolboy before a final examination."

"But maybe not, Chaim. Maybe he has done so much research that he could talk about this for an hour without notes. Maybe he's ready now and is looking for something to occupy him so he doesn't overprepare or stress out waiting for his big moment."

There was silence on the other end, and Buck prayed Rosenzweig would yield. "I don't know, Cameron. I would not want to be bothered so close to a big moment."

"Would you do this, Chaim—just call and wish him the best and feel him out about his schedule this weekend? I'll come anywhere at any time if he can get me close to the Wall."

"Only if he is looking for a diversion," Rosenzweig said. "If I sense he is buried in his work, I won't even broach the subject."

"Thank you, sir! You'll call me back?"

"Either way. And Cameron, please don't get your hopes up, and don't hold it against me if he is unavailable."

"I would never do that."

"I know. But I also sense how important this is to you."

* * *

Buck was dead to the world and had no idea how long his phone had been ringing. He sat straight up in bed and noticed the Sunday afternoon sun turning orange, the stream of light making a weird pattern on the bed. Buck caught a glimpse of himself in the mirror as he reached for the phone. His cheek was red and creased, his eyes puffy and half open, his hair shooting out in all directions. His mouth tasted horrible, and he had slept in his clothes.

"Hello?"

"Ees dis Chamerown Weeleeums?" came the thick Hebrew accent.

"Yes, sir."

"Dees ist Dochtor Tsion Ben-Judah."

Buck jumped to his feet as if the respected scholar were in the room. "Yes, Dr. Ben-Judah. A privilege to hear from you, sir!"

"Thank you," the doctor managed. "I am calling you from out front of your hotel."

Buck fought to understand him. "Yes?"

"I have a car and a driver."

"A car and driver, yes sir."

"Are you ready to go?"

"To go?"

"To the Wall."

"Oh, yes, sir—I mean, no, sir. I'm going to need ten minutes. Can you wait ten minutes?"

"I should have called before arriving. I was under the impression from our mutual friend that this was a matter of some urgency to you."

Buck ran the strange-sounding English through his mind again. "A matter of urgency, yes! Just give me ten minutes! Thank you, sir!"

Buck tore off his clothes and jumped in the shower. He didn't give the water time to heat. He lathered up and rinsed off, then dragged his razor across his face.

He didn't take the time to find the electrical adapter for his hair dryer but just yanked a towel off the rack and attacked his long hair, feeling as if he were pulling half of it out of his scalp.

He jerked the comb through his hair and brushed his teeth. What did one wear to the Wailing Wall? He knew he wouldn't be getting inside, but would he offend his host if he was not wearing a coat and tie? He hadn't brought one. He hadn't planned on dressing up even for the treaty signing the next morning.

Buck chose his usual denim shirt, dressy jeans, ankle-high boots, and leather jacket. He dropped his tape recorder and camera into his smallest leather bag and ran down three flights of stairs. When he burst from the door he stopped. He had no idea what the rabbi looked like. Would he look like Rosenzweig, or Feinberg, or neither?

Neither, it turned out. Tsion Ben-Judah, in a black suit and black felt hat, stepped from the front passenger seat of an idling white Mercedes and waved shyly. Buck hurried to him. "Dr. Ben-Judah?" he said, shaking his hand. The man was middle-aged, trim, and youthful with strong, angular features and only a hint of gray in his dark brown hair.

In his labored English, the rabbi said, "In your dialect, my first name sounds like the city, Zion. You may call me that."

"Zion? Are you sure?"

"Sure of my own name?" The rabbi smiled. "I am sure."

"No, I meant are you sure I can call you—"

"I know what you meant, Mr. Williams. You may call me Zion."

To Buck, *Zion* didn't sound too much different from *Tsion* in Dr. Ben-Judah's accent. "Please call me Buck."

"Buck?" The rabbi held open the front door as Buck slid in next to the driver.

"It's a nickname."

"All right, Buck. The driver understands no English."

Buck turned to see the driver with his hand extended. Buck shook it and the man said something totally unintelligible. Buck merely smiled and nodded. Dr. Ben-Judah spoke to the driver in Hebrew, and they pulled away.

"Now, Buck," the rabbi said as Buck turned in his seat to face him, "Dr. Rosenzweig said you wanted access to the Wailing Wall, which you understand is impossible. I can get you close enough to the two witnesses so that you can get their attention if you dare."

"The two witnesses? You call them the two witnesses? That's what my friends and I—"

Dr. Ben-Judah held up both hands and turned his head away, as if to indicate that was a question he would not answer or comment on. "The question is, do you dare?"

"I dare."

"And you will not hold me personally responsible for anything that might happen to you."

"Of course not, but I would like to interview you, too."

The hands came up yet again. "I made quite clear to the press, and to Dr. Rosenzweig, that I am not granting any interviews."

"Just some personal information, then. I won't ask about your research, because I am sure after boiling down three years into a one-hour presentation, you'll explain your conclusions fully tomorrow afternoon."

"Precisely. As for personal information, I am forty-four years old. I grew up in Haifa, the son of an Orthodox rabbi. I have two doctorates, one in Jewish history and one in ancient languages. I have studied and taught my whole life and consider myself more of a scholar and historian than an educator, though my students have been most kind in their evaluations. I think and pray and read mostly in Hebrew, and I am embarrassed to speak English so poorly, especially in an egalitarian country like this. I know English grammar and syntax better than most Englishmen and certainly most Americans, present company excepted I'm sure, but I have never had the time to practice, let alone perfect, my diction. I married only six years ago and have two teenage stepchildren, a boy and a girl.

"A little over three years ago, I was commissioned by a state agency to conduct an exhaustive study of the messianic passages so the Jews would recognize Messiah when he comes. This has been the most rewarding work of my life. In the process I added Greek and Aramaic to the list of my mastered languages, which now number twenty-two. I am excited about the completion of the work and eager to share my findings with the world by television. I don't pretend that the program will compete with anything containing sex, violence, or humor, but I expect it will be controversial nonetheless."

"I don't know what else to ask," Buck admitted.

"Then we can be done with the interview and get on with the business at hand."

"I am curious about your taking the time to do this."

"Dr. Rosenzweig is a mentor, one of my most beloved colleagues. A friend of his is a friend of mine."

"Thank you."

"I admire your work. I read the articles about Dr. Rosenzweig that you have done, and many others, too. Besides, the men at the Wall intrigue me as well. Perhaps with my language proficiency we will be able to communicate with them. So far, all I have seen them do is communicate with the masses who assemble. They speak to people who threaten them, but otherwise, I know of no individual who has spoken with them."

The Mercedes parked near some tour buses, and the driver waited as Dr. Ben-Judah and Buck mounted a set of stairs to take in the view of the Wailing Wall, the Temple Mount, and everything in between. "These are the largest crowds I have seen," the rabbi said.

"But they are so quiet," Buck whispered.

"The two preachers do not use microphones," Dr. Ben-Judah explained. "People make noise at their own peril. So many want to hear what the men have to say that others threaten those who cause any distraction."

"Do the two ever take a break?"

"Yes, they do. Occasionally one will move around the side of that little building there and lie on the ground near the fence. They will often trade off resting and speaking. The men who were consumed by fire recently actually tried to attack them there from outside the fence when they both rested. That is why no one approaches them there."

"That might be my best opportunity," Buck said.

"That was my thinking."

"You will go with me?"

"Only if we make it plain we mean them no harm. They have killed at least six and have threatened many more. A friend of mine stood on this very spot the day they burned up four attackers, and he swears the fire came from their mouths."

"Do you believe that?"

"I have no reason to doubt my friend, though he was several hundred feet away."

"Is there a better time than another to approach, or should we just play that by ear?"

"I propose we join the crowds first."

They descended the stairs and moved toward the Wall. Buck was impressed that the crowd seemed so reverential. Within forty or fifty feet of the preachers were Orthodox rabbis, bowing, praying, sliding written prayers into the cracks between the stones in the Wall. Occasionally one of the rabbis would turn toward the witnesses and shake his fist, crying out in Hebrew, only to be shushed by the crowd. Sometimes one of the preachers would respond directly.

As Buck and Dr. Ben-Judah reached the edge of the crowd, a rabbi at the Wall fell to his knees, his eyes toward heaven, and howled out a prayer in anguish.

"Silence!" shouted one of the preachers, and the rabbi wept bitterly. The preacher turned to the crowd. "He beseeches almighty God to strike us dead for blaspheming his name! But he is as the Pharisees of old! He does not recognize the one who was God and is God and shall be God now and forevermore! We come to bring witness to the Godship of Jesus Christ of Nazareth!"

With that, the crying rabbi prostrated himself and hid his face, rocking in humiliation at the wickedness of what he heard.

Dr. Ben-Judah whispered to Buck, "Would you like me to translate?"

"Translate what? The prayer of the rabbi?"

"And the response of the preacher."

"I understood the preacher."

Dr. Ben-Judah looked puzzled. "If I had known you were fluent in Hebrew, it would have been much easier for me to communicate with you."

"I'm not. I didn't understand the prayer, but the preacher spoke to the crowd in English."

Ben-Judah shook his head. "My mistake," he said. "Sometimes I forget what language I'm in. But there! Right now! He's speaking in Hebrew again. He's saying—"

"Sir, sorry to interrupt. But he is speaking in English. There is a Hebraic accent, but he is saying, 'And now unto Him who is able to keep you from falling . . .'"

"You understand that?!"

"Of course."

The rabbi looked shaken. "Buck," he whispered ominously, "he is speaking in Hebrew."

Buck turned and stared at the two witnesses. They took turns speaking, sentence by sentence. Buck understood every word in English. Ben-Judah touched him lightly and he followed the rabbi deeper into the crowd. "English?" Ben-Judah asked a Hispanic-looking man who stood with a woman and three teenagers.

"Español," the man responded apologetically.

Dr. Ben-Judah immediately began conversing with him in Spanish. The man kept nodding and answering in the affirmative. The rabbi thanked him and moved on. He found a Norwegian and spoke to him in his native tongue, then some Asians. He grabbed Buck's arm tight and pulled him away from the crowd and closer to the preachers. They stopped about thirty feet from the two men, separated by a fence of wrought-iron bars.

"These people are hearing the preachers in their own languages!" Ben-Judah shuddered. "Truly this is of God!"

"Are you sure?"

"No question. I hear them in Hebrew. You hear them in English. The family from Mexico knows only a little English but no Hebrew. The man from Norway knows some German and some English, but no Hebrew. He hears them in Norwegian. Oh God, oh God," the rabbi added, and Buck knew it was out of reverence. He was afraid Ben-Judah might collapse.

"Ayeee!" A young man wearing boots, khaki slacks, and a white T-shirt came screaming through the crowd. People fell to the ground when they saw his automatic weapon. He wore a gold necklace, and his black hair and beard were unkempt. His dark eyes were ablaze as he rattled off a few rounds into the air, which cleared a path for him directly to the preachers.

He shouted something in an Eastern dialect Buck did not understand, but as he lay on the pavement peeking out from under his arms, Rabbi Ben-Judah whispered, "He says he's on a mission from Allah."

Buck reached into his bag and turned on the tape recorder as the man ran to the front of the crowd. The two witnesses stopped preaching and stood shoulder to shoulder, glaring at the gunman as he approached. He ran full speed, firing as he ran, but the preachers stood rock solid, not speaking, not moving, arms crossed over their ragged robes. When the young man got to within five feet of them, he seemed to hit an invisible wall. He recoiled and flipped over backward, his weapon clattering away. His head smacked the ground first, and he lay groaning.

Suddenly one of the preachers shouted, "You are forbidden to come nigh to the servants of the Most High God! We are under his protection until the due time, and woe to anyone who approaches without the covering of Yahweh himself." And as he finished, the other breathed from his mouth a column of fire that incinerated the man's clothes, consumed his flesh and organs, and in seconds left a charred skeleton smoking on the ground. The weapon melted and was fused to the cement, and the man's molten necklace dripped gold through the cavity in his chest.

Buck lay on his stomach, his mouth agape, his hand on the back of the rabbi, who shuddered uncontrollably. In the distance families ran screaming toward their cars and buses while Israeli soldiers approached the Wall slowly, weapons at the ready.

One of the preachers spoke. "No one need fear us who comes to listen to our testimony to the living God! Many have believed and received our report. Only those who seek to do us harm shall die! Fear not!"

Buck believed him. He wasn't sure the rabbi did. They stood and began to move away, but the eyes of the witnesses were on them. Israeli soldiers shouted at them from the edge of the plaza. "The soldiers are telling us to move away slowly," Dr. Ben-Judah translated.

"I want to stay," Buck said. "I want to talk to these men."

"Did you not see what just happened?"

"Of course, but I also heard them say they meant no harm to sincere listeners."

"But *are* you a sincere listener, or are you just a journalist looking for a scoop?"

"I'm both," Buck admitted.

"God bless you," the rabbi said. He turned and spoke in Hebrew to the two witnesses as Israeli soldiers shouted at him and Buck all the more. Buck and Ben-Judah backed away from the preachers, who now stood silent.

"I told them we would meet them at ten o'clock tonight behind the building where they occasionally rest. Will you be able to join me?"

"Like I would pass that up," Buck said.

\+ + +

Rayford returned from a quiet dinner with part of his new crew to an urgent message from Chloe. It took him a few minutes to get through, wishing she had given him some indication of what was wrong. It wasn't like her to say something was urgent unless it really was. She picked up the phone on the first ring.

"Hello?" she said. "Buck? Dad?"

"Yeah, what's up?"

"How's Buck?"

"I don't know. I haven't seen him yet."

"Are you going to?"

"Well, sure, I suppose."

"Do you know what hospital he's in?"

"What?"

"You didn't see it?"

"See what?"

"Dad, it was just on the morning news here. The two witnesses at the Wailing Wall burned some guy to death, and everybody around hit the ground. One of the last two lying there was Buck."

"Are you sure?"

"No question."

"Do you know for certain he was hurt?"

"No! I just assumed. He was just lying there next to a guy in a black suit whose hat had fallen off."

"Where's he staying?"

"At the King David. I left a message for him. They said they had his key, so he was out. What does that mean?"

"Some people leave their keys at the desk whenever they go out. It doesn't mean anything special. I'm sure he'll call you."

"Isn't there some way you can find out if he was hurt?"

"I'll try. Let's leave it this way: If I find out anything either way, I'll call you. No news will be good news, at least."

\+ + +

Buck's knees felt like jelly. "Are you all right, Rabbi?"

"I'm fine," Dr. Ben-Judah said, "but I am nearly overcome."

"I know the feeling."

"I want to believe those men are of God."

"I believe they are," Buck said.

"Do you? Are you a student of the Scriptures?"

"Only recently."

"Come. I want to show you something."

When they got back to the car, the rabbi's driver stood with his door open, ashen-faced. Tsion Ben-Judah spoke reassuringly to him in Hebrew, and the man kept looking past him to Buck. Buck tried to smile.

Buck got into the front seat, and Ben-Judah quietly guided the driver to park as close as possible to the Golden Gate at the east of the Temple Mount. He invited Buck to walk with him to the gate so he could interpret the Hebrew graffiti. "See here," he said. "It says, 'Come Messiah.' And here, 'Deliver us.' And there, 'Come in triumph.'

"My people have longed for and prayed for and watched and waited for our Messiah for centuries. But much of Judaism, even in the Holy Land, has become secular and less biblically oriented. My research project was assigned almost as an inevitability. People have lost sight of exactly what or whom they are looking for, and many have given up.

"And to show you how deep runs the animosity between the Muslim and the Jew, look at this cemetery the Muslims have built just outside the fence here."

"What's the significance?"

"Jewish tradition says that in the end times, Messiah and Elijah will lead the Jews to the temple in triumph through the gate from the east. But Elijah is a priest, and walking through a graveyard would defile him, so the Muslims have put one here to make the triumphal entry impossible."

Buck reached for his tape recorder and was going to ask the rabbi to repeat that tidbit of history, but he noticed it was still running. "Look at this," Buck said. "I got the attack on tape."

He rewound the machine to where they heard gunfire and screaming. Then the man fell and the weapon clattered. In his mind's eye, Buck recalled the blast of fire coming from the witness's mouth. On the tape it sounded like a strong gust of wind. More screaming. Then the preachers shouted loudly in a language Buck couldn't understand.

"That's Hebrew!" Rabbi Ben-Judah said. "Surely you hear that!"

"They spoke in Hebrew," Buck acknowledged, "and the tape recorder picked it up in Hebrew. But I heard it in English as sure as I'm standing here."

"You did say you heard them promise no harm to anyone who came only to listen to their testimony."

"I understood every word."

The rabbi closed his eyes. "The timing of this is very important to my presentation."

Buck walked back to the car with him. "I need to tell you something," he said. "I believe your Messiah has already come."

"I know you do, young man. I will be interested to hear what the two preachers say when you tell them that."

* * *

Rayford checked with Steve Plank to see if his people had heard any more about another death at the Wailing Wall. He didn't ask specifically about Buck, still not wanting to let on about their friendship.

"We heard all about it," Plank said angrily. "The secretary-general believes those two should be arrested and tried for murder. He doesn't understand why the Israeli military seems so impotent."

"Maybe they're afraid of being incinerated."

"What chance would those two have against a sniper with a high-powered weapon? You close the place down, clear out the innocent bystanders, and shoot those two dead. Use a grenade or even a missile if you have to."

"That's Carpathia's idea?"

"Straight from the horse's mouth," Plank said.

"Spoken like a true pacifist."

15

RAYFORD WATCHED the news and was certain Chloe had been correct. It had indeed been Buck Williams, not more than thirty feet from the witnesses and even closer to the gunman, who was now little more than charred bones on the pavement. But Israeli television stayed with the images longer, and after watching the drama a few times, Rayford was able to take his eyes from the fire-breathing witnesses and watch the edge of the screen. Buck rose quickly and helped the dark-suited man next to him. Neither appeared hurt.

Rayford dialed the King David Hotel. Buck was still out, so Rayford took a cab to the King David and sat waiting in the lobby. Knowing better than to be seen with Buck, he planned to slip away to a house phone as soon as he saw him.

* * *

"In the long history of Judaism," Rabbi Ben-Judah was saying, "there have been many evidences of the clear hand of God. More during Bible times, of course, but the protection of Israel against all odds in modern wars is another example. The destruction of the Russian Air Force, leaving the Holy Land unscathed, was plainly an act of God."

Buck turned in the seat of the car. "I was here when it happened."

"I read your account," Ben-Judah said. "But by the same token, Jews have learned to be skeptical of what appears to be divine intervention in their lives. Those who know the Scriptures know that while Moses had the power to turn a stick into a snake, so did Pharaoh's magicians. They could also imitate Moses' turning water into blood. Daniel was not the only dream-interpreter in the king's court. I tell you this only to explain why these two preachers are being looked upon with such suspicion. Their acts are mighty and terrible, but their message an anathema to the Jewish mind."

"But they are talking about the Messiah!" Buck said.

"And they seem to have the power to back up their statements," Ben-Judah said. "But the idea of Jesus having been the Jewish Messiah is thousands of years old. His very name is as profane to the Jew as racial slurs and epithets are to other minorities."

"Some have become believers here," Buck said. "I've seen it on the news, people bowing and praying before the fence, becoming followers of Christ."

"At great cost," the rabbi said. "And they are very much in the minority. No matter how impressive are these witnesses of Christ, you will not see significant numbers of Jews convert to Christianity."

"That's the second time you have referred to them as witnesses," Buck said. "You know that this is what the Bible—"

"Mr. Williams," Rabbi Ben-Judah interrupted, "do not mistake me for a scholar of only the Torah. You must realize that my study has included the sacred works of all the major religions of the world."

"But what do you make of it, then, if you know the New Testament?"

"Well, first of all, you may be overstating it to say that I 'know' the New Testament. I cannot claim to know it the way I know my own Bible, having become steeped in the New Testament mostly only within the last three years. But secondly, you have now crossed over the line journalistically."

"I'm not asking as a journalist!" Buck said. "I'm asking as a Christian!"

"Don't mistake being a Gentile for being a Christian," the rabbi said. "Many, many people consider themselves Christians because they are not Jewish."

"I know the difference," Buck said. "Friend to friend, or at least acquaintance to acquaintance, with all your study, you must have come to some conclusions about Jesus as the Messiah."

The rabbi spoke carefully. "Young man, I have not released one iota of my findings to anyone in three years. Even those who commissioned and sponsored my study do not know what conclusions I have drawn. I respect you. I admire your courage. I will take you back to the two witnesses tonight as I promised. But I will not reveal to you any of what I will say on television tomorrow."

"I understand," Buck said. "More people may be watching than you think."

"Perhaps. And maybe I was being falsely modest when I said the program would not likely compete with the normal fare. CNN and the state agency that commissioned my study have cooperated in an international effort to inform Jews on every continent of the coming program. They tell me the audience in Israel will be only a fraction of the Jewish viewers around the world."

* * *

Rayford was reading the *International Tribune* when Buck hurried past him to the desk and retrieved his key and a message. Rayford loudly rattled the paper as he lowered it, and when Buck glanced his way Rayford motioned he would call him. Buck nodded and went upstairs.

"You'd better call Chloe," Rayford said when he reached Buck on the house phone a couple of minutes later. "Are you all right?"

"I'm fine. Rayford, I was right there!"

"I saw you."

"The rabbi I was with is a friend of Rosenzweig. He's the one who'll be on TV tomorrow afternoon. Get anyone you can to watch that. He's a really interesting guy."

"Will do. I promised Chloe one of us would call her as soon as I knew anything."

"She saw it?"

"Yeah, on the morning news."

"I'll call her right now."

* * *

Buck placed the call through the hotel operator and hung up, waiting for the call that would tell him his party was on the line. Meanwhile he slumped on the edge of the bed and lowered his head. He shuddered at what he had seen. How could the rabbi have seen the same, heard the same, and then imply that these men could just as easily be magicians or seers as from God?

The phone rang. "Yes!"

"Buck!"

"I'm here, Chloe, and I'm fine."

"Oh, thank God."

"Well, thank you!"

Chloe sounded emotional. "Buck, those witnesses know the difference between believers and their enemies, don't they?"

"I sure hope so. I'll find out tonight. The rabbi is taking me back to see them."

"Who's the rabbi?"

Buck told her.

"Are you sure it's wise?"

"Chloe, it's the chance of a lifetime! No one has spoken to them individually."

"Where does the rabbi stand?"

"He's Orthodox, but he knows the New Testament, too, at least intellectually. Be sure you and Bruce watch tomorrow afternoon—well, it would be six hours earlier for you, of course. Tell everybody in the church to watch. It should be interesting. If you want to watch the covenant signing first, you're going to have to be up early."

"Buck, I miss you."

"I miss you too. More than you know."

\+ + +

Rayford returned to his hotel to find an envelope from Hattie Durham. The note inside read:

> *Captain Steele, this is no practical joke. The secretary-general wanted you to have the enclosed ticket to the festivities tomorrow morning and to express to you how impressed he was with the service on* Global Community One. *While he may not be able to speak with you personally until tomorrow afternoon on the way to Baghdad, he thanks you for your service. And so do I. Hattie D.*

Rayford slid the ticket into his passport wallet and threw the note in the trash.

\+ + +

Buck, still out of kilter with the time change and the trauma of the morning, tried to get a few hours sleep before dinner. He dined alone, eating lightly and wondering if there had ever been such a thing as protocol for meeting with two men sent from God. Were they human? Were they spirits? Were they, as Bruce believed, Elijah and Moses? They called each other Eli and Moishe. Could they be thousands of years old? Buck was more anxious about talking with them than he had ever been about interviewing a head of state or even Nicolae Carpathia.

The evening would be chilly. Buck put on a wool sport coat with a heavy lining and pockets big enough that he wouldn't need a bag. He took only pen and pad and tape recorder and reminded himself to check with Jim Borland and others at the *Weekly* to be sure photographers were at least getting long shots of the two when they preached.

\+ + +

At 9:45 Rayford sat straight up in his bed. He had dozed in his clothes with the television droning, but something had caught his attention. He'd heard the word *Chicago*, maybe *Chicago Tribune*, and it roused him. He began changing to his pajamas as he listened. The newscaster was summarizing a major story out of the United States.

"The secretary-general is out of the country this weekend and unavailable for comment, but media moguls from around the world are corroborating this report. The surprising legislation allows a nonelected official and an international nonprofit organization unrestricted ownership of all forms of media and opens the door to the United Nations, soon to be known as Global Community, to purchase and control newspapers, magazines, radio, television, cable, and satellite communications outlets.

"The only limit will be the amount of capital available to Global Community, but the following media are among many rumored to be under consideration by a buyout team from Global Community: *New York Times*, *Long Island News Day*, *USA Today*, *Boston Globe*, *Baltimore Sun*, *Washington Post*, *Atlanta Journal and Constitution*, *Tampa Tribune*, *Orlando Sentinel*, *Houston* . . ."

Rayford sat on the edge of the bed and listened in disbelief. Nicolae Carpathia had done it—put himself in a position to control the news and thus control the minds of most of the people within his sphere of influence.

The newscaster droned on with the list: Turner Network News, the Cable News Network, the Entertainment and Sports Network, the Columbia Broadcast System, the American Broadcasting Corporation, the Fox Television Network, the National Broadcasting Corporation, the Christian Broadcasting Network, the Family Radio Network, Trinity Broadcasting Network, Time-Warner, Disney, *U.S. News and World Report*, *Global Weekly*, *Newsweek*, *Reader's Digest*, and a host of other news and feature syndicates and magazine groups.

"Most shocking is the initial reaction from current owners, most of whom seem to welcome the new capital and say they take Global Community leader Nicolae Carpathia at his word when he pledges no interference."

Rayford thought about calling Buck. But surely he had heard the news before it had come over television. Someone from the *Global Weekly* staff would have had to have informed him, or at least he would have heard it from one of the hundreds of other media employees in Israel for the signing. But maybe everybody thought everybody else was calling Buck. Rayford didn't want him to be the last to find out.

He reached for the phone. But there was no answer in Buck's room.

\+ \+ \+

A tentative crowd milled about in the darkness, some fifty yards from the Wailing Wall. Remains of the would-be assassin had been removed, and the local military commander told the news media that he and his charges were unable to take action "against two people who have no weapons, have touched no one, and who have themselves been attacked."

No one from the crowd seemed willing to move any closer, though the two preachers could be seen in the faint light, standing near one end of the Wall. They neither advanced nor spoke.

As Rabbi Tsion Ben-Judah's driver pulled into a nearly empty parking area, Buck was tempted to ask if the rabbi believed in prayer. Buck knew the rabbi would say he did, but Buck wanted to pray aloud for the protection of Christ, and that was simply something one would not ask an Orthodox rabbi to pray for. Buck prayed silently.

He and Tsion left the car and walked slowly and carefully, far around the small crowd. The rabbi walked with his hands clasped in front of him, and Buck couldn't help doing a double take when he noticed. It seemed an unusually pious and almost showy gesture—particularly because Ben-Judah had seemed disarmingly humble for one holding such a lofty position in religious academia.

"I am walking in a traditional position of deference and conciliation," the rabbi explained. "I want no mistakes, no misunderstanding. It is important to our safety that these men know we come in humility and curiosity. We mean them no harm."

Buck looked into the rabbi's eyes. "The truth is we are scared to death and don't want to give them any reason to kill us."

Buck thought he saw a smile. "You have a way of knifing to the truth," Ben-Judah said. "I am praying that we will both be healthy on the way back as well and able to discuss our shared experience here."

Me too, Buck thought, but he said nothing.

Three Israeli soldiers stepped in front of Buck and the rabbi, and one spoke sharply in Hebrew. Buck began to reach for his press pass, then realized it carried no weight here. Tsion Ben-Judah moved forward and spoke earnestly and quietly to the leader, again in Hebrew. The soldier asked a few questions, sounding less hostile and more curious than at first. Finally he nodded, and they were able to pass.

Buck glanced back. The soldiers had not moved. "What was that all about?" he asked.

"They said only the Orthodox are allowed past a certain point. I assured them you were with me. I am always amused when the secular military tries to enforce religious laws. He warned me of what had happened earlier, but I told him we had an appointment and were willing to take the risk."

"Are we?" Buck asked lightly.

The rabbi shrugged. "Perhaps not. But we are going to proceed anyway, are we not? Because we said we would, and neither of us would miss this opportunity."

As they continued, the two witnesses stared at them from the end of the Wailing Wall, some fifty or so feet away. "We are headed for the fence over there," Ben-Judah said, pointing to the other side of the small building. "If they are still willing to meet us, they will come there, and we will have the fence between us."

"After what happened to the assassin today, that wouldn't be much help."

"We are not armed."

"How do they know?"

"They don't."

When Buck and Ben-Judah were within about fifteen feet of the fence, one of the witnesses held up a hand, and they stopped. He spoke, not at the top of his voice as Buck had always heard him before, but still in a sonorous tone. "We will approach and introduce ourselves," he said. The two men walked slowly and stood just inside the iron bars. "Call me Eli," he said. "And this is Moishe."

"English?" Buck whispered.

"Hebrew," Ben-Judah responded.

"Silence!" Eli said in a hoarse whisper.

Buck jumped. He recalled one of the two shouting at a rabbi to be silent earlier that day. A few minutes later another man lay dead and charred.

Eli motioned that Buck and Tsion could approach. They advanced to within a couple feet of the fence. Buck was struck by their ragged robes. The scent of ashes, as from a recent fire, hung about them. In the dim light from a distant lamp their long, sinewy arms seemed muscled and leathery. They had large, bony hands and were barefoot.

Eli said, "We will answer no questions as to our identities or our origin. God will reveal this to the world in his own time."

Tsion Ben-Judah nodded and bowed slightly from the waist. Buck reached into his pocket and turned on the tape recorder. Suddenly Moishe stepped close and put his bearded face between the bars. He stared at the rabbi with hooded eyes and a sweat-streaked face.

He spoke very quietly and in a low, deep voice, but every word was distinct to Buck. He couldn't wait to ask Tsion whether he had heard Moishe in English or Hebrew.

Moishe spoke as if he had just thought of something very interesting, but the words were familiar to Buck.

"Many years ago, there was a man of the Pharisees named Nicodemus, a ruler of the Jews. Like you, this man came to Jesus by night."

Rabbi Ben-Judah whispered, "Eli and Moishe, we know that you come from God; for no one can do these signs that you do unless God is with him."

Eli spoke. "Most assuredly, I say to you, unless one is born again, he cannot see the kingdom of God."

"How can a man be born when he is old?" Rabbi Ben-Judah said, and Buck realized he was quoting New Testament Scripture. "Can he enter a second time into his mother's womb and be born?"

Moishe answered, "Most assuredly, I say to you, unless one is born of water and the Spirit, he cannot enter the kingdom of God. That which is born of the flesh is flesh, and that which is born of the Spirit is spirit. Do not marvel that I said to you, 'You must be born again.'"

Eli spoke up again: "The wind blows where it wishes, and you hear the sound of it, but cannot tell where it comes from and where it goes. So is everyone who is born of the Spirit."

Right on cue, the rabbi said, "How can these things be?"

Moishe lifted his head. "Are you the teacher of Israel, and do not know these things? Most assuredly, I say to you, we speak what we know and testify what we have seen, and you do not receive our witness. If we have told you earthly things and you do not believe, how will you believe if we tell you heavenly things?"

Eli nodded. "No one has ascended to heaven but He who came down from heaven, that is, the Son of Man who is in heaven. And as Moses lifted up the serpent in the wilderness, even so must the Son of Man be lifted up, that whoever believes in Him should not perish but have eternal life. For God so loved the world that He gave His only begotten Son, that whoever believes in Him should not perish but have everlasting life."

Buck was light-headed with excitement. He felt as if he had been dropped back into ancient history and was a spectator at one of the most famous nighttime conversations ever. Not for an instant did he forget that his companion was not Nicodemus of old, or that the other two men were not Jesus. He was new to this truth, new to this Scripture, but he knew what was coming as Moishe concluded, "For God did not send His Son into the world to condemn the world, but that the world through Him might be saved. He who believes in Him is not condemned; but he who does not believe is condemned already, because he has not believed in the name of the only begotten Son of God."

Suddenly the rabbi became animated. He gestured broadly, raising his hands and spreading them wide. As if in some play or recital, he set the witnesses up for their next response. "And what," he said, "is the condemnation?"

The two answered in unison, "That the Light has already come into the world."

"And how did men miss it?"

"Men loved darkness rather than light."

"Why?"

"Because their deeds were evil."

"God forgive us," the rabbi said.

And the two witnesses said, "God forgive you. Thus ends our message."

"Will you speak with us no more?" Ben-Judah asked.

"No more," Eli said, but Buck did not see his mouth move. He thought he had been mistaken, that perhaps Moishe had said it. But Eli continued, speaking clearly but not aloud. "Moishe and I will not speak again until dawn when we will continue to testify to the coming of the Lord."

"But I have so many questions," Buck said.

"No more," they said in unison, neither opening his mouth. "We wish you God's blessing, the peace of Jesus Christ, and the presence of the Holy Spirit. Amen."

Buck's knees went weak as the men backed away. As he and the rabbi stared, Eli and Moishe merely moved against the building and sat, leaning back against the wall. "Good-bye and thank you," Buck said, feeling foolish.

Rabbi Ben-Judah sang a beautiful chant, a blessing of some sort that Buck did not understand. Eli and Moishe appeared to be praying, and then it seemed they slept where they sat.

Buck was speechless. He followed as Ben-Judah turned and walked toward a low chain fence. He stepped over it and moved away from the Temple Mount and across the road to a small grove of trees. Buck wondered if perhaps the rabbi wished to be alone, but his body language indicated he wanted Buck to stay with him.

When they reached the edge of the trees, the rabbi simply stood gazing into the sky. He covered his face with his hands and wept, his crying becoming great sobs. Buck, too, was overcome and could not stop the tears. They had been on holy ground, he knew. What he did not know was how the rabbi interpreted all this. Could he have missed the message of the conversation between Nicodemus and Jesus when he had read it from the Scriptures, and again now when he had been part of its re-creation?

Buck certainly hadn't missed it. The Tribulation Force would not be able to believe his privilege. He would not hoard it, would not be jealous of it. In fact, he wished they could have all been there with him.

As if sensing that Buck wanted to talk, Ben-Judah precluded him. "We must not debase the experience by reducing it to words," he said. "Until tomorrow, my friend."

The rabbi turned, and there at the roadside was his car and driver. He moved to the front passenger door and opened it for Buck. Buck slid in and whispered his thanks. The rabbi went around the front of the car and whispered to the driver, who pulled away, leaving Ben-Judah at the side of the road.

"What's up?" Buck said, craning to watch the black suit fade into the night. "Is he finding his own way back?"

The driver said nothing.

"I hope I haven't offended him."

The driver looked to Buck apologetically and shrugged. "No Englees," he said, and drove Buck back to the King David Hotel.

The man at the counter handed Buck a message from Rayford, but since it was not marked urgent, he decided not to call him until morning. If he didn't reach Rayford, he would look for him at the signing of the covenant.

Buck left the light off in his room and stepped out the glass door to the tiny balcony in the trees. Through the branches he saw the full moon in a cloudless sky. The wind was still, but the night had grown colder. He raised his collar and gazed at the beauty of the night. He felt as privileged as any man on earth. Besides his charmed professional life and the gift he had honed, he had been eyewitness to some of the most astounding works of God in the history of the world.

He had been in Israel when the Russians attacked less than a year and a half before. God had clearly destroyed the threat to his chosen people. Buck had been in the air when the Rapture had occurred, in a plane flown by a man he had never met, served by a senior flight attendant whose future now seemed his responsibility. And the daughter of that pilot? He believed he was in love with her, if he knew what love was.

Buck hunched his shoulders and let his sleeves cover his hands, then folded his arms. He had been spared a car bombing in London, had received Christ on the cusp of the end of the world, and had been supernaturally protected while witnessing two murders by the Antichrist himself. This very day he had seen Scripture fulfilled when a would-be killer was thwarted by fire from the throat of one of the two witnesses.

And then, to have heard these two recite Jesus' words to Nicodemus! Buck wanted to humble himself, to communicate to his Creator and his Savior how unworthy he felt, how grateful he was. "All I can do," he whispered huskily into the night air, "is to give you all of me for as long as I have left. I will do what you want, go where you send me, obey you regardless."

He pulled from his pocket the tape recorder and rewound it. When he played the conversation he had witnessed that evening, he was stunned to hear no English. It shouldn't have been a surprise, he realized. It had been typical of the day. But he heard at least three languages. He recognized Hebrew, though he didn't understand it. He recognized Greek, but didn't understand that either. The other language, which he was sure he had never heard before, was used when the witnesses had directly quoted Jesus. That had to be Aramaic.

At the end of the tape, Buck heard Dr. Ben-Judah ask something in Hebrew, which he remembered having heard in English as "Will you speak with us no more?" But he heard no response.

Then he heard himself say, "But I have so many questions." And then after a pause, "Good-bye and thank you." What the men had spoken to his heart had not been recorded.

Buck took a pen and punched out the tabs, making it impossible to record over his priceless cassette.

The only thing that could make this even more perfect would be to share it with Chloe. He looked at his watch. It was just after midnight in Israel, making it around six in Chicago. But when Buck reached Chloe, he could barely speak. He managed to work out the story of the evening between his tears, and Chloe wept with him.

"Buck," she concluded at last, "we wasted so many years without Christ. I'll pray for the rabbi."

\+ + +

A few minutes later, Rayford was awakened by his phone. He was certain it would be Buck and hoped he had not heard the news of Carpathia's media plans from someone else.

"Daddy, it's Chloe," she said. "I just talked to Buck, but I didn't have the heart to tell him about the media stuff. Have you heard?"

Rayford told her he had and asked if she was sure Buck didn't know. She related everything Buck had told her about his evening. "I'll try to reach him in the morning," Rayford said. "He's sure to hear it from someone else if I don't get to him first."

"He was so overcome, Dad. It wasn't the time to give him that news. I didn't know how he'd react. What do you think will happen to him?"

"Buck will survive. He'll have to swallow a lot of pride, having to work for Carpathia wherever he goes. But he'll be all right. Knowing him, he'll find a way to get the truth to the masses, either by camouflaging it in Carpathia's own publications or by operating some sort of bootleg production that is sold under the counter."

"It sounds like Carpathia is going to control everyhing."

"It sure does."

Rayford tried calling Buck at six-thirty the next morning, but he had already left the hotel.

\+ + +

It had been ages since Buck had seen Steve Plank so harried. "This job was fun and interesting until today," Steve said as the entourage at his hotel began assembling for the short trip to the Old City. "Carpathia's got a burr in his saddle, and I'm the one who takes the heat."

"What's up?"

"Oh, nothing special. We just have to have everything perfect, that's all."

"And you're trying to talk me into working for him? I don't think so."

"Well, that'll be a moot question in a couple of weeks anyway, won't it?"

"It sure will." Buck smiled to himself. He had decided to turn the *Tribune* offer down flat and stay with *Global Weekly*.

"You're going with us to Baghdad, right?"

"I'm trying to find a way there, but not with you, no."

"Buck, there aren't going to be too many ways to get there. We've got the room, and for all practical purposes, you work for Carpathia anyway. Just come along. You'll love what he has in mind for New Babylon, and if the reports can be believed, it's already coming along nicely."

"I work for Carpathia? I thought we were pretty clear on that."

"It's just a matter of time, my boy."

"Dream on," Buck said, but wondered about Plank's puzzled look. Buck found Jim Borland organizing his notes. "Hey, Jim," he said. Borland hardly looked up. "Interview Carpathia yet?"

"Yep," Borland said. "No big deal. Right now all he's concerned about is moving the signing."

"Moving it?"

"He's afraid of those weirdos at the Wailing Wall. The soldiers can keep the place clear of tourists, but the guys at the Wall will have an audience of the covenant-signing crowd."

"Pretty big crowd," Buck said.

"No kidding. I don't know why they don't just keep those two homeless guys away."

"You don't?"

"What, Buck? You think those old coots are going to breathe their fire on the army? Get serious. You believe that fire story?"

"I saw the guy, Jimmy. He was toast."

"A million-to-one he set himself on fire."

"This was no immolation, Jim. He hit the ground, and one of those two incinerated him."

"With fire from his mouth."

"That's what I saw."

"It's a good thing you're off the cover story, Buck. You're losing it. So did you also get an exclusive interview with them?"

"Not entirely exclusive and not exactly an interview."

"In other words, no, you struck out, right?"

"No. I was with them late last night. I did not get into a give-and-take, that's all I'll say."

"I'd say if you're going to write fiction, you ought to get a novel deal and go for it. You'd still wind up publishing with Carpathia, but you might have a little more latitude."

"I wouldn't work for Carpathia," Buck said.

"Then you won't be in communications."

"What are you talking about?"

Borland told him of the announcement.

Buck blanched. "*Global Weekly*'s included?"

"*Included?* If you ask me, it's one of the plums."

Buck shook his head. So he was writing his stories for Carpathia after all. "No wonder everybody looks shell-shocked. So, if the signing isn't near the Wall, where will it be?"

"The Knesset."

"Inside?"

"Don't think so."

"Is the outside conducive?"

"Don't think so."

"Listen, Jimmy, are you going to watch Rabbi Ben-Judah this afternoon?"

"If they show it on the plane to Baghdad."

"You got a flight?"

"I'm going on *Global Community One*."

"You've sold out?"

"You can't sell out to your boss, Buck."

"He's not your boss yet."

"It's only a matter of time, pal."

Chaim Rosenzweig came scurrying by and slid to a stop. "Cameron!" he said. "Come, come!" Buck followed the stooped old man to a corner. "Stay with me, please! Nicolae is not happy this morning. We're moving to the Knesset, everything is in an uproar, he wants everybody to go to Babylon, and some are resisting. To tell you the truth, I think he would kill those two at the Wailing Wall himself if he had the opportunity. All morning they have been howling about the injustice of the signing, about how the covenant signals an unholy alliance between a people who missed their Messiah the first time and a leader who denies the existence of God. But, Cameron, Nicolae is not an atheist. An agnostic at best—but so am I!"

"You're not an agnostic since the Russian invasion!"

"Well, maybe not, but those are strong words against Nicolae."

"I thought no one was allowed into the area in front of the Wall this morning. Who are they saying this to?"

"The press is there with their long-range directional microphones, and those men have lungs! Nicolae has been on the phone to CNN all morning, insisting that they give the two no more coverage today of all days. CNN has resisted, of course. But when he owns them, they will do what he says. That will be a relief."

"Chaim! You *want* that kind of leadership? Control of the media?"

"I am so tired of most of the press, Cameron. You must know that I hold you in the highest regard. You are one of few I trust. The rest are so biased, so critical, so negative. We must pull the world together once and for all, and a credible, state-run news organization will finally get it right."

"That's scary," Buck said. And quietly he grieved for his old friend who had seen so much and was now willing to surrender so much to a man he should not trust.

16

RAYFORD'S DAY—and, he felt, his future—were both set. He would attend the gala festivities, then get a cab back to Ben Gurion International Airport at Lod, nine miles southeast of Tel Aviv. By the time he arrived, the crew should have the 777 shipshape, and he would begin preflight safety checklists. The schedule called for an afternoon flight to Baghdad and then a nonstop to New York. By flying west at that time of day, he would go against conventional schedules and wisdom, but for this trip, and maybe for the rest of Rayford's career, Carpathia was the boss.

Rayford would spend the night in New York before heading back home to decide whether it was really feasible to do this job from Chicago. Maybe he and Chloe would move to New York. Clearly the piloting of *Air Force One* for the president was a ruse. His job was ferrying Nicolae Carpathia wherever he wanted to go, and for some reason, Rayford felt compelled to sublimate his wishes, his desires, his will, and his logic. God had laid this in his lap for some reason, and as long as he didn't have to live a lie, at least for now he would do it.

What he had been learning from Bruce and his own study of prophecy indicated that the day would come when the Antichrist would no longer be a deceiver. He would show his colors and rule the world with an iron fist. He would smash his enemies and kill anyone disloyal to his regime. That would put every follower of Christ at risk of martyrdom. Rayford foresaw the day when he would have to leave Carpathia's employ and become a fugitive, merely to survive and help other believers do the same.

* * *

Buck saw an American Secret Service agent making a beeline toward him. "Cameron Williams?"

"Who's asking?"

"Secret Service, and you know it. Can I see some ID please?"

"I've been cleared a hundred times over." Buck reached for his credentials.

"I know that." The agent peered at Buck's identification. "Fitz wants to see you, and I've got to be sure I bring him the right guy."

"The president wants to see me?"

The agent snapped Buck's wallet shut and handed it back, nodding. "Follow me."

In a small office at the back of the Knesset Building, more than two dozen members of the press fought for position by the door, waiting to pounce on President Gerald Fitzhugh the moment he headed for the ceremonies. Two more agents—lapel pins showing, earpieces in place, hands clasped in front—stood guarding the door.

"When can we expect him?" they were asked.

But the agents didn't respond. The media were not their responsibility, except to keep them away when necessary. The agents knew better than the press secretary when the president would move from one location to another, but that was certainly nobody else's business.

Buck looked forward to seeing the president again. It had been a few years since he had done the Newsmaker of the Year story on Fitzhugh, the year Fitz had been reelected and also the second time the man had won *Global Weekly*'s honor. Buck seemed to have hit it off with the president, who was a younger version of Lyndon Johnson. Fitzhugh had been just fifty-two when elected the first time and was now pushing fifty-nine. He was robust and youthful, an exuberant, earthy man. He used profanity liberally, and though Buck had never been in his presence when Fitz was angry, his outbursts were legendary among staffers.

Buck's lack of exposure to the presidential temper ended that Monday morning.

As Buck's escort maneuvered him through the throng before the door, the agents recognized their colleague and stepped aside so Buck could enter. American members of the press corps expressed their displeasure with Buck's easy access.

"How does he *do* that?"

"It never fails!"

"It's not what you know or how much you hustle! It's who you know!"

"The rich get richer!"

Buck only wished they were right. He wished he had somehow talked his way into a scoop, an exclusive with the president. But he was as much in the dark as they were about what he was doing there.

Buck's Secret Service escort handed him off to a presidential aide, who grasped his sleeve and dragged him to a corner of the room where the president sat on the edge of a huge side chair. His suit jacket was open, his tie loose, and he was whispering with a couple of advisers. "Mr. President, Cameron Williams of *Global Weekly*," the aide announced.

"Give me a minute," Fitzhugh said, and the aide and the two advisers began to move away. The president grabbed one of the advisers. "Not you, Rob! How long do you have to work for me before you catch on? I need you here. When I say to give me a minute, I don't mean you."

"Sorry, sir."

"And quit apologizing."

"Sorry."

As soon as he had said that, Rob realized he shouldn't have apologized for apologizing. "Sorry, well, sorry. OK."

Fitzhugh rolled his eyes. "Somebody get Williams a chair, will ya? For crying out loud, let's get with it here. We've only got a few minutes."

"Eleven," Rob said apologetically.

"Fine. Eleven it is."

Buck stuck out his hand. "Mr. President," he said. Fitzhugh gave his hand a perfunctory squeeze, not making eye contact.

"Sit down here, Williams." Fitzhugh's face was red, and sweat had begun to bead on his forehead. "First off, this is totally off the record, all right?"

"Whatever you say, sir."

"No, not whatever I say! I've heard that before and been burned."

"Not by me, sir."

"No, not by you, but I remember once I told you something and then said it was off the record and you gave me that cockamamie stuff about when it is and when it isn't off the record legally."

"As I recall, sir, I cut you some slack on that."

"So you said."

"Technically, you can't say something's off the record after the fact. Only before you say it."

"Yeah, I think I've learned that a few times. So, we're clear this is all off the record from the git-go, right?"

"Loud and clear, sir."

"Williams, I want to know what in blazes is going on with Carpathia. You've spent some time with him. You've interviewed him. Word is he's trying to hire you. You know the man?"

"Not well, sir."

"I'm getting pretty steamed by him, to tell you the truth, but he's the most popular guy in the world since Jesus himself, so who am I to squawk?"

Buck was staggered by the truth of that statement. "I thought you were a big supporter of his, sir—America showing the way, and all that."

"Well, I am! I mean, I was. I invited him to the White House! He spoke to the joint session. I like his ideas. I wasn't a pacifist till I heard him talk about it, and by George I think he can pull this off. But the polls say he would double me in a run for the presidency right now! Only he doesn't want that. He wants me to stay in office and be my boss!"

"He told you that?"

"Don't be naive, Williams. I wouldn't have brought you in here if I thought you were going to take everything literally. But look, he weasels me out of *Air Force One*, and now have you seen the thing? He's got *Global Community One* painted on it and is issuing a statement this afternoon thanking the citizens of the United States for giving it to him. I've got a mind to call him a liar to his face and try to turn some of his good press around."

"It would never work, sir," the obsequious Rob interjected. "I mean, I know you didn't ask, but the statement going out makes it appear he tried to refuse, you insisted, and he reluctantly agreed."

The president turned back to Buck. "There you go, Williams, you see? You see what he does? Now am I getting myself in hotter water by sharing this stuff with you? Are you already on his payroll and going to blow the whistle on me?"

Buck wanted to tell him what he had seen, what he really knew about Carpathia, who the Bible proved he was. "I can't say I'm a Carpathia fan," Buck said.

"Well, are you a Fitzhugh fan? I'm not going to ask you how you voted—"

"I don't mind telling you. The first time you ran, I voted for your opponent. The second time I voted for you."

"Won you over, did I?"

"You did."

"So what's *your* problem with Carpathia? He's so smooth, so persuasive, so believable. I think he's got almost all of the people fooled most of the time."

"I guess that's one of my problems," Buck said. "I'm not sure what he's using for leverage, but it seems to work. He gets what he wants when he wants it, and he looks like a reluctant hero."

"That's it!" the president said, slapping Buck's knee hard enough to make it sting. "That's what gets me too!" He swore. And then he swore again. Soon he was lacing every sentence with profanity. Buck was afraid the man would burst a blood vessel.

"I've got to put a stop to it," he raged. "This is really ticking me off. He's going to come off sacrosanct today, making me look like an overgrown wuss. I mean, it's one thing for the United States to model leadership to the world, but what we look like now is one of his puppets. I'm a strong guy, a strong leader, decisive. And somehow he's succeeded in making me look like his sycophant." He took a deep breath. "Williams, do you know the trouble we've got with the militia?"

"I can only imagine."

"I'll tell you, they've got a point, and I can't argue with them! Our intelligence is telling us they're starting to hoard and hide some major weaponry, because they're so against my plan to join this destroy-90-give-10-to-the-U.N. or Global Community or whatever he's calling it this week. I'd like to believe his motives are pure and that this is the last step toward true peace, but it's the little things that make me wonder. Like this airplane deal.

"We got the new plane, we needed a new pilot. I don't care who flies the thing as long as he's qualified. We get a list from people we trust, but all of a sudden there's only one name on that list acceptable to the Grand Potentate of the World, and he's going to get the job. Now I should care even less, because I guess I've given the plane *and* the crew to Carpathia!" And he swore some more.

"Well, sir, I don't know what to tell you, but it is a pity you're not getting the services of the new pilot. I know him and he's tops."

"Well, great. Wouldn't you think I'd get the best pilot in my own country? No! And I wasn't exaggerating about that new title for Carpathia. There's some resolution in the U.N., excuse me, Global Community, and the Security Council is supposed to vote on it soon. It calls for a 'more appropriate title' for the secretary-general, given that he will soon become the commander in chief of the world's remaining military power and the chief financial officer of the global bank. The worst part is, that resolution came from our own ambassador, and I didn't know a thing about it until it went to committee. The only recourse I have is to insist he vote against his own proposal, withdraw it, or resign. How would that make me look, firing a guy because he wants to give the head of the Global Community, whom the whole world loves, a better title?"

The president wasn't giving Buck an opportunity to respond, which was all right with him, because he had no idea what to say.

Fitzhugh leaned forward and whispered, "And this media thing! We agreed with him that our conflict of interest laws were a little restrictive, along with those of most of the rest of the world. We didn't want to keep the U.N. or whatever from having the right to publish more widely when they were so close to world peace. So we make a little loophole for him and now look what we've got. He'll have bought up all the newspapers and magazines and radio and TV networks before we can change our minds!

"Where's he getting the money, Williams? Can you tell me that?"

Cameron had a crisis of conscience. He had implied to Carpathia that he would not tell about the inheritance from Stonagal. And yet were promises made to devils required to be kept? Wouldn't that be on the same order as lying to an intruder when he asks where your loved ones are?

"I couldn't tell you," Buck said. He felt no loyalty to Carpathia, but he couldn't afford having it get back to Carpathia that he had broken a confidence as significant as this. He had to hold on to his own ability to function—for as long as he could.

"You know what our intelligence people are telling us?" Fitzhugh continued. "That the eventual plan is for the heads of countries represented by the ten members of the Security Council to actually report as subordinates to their ambassadors. That would make those ten ambassadors kings of the world under Carpathia's rule."

Buck scowled. "In other words, you and the Mexican president and the Canadian prime minister would report to the U.N. ambassador of North America?"

"That's it, Williams. But you've got to forget the United Nations. It's the Global Community now."

"My mistake."

"Well, it's a mistake all right, but it's not yours."

"Sir, is there something I can do to help?"

President Fitzhugh looked to the ceiling and wiped his sweaty face with his hand. "I don't know. I just wanted to unload, I guess, and I thought maybe you had some insight. Anything we can get on this guy to slow him down a little. There's got to be a chink in his armor somewhere."

"I wish I could be of more help," Buck said, suddenly realizing what an understatement that was. What he wouldn't give to expose Nicolae Carpathia as a lying murderer, the hypnotic Antichrist! And though Buck would oppose him, anyone without Christ would never understand or agree. Besides, Scripture didn't seem to indicate that even Christ's followers would be able to do more than simply bear up against him. The Antichrist was on a course foretold centuries before, and the drama would be played out to the end.

Nicolae Carpathia was going to swallow up the president of the United States and everyone else in his path. He would gain ultimate power, and then the true battle would begin, the war between heaven and hell. The ultimate cold war would become a battle to the death. Buck took comfort in the assurance that the end had been known from the beginning . . . even if he had known it for only a few weeks.

The aide who had announced Buck to President Fitzhugh politely interrupted.

"Excuse me, Mr. President, but the secretary-general is asking for five minutes before the ceremony."

Fitzhugh swore again. "I guess we're through, Williams. I appreciate the ear anyway, and I'm grateful for your confidence."

"Certainly, sir. Ah, it would be really good if Carpathia did not see me in here. He will ask what this was about."

"Yeah, OK, listen, Rob. Go out there and tell Carpathia's people that this room is not conducive and that we'll meet him anywhere else he says in one minute. And get me Pudge."

Pudge was apparently the nickname of the agent who had accompanied Buck in the first place. The moniker didn't fit the trim young man. "Pudge, get Williams out of here without Carpathia's people seeing him."

The president knotted his tie and buttoned his coat, then was escorted to another room for his meeting with Carpathia. Buck was shielded by Pudge, the Secret Service agent, until the coast was clear. Then he made his way to the staging area, where he would be introduced as part of the American delegation.

+ + +

Rayford's credentials gave him a seat near the front with the American dignitaries. He was one of few people who knew that the witnesses at the Wailing Wall were right—that this was the celebration of an unholy alliance. He knew, but he felt helpless. No one could stem the tide of history.

Bruce Barnes had taught him that much.

Rayford missed Bruce already. He had begun to enjoy the nightly meetings and all the insight he was gaining. And Bruce's intuition was right. The Holy Land was the place to be right now. If this was where the first of 144,000 Jewish converts would come from, Bruce would want to be here.

According to what Bruce had taught Rayford and Chloe and Buck from the Scriptures, the converts would come from every part of the globe and would reap an incredible harvest—perhaps a billion souls. The 144,000 would be Jews, 12,000 from each of the original twelve tribes, but they would be gathered from all over the world, a restoration of the dispersion of Jews throughout history. Imagine, Rayford thought, Jews ministering in their own lands and their own tongues, drawing millions to Jesus the Messiah.

Despite all the mayhem and heartache to come, there would be many mighty victories, and Rayford looked forward to them. But he was not excited about the breaking up and dispersing of the Tribulation Force. Who knew where Buck would land if Carpathia really bought up all the media? If the relationship between Buck and Chloe blossomed, they might end up together somewhere far away.

He turned in his chair and surveyed the crowd. Hundreds were filing into their seats. Security was heavy and tight. At the top of the hour he saw the red lights on the TV cameras come on. Music swelled, news reporters whispered into their microphones, and the crowd hushed. Rayford sat tall and straight, his cap in his lap, wondering if Chloe could see him from their home in suburban Chicago. It was the middle of the night there, and she would not be looking for him as much as for Buck. Buck would be easy to spot. He had a position on the dais directly behind the chair of one of the signers, Dr. Chaim Rosenzweig.

To polite applause, the dignitaries were announced—veteran members of the Knesset, ambassadors from around the world, American statesmen and former presidents, Israeli leaders.

Finally came the second tier, those who would stand behind the chairs. Buck was introduced as "Mr. Cameron 'Buck' Williams, former senior staff writer and current Midwest bureau writer for *Global Weekly*, of the United States of America." Rayford smiled as Buck did at the lukewarm response. Obviously everybody wondered who he was and why he was considered a dignitary.

The loudest applause was reserved for the last five men: the chief rabbi of Israel, the Nobel Prize–winning botanist Chaim Rosenzweig of Israel, the prime minister of Israel, the president of the United States, and the secretary-general of the Global Community.

By the time Carpathia was announced and entered with his trademark shy confidence, the audience was standing. Rayford rose reluctantly and clapped without making a sound, his cap tucked under his arm. He found it difficult to reconcile the appearance of applauding the enemy of Christ.

+ + +

Chaim Rosenzweig turned to beam at Buck, who smiled at him. Buck wished he could rescue his friend from this debacle, but the time was not right. All he could do was let the man enjoy the moment, for he would not have too many more to enjoy.

"This is a great day, Cameron," he whispered, reaching for Buck's hand with both of his. He patted Buck's hand as if Buck were his son.

For a fleeting instant, Buck almost wished God couldn't see him. Flash units were erupting all over, recording for posterity the dignitaries lending their support to this historic covenant. And Buck was the only one in the picture who knew who Carpathia was, who knew that the signing of the treaty would officially usher in the Tribulation.

Suddenly Buck remembered the Velcro-backed *Global Weekly* patch in his side pocket. As he pulled it out to apply it to his breast pocket, the Velcro caught the flap over the side pocket and held fast. As Buck lifted, his entire jacket pulled up over his belt, and when he let go, the hem stayed up by his shirt. By the time he smoothed out his jacket and used both hands to yank the patch free, he had been photographed a dozen times looking like a contortionist.

When the applause died and the crowd resumed their seats, Carpathia stood, microphone in hand. "This is an historic day," he began with a smile. "While all this has come about in record time, it has been nonetheless a herculean effort to pull together all the resources necessary to make it happen. Today we honor many individuals. First, my beloved friend and mentor, a father figure to me, the brilliant Dr. Chaim Rosenzweig of Israel!"

The crowd responded with enthusiasm, and Chaim rose unsteadily, waving his little wave and smiling like a small boy. Buck wanted to pat him on the back, to congratulate him for his accomplishments, but he grieved for his friend. Rosenzweig was being used. He was a small part of a devious plot that would make the world unsafe for him and his loved ones.

Carpathia sang the praises of the chief rabbi, of the Israeli prime minister, and finally of "the Honorable Gerald Fitzhugh, president of the United States of America, the greatest friend Israel has ever had."

More thunderous applause. Fitzhugh rose a few inches from his chair to acknowledge the response, and just when it was about to die down, Carpathia himself kept it going, tucking the microphone under his arm and stepping back to applaud loudly himself.

Fitzhugh appeared embarrassed, almost flustered, and looked to Carpathia as if wondering what to do. Carpathia beamed, as if thrilled for his friend the president. He shrugged and offered the microphone to Fitzhugh. At first the president didn't react, then he seemed to wave it off. Finally he accepted it to the roar of the audience.

Buck was amazed at Carpathia's ability to control the crowd. Clearly this was something he had choreographed. But what would Fitzhugh do now? Surely the only appropriate reaction would be to thank the people and toss a few bouquets at his good friends the Israelis. And despite Fitzhugh's dawning awareness of the devious agenda of Nicolae Carpathia, he would have to acknowledge Nicolae's role in the peace process.

Fitzhugh's chair scraped noisily as he stood, pushing back awkwardly against his own secretary of state. He had to wait for the crowd to quiet, and the process seemed to take forever. Carpathia rushed to Fitzhugh and thrust his hand aloft, the way a referee does with the winning boxer, and the Israeli crowd cheered all the more.

Finally, Carpathia stepped into the background and President Fitzhugh stood in the center of the dais, obligated to say a few words. As soon as Fitzhugh began to speak, Buck knew Carpathia was at work. And while he didn't expect to witness a murder, as he had in New York, Buck became immediately convinced that Carpathia had somehow caused something every bit as sinister. For the Gerald Fitzhugh speaking to the enthusiastic throng was anything but the frustrated president Buck had met with just minutes before.

Buck felt his neck grow warm and his knees weaken as Fitzhugh spoke. He leaned forward and gripped the back of Rosenzweig's chair, trying in vain to keep from trembling. Buck felt the clear presence of evil, and nausea nearly overtook him.

"The last thing I want to do at a moment like this," President Fitzhugh said, "is to detract in any way from the occasion at hand. However, with your kind indulgence and that of our great leader of the aptly renamed Global Community, I would like to make a couple of brief points.

"First, it has been a privilege to see what Nicolae Carpathia has done in just a few short weeks. I am certain we all agree that the world is a more loving, peaceful place because of him."

Carpathia made an effort to take back the microphone, but President Fitzhugh resisted. "Now I have the floor, sir, if you don't mind!" This brought a peal of laughter. "I've said it before, and I'll say it again, the secretary-general's idea for global disarmament is a stroke of genius. I support it without reservation and am proud to lead the way to the rapid destruction of 90 percent of our weapons and the donation of the other 10 percent to Global Community, under Mr. Carpathia's direction."

Buck's head swam and he fought to keep his equilibrium.

"As a tangible expression of my personal support and that of our nation as a whole, we have also gifted Global Community with the brand-new *Air Force One*. We have financed its repainting and titling, and it can be viewed at Ben Gurion International.

"Now I surrender the microphone to the man of destiny, the leader whose current title does not do justice to the extent of his influence, to my personal friend and compatriot, Nicolae Carpathia!"

Nicolae appeared to accept the microphone reluctantly and seemed embarrassed by all the attention. He looked bemused, as if helpless to know what to do with such a recalcitrant U.S. president who didn't know when enough was enough.

When the applause finally died down, Carpathia affected his humblest tone and said, "I apologize for my overexuberant friend, who has been too kind and too generous, and to whom the Global Community owes a tremendous debt."

* * *

Rayford kept a close eye on Buck. The man did not look well. Buck had seemed to nearly topple, and Rayford wondered if it was the heat or merely the nauseating mutual-admiration-society speeches that were turning Buck green around the gills.

The Israeli dignitaries, except Rosenzweig of course, looked vaguely uncomfortable with all the talk of destroying weapons and disarming. A strong military had been their best defense for decades, and without the covenant with Global Community, they would have been loath to agree to Carpathia's disarmament plan.

The rest of the ceremony was anticlimactic to the rousing—and, in Rayford's mind, disturbing—speech of the president. Fitzhugh seemed more enamored of Carpathia every time they were together. But his view only mirrored that of most of the populace of the world. Unless one was a student of Bible prophecy and read between the lines, one would easily believe that Nicolae Carpathia was a gift from God at the most crucial moment in world history.

* * *

Buck recovered control as other leaders made innocuous speeches and rattled on about the importance and historicity of the document they were about to sign. Several decorative pens were produced as television, film, video, and still cameras zeroed in on the signers. The pens were passed back and forth, the poses struck, and the signatures applied. With handshakes, embraces, and kisses on both cheeks all around, the treaty was inaugurated.

And the signers of this treaty—all except one—were ignorant of its consequences, unaware they had been party to an unholy alliance.

A covenant had been struck. God's chosen people, who planned to rebuild the temple and reinstitute the system of sacrifices until the coming of their Messiah, had signed a deal with the devil.

Only two men on the dais knew this pact signaled the beginning of the end of time. One was maniacally hopeful; the other trembled at what was to come.

* * *

At the famed Wall, the two witnesses wailed the truth. At the tops of their voices, the sound carrying to the far reaches of the Temple Mount and beyond, they called out the news: *"Thus begins the last terrible week of the Lord!"*

The seven-year "week" had begun.

The Tribulation.

17

RAYFORD STEELE sat in a phone booth at Ben Gurion Airport. He was early, preceding the Carpathia delegation by more than an hour. His crew was busy on *Global Community One*, and he had time to wait for an international operator to try to get through to Chloe.

"I saw you, Dad!" she laughed. "They tried to flash names with each shot. They had yours almost right. It said you were Raymond Steel, no *e* on the end, and that you were the pilot of *Air Force One*."

Rayford smiled, warmed by the sound of his daughter's voice. "Close. And the press wonders why no one trusts them."

"They didn't know what to do with Buck," Chloe said. "The first few times they panned to him, they didn't put anything on the screen. Then somebody must have heard the announcement when he was introduced and they came up with 'Duke Wilson, former writer, *Newsweek*.'"

"Perfect," Rayford said.

"Buck's all excited about this rabbi who's going to be on international CNN in a couple of hours. You going to get a chance to watch?"

"We'll have it on the plane."

"You can get it that far away and that far up?"

"You should see the technology, Chlo'. The reception will be better than we get on cable at home. At least as good, anyway."

* * *

Buck felt an overwhelming sadness. Chaim Rosenzweig had embraced him at least three times after the ceremony, exulting that this was one of the happiest days of his life. He pleaded with Buck to come along on the flight to Baghdad. "You will be working for Nicolae in a month regardless," Chaim said. "No one will see this as conflict of interest."

"I will, especially in a month when he owns whatever rag I work for."

"Don't be negative today, of all days," Chaim said. "Come along. Marvel. Enjoy. I have seen the plans. New Babylon will be magnificent."

Buck wanted to weep for his friend. When would it all come crashing down on Chaim? Might he die before he realized he'd been duped and used? Maybe that would be best. But Buck also feared for Chaim's soul. "Will you watch Dr. Ben-Judah on live television today?"

"Of course! Wouldn't miss it! He has been my friend since Hebrew University days. I understand they will have it on the plane to Baghdad. Another reason for you to come along."

Buck shook his head. "I will be watching from here. But once your friend outlines his findings, you and I should talk about the ramifications."

"Ah, I am not a religious man, Cameron. You know this. I likely should not be surprised with what Tsion comes up with today. He is an able scholar and careful researcher, brilliant really, and an engaging speaker. He reminds me somewhat of Nicolae."

Please, Buck thought. *Anything but that!*

"What do you think he'll say?"

"Like most Orthodox Jews, he will come to the conclusion that Messiah is yet to come. There are a few fringe groups, as you know, who believe Messiah already came, but these so-called Messiahs are no longer in Israel. Some are dead. Some have moved to other countries. None brought the justice and peace the Torah predicts. So, like all of us, Tsion will outline the prophecies and encourage us to keep waiting and watching. It will be uplifting and inspirational, which I believe was the point of the research project in the beginning.

"He may talk about hastening the coming of Messiah. Some groups moved into ancient Jewish dwellings, believing they had a sacred right to do so and that this would help fulfill some prophecies, clearing the way for the coming of Messiah. Others are so upset at the Muslim desecration of the Temple Mount that they have reopened synagogues in the same vicinity, as close as they can to the original site of the temple."

"You know there are Gentiles who also believe Messiah has already come," Buck said carefully.

Chaim was looking over Buck's shoulder, making sure he was not left behind when the entourage moved toward transportation back to the hotels and eventually to Ben Gurion for the flight to Baghdad. "Yes, yes, I know, Cameron. But I would sooner believe Messiah is not a person but more of an ideology."

He began moving away and Buck suddenly felt desperate. He held Chaim's arm. "Doctor, Messiah is more than an ideology!"

Rosenzweig stopped and looked his friend in the face. "Cameron, we can discuss this, but if you are going to be so literal about it, let me tell you something.

If Messiah is a person, if he is to come to bring peace and justice and hope to the world, I agree with those who believe he is already here."

"You do?"

"Yes, don't you?"

"You believe in Messiah?"

"I said *if*, Cameron. That is a big if."

"If Messiah is real and is to come, what?" Buck pleaded as his friend pulled away.

"Don't you see, Cameron? Nicolae himself fulfills most of the prophecies. Maybe all, but this is not my area of scholarship. Now I must go. I will see you in Babylon?"

"No, I told you—"

Rosenzweig stopped and returned. "I thought you just meant you were finding your own way there so as not to accept any favors from an interview subject."

"I was, but I have changed my mind. I'm not going. If I do wind up working for a Carpathia-owned publication, I imagine I'll tour New Babylon soon enough."

"What will you do? Are you returning to the States? Will I see you there?"

"I don't know. We'll see."

"Cameron! Give me a smile on this historic day!"

But Buck could not muster one. He walked all the way back to the King David Hotel, where the clerk asked if he still wanted information on commercial flights to Baghdad. "No, thanks," he said.

"Very good, sir. A message for you."

The envelope bore the return address of Dr. Tsion Ben-Judah. Buck trotted up to his room before tearing it open. It read, "Sorry to abandon you last night. Would not have been able to converse. Would you do me the honor of joining me for lunch and accompanying me to the ICNN studio? I will await your call."

Buck looked at his watch. Surely it was too late. He placed the call, only to get a housekeeper who said that the rabbi had left twenty minutes before. Buck slammed his hand on the dresser. What a privilege he would miss, just because he had walked back to the hotel instead of taking a cab! Perhaps he would take a cab to the TV studio and meet Tsion there after lunch. But did the rabbi want to talk before going on the air; was that it?

Buck lifted the receiver, and the front desk answered. "Can you get me a cab, please?"

"Certainly, sir, but a call has just come in for you. Would you like to take it now?"

"Yes, and hold onto that cab until I get back to you."

"Yes, sir. Hang up, please, and I will ring your call through."

It was Tsion. "Dr. Ben-Judah! I'm so glad you called! I just got back."

"I was at the signing, Buck," Tsion said in his thick Hebrew accent, "but I did not make myself visible or available."

"Is your lunch invitation still open?"

"It is."

"When shall I meet you, and where?"

"How about now, out in front?"

"I'm there."

Thank you, Lord, Buck breathed as he ran down the stairs. *Give me the opportunity to tell this man that you are the Messiah.*

At the car the rabbi shook Buck's hand with both of his and pulled him close. "Buck, we have shared an incredible experience. I feel a bond. But now I am nervous about informing the world of my findings, and I need to talk over lunch. May we?"

The rabbi directed his driver to a small cafe in a busy section of Jerusalem. Tsion, a huge black three-ring binder under his arm, spoke quietly to the waiter in Hebrew, and they were directed to a window table surrounded by plants. When menus were brought, Ben-Judah looked at his watch, waved off the menus, and spoke again in his native tongue. Buck assumed he was ordering for both of them.

"Do you still need your patch, identifying yourself as a reporter from the magazine?"

Buck quickly yanked the patch off his pocket.

"It came off much easier than it went on, did it not?"

Buck laughed.

As Tsion joined in the laughter, the waiter brought an unsliced loaf of warm bread, butter, a wheel of cheese, a mayonnaise-like sauce, a bowl of green apples, and fresh cucumbers.

"If you will allow me?" Ben-Judah pointed to the plate.

"Please."

The rabbi sliced the warm bread in huge sections, slathered them with butter and the sauce, applied slices of the cucumber and cheese, then put apple slices on the side and slid a plate in front of Buck.

Buck waited as the rabbi prepared his own plate. "Please do not wait for me. Eat while the bread is warm."

Buck bowed his head briefly, praying again for Tsion Ben-Judah's soul. He raised his eyes and lifted the delicacy.

"You are a man of prayer," Tsion observed as he continued to prepare his meal.

"I am." Buck continued to pray silently, wondering if now was the time to jump in with a timely word. Could this man be influenced within an hour of revealing his scholarly research to the world? Buck felt foolish. The rabbi was smiling.

"What is it, Tsion?"

"I was just recalling the last American with whom I shared a meal here. He was on a junket, sightseeing, and I was asked to entertain him. He was some sort of a religious leader, and we all take turns here, you know, making the tourists feel welcome." Buck nodded.

"I made the mistake of asking if he wanted to try one of my favorites, a vegetable and cheese sandwich. Either my accent was too difficult for him or he understood me and the offering did not appeal. He politely declined and ordered something more familiar, something with pita bread and shrimp, as I recall. But I asked the waiter, in my own language, to bring extra of what I was having, due to what I call the jealousy factor. It was not long before the man had pushed his plate aside and was sampling what I had ordered."

Buck laughed. "And now you simply order for your guests."

"Exactly."

And before the rabbi ate, he prayed silently too.

"I skipped breakfast," Buck said, lifting the bread in salute.

Tsion Ben-Judah beamed with delight. "Perfect!" he said. "An international adage says that hunger is the best seasoning."

Buck found it true. He had to slow down to keep from overeating, which had rarely been a problem for him. "Tsion," he began finally, "did you just want company before going on the air, or was there something specific you wanted to talk about?"

"Something specific," the rabbi said, looking at his watch. "How does my hair look, by the way?"

"Fine. They'll probably comb out the hat line there in makeup."

"Makeup? I had forgotten that part. No wonder they want me so early."

Ben-Judah checked his watch, then pushed his plates aside and hefted the notebook onto the table. It contained a four-inch stack of manuscript pages. "I have several more of these in my office," he said, "but this is the essence, the conclusion, the result of my three years of exhaustive—and exhausting—work with a team of young students who were of incalculable help to me."

"You're not dreaming of reading that aloud in an hour, are you?"

"No, no!" Ben-Judah said, laughing. "This is what you would call my security blanket. If I draw a blank, I pick up the blanket. No matter where I turn, there is something I should say. You might be interested to know that I have memorized what I will say on television."

"An hour's worth?"

"That might have seemed daunting to me, too, three years ago. Now I know I could go on for many more hours, and without notes. But I must stick to my plan to redeem the time. If I get off on tangents, I will never finish."

"And yet you'll take your notes with you."

"I am confident, Buck, but I am no fool. Much of my life has consisted of speaking publicly, but about half the time that has been in Hebrew. Naturally, with their worldwide audience, CNN prefers English. That makes it more difficult for me, and I don't want to compound that by losing my way."

"I'm sure you'll do fine."

"You have just satisfied the requirements of your end of the conversation!" the rabbi said, grinning. "Treating you to lunch is already a profitable proposition."

"So you just needed a little cheerleading."

The rabbi seemed to think about the word for a moment. Though it was an American term, Buck assumed it was self-explanatory. "Yes," Ben-Judah said. "Cheerleading. And I want to ask you a question. If it is too personal, you may decline to answer."

Buck held his hands apart as if open to any question.

"Last night you asked me my conclusions on the Messiah question, and I told you, in essence, that you would have to wait until the rest of the world heard it. But let me pose the same question to you."

Praise the Lord, Buck thought. "How much time do we have?"

"About twenty minutes. If it takes longer, we can continue in the car on the way to the studio. Maybe even into makeup."

The rabbi smiled at his own humor, but Buck was already formulating his story. "You already know about my being at a kibbutz when the Russians attacked Israel."

Ben-Judah nodded. "The day you lost your agnosticism."

"Right. Well, I was on an airplane, headed for London, the day of the disappearances."

"You don't say."

And Buck was off and running with the story of his own spiritual journey. He wasn't finished until the rabbi was out of makeup and sitting nervously in the green room. "Did I go on too long?" Buck asked. "I realize it was asking a lot for you to even pretend to pay attention with your mind on your own presentation."

"No, Buck," the rabbi said, deep emotion in his voice. "I should be able to do this in my sleep. If I tried to push any more into my head at this late date, I would lose it all."

So that was it? No response? No thank you? No "you're a fool"?

Finally, after a long silence, Tsion spoke again. "Buck, I deeply appreciate your sharing that with me."

A young woman with a battery pack on her hip, earphones and mouthpiece in place, slipped in. "Dr. Ben-Judah," she said. "We are ready for you in the studio for sound check, and ninety seconds to air."

"I am ready." Ben-Judah did not move.

The young woman hesitated, looking doubtful. Apparently she was not used to guests who didn't simply nervously follow her to the set. She left.

Tsion Ben-Judah rose with his notebook under his arm and opened the door, standing there with his free hand on the knob. "Now, Buck Williams, if you would be so kind as to do me a favor while you wait here."

"Sure."

"As you are a man of prayer, would you pray that I will say what God wants me to say?"

Buck raised a fist of encouragement to his new friend and nodded.

+ + +

"Want to take over?" Rayford asked his first officer. "I wouldn't mind catching this special CNN report."

"Roger. That rabbi thing?"

"Right."

The first officer shook his head. "That would put me right to sleep."

Rayford made his way out of the cockpit but was disappointed to see that the television was not on in the main cabin. He moved toward the back where other dignitaries and press were gathering around another TV. But before Rayford was completely out of Carpathia's conference room, Nicolae noticed him. "Captain Steele! Please! Spend a few minutes with us!"

"Thank you, sir, but I was hoping to catch the—"

"The Messiah broadcast, yes, of course! Turn it on!"

Someone turned on the set and tuned in ICNN. "You know," Carpathia announced to all within earshot, "our captain believes Jesus was the Messiah."

Chaim Rosenzweig said, "Frankly, as a nonreligious Jew, I think Nicolae fulfills more of the prophecies than Jesus did."

Rayford recoiled. *What blasphemy!* He knew Buck liked and respected Rosenzweig, but what a statement! "No offense, sir, but I doubt many Jews could believe in a Messiah—even if they think he is yet to come—who was born other than in the Holy Land."

"Ah, well, you see?" Rosenzweig said. "I am not that much a student. Now this man," he added, pointing to the TV screen where Tsion Ben-Judah was being introduced, "here is your religious scholar. After three years of intensive research, he ought to be able to outline the qualifications of Messiah."

I'll bet, Rayford thought. He stood in a corner and leaned against the wall to keep out of the way. Carpathia slipped off his suit jacket, and a flight attendant immediately hung it for him. He loosened his tie, rolled up his sleeves, and sat down in front of the television holding a fresh seltzer with a twist. Carpathia obviously considered this a good hour's diversion, Rayford thought.

An off-camera announcer clarified that "the views and opinions expressed on this broadcast do not necessarily reflect the views of the International Cable News Network or its subscribing stations."

Rayford found Dr. Ben-Judah a most engaging communicator. He looked directly into the camera, and though his accent was thick, he spoke slowly and distinctly enough to be easily understood. Most of all, Rayford sensed an enthusiasm and a passion for his subject. This was not at all what Rayford had expected. He would have imagined an ancient rabbi with a long white beard, hunched over some musty manuscripts with a magnifying glass, comparing jots and tittles.

Ben-Judah, however, after a brief introduction of himself and the process through which he and his team did their research, began with a promise. "I have come to the conclusion that we may know beyond all shadow of doubt the identity of our Messiah. Our Bible has given clear prophecies, prerequisites, and predictions that only one person in the human race could ever fulfill. Follow along with me and see if you come to the same conclusion I have, and we shall see whether Messiah is a real person, whether he has already come, or whether he is yet to come."

Rabbi Ben-Judah said he and his team spent almost the entire first year of their project confirming the accuracy of the late Alfred Edersheim, a teacher of languages and Grinfield Lecturer on the Septuagint. Edersheim had postulated that there were 456 messianic passages in Scripture, supported by more than 558 references from the most ancient rabbinical writings.

"Now," the rabbi said, "I promise to not bore you with statistics, but let me just say that many of those prophetic passages are repetitive and some are obscure. But based on our careful study, we believe there are at least 109 separate and distinct prophecies Messiah must fulfill. They require a man so unusual and a life so unique that they eliminate all pretenders.

"I do not have time in this brief hour to cover all 109, of course, but I will deal with some of the most clearly obvious and specific ones. We consulted a mathematician and asked him to calculate the probability of even 20 of the 109 prophecies being fulfilled in one man. He came up with odds of one in one quadrillion, one hundred and twenty-five trillion!"

Dr. Ben-Judah gave what Rayford considered a brilliant example of how to easily identify someone with just a few marks. "Despite the billions of people who still populate this planet, you can put a postcard in the mail with just a few distinctions on it, and I will be the only person to receive it. You eliminate much of the world when you send it to Israel. You narrow it more when it comes to Jerusalem. You cut the potential recipients to a tiny fraction when it goes to a certain street, a certain number, a certain apartment. And then, with my first and last name on it, you have singled me out of billions. That, I believe, is what these prophecies of Messiah do. They eliminate, eliminate, eliminate, until only one person could ever fulfill them."

Dr. Ben-Judah was so engaging that everyone on the plane had stopped talking, moving, even shifting in their seats. Even Nicolae Carpathia, despite the occasional sip from his glass and the tinkling of the ice, barely moved. It seemed to Rayford that Carpathia was almost embarrassed by the attention Ben-Judah had commanded.

Trying not to cause a distraction, Rayford excused himself and quickly slipped back into the cockpit. He put a hand on his first officer's shoulder and leaned down to talk to him. The first officer lifted his left earphone.

"I want this plane to not touch the ground before five minutes after the hour."

"We're scheduled for about two minutes to, Cap, and we're making good time."

"Make whatever adjustments you have to make."

"Roger." He reached for the radio. "Baghdad tower, this is *Global Community One*, over."

"Baghdad tower, go ahead *One*."

"We're reducing speed a few knots and are setting a new ETA of five minutes after the hour."

"Roger, *Global*. Problems?"

"Negative. Just experimenting with the new plane."

The first officer glanced up at Rayford to see if that was all right. Rayford gave him the thumbs-up and hurried back to the television.

\+ \+ \+

Buck prayed as he watched. Other staffers had gathered around monitors. There was none of the usual behind-the-scenes banter. People were glued to the broadcast. To keep from jumping out of his skin, Buck dug out his notebook and pen and tried to keep copious notes. It was nearly impossible to keep up with the rabbi, who rolled on and on with prophecy after prophecy.

"Messiah is not limited to just a few identifying marks," Ben-Judah said. "We Jews have been looking for him, praying for him, longing for him for centuries, and yet we have stopped studying the many identification hallmarks in our Scriptures. We have ignored many and made favorites of others, to the point that we are now looking for a political leader who will right wrongs, bring justice, and promise peace."

Chaim Rosenzweig stepped over to Carpathia and clapped him on the back, turning to beam at everyone. He was largely ignored, especially by Carpathia.

"Some believe Messiah will restore things as they were in the glorious days of Solomon," Rabbi Ben-Judah continued. "Others believe Messiah will make all things new, ushering in a kingdom unlike anything we have ever seen. And yet the prophecies themselves tell us what Messiah will do. Let us examine just a few of them in the remaining time."

\+ + +

Buck was getting a glimpse of what was to come. Jesus was either the Messiah, the chosen one, the fulfillment of God's Word, or he could not stand up to the scrutiny of the record. If only one man could possibly fulfill the prophecies, it had to be Jesus. It didn't appear the rabbi was going to use the New Testament to try to convince his first and primary audience, the Jews. So the prophecies from hundreds of years before the birth of Christ would have to be clear enough to make the point—if indeed that was where Tsion was going.

Dr. Ben-Judah was sitting on the edge of the table where he had displayed the several-hundred-page conclusion to his research study. The camera zoomed in on his expressive features. "The very first qualification of Messiah, accepted by our scholars from the beginning, is that he should be born the seed of a woman, not the seed of a man like all other human beings. We know now that women do not possess 'seed.' The man provides the seed for the woman's egg. And so this must be a supernatural birth, as foretold in Isaiah 7:14, 'Therefore the Lord Himself will give you a sign: Behold, the virgin shall conceive and bear a Son, and shall call His name Immanuel.'

"Our Messiah must be born of a woman and not of a man because he must be righteous. All other humans are born of the seed of their father, and thus the sinful seed of Adam has been passed on to them. Not so with the Messiah, born of a virgin.

"Our Messiah must be born of an extremely rare bloodline. While he must be born of a woman, that woman must be of a bloodline that includes many of the fathers of Israel. God himself eliminated billions of people from this select bloodline so Messiah's identity would be unmistakable.

"First God eliminated two-thirds of the world's population by choosing Abraham, who was from the line of Shem, one of Noah's three sons. Of Abraham's two sons, God chose only Isaac, eliminating half of Abraham's progeny. One of the two sons of Isaac, Jacob, received the blessing but passed it on to only one of his twelve sons, Judah. That eliminated millions of other sons in Israel. The prophet Isaiah years later singled out King David as another through whom Messiah would come, predicting that he would be a 'root out of Jesse.' David's father, Jesse, was a son of Judah.

"Messiah, according to the prophet Micah, must be born in Bethlehem." The rabbi turned to the passage in his notes and read, "'But you, Bethlehem Ephrathah, though you are little among the thousands of Judah, yet out of you shall come forth to Me the One to be Ruler in Israel, whose goings forth are from of old, from everlasting.'"

* * *

Chaim Rosenzweig was moving nervously, the only one on the plane not perfectly still. Rayford felt the old man had made a fool of himself and hoped he wouldn't compound it. But he did. "Nicolae," he said. "You were born in Bethlehem and moved to Cluj, right? Ha, ha!"

Others shushed him, but Carpathia finally sat back as if he had just realized something. "I know where this man is going!" he said. "Can you not see it? It is as plain as the nose on his face."

I can, Rayford thought. *It should be obvious to more than Carpathia by now.*

"He is going to claim to be the Messiah himself!" Carpathia shouted. "He was probably born in Bethlehem, and who knows what his bloodline is. Most people deny being born out of wedlock, but maybe that is his history. He can claim his mother was never with a man before he was born, and *voilà*, the Jews have their Messiah!"

"Ach!" Rosenzweig said. "You are speaking of a dear friend of mine. He would never claim such a thing."

"You watch and see," Carpathia said.

A steward leaned in and whispered, "Phone for you, Mr. Secretary-General."

"Who is it?"

"Your assistant calling from New York."

"Which one?"

"Ms. Durham."

"Take a message."

Carpathia turned back to the screen as Rabbi Ben-Judah continued. "As a child, Messiah will go to Egypt, because the prophet Hosea says that out of Egypt God will call him. Isaiah 9:1-2 indicates that Messiah will minister mostly in Galilee.

"One of the prophecies we Jews do not like and tend to ignore is that Messiah will be rejected by his own people. Isaiah prophesied, 'He is despised and rejected by men, a Man of sorrows and acquainted with grief. And we hid, as it were, our faces from Him; He was despised, and we did not esteem Him.'"

The rabbi looked at his watch. "My time is fleeting," he said, "so I want to speed through a few more clear prophecies and tell you what conclusion I have drawn. Isaiah and Malachi predict that Messiah will be preceded by a forerunner. The Psalmist said Messiah would be betrayed by a friend. Zechariah said that he would be betrayed for thirty pieces of silver. He adds that people will look on the one whom they have pierced.

"The Psalmist prophesied that people would 'look and stare at Me. They divide My garments among them, and for My clothing they cast lots.' And later it is prophesied that 'He guards all his bones; not one of them is broken.'

"Isaiah says 'they made His grave with the wicked; but with the rich at His death, because He had done no violence, nor was any deceit in His mouth.' The Psalms say he was to be resurrected.

"If I had more time, I could share with you dozens more prophecies from the Hebrew Scriptures that point to the qualifications of the Messiah. I will broadcast a phone number at the end of this broadcast so you can order all the printed material from our study. The study will convince you that we can be absolutely sure only one person could ever be qualified to be the special Anointed One of Jehovah.

"Let me close by saying that the three years I have invested in searching the sacred writings of Moses and the prophets have been the most rewarding of my life. I expanded my study to books of history and other sacred writings, including the New Testament of the Gentiles, combing every record I could find to see if anyone has ever lived up to the messianic qualifications. Was there one born in Bethlehem of a virgin, a descendant of King David, traced back to our father Abraham, who was taken to Egypt, called back to minister in Galilee, preceded by a forerunner, rejected by God's own people, betrayed for thirty pieces of silver, pierced without breaking a bone, buried with the rich, and resurrected?

"According to one of the greatest of all Hebrew prophets, Daniel, there would be exactly 483 years between the decree to rebuild the wall and the city of Jerusalem 'in troublesome times' before the Messiah would be cut off for the sins of the people."

Ben-Judah looked directly into the camera. "Exactly 483 years after the rebuilding of Jerusalem and its walls, Jesus Christ of Nazareth offered himself to the nation of Israel. He rode into the city on a donkey to the rejoicing of the people, just as the prophet Zechariah had predicted: 'Rejoice greatly, O daughter of Zion! Shout, O daughter of Jerusalem! Behold, your King is coming to you; He is just and having salvation, lowly and riding on a donkey, a colt, the foal of a donkey.'"

* * *

Buck leaped from the couch in the green room, standing now, watching the monitor. Others had gathered, but he couldn't help himself. He shouted, "Yes! Go, Tsion! Amen!" Buck heard phones ringing down the hall, and the rabbi hadn't even flashed the number yet.

"Jesus Christ is the Messiah!" the rabbi concluded. "There can be no other option. I had come to this answer but was afraid to act on it, and I was almost too late. Jesus came to rapture his church, to take them with him to heaven as he said he would. I was not among them, because I wavered. But I have since received him as my Savior. He is coming back in seven years! Be ready!"

Suddenly the TV studio was crawling with activity. Orthodox rabbis called, angry Israelis pounded on the doors, studio technicians looked for the cue to pull the plug.

"Here is the number to call to obtain more information!" the rabbi said. "If they will not flash it, let me quote it for you!" And he did, as directors signaled the cameramen to shut down. "Yeshua ben Yosef, Jesus son of Joseph, is Yeshua Hamashiac!" the rabbi shouted quickly. "Jesus is the Messiah!" And the screen went blank.

Rabbi Ben-Judah gathered up his notebook and looked frantically for Buck.

"I'm here, brother!" Buck said, running into the studio. "Where's the car?"

"Hidden around back, and my driver still doesn't know why!"

Executives burst into the studio. "Wait! People need to see you!"

The rabbi hesitated, looking to Buck. "What if they are seeking Christ?"

"They can call!" Buck said. "I'm getting you out of here!"

They ran through the back door and skipped into the employee parking lot. No sign of the Mercedes. Suddenly, from across the road, the driver jumped from the car, waving and shouting. Buck and Tsion sprinted toward him.

* * *

"Now *that* was anticlimactic." Nicolae Carpathia concluded. "I would have liked him saying *he* was the Messiah better. This is old news. Lots of people believe this myth. So they have a primo Hebrew rabbi convert. Big deal."

It sure is, Rayford thought, moving back to the cockpit for the landing.

* * *

Buck felt awkward in the small home of Tsion Ben-Judah, whose wife embraced him tearfully and then sat with her children in another room, sobbing loudly. "I support you, Tsion," she called out. "But our lives are ruined!"

Tsion answered the phone and motioned for Buck to pick up the extension in the other room. Mrs. Ben-Judah tried to quiet herself while Buck was listening in.

"Yes, this is Rabbi Ben-Judah."

"This is Eli. I spoke to you last night."

"Of course! How did you get my number?"

"I called the one you mentioned on the broadcast, and the student who answered gave it to me. Somehow I convinced her who I was."

"It's good to hear from you."

"I rejoice with you, Tsion my brother, in the fellowship of Jesus Christ. Many have received him under our preaching here in Jerusalem. We have arranged for a meeting of new believers in Teddy Kollek Stadium. Would you come and address us?"

"Frankly, brother Eli, I fear for the safety of my family and myself."

"Have no fear. Moishe and I will make clear that anyone who threatens harm to you will answer to us. And I think our record is plain on that account."

18

Eighteen months later

IT WAS FRIGID in Chicago. Rayford Steele pulled his heavy parka out of the closet. He hated lugging it through the airport, but he needed it just to get from the house to the car and from the car to the terminal. For months it had been all he could do to look at himself in the mirror while dressing for work. Often he packed his *Global Community One* captain's uniform, with its gaudy gold braids and buttons on a background of navy. In truth, it would have been a snappy-looking and only slightly formal and pompous uniform, had it not been such a stark reminder that he was working for the devil.

The strain of living in Chicago while flying out of New York showed on Rayford's face. "I'm worried about you, Dad," Chloe had said more than once. She had even offered to move with him to New York, especially after Buck had relocated there a few months before. Rayford knew Chloe and Buck missed each other terribly, but he had his own reasons for wanting to stay in Chicago for as long as possible. Not the least of which was Amanda White.

"I'll be married before you will if Buck doesn't get on the ball. Has he even held your hand yet?"

Chloe blushed. "Wouldn't you like to know? This is just all new to him, Dad. He's never been in love before."

"And you have?"

"I thought I had been, until Buck. We've talked about the future and everything. He just hasn't popped the question."

Rayford put on his cap and stood before the mirror, parka slung over his shoulder. He made a face, sighed, and shook his head. "We close on this house two weeks from tomorrow," he said. "And then you either come with me to New Babylon or you're on your own. Buck could sure make life easier for all of us by being a little decisive."

"I'm not going to push him, Dad. Being apart has been a good test. And I hate the idea of leaving Bruce alone at New Hope."

"Bruce is hardly alone. The church is bigger than it's ever been, and the underground shelter won't be much of a secret for long. It must be bigger than the sanctuary."

Bruce Barnes had done his share of traveling, too. He had instituted a program of house churches, small groups that met all over the suburbs and throughout the state in anticipation of the day when the assembling of the saints would be outlawed. It wouldn't be long. Bruce had gone all over the world, multiplying the small-group ministry, starting in Israel and seeing the ministry of the two witnesses and Rabbi Tsion Ben-Judah swell to fill the largest stadiums on the globe.

The 144,000 Jewish evangelists were represented in every country, often infiltrating colleges and universities. Millions and millions had become believers, but as faith had grown, crime and mayhem had increased as well.

Already there was pressure from the Global Community North American government outpost in Washington D.C. to convert all churches into official branches of what was now called Enigma Babylon One World Faith. The one-world religion was headed by the new Pope Peter, formerly Peter Mathews of the United States. He had ushered in what he called "a new era of tolerance and unity" among the major religions. The biggest enemy of Enigma Babylon, which had taken over the Vatican as its headquarters, were the millions of people who believed that Jesus was the only way to God.

To say arbitrarily, Pontifex Maximus Peter wrote in an official Enigma Babylon declaration, *that the Jewish and Protestant Bible, containing only the Old and New Testaments, is the final authority for faith and practice, represents the height of intolerance and disunity. It flies in the face of all we have accomplished, and adherents to that false doctrine are hereby considered heretics.*

Pontifex Maximus Peter had lumped the Orthodox Jews and the new Christian believers together. He had as much problem with the newly rebuilt temple and its return to the system of sacrifices as he did with the millions and millions of converts to Christ. And ironically, the supreme pontiff had strange bedfellows in opposing the new temple. Eli and Moishe, the now world-famous witnesses whom no one dared oppose, often spoke out against the temple. But their logic was an anathema to Enigma Babylon.

"Israel has rebuilt the temple to hasten the return of their Messiah," Eli and Moishe had said, "not realizing that she built it apart from the true Messiah, who has already come! Israel has constructed a temple of rejection! Do not wonder why so few of the 144,000 Jewish evangelists are from Israel! Israel remains largely unbelieving and will soon suffer for it!"

The witnesses had been ablaze with anger the day the temple was dedicated and presented to the world. Hundreds of thousands began streaming to

Jerusalem to see it, nearly as many as had begun pilgrimages to New Babylon to see the magnificent new Global Community headquarters Nicolae Carpathia had designed.

Eli and Moishe had angered everyone, including the visiting Carpathia, the day of the celebration of the reopening of the temple. For the first time they had preached other than at the Wailing Wall or at a huge stadium. That day they waited until the temple was full and thousands more filled the Temple Mount shoulder to shoulder. Moishe and Eli made their way to the temple side of the Golden Gate, much to the consternation of the crowd. They were jeered and hissed and booed, but no one dared approach, let alone try to harm them.

Nicolae Carpathia had been among the cadre of dignitaries that day. He railed against the interlopers, but Eli and Moishe silenced even him. Without the aid of microphones, the two witnesses spoke loudly enough for all to hear, crying out in the courtyard, "Nicolae! You yourself will one day defile and desecrate this temple!"

"Nonsense!" Carpathia had responded. "Is there not a military leader in Israel with the fortitude to silence these two?"

The Israeli prime minister, who now reported to the Global Community ambassador of the United States of Asia, was caught on microphone and news tape. "Sir, we have become a weaponless society, thanks to you."

"These two are weaponless as well!" Carpathia had thundered. "Subdue them!"

But Eli and Moishe continued to shout, "God does not dwell in temples made with hands! The body of believers is the temple of the Holy Spirit!"

Carpathia, who had been merely trying to support his friends in Israel by honoring them for their new temple, asked the crowd, "Do you wish to listen to me or to them?"

The crowd had shouted, "You, Potentate! You!"

"There is no potentate but God himself!" Eli responded.

And Moishe added, "Your blood sacrifices shall turn to water, and your water-drawing to blood!"

Buck had been there that day as the new publisher of the renamed *Global Community Weekly*. He resisted Carpathia's urging him to editorialize about what Nicolae called the intrusion of the two witnesses, and he persuaded the Global Community potentate that the coverage could not ignore the facts. The blood let from a sacrificed heifer had indeed turned to water. And the water drawn in another ceremony turned to blood in the pail. The Israelis blamed the two witnesses for debasing their celebration.

Buck hated the money he was making. Not even an outrageous salary could make his life easier. He had been forced to move back to New York. Much of the old guard at *Global Weekly* had been fired, including Stanton Bailey and Marge Potter, and even Jim Borland. Steve Plank was now publisher of the *Global Community East Coast Daily Times*, a newspaper borne out of the merger of the *New York Times*, the *Washington Post*, and the *Boston Globe*. Though Steve wouldn't admit it, Buck believed the luster had faded from Steve's relationship to the potentate too.

The only positive factor about Buck's new position was that he now had the means to isolate himself somewhat against the terrible crime wave that had broken all records in North America. Carpathia had used it to sway public opinion and get the populace behind the idea that the North American ambassador to the Global Community should supplant the sitting president. Gerald Fitzhugh and his vice president were now headquartered in the old Executive Office Building in Washington, in charge of enforcing Potentate Carpathia's global disarmament plan in America.

Buck's one act of resistance to Carpathia was to ignore the rumors about Fitzhugh plotting with the militia to oppose the Global Community regime by force. Buck was all for it and had secretly studied the feasibility of producing an anti–Global Community Web site on the Internet. As soon as he could figure out a way to do it without its being traced back to his penthouse apartment on Fifth Avenue, he would do it.

At least Buck had convinced Potentate Carpathia that Buck's moving to New Babylon would be a mistake. New York was still the world publishing capital, after all. He was already heartbroken that Chloe's father was being required to relocate to New Babylon. The new city was palatial, but unless a person lived indoors twenty-four hours a day, the weather in Iraq was unbearable. And despite Carpathia's unparalleled popularity and his emphasis on the new one-world government and one-world religion, there were still enough vestiges of the old ways in the Middle East that a western woman would feel totally out of place there.

Buck had been thrilled at how Rayford and Amanda White had taken to each other. That took pressure off Buck and Chloe, wondering about the future, worrying about leaving her father alone if they were ever to marry. But how could Rayford expect an American woman to live in New Babylon? And how long could they live there before the potentate began to step up his attacks on Christian believers? According to Bruce Barnes, the days of persecution were not far off.

Buck missed Bruce more than he thought possible. Buck tried to see him every time he got back to Chicago to see Chloe. Anytime Bruce came through

New York or they happened to run into each other in a foreign city, Bruce tried to make the time for a private study session. Bruce was fast becoming one of the leading prophecy scholars among new believers. The year or year and a half of peace, he said, was fast coming to a close. Once the next three horsemen of the Apocalypse appeared, seventeen more judgments would come in rapid succession, leading to the glorious appearing of Christ seven years from the signing of the covenant between Israel and the Antichrist.

Bruce had become famous, even popular. But many believers were growing tired of his dire warnings.

* * *

Rayford was going to be out of town until the day before he and Chloe and the new buyers were to close on the house. He smiled at the idea of buyers securing a thirty-year mortgage. Someone was going to lose on that deal.

With Rayford gone, Chloe would be left with much of the work, selling stuff off, putting furniture into storage, and arranging with a moving company to ship her things to a local apartment and his all the way to Iraq.

For the past couple of months, Amanda had been driving Rayford to O'Hare for these long trips, but she had recently taken a new position and couldn't get away. So today, Chloe would take Rayford by Amanda's new office, where she was chief buyer for a retail clothier. When they had said their good-byes, Chloe would drive him to the airport and bring the car back home.

"So how's it going with you two?" Chloe asked in the car.

"We're close."

"I know you're close. That's obvious to everybody. Close to what, is the question."

"Close," he said.

* * *

As they drove, Rayford's mind drifted to Amanda. Neither he nor Chloe had known what to make of her at first. A tall, handsome woman a couple of years Rayford's senior, she had streaked hair and impeccable taste in clothes. A week after Rayford had returned from his first assignment flying *Global Community One* to the Middle East, Bruce had introduced her to the Steeles after a Sunday morning service. Rayford was tired and none too happy about his reluctant decision to leave Pan-Con for the employ of Nicolae Carpathia, and he was not really in the mood to be sociable.

Mrs. White, however, seemed oblivious to Rayford and Chloe as people. To her they had been just names associated with a former acquaintance, Irene

Steele, who had left an indelible impression on her. Amanda had insisted on taking them to dinner that Sunday noon and was adamant about paying. Rayford had not felt much like talking, but that seemed not to be an issue for Amanda. She had a lot to say.

"I've wanted to meet you, Captain Steele, because—"

"Rayford, please."

"Well, I'll call you Mr. Steele for now, then, if *captain* is too formal. Rayford is a little too familiar for me, though that is what Irene called you. Anyway, she was the sweetest little woman, so soft-spoken, so totally in love and devoted to you. She was the sole reason I came as close as I did to becoming a Christian before the Rapture, and—second only to the vanishings themselves—she was the reason I finally did come to the Lord. Then I couldn't remember her name, and none of the other ladies from that Bible study were still around. That made me feel lonely, as you can imagine. And I lost my family, too, I'm sure Bruce told you. So it's been hard.

"Bruce has certainly been a godsend though. Have you learned as much from him as I have? Well, of course you have. You've been with him for weeks."

Eventually Amanda slowed down and shared her own story of the loss of her family. "We had been in a dead church all our lives. Then my husband got invited to some outing at a friend's church, came home, and insisted that we at least check out the Sunday services there. I don't mind telling you, I was not comfortable. They made a big deal all the time about being saved.

"Well, before I could get my little mind around the idea, I was the only one in my family who *wasn't* saved. To tell you the truth, the whole thing sounded a little white trashy to me. I didn't know I had a lot of pride. Lost people never know that, do they? Well, I pretended I was right there with my family, but they knew. They kept encouraging me to go to this women's Bible study, so finally I went. I was just sure it was going to be more of the same—frumpy middle-aged women talking about being sinners saved by grace."

Somehow, Amanda White managed to finish her meal while talking, but when she got to this part of her story she clouded up and had to excuse herself for a few minutes. Chloe rolled her eyes. "Dad!" she said. "What planet would you guess she's from?"

Rayford had chuckled. "I do want to hear her impressions of your mother," he said. "And she certainly sounds 'saved' now, doesn't she?"

"Yeah, but she's a long way from frumpy white trash."

When Amanda returned, she apologized and said she was "determined to get this said." Rayford smiled encouragingly at her while Chloe made faces at him behind her back, trying to get him to laugh.

"I'm not going to bother you anymore," she said. "I'm an executive and not the type to insert myself into people's lives. I just wanted to get together with you one time to tell you what your wife, and your mother, meant in my life. You know, I had only one brief conversation with her. It came after that one meeting, and I was glad I got the chance to tell her how she had impressed me.

"If you're interested, I'll tell you about it. But if I've already rattled on too long, tell me that, too, and I'll let you go with just the knowledge that Mrs. Steele was a wonderful lady."

Rayford actually considered saying that they had had a tiring week and needed to get home, but he would never be that rude. Even Chloe would likely chastise him for a move like that, so he said, "Oh, by all means, we'd love to hear it. The truth is," he added, "I love to talk about Irene."

"Well, I don't know why I forgot her name for so long, because I was so struck by it at first. Besides sounding a little like *iron* and *steel*, I remember thinking that Irene sounded more like a name of someone many years older than your wife. She was about forty, right?"

Rayford nodded.

"Anyway, I took the morning off, and I arrived at this home where the ladies were meeting that week. They all looked so normal and were wonderful to me. I noticed your wife right off. She was just radiant—friendly and smiling and talking with everyone. She welcomed me and asked about me. And then during the Bible study, prayer, and discussion, I was just impressed by her. What more can I say?"

A lot, Rayford hoped. But he didn't want to interview the woman. What had so impressed her? He was glad when Chloe jumped in.

"I'm glad to hear that, Mrs. White, because I was never more impressed with my mother than after I had left home. I had always thought her a little too religious, too strict, too rigid. Only when we were apart did I realize how much I loved her because of how much she cared for me."

"Well," Amanda said, "it was her own story that moved me, but more than that, it was her carriage, her countenance. I don't know if you knew this, but she had not been a Christian long either. Her story was the same as mine. She said her family had been going to church sort of perfunctorily for years. But when she found New Hope Village Church, she found Christ.

"There was a peace, a gentleness, a kindness, a serenity about her that I had never seen in anyone else. She had confidence, but she was humble. She was outgoing, yet not pushy or self-promoting. I loved her immediately. She grew emotional when she talked about her family, and she said that her husband and her daughter were at the top of her prayer list. She loved you both so deeply. She said her greatest fear was that she would reach you too late and that you would not go to heaven with her and her son. I don't remember his name."

"Rayford, Junior," Chloe said. "She would have called him Raymie."

"After the meeting I sought her out and told her that my family was the opposite. They were all worried that they would go to heaven without me. She told me how to receive Christ. I told her I wasn't ready, and she warned me not to put it off and said she would pray for me. That night my family disappeared from their beds. Almost everyone was gone from our new church, including all the Bible study ladies. Eventually I tracked down Bruce and asked if he knew Irene Steele."

Rayford and Chloe had returned home chagrined and a little ashamed of themselves. "That was nice," Rayford said. "I'm glad we took the time for that."

"I just wish I hadn't been such a creep," Chloe said. "For hardly having known her, that woman had a lot of insight into Mom."

For nearly a year after that, Rayford saw Amanda White only on Sundays and at an occasional midweek meeting of the larger core study group. She was always cordial and friendly, but what impressed him most was her servant's attitude. She continually prayed for people, and she was busy in the church all the time. She studied, she grew, she learned, she talked to people about their standing with God.

As Rayford watched her from afar, she became more and more attractive to him. One Sunday he told Chloe, "You know, we never reciprocated on Amanda White's dinner invitation."

"You want to have her over?" Chloe asked.

"I want to ask her out."

"Pardon me?"

"You heard me."

"Dad! You mean like on a date?"

"A double date. With you and Buck."

Chloe had laughed, then apologized. "It's not funny. I'm just surprised."

"Don't make a big deal of it," he said. "I just might ask her."

"Don't *you* make a big deal of it," Chloe said.

+ + +

Buck was not surprised when Chloe told him her Dad wanted them to double-date with Amanda White. "I wondered when he'd get around to it."

"To dating?"

"To dating Amanda White."

"You noticed something there? You never said anything."

"I didn't want to risk your mentioning it and planting an idea in his head that wasn't his own."

"That rarely happens."

"Anyway, I think they'll be good for each other," Buck said. "He needs companionship his own age, and if something comes of it, so much the better."

"Why?"

"Because he's not going to want to be alone if we decide to get more serious."

"Seems to me we've already decided." Chloe slipped her hand into Buck's.

"I just don't know what to do about timing and geography, with everything breaking the way it has."

Buck was hoping for some hint from Chloe that she would be willing to follow him anywhere, that she was either ready for marriage or that she needed more time. Time was getting away from them, but still Buck hesitated.

\+ \+ \+

"I'm ready when he is," Chloe told Rayford. "But I'm not going to say a word."

"Why not?" Rayford said. "Men need a few signals."

"He's getting all the signals he needs."

"So you've held his hand by now?"

"Dad!"

"Bet you've even kissed him."

"No comment."

"That's a *yes* if I ever heard one."

"Like I said, he's getting all the signals he needs."

\+ \+ \+

In fact, Buck would never forget the first time he had kissed Chloe. It had been the night he left for New York by car, about a year before. Carpathia had bought up the *Weekly* as well as any of the competition worth working for, and Buck seemed to have less choice than ever over his own career. He could try bootlegging copy over the Internet, but he still needed to make a living. And Bruce, who was at the church less and less all the time due to his ministry all over the world, had encouraged him to stay with *Global Weekly*, even after the name was changed to *Global Community Weekly*. "I wish we could change the last word one more time," Buck said. "To *Weakly.*"

Buck had resigned himself to doing the best he could for the kingdom of God, just as Chloe's father had done. But he still hid his identity as a believer. Whatever freedom and perceived objectivity he had would soon be gone if that truth was known to Carpathia.

That last night in Chicago, he and Chloe were in his apartment packing the last of his personal things. His plan was to leave by nine o'clock that night and drive all the way to New York City in one marathon stretch. As they worked, they talked about how much they would hate being apart, how much they would miss each other, how often they would phone and e-mail each other.

"I wish you could come with me," Buck said at one point.

"Yeah, that would be appropriate," she said.

"Someday," he said.

"Someday what?"

But he would not bite. He carried a box to the car and came back in, passing her as she taped another. Tears ran down her face.

"What's this?" he said, stopping to wipe her face with his fingers. "Don't get *me* started now."

"You'll never miss me as much as I'll miss you," she said, trying to continue to work with him hovering, a hand on her face.

"Stop it," he whispered. "Come here."

She set down the tape and stood to face him. He embraced her and pulled her close. Her hands were at her sides, and her cheek was on his chest. They had held each other before, and they had walked hand in hand, sometimes arm in arm. They had expressed their deep feelings for each other without mentioning love. And they had agreed not to cry and not to say anything rash in the moment of parting.

"We'll see each other often," he said. "You'll rendezvous with your dad when he comes through New York. And I'll have reasons to come here."

"What reason? The Chicago office is closing."

"This reason," he said, holding her tighter. And she began to sob.

"I'm sorry," she said. "This is going to be so hard."

"I know."

"No you don't. Buck, you can't say you care for me as much as I care for you."

Buck had already planned his first kiss. He had hoped to find a reason to simply brush her lips with his at the end of an evening, say good night, and slip away. He didn't want to have to deal with her reaction, or deal with kissing her again just then. It was going to be meaningful and special, but quick and simple, something they could build on later.

But now he wanted her to know how he felt. He was angry at himself for being so good at writing but so incompetent at telling her to her face how much she meant to him.

He stepped back and took her face in his hands. She resisted at first and tried to hide her face in his chest again, but he insisted she look at him. "I don't ever want to hear you say that again," he said.

"But, Buck, it's true—"

He lowered his head until his eyes were inches from hers. "Did you hear me?" he said. "Don't say it again. Don't imply it, don't even think it. There's no possible way you could care for me more than I care for you. You are my whole life. I *love* you, Chloe. Don't you know that?"

He felt her nearly recoil at that first declaration of his love. Her tears rolled over his hands, and she began to say, "How would I—?" But he lowered his mouth to hers, cutting off her words. And it was no quick touch of the lips. She raised her hands between his arms, wrapped them around his neck, and held him tight as they kissed.

She pulled away briefly and whispered, "Did you only say that because you're leaving and—" But he covered her mouth again with his.

A moment later he touched her nose with the tip of his own and said, "Don't doubt my love for you ever again. Promise."

"But, Buck—"

"Promise."

"I promise. And I love you, too, Buck."

+ + +

Rayford was not sure just when his respect and admiration for Amanda White had developed into love. He had grown fond of her, liked her, loved being with her. They had become comfortable enough with each other to touch each other when they spoke, to hold hands, to embrace. But when he found himself missing her after only a day away and needing to call her when he was gone more than a few days, he knew something was developing.

She actually started kissing Rayford before he kissed her. Twice when he returned to Chicago after several days away, Amanda greeted him with a hug and a peck on the cheek. He had liked it, but had also been embarrassed. But the third time he returned from such a trip, she merely embraced him and did not attempt to kiss him.

His timing had been perfect. He had decided that if she tried to kiss him on the cheek this time, he would turn and take it on the lips. He had brought her a gift from Paris, an expensive necklace. When she did not try to kiss him, he just held her embrace longer and said, "Come here a minute."

As passengers and crew passed them in the corridor, Rayford had Amanda sit next to him in the waiting area. It was awkward with an armrest between them. Both were bundled up, Amanda in a fur coat and Rayford with his uniform coat over his arm. He pulled the jewelry box from the sack in his flight bag. "This is for you."

Amanda, knowing where he had been, made a big deal over the bag, the name of the store, and the box. Finally, she opened it and appeared to stop breathing. It was a magnificent piece, gold with diamonds. "Rayford!" she said. "I don't know what to say."

"Don't say anything," he said. And he took her in his arms, the package in her hands nearly crushed between them, and kissed her.

"I still don't know what to say," she said with a twinkle in her eye, and he kissed her again.

Now, two weeks before his move to New Babylon, Rayford had been on the phone with Buck more often than Chloe had. While she was warming up the car, he sneaked in one last call.

"Everything set?" he asked Buck.

"Everything. I'll be there."

"Good."

In the car he asked Chloe, "What's the status on your apartment?"

"They promised it'll be ready," she said. "But I'm getting a little skittish because they keep stalling me on the paperwork."

"You're going to be all right here with me in New Babylon and Buck in New York?"

"It's not my first choice, but I have no interest living anywhere near Carpathia, and certainly not in Iraq."

"What's Buck saying?"

"I haven't been able to reach him today. He must be on assignment somewhere. I know he wanted to see Fitzhugh in D.C. soon."

"Yeah, maybe that's where he is."

Chloe stopped at Amanda's clothing store in Des Plaines and waited in the car as Rayford hurried in to say good-bye.

"Is he here?" he asked her secretary.

"He is, and she is," the secretary said. "She's in her office, and he's in that one." She pointed to a smaller office next to Amanda's.

"As soon as I'm in there, would you run out to the car and tell my daughter she has a call she can take in there?"

"Sure."

Rayford knocked and entered Amanda's office. "I hope you're not expecting me to be cheery, Ray," she said. "I've been trying to work up a smile all day, and it's not working."

"Let me see what I can do to make you smile," he said, pulling her from her chair and kissing her.

"You know Buck's here," she said.

"Yeah. It'll be a nice surprise for Chloe."

"Are you going to come and surprise me like that sometime?"

"Maybe I'll surprise you right now," he said. "How do you like your new job?"

"I hate it. I'd leave in a New York minute if the right guy came along."

"The right guy just came along," Rayford said, slipping a small box from his side pocket and pressing it into Amanda's back.

She pulled away. "What *is* that?"

"What? This? I don't know. Why don't you tell me?"

\+ + +

Buck had heard Rayford outside the door and knew Chloe wouldn't be far behind. He turned the light off and felt his way back to the chair behind the desk. In a few minutes he heard Chloe. "In here?" she said.

"Yes, ma'am," the secretary said. "Line one."

The door opened slowly, and Chloe turned on the light. She jumped when she saw Buck behind the desk, then squealed and ran to him. As soon as he stood, she leaped into his arms and he held her, twirling her around.

"Shhh," he said. "This is a business!"

"Did Daddy know about this? Of course he did! He had to."

"He knew," Buck said. "Surprised?"

"Of course! What are you doing in town? How long can you stay? What are we doing?"

"I'm in town only to see you. I leave on a red-eye tonight for Washington. And we're going to dinner after we drop your dad off at the airport."

"Yeah, you came only to see me."

"I told you a long time ago to never doubt my love for you."

"I know."

He turned and lowered her into the chair he had been sitting in, then knelt before her and pulled a ring box from his pocket.

\+ + +

"Oh, Ray!" Amanda said, gazing at the ring on her finger. "I love you. And for the few years we have left, I will love being yours."

"There's one more thing," he said.

"What?"

"Buck and I have been talking. He's proposing in the next room right now, and we were wondering if you two might be open to a double ceremony with Bruce officiating."

Rayford wondered how she would react. She and Chloe were friends, but not close.

"That would be wonderful! But Chloe might not go for it, so let's leave it up to her, no hard feelings either way. If she wants her own day, fine. But I love the idea. When?"

"The day before we close on the house. You give two weeks' notice here and move with me to New Babylon."

"Rayford Steele!" she said. "It takes a while to get your temperature up, but not long to make you boil. I'll write my resignation before your plane leaves the ground."

\+ + +

"Have you wondered why you never got the paperwork on the apartment?" Buck asked.

Chloe nodded.

"Because that deal's not going to happen. If you'll have me, I want you to move in with me in New York."

\+ + +

"Rayford," Amanda said. "I didn't think I would ever be truly happy again. But I am."

\+ + +

"A double ceremony?" Chloe swiped at her tears. "I'd love it. But do you think Amanda would stand for it?"

19

SOMETHING BIG was brewing. In a clandestine meeting, Buck went to see American President Gerald Fitzhugh. The president had become a tragic figure, reduced to a mere token. After serving his country for most of two terms in office, he now was relegated to a suite in the Executive Office Building and had lost most of the trappings from his previous role. Now his Secret Service protection consisted of three men rotating every twenty-four hours, and they were financed by the Global Community.

Buck met with Fitzhugh shortly after he proposed to Chloe, two weeks before the scheduled wedding. The president groused that his bodyguards were really there to make sure Carpathia knew his every move. But the most shattering thing, in Fitzhugh's mind, was that the U.S. public had so easily accepted the president's demotion. Everyone was enamored of Nicolae Carpathia, and no one else mattered.

Fitzhugh pulled Buck into a secure room and left his Secret Service agent out of earshot. The worm was about to turn, Fitzhugh told Buck. At least two other heads of state believed it was time to throw off the shackles of the Global Community. "I'm risking my life telling this to an employee of Carpathia," Fitzhugh said.

"Hey, we're *all* employees of Carpathia," Buck said.

Fitzhugh confided to Buck that Egypt, England, and patriotic militia forces in the U.S. were determined to take action "before it was too late."

"What does that mean?" Buck asked.

"It means soon," Fitzhugh said. "It means stay out of the major East Coast cities."

"New York?" Buck said, and Fitzhugh nodded. "Washington?"

"Especially Washington."

"That's not going to be easy," Buck said. "My wife and I are going to be living in New York when we're married."

"Not for long you're not."

"Can you give me an idea of timing?"

"That I cannot do," Fitzhugh said. "Let's just say I should be back in the Oval Office within a couple of months."

Buck desperately wanted to tell Fitzhugh that he was merely playing into Carpathia's hands. This was all part of the foretold future. The uprising against Antichrist would be crushed and would initiate World War III, from which would come worldwide famine, plagues, and the death of a quarter of the earth's population.

* * *

The double ceremony in Bruce's office two weeks later was the most private wedding anyone could imagine. Only the five of them were in the room. Bruce Barnes concluded by thanking God for all the smiles, the embraces, the kisses, and the prayer.

Buck asked if he could see the underground shelter Bruce had constructed. "It was barely under way when I moved to New York," he said.

"It's the best-kept secret in the church," Bruce said as they made their way down past the furnace room and through a secret doorway.

"You don't want church members to use it?" Buck asked.

"You'll see how small it is," Bruce said. "I'm encouraging families to build their own. It would be chaos if the church body showed up here in a time of danger."

Buck was astounded at how small the shelter was, but it seemed to have everything they would need to survive for a few weeks. The Tribulation Force was not made up of people who would hide out for long.

The five huddled to compare schedules and discuss when they might see each other again. Carpathia had devised a minute-by-minute schedule for the next six weeks that would have Rayford flying him all over the world, finally to Washington. Then Rayford would have a few days off before flying back to New Babylon. "Amanda and I could get here from Washington during that break," he said.

Buck said he and Chloe would come to Chicago then, too. Bruce would be back from a swing through Australia and Indonesia. They set the date, four in the afternoon, six weeks later. They would have a two-hour intensive Bible study in Bruce's office and then enjoy a nice dinner somewhere.

Before they parted, they held hands in a circle and prayed yet again. "Father," Bruce whispered, "for this brief flash of joy in a world on the brink of disaster, we thank you and pray your blessing and protection on us all until we meet back here again. Bind our hearts as brothers and sisters in Christ while we are apart."

\+ + +

Nicolae Carpathia seemed thrilled about Rayford's marriage and insisted upon meeting his new wife. He took both her hands in greeting and welcomed her and Rayford to his opulent offices, which covered the entire top floor of the Global Community headquarters in New Babylon. The suite also included conference rooms, private living quarters, and an elevator to the helipad. From there, one of Rayford's crew could ferry the potentate to the new airstrip.

Rayford could tell that Amanda's heart was in her throat. Her speech was constricted and her smile pasted on. Meeting the most evil man on the face of the earth was clearly out of her sphere of experience, though she had told Rayford she knew a few garment wholesalers who might have fit the bill.

After pleasantries, Nicolae immediately approved Rayford's request that Amanda accompany them on the next trip to the U.S. to see his daughter and new son-in-law. Rayford did not say who that son-in-law was, not even mentioning that the young newlyweds lived in New York City. He said, truthfully, that he and Amanda would visit the couple in Chicago.

"I will be in Washington at least four days," Carpathia said. "Enjoy whatever of that time you can. And now I have some news for you and your bride." Carpathia pulled a tiny remote control from his pocket and pointed it at the intercom on his desk across the room. "Darling, would you join us a moment, please?"

Darling? Rayford thought. *No pretense anymore.*

Hattie Durham knocked and entered. "Yes, sweetie?" she said. Rayford thought he would gag.

Carpathia leaped to his feet and embraced her gently as if she were a porcelain doll. Hattie turned to Rayford. "I'm so happy for you and Amelia," she said.

"Amanda," Rayford corrected, noticing his wife stiffen. He had told Amanda all about Hattie Durham, and apparently the two were not going to become soul mates.

"We have an announcement too," Carpathia said. "Hattie will be leaving the employ of Global Community to prepare for our new arrival."

Carpathia was beaming, as if expecting a joyous reaction. Rayford did what he could to not betray his disgust and loathing. "A new arrival?" he said. "When's the big day?"

"We just found out." Nicolae gave him a broad wink.

"Well, isn't that something?" Rayford said.

"I didn't realize you were married," Amanda said sweetly, and Rayford fought to keep his composure. She knew full well they were not.

"Oh, we will be," Hattie said, beaming. "He's going to make an honest woman of me yet."

* * *

Chloe broke down when she read her father's e-mail about Hattie. "Buck, we have failed that woman. We have all failed her."

"Don't I know it," Buck said. "I introduced her to him."

"But I know her too, and I know she knows the truth. I was right there when Daddy was sharing it with you, and she was at the same table. He tried, but we have to do more. We have to get to her somehow, talk to her."

"And have her know that I'm a believer, just like your dad is? It doesn't seem to matter that Nicolae's pilot is a Christian, but can you imagine how long I would last as his magazine publisher if he knew I was?"

"One of these days we have to get to Hattie, even if it means going to New Babylon."

"What are you going to do, Chloe? Tell her she's carrying the Antichrist's child and that she ought to leave him?"

"It may come to that."

Buck stood over Chloe's shoulder as she tapped out an e-mail message back to Rayford and Amanda. Both couples had taken to writing obscurely, not using names. "Any chance," Chloe wrote, "that she will come with him on the next trip to the capital?"

It was seven hours later, New Babylon time, when the message was sent, and the next day they received a reply: "None."

"Someday, somehow," Chloe told Buck. "And before that baby is born."

* * *

Rayford found it difficult to take in the incredible change in New Babylon since the first time he had visited following the treaty signing in Israel. He had to hand it to Carpathia and his sea of money. A lavish world capital had sprung up out of the ruins, and now it teemed with commerce, industry, and transportation. The center of global activity was moving east, and Rayford's homeland seemed headed for obsolescence.

The week before his and Amanda's flight to Washington with Nicolae and his entourage, Rayford e-mailed Bruce at New Hope, welcoming him back from his trip and asking some questions.

A few things still puzzle me about the future—a lot, actually. Could you explain for us the fifth and seventh?

He didn't write *seals*, not wanting to tip off any interloper. Bruce would know what he meant.

> *I mean, the second, third, fourth, and sixth are self-explanatory, but I'm still in the dark about five and seven. We can't wait to see you. "A" sends her love.*

* * *

Buck and Chloe had settled in Buck's beautiful Fifth Avenue penthouse, but any joy normal newlyweds might have received from a place like that was lost on them. Chloe kept up her research and study on the Internet, and she and Buck kept in touch with Bruce daily via e-mail. Bruce was lonely and missed his family more than ever, he wrote, but he was thrilled that his four friends had found love and companionship. They all expressed great anticipation of the pleasure they would enjoy in each other's company at their upcoming reunion.

Buck had been praying about whether to tell Chloe of President Fitzhugh's warning about New York City and Washington. Fitzhugh was well connected and undoubtedly accurate, but Buck couldn't spend his life running from danger. Life was perilous these days, and war and destruction could break out anywhere. His job had taken him to the hottest hazard spots in the world. He didn't want to be reckless or foolishly put his wife in harm's way, but every member of the Tribulation Force knew the risks.

Rayford was grateful that Chloe had begun getting to know Amanda better by e-mail. When Rayford and Amanda were dating, he had monopolized most of Amanda's time, and while the women seemed to like each other, they had not bonded other than as believers. Now, communicating daily, Amanda seemed to be growing in her knowledge of Scripture. Chloe was passing along everything she was studying.

Between Bruce and Chloe, Rayford found his answers about the fifth and seventh seals. It was not pleasant news, but he hadn't expected any different. The fifth seal referred to the martyrdom of Tribulation saints. In a secured mail package, Bruce sent to Chloe—who forwarded it on to Rayford—his careful study and explanation of the passage from Revelation which referred to that fifth seal.

> *John sees under the altar the souls of those who had been slain for the Word of God and for the testimony which they held. They ask God how long it will be until he avenges their deaths. He gives them white robes and tells them that first some of their fellow servants and their brethren will also be martyred.*

So the fifth Seal Judgment costs people their lives who have become believers since the Rapture. That could include any one or all of us. I say before God, that I would count it a privilege to give my life for my Savior and my God.

Bruce's explanation of the seventh seal made it clear that it was still a mystery even to him.

The seventh seal is so awesome that when it is revealed in heaven, there is silence for half an hour. It seems to progress from the sixth seal, the greatest earthquake in history, and serves to initiate the seven Trumpet Judgments, which, of course, are progressively worse than the Seal Judgments.

Amanda tried to summarize for Rayford: "We're looking at a world war, famine, plagues, death, the martyrdom of the saints, an earthquake, and then silence in heaven as the world is readied for the next seven judgments."

Rayford shook his head, then cast his eyes down. "Bruce has been warning us of this all along. There are times I think I'm ready for whatever comes and other times when I wish the end would simply come quickly."

"This is the price we pay," she said, "for ignoring the warnings when we had the chance. And you and I were warned by the same woman."

Rayford nodded.

"Look here," Amanda said. "Bruce's last line says, 'Check your e-mail Monday at midnight. Lest you find this all as depressing as I have, I am uploading a favorite verse to comfort your hearts.'"

Bruce had sent it so it would be available to both couples just before they left for their trips to Chicago to meet up with him. It read simply, "He who dwells in the secret place of the Most High shall abide under the shadow of the Almighty."

Rayford shifted in the pilot's seat, eager to talk to Amanda and find out how she was faring on the grueling nonstop flight from New Babylon to Dulles International. She was spending as much of the time as she could in Rayford's private quarters behind the cockpit, but she had to be sociable enough with the rest of the contingent so as not to appear rude. That, Rayford knew, meant hours of small talk.

She had already been asked about the new import/export business she was starting, but then the mood in *Global Community One* seemed to shift. During one of the few breaks Rayford shared alone with her, she said, "Something's up. Someone keeps bringing Carpathia printouts. He studies them and scowls and has private, heated meetings."

"Hmph," Rayford said. "Could be something. Could be anything. Could be nothing."

Amanda smirked. "Don't doubt my intuition."

"I've learned that," he said.

* * *

Buck and Chloe arrived in Chicago the night before the scheduled rendezvous with the Tribulation Force. They checked into the Drake Hotel and called New Hope to leave a message for Bruce, telling him they had arrived and that they would see him the following afternoon at four. They knew from his e-mails that he was back in the States from his Australia/Indonesia trip, but they had heard nothing from him since.

They also e-mailed him that Rayford and Amanda were going to come to the Drake for lunch the next day and that the four of them would travel to Mount Prospect together that afternoon. *If you want to join us for lunch in the Cape Cod Room, we'd be delighted,* Buck had written.

A couple of hours later, when they still had received no response to either the e-mail or the phone message, Chloe said, "What do you think it means?"

"It means he's going to surprise us at lunch tomorrow."

"I hope you're right."

"Count on it," Buck said.

"Then it won't really be a surprise, will it?"

The phone rang. "So much for surprises," Buck said. "That has to be him."

But it wasn't.

* * *

Rayford had illuminated the Fasten Seat Belt sign and was five minutes from touchdown at Dulles when he was contacted through his earphones by one of Carpathia's communications engineers. "The potentate would like a word with you."

"Right now? We're close to final approach."

"I'll ask." A few seconds later he came back on. "In the cockpit with you alone after engine shutdown."

"We have a postflight checklist with the first officer and the navigator."

"Just a minute!" The engineer sounded peeved. When he came back on, he said, "Run the other two out of there after shutdown and do the postflight jazz after your meeting with the potentate."

"Roger," Rayford muttered.

* * *

"If you recognize my voice and will talk to me, call me at this pay phone number, and make sure you call from a pay phone."

"Affirmative," Buck said. He hung up and turned to Chloe. "I've got to run out for a minute."

"Why? Who was that?"

"Gerald Fitzhugh."

* * *

"Thank you, gentlemen, and forgive me for the intrusion," Carpathia said as he passed the first officer and navigator on his way into the cockpit. Rayford knew they were as annoyed as he at the breach of procedural protocol, but then Carpathia was the boss. Was he ever.

Carpathia slipped deftly into the copilot chair. Rayford imagined that along with all his other gifts, the man could probably learn to fly a jet in an afternoon.

"Captain, I feel the need to take you into my confidence. Our intelligence has discovered an insurrection plot, and we are being forced to circulate false itineraries for me in the United States." Rayford nodded, and Carpathia continued. "We suspect militia involvement and even collusion between disgruntled American factions and at least two other countries. To be on the safe side, we are scrambling our radio communications and telling the press conflicting stories of my destinations."

"Sounds like a plan," Rayford said.

"Most people think I will be in Washington for at least four days, but we are now announcing that I will also be in Chicago, New York, Boston, and perhaps even Los Angeles over the next three days."

"Do I hear my little vacation slipping away?" Rayford said.

"On the contrary. But I do want you available on a moment's notice."

"I will leave word where I can be reached."

"I would like you to fly the plane to Chicago and have someone you trust return it to New York the same day."

"I know just the person," Rayford said.

"I'll get to New York somehow, and we can leave the country from there on schedule. We're just trying to keep the insurrectionists off balance."

* * *

"Hey," Buck said when President Fitzhugh picked up on the first ring. "It's me."

"I'm glad you're not at home," Fitzhugh said.

"Can you tell me more?"

"Just that it's good you're not at home."

"Gotcha. When can I return home?"

"That could be problematic, but you'll know before you head back that way. How long are you away from home?"

"Four days."

"Perfect."

Click.

* * *

"Hello? Mrs. Halliday?"

"Yes. Who's—?"

"This is Rayford Steele calling for Earl, but please don't tell him it's me. I have a surprise for him."

* * *

In the morning Buck took a call from one of the women who helped out in the office at New Hope. "We're a little worried about Pastor Barnes," she said.

"Ma'am?"

"He was gonna surprise y'all by comin' down there for lunch."

"We thought he might."

"But he picked up some kinda bug in Indonesia and we had to get him to the emergency room. He didn't want us to tell anyone, because he was sure it was something they could fix real quick and he could still get down there. But he's slipped into a coma."

"A coma!?"

"Like I say, we're a little worried about him."

"As soon as the Steeles get here, we'll head out there. Where is he?"

"Northwest Community Hospital in Arlington Heights."

"We'll find it," Buck said.

* * *

Rayford and Amanda met Earl Halliday at O'Hare at ten that morning. "I'll never forget this, Ray," Earl said. "I mean, it's not like carting around the potentate himself, or even the president, but I can pretend."

"They're expecting you at Kennedy," Rayford said. "I'll give you a call later to see how you liked flying her."

Rayford rented a car, and Amanda answered a page from Chloe. "We have to pick them up and go straight to Arlington Heights."

"Why? What's up?"

\+ + +

Buck and Chloe were waiting at the curb in front of the Drake when Rayford and Amanda pulled up. After quick embraces all around, they piled into the car.

"Northwest Community is on Central, right, Chlo'?" Rayford said.

"Right. Let's hurry."

Despite their concern for Bruce, Rayford felt a little more whole. He had a four-person family again, albeit a new wife and a new son. They discussed Bruce's situation and brought each other up to date, and though they were all aware that they were living in a time of great danger, for the moment they simply enjoyed being together again.

\+ + +

Buck sat in the backseat with Chloe, listening. How refreshing to be with people who were related and yet loved each other, cared about each other, respected one another. He didn't even want to think about the small-minded family he had come from. Somehow, someday, he would convince them they were not the Christians they thought they were. Had they been, they would not have been left behind, as he was.

Chloe leaned against Buck and slipped her hand into his. He was grateful she was so casual, so matter-of-fact, about her devotion to him. She was the greatest gift God could have granted him since his salvation.

"What's this?" he heard Rayford say. "And we've been making such good time."

Rayford was trying to exit onto Arlington Heights Road off the Northwest Tollway. Chloe had told him that would put them close to Northwest Community Hospital. But now local and state police and Global Community peacekeepers were directing a snarl of traffic past the exits. Everything came to a standstill.

After a few minutes they were able to creep forward a little. Rayford rolled down his window and asked a cop what was happening.

"Where've you been, pal? Keep it moving."

"What does he mean?" Amanda reached for the radio. "What are the news stations on, Chloe?"

Chloe moved away from Buck and leaned forward. "Hit *AM*, then try *1*, *2*, and *3*," she said. "One of those should be WGN or 'MAQ."

They stopped again, this time with a Global Community peacekeeper right next to Buck's window. Buck lowered it and flashed his *Global Community Weekly* press pass. "What's the trouble down there?"

"Militia had taken over an old Nike base to store contraband weapons. After the attack on Washington, our boys wiped them out."

"The attack on Washington?" Rayford said, craning his neck to talk to the officer. "Washington, D.C.?"

"Keep moving," the officer said. "If you need to get back this way you can get off at Route 53 and try the side streets, but don't expect to get near that old Nike base."

Rayford had to keep driving, but he and Buck hollered questions at every officer they passed while Amanda kept looking for a local station. Every one she tried carried the Emergency Broadcast System tone. "Put it on 'scan,'" Chloe suggested. Finally the radio found an EBS station and Amanda locked it in.

A Cable News Network/Global Community Network radio correspondent was broadcasting live just outside Washington, D.C. "The fate of Global Community Potentate Nicolae Carpathia remains in question at this hour as Washington lies in ruins," he said. "The massive assault was launched by east coast militia, with the aid of the United States of Britain and the former sovereign state of Egypt, now part of the Middle Eastern Commonwealth.

"Potentate Carpathia arrived here last night and was thought to be staying in the presidential suite of the Capital Noir, but eyewitnesses say that luxury hotel was leveled this morning.

"Global Community peacekeeping forces immediately retaliated by destroying a former Nike center in suburban Chicago. Reports from there indicate that thousands of civilian casualties have been reported in surrounding suburbs, and a colossal traffic tie-up is hampering rescue efforts."

"Oh, dear God!" Amanda prayed.

"Other attacks we know about at this moment," the reporter went on, "include a foray of Egyptian ground forces toward Iraq, obviously intending a siege upon New Babylon. That effort was quickly eliminated by Global Community air forces, which are now advancing on England. This may be a retaliatory strike for Britain's part in the American militia action against Washington. Please hold. Ah, please stand by. . . . Potentate Carpathia is safe! He will address the nation via radio. We will stand by here and bring that to you as we receive it."

"We've got to get to Bruce," Chloe said, as Rayford inched along. "Everybody's going to be taking 53 north, Dad. Let's go south and double back."

"It'll be another few moments before Potentate Carpathia comes on," the reporter said. "Apparently the GCN is ensuring that his transmission cannot be traced. Meanwhile, this news out of Chicago regarding the strike against the former Nike base: It appears to have been preemptive as well as retaliatory. Global Community intelligence today uncovered a plot to destroy Potentate

Carpathia's plane, which may or may not have contained Carpathia when it was flown to O'Hare International this morning. That plane is now airborne, destination unknown, though Global Community forces are marshaling in New York City."

Amanda grabbed Rayford's arm. "We could have been killed!"

When Rayford spoke, Buck thought he might break down. "Let's just hope I didn't fulfill Earl's dream by getting *him* killed," he said.

"You want me to drive, Rayford?" Buck asked.

"No, I'll be all right."

The radio announcer continued: "We're on standby for a lie feed, excuse me, a *live* feed from Global Community Potentate Nicolae Carpathia. . . ."

"He had *that* right the first time," Chloe said.

". . . Meanwhile, this word from Chicago. GC peacekeeping forces spokesmen say the destruction of the old Nike base was effected without the use of nuclear weapons, and though they regret heavy civilian casualties in nearby suburbs, they have issued the following statement: 'Casualties should be laid at the feet of the militia underground. Unauthorized military forces are illegal to start with, but the folly of mustering arms in a civilian area has literally blown up in their faces.' There is, we repeat, no danger of radiation fallout in the Chicago area, though peacekeeping forces are not allowing automobile traffic near the site of the destruction. Please stand by now for this live feed from Potentate Nicolae Carpathia."

Rayford had finally exited south onto Route 53, snaked his way through an Authorized Vehicles Only turnaround, and was heading north toward Rolling Meadows.

"Loyal citizens of the Global Community," came the voice of Carpathia, "I come to you today with a broken heart, unable to tell you even from where I speak. For more than a year we have worked to draw this Global Community together under a banner of peace and harmony. Today, unfortunately, we have been reminded again that there are still those among us who would pull us apart.

"It is no secret that I am, always have been, and always will be, a pacifist. I do not believe in war. I do not believe in weaponry. I do not believe in bloodshed. On the other hand, I feel responsible for you, my brother or my sister in this global village.

"Global Community peacekeeping forces have already crushed the resistance. The death of innocent civilians weighs heavy on me, but I pledge immediate judgment upon all enemies of peace. The beautiful capital of the United States of North America has been laid waste, and you will hear stories of more destruction and death. Our goal remains peace and reconstruction. I will be back at the secure headquarters in New Babylon in due time and will communicate with you frequently.

"Above all, do not fear. Live in confidence that no threat to global tranquility will be tolerated, and no enemy of peace will survive."

As Rayford looked for a route that would get him near Northwest Community Hospital, the CNN/GCN correspondent came back on. "This late word: Anti–Global Community militia forces have threatened nuclear war on New York City, primarily Kennedy International Airport. Civilians are fleeing the area and causing one of the worst pedestrian and auto traffic jams in that city's history. Peacekeeping forces say they have the ability and technology to intercept missiles but are worried about residual damage to outlying areas.

"And now this from London: A one-hundred-megaton bomb has destroyed Heathrow Airport, and radiation fallout threatens the populace for miles. The bomb was apparently dropped by peacekeeping forces after contraband Egyptian and British fighter-bombers were discovered rallying from a closed military airstrip near Heathrow. The warships, which have all been shot from the sky, were reportedly nuclear-equipped and en route to Baghdad and New Babylon."

"It's the end of the world," Chloe whispered. "God help us."

"Maybe we should just try to get to New Hope," Amanda suggested.

"Not till we check on Bruce," Rayford said. He asked stunned passersby if it was possible to get to Northwest Community Hospital on foot.

"It's possible," a woman said. "It's right past that field and over the rise. But I don't know how close they'll let you get to what's left of it."

"It was hit?"

"Was it hit? Mister, it's just up the road and across the street from the old Nike base. Most people think it got hit first."

"I'm going," Rayford said.

"Me too," Buck said.

"We're all going," Chloe insisted, but Rayford held up a hand.

"We're not all going. It's going to be hard enough for one of us to get past security. Buck or I will have a better chance because we have Global Community identification. I think one of us with an ID should go, and the other should stay with the wives. We all have to be with someone who can get past the red tape if necessary."

"I want to go," Buck said, "but you make the call."

"Stay and make sure the car is positioned so we can get out of here and get to Mount Prospect. If I'm not back in half an hour, take the risk and come looking for me."

"Daddy, if Bruce is any better, try to bring him with you."

"Don't worry, Chloe," Rayford said. "I'm ahead of you."

As soon as Rayford had jogged through the muddy weeds and out of sight, Buck regretted agreeing to stay behind. He had always been a person of action, and as he watched shell-shocked citizens milling about and commiserating, he could hardly stand still.

\+ \+ \+

Rayford's heart sank as he came over the rise and saw the hospital. Part of the full height of the structure was still intact, but much of it was rubble. Emergency vehicles surrounded the mess, with white-uniformed rescue workers scurrying about. A long stretch of police barrier tape had been stretched around the hospital campus. As Rayford lifted it to duck under, a security guard, weapon ready, ran toward him.

"Halt!" he called out. "This is a restricted area!"

"I have clearance!" Rayford shouted, waving his ID wallet.

"Stay right there!" the guard hollered. When he got to Rayford he took the wallet and studied it, comparing the photo to Rayford's face. "Wow! Clearance level 2-A. You work for Carpathia himself?"

Rayford nodded.

"What's your job?"

"Classified."

"Is he around here?"

"No, and I wouldn't tell you if he was."

"You're all good," the guard said, and Rayford headed toward what had been the front of the building. He was largely ignored by people too busy to care who did or did not have clearance to be there. Body after body was laid out in a neat row and covered. "Any survivors?" Rayford asked an emergency medical technician.

"Three so far," the man said. "All women. Two nurses and a doctor. They were outside for a smoke."

"No one inside?"

"We hear voices," the man said. "But we haven't gotten to anyone in time yet."

Breathing a prayer, Rayford folded his wallet so his ID was facing out. He slid it into his breast pocket. He strode to the makeshift outdoor morgue where several EMTs moved among the remains, lifting sheets and taking notes, trying to reconcile patient and employee lists with body parts and ID bracelets.

"Help or get out of the way," a heavyset woman said as she brushed past Rayford.

"I'm looking for a Bruce Barnes," Rayford said.

The woman, whose nameplate read *Patricia Devlin*, stopped and squinted, cocked her head, and checked her clipboard. She flipped through the three top pages, shaking her head. "Staff or patient?" she asked.

"Patient. Brought into the emergency room. He was in a coma last we heard."

"Probably ICU then," she said. "Check over there." Patricia pointed to six bodies at the end of a row. "Just a minute," she added, flipping to yet one more page. "Barnes, ICU. Yep, that's where he was. There's still more inside, you know, but ICU was just about vaporized."

"So he might be here and he might still be inside?"

"If he's out here, hon, he's confirmed dead. If he's still inside, they may never find him."

"No chance for anybody in ICU?"

"Not so far. Relative?"

"Closer than a brother."

"You want I should check for you?"

Rayford's face contorted, and he could hardly speak. "I'd be grateful."

Patricia Devlin moved quickly, surprisingly agile for her size. Her thick, white-soled shoes were muddy. She knelt by the bodies one by one, checking, as Rayford stood ten feet away, his hand covering his mouth, a sob rising in his throat.

At the fourth body, Miss Devlin began to lift the sheet when she hesitated and checked the still-intact wristband. She looked back at Rayford, and he knew. The tears began to roll. She rose and approached. "Your friend is presentable," she said. "Some of these I wouldn't dare show you, but you could see him."

Rayford forced himself to put one foot in front of the other. The woman reached down and slowly pulled back the sheet, revealing Bruce, eyes open, lifeless and still. Rayford fought for composure, his chest heaving. He reached to close Bruce's eyes, but the nurse stopped him. "I can't let you do that." She reached with a gloved hand. "I'll do it."

"Could you check for a pulse?" Rayford managed.

"Oh, sir," she said, deep sympathy in her voice, "they don't bring them out here unless they've been pronounced."

"Please," he whispered, crying openly now. "For me."

And as Rayford stood in the bluster of suburban Chicago's early afternoon, his hands to his face, a woman he had never met before and would never see again placed a thumb and forefinger at the pressure points under his pastor's jaw.

Without looking at Rayford, she took her hand away, replaced the sheet over Bruce Barnes's head, and went back about her business. Rayford's legs buckled, and he knelt on the muddy pavement. Sirens blared in the distance, emergency lights flashed all around him, and his family waited less than half a mile away. It was just him and them now. No teacher. No mentor. Just the four of them.

As he rose and trudged back down the rise with his awful news, Rayford heard the Emergency Broadcast System station blaring from every vehicle he passed. Washington had been obliterated. Heathrow was gone. There had been death in the Egyptian desert and in the skies over London. New York was on alert.

+ + +

Buck was nearly ready to go after Rayford when he saw a tall form appear on the horizon. From his gait and the slump of his shoulders, Buck knew.

"Oh, no," he whispered, and Chloe and Amanda began to cry. The three of them rushed to meet Rayford and walk him back to the car.

The Red Horse of the Apocalypse was on the rampage.

NICOLAE

✢ ✢ ✢

To Beverly and to Dianna

1

IT WAS THE WORST OF TIMES; it was the worst of times.

Rayford Steele's knees ached as he sat behind the wheel of the rented Lincoln. He had dropped to the pavement at the crushing realization of his pastor's death. The physical pain, though it would stay with him for days, would prove minor compared to the mental anguish of having yet again lost one of the dearest people in his life.

Rayford felt Amanda's eyes on him. She laid one comforting hand on his thigh. In the backseat his daughter, Chloe, and her husband, Buck, each had a hand on his shoulder.

What now? Rayford wondered. *What do we do without Bruce? Where do we go?*

The Emergency Broadcast System station droned on with the news of chaos, devastation, terror, and destruction throughout the world. Unable to speak over the lump in his throat, Rayford busied himself maneuvering his way through the incongruous traffic jams. Why were people out? What did they expect to see? Weren't they afraid of more bombs, or fallout?

"I need to get to the Chicago bureau office," Buck said.

"You can use the car after we get to the church," Rayford managed. "I need to get the word out about Bruce."

Global Community peacekeeping forces supervised local police and emergency relief personnel directing traffic and trying to get people to return to their homes. Rayford relied on his many years in the Chicago area to use back roads and side streets to get around the major thoroughfares, which were hopelessly clogged.

Rayford wondered if he should have taken Buck up on his offer to drive. But Rayford had not wanted to appear weak. He shook his head. *There's no limit to the pilot's ego!* He felt as if he could curl into a ball and cry himself to sleep.

Nearly two years since the vanishing of his wife and son, along with millions of others, Rayford no longer harbored illusions about his life in the twilight of history. He had been devastated. He lived with deep pain and regret. This was so hard. . . .

Rayford knew his life could be even worse. Suppose he had not become a believer in Christ and was still lost forever. Suppose he had not found a new love and was alone. Suppose Chloe had also vanished. Or he had never met Buck. There was much to be grateful for. Were it not for the physical touch of the other three in that car, Rayford wondered if he would have had the will to go on.

He could hardly imagine not having come to know and love Bruce Barnes. He had learned more and been enlightened and inspired more by Bruce than anyone else he'd ever met. And it wasn't just Bruce's knowledge and teaching that made the difference. It was his passion. Here was a man who immediately and clearly saw that he had missed the greatest truth ever communicated to mankind, and he was not about to repeat the mistake.

"Daddy, those two guards by the overpass seem to be waving at you," Chloe said.

"I'm trying to ignore them," Rayford said. "All these nobodies-trying-to-be-somebodies think they have a better idea about where the traffic should go. If we listen to them, we'll be here for hours. I just want to get to the church."

"He's hollering at you with a bullhorn," Amanda said, and she lowered her window a few inches.

"You in the white Lincoln!" came the booming voice. Rayford quickly turned off the radio. "Are you Rayford Steele?"

"How would they know that?" Buck said.

"Is there any limit to the Global Community intelligence network?" Rayford said, disgusted.

"If you're Rayford Steele," came the voice again, "please pull your vehicle to the shoulder!"

Rayford considered ignoring even that but thought better of it. There would be no outrunning these people if they knew who he was. But how did they know?

He pulled over.

* * *

Buck Williams pulled his hand from Rayford's shoulder and craned his neck to see two uniformed soldiers scampering down the embankment. He had no idea how Global Community forces had tracked down Rayford, but one thing was certain: it would not be good for Buck to be discovered with Carpathia's pilot.

"Ray," he said quickly, "I've got one set of phony IDs in the name of Herb Katz. Tell 'em I'm a pilot friend of yours or something."

"OK," Rayford said, "but my guess is they'll be deferential to me. Obviously, Nicolae is merely trying to reconnect with me."

Buck hoped Rayford was right. It made sense that Carpathia would want to make sure his pilot was all right and could somehow get him back to New Babylon. The two uniforms now stood behind the Lincoln, one speaking into a walkie-talkie, the other on a cell phone. Buck decided to go on the offensive and opened his door.

"Please remain in the vehicle," Walkie-Talkie said.

Buck slumped back into his seat and switched his phony papers with his real ones. Chloe looked terrified. Buck put his arm around her and drew her close. "Carpathia must have put out an all points bulletin. He knew your dad had to rent a car, so it didn't take long to track him down."

Buck had no idea what the two GC men were doing behind the car. All he knew was that his entire perspective on the next five years had changed in an instant. When global war broke out an hour before, he wondered if he and Chloe would survive the rest of the Tribulation. Now with the news of Bruce's death, Buck wondered if they *wanted* to survive. The prospect of heaven and being with Christ sure seemed better than living in whatever remained of this world, even if Buck had to die to get there.

Walkie-Talkie approached the driver's-side window. Rayford lowered it. "You *are* Rayford Steele, are you not?"

"Depends on who's asking," Rayford said.

"This car, with this license number, was rented at O'Hare by someone claiming to be Rayford Steele. If that's not you, you're in deep trouble."

"Wouldn't you agree," Rayford said, "that regardless who I am, we're all in deep trouble?"

Buck was amused at Rayford's feistiness, in light of the situation.

"Sir, I need to know if you are Rayford Steele."

"I am."

"Can you prove that, sir?"

Rayford appeared as agitated as Buck had ever seen him. "You flag me down and holler at me through a bullhorn and tell me I'm driving Rayford Steele's rental car, and now you want me to prove to you that I'm who you think I am?"

"Sir, you must understand the position I'm in. I have Global Community potentate Carpathia himself patched through to a secure cell phone here. I don't even know where he's calling from. If I put someone on the phone and tell the potentate it's Rayford Steele, it had blamed better be Rayford Steele."

Buck was grateful that Rayford's cat-and-mouse game had taken the spotlight off the others in the car, but that didn't last. Rayford slipped from his breast pocket his ID wallet, and as the GC man studied it, he asked idly, "And the others?"

"Family and friends," Rayford said. "Let's not keep the potentate waiting."

"I'm going to have to ask you to take this call outside the car, sir. You understand the security risks."

Rayford sighed and left the car. Buck wished Walkie-Talkie would disappear too, but he merely stepped out of Rayford's way and pointed him toward his partner, the one with the phone. Then he leaned in and spoke to Buck. "Sir, in the event that we transport Captain Steele to a rendezvous point, would you be able to handle the disposition of this vehicle?"

Do all uniformed people talk this way? Buck wondered. "Sure."

Amanda leaned over. "I'm Mrs. Steele," she said. "Wherever Mr. Steele is going, I'm going."

"That will be up to the potentate," the guard said, "and providing there's room in the chopper."

"Yes, sir," Rayford said into the phone, "I'll see you soon then."

Rayford handed the cell phone to the second guard. "How will we get to wherever we're supposed to go?"

"A copter should be here momentarily."

Rayford motioned for Amanda to pop the trunk but to stay in the car. As he shouldered both their bags, he leaned in her window and whispered. "Amanda and I have to rendezvous with Carpathia, but he couldn't even tell me where he was or where we would meet. That phone is only so secure. I get the feeling it's not far away, unless they're coptering us to an airfield from which we'll fly somewhere else. Buck, you'd better get this car back to the rental company soon. It'll be too easy to connect you with me otherwise."

Five minutes later Rayford and Amanda were airborne. "Any idea where we're going?" Rayford shouted to one of the Global Community guards.

The guard clapped the chopper pilot on the shoulder and shouted, "Are we at liberty to say where we're going?"

"Glenview!" the pilot hollered.

"Glenview Naval Air Station has been closed for years," Rayford said.

The chopper pilot turned to look at him. "The big runway's still open! The man's there now!"

Amanda leaned close to Rayford. "Carpathia's in Illinois already?"

"He must have been out of Washington before the attack. I thought they might have taken him to one of the bomb shelters at the Pentagon or the National Security Administration, but his intelligence people must have figured those would be the first places the militia would attack."

* * *

"This reminds me of when we were first married," Buck said as Chloe snuggled close to him.

"What do you mean 'when we were first married'? We're still newlyweds!"

"Shh!" Buck said quickly. "What're they saying about New York City?"

Chloe turned up the radio. ". . . devastating carnage everywhere here in the heart of Manhattan. Bombed-out buildings, emergency vehicles picking their way through debris, Civil Defense workers pleading with people over loudspeakers to stay underground."

Buck heard the panic in the reporter's voice as he continued. "I'm seeking shelter myself now, probably too late to avoid the effects of radiation. No one knows for certain if the warheads were nuclear, but everyone is being urged to take no risks. Damage estimates will be in the billions of dollars. Life as we know it here may never be the same. There's devastation as far as the eye can see.

"All major transportation centers have been closed if not destroyed. Huge traffic jams have snarled the Lincoln Tunnel, the Triborough Bridge, and every major artery out of New York City. What has been known as the capital of the world looks like the set of a disaster movie. Now back to the Cable News/Global Community News Network in Atlanta."

"Buck," Chloe said, "our home. Where will we live?"

Buck didn't answer. He stared at the traffic and wondered at the billowing clouds of black smoke and intermittent balls of orange flame that seemed to hover directly over Mt. Prospect. It was like Chloe to worry about her home. Buck was less concerned about that. He could live anywhere and seemed to *have* lived everywhere. As long as he had Chloe and shelter, he was all right. But she had made their ridiculously expensive Fifth Avenue penthouse flat her own.

Finally, Buck spoke. "They won't let anybody back into New York for days, maybe longer. Even our vehicles, if they survived, won't be available to us."

"What are we going to do, Buck?"

Buck wished he knew what to say. He usually had an answer. Resourcefulness had been the trademark of his career. Regardless of the obstacle, he had somehow made do in every imaginable situation or venue in the world at one time or another. Now, with his new, young wife beside him, not knowing where she would live or how they would manage, he was at a loss. All he wanted to do was to make sure his father-in-law and Amanda were safe, in spite of the danger of Rayford's work, and to somehow get to Mt. Prospect to assess what was happening to the people of New Hope Village Church and to inform them of the tragedy that had befallen their beloved pastor.

Buck had never had patience for traffic jams, but this was ridiculous. His jaw tightened and his neck stiffened as his palms squeezed the wheel. The late-model car was a smooth ride, but inching along in near gridlock made the huge automotive power plant feel like a stallion that wanted to run free.

Suddenly an explosion rocked their car and nearly lifted it off its tires. Buck wouldn't have been surprised had the windows blown in around them. Chloe shrieked and buried her head in Buck's chest. Buck scanned the horizon for what might have caused the concussion. Several cars around them quickly pulled off the road. In the rearview mirror Buck saw a mushroom cloud slowly rise and assumed it was in the neighborhood of O'Hare International Airport, several miles away.

CNN/GCN radio almost immediately reported the blast. "This from Chicago: Our news base there has been taken out by a huge blast. No word yet on whether this was an attack by militia forces or a Global Community retaliatory strike. We have so many reports of warfare, bloodshed, devastation, and death in so many major cities around the globe that it will be impossible for us to keep up with all of it. . . ."

Buck looked quickly behind him and out both side windows. As soon as the car ahead gave him room, he whipped the wheel left and punched the accelerator. Chloe gasped as the car jumped the curb and went down through a culvert and up the other side. Buck drove on a parkway and passed long lines of creeping vehicles.

"What are you doing, Buck?" Chloe said, bracing herself on the dashboard.

"I don't know what I'm doing, babe, but I know one thing I'm not doing: I'm not poking along in a traffic jam while the world goes to hell."

+ + +

The guard who had flagged down Rayford from the overpass now lugged his and Amanda's baggage out of the helicopter. He led the Steeles, ducking under the whirring blades, across a short tarmac and into a single-story brick building at the edge of a long airstrip. Weeds grew between the cracks in the runway. A small Learjet sat at the end of the strip close to the chopper, but Rayford noticed no one in the cockpit and no exhaust from the engine. "I hope they don't expect me to fly that thing!" he hollered at Amanda as they hurried inside.

"Don't worry about that," their escort said. "The guy who flew it here will get you as far as Dallas and the big plane you'll be flying."

Rayford and Amanda were ushered to garishly colored plastic chairs in a small, shabbily appointed military office, decorated in early Air Force. Rayford sat, gingerly massaging his knees. Amanda paced, stopping only when their escort motioned that she should sit down. "I am free to stand, am I not?" she said.

"Suit yourself. Please wait here a few moments for the potentate."

\+ + +

Buck was waved at, pointed at, and hollered at by traffic cops, and he was honked at and obscenely gestured at by other motorists. He was not deterred. "Where are you going?" Chloe insisted.

"I need a new car," he said. "Something tells me it's going to be our only chance to survive."

"What are you talking about?"

"Don't you see, Chlo'?" he said. "This war has just broken out. It's not going to end soon. It's going to be impossible to drive a normal vehicle anywhere."

"So what're you gonna do, buy a tank?"

"If it wasn't so conspicuous, I just might."

Buck cut across a huge grassy field, through a parking lot, and beside a sprawling suburban high school. He drove between tennis courts and across soccer and football fields, throwing mud and sod in the air as the big car fishtailed. Radio reports continued from around the world with news of casualties and mayhem while Buck Williams and his bride careened on, speeding through yield signs and sliding around curves. Buck hoped he was somehow pointed in the right direction. He wanted to wind up on Northwest Highway, where a series of car dealerships comprised a ghetto of commercialism.

A last sweeping turn led Buck out of the subdivision, and he saw what his favorite traffic reporter always said was "heavy, slow, stop-and-go" traffic all along Northwest Highway. He was in a mood and in a groove, so he just kept going. Pulling around angry drivers, he rode along a soft shoulder for more than a mile until he came upon those car dealerships. "Bingo!" he said.

\+ + +

Rayford was stunned, and he could tell Amanda was too, at the demeanor of Nicolae Carpathia. The dashing young man, now in his mid-thirties, had seemingly been thrust to world leadership against his own will overnight. He had gone from being nearly an unknown in the lower house of Romanian government to president of that country, then almost immediately had displaced the secretary-general of the United Nations. After nearly two years of peace and a largely successful campaign to charm the masses following the terror-filled chaos of the global vanishings, Carpathia now faced significant opposition for the first time.

Rayford had not known what to expect from his boss. Would Carpathia be hurt, offended, enraged? He seemed none of the above. Ushered by Leon Fortunato, a sycophant from the New Babylon office, into the long-unused administrative office at the former Glenview Naval Air Station, Carpathia seemed excited, high.

"Captain Steele!" Carpathia exalted. "Al—, uh, An—, uh, Mrs. Steele, how good to see you both and to know that you are well!"

"It's Amanda," Amanda said.

"Forgive me, Amanda," Carpathia said, reaching for her hand with both of his. Rayford noticed how slow she was to respond. "In all the excitement, you understand . . ."

The excitement, Rayford thought. *Somehow World War III seems more than excitement.*

Carpathia's eyes were ablaze, and he rubbed his hands together, as if thrilled with what was going on. "Well, people," he said, "we need to get headed home."

Rayford knew Carpathia meant home to New Babylon, home to Hattie Durham, home to Suite 216, the potentate's entire floor of luxuriously appointed offices in the extravagant and sparkling Global Community headquarters. Despite Rayford and Amanda's sprawling, two-story condo within the same four-block complex, neither had ever remotely considered New Babylon home.

Still rubbing his hands as if he could barely contain himself, Carpathia turned to the guard with the walkie-talkie. "What is the latest?"

The uniformed GC officer had a wire plugged in his ear and appeared startled that he had been addressed directly by Carpathia himself. He yanked out the earplug and stammered, "What? I mean, pardon me, Mr. Potentate, sir."

Carpathia leveled his eyes at the man. "What is the news? What is happening?"

"Uh, nothing much different, sir. Lots of activity and destruction in many major cities."

It seemed to Rayford that Carpathia was having trouble manufacturing a look of pain. "Is this activity largely centered in the Midwest and East Coast?" the potentate asked.

The guard nodded. "And some in the South," he added.

"Virtually nothing on the West Coast then," Carpathia said, more a statement than a question. The guard nodded. Rayford wondered if anyone other than those who believed Carpathia was Antichrist himself would have interpreted Carpathia's look as one of satisfaction, almost glee. "How about Dallas/Ft. Worth?" Carpathia asked.

"DFW suffered a hit," the guard said. "Only one major runway is still open. Nothing's coming in, but lots of planes are heading out of there."

Carpathia glanced at Rayford. "And the military strip nearby, where my pilot was certified on the 777?"

"I believe that's still operational, sir," the guard said.

"All right then, very good," Carpathia said. He turned to Fortunato. "I am certain no one knows our whereabouts, but just in case, what do you have for me?"

The man opened a canvas bag that seemed incongruous to Rayford. Apparently he had gathered Air Force leftovers for a disguise for Carpathia. He produced a cap that didn't match a huge, dress overcoat. Carpathia quickly donned the getup and motioned that the four others in the room should gather around him. "The jet pilot is where?" he asked.

"Waiting just outside the door, per your instructions, sir," Fortunato said.

Carpathia pointed to the armed guard. "Thank you for your service. You may return to your post via the helicopter. Mr. Fortunato and the Steeles and I will be flown to a new plane, on which Captain Steele will transport me back to New Babylon."

Rayford spoke up. "And that is in—?"

Carpathia raised a hand to silence him. "Let us not give our young friend here any information he would have to be responsible for," he said, smiling at the uniformed guard. "You may go." As the man hurried away, Carpathia spoke quietly to Rayford. "The Condor 216 awaits us near Dallas. We will then fly west to go east, if you know what I mean."

"I've never heard of a Condor 216," Rayford said. "It's unlikely I'm qualified to—"

"I have been assured," Carpathia interrupted, "that you are more than qualified."

"But what *is* a Condor 2—"

"A hybrid I designed and named myself," Carpathia said. "Surely you do not think what has happened here today was a surprise to me."

"I'm learning," Rayford said, sneaking a glance at Amanda, who appeared to be seething.

"You are learning," Carpathia repeated, smiling broadly. "I like that. Come, let me tell you about my spectacular new aircraft as we travel."

Fortunato raised a forefinger. "Sir, my recommendation is that you and I run together to the end of the airstrip and board the jet. The Steeles should follow when they see us get on board."

Carpathia held the oversized hat down onto his styled hair and slipped in behind Fortunato as the aide opened the door and nodded to the waiting jet pilot. The pilot immediately took off running toward the Learjet as Fortunato and Carpathia jogged several yards behind. Rayford slipped an arm around Amanda's waist and drew her close.

"Rayford," Amanda said, "have you ever once in your life heard Nicolae Carpathia misspeak?"

"Misspeak?"

"Stutter, stammer, have to repeat a word, forget a name?"

Rayford suppressed a smile, amazed he could find anything humorous on what could easily be the last day of his life on earth. "Besides your name, in other words?"

"He does that on purpose, and you know it," she said.

Rayford shrugged. "You're probably right. But with what motive?"

"I have no idea," she said.

"Hon, do you see no irony in your being offended by the man we're convinced is the Antichrist?" Amanda stared at him. "I mean," he continued, "listen to yourself. You expect common courtesy and decency from the most evil man in the history of the universe?"

Amanda shook her head and looked away. "When you put it that way," she muttered, "I suppose I am being oversensitive."

\+ \+ \+

Buck sat in the sales manager's office of a Land Rover dealership. "You never cease to amaze me," Chloe whispered.

"I've never been conventional, have I?"

"Hardly, and now I suppose any hope of normalcy is out the window."

"I don't need any excuse for being unique," he said, "but everyone everywhere will be acting impulsively soon enough."

The sales manager, who had busied himself with paperwork and figuring a price, turned the documents and slid them across the desk toward Buck. "You're not trading the Lincoln, then?"

"No, that's a rental," Buck said. "But I am going to ask you to return that to O'Hare for me." Buck looked up at the man without regard to the documents.

"That's highly unusual," the sales manager said. "I'd have to send two of my people and an extra vehicle so they could get back."

Buck stood. "I suppose I am asking too much. Another dealer will be willing to go the extra mile to sell me a vehicle, I'm sure, especially when no one knows what tomorrow may bring."

"Sit back down, Mr. Williams. I won't have any trouble getting my district manager to sign off on throwing in that little errand for you. As you can see, you're going to be able to drive your fully loaded Range Rover out of here within an hour for under six figures."

"Make it half an hour," Buck said, "and we've got a deal."

The sales manager rose and thrust out his hand. "Deal."

2

THE LEARJET WAS a six-seater. Carpathia and Fortunato, deep in conversation, ignored Rayford and Amanda as the couple passed. The Steeles ducked into the last two seats and held hands. Rayford knew global terror was entirely new to Amanda. It was new to *him*. On this scale, it was new to everyone. She gripped his hands so tight his fingers turned white. She was shuddering.

Carpathia turned in his seat to face them. He had that fighting-a-grin look Rayford found so maddening in light of the situation. "I know you are not certified on these little speedsters," Carpathia said, "but you might learn something in the copilot's chair."

Rayford was much more worried about the plane he would be expected to fly out of Dallas, something he had never seen or even heard of. He looked at Amanda, hoping she would plead with him to stay with her, but she quickly let go of his hand and nodded. Rayford climbed toward the cockpit, which was separated from the other seats by a thin panel. He strapped himself in and looked apologetically at the pilot, who offered his hand and said, "Chico Hernandez, Captain Steele. Don't worry, I've already done the preflight check, and I don't really need any help."

"I wouldn't be of any help anyway," Rayford said. "I haven't flown anything smaller than a 707 for years."

"Compared to what you usually fly," Hernandez said, "this will seem like a motorbike."

And that's exactly what it seemed to Rayford. The Learjet screamed and whined as Hernandez carefully lined it up on the runway. They seemed to hit top ground speed in seconds and quickly lifted off, banking hard to the right and setting a course for Dallas. "What tower do you connect with?" Rayford asked.

"The tower's empty at Glenview," Hernandez said.

"I noticed."

"I'll let a few towers know I'm coming along the way. The weather people tell us we're clear all the way, and Global Community intelligence spots no enemy aircraft between here and touchdown."

Enemy aircraft, Rayford thought. *There's an interesting way to refer to American militia forces.* He recalled not liking the militias, not understanding them, assuming them criminals. But that had been when the American government was also their enemy. Now they were allies of lame duck United States President Gerald Fitzhugh, and their enemy was Rayford's enemy—his boss, of all things, but his enemy nonetheless. Rayford had no idea where Hernandez came from, what his background was, whether he was sympathetic and loyal to Carpathia or had been pressed into reluctant service as Rayford himself had. Rayford slipped on earphones and found the proper dials so he could communicate to the pilot without allowing for anyone else to hear. "This is your pretend first officer," he said softly. "Do you read me?"

"Loud and clear, 'Copilot'," Hernandez said. And as if reading Rayford's mind, Hernandez added, "This channel is secure."

Rayford took that to mean that no one else, inside or outside the plane, could hear their conversation. That made sense. But why had Hernandez said that? Had he realized that Rayford wanted to talk? And how comfortable would Rayford be talking to a stranger? Just because they were fellow pilots didn't mean he could bare his soul to this man. "I'm curious about *Global Community One,*" Rayford said.

"You haven't heard?" Hernandez asked.

"Negative."

Hernandez shot a glance behind him at Carpathia and Fortunato. Rayford chose not to turn, so as not to arouse any suspicion. Apparently, Hernandez had found Carpathia and Fortunato in earnest discussions again, because he told what he knew about Rayford's former plane.

"I suppose the potentate would have told you himself if he had had the chance," Hernandez said. "There's not good news out of New York."

"I heard that," Rayford said. "But I hadn't heard how widespread the damage was at the major airports."

"Just about total destruction, I understand. We know for sure that the hangar where she was located was virtually vaporized."

"And the pilot?"

"Earl Halliday? He was long gone by the time of the attack."

"He's safe then?" Rayford said. "That's a relief! Do you know him?"

"Not personally," Hernandez said. "But I've heard a lot about him in the past few weeks."

"From Carpathia?" Rayford said.

"No. From the North American delegation to the Global Community."

Rayford was lost, but he didn't want to admit it. Why would the North

American delegation be talking about Earl Halliday? Carpathia had asked Rayford to find someone to fly the *Global Community One* 777 to New York while Rayford and Amanda were taking a brief vacation in Chicago. Carpathia was to spend a few days confusing the press and the insurrectionists (President Fitzhugh and several American militia groups) by ignoring his published itinerary and being shuttled from place to place. When the militia attacked and the Global Community retaliated, Rayford had assumed that at least the timing was a surprise. He also assumed that his selection of his old friend and boss at Pan-Continental Airlines as the one to ferry the empty 777 to New York was of little consequence to Nicolae Carpathia. But apparently Carpathia and the North American delegation had known exactly whom he would choose. What was the point of that? And how did Halliday know to get out of New York in time to avoid being killed?

"Where is Halliday now?" Rayford asked.

"You'll see him in Dallas."

Rayford squinted, trying to make it all compute. "I will?"

"Who did you think was going to take you through the paces of the new aircraft?"

When Carpathia had told Rayford he might learn a few things by sitting in the copilot's chair, Rayford had had no idea it would entail more than a few interesting tidbits about this quick, small jet. "Let me get this straight," he said. "Earl Halliday knew about the new plane and is conversant enough to teach me to drive it?"

Hernandez smiled as he scanned the horizon and maneuvered the Learjet. "Earl Halliday practically built the Condor 216 himself. He helped design it. He made sure anyone who was certified on a seven-seven-seven would be able to fly it, even though it's much bigger and a whole sight more sophisticated than *Global Community One*."

Rayford felt an ironic emotion rise within him. He hated Carpathia and knew precisely who he was. But as strange as his wife's taking offense at Carpathia's insistence on getting her name wrong, Rayford suddenly felt left out of the loop. "I wonder why I would not have been informed of a new plane, especially if I am supposed to be its pilot," he said.

"I can't say for sure," Hernandez said, "but you know the potentate tends to be very wary, very careful, and very calculating."

Don't I know it? Rayford thought. *Conniving and scheming is more like it.* "So he apparently doesn't trust me."

"I'm not sure he trusts anyone," Hernandez said. "If I were in his shoes, I wouldn't either. Would you?"

"Would I what?"

"Would you trust anyone if you were Carpathia?" Hernandez said.

Rayford did not respond.

* * *

"Do you feel like you just spent the devil's money?" Chloe asked Buck as he carefully pulled the beautiful, new, earth-toned Range Rover out of the dealership and into traffic.

"I *know* I did," Buck said. "And the Antichrist has never invested a better dollar for the cause of God."

"You consider spending almost a hundred thousand dollars on a toy like this an investment in our cause?"

"Chloe," Buck said carefully, "look at this rig. It has everything. It will go anywhere. It's indestructible. It comes with a phone. It comes with a citizen's band radio. It comes with a fire extinguisher, a survival kit, flares, you name it. It has four-wheel drive, all-wheel drive, independent suspension, a CD player that plays those new two-inch jobs, electrical outlets in the dashboard that allow you to connect whatever you want directly to the battery."

"But Buck, you slapped down your *Global Community Weekly* credit card as if it were your own. What kind of a limit do you have on that thing?"

"Most of the cards Carpathia issues like this have a quarter-of-a-million-dollar limit," Buck said. "But those of us at senior levels have a special code built into ours. They're unlimited."

"Literally unlimited?"

"Didn't you see the eyes of that sales manager when he phoned for verification?"

"All I saw," Chloe said, "was a smile and a done deal."

"There you go."

"But doesn't somebody have to approve purchases like that?"

"I report directly to Carpathia. He might want to know why I bought a Range Rover. But it should certainly be easy enough to explain, what with the loss of our apartment, our vehicles, and the need to be able to get wherever we have to go."

Once again, Buck soon grew impatient with the traffic. This time, when he left the road and made his way through ditches, gullies, parkways, alleys, and yards, the ride was sure and, if not smooth, purposeful. That vehicle was made for this kind of driving.

"Look what else this baby has," Buck said. "You can switch between automatic or manual transmission."

Chloe leaned down to look at the floorboard. "What do you do with the clutch when you're in automatic?"

"You ignore it," Buck said. "You ever drive a stick?"

"A friend in college had a little foreign sports car with a stick shift," she said. "I loved it."

"You wanna drive?"

"Not on your life. At least not now. Let's just get to the church."

\+ + +

"Anything else I should know about what we're going to encounter in Dallas?" Rayford asked Hernandez.

"You're gonna be ferrying a lot of VIPs back to Iraq," Hernandez said. "But that's nothing new for you, is it?"

"Nope. I'm afraid it's lost its luster by now."

"Well, for what it's worth, I envy you."

Rayford was stunned to silence. Here he was, what Bruce Barnes referred to as a tribulation saint, a believer in Christ during the most horrifying period in human history, serving Antichrist himself against his own will and certainly at the peril of his wife, his daughter, her husband, and himself. And yet he was envied.

"Don't envy me, Captain Hernandez. Whatever you do, don't envy me."

\+ + +

As Buck neared the church, he noticed yards full of people. They stared at the sky and listened to radios and TVs that blared from inside their houses. Buck was surprised to see one lone car in the parking lot at New Hope. It belonged to Loretta, Bruce's assistant.

"I don't look forward to this," Chloe said.

"I hear you," Buck said.

They found the woman, now nearly seventy, sitting stiffly in the outer office staring at the television. Two balled-up tissues rested in her lap, and she riffled a third in her bony fingers. Her reading glasses rode low on her nose, and she peered over the top of them at the television. She did not seem to look Buck and Chloe's way as they entered, but it soon became clear she knew they were there. From the inner office, Buck heard a computer printer producing page after page after page.

Loretta had been a southern belle in her day. Now she sat red-eyed and sniffling, fingers working that tissue as if creating some piece of art. Buck glanced up to see a helicopter view of the bombed-out Northwest Community Hospital.

"People been callin'," Loretta said. "I don't know what to tell 'em. He couldn't survive that, could he? Pastor Bruce, I mean. He couldn't still be alive now, could he? Did y'all see him?"

"We didn't see him," Chloe said carefully, kneeling next to the old woman. "But my dad did."

Loretta turned quickly to stare at her. "Mr. Steele saw him? And is he all right?"

Chloe shook her head. "I'm sorry, ma'am, he's not. Bruce is gone."

Loretta lowered her chin to her chest. Tears gathered and pooled in her half-glasses. She spoke hoarsely. "Would y'all mind turnin' that off then, please. I was just praying I'd catch a glimpse of Pastor Bruce. But if he's under one of those sheets, I don't care to see that."

Buck turned off the TV as Chloe embraced the old woman. Loretta broke down and sobbed. "That young man was like family to me, you know."

"We know," Chloe said, crying herself now. "He was family to us, too."

Loretta pulled back to look at Chloe. "But he was my *only* family. You know my story, don't you?"

"Yes, ma'am—"

"You know I lost everybody."

"Yes, ma'am."

"I mean, everybody. I lost every living relative I had. More than a hundred. I came from one of the most devout, spiritual heritages a woman could come from. I was considered a pillar of this church. I was active in everythin', a church woman. I just never really knew the Lord."

Chloe held her close and cried with her.

"That young man taught me everythin'," Loretta continued. "I learned more from him in two years than I learned in more than sixty years in Sunday school and church before that. I'm not blamin' anybody but myself. I was deaf and blind spiritually. My daddy had gone on before, but I lost Mama, all six of my brothers and sisters, all of their kids, their kids' husbands and wives. I lost my own children and grandchildren. Everybody. If somebody had made a list of who in this church would be most likely to go to heaven when they died, I would have been at the top of the list, right up there with the pastor."

This was as painful for Buck as it seemed for Chloe and Loretta. He would grieve in his own way and his own time, but for now he didn't want to dwell on the tragedy. "What're you working on in the office, ma'am?" he said.

Loretta cleared her throat. "Bruce's stuff, of course," she managed.

"What is it?"

"Well, you know when he got back from that big teaching trip of his in

Indonesia, he had some sort of a virus or something. One of the men rushed him to the hospital so fast that he left his laptop computer here. You know he took that thing with him everywhere he went."

"I know he did," Chloe said.

"Well, as soon as he was settled into that hospital, he called me. He asked me to bring that laptop to him if I could. I would've done anythin' for Bruce, of course. I was on my way out the door with it when the phone rang again. Bruce told me they were taking him out of the emergency room and straight to intensive care, so he wouldn't be able to have any visitors for a while. I think he had a premonition."

"A premonition?" Buck said.

"I think he knew he might die," she said. "He told me to keep in touch with the hospital for when he could have visitors. He was fond of me, but I know he wanted that laptop more than he wanted to see me."

"I'm not so sure about that," Chloe said. "He loved you like a mother."

"I know that's true," Loretta said. "He told me that more than once. Anyway, he asked if I would print out everything he had on his hard drive off his computer, you know, everything except what he called program files and all that."

"What?" Chloe asked. "His own Bible studies and sermon preparation, stuff like that?"

"I guess," Loretta said. "He told me to make sure I had plenty of paper. I thought he meant like just a ream or something."

"It's taken more than that?" Buck said.

"Oh, yes sir, much more than that. I stood there feeding that machine every two hundred pages or so until I'd finished up two reams. I'm scared to death of those computers, but Bruce talked me through how to print out everything that had a file name that began with his initials. He told me if I just typed in 'Print BB*.*' that it should spit out everything he wanted. I sure hope I did the right thing. It's given him more than he could ever want. I suppose I should just shut it down now."

"You've got a third ream going in there?" Chloe said.

"No. I got some help from Donny."

"The phone guy?" Buck said.

"Oh, Donny Moore is a whole lot more than just a phone guy," Loretta said. "There's hardly anything electronic he can't fix or make better. He showed me how I can use those old boxes of continuous-feed computer paper in our laser printer. He just hauled a box out and fed it in one end and it comes out the other so I don't have to keep feeding it."

"I didn't know you could do that," Buck said.

"Neither did I," Loretta said. "There's a lot of stuff Donny knows that I don't.

He said our printer was pretty new and fancy and should be kicking out close to fifteen pages a minute."

"And you've been doing this how long?" Chloe said.

"Just about ever since I talked to Bruce from the hospital this morning. There was probably a five- or ten-minute break after those first two reams and before Donny helped me get that big box of paper under there."

Buck slipped into the inner office and stood watching in amazement as the high-tech printer drew page after page from the paper box through its innards and out the other side into a stack that was threatening to topple. He straightened the stack and stared at the box. The first two reams of printed material, all single-spaced, lay neatly on Bruce's desk. The old paper box, the likes of which Buck hadn't seen in years, noted that it contained five thousand sheets. He guessed that it had already used 80 percent of its total. Surely, there must be some mistake. Could Bruce have produced more than five thousand pages of notes? Perhaps there was a glitch and Loretta had mistakenly printed everything, including program files, Bibles and concordances, dictionaries, and the like.

But there had been no glitch. Buck casually fanned through first one ream and then the other, looking for something other than Bruce's own notes. Every page Buck glanced at contained personal writing from Bruce. This included his own commentary on Bible passages, sermon notes, devotional thoughts, and letters to friends and relatives and churchmen from around the globe. At first Buck felt guilty, as if he were invading Bruce's privacy. And yet why had Bruce urged Loretta to print all this stuff? Was he afraid he might be gone? Had he wanted to leave it for their use?

Buck bent over the fast-rising stack of continuous-feed sheets. He lifted it from the bottom and allowed the pages to drop before his eyes one at a time. Again, page after page of single-spaced copy, all from Bruce. He must have written several pages a day for more than two years.

When Buck rejoined Chloe and Loretta, Loretta said again, "We might as well shut it off and throw the pages away. He'll have no use for all that stuff now."

Chloe had risen and now sat, looking exhausted, in a side chair. It was Buck's turn to kneel before Loretta. He placed his hands on her shoulders and spoke earnestly. "Loretta, you can still serve the Lord by serving Bruce." She began to protest, but he continued. "He's gone, yes, but we can rejoice that he's with his family again, can't we?" Loretta pressed her lips together and nodded. Buck continued. "I need your help on a big project. There's a gold mine in that room. From just glancing at those pages, I can see that Bruce is still with us. His knowledge, his teaching, his love and compassion, they are all there. The best we can do for this little flock that has lost its shepherd is to get those pages reproduced. I don't know what this place will do for a pastor or a teacher, but in the meantime, people need access to what Bruce has written. Maybe they've heard him preach it, maybe they've seen it in other forms before. But this is a treasure that everyone can use."

Chloe spoke up. "Buck, shouldn't you try to edit it or shape it into some sort of book form first?"

"I'll take a look at it, Chloe, but there's a certain beauty in simply reproducing it in the form it's in. This was Bruce off-the-cuff, in the middle of his study, writing to fellow believers, writing to friends and loved ones, writing to himself. I think Loretta ought to take all those pages to a quick-print shop and get them started. We need a thousand copies of all that stuff, printed on two sides and bound simply."

"That'll cost a fortune," Loretta said.

"Don't worry about that now," Buck said. "I can't think of a better investment."

+ + +

As the Learjet made its initial descent into the Dallas/Ft. Worth area, Fortunato ducked into the cockpit and knelt between Hernandez and Rayford. Each slipped the headphone off the ear closest to Carpathia's aide. "Anybody hungry?" he said.

Rayford hadn't even thought of food. For all he knew, the world was blowing itself to bits and no one would survive this war. The very mention of hunger, however, triggered something in him. He realized he was famished. He knew Amanda would be as well. She was a light eater, and he often had to make sure she remembered to eat.

"I could eat," Hernandez said. "In fact, I could eat a lot."

"Potentate Carpathia would like you to contact DFW tower and have something nice waiting for us."

Hernandez suddenly looked panicky. "What do you think he means by 'something nice'?"

"I'm sure you'll arrange for something appropriate, Captain Hernandez."

Fortunato backed out of the cockpit and Hernandez rolled his eyes at Rayford. "DFW tower, this is *Global Community Three*, over."

Rayford glanced back as Fortunato took his seat. Carpathia had swung around and was in deep conversation with Amanda.

+ + +

Chloe worked with Loretta in fashioning a terse, two-sentence statement that was sent out by phone to the six names at the top of the prayer chain list. Each would call others who would call others, and the news would quickly spread throughout the New Hope body. Meanwhile, Buck recorded a brief message on the answering machine that simply said: "The tragic news of Pastor Bruce's death is true. Elder Rayford Steele saw him and believes he may have died before any explosives hit the hospital. Please do not come to the church, as there will be no meetings or services or further announcements until Sunday at the regular time." Buck turned the ringer off on the phone and directed all calls to the answering machine, which soon began clicking every few minutes, as more and more parishioners called in for confirmation. Buck knew Sunday morning's meeting would be packed.

Chloe agreed to follow Loretta home and make sure she was all right while Buck was calling Donny Moore. "Donny," Buck said, "I need your advice, and I need it right away."

"Mr. Williams, sir," came Donny's characteristic staccato delivery, "advice is my middle name. And as you know, I work at home, so I can come to you or you can come to me and we can talk whenever you want."

"Donny, I'm not mobile just now, so if you could find your way clear to visiting me at the church, I'd sure appreciate it."

"I'll be right over, Mr. Williams, but could you tell me something first? Did Loretta have the phones off the hook there for a while?"

"Yes, I believe she did. She didn't have answers for people who were calling about Pastor Bruce. With nothing to tell people, she just turned off the phones."

"That's a relief," Donny said. "I just got her set up with a new system a few weeks ago, so I hope nothing was wrong. How is Bruce, by the way?"

"I'll tell you all about that when you get here, Donny, OK?"

+ + +

Rayford saw billowing black clouds over the Dallas/Ft. Worth commercial airport and thought of the many times he had landed big craft on those long runways. How long would it take to rebuild here? Captain Hernandez guided the Learjet to a nearby military strip, the one Rayford had visited so recently. He saw no other aircraft on the ground. Clearly, someone had moved all the planes to keep the strip from being a target.

Hernandez landed the Learjet as smoothly as a man can land a plane that small, and they immediately taxied to the end of the runway and directly into a large hangar. Rayford was surprised that, indeed, the rest of the hangar was empty, too. Hernandez shut down the engines, and they deplaned. As soon as Carpathia had room, he put back on his disguise. He whispered something to

Fortunato, who asked Hernandez where they would find the food. "Hangar three," Hernandez said. "We're in hangar one. The plane's in hangar four."

The disguise proved unnecessary. There was not much space between the hangars, and the small contingent moved quickly into and out of small doors at the sides of the buildings. Hangars two and three were also empty, except for a table piled with catered lunches near the side door that led to hangar four.

They approached the tables, and Carpathia turned to Rayford. "Say good-bye to Captain Hernandez," he said. "After he has eaten, he will be on assignment for me near the old National Security Agency building in Maryland. It is unlikely you will see him again. He flies only the small craft."

It was all Rayford could do to keep from shrugging. What did he care? He had just met the man. Why was it so important for Carpathia to keep him updated on personnel? He had not told Rayford of Earl Halliday's involvement in helping design a new plane. He had not told Rayford that he expected to need a new plane. He had not even sought Rayford's input about the plane he would be flying. Rayford would never understand the man.

Rayford ate ravenously and tried to encourage Amanda to eat more than usual. She did not. As the group made its last move between hangars, Rayford heard the characteristic whine of the Learjet and realized Hernandez was already airborne. Interestingly, Fortunato disappeared soon after they entered hangar four. There, standing at attention in a neat row, were four of the ten international ambassadors who represented huge land masses and populations and reported directly to Carpathia. Rayford had no idea where they had been or how they had gotten here. All he knew was that it was his job to get them all to New Babylon for emergency meetings in light of the outbreak of World War III.

At the end of the row was Earl Halliday, standing stiffly and staring straight ahead. Carpathia shook hands with each of the four ambassadors in turn and ignored Halliday, who seemed to expect that. Rayford walked directly to Halliday and stuck out his hand. Halliday ignored it and spoke under his breath. "Get away from me, Steele, you scum!"

"Earl!"

"I mean it, Rayford. I have to bring you up to speed on this plane, but I don't have to pretend to like it."

Rayford backed away, feeling awkward, and joined Amanda, who had been left alone and looked out of place herself.

"Rayford, what in the world is Earl doing here?" she asked.

"I'll tell you later. He's not happy, I can tell you that. What was Carpathia talking to you about on the plane?"

"He wanted to know what I wanted to eat, of all things. That man!"

Two aides from New Babylon entered and greeted Carpathia with embraces. One motioned for Earl and Rayford to join him in a corner of the hangar as far from the Condor 216 as they could get. Rayford had purposely avoided staring at the monstrous aircraft. Though it sat facing the door that would open to the runway and was more than 150 feet from where they stood, still the Condor seemed to dominate the hangar. Rayford had known from a glance that here was a plane that had been in development for years, not just months. It was clearly the biggest passenger plane he had ever seen, and it was painted such a brilliant white that it seemed to disappear against the light walls in the dimly lit hangar. He could only imagine how difficult it would be to spot in the sky.

Carpathia's aide, dressed just like Carpathia in a natty black suit, white shirt, and bloodred tie with a gold stickpin, leaned in close to Rayford and Earl and spoke earnestly. "Potentate Carpathia would like to be airborne as soon as possible. Can you give us an estimated time of departure?"

"I've never even seen this plane," Rayford said, "and I have no idea—"

"Rayford," Earl interrupted, "I'm telling you, you can fly this plane within half an hour. I know you; I know planes. So trust me."

"Well, that's interesting, Earl, but I won't make any promises until I've been put through the paces."

The Carpathia wannabe turned to Halliday. "Are you available to fly this plane, at least until Steele here feels he's—"

"No sir, I am not!" Halliday said. "Just let me have Steele for thirty minutes and then let me get back to Chicago."

* * *

Donny Moore proved more of a talker than Buck appreciated, but he decided feigning interest was a small price for the man's expertise. "So, you're a phone systems guy, but you sell computers—"

"On the side, right, yes sir. Just about double my income that way. Got a trunk full of catalogs, you know."

"I'd like to see those," Buck said.

Donny grinned. "I thought you might." He opened his briefcase and pulled out a stack, apparently one of each of the manufacturers he represented. He spread six out before Buck on the coffee table.

"Whoa," Buck said, "I can see already there are going to be too many choices. Why don't you just let me tell you what I'm looking for, and you tell me if you can deliver?"

"I can tell you right now I can deliver," Donny said. "Last week I sold a guy thirty sub-notebooks with more power than any desktop anywhere, and—"

"Excuse me a moment, Donny," Buck said. "Did you hear that printer quit?"

"I sure did. It just stopped now. It's either out of paper, out of ink, or done with whatever it was doing. I sold that machine to Bruce, you know. Top of the line. Prints regular paper, continuous feed—whatever you need."

"Let me just check on it," Buck said. He rose and peeked into the inner office. The screen on Bruce's laptop had already suspended itself. No warning lights on the printer told of shortages of ink or paper. Buck pushed a button on the laptop and the screen came alive. It indicated the print job was finally over. Buck guessed there were about a hundred pages left from the five-thousand-page box Loretta had run through the printer. *What a treasure,* Buck thought.

"When's Bruce gonna be back here?" Buck heard Donny ask from the other room.

* * *

Rayford and Earl boarded the Condor alone. Earl held a finger to his lips and Rayford assumed he was looking for bugs. He checked the intercom system thoroughly before speaking. "You never know," he said.

"Tell me about it," Rayford said.

"*You* tell *me* about it, Rayford!"

"Earl, I'm much more in the dark than you are. I didn't even know you were involved in this project. I had no idea you were working for Carpathia. You knew I was, so why didn't you tell me?"

"I'm not working for Carpathia, Rayford. I was pressed into service. I'm still a Pan-Con chief pilot at O'Hare, but when duty calls—"

"Why didn't Carpathia tell me he was aware of you?" Rayford said. "He asked me to find somebody to fly *Global Community One* into New York. He didn't know I would choose you."

"He must have," Earl said. "Who else would you pick? I was asked to help design this new plane, and I thought it would be fun just to test it a little bit. Then I get asked to fly the original plane to New York. Since the request came from you, I was flattered and honored. It was only when I got on the ground and realized the plane and I were targets that I got out of New York and headed back to Chicago as fast as I could. I never got there. I got word from Carpathia's people while I was in the air that I was needed in Dallas to brief you on this plane."

"I'm lost," Rayford said.

"Well, I don't know much either," Earl said. "But it's clear Carpathia wanted my going to New York and winding up dead to look like your decision, not his."

"Why would he want you dead?"

"Maybe I know too much."

"I've been flying him all over the place," Rayford said. "I have to know more than you, and yet I don't sense he's thinking about doing me in."

"Just watch your back, Rayford. I've heard enough to know this is not all what it seems to be and that this man does not have the world's best interests at heart."

There's the understatement of the ages, Rayford thought.

"I don't know how you got me into this, Rayford, but—"

"*I* got *you* into this? Earl, you have a short memory. You're the one who encouraged me to become the pilot of *Air Force One*. I wasn't looking for that job, and I certainly never dreamed it would turn into this."

"Piloting *Air Force One* was a plum assignment," Earl said, "whether you recognized that at the time or not. How was I to know what would come of it?"

"Let's stop blaming each other and decide what we're supposed to do now."

"Ray, I'm gonna bring you up to speed on this plane, but then I think I'm a dead man. Would you tell my wife that—"

"Earl, what are you talking about? Why do you think you won't make it back to Chicago?"

"I have no idea, Ray. All I know is that I was supposed to be in New York with that plane when it got obliterated. I don't see myself as any threat to the Carpathia administration, but if they cared a whit about me, they would have gotten me out of New York before I had the idea I'd better get out of there."

"Can't you get yourself some sort of emergency assignment at DFW? There has to be a huge need for Pan-Con personnel over there, in light of everything."

"Carpathia's people have arranged a ride back to Chicago for me. I just have this feeling I'm not safe."

"Tell them you don't want to put them out. Tell them you've got plenty of work to do at DFW."

"I'll try. Meanwhile, let me show you this rig. And Ray, as an old friend, I want you to promise me that if anything does happen to me—"

"Nothing is going to happen to you, Earl. But of course I'll keep in touch with your wife either way."

\+ + +

Donny Moore fell silent at the tragic news. He sat staring, eyes wide, seemingly unable to form words. Buck busied himself leafing through the catalogs. He couldn't concentrate. He knew there would be more questions. He didn't know what to tell Donny. And he needed this man's help.

Donny's voice came hoarse with emotion. "What's gonna happen to this church?"

"I know this sounds like a cliché," Buck said, "but I believe God will provide."

"How will God provide anybody like Pastor Bruce?"

"I know what you mean, Donny. Whoever it is won't be another Pastor Bruce. He was unique."

"I'm still having trouble believing it," Donny said. "But I don't guess anything should surprise me anymore."

* * *

Rayford sat behind the controls of the Condor 216. "What am I supposed to do for a first officer?" he asked Earl.

"They've got somebody on his way over from one of the other airlines. He'll fly with you as far as San Francisco, where McCullum will join you."

"McCullum? He copiloted for me from New Babylon to Washington, Earl. When I went to Chicago, he was supposed to go back to Iraq."

"I only know what I'm told, Rayford."

"And why are we flying west to go east, as Carpathia says?"

"I have no idea what's going on here, Rayford. I'm new to this. Maybe you know better than I do. The fact is, most of the war and devastation seems to be east of the Mississippi. Have you noticed that? It's almost as if it was planned. This plane was designed and built here in Dallas, but not at DFW where it might have been destroyed. It's ready for you just when you need it. As you can see it has the controls of a seven-seven-seven and yet it's a much bigger plane. If you can fly a 'seventy-seven, you can fly this. You just need to get used to the size of it. The people you need are where you need them when you need them. Figure it out, boy. None of this seems a surprise to Carpathia, does it?"

Rayford had no idea what to say. It didn't take long to catch on.

Halliday continued, "You'll fly on a straight line from Dallas to San Francisco, and my guess is you won't see any devastation from the air, and you won't be threatened from attack heading that way either. There might be militia people somewhere out west who would like to shoot rockets at Carpathia, but there are precious few people who know he's heading that way. You'll stop in San Francisco just long enough to get rid of this copilot and pick up your usual one."

* * *

Buck touched Donny's arm, as if rousing him from sleep. Donny looked at him blankly. "Mr. Williams, this has all been hard enough even with Pastor Bruce here. I don't know what we're going to do now."

"Donny," Buck said gravely, "you have an opportunity here to do something for God, and it's the greatest memorial tribute you could ever give to Bruce Barnes."

"Well then, sir, whatever it is, I want to do it."

"First, Donny, let me assure you that money is no object."

"I don't want any profit off something that will help the church and God and Bruce's memory."

"Fine. Whatever profit you build in or don't build in is up to you. I'm just telling you that I need five of the absolute best, top-of-the-line computers, as small and compact as they can be, but with as much power and memory and speed and communications abilities as you can wire into them."

"You're talking my language, Mr. Williams."

"I hope so, Donny, because I want a computer with virtually no limitations. I want to be able to take it anywhere, keep it reasonably concealed, store everything I want on it, and most of all, be able to connect with anyone anywhere without the transmission being traced. Is that doable?"

"Well, sir, I can put together something for you like those computers that scientists use in the jungle or in the desert when there's no place to plug in or hook up to."

"Yeah," Buck said. "Some of our reporters use those in remote areas. What do they have, built-in satellite dishes?"

"Believe it or not, it *is* something like that. And I can add another feature for you, too."

"What's that?"

"Videoconferencing."

"You mean I can see the person I'm talking to while I'm talking to him?"

"Yes, if he has the same technology on his machine."

"I want all of it, Donny. And I want it fast. And I need you to keep this confidential."

"Mr. Williams, these machines could run you more than twenty thousand dollars apiece."

Buck had thought money would be no object, but this was one expense he could not lay off on Carpathia. He sat back and whistled through his teeth.

3

"CALL IT A HUNCH, Rayford, but I put something in here just for you."

Rayford and Earl were finished in the cockpit. He trusted Earl. He knew that if Earl thought he could fly this thing, then he could. He still was going to insist on his and his temporary first officer's taking off, staging, and landing before he risked flying anyone else. It wouldn't have bothered Rayford to crash and kill himself along with the Antichrist, but he didn't want to be responsible for innocent lives, particularly that of his own wife.

"So, what did you do for me, Earl?"

"Just look at this," Earl said. He pointed to the button that allowed the captain to speak to the passengers.

"Captain's intercom," Rayford said. "So what?"

"Reach under your seat with your left hand and run your fingers along the side edge of the bottom of your chair," Earl said.

"I feel a button."

"I'm going to step back into the cabin now," Earl said. "You mash the normal intercom button and make an announcement. Wait for a count of three, and then push that button under your seat. Make sure your headphones are still on."

Rayford waited until Halliday had left and latched the cockpit door. Rayford got on the intercom. "Hello, hello, hey Earl yada yada yada." Rayford counted silently to himself, then pushed the button under his seat. He was amazed to hear through his earphones Earl Halliday speaking in just above a whisper. "Rayford, you can tell I'm speaking in lower than even conversational tones. If I did my job right, you can hear me plain as day from all over this plane. Every one of the speakers is also a transmitter and leads back to only your headphone jack. I wired it in such a way that it's undetectable, and this plane has been gone over by Global Community's best bug finders. If it's ever detected, I'll just tell them I thought that was what they wanted."

Rayford came hustling out of the cockpit. "Earl, you're a genius! I'm not sure what I'll hear, but it has to be an advantage to know what's going on out here."

* * *

Buck was boxing up all the pages from Bruce's printout when he heard the Range Rover in the parking lot. By the time Chloe reached the office, he had packaged pages and Bruce's computer into one huge carton. As he lugged it out, he told Chloe, "Drop me off at the Chicago bureau office, and then you'd better check with The Drake and be sure our stuff is still there. We'll want to keep that room until we find a place to live closer to here."

"I was hoping you'd say that," Chloe said. "Loretta is devastated. She's going to need a lot of help here. What are we going to do about a funeral?"

"You're going to have to help handle that, Chlo'. You'll want to check with the coroner's office, have the body delivered to a funeral home nearby here, and all that. With so many casualties, it's going to be a mess, so they'll probably be glad to know that at least one body has been claimed. We're each going to need a vehicle. I have no idea where I'll be expected to go. I can work out of the Chicago office in light of the fact that no one will be going to New York for a long time, but I can't promise I'll be around here all the time."

"Loretta, bless her heart, thought of the same thing in spite of all she's going through. She reminded me that there's a fleet of extra cars among the congregation and has been ever since the Rapture. They lend these out for just such crises as this one."

"Good," Buck said. "Let's get you fixed up with one of those. And remember, we're going to need to get this material reproduced for members of the congregation."

"You're not going to have time to go through all that, are you, Buck?"

"No, but I'm confident that anything in here will be profitable for all."

"Buck, wait a minute. There's no way we can reproduce that until someone has read all of it. There's got to be private, personal stuff in there. And you know there will be direct references to Carpathia and to the Tribulation Force. We can't risk being exposed like that."

Buck had an ego crisis. He loved this woman, but she was ten years his junior and he hated when it seemed as if she was telling him what to do, especially when she was right. As he lay the heavy box of pages and the computer in the back of the Range Rover, Chloe said, "Just entrust it to me, hon. I'll spend every day between now and Sunday poring over it line by line. By then we'll have something to share with the rest of New Hope, and we can even announce that we might have something in copied form for them within a week or so."

"When you're right, you're right. But where will you do this?"

"Loretta has offered to let us stay with her. She's got that big old house, you know."

"That would be perfect, but I hate to impose."

"Buck, we would hardly be imposing. She'll hardly know we're there. Anyway, I sense she's so lonely and beside herself with grief that she really needs us."

"You know it's unlikely I'll be there much," Buck said.

"I'm a big girl. I can take care of myself."

They were in the Range Rover now. "Then what do you need me for?" Buck said.

"I keep you around because you're cute."

"But seriously, Chloe, I'll never forgive myself if I'm in some other city or country and the war comes right here to Mt. Prospect."

"You've forgotten the shelter under the church."

"I haven't forgotten it, Chloe. I'm just praying it'll never come to that. Does anybody else know about that place except the Tribulation Force?"

"No. Not even Loretta. It's an awfully small place. If Daddy and Amanda and you and I had to stay there for any length of time, it wouldn't be much fun."

Half an hour later, Buck pulled into the Chicago area office of *Global Community Weekly* magazine. "I'm going to get us a couple of cell phones," Chloe said. "I'll call The Drake and then get down there and get our stuff. I'll also talk with Loretta about a second vehicle."

"Get five of those cell phones, Chloe, and don't scrimp."

"Five?" she said. "I don't know if Loretta would even know how to use one."

"I'm not thinking of Loretta. I just want to make sure we have a spare."

* * *

The Condor 216 was outfitted even more lavishly than *Global Community One* had been, if that was possible. No detail had been missed, and the latest communications devices had been installed. Rayford had bidden farewell to Earl Halliday, urging Earl to let him know that his home was intact and his wife was safe, as soon as he knew. "You're not going to like what's happened to our airport," Rayford had told him. "You won't be landing at O'Hare."

Rayford and his temporary copilot had irritated Carpathia by making a trial takeoff and fly-around before letting the others board the plane. Rayford was glad he had. While it was true that everything in the cockpit was identical to a 777, the bigger, heavier plane behaved more like a 747, and it took some getting used to. Now that the loaded and airborne Condor 216 was streaking toward San Francisco at thirty-three thousand feet and at more than seven hundred miles per hour, Rayford put the craft on autopilot and urged his first officer to stay alert.

"What are you going to be doing, sir?" the younger man asked.

"Just sitting here," Rayford said. "Thinking. Reading."

Rayford had cleared his flight path with an Oklahoma tower and now pushed the button to communicate with his passengers. "Potentate Carpathia and guests, this is Captain Steele. Our estimated time of arrival in San Francisco is 5:00 p.m., Pacific Standard Time. We expect clear skies and smooth flying."

Rayford sat back and pulled his earphone band toward the back of his head, as if pulling the phones off. However, they were still close enough to his ears so that he could hear and his copilot, because his own earphones were on, could not. Rayford pulled from his flight bag a book and opened it, resting it on the controls before him. He would have to remember to turn a page occasionally. He would not really be reading. He would be listening. He slipped his left hand under the seat and quietly depressed the hidden button.

The first voice he heard, clear as if she were talking to him on the phone, was Amanda's. "Yes, sir, I understand. You need not worry about me, no sir."

Now Carpathia spoke: "I trust everyone got enough to eat in Dallas. We will have an entire flight crew joining us in San Francisco, and we will be well taken care of throughout our flight to Baghdad and then on to New Babylon."

Another voice: "Baghdad?"

"Yes," Carpathia said. "I have taken the liberty of flying into Baghdad the remaining three loyal ambassadors. Our enemies might have assumed we would fly them directly into New Babylon. We will pick them up and begin our meetings on the short hop from Baghdad to New Babylon.

"Mrs. Steele, if you would excuse us—"

"Certainly," Amanda said.

"Gentlemen," Carpathia spoke more quietly now, but still clearly enough that Rayford could understand every word. Someday he would have to thank Earl Halliday on behalf of the kingdom of Christ. Earl had no interest in serving God, at least not yet, but whatever motivated him to do Rayford a favor like that, it was certainly going to benefit the enemies of the Antichrist.

Carpathia was saying: "Mr. Fortunato remained in Dallas briefly to arrange my next radio broadcast from there. I will do it from here; however, it will be patched to Dallas and broadcast, again to throw off any enemies of the Global Community. I do need him in on our talks in the night, so we will wait on the ground in San Francisco until he is able to join us. As soon as we leave the ground out of San Francisco, we will trigger both L.A. and the Bay Area."

"The Bay Area?" came a heavily accented voice.

"Yes, that is San Francisco and the Oakland area."

"What do you mean by 'trigger'?"

Carpathia's tone became grave. "'Trigger' means just what it sounds like it means," he said. "By the time we land in Baghdad, more than Washington, New York, and Chicago will have been decimated. Those are just three of the North American cities that will suffer the most. So far, only the airport and one suburb have suffered in Chicago. That will change within the hour. You already know about London. Do you gentlemen understand the significance of a one-hundred-megaton bomb?"

There was silence. Carpathia continued. "To put it in perspective, history books tell us that a twenty-megaton bomb carries more power than all those dropped in World War II, including the two that fell on Japan."

"The United States of Great Britain had to be taught," came the accented voice again.

"Indeed they did," Carpathia said. "And in North America alone, Montreal, Toronto, Mexico City, Dallas, Washington, D.C., New York, Chicago, San Francisco, and Los Angeles will become object lessons to those who would oppose us."

Rayford whipped off his earphones and unbuckled himself. He stepped through the cockpit door and made eye contact with Amanda. He motioned for her to come to him. Carpathia looked up and smiled. "Captain Steele," he greeted him, "is everything well?"

"Our flight is uneventful, sir, if that's what you're asking. That's the best kind of flight. I can't say much for what's happening on the ground, however."

"True enough," Carpathia said, suddenly sober. "I will soon address the global community with my condolences."

Rayford pulled Amanda into the galley way. "Were Buck and Chloe going to stay at The Drake again tonight?"

"There wasn't time to talk about it, Ray," she said. "I can't imagine what other choice they'd have. It sounds like they may never get back to New York."

"I'm afraid Chicago is a certain someone's next target," Rayford said.

"Oh, I can't imagine," Amanda said.

"I have to warn them."

"Do you want to risk a phone call that could be traced?" she asked.

"Saving their lives would be worth any risk."

Amanda embraced him and went back to her seat.

Rayford used his own cell phone after making sure his first officer had his own earphones on and was otherwise engaged. Reaching The Drake Hotel in Chicago, Rayford asked for the Williamses. "We have three guests named Williams," he was told. "None with the first name of Cameron or Buck or Chloe."

Rayford racked his brain. "Uh, just put me through to Mr. Katz then," he said.

"Herbert Katz?" the operator said.

"That's the one."

After a minute: "No answer, sir. Would you like to leave a message on their voice mail?"

"I would," Rayford said, "but I would also like to be sure that the message light is lit and that they are flagged down for an urgent message should they visit the front desk."

"We'll certainly do that, sir. Thank you for calling The Drake."

When the voice mail tone came on, Rayford spoke quickly. "Kids, you know who this is. Don't take the time to do anything. Get as far away from downtown Chicago as you can. Please trust me on this."

* * *

Buck had had innumerable run-ins with Verna Zee in the Chicago office. Once he felt she had overstepped her bounds and had moved too quickly into her former boss's office after Lucinda Washington disappeared in the Rapture. Then, when Buck himself was demoted for ostensibly missing the most important assignment of his life, Verna did become Chicago bureau chief and lorded it over him. Now that he was the publisher, he had been tempted to fire her. But he had let her remain, provided she did the job and kept her nose clean.

Even feisty Verna seemed shell-shocked when Buck swept into the office late that afternoon. As usual in times of international crisis, the staff was huddled around the TV. A couple of employees looked up when Buck came in. "What do you think of this, chief?" one said, and several others noticed him. Verna Zee made a beeline for Buck.

"You have several urgent messages," she said. "Carpathia himself has been trying to reach you all day. There's also an urgent message from a Rayford Steele."

Now there was a choice for all time. Whom should Buck call? He could only guess what spin Carpathia wanted to put on World War III. He had no idea what Rayford might want. "Did Mr. Steele leave a number?"

"You're returning *his* call first?"

"Excuse me?" he said. "I believe I asked you a question."

"His message was simply that you should call your hotel room."

"Call my hotel room?"

"I would have done it for you myself, boss, but I didn't know where you were staying. Where *are* you staying?"

"None of your business, Verna."

"Well, pardon me!" she said and marched away, which was Buck's hope.

"I'll be borrowing your office temporarily," Buck called after her.

She stopped and spun around. "For how long?"

"For as long as I need it," he said. She scowled.

Buck rushed in and shut the door. He dialed The Drake and asked for his own room. Hearing the fear in Rayford's voice, not to mention the message itself, made the color drain from his face. Buck called information for the number of the Land Rover dealership in Arlington Heights. He asked for the sales manager and said it was an emergency.

Within a minute, the man was on the line. As soon as Buck identified himself, the man said, "Everything all right with the—"

"The car is fine, sir. But I need to reach my wife, and she's driving it right now. I need the phone number on that built-in phone."

"That would take a little digging."

"I can't tell you how urgent this is, sir. Let me just say that it's worth my developing a quick case of buyer's remorse and returning the vehicle if I can't get that number right now."

"One moment."

A couple of minutes later Buck dialed the number. It rang four times. "The mobile customer you have dialed is either away from the vehicle or out of the calling zone. Please try your call—"

Buck slammed down the phone, picked it up, and hit the redial button. While listening to the ring, he was startled when the door burst open and Verna Zee mouthed, "Carpathia on the line for you."

"I'm gonna have to call him back!" Buck said.

"You're what?!"

"Take a number!"

"Dial 1-800-FIRED," she said.

* * *

Rayford was frantic. He forgot any pretense of doing anything but sitting there, and he stared straight ahead into the late afternoon sky, earphones firmly engaged and his left hand pressing the hidden button hard. He heard Carpathia's aide: "Well, of all the—"

"What?" Carpathia said.

"I'm trying to get this Williams character on the line for you, and he's told his girl there to take a number."

It was all Rayford could do to keep from calling Buck again himself, knowing for sure now that he was at the Chicago office. But if someone told Carpathia Buck couldn't talk to him because he was on with Rayford Steele, that would be disastrous. He heard Carpathia's reassuring voice again. "Just give him the number, my friend. I trust this young man. He is a brilliant journalist and would not keep me waiting without good reason. Of course, he is trying to cover the story of a lifetime, would you not agree?"

* * *

Buck ordered Verna Zee to shut the door on her way out and to leave him alone until he was off the phone. She sighed heavily and shook her head, slamming the door. Buck continued to hit the redial button, hating the sound of that recorded announcement more than anything he had ever heard in his life.

Suddenly the intercom came alive. "I'm sorry to bother you," Verna said in a sickly sweet, singsong voice, "but you have yet another urgent phone call. Chaim Rosenzweig from Israel."

Buck punched the intercom button. "I'm afraid I'm gonna have to call him back, too. Tell him I'm very sorry."

"You should tell *me* you're very sorry," Verna said. "I'm tempted to patch him through anyway."

"I'm very sorry, Verna," Buck said with sarcasm. "Now leave me alone, please!"

The car phone kept ringing. Buck hung up on the recorded message several times. Verna punched back in. "Dr. Rosenzweig says it's a matter of life and death, Cameron."

Buck quickly punched into the blinking line. "Chaim, I'm very sorry, but I'm in the middle of an urgent matter here myself. Can't I call you back?"

"Cameron! Please don't hang up on me! Israel has been spared the terrible bombings that your country has suffered, but Rabbi Ben-Judah's family was abducted and slaughtered! His house has burned to the ground. I pray he is safe, but no one knows where he is!"

Buck was speechless. He hung his head. "His family is gone? Are you sure?"

"It was a public spectacle, Cameron. I was afraid it would come sooner or later. Why, oh why did he have to go public with his views about Messiah? It's one thing to disagree with him, as I do, a respected and trusted friend. But the religious zealots in this country hate a person who believes that Jesus is Messiah. Cameron, he needs our help. What can we do? I have not been able to get through to Nicolae."

"Chaim, do me one huge favor and leave Nicolae out of this, please!"

"Cameron! Nicolae is the most powerful man in the world, and he has pledged to help me and to help Israel and to protect us. Surely, he will step in and preserve the life of a friend of mine!"

"Chaim, I'm begging you to trust me on this. Leave Nicolae out of it. Now I must call you back. I have family members in trouble myself!"

"Forgive me, Cameron! Get back to me as soon as you can."

Buck punched in on his original line and hit redial again. As the numbers sounded in his ear, Verna came on the intercom. "Someone's on the line for you, but since you don't want to be bothered—"

Chloe's car phone was busy! Buck slammed the phone down and punched in on the intercom. "Who is it?"

"I thought you didn't want to be bothered."

"Verna, I have no time for this!"

"If you must know, it was your wife."

"Which line?"

"Line two, but I told her you were probably on the phone with Carpathia or Rosenzweig."

"Where was she calling from?"

"I don't know. She said she would wait for your call."

"Did she leave a number?"

"Yes. It's—"

When Buck heard the first two numbers, he knew it was the car phone. He turned off the intercom and hit the redial button. Verna poked her head in the door and said, "I'm not a secretary, you know, and I'm certainly not *your* secretary!"

Buck had never been angrier with anyone. He stared at Verna. "I'm coming across this desk to kick that door shut. You had better not be in the way."

The car phone was ringing. Verna still stood there. Buck rose from his chair, phone still to his ear, and stepped up onto the desk and across Verna's mess of papers. Her eyes grew wide as he lifted his leg, and she ducked out of the way as he kicked the door shut with all his might. It sounded like a bomb and nearly toppled the wall partitions. Verna screamed. Buck almost wished she'd been in the doorway.

"Buck!" came Chloe's voice from the phone.

"Chloe! Where are you?"

"I'm on my way out of Chicago," she said. "I got the phones and went to The Drake, but there was a message for me at the desk."

"I know."

"Buck, something in Daddy's voice made me not even take the time to get anything from our room."

"Good!"

"But your laptop and all your clothes and all your toiletries and everything I brought from New York—"

"But your dad sounded serious, didn't he?"

"Yes. Oh, Buck, I'm being pulled over by the police! I made a U-turn and I was speeding, and I went through a light, and I was even on the sidewalk for a while."

"Chloe, listen! You know the old saying about how it's easier to ask forgiveness than permission?"

"You want me to try to outrun him?"

"You'll probably be saving his life! There's only one reason your father would want us out of Chicago as far and as fast as possible!"

"OK, Buck, pray for me! Here goes nothing!"

"I'll stay on the line with you, Chloe."

"I need both hands to drive!"

"Hit the speaker button and hang that phone up!" Buck said.

But then he heard an explosion, tires squealing, a scream, and silence. Within seconds the electricity went off in the *Global Community Weekly* office. Buck felt his way out into the hall where battery-operated emergency lights near the ceiling illuminated the doors. "Look at that!" someone shouted, and the staff pushed its way through the front doors and began climbing atop their own cars to watch a huge aerial attack on the city of Chicago.

* * *

Rayford clandestinely listened in horror as Carpathia announced to his compatriots, "Chicago should be under retaliatory attack, even as we speak. Thank you for your part in this, and for the strategic nonuse of radioactive fallout. I have many loyal employees in that area, and though I expect to lose some in the initial attack, I need not lose any to radiation to make my point."

Someone else spoke up. "Shall we watch the news?"

"Good idea," Carpathia said.

Rayford could remain seated no longer. He didn't know what he would say or do, if anything, but he simply could not stay in that cockpit, not knowing whether his loved ones were safe. He entered the cabin as the television was coming on, showing the first images from Chicago. Amanda gasped. Rayford went and sat with her to watch. "Would you go to Chicago for me?" Rayford whispered.

"If you think I would be safe."

"There's no radiation."

"How do you know that?"

"I'll tell you later. Just tell me you'll go if I can get permission from Carpathia to have you fly out of San Francisco."

"I'll do anything for you, Rayford. You know that."

"Listen to me, sweetheart. If you can't get an immediate flight, and I mean before this plane leaves the ground again, you must reboard the Condor. Do you understand?"

"I understand, but why?"

"I can't tell you now. Just get an immediate flight to Milwaukee if I can get it cleared. If the plane is not airborne before we are—"

"What?"

"Just be sure, Amanda. I couldn't bear losing you."

Following the news from Chicago, the cable news channel broke for a commercial, and Rayford approached Carpathia. "Sir, may I have a moment?"

"Certainly, Captain. Awful news out of Chicago, is it not?"

"Yes, sir, it is. In fact, that's what I wanted to talk to you about. You know I have family in that area."

"Yes, and I hope they are all safe," Carpathia said.

Rayford wanted to kill him where he sat. He knew full well the man was the Antichrist, and he also knew that this very person would be assassinated one day and be resurrected from the dead by Satan himself. Rayford had never dreamed he might be an agent in that assassination, but at that instant he would have applied for the job. He fought for composure. Whoever killed this man would be merely a pawn in a huge cosmic game. The assassination and resurrection would only make Carpathia more powerful and satanic than ever.

"Sir," Rayford continued, "I was wondering if it would be possible for my wife to deplane in San Francisco and head back to Chicago to check on my people."

"I would be happy to have my staff check on them," Carpathia said, "if you will simply give me their addresses."

"I would really feel a lot better if she could be there with them to help as needed."

"As you wish," Carpathia said, and it was all Rayford could do not to breathe a huge sigh of relief in the man's face.

* * *

"Who's got a cell phone I can borrow?" Buck shouted over the din in the parking lot of *Global Community Weekly*.

A woman next to him thrust one into his hands, and he was shocked to realize she was Verna Zee. "I need to make some long-distance calls," he said quickly. "Can I skip all the codes and just pay you back?"

"Don't worry about it, Cameron. Our little feud just got insignificant."

"I need to borrow a car!" Buck shouted. But it quickly became clear that everyone was heading to their own places to check on loved ones and assess the damage. "How about a ride to Mt. Prospect?"

"I'll take you," Verna muttered. "I don't even want to see what's happening in the other direction."

"You live in the city, don't you?" Buck said.

"I did until about five minutes ago," Verna said.

"Maybe you got lucky."

"Cameron, if that big blast was nuclear, none of us will last the week."

"I might know a place you can stay in Mt. Prospect," Buck said.

"I'd be grateful," she said.

Verna went back inside to gather up her stuff. Buck waited in her car, making his phone calls. He started with his own father out west. "I'm so glad you called," his father said. "I tried calling New York for hours."

"Dad, it's a mess here. I'm left with the clothes on my back, and I don't have much time to talk. I just called to make sure everybody was all right."

"Your brother and I are doing all right here," Buck's dad said. "He's still grieving the loss of his family, of course, but we're all right."

"Dad, the wheels are coming off of this country. You're not gonna really be all right until—"

"Cameron, let's not get into this again, OK? I know what you believe, and if it gives you comfort—"

"Dad! It gives me little comfort right now. It kills me that I was so late coming to the truth. I've already lost too many loved ones. I don't want to lose you too."

His father chuckled, maddening Buck. "You're not going to lose me, big boy. Nobody seems to want to even attack us out here. We feel a little neglected."

"Dad! Millions are dying. Don't be glib about this."

"So, how's that new wife of yours? Are we ever gonna get to meet her?"

"I don't know, Dad. I don't know exactly where she is right now, and I don't know whether you'll ever get the chance to meet her."

"You ashamed of your own father?"

"It's not that at all, Dad. I need to make sure she's all right, and we're going to have to try to get out that way somehow. Find a good church there, Dad. Find somebody who can explain to you what's going on."

"I can't think of anybody more qualified than you, Cameron. And you're just gonna have to let me ruminate on this myself."

4

RAYFORD HEARD Carpathia's people setting up for his broadcast. "Is there any way anyone will be able to tell we are airborne?" Carpathia asked.

"None," he was assured. Rayford wasn't so sure, but certainly, unless Carpathia made some colossal error, no one would have a clue precisely where in the air he was.

At the sound of a knock on the cockpit door, Rayford shut off the hidden button and turned expectantly. It was a Carpathia aide. "Do whatever you have to do to shut down all interference and patch us back through to Dallas. We go live on satellite in about three minutes, and the potentate should be able to be heard everywhere in the world."

Yippee, Rayford thought.

⁂

Buck was on the phone with Loretta when Verna Zee slipped behind the wheel. She slung her oversized bag onto the seat behind her, then had trouble fastening her seat belt, she was shaking so. Buck shut off the phone. "Verna, are you all right? I just talked with a woman from our church who has a room and private bath for you."

A mini traffic jam dissipated as Verna and Buck's coworkers wended their way out of the small parking lot. Headlights provided the only illumination in the area.

"Cameron, why are you doing this for me?"

"Why not? You lent me your phone."

"But I've been so awful to you."

"And I've responded in kind. I'm sorry, Verna. This is the last time in the world we should care so much about getting our own way."

Verna started the car but sat with her face in her hands. "You want me to drive?" Buck asked.

"No, just give me a minute."

Buck told her of his urgency to locate a vehicle and try to find Chloe.

"Cameron! You must be frantic!"

"Frankly, I am."

She unlatched her seat belt and reached for the door handle. "Take my car, Cameron. Do whatever you have to do."

"No," Buck said. "I'll let you lend me your car, but let's get you settled first."

"You may not have a minute to spare."

"All I can do is trust God at this point," Buck said.

He pointed Verna in the right direction. She sped to the edge of Mt. Prospect and slid up to the curb in front of Loretta's beautiful, rambling, old home. Verna did not allow Buck to even take the time to make introductions. She said, "We all know who each other is, so let's let Cameron get going."

"I arranged for a car for you," Loretta said. "It should be here in a few minutes."

"I'll take Verna's for now, but I sure appreciate it."

"Keep the phone as long as you need it," Verna said, as Loretta welcomed her.

Buck pushed the driver's seat all the way back and adjusted the mirror. He punched in the number he'd been given for Nicolae Carpathia and tried to return that call. The phone was answered by an aide. "I'll tell him you returned his call, Mr. Williams, but he's conducting an international broadcast just now. You might want to tune it in."

Buck whipped on the radio while racing toward the only route he could imagine Chloe taking to escape Chicago.

\+ \+ \+

"Ladies and gentlemen, from an unknown location, we bring you, live, Global Community Potentate Nicolae Carpathia."

Rayford swung around in his chair and propped open the cockpit door. The plane was on autopilot, and both he and his first officer sat watching as Carpathia addressed the world. The potentate looked amused as he was being introduced and winked at a couple of his ambassadors. He pretended to lick his finger and smooth his eyebrows, as if primping for his audience. The others stifled chuckles. Rayford wished he had a weapon.

On cue, Carpathia mustered his most emotional voice. "Brothers and sisters of the Global Community, I am speaking to you with the greatest heaviness of heart I have ever known. I am a man of peace who has been forced to retaliate with arms against international terrorists who would jeopardize the cause of harmony and fraternity. You may rest assured that I grieve with you over the loss of loved ones, of friends, of acquaintances. The horrible toll of civilian lives should haunt these enemies of peace for the rest of their days.

"As you know, most of the ten world regions that comprise the Global Community destroyed 90 percent of their weapon hardware. We have spent nearly the last two years breaking down, packaging, shipping, receiving, and reassembling this hardware in New Babylon. My humble prayer was that we would never have had to use it.

"However, wise counselors persuaded me to stockpile storehouses of technologically superior weapons in strategic locations around the globe. I confess I did this against my will, and my optimistic and overly positive view of the goodness of mankind has proven faulty.

"I am grateful that somehow I allowed myself to be persuaded to keep these weapons at the ready. In my wildest dreams, I never would have imagined that I would have to make the difficult decision to turn this power against enemies on a broad scale. By now you must know that two former members of the exclusive Global Community executive council have viciously and wantonly conspired to revolt against my administration, and another carelessly allowed militia forces in his region to do the same. These forces were led by the now late president of the United States of North America Gerald Fitzhugh, trained by the American militia, and supported also by secretly stored weapons from the United States of Great Britain and the formerly sovereign country of Egypt.

"While I should never have to defend my reputation as an antiwar activist, I am pleased to inform you that we have retaliated severely and with dispatch. Anywhere that Global Community weaponry was employed, it was aimed specifically at rebel military locations. I assure you that all civilian casualties and the destruction of great populated cities in North America and around the world was the work of the rebellion.

"There are no more plans for counterattacks by Global Community forces. We will respond only as necessary and pray that our enemies understand that they have no future. They cannot succeed. They will be utterly destroyed.

"I know that in a time of global war such as this, most of us live in fear and grief. I can assure you that I am with you in your grief but that my fear has been overcome by confidence that the majority of the global community is together, heart and soul, against the enemies of peace.

"As soon as I am convinced of security and safety, I will address you via satellite television and the Internet. I will communicate frequently so you know exactly what is going on and will see that we are making enormous strides toward rebuilding our world. You may rest assured that as we reconstruct and reorganize, we will enjoy the greatest prosperity and the most wonderful home this earth can afford. May we all work together for the common goal."

While Carpathia's aides and ambassadors nodded and clapped him on the back, Rayford caught Amanda's eye and resolutely shut the cockpit door.

* * *

Verna Zee's car was a junky old import. It was rattly and drafty, a four-cylinder automatic. In short, it was a dog. Buck decided to test its limits and reimburse Verna later, if necessary. He sped to the Kennedy and headed toward the Edens junction, trying to guess how far Chloe might have gotten from The Drake in heavy traffic that would now be impassable.

What he didn't know was whether she would take Lake Shore Drive (which locals referred to as the LSD) or the Kennedy. This was more her bailiwick than his, but his question soon became moot. Chicago was in flames, and most of the drivers of cars that clogged the Kennedy in both directions stood on the pavement gaping at the holocaust. Buck would have given anything to have had the Range Rover at that moment.

When he whipped Verna's little pile of junk onto the shoulder, he found he wasn't alone. Traffic laws and civility went out the window at a time like this, and there was almost as much traffic off the road as on. He had no choice. Buck had no idea whether he was destined to survive the entire seven years of the Tribulation anyway, and he could think of only one better reason to die than trying to rescue the love of his life.

Ever since he had become a believer, Buck had considered the privilege of giving his life in the service of God. In his mind, regardless of what really killed Bruce, he believed Bruce was a martyr to the cause. Risking his life in traffic may not have been as altruistic as that, but one thing he was sure of: Chloe would not have hesitated had the shoe been on the other foot.

The biggest jam-ups came at the bridge overpasses where the shoulders ended and those fighting to go around stalled traffic had to take turns picking their way through. Angry motorists rightfully tried to block their paths. Buck couldn't blame them. He would have done the same in their places.

He had stored the number of the phone in the Range Rover and continued to redial every chance he got. Every time he first heard a hint of the message "The mobile customer you have called—", he disconnected and tried again.

* * *

Just before the initial descent into San Francisco, Rayford huddled with Amanda. "I'm gonna get that door open and get you off this plane as soon as possible," he said. "I'm not going to wait for the postflight checklist or anything. Don't forget, it's imperative that whatever flight you find is off the ground before we are."

"But why, Ray?"

"Just trust me, Amanda. You know I have your best interests in mind. As soon as you can, call me on my universal cell phone and let me know Chloe and Buck are all right."

\+ + +

Buck left the expressway and picked his way through side streets for more than an hour until reaching Evanston. By the time he got to Sheridan Road along the lake, he found it barricaded but not guarded. Apparently every law enforcement officer and emergency medical technician was busy. He thought about ramming one of the construction horses, but didn't want to do that to Verna's car. He stepped out and moved the horse enough to drive through. He was going to leave the opening there, but someone hollered from an apartment, "Hey! What are you doing?"

Buck looked up and waved in the direction of the voice. "Press!" he shouted.

"All right, then! Carry on!"

To make himself look more legitimate, Buck took the time to get out of the car and replace the barrier before driving on. He saw the occasional police car with lights flashing and some uniformed men standing at side streets. Buck merely put on his emergency flashers and kept going. No one stood in his way. No one drew down on him. No one so much as shined a light at him. To Buck it seemed as if they assumed that if he had gone to the trouble of getting so deep into a prohibited area and was now proceeding with such confidence, he must be all right. He could hardly believe how clear the sailing was with all the arteries leading into Sheridan Road blocked off. The question now was what he would find on Lake Shore Drive.

\+ + +

Frustrated was too mild a word for the way Rayford felt as he landed the Condor 216 in San Francisco and taxied to a private jetway. There he sat with the unenviable task of carrying Antichrist himself wherever he wanted to go. Carpathia had just told bald-faced lies to the largest audience that had ever listened to a single radio broadcast. Rayford knew beyond doubt that shortly after take-off toward New Babylon, San Francisco would be devastated from the air the same way Chicago had been. People would die. Business and industry would crumble. Transportation centers would be destroyed, including that very airport. Rayford's first order of business was to get Amanda off that plane and out of that airport and into the Chicago area. He didn't even want to wait for the jetway to be maneuvered out to the plane. He opened the door himself and lowered the telescoping stairs to the runway. He motioned for Amanda to hurry. Carpathia made some farewell small talk as she hurried past, and Rayford was grateful that she merely thanked the man and kept moving. Ground personnel waved at Rayford and tried to get him to pull the stairs back up. He shouted, "We have one passenger who needs to make a connection!"

Rayford embraced Amanda and whispered, "I checked with the tower. There's a flight to Milwaukee leaving from a gate at the end of this corridor in less than twenty minutes. Make sure you're on it." Rayford kissed Amanda and she hurried down the steps.

He saw the ground crew waiting for him to pull the stairs back up so they could get the jetway into position. He could think of no legitimate reason to stall, so he simply ignored them, walked back into the cockpit, and began post-flight checks.

"What's going on?" his copilot asked. "I want to switch places with your guy as soon as I can."

If you only knew what you were walking into, Rayford thought. "Where are you headed tonight?"

"What possible business is that of yours?" the young man said.

Rayford shrugged. He felt like the little Dutch boy with his thumb in the dike. He couldn't save everyone. Could he save *anyone*? A Carpathia aide poked his head into the cockpit. "Captain Steele, you're being summoned by the ground crew."

"I'll handle it, sir. They'll have to wait for our postflight check. You realize that with a new plane there's a lot we need to be sure of before we attempt a trans-Pacific flight."

"Well, we've got McCullum waiting to board, and we've got a full flight crew waiting besides. We'd kind of like to have some service."

Rayford tried to sound cheery. "Safety first."

"Well, hurry it up!"

While the first officer double-checked items on his clipboard, Rayford checked with the tower on the status of the outbound flight to Milwaukee. "Behind schedule about twelve minutes, Condor 216. It shouldn't affect you."

But it will, Rayford thought.

Rayford stepped into the cabin. "Excuse me, sir, but isn't Mr. Fortunato joining us for the next leg of the flight?"

"Yes," an aide said. "He left Dallas half an hour after we did, so he shouldn't be long."

He will be if I can help it.

* * *

Buck finally hit the brick wall he knew would be inevitable. He had bounced over a couple of curbs and couldn't avoid smashing one traffic barrier where Sheridan Road jogged to meet Lake Shore Drive. All along the Drive he saw cars off the road, emergency vehicles with lights flashing, and disaster relief specialists trying to flag him down. He floored Verna Zee's little car, and no one dared step in front of him. He had most of the lanes open all the way down the Drive, but he heard people shouting, "Stop! Road closed!"

The radio told him that gridlock within the city proper had ground all fleeing traffic to a halt. One report said it had been that way since the moment of the first blast. Buck wished he had time to scan the exits that led to the beach. There were plenty of places where a Range Rover might have left the road, crashed, or been hidden. If it became clear to Chloe that she could not have made any decent time by heading to the Kennedy or the Eisenhower from The Drake, she might have tried the LSD. But as Buck got to the Michigan Avenue exit that would have taken him within sight of The Drake, he would have had to kill someone or go airborne to go any farther. The barricade that shut down Lake Shore Drive and the exit looked like something from the set of *Les Misérables*. Squad cars, ambulances, fire trucks, construction and traffic horses, caution lights, you name it, were stretched across the entire area, manned by a busy force of emergency workers. Buck came to a screeching halt, swerving and sliding about fifty feet before his right front tire blew. The car spun as emergency workers danced out of the way.

Several swore at him, and a woman police officer advanced, gun drawn. Buck started to get out, but she said, "Stay right where you are, pal!" Buck lowered the window with one hand and reached for his press credentials with the other. The policewoman would have none of that. She thrust her weapon through the window and pressed it to his temple. "Both hands where I can see 'em, scumbag!" She opened the door, and Buck executed the difficult procedure of getting out of a small car without the use of his hands. She made him lie flat on the pavement, spread-eagle.

Two other officers joined the first and roughly frisked Buck.

"Any guns, knives, needles?"

Buck went on the offensive. "Nope, just two sets of IDs."

The cops pulled a wallet out of each of his back pockets, one containing his own papers, the other the documents of the fictitious Herb Katz.

"So, which one are you, and what's the deal?"

"I'm Cameron Williams, publisher of *Global Community Weekly.* I report directly to the potentate. The phony ID is to help me get into unsympathetic countries."

A young, slender cop pulled Buck's real ID wallet from the hands of the woman officer. "Let me just have a look at this," he said with sarcasm. "If you really report to Nicolae Carpathia, you'd have level 2-A clearance, and I don't see—oops, I guess I do see level 2-A security clearance here."

The three officers huddled to peer at the unusual identification card. "You know, carrying phony 2-A security clearance is punishable by death—"

"Yes, I do."

"We aren't even going to be able to run your license plate, with the computers so jammed."

"I can tell you right now," Buck said, "that I borrowed this car from a friend named Zee. You can check that for sure before you have it junked."

"You can't leave this car here!"

"What am I gonna do with it?" Buck said. "It's worthless, it's got a flat tire, and there's no way we're gonna find help for that tonight."

"Or for the next two weeks, most likely," one of the cops said. "So, where were you goin' in such an all-fired hurry?"

"The Drake."

"Where have you been, pal? Don't you listen to the news? Most of Michigan Avenue is toast."

"Including The Drake?"

"I don't know about that, but it can't be in too good a shape by now."

"If I walk up over that rise and get onto Michigan Avenue on foot, am I gonna die of radiation poisoning?"

"Civil Defense guys tell us there's no fallout readings. That means this must have been done by the militia, trying to spare as much human life as possible. Anyway, if those bombs had been nuclear, the radiation would have traveled a lot farther than this already."

"True enough," Buck said. "Am I free to go?"

"No guarantees you'll get past the guards on Michigan Avenue."

"I'll take my chances."

"Your best bet is with that clearance card. I sure hope it's legit, for your sake."

* * *

Rayford couldn't stall the ground crew any longer, at least by merely ignoring them. He pulled the stairs in as if to receive the jetway, but did not fully move them out of the way, knowing that the jetway would never connect. Rather than stay and watch, he returned to the cockpit and busied himself. *I don't even want fuel before Amanda's plane is off the ground.*

It was a full fifteen minutes before Rayford's usual copilot switched places with his temporary one, and a full flight service crew entered the plane. Every time the ground crew radioed Rayford that they were ready to begin refueling, he told them he wasn't ready. Finally, an exasperated laborer barked into his radio, "What's the holdup up there, chief? I was told this was a VIP plane that needed fast service."

"You were told wrong. This is a cargo plane, and it's a new one. We've got a learning curve in the cockpit, plus we're switching crews. Just hold tight. Don't call us, we'll call you."

Rayford breathed a sigh of relief twenty minutes later when he discovered that Amanda's plane was en route to Milwaukee. Now he could refuel, play it by the book, and settle in for the long flight over the Pacific.

"Some plane, huh?" McCullum said as he checked out the cockpit.

"Some plane," Rayford agreed. "It's been a long day for me, Mac. I'd appreciate a good, long snooze once we get her on course."

"My pleasure, Cap. You can sleep the night away for all I care. You want me to come in and wake you for initial descent?"

"I'm not quite confident enough to leave the cockpit," Rayford said. "I'll be right here if you need me."

* * *

It suddenly hit Buck that he had taken a huge risk. It wouldn't be long before Verna Zee learned that he had, at least at one time, been a full-fledged member of New Hope Village Church. He had been so careful about not taking a leadership role there, not speaking in public, not being known to very many people. Now, one of his own employees—and a long-standing enemy at that—would have knowledge that could ruin him, even cost him his life.

He called Loretta's home on Verna's phone. "Loretta," he said, "I need to speak with Verna."

"She's quite distraught just now," Loretta said. "I hope you're prayin' for this girl."

"I certainly will," Buck said. "How are you two getting along?"

"As well as can be expected for two complete strangers," Loretta said. "I'm just tellin' her my story, as I assumed you wanted me to."

Buck was silent. Finally, he said, "Put her on, would you, Loretta?"

She did, and Buck got straight to the point. "Verna, you need a new car."

"Oh no! Cameron, what happened?"

"It's only a flat tire, Verna, but it's going to be impossible to get fixed for several days, and I don't think your car is worth worrying about."

"Well, thanks a lot!"

"How 'bout I replace it with a better car?"

"I can't argue with that," she muttered.

"I promise. Now, Verna, I'm going to abandon this vehicle. Is there anything you need out of it?"

"Nothing I can think of. There is a hairbrush I really like in the glove box."

"Verna!"

"That does seem a little trivial in light of everything."

"No documents, personal belongings, hidden money, anything like that?"

"No. Just do what you gotta do. It would be nice if I didn't get in trouble for this."

"I'll leave word with the authorities that when they get around to it they can tow this car to any junkyard and trade whatever the yard gives them for it for the towing fee."

"Cameron," Verna whispered, "this woman is one strange, old bird."

"I don't have time to discuss that with you now, Verna. But give her a chance. She's sweet. And she *is* providing shelter."

"No, you misunderstand. I'm not saying she isn't wonderful. I'm just saying she's got some really strange ideas."

As Buck scrambled over an embankment to bring Michigan Avenue into view, he fulfilled his promise to Loretta that he would pray for Verna. Exactly how to pray, he didn't know. *Either she becomes a believer, or I'm dead.*

All Buck could think of as he came into sight of the dozens of bombed-out buildings along Michigan Avenue and knew that they continued almost the entire length of the Magnificent Mile, was his experience in Israel when Russia had attacked. He could imagine the sound of the bombs and the searing heat of the flames, but in that instance the Holy Land had been miraculously delivered from damage. There was no such intervention here. He hit the redial button on Verna's phone, forgetting that he had last called Loretta, not the cell phone in the Range Rover.

When he did not get the usual recording about the "mobile customer you have called," he stood still and prayed Chloe would answer. When it was Loretta, he was speechless at first.

"Hello? Is anyone there?"

"I'm sorry, Loretta," he said. "Wrong number."

"I'm glad you called, Buck. Verna was about to call you."

"About what?"

"I'll let her tell you."

"Cameron, I called the office. A few people are still there, monitoring things and promising to lock up when they're finished. Anyway, there were a couple of phone messages for you."

"From Chloe?"

"No, I'm sorry. There was one from Dr. Rosenzweig in Israel. Another was from a man claiming to be your father-in-law. And another from a Miss White, who says she needs to be picked up at Mitchell Field in Milwaukee at midnight."

Miss White? Buck thought. *Crafty of Amanda to keep hidden how connected our little family has become.*

"Thanks, Verna. Got it."

"Cameron, how are you going to pick anyone up in Milwaukee without a vehicle?"

"I've still got a few hours to figure that out. Right now that much time seems like a luxury."

"Loretta has offered her car, provided I'm willing to drive," Verna said.

"I hope that won't be necessary," Buck said. "But I appreciate it. I'll let you know."

Buck didn't feel much like a journalist, standing in the midst of the chaos. He should have been drinking it all in, impressing it upon his brain, asking questions of people who seemed to be in charge. But no one seemed in charge. Everyone was working. And Buck didn't care whether he could translate this into a story or not. His magazine, along with every other major media outlet, was controlled, if not owned, by Nicolae Carpathia. As much as he strived to keep things objective, everything seemed to come out with the spin of the master deceiver. The worst part was, Nicolae was good at it. Of course, he had to be. It was his very nature. Buck just hated the idea that he himself was being used to spread propaganda and lies that people were eating like ice cream.

Most of all though, right now, right here, he cared about nothing but Chloe. He had allowed the thought to invade his mind that he might have lost her. He knew he would see her again at the end of the Tribulation, but would he have the will to go on without her? She had become the center of his life, around which everything else revolved. During the short time they had been together, she had proved more than he ever could have hoped for in a wife. It was true they were bound in a common cause that made them look past the insignificant and the petty, which seemed to get in so many other couples' way. But he sensed she would never have been catty or a nag anyway. She was selfless and loving. She trusted him and supported him completely. He would not stop until he found her. And until he knew for sure, he would never believe her dead.

Buck dialed the number in the Range Rover. How many dozens of times had he done this now? He knew the routine by heart. When he got a busy signal, his knees nearly buckled. Had he dialed the right number? He'd had to punch it in anew because redial would have given him Loretta's home again. He stopped dead on the sidewalk, mayhem all around him, and with fingers shaking, carefully and resolutely punched in the numbers. He pressed the phone to his ear. "The mobile customer you have called—" Buck swore and gripped Verna's phone so tightly he thought it might break. He took a step and pulled his arm back as if to fire the blasted machine into the side of a building. He followed through but hung onto the phone, realizing it would be the stupidest thing he had ever done. He shook his head at the word that had burst from his lips when that cursed recording had come on. *So, the old nature is still just under the surface.*

He was mad at himself. How, in such dire circumstances, could he have dialed the wrong number?

Though he knew he would hear that recording again and that he would hate it as never before, he couldn't keep himself from hitting the redial button yet again. Now the line was busy! Was it a malfunction? Some cruel cosmic joke? Or was somebody, somewhere, trying to use that phone?

There was no guarantee it was Chloe. It could be anyone. It could be a cop. It could be an emergency worker. It could be someone who found her wrecked Range Rover.

No, he would not allow himself to believe that. Chloe was alive. Chloe was trying to call him. But where would she call? No one was at the church. For all he knew, no one was still at the *Global Community Weekly* office. Did Chloe know Loretta's number? It would be easy enough to get. The question was whether he should try calling the places she might have called, or just keep redialing her number in hopes of catching her between calls.

✢ ✢ ✢

The senior flight attendant of a crew that was two-thirds as many people as the entire passenger list rapped on the cockpit door and opened it as Rayford taxied slowly down the runway. "Captain," she said as he lifted the headphone from his right ear, "not everyone is seated and buckled in."

"Well, I'm not going to stop," he said. "Can't you handle it?"

"The offending party, sir, is Mr. Carpathia himself."

"I don't have jurisdiction over him," Rayford said. "And neither do you."

"Federal Aviation Administration rules require that—"

"In case you haven't noticed, 'federal anything' means nothing anymore. Everything is global. And Carpathia is above global. If he doesn't want to sit down, he can stand. I've made my announcement, and you have given your instructions, right?"

"Right."

"Then you go get strapped in and let the potentate worry about himself."

"If you say so, Captain. But if this plane is as powerful as a 777, I wouldn't want to be standing when you accelerate—"

But Rayford had replaced his earphones and was getting the plane into position for takeoff. As he awaited instructions from the tower, Rayford surreptitiously slipped his left hand beneath the seat and depressed the intercom button. Someone was asking Carpathia if he didn't want to sit down. Rayford was aware of McCullum looking at him expectantly, as if he had heard something through his earphones that Rayford had not. Rayford quickly released the intercom button and heard McCullum say, "We have clearance, Cap. We can roll." Rayford could have begun gradually and slowly picked up enough speed to go airborne. But everybody enjoyed a powerful takeoff once in a while, right? He throttled up and took off down the runway with such speed and power that he and McCullum were driven back into their seats.

"Yeehah!" McCullum cried. "Ride 'em cowboy!"

Rayford had a lot to think about, and taking off for only the second time in a new aircraft, he should have remained focused on the task at hand. But he couldn't resist pressing that intercom button again and hearing what he might have done to Carpathia. In his mind's eye he pictured the man somersaulting all the way to the back of the plane, and he only wished there was a back door he could open from the cockpit.

"Oh, my goodness!" he heard over the intercom. "Potentate, are you all right?"

Rayford heard movement, as if others were trying to unstrap themselves to help Carpathia, but with the plane still hurtling down the runway, those people would be pinned in their seats by centrifugal force.

"I am all right," Carpathia insisted. "It is my own fault. I will be fine."

Rayford turned off the intercom and concentrated on his takeoff. Secretly, he hoped Carpathia had been leaning against one of the seats at the time of the initial thrust. That would have spun him around and nearly flipped him over. *Probably my last chance to inflict any justice.*

+ + +

No one paid attention to Buck anyway, but still, he didn't want to be conspicuous. He ducked around a corner and stood in the shadows, punching the redial button over and over, not wanting a second to pass between calls if Chloe was using her phone. Somehow, in the brief moment it took between hearing that busy signal and hanging up and punching redial again, his own phone rang. Buck shouted, "Hello! Chloe?" before he had even hit the receive button. His fingers were shaking so badly he nearly dropped the phone. He pushed the button and shouted, "Chloe?"

"No, Cameron, it's Verna. But I just heard from the office that Chloe tried to reach you there."

"Did somebody give her the number of this phone?"

"No. They didn't know you had my phone."

"I'm trying to call her now, Verna. The line is busy."

"Keep trying, Cameron. She didn't say where she was or how she was, but at least you know she's alive."

"Thank God for that!"

5

BUCK WANTED TO jump or shout or run somewhere, but he didn't know where to go. Knowing Chloe was alive was the best news he'd ever had, but now he wanted to act on it. He kept pushing the redial button and getting that busy signal.

Suddenly his phone rang again.

"Chloe!"

"No, sorry, Cameron, it's Verna again."

"Verna, please! I'm trying to reach Chloe!"

"Calm down, big boy. She got through to the *Weekly* office again. Now, listen up. Where are you now and where have you been?"

"I'm on Michigan Avenue near Water Tower Place, or what used to be Water Tower Place."

"How did you get there?"

"Sheridan to Lake Shore Drive."

"OK," Verna said. "Chloe told somebody in our office that she's the other way on Lake Shore Drive."

"The other way?"

"That's all I know, Cameron. You're gonna need to look off the road, lakeside, the other way from where you might expect on Lake Shore Drive."

Buck was already moving that way as he spoke. "I don't see how she could have gotten onto the lakeside if she was heading south on the Drive."

"I don't know either," Verna said. "Maybe she was hoping to go around everything by heading that way, saw that she couldn't, and popped a U-turn."

"Tell anybody who hears from her that she should stay off the phone until I can connect. She's gonna have to direct me right to her, if possible."

* * *

Any remaining doubts Rayford Steele had about the incredible and instant evil power that Nicolae Carpathia wielded were eradicated a few minutes after the Condor 216 left the ground at San Francisco International. Through the privately bugged intercom he heard one of Carpathia's aides ask, "Now, sir, on San Francisco?"

"Trigger," came the whispered reply.

The aide, obviously speaking into a phone, said simply, "It's a go."

"Look out the window on that side," Carpathia said, the excitement obvious in his voice. "Look at that!"

Rayford was tempted to turn the plane so he could see too, but this was something he would rather try to forget than have visually burned into his memory. He and McCullum looked at each other as their earphones came alive with startled cries from the control tower. "Mayday! Mayday! We're being attacked from the air!" The concussions knocked out communications, but Rayford knew the bombs themselves would easily take out that whole tower, not to mention the rest of the airport and who knew what portion of the surrounding area.

Rayford didn't know how much longer he could take being the devil's own pilot.

* * *

Buck was in reasonably good shape for a man in his early thirties, but now his joints ached and his lungs pleaded for air as he sprinted to Chicago Avenue and headed east toward the lake. How far south might Chloe have gotten before turning around? She had to turn around. Otherwise, how could she have gone off the road and wound up on that side?

When he finally got to the Drive, he found it empty. He knew it was barricaded from the north at the Michigan Avenue exit. It had to have been blocked from the far south end too. Gasping, he hurdled the guardrail, jogged to the middle, heard the clicking of meaningless traffic lights, and raced across to the other side. He jogged south, knowing Chloe was alive but not knowing what he might find. The biggest question now, assuming Chloe didn't have some life-threatening injury, was whether those printouts of Bruce's personal commentaries—or worse, the computer itself—might have fallen into the wrong hands. Surely, parts of that narrative were quite clear about Bruce's belief that Nicolae Carpathia was Antichrist.

Buck didn't know how he was able to put one foot in front of the other, but on he ran, pushing redial and holding the phone to his ear as he went. When he could go no further, he slumped into the sand and leaned back against the outside of the guardrail, gasping. Finally, Chloe answered her phone.

Having not planned what to say, Buck found himself majoring on the majors. "Are you all right? Are you hurt? Where are you?" He hadn't told her he loved her or that he was scared to death about her or that he was glad she was alive. He would assume she knew that until he could tell her later.

She sounded weak. "Buck," she said, "where are you?"

"I'm heading south on Lake Shore Drive, south of Chicago Avenue."

"Thank God," she said. "I'm guessing you've got about another mile to go."

"Are you hurt?"

"I'm afraid I am, Buck," she said. "I don't know how long I was unconscious. I'm not even sure how I got where I am."

"Which is where, exactly?"

Buck had risen and was walking quickly. There was no running left in him, despite his fear that she might be bleeding or in shock.

"I'm in the strangest place," she said, and he sensed her fading. He knew she had to still be in the vehicle because that phone was not removable. "The airbag deployed," she added.

"Is the Rover still driveable?"

"I have no idea, Buck."

"Chloe, you're gonna have to tell me what I'm looking for. Are you out in the open? Did you elude that cop?"

"Buck, the Range Rover seems to be stuck between a tree and a concrete abutment."

"What?"

"I was doing about sixty," she said, "when I thought I saw an exit ramp. I took it, and that's when I heard the bomb go off."

"The bomb?"

"Yes, Buck, surely you know a bomb exploded in Chicago."

One bomb? Buck thought. *Maybe it was merciful she was out for all the bombs that followed.*

"Anyway, I saw the squad car pass me. Maybe he wasn't after me after all. All the traffic on Lake Shore Drive stopped when they saw and heard the bomb, and the cop slammed into someone. I hope he's all right. I hope he doesn't die. I'll feel responsible."

"So, where did you wind up then, Chloe?"

"Well, I guess what I thought was an exit wasn't really an exit. I never hit the brake, but I did take my foot off the gas. The Range Rover was in the air for a few seconds. I felt like I was floating for a hundred feet or so. There's some sort of a dropoff next to me, and I landed on the tops of some trees and turned sideways. The next thing I knew, I woke up and I was alone here."

"Where?" Buck was exasperated, but he certainly couldn't blame Chloe for not being more specific.

"Nobody saw me, Buck," she said dreamily. "Something must have turned my lights off. I'm stuck in the front seat, kind of hanging here by the seat belt. I can reach the rearview mirror, and all I saw was traffic all racing away and then no more traffic. No more emergency lights, no nothing."

"There's nobody around you?"

"Nobody. I had to turn the car off and then back on to get the phone to turn on. I was just praying you'd come looking for me, Buck."

She sounded as if she were about to fall asleep. "Just stay on the line with me, Chloe. Don't talk, just keep the line open so I can be sure I don't miss you."

The only lights Buck saw were emergency flashers far in the distance toward the inner city, fires still blazing here and there, and a few tiny lights from the boats on the lake. Lake Shore Drive was dark as midnight. All the streetlights were out north of where he had seen the traffic light flashing. He came around a long bend and squinted into the distance. From the faint light of the moon he thought he saw a torn up stretch of guardrail, some trees, and a concrete abutment, one of those that formed an underpass to get to the beach. He moved slowly forward and then stopped to stare. He guessed he was two hundred yards from the spot. "Chloe?" he said into the phone.

No response.

"Chloe? Are you there?"

He heard a sigh. "I'm here, Buck. But I don't feel so good."

"Can you reach your lights?"

"I can try."

"Do. Just don't hurt yourself."

"I'll try to pull myself up that way by the steering wheel."

Buck heard her groan painfully. Suddenly in the distance, he saw the crazy, vertical angle of headlights shining out onto the sand.

"I see you, Chloe. Hang on."

* * *

Rayford assumed that McCullum assumed that Rayford was sleeping. He was slouched in his pilot's chair, chin to his chest, breathing evenly. But his headphones were on, and his left hand had depressed the intercom receiver. Carpathia was talking in low tones, thinking he was keeping his secrets from the flight crew.

"I was so excited and so full of ideas," the potentate said, "that I could not stay seated. I hope I do not have a bruise to show for it." His lackeys all roared with laughter.

Nothing funnier than the boss's joke, Rayford thought.

"We have so much to talk about, so much to do," Carpathia continued. "When our compatriots join us in Baghdad, we will get right to work."

The destruction of the San Francisco airport and much of the Bay Area had already made the news. Rayford saw the fear in McCullum's eyes. Maybe the man would have felt more confident had he known that his ultimate boss, Nicolae Carpathia, had most everything under control for the next few years.

Suddenly Rayford heard the unmistakable voice of Leon Fortunato. "Potentate," he whispered, "we'll need replacements for Hernandez, Halliday, and your fiancée, will we not?"

Rayford sat up. Was it possible? Had they already eliminated those three, and why Hattie Durham? He felt responsible that his former senior flight attendant was now not only in Carpathia's employ, but was also his lover and the soon-to-be mother of his child. So, was he not going to marry her? Did he not want a child? He had put on such a good front before Rayford and Amanda when Hattie had announced the news.

Carpathia chuckled. "Please do not put Ms. Durham in the same category as our late friends. Hernandez was expendable. Halliday was a temporary necessity. Let us replace Hernandez and not worry about replacing Halliday. He served a purpose. The only reason I asked you to replace Hattie is that the job has passed her by. I knew that her clerical skills were suspect when I brought her on. I needed an assistant, and of course I wanted her. But I will use the excuse of her pregnancy to get her out of the office."

"Did you want me to handle that for you?" Fortunato said.

"I will tell her myself, if that is what you mean," Carpathia said. "I would like you to handle finding new secretarial personnel."

Rayford fought for composure. He did not want to give anything away to McCullum. No one could ever know Rayford could hear those conversations. But now he was hearing things he never wanted to hear. Maybe there was some advantage to knowing this stuff, and perhaps it might be useful to the Tribulation Force. But life had become so cheap that in a matter of hours he had lost a new acquaintance, Hernandez, and a dear old mentor and friend, Earl Halliday. He had promised Earl he would communicate with Earl's wife should anything happen. He did not look forward to that.

Rayford shut off the intercom. He flipped the switch that allowed him to speak to his first officer through the headphones. "I think I *will* take a break in my quarters," he said. McCullum nodded, and Rayford made his way out of the cockpit and into his chamber, which was even more lavishly appointed than his area on the now-destroyed *Global Community One*. Rayford removed his shoes and stretched out on his back. He thought about Earl. He thought about Amanda. He thought about Chloe and Buck. And he worried. And it all started with the loss of Bruce. Rayford turned on his side and buried his face in his hands and wept. How many close to him might he lose today alone?

* * *

The Range Rover was lodged between the trunk and lower branches of a large tree and the concrete abutment. "Turn those lights off, hon!" Buck called out. "Let's not draw attention to ourselves now."

The wheels of the vehicle pressed almost flat against the wall, and Buck was amazed that the tree could sustain the weight. Buck had to climb into the tree to look down through the driver's-side window. "Can you reach the ignition?" he asked.

"Yes, I had to turn the car off because the wheels were spinning against the wall."

"Just turn the key halfway and lower the window so I can help you."

Chloe seemed to be dangling from the seat belt. "I'm not sure I can reach the window button on that side."

"Can you unlatch your seat belt without hurting yourself?"

"I'll try, Buck, but I hurt all over. I'm not sure what's broken and what isn't."

"Try to brace yourself somehow and get loose of that thing. Then you can stand on the passenger's-side window and lower this one." But Chloe was so hopelessly entangled in the strap that it was all she could do to swing her body around and turn the ignition switch halfway. She pulled herself up with her right hand to reach the window button. When the window was open, Buck reached down with both hands to try to support her. "I was so worried about you," he said.

"I was worried about me too," Chloe said. "I think I took all the damage to my left side. I think my ankle's broken, my wrist is sprained, and I feel pain in my left knee and shoulder."

"Makes sense, from the looks of things," Buck said. "Does it hurt if I hold you this way so you can put your good foot down on the passenger's-side window?"

Buck lay across the side of the nearly upended Range Rover and reached way down in to put one forearm under Chloe's right arm and grab her waistband at the back with the other. He lifted as she pushed the seat belt button. She was petite, but with no foundation or way to brace himself it was all Buck could do to keep from dropping her. She moved her feet out from under the dashboard and stood gingerly. Her feet were on the passenger's-side door, and her head now was near the steering wheel.

"You're not bleeding anywhere?"

"I don't think so."

"I hope you're not bleeding internally."

"Buck, I'm sure I'd be long gone by now if I were bleeding internally."

"So you're basically all right if I can get you out of there?"

"I really want out of here in a bad way, Buck. Can we get that door open, and can you help me climb?"

"I just have one question for you first. Is this how our married life is going to be? I'm going to buy you expensive cars, and you're going to ruin them the first day?"

"Normally that would be funny—"

"Sorry."

Buck directed Chloe to use her good foot as a base and her good arm to push as he pulled open the door. The bottom of the door scraped on the abutment, and Buck was struck with how relatively little other damage there was to the vehicle, from what he could see in the dim light. "There should be a flashlight in the glove box," he said. Chloe handed it up to him. He looked all around the vehicle. The tires were still good. There was some damage to the front grille, but nothing substantial. He turned off the flashlight and slid it into his pocket. With much groaning and whimpering, Chloe came climbing out of the car, with Buck's help.

As they both sat on the upturned driver's side, Buck felt the heavy machine moving in its precarious position.

"We have to get you down from here," he said.

"Let me see that flashlight for a second," Chloe said. She shined it above her. "It would be easier to go two feet up to the top of the abutment," she said.

"You're right," he said. "Can you make it?"

"I think I can," she said. "I'm the little engine who could."

"Tell me about it."

Chloe hopped to where she could reach the top of the wall with her good hand, and she asked Buck to push until she had most of her weight atop the wall. When she made the last thrust with her good leg, the Range Rover shifted just enough to loosen itself from the wickedly bent tree branches. The tree and the Range Rover shuddered and began to move. "Buck! Get out of there! You're going to be crushed!"

Buck was spread-eagled on the side of the Range Rover that had been facing up. Now it was shifting toward the abutment, the tires scraping and leaving huge marks on the concrete. The more Buck tried to move, the faster the vehicle shifted, and he realized he had to stay clear of that wall to survive. He grabbed the luggage rack as it moved toward him and pulled himself to the actual top of the Range Rover. Branches snapped free from under the vehicle and smacked him in the head, scraping across his ear. The more the car moved, the more it seemed to want to move, and to Buck that was good news—provided he could keep from falling. First the car moved, then the tree moved, then both seemed to readjust themselves at once. Buck guessed that the Range Rover, once free of the pressure from the branches, had about three feet to drop to the ground. He only hoped it would land flat. It didn't.

The heavy vehicle, left tires pressed against the concrete and several deeply bowed branches pushing it from the right side, began slipping to the right. Buck buried his head in his hands to avoid the springing out of those branches as the Range Rover fell clear of them. They nearly knocked him into the wall again. Once the Range Rover was free of the pressure of the branches, it lurched down onto its right side tires and nearly toppled. Had it rolled that way, it would have crushed him into the tree. But as soon as those tires hit the ground, the whole thing bounced and lurched, and the left tires landed just free of the concrete. The momentum made the left side of the vehicle smash into the concrete, and finally it came to rest. Less than an inch separated the vehicle from the wall now, but there the thing sat on uneven ground. Damaged branches hung above it. Buck used the flashlight to illuminate the violated car. Except for the damage to the front grille and the scrapes on both sides, one from concrete and one from tree branches, the car looked little the worse for wear.

Buck had no idea how to reset an airbag, so he decided to cut it off and worry about that later if he could get the Range Rover to run. His side ached, and he was certain he had cracked a rib when the Rover had finally hit bottom. He gingerly climbed down and stood under the tree, the branches now blocking his view of Chloe.

"Buck? Are you all right?"

"Stay right where you are, Chloe. I'm gonna try something."

Buck climbed in the passenger side, strapped himself behind the wheel, and started the engine. It sounded perfect. He carefully watched the gauges to make sure nothing was empty, dry, or overheated. The Rover was in automatic and four-wheel drive. When he tried to go forward it seemed he was in a rut. He quickly switched to stick shift and all-wheel drive, gunned the engine, and popped the clutch. Within seconds he was free of the tree and out onto the sand. He took a sharp right and moved back up next to the guardrail that separated the sand from Lake Shore Drive. He drove about a quarter of a mile until he found a spot he could slip through the guardrail and turn around. He headed back up toward the overpass where Chloe stood, favoring one foot and holding her left wrist in her other hand. To Buck she had never looked better.

He pulled up next to her and ran around to help her into the car. He fastened her seat belt and was on the phone before he got back into the car. "Loretta? Chloe is safe. She's banged up a little, and I'd like to get her checked out as soon as possible. If you could call around and find any doctor in the church who has not been pressed into service, I'd sure appreciate it."

Buck tried to drive carefully so as not to exacerbate Chloe's pain. However, he knew the shortest way home. When he got to the huge barrier at Michigan Avenue on the LSD, he swung left and went up over the embankment he had previously walked. He saw Verna's now deceased automobile and ignored the waves and warnings of the cops he had talked to not so long ago. He sped up Lake Shore Drive, went around the barriers at Sheridan, followed Chloe's directions to Dempster, and was soon back into the northwest suburbs.

Loretta and Verna were watching from the window as he pulled into the drive. Only then did he smack himself in the head and remember. He jumped out of the car and raced around to the back. Fumbling with the keys, he opened the back latch and found, strewn all over, Bruce's pages. The computer was there too, along with the phones Chloe had bought. "Chloe," he said, and she turned gingerly. "As soon as we get you inside, I'd better get back to Carpathia."

* * *

Rayford was back in the cockpit. As the night wore on, the cabin grew more and more quiet. The conversation deteriorated into small talk. The dignitaries were well fed by the crew, and Rayford got the impression they were settling in for the long haul.

Rayford awakened with a start and realized his finger had slipped off the intercom button. He pressed it again and still heard nothing. He had heard more than he wanted to hear already anyway. He decided to stretch his legs.

As he walked back through the main cabin to watch one of the televisions in the back of the plane, everyone except Carpathia ignored him. Some dozed and some were being attended to by the flight crew, who were clearing trays and finding blankets and pillows.

Carpathia nodded and smiled and waved to Rayford.

How can he do that? Rayford wondered. *Bruce said the Antichrist would not be indwelt by Satan himself until halfway into the Tribulation, but surely this man is the embodiment of evil.*

Rayford could not let on that he knew the truth, despite the fact that Carpathia was well aware of his Christian beliefs. Rayford merely nodded and walked on. On television he saw live reports from around the world. Scripture had come to life. This was the Red Horse of the Apocalypse. Next would come more death by famine and plagues until a quarter of the population of the earth that remained after the Rapture was wiped out. His universal cell phone vibrated in his pocket. Few people not on that plane knew his number. *Thank God for technology,* he thought. He didn't want anyone to hear him. He slipped deeper into the back of the plane and stood near a window. The night was as black as Carpathia's soul.

"This is Rayford Steele," he said.

"Daddy?"

"Chloe! Thank God! Chloe, are you all right?"

"I had a little car accident, Dad. I just wanted you to know that you saved my life again."

"What do you mean?"

"I got that message you left at The Drake," she said. "If I had taken the time to go to our room, I probably wouldn't be here."

"And Buck's OK?"

"He's fine. He's late returning a call to you-know-who, so he's trying to do that right now."

"Let me excuse myself, then," Rayford said. "I'll get back to you."

Rayford strode back to the cockpit, trying not to appear in a hurry. As he passed Fortunato, Leon was handing a phone to Carpathia. "Williams from Chicago," he said. "It's about time."

Carpathia made a face as if he felt Leon was overreacting. As Rayford reached the cockpit, he heard Carpathia exalt, "Cameron, my friend! I have been worried about you."

Rayford quickly settled in and set his earphones. McCullum looked at him expectantly, but Rayford ignored him and closed his eyes, pressing the secret button.

"I am curious about coverage," Carpathia was saying. "What is happening there in Chicago? Yes—yes—devastation, I understand—yes. Yes, a tragedy—"

Sickening, Rayford thought.

"Cameron," Carpathia said, "would it be possible for you to get to New Babylon within the next few days? Ah, I see—Israel? Yes, I see the wisdom of that. The so-called holy lands were spared again, were they not? I would like pooled coverage of high-level meetings in Baghdad and New Babylon. I would like to have your pen on it, but Steve Plank, your old friend, can run the point. You and he can work together to see that the appropriate coverage is carried in all our print media. . . ."

Rayford would be eager to talk to Buck. He admired his son-in-law's moxie and ability to set his own agenda and even gracefully decline suggested directives from Carpathia. Rayford wondered how long Carpathia would stand for that. For now, he apparently respected Buck enough and was, Rayford hoped, still unaware of Buck's true loyalties.

"Well," Carpathia was saying, "of course I am grieving. You will keep in touch then, and I will hear from you from Israel."

6

BUCK SAT BLEARY-EYED at the breakfast table, his ear stinging and his rib cage tender. Only he and Loretta were up. She was heading to the church office after having been assured she would not have to handle the arrangements for Bruce's body or for the memorial service, which would be part of Sunday morning's agenda. Verna Zee was asleep in a small bedroom in the finished basement. "It feels so good to have people in this place again," Loretta said. "Y'all can stay as long as you need to or want to."

"We're grateful," Buck said. "Amanda may sleep till noon, but then she'll get right on those arrangements with the coroner's office. Chloe didn't sleep much with that ankle cast. She's dead to the world now, though, so I expect her to sleep a long time."

Buck had used the dining-room table to put back in order all the pages from Bruce's transcripts that had been strewn throughout the back of the Range Rover. He had a huge job ahead of him, checking the text and determining what would be best for reproduction and distribution. He set the stacks to one side and laid out the five deluxe universal cell phones Chloe had bought. Fortunately, they had been packed in spongy foam and had survived her accident.

He had told her not to scrimp, and she certainly hadn't. He didn't even want to guess the total price, but these phones had everything, including the ability to take calls anywhere in the world, due to a built-in satellite chip.

After Loretta left for the church, Buck rummaged for batteries, then quickly taught himself the basics from the instruction manual and tried his first phone call. For once, he was glad he had always been manic about hanging onto old phone numbers. Deep in his wallet was just the one he needed. Ken Ritz, a former commercial pilot and now owner of his own jet charter service, had bailed out Buck before. He was the one who had flown Buck from a tiny airstrip in Waukegan, Illinois, to New York the day after the vanishings. "I know you're busy, Mr. Ritz, and probably don't need my business," Buck said, "but you also know I'm on a big, fat expense account and can pay more than anyone else."

"I'm down to one jet," Ritz said. "It's at Palwaukee, and right now both it and I are available. I'm charging two bucks a mile and a thousand dollars a day for down time. Where do you want to go?"

"Israel," Buck said. "And I have to be back here by Saturday night at the latest."

"Jet lag city," Ritz said. "It's best to fly that way early evening and land there the next day. Meet me at Palwaukee at seven, and we've got a deal."

+ + +

Rayford had finally fallen off to sleep for real, snoring, according to McCullum, for several hours.

About an hour outside Baghdad, Leon Fortunato entered the cockpit and knelt next to Rayford. "We're not entirely sure of security in New Babylon," he said. "No one expects us to land in Baghdad. Let's keep maintaining with the New Babylon tower that we're on our way directly there. When we pick up our other three ambassadors, we may just stay on the ground for a few hours until our security forces have had a chance to clear New Babylon."

"Will that affect your meetings?" Rayford said, trying to sound casual.

"I don't see how it concerns you one way or the other. We can easily meet on the plane while it is being refueled. You can keep the air-conditioning on, right?"

"Sure," Rayford said, trying to think quickly, "there is still a lot I'd like to teach myself about this craft. I'll stay in the cockpit or in my quarters and keep out of your way."

"See that you do."

+ + +

Buck checked in with Donny Moore, who said he had found some incredible deals on individual components and was putting together the five mega-laptops himself. "That'll save you a little money," he said. "Just a little over twenty thousand apiece, I figure."

"And I can have these when I get back from a trip, on Sunday?"

"Guaranteed, sir."

Buck told key people at *Global Community Weekly* his new universal cell phone number and asked that they keep it confidential except from Carpathia, Plank, and Rosenzweig. Buck carefully packed his one big, leather shoulder bag and spent the rest of the day working on Bruce's transcripts and trying to reach Rosenzweig. The old man had seemed to be trying to tell him, not in so many words, that he knew Dr. Ben-Judah was alive and safe somewhere. He just hoped Rosenzweig had followed his advice and was keeping Carpathia out of the picture. Buck had no idea where Tsion Ben-Judah might be hiding out. But if Rosenzweig knew, Buck wanted to talk with him before he and Ken Ritz hit the ground at Ben Gurion Airport.

How long, he wondered, before he and his loved ones would be hiding out in the shelter under the church?

* * *

Security was tight at Baghdad. Rayford had been instructed not to communicate with the tower there so as not to allow enemy aircraft to know where they were. Rayford was convinced that the retaliatory strikes by Global Community forces in London and Cairo, not to mention North America, would have kept all but the suicidal out of Iraq. However, he did what he was told.

Leon Fortunato communicated by phone with both Baghdad and New Babylon towers. Rayford phoned ahead to be sure there was a place he and McCullum could stretch their legs and relax inside the terminal. Despite his years of flying, there came certain points even for him when he became claustrophobic aboard a plane.

A ring of heavily armed GC soldiers surrounded the plane as it slowly rolled to a stop at the most secure end of the Baghdad terminal. The six-member crew of stewards and flight attendants were the first to get off. Fortunato waited until Rayford and McCullum had run through their postflight checklist. He got off with them. "Captain Steele," he said, "I will be bringing the three other ambassadors back on board within the hour."

"And when would you like to leave for New Babylon?"

"Probably not for another four hours or so."

"International aviation rules prohibit me from flying again for twenty-four hours."

"Nonsense," Fortunato said. "How do you feel?"

"Exhausted."

"Nevertheless, you're the only one qualified to fly this plane, and you'll be flying it when we say you'll be flying it."

"So international aviation rules go out the window?"

"Steele, you know that international rules on everything are embodied in the man sitting on that plane. When he wants to go to New Babylon, you'll fly him to New Babylon. Understood?"

"And if I refuse?"

"Don't be silly."

"Let me remind you, Leon, that once I've gotten a break, I'll want to be on that plane, familiarizing myself with all its details."

"Yeah, yeah, I know. Just stay out of our way. And I would appreciate it if you would refer to me as Mr. Fortunato."

"That means a lot to you, does it, Leon?"

"Don't push me, Steele."

As they entered the terminal, Rayford said, "As I am the only one who can fly that plane, I would appreciate it if you would call me Captain Steele."

* * *

Late in the afternoon, Chicago time, Buck broke from the fascinating reading of Bruce Barnes's writing and finally got through to Chaim Rosenzweig.

"Cameron! I have finally talked live with our mutual friend. Let us not mention his name on the phone. He did not speak to me long, but he sounded so empty and hollow that it moved me to my very soul. It was a strange message, Cameron. He simply said that you would know whom to talk with about his whereabouts."

"That *I* would know?"

"That's what he said, Cameron. That you would know. Do you suppose he means N.C.?"

"No! No! Chaim, I'm still praying you're keeping him out of this."

"I am, Cameron, but it is not easy! Who else can intercede for the life of my friend? I am frantic that the worst will happen, and I will feel responsible."

"I'm coming there. Can you arrange a car for me?"

"Our mutual friend's car and driver are available, but dare I trust him?"

"Do you think he had anything to do with the trouble?"

"I should think he had more to do with getting our friend to safety."

"Then he is probably in danger," Buck said.

"Oh, I hope not," Rosenzweig said. "Anyway, I will meet you at the airport myself. Somehow we will get you where you need to go. Can I arrange a room for you somewhere?"

"You know where I've always stayed," Buck said, "but I think I'd better stay somewhere else this time."

"Very well, Cameron. There's a nice hotel within driving distance of your usual, and I am known there."

* * *

Rayford stretched and stood watching the Cable News Network/Global Community Network television broadcast originating in Atlanta and beamed throughout the world. It was clear Carpathia had completely effected his will and spin onto the news directors at every venue. While the stories carried the horrifying pictures of war, bloodshed, injury, and death, each also spoke glowingly of the swift and decisive action of the potentate in responding to the crisis and crushing the rebellion. Water supplies had been contaminated, power was out in many areas, millions were instantly homeless.

Rayford noticed activity outside the terminal. A dolly carrying television equipment, including a camera, were wheeled toward the Condor 216. Soon enough, CNN/GCN announced the impending live television broadcast from Potentate Carpathia at an unknown location. Rayford shook his head and went to a desk in the corner, where he found stationery from a Middle Eastern airline and began composing a letter to Earl Halliday's wife.

Logic told Rayford he should not feel responsible. Apparently Halliday had been cooperating with Carpathia and his people on the Condor 216 long before Rayford was even aware of it. However, there would be no way Mrs. Halliday would know or understand anything except that it appeared Rayford had led his old friend and boss directly to his death. Rayford didn't even know yet how Earl had been killed. Perhaps everyone on his flight to Glenview had perished. All he knew was that the deed had been done, and Earl Halliday was no more. As he sat trying to compose a letter with words that could never be right, he felt a huge, dark cloud of depression begin to settle on him. He missed his wife. He missed his daughter. He grieved over his pastor. He mourned the loss of friends and acquaintances, new and old. How had it come to this?

Rayford knew he was not responsible for what Nicolae Carpathia meted out against his enemies. The terrible, dark judgment on the earth rendered by this evil man would not stop if Rayford merely quit his job. Hundreds of pilots could fly this plane. He himself had learned in half an hour. He didn't need the job, didn't want the job, didn't ask for the job. Somehow, he knew God had placed him there. For what? Was this surprising bugging of the intercom system by Earl Halliday a gift directly from God that allowed Rayford to somehow protect a few from the wrath of Carpathia?

Already he believed it had saved his daughter and son-in-law from certain death in the Chicago bombings, and now, as he looked at television reports from America's West Coast, he wished there had been something he could have done to have warned people in San Francisco and Los Angeles of their impending doom. He was fighting an uphill battle, and in himself he didn't have the strength to carry on.

He finished the brief note of condolence and regret to Mrs. Halliday, lowered his head to his arms on the desk, felt a lump in his throat, but was unable to produce tears. He knew he could cry twenty-four hours a day from now until the end of the Tribulation, when his pastor had promised that Christ would return yet again in what Bruce had called "the Glorious Appearing." How he longed for that day! Would he or his loved ones survive to see it, or would they be "tribulation martyrs," as Bruce had been? At times like this Rayford wished for some quick, painless death that would take him directly to heaven to be with Christ. It was selfish, he knew. He wouldn't really want to leave those he loved and who loved him, but the prospect of five more years of this was nearly unbearable.

And now came a brief address from Global Community Potentate Nicolae Carpathia. Rayford knew he was sitting within two hundred feet of the man, and yet he watched it on television, as did millions of others across the globe.

+ + +

It was nearly time for Buck to head for Palwaukee Airport. Verna Zee was back at the *Global Community Weekly* office with the new (to her) used car Buck had promised to buy her from the fleet of leftovers from New Hope. Loretta was at the church office fielding the constant phone calls about Sunday's memorial service. Chloe hobbled around on a cane, needing crutches but unable to manage them with her sprained wrist in a sling. That left Amanda to take Buck to the airport.

"I want to ride along," Chloe said.

"Are you sure you're up to it, hon?" Buck said.

Chloe's voice was quavery. "Buck, I hate to say it, but in this day and age we never know when we might or might not ever see each other again."

"You're being a little maudlin, aren't you?" he said.

"Buck!" Amanda said in a scolding tone. "You cater to her feelings now. I had to kiss my husband good-bye in front of the Antichrist. You think that gives me confidence about whether I'll ever see *him* again?"

Buck was properly chastised. "Let's go," he said. He jogged out to the Range Rover and swung his bag into the back, returning quickly to help Chloe to the car. Amanda sat in the backseat and would drive Chloe home later.

Buck was amazed that the built-in TV had survived Chloe's crash. He was not in a position to see it, but he listened as Amanda and Chloe watched. Nicolae Carpathia, in his usual overly humble manner, was holding forth:

"Make no mistake, my brothers and sisters, there will be many dark days ahead. It will take tremendous resources to begin the rebuilding process, but because of the generosity of the seven loyal global regions and with the support of those citizens in the other three areas who were loyal to the Global Community and not to the insurrectionists, we are amassing the largest relief fund in the history of mankind. This will be administered to needy nations from New Babylon and the Global Community headquarters under my personal supervision. With the chaos that has resulted from this most sinister and unwise rebellion, local efforts to rebuild and care for the displaced will likely be thwarted by opportunists and looters. The relief effort carried out under the auspices of the Global Community will be handled in a swift and generous way that will allow as many loyal members of the Global Community as possible to return to their prosperous standard of living.

"Continue to resist naysayers and insurrectionists. Continue to support the Global Community. And remember that though I did not seek this position, I accept it with gravity and with resolve to pour out my life in service to the brotherhood and sisterhood of mankind. I appreciate your support as we set about to sacrificially stand by each other and pull ourselves out of this morass and to a higher plane than any of us could reach without the help of the other."

Buck shook his head. "He sure tells 'em what they wanna hear, doesn't he?"

Chloe and Amanda were silent.

* * *

Rayford told First Officer McCullum to hang loose and be ready to depart for New Babylon whenever they were asked. He guessed it would be several hours yet. "But, at least stay available," Rayford told him.

When Rayford boarded the plane, ostensibly to familiarize himself better with all the new whistles and bells, he went first to the pilot's quarters, noticing that Carpathia and his aides were merely greeting and small-talking with the seven loyal ambassadors to the Global Community.

When Rayford moved from his quarters into the cockpit, he noticed Fortunato look up. He whispered something to Carpathia. Carpathia agreed, and the entire meeting was moved back one compartment in the middle of the aircraft. "This will be more comfortable anyway," Carpathia was saying. "There is a nice conference table in here."

Rayford shut the cockpit door and locked it. He pulled out pre- and post-flight checklists and put them on a clipboard with other blank sheets, just to make it look good in case someone knocked. He sat in his chair, applied his headphones, and hit the intercom button.

The Middle Eastern ambassador was speaking. "Dr. Rosenzweig sends his most heartfelt and loyal greetings to you, Potentate. There is an urgent personal matter he wants me to share with you."

"Is it confidential?" Carpathia said.

"I don't believe so, sir. It concerns Rabbi Tsion Ben-Judah."

"The scholar who has been creating such a furor with his controversial message?"

"One and the same," the Middle Eastern ambassador said. "Apparently his wife and two stepchildren have been murdered by zealots, and Dr. Ben-Judah himself is in hiding somewhere."

"He should have expected no better," Nicolae said.

Rayford shuddered as he always did when Carpathia's voice waxed grave.

"I couldn't agree with you more, Potentate," the ambassador said. "I can't believe those zealots let him slip through their fingers."

"So, what does Rosenzweig want from me?"

"He wants you to intercede on Ben-Judah's behalf."

"With whom?"

"I suppose with the zealots," the ambassador said, bursting into laughter.

Rayford recognized Carpathia's laughter as well, and soon the others joined in.

"OK, gentlemen, calm down," Carpathia said. "Perhaps what I should do is accede to Dr. Rosenzweig's request and speak directly with the head of the zealot faction. I would give him my full blessing and support and perhaps even supply some technology that would help him find his prey and eliminate him with dispatch."

The ambassador responded, "Seriously, Potentate, how shall I respond to Dr. Rosenzweig?"

"Stall him for a while. Be hard to reach. Then tell him that you have not found the proper moment to raise the issue with me. After an appropriate lapse, tell him I have been too busy to pursue it. Finally, you can tell him that I have chosen to remain neutral on the subject."

"Very good, sir."

But Carpathia was not neutral. He had just begun to warm to the subject. Rayford heard the squeak of a leather seat and imagined Carpathia leaning forward to speak earnestly to his cadre of international henchmen. "But let me tell you this, gentlemen. A person such as Dr. Ben-Judah is much more dangerous to our cause than an old fool like Rosenzweig. Rosenzweig is a brilliant scientist, but he is not wise in the ways of the world. Ben-Judah is more than a brilliant scholar. He has the ability to sway people, which would not be a bad thing if he served our cause. But he wants to fill his countrymen's minds with this blather about the Messiah having already returned. How anyone can still insist on taking the Bible literally and interpreting its prophecies in that light is beyond me, but tens of thousands of converts and devotees have sprung up in Israel and around the world due to his preaching at Teddy Kollek Stadium and in other huge venues. People will believe anything. And when they do, they are dangerous. Ben-Judah's time is short, and I will not stand in the way of his demise. Now, let us get down to business."

Rayford pulled up the top two sheets on his clipboard and began to take notes, as Carpathia outlined immediate plans.

"We must act swiftly," he was saying, "while the people are most vulnerable and open. They will look to the Global Community for help and aid, and we will give it to them. However, they will give it to us first. We had an enormous storehouse of income before the rebuilding of Babylon. We will need much more to effect our plan of raising the level of Third World countries so that the entire globe is on equal footing. I tell you, gentlemen, I was so excited and full of ideas last night that I could not sit down for our takeoff out of San Francisco. I was nearly thrown into this room from the forward cabin when we started down the runway. Here is what I was thinking about:

"You all have been doing a wonderful job of moving to the one-world currency. We are close to a cashless society, which can only help the Global Community administration. Upon your return to your respective areas, I would like you to announce, simultaneously, the initiation of a ten-cent tax on all electronic money transfers. When we get to the totally cashless system, you can imagine that every transaction will be electronic. I estimate that this will generate more than one and a half trillion dollars annually.

"I am also initiating a one-dollar-per-barrel tax on oil at the well, plus a ten-cents-per-gallon tax at the pump on gasoline. My economic advisers tell me this could net us more than half a trillion dollars every year. You knew the time would come for a tax to the Global Community on each area's gross national product. That time has come. While the insurrectionists from Egypt, Great Britain, and North America have been devastated militarily, they must also be disciplined with a 50 percent tax on their GNP. The rest of you will pay 30 percent.

"Now do not give me those looks, gentlemen. You understand that everything you pay in will be returned to you in multiplied benefits. We are building a new global community. Pain is part of the process. The devastation and death of this war will blossom into a utopia unlike any the world has ever seen. And you will be in the forefront of it. Your countries and regions will benefit, and you personally most of all.

"Here is what else I have in mind. As you know, our intelligence sources quickly became convinced that the attack on New York had been planned by American militia under the clandestine leadership of President Fitzhugh. This only confirmed my earlier decision to virtually strip him of executive power. We now know that he was killed in our retaliatory attack on Washington, D.C., which we have been able to effectively lay at the feet of the insurrectionists. Those limited few who remain loyal to him will likely turn against the rebels and see that they were bumbling fools.

"As you know, the second largest pool of oil, second only to the one in Saudi Arabia, was discovered above the Prudhoe Bay in Alaska. During the state of this leadership vacuum in North America, the Global Community will appropriate the vast oil fields in Alaska, including that huge pool. Years ago it was capped off to satisfy environmentalists; however, I have ordered teams of laborers into the region to install a series of sixteen-inch pipelines that would route that oil through Canada and to waterways where it could be barged to international trade centers. We already own the rights to oil in Saudi Arabia, Kuwait, Iraq, Iran, and the rest of the Middle East. That gives us control of two-thirds of the world's oil supply.

"We will gradually but steadily raise the price of oil, which will further finance our plans to inject social services into underprivileged countries and make the world playing field equal for everyone. From oil alone, we should be able to profit at a rate of about one trillion dollars per year.

"I will soon be appointing leaders to replace the three ambassadors of the regions that turned against us. That will bring the Global Community administration back to its full complement of ten regions. While you are now known as ambassadors to the Global Community, forthwith I will begin referring to you as sovereign heads of your own kingdoms. You will each continue to report directly to me. I will approve your budgets, receive your taxes, and give you bloc grants. Some will criticize this as making it appear that all nations and regions are dependent upon the Global Community for their income and thus assuring our control over the destiny of your people. You know better. You know that your loyalty will be rewarded, that the world will be a better place in which to live, and that our destiny is a utopian society based on peace and brotherhood.

"I am sure you all agree that the world has had enough of an antagonistic press. Even I, who have no designs on personal gain and certainly only altruistic motives for humbly and unwillingly accepting the heavy mantle of responsibility for world leadership, have been attacked and criticized by editorialists. The Global Community's ability to purchase all the major media outlets has virtually eliminated that. While we may have been criticized for threatening freedom of speech or freedom of the press, I believe the world can see that those unchecked freedoms led to excesses that stifled the ability and creativity of any leader. While they may once have been necessary to keep evil dictators from taking over, when there is nothing to criticize, such oppositional editorialists are anachronistic."

Rayford felt a tingle up his spine and nearly turned, convinced someone was standing right outside the cockpit door. Finally the feeling became so foreboding and pervasive that he whipped off his headphones and stood, leaning to peek through the fish-eye peephole. No one was there. Was God trying to tell him something? He was reminded of the same sense of fear that had overcome him when Buck had told his terrifying story of sitting through a meeting where Carpathia had single-handedly hypnotized and brainwashed everyone in the room except Buck.

Rayford sat back in his seat and put the headphones on. When he depressed the intercom button, it was as if he were hearing a new Carpathia. Nicolae spoke very softly, very earnestly, in a monotone. None of the flourishes and inflections that usually characterized his speech were evident. "I want to tell you all something, and I want you to listen very carefully and understand fully. This same control that we now have over all media, we also need over industry and commerce. It is not necessary for us to buy or own all of it. That would be too obvious and too easily opposed. Ownership is not the issue. Control is. Within the next few months we shall all announce unanimous decisions allowing us to control business, education, health care, and even the way your individual kingdoms choose their leaders. The fact is, democracy and voting will be suspended. They are inefficient and not in the best interests of the people. Because of what we will provide people, they will quickly understand that this is correct. Each of you can go back to your subjects and honestly tell them that this was your idea, you raised it, you sought support of your colleagues and me for it, and you prevailed. I will publicly reluctantly accede to your wishes, and we will all win."

Rayford listened to a long silence, wondering if his bugging device was malfunctioning. He released and depressed it several times, finally deciding that no one was saying anything in the conference area. So this was the mind control Buck had witnessed firsthand. Finally, Leon Fortunato spoke up. "Potentate Carpathia," he began deferentially, "I know I am merely your aide and not a member of this august body. However, may I make a suggestion?"

"Why, yes, Leon," Carpathia said, seeming pleasantly surprised. "You are in a significant position of trust and confidence, and we all value your input."

"I was just thinking, sir," Fortunato said, "that you and your colleagues here might consider suspending popular voting as inefficient and not in the best interests of the people, at least temporarily."

"Oh, Mr. Fortunato," Carpathia said, "I do not know. How do you feel people would respond to such a controversial proposal?"

The others seemed unable to keep from talking over each other. Rayford heard them all agreeing with Fortunato and urging Carpathia to consider this. One repeated Carpathia's statement about how much healthier the press was now that the Global Community owned it and added that ownership of industry and commerce was not as necessary as ownership of the press, as long as it was Carpathia controlled and Global Community led.

"Thank you very much for your input, gentlemen. It has been most stimulating and inspiring. I will take all these matters to heart and let you know soon of their disposition and implementation."

The meeting lasted another couple of hours and consisted mostly of Carpathia's so-called kings parroting back to him everything he had assured them that they would find brilliant when they thought about it. Each seemed to raise these as new and fresh ideas. Not only had Carpathia just mentioned them, but often the ambassadors would repeat each other as if not having heard.

"Now, gentlemen," Carpathia concluded, "in a few hours we will be in New Babylon, and I will soon appoint the three new ambassador rulers. I want you to be aware of the inevitable. We cannot pretend that the world as we know it has not been almost destroyed by this outbreak of global war. It is not over yet. There will be more skirmishes. There will be more surreptitious attacks. We will have to reluctantly access our power base of weaponry, which you all know I am loath to do, and many more thousands of lives will be lost in addition to the hundreds of thousands already taken. In spite of all of our best efforts and the wonderful ideas you have shared with me today, we must face the fact that for a long time we will be fighting an uphill battle.

"Opportunists always come to the fore at a time such as this. Those who would oppose us will take advantage of the impossibility of our peacekeeping forces to be everywhere at once, and this will result in famine, poverty, and disease. In one way, there is a positive side to this. Due to the incredible cost of rebuilding, the fewer people we must feed and whose standard of living we must raise, the more quickly and economically we can do this. As the population level decreases and then stabilizes, it will be important for us to be sure that it does not then explode again too quickly. With proper legislation regarding abortion, assisted suicide, and the reduction of expensive care for the defective and handicapped, we should be able to get a handle on worldwide population control."

All Rayford could do was pray. "Lord," he said silently, "I wish I was a more willing servant. Is there no other role for me? Could I not be used in some sort of active opposition or judgment against this evil one? I can only trust in your purpose. Keep my loved ones safe until we see you in all your glory. I know you have long since forgiven me for my years of disbelief and indifference, but still it weighs heavily on me. Thank you for helping me find the truth. Thank you for Bruce Barnes. And thank you for being with us as we fight this ultimate battle."

7

BUCK HAD ALWAYS HAD the ability to sleep well, even when he couldn't sleep long. He could have used a dozen or more hours the night before, after the day he had had. However, seven-plus hours had been just enough because when he was out, he was out. He knew Chloe had slept fitfully only because she told him in the morning. Her tossing and turning and winces of pain had not affected his slumber.

Now, as Ken Ritz landed the Learjet in Easton, Pennsylvania, "just to top off the tank before headin' to Tel Aviv," Buck was alert. He and the lanky, weathered, veteran pilot in his late fifties seemed to have picked up where they left off the last time he had employed this freelance charter service. Ritz was a talker, a raconteur, opinionated, interesting, and interested. He was as eager to know Buck's latest thoughts on the vanishings and the global war as he was in sharing his own views.

"So, what's new with the jet-setting young magazine writer since I saw you last, what, almost two years ago?" Ritz had begun.

Buck told him. He recalled that Ritz had been forthright and outspoken when they first met, admitting that he had no more idea than anyone else what might have caused the vanishings but coming down on the side of aliens from outer space. It had hit Buck as a wild idea for a buttoned-down pilot, but Buck hadn't come to any conclusions at that time either. One theory was as good as the next. Ritz had told him of many strange encounters in the air that made it plausible that an airman might believe in such things.

That gave Buck the confidence to tell his own story without apology. It didn't seem to faze Ritz, at least negatively. He listened quietly, and when Buck was through, Ritz simply nodded.

"So," Buck said, "do I seem as weird to you now as you did to me when you were propounding the space aliens theory?"

"Not really," Ritz said. "You'd be amazed at the number of people just like you that I've run into since the last time we talked. I don't know what it all means, but I'm beginning to believe there are more people who agree with you than agree with me."

"I'll tell you one thing," Buck said, "if I'm right, I'm still in big trouble. We are all gonna go through some real horror. But people who don't believe are going to be in worse trouble than they could ever imagine."

"I can't imagine worse trouble than we're in right now."

"I know what you mean," Buck said. "I used to apologize and try to make sure I wasn't coming on too strong or being obnoxious, but let me just urge you to investigate what I've said. And don't assume you've got a lot of time to do it."

"That's all part of the belief system, isn't it?" Ritz said. "If what you say is true, the end isn't that far off. Just a few years."

"Exactly."

"Then, if a fella was gonna check it out, he better get to it."

"I couldn't have said it better myself," Buck said.

After refueling in Easton, Ritz spent the hours over the Atlantic asking "what if" questions. Buck had to keep assuring him he was not a student or a scholar, but he amazed even himself at what he remembered from Bruce's teaching.

"It must have hurt like everything to lose a friend like that," Ritz said.

"You can't imagine."

* * *

Leon Fortunato instructed everyone on the plane when to get off and where to stand for the cameras when they finally reached New Babylon.

"Mr. Fortunato," Rayford said, careful to follow Leon's wishes, at least in front of others, "McCullum and I don't really need to be in the photograph, do we?"

"Not unless you'd like to go against the wishes of the potentate himself," Fortunato said. "Please just do what you're told."

The plane was on the ground and secure in New Babylon for several minutes before the doors were opened and the Carpathia-controlled press was assembled. Rayford sat in the cockpit, still listening over the two-way intercom. "Remember," Carpathia said, "no smiles. This is a grave, sad day. Appropriate expressions, please."

Rayford wondered why anyone would have to be reminded not to smile on a day like this.

Next came Fortunato's voice: "Potentate, apparently there's a surprise waiting for you."

"You know I do not like surprises," Carpathia said.

"It seems your fiancée is waiting with the crowd."

"That is totally inappropriate."

"Would you like me to have her removed?"

"No, I am not sure how she might react. We certainly would not like a scene. I just hope she knows how to act. This is not her strength, as you know."

Rayford thought Fortunato was diplomatic to not respond to that.

There was a rap at the cockpit door. "Pilot and copilot first," Fortunato called out. "Let's go!"

Rayford buttoned his dress uniform jacket and put his hat on as he stepped out of the cockpit. He and McCullum trotted down the steps and began the right side of a V of people who would flank the potentate, the last to disembark.

Next came the flight service crew, who seemed awkward and nervous. They knew enough not to giggle, but simply looked down and walked directly to their spots. Fortunato and two other Carpathia aides led the seven ambassadors down the steps. Rayford turned to watch Carpathia appear in the opening at the top of the stairs.

The potentate always seemed taller than he really was in these situations, Rayford thought. He appeared to have just shaved and washed his hair, though Rayford had not been aware he had the time for that. His suit, shirt, and tie were exquisite, and he was understatedly elegant in his accessories. He waited ever so briefly, one hand in his right suit pocket, the other carrying a thin, glove-leather portfolio. *Always looking as if he's busily at the task at hand,* Rayford thought.

Rayford was amazed at Carpathia's ability to strike just the right pose and expression. He appeared concerned, grave, and yet somehow purposeful and confident. As lights flashed all around him and cameras whirred, he resolutely descended the steps and approached a bank of microphones. Every network insignia on each microphone had been redesigned to include the letters "GCN," the Global Community Network.

The only person he couldn't fully control chose that moment to burst Carpathia's bubble of propriety. Hattie Durham broke from the crowd and ran directly for him. Security guards who stepped in her way quickly realized who she was and let her through. She did everything, Rayford thought, except squeal in delight. Carpathia looked embarrassed and awkward for the first time in Rayford's memory. It was as if he had to decide which would be worse: to brush her off or to welcome her to his side.

He chose the latter, but it was clear he was holding her at bay. She leaned in to kiss him and he bent to brush her cheek with his lips. When she turned to plant an open-mouthed kiss on his lips, he pulled her ear to his mouth and whispered sternly. Hattie looked stricken. Near tears, she began to pull away from him, but he grabbed her wrist and kept her standing next to him there at the microphones.

"It is so good to be back where I belong," he said. "It is wonderful to reunite with loved ones. My fiancée is overcome with grief, as I am, at the horrible events that began so relatively few hours ago. This is a difficult time in which we live, and yet our horizons have never been wider, our challenges so great, our future so potentially bright.

"That may seem an incongruous statement in light of the tragedy and devastation we have all suffered, but we are all destined for prosperity if we commit to standing together. We will stand against any enemy of peace and embrace any friend of the Global Community."

The crowd, including the press, applauded with just the right solemnity. Rayford was sick to his stomach, eager to get to his own apartment, and desperate to phone his wife as soon as he was sure it was daytime in the States.

* * *

"Don't worry about me, buddy boy," Ken Ritz told Buck as he helped him off the Learjet. "I'll hangar this baby and find a place to crash for a few days. I've always wanted to tour this country, and it's nice to be in a place that hasn't been blown to bits. You know how to reach me. When you're ready to head back, just leave a message here at the airport. I'll be checking in frequently."

Buck thanked him and grabbed his bag, slinging it over his shoulder. He headed toward the terminal. There, beyond the plate-glass window, he saw the enthusiastic wave of the wispy little old man with the flyaway hair, Chaim Rosenzweig. How he wanted this man to become a believer! Buck had come to love Chaim. That was not an expression he would have used about the other man back when he first met the scientist. It had been only a few years, but it seemed so long ago. Buck had been the youngest senior writer in the history of *Global Weekly*—in fact, in the history of international journalism. He had unabashedly campaigned for the job of profiling Dr. Rosenzweig as the *Weekly*'s "Man of the Year."

Buck had first met the man a little more than a year before that assignment, after Rosenzweig had won a huge international prize for his invention (Chaim himself always called it more of a discovery) of a botanic formula. Rosenzweig's concoction, some said without much exaggeration, allowed flora to grow anywhere—even on concrete.

The latter had never been proven; however, the desert sands of Israel soon began to blossom like a greenhouse. Flowers, corn, beans, you name it, every spare inch of the tiny nation was quickly cleared for agriculture. Overnight, Israel had become the richest nation in the world.

Other nations had been jealous to get hold of the formula. Clearly, this was the answer to any economic woes. Israel had gone from vulnerable, geographically defenseless country to a world power—respected, feared, envied.

Rosenzweig had become the man of the hour and, according to *Global Weekly*, "Man of the Year."

Buck had enjoyed meeting him more than any powerful politician he had ever interviewed. Here was a brilliant man of science, humble and self-effacing, naive to the point of childlikeness, warm, personable, and unforgettable. He treated Buck like a son.

Other nations wanted Rosenzweig's formula so badly that they assigned high-level diplomats and politicians to court him. He acceded to audiences from so many dignitaries that his life's work had to be set aside. He was past retirement age anyway, but clearly here was a man more comfortable in a laboratory or a classroom than in a diplomatic setting. The darling of Israel had become the icon of world governments, and they all came calling.

Chaim had told Buck at one point that each suitor had his own not-so-hidden agenda. "I did my best to remain calm and diplomatic," he told Buck, "but only because I was representing my mother country. I grew almost physically ill," he added with his charming Hebrew-accented dialect, "when each began trying to persuade me that I would personally become the wealthiest man in the world if I would condescend to rent them my formula."

The Israeli government was even more protective of the formula. They made it so clear that the formula was not for sale or rent that other countries threatened war over it, and Russia actually attacked. Buck had been in Haifa the night the warplanes came screaming in. The miraculous delivery of that country from any damage, injury, or death—despite the incredible aerial assault—made Buck a believer in God, though not yet in Christ. There was no other explanation for bombs, missiles, and warships crashing and burning all over the nation, yet every citizen and building escaping unscathed.

That had sent Buck, who had feared for his life that night, on a quest for truth that was satisfied only after the vanishings and his meeting Rayford and Chloe Steele.

It had been Chaim Rosenzweig who had first mentioned the name Nicolae Carpathia to Buck. Buck had asked the old man if any of those who had been sent to court him about the formula had impressed him. Only one, Rosenzweig had told him; a young midlevel politician from the little country of Romania. Chaim had been taken with Carpathia's pacifist views, his selfless demeanor, and his insistence that the formula had the potential to change the world and save lives. It still rang in Buck's ears that Chaim Rosenzweig had once told him, "You and Carpathia must meet one day. You would like each other."

Buck could hardly remember when he had not been aware of Nicolae Carpathia, though his first exposure even to the name had been in that interview with Rosenzweig. Within days after the vanishings, the man who had seemingly overnight become president of Romania was a guest speaker at the United Nations. His brief address was so powerful, so magnetic, so impressive, that he had drawn a standing ovation even from the press—even from Buck. Of course, the world was in shock, terrified by the disappearances, and the time had been perfect for someone to step to the fore and offer a new international agenda for peace, harmony, and brotherhood.

Carpathia was thrust, ostensibly against his will, into power. He displaced the former secretary-general of the United Nations, reorganized it to include ten international mega-territories, renamed it the Global Community, moved it to Babylon (which was rebuilt and renamed New Babylon), and then set about disarming the entire globe.

It had taken more than Carpathia's charismatic personality to effect all this. He had a trump card. He had gotten to Rosenzweig. He had convinced the old man and his government that the key to the new world was Carpathia's and Global Community's ability to broker Rosenzweig's formula in exchange for compliance with international rules for disarmament. In exchange for a Carpathia-signed guarantee of at least seven years of protection from her enemies, Israel licensed to him the formula that allowed him to extract any promise he needed from any country in the world. With the formula, Russia could grow grain in the frozen tundra of Siberia. Destitute African nations became hothouses of domestic food sources and agricultural exports.

The power the formula allowed Carpathia to wield made it possible for him to bring the rest of the world willingly to its knees. Under the guise of his peacenik philosophies, member nations of the Global Community were required to destroy 90 percent of their weaponry and to donate the other 10 percent to Global Community headquarters. Before anyone realized what had happened, Nicolae Carpathia, now called the grand potentate of the Global Community, had quietly become the most militarily powerful pacifist in the history of the globe. Only those few nations that were suspicious of him kept back any firepower. Egypt, the new United States of Great Britain, and a surprisingly organized underground group of American militia forces had stockpiled just enough firepower to become a nuisance, an irritant, a trigger for Carpathia's angry retaliation. In short, their insurrection and his incredible overreaction had been the recipe for World War III, which the Bible had symbolically foretold as the Red Horse of the Apocalypse.

The irony of all this was that the sweet-spirited and innocent Chaim

Rosenzweig, who always seemed to have everyone else's interests at heart, became an unabashed devotee of Nicolae Carpathia. The man whom Buck and his loved ones in the Tribulation Force had come to believe was Antichrist himself played the gentle botanist like a violin. Carpathia included Rosenzweig in many visible diplomatic situations and even pretended Chaim was part of his elite inner circle. It was clear to everyone else that Rosenzweig was merely tolerated and humored. Carpathia did what he wanted. Still, Rosenzweig nearly worshiped the man, once intimating to Buck that if anyone embodied the qualities of the long-sought Jewish Messiah, it was Nicolae himself.

That had been before one of Rosenzweig's younger protégés, Rabbi Tsion Ben-Judah, had broadcast to the world the findings of his government-sanctioned quest for what Israel should look for in the Messiah.

Rabbi Ben-Judah, who had conducted a thorough study of ancient manuscripts, including the Old and New Testaments, had come to the conclusion that only Jesus Christ had fulfilled all the prophecies necessary to qualify for the role. To his regret, Rabbi Ben-Judah had come just short of receiving Christ and committing his life to him when the Rapture occurred. That sealed for sure his view that Jesus was Messiah and had come for his own. The Rabbi, in his mid-forties, had been left behind with a wife of six years and two teenage stepchildren, a boy and a girl. He had shocked the world, and especially his own nation, when he withheld the conclusion of his three-year study until a live international television broadcast. Once he had clearly stated his belief, he became a marked man.

Though Ben-Judah had been a student, protégé, and eventually a colleague of Dr. Rosenzweig, the latter still considered himself a nonreligious, nonpracticing Jew. In short, he did not agree with Ben-Judah's conclusion about Jesus, but mostly it was simply something he didn't want to talk about.

That, however, made him no less a friend of Ben-Judah's and no less an advocate. When Ben-Judah, with the encouragement and support of the two strange, otherworldly preachers at the Wailing Wall, began sharing his message, first at Teddy Kollek Stadium and then in other similar venues around the world, everyone knew it was just a matter of time before he would suffer for it.

Buck knew that one reason Rabbi Tsion Ben-Judah was still alive was that any attempt on his life was treated by the two preachers, Moishe and Eli, as attempts on their own. Many had died mysterious and fiery deaths trying to attack those two. Most everyone knew that Ben-Judah was "their guy," and thus he had so far eluded mortal harm.

That safety seemed at an end now, and that was why Buck was in Israel. Buck was convinced that Carpathia himself was behind the horror and tragedy that had come to Ben-Judah's family. News reports said black-hooded thugs pulled up to Ben-Judah's home in the middle of a sunny afternoon when the teenagers had just returned from Hebrew school. Two armed guards were shot to death, and Mrs. Ben-Judah and her son and daughter were dragged out into the street, decapitated, and left in pools of their own blood.

The murderers had driven away in a nondescript and unmarked van. Ben-Judah's driver had raced to the rabbi's university office as soon as he heard the news, and he had reportedly driven Ben-Judah to safety. Where, no one knew. Upon his return, the driver denied knowledge of Ben-Judah's whereabouts to the authorities and the press, claiming he had not seen him since before the murders and that he merely hoped to hear from him at some point.

8

RAYFORD THOUGHT he had had enough sleep, catching catnaps on his long journey. He had not figured the toll that tension and terror and disgust would exact on his mind and body. In his and Amanda's own apartment, as comfortable as air-conditioning could make a place in Iraq, Rayford disrobed to his boxers and sat on the end of his bed. Shoulders slumped, elbows on knees, he exhaled loudly and realized how exhausted he truly was. He had finally heard from home. He knew Amanda was safe, Chloe was on the mend, and Buck—as usual—was on the move. He didn't know what he thought about this Verna Zee threatening the security of the Tribulation Force's new safe house (Loretta's). But he would trust Buck, and God, in that.

Rayford stretched out on his back atop the bedcovers. He put his hands behind his head and stared at the ceiling. How he'd love to get a peek at the treasure trove of Bruce's computer archives. But as he drifted off to a sound sleep, he was trying to figure a way to get back to Chicago by Sunday. Surely there had to be some way he could make it to Bruce's memorial service. He was pleading his case with God as sleep enveloped him.

* * *

Buck had often been warmed by Chaim Rosenzweig's ancient-faced smile of greeting. There was no hint of that now. As Buck strode toward the old man, Rosenzweig merely opened his arms for an embrace and said hoarsely, "Cameron! Cameron!"

Buck bent to hug his tiny friend, and Rosenzweig clasped his hands behind Buck and squeezed tightly as a child. He buried his face in Buck's neck and wept bitterly. Buck nearly lost his balance, the weight of his bag pulling him one way and Chaim Rosenzweig's vice-grip pulling him forward. He felt as if he might stumble and fall atop his friend. He fought to stay upright, holding Chaim and letting him cry.

Finally Rosenzweig released his grip and pulled Buck toward a row of chairs. Buck became aware of Rosenzweig's tall, dark-complected driver standing about ten feet away with his hands clasped before him. He appeared concerned for his employer, and embarrassed.

Chaim nodded toward him. "You remember Andre," Rosenzweig said.

"Yeah," Buck said, nodding, "how ya doin'?"

Andre responded in Hebrew. He neither spoke nor understood English. Buck knew no Hebrew.

Rosenzweig spoke to Andre and he hurried away. "He'll bring the car around," Chaim said.

"I have only a few days here," Buck said. "What can you tell me? Do you know where Tsion is?"

"No! Cameron, it's so terrible! What a hideous, horrible defiling of a man's family and of his name!"

"But you heard from him—"

"One phone call. He said you would know where to begin looking for him. But, Cameron, have you not heard the latest?"

"I can't imagine."

"The authorities are trying to implicate him in the murders of his own family."

"Oh, come on! No one is going to buy that! Nothing even points in that direction. Why would he do that?"

"Of course, you and I know he would never do such a thing, Cameron, but when evil elements are out to get you, they stop at nothing. You heard, of course, about his driver."

"No."

Rosenzweig shook his head and lowered his chin to his chest.

"What?" Buck asked. "Not him too?"

"I'm afraid so. A car bombing. His body was barely recognizable."

"Chaim! Are you sure you're safe? Does your driver know how to—"

"Drive defensively? Check for car bombs? Defend himself or me? Yes to all of those. Andre is quite skilled. It makes me no less terrified, I admit, but I feel I am protected the best I can be."

"But you are associated with Dr. Ben-Judah. Those looking for him will try to follow you to him."

"Which means you should not be seen with me either," Rosenzweig said.

"It's too late for that," Buck said.

"Don't be too sure. Andre assured me we were not followed here. It wouldn't surprise me if someone picked us up at this point and followed us, but for the instant, I believe we are here undetected."

"Good! I cleared customs with my phony passport. Did you use my name when booking me a room?"

"Unfortunately I did, Cameron. I'm sorry. I even used my own name to secure it."

Buck had to suppress a smile at the man's sweet naiveté. "Well, friend, we'll just use that to keep them off our trail, hm?"

"Cameron, I'm afraid I'm not too good at all this."

"Why don't you have Andre drive you directly to that hotel. Tell them my plans have changed and that I will not be in until Sunday."

"Cameron! How do you think of such things so quickly?"

"Hurry now. And we must not be seen together anymore. I will leave here no later than Saturday night. You can reach me at this number."

"Is it secure?"

"It's a satellite phone, the latest technology. No one can tap into it. Just don't put my name next to that number, and don't give that number to anyone else."

"Cameron, where will you begin looking for Tsion?"

"I have a couple of ideas," Buck said. "And you must know, if I can get him out of this country, I'll do it."

"Excellent! If I were a praying man, I'd pray for you."

"Chaim, one of these days soon, you *need* to become a praying man."

Chaim changed the subject. "One more thing, Cameron. I have placed a call to Carpathia for his assistance in this."

"I wish you hadn't done that, Chaim. I don't trust him the way you do."

"I've sensed that, Buck," Rosenzweig said, "but you need to get to know the man better."

If you only knew, Buck thought. "Chaim, I'll try to communicate with you as soon as I know anything. Call me only if you need to."

Rosenzweig embraced him fiercely again and hurried off. Buck used a pay phone to call the King David Hotel. He booked a room for two weeks under the name of Herb Katz. "Representing what company?" the clerk said.

Buck thought a moment. "International Harvester," he said, deciding that that would have been a great description of both Bruce Barnes and Tsion Ben-Judah.

\+ \+ \+

Rayford's eyes popped open. He had not moved a muscle. He had no idea how long he had slept, but something had interrupted his reverie. The jangling phone on the bedside table made him jump. Reaching for it, he realized his arm was asleep. It didn't want to go where he wanted it to. Somehow he forced himself to grasp the receiver. "Steele here," he gargled.

"Captain Steele? Are you all right?" It was Hattie Durham.

Rayford rolled onto his side and tucked the receiver under his chin. Leaning on his elbow, he said, "I'm all right, Hattie. How are you?"

"Not so good. I'd like to see you if I could."

Despite the closed curtains, the brilliant afternoon sun forced its way into the room. "When?" Rayford said.

"Dinner tonight?" she said. "About six?"

Rayford's mind was reeling. Had she already been told of her lessened role in the Carpathia administration? Did he want to be seen in public with her while Amanda was away? "Is there a rush, Hattie? Amanda's in the States, but she'll be back in a week or so—"

"No, Rayford, I really need to talk to you. Nicolae has meetings from now until midnight, and their dinner is being catered. He said he didn't have a problem with my talking with you. I know you want to be appropriate and all that. It's not a date. Let's just have dinner somewhere where it will be obvious that we're just old friends talking. Please?"

"I guess," Rayford said, curious.

"My driver will pick you up at six then, Rayford."

"Hattie, do me a favor. If you agree this shouldn't look like a date, don't dress up."

"Captain Steele," she said, suddenly formal, "stepping out is the last thing on my mind."

\+ + +

Buck settled into his room on the third floor of the King David Hotel. On a hunch he called the offices of the *Global Community East Coast Daily Times* in Boston and asked for his old friend, Steve Plank. Plank had been his boss at *Global Weekly* what seemed eons ago. He had abruptly left there to become Carpathia's press secretary when Nicolae became secretary-general of the United Nations. It wasn't long before Steve was tabbed for the lucrative position he now held.

It was no surprise to Buck to find that Plank was not in the office. He was in New Babylon at the behest of Nicolae Carpathia and no doubt feeling very special about it.

Buck showered and took a nap.

\+ + +

Rayford felt as if he could use another several hours' sleep. He certainly didn't intend to stay out long with Hattie Durham. He dressed casually, just barely presentable enough for a place like Global Bistro, where Hattie and Nicolae were often seen.

Of course, Rayford would not be able to let on that he had known about Hattie's demotion before she did. He would have to let her play the story out with all her characteristic emotion and angst. He didn't mind. He owed her that much. He still felt guilty about where she was, both geographically and in her life. It didn't seem that long ago that she had been the object of his lust.

Rayford had never acted on it, of course, but it was Hattie whom he was thinking of the night of the Rapture. How could he have been so deaf, so blind, so out of touch with reality? A successful professional man, married more than twenty years with a college-age daughter and a twelve-year-old son, daydreaming about his senior flight attendant and justifying it because his wife had been on a religious kick! He shook his head. Irene, the lovely little woman he had for so long taken for granted, the one with the name of an aunt many years her senior, had known real truth with a capital *T* long before any of them.

Rayford had always been a churchgoer and would have called himself a Christian. But to him church was a place to see and be seen, to network, to look respectable. When preachers got too judgmental or too literal, it made him nervous. And when Irene had found a new, smaller congregation that seemed much more aggressive in their faith, he had begun finding reasons not to go with her. When she started talking about the salvation of souls, the blood of Christ, and the return of Christ, he became convinced she was off her nut. How long before she had him traipsing along behind her, passing out literature door-to-door?

That was how he had justified the dalliance, only in his mind, with Hattie Durham. Hattie was fifteen years his junior, and she was a knockout. Though they had enjoyed dinner together a few times and drinks several times, and despite the silent language of the body and the eyes, Rayford had never so much as touched her. It had not been beyond Hattie to grab his arm as she brushed past him or even to put her hands on his shoulders when speaking to him in the cockpit, but Rayford had somehow kept from letting things go further. That night over the Atlantic, with a fully loaded 747 on autopilot, he had finally worked up the courage to suggest something concrete to her. Ashamed as he was now to admit it even to himself, he had been ready to take the next, bold, decisive step toward a physical relationship.

But he had never gotten the words out of his mouth. When he left the cockpit to find her, she had nearly bowled him over with the news that about a quarter of his passengers had disappeared, leaving everything material behind. The cabin, which was normally a black, humming, sleep chamber at four o'clock in the morning, quickly became a beehive of panic as people realized what was happening. That was the night Rayford told Hattie he didn't know what was happening any more than she did. The truth was that he knew all too well. Irene had been right. Christ had returned to rapture his church, and Rayford, Hattie, and three-fourths of their passengers had been left behind.

Rayford had not known Buck Williams at that time, didn't know Buck was a first class passenger on that very flight. He couldn't know that Buck and Hattie had chatted, that Buck had used his computer and the Internet to try to reach her people to see if they were OK. Only later would he discover that Buck had introduced Hattie to the new, sparkling international celebrity leader, Nicolae Carpathia. Rayford had met Buck in New York. Rayford was there to apologize to Hattie for his inappropriate actions toward her in the past and to try to convince her of the truth about the vanishings. Buck was there to introduce her to Carpathia, to interview Carpathia, and to interview Rayford—Hattie's captain. Buck was merely trying to put a story together about various views of the disappearances.

Rayford had been earnest and focused in his attempts to persuade Buck that he had found the real truth too. That was the night Buck met Chloe. So much had happened in so short a time. Less than two years later, Hattie was the personal assistant and lover of Nicolae Carpathia, the Antichrist. Rayford, Buck, and Chloe were believers in Christ. And all three of them agonized over the plight of Hattie Durham.

Maybe tonight, Rayford thought, he could finally have some positive influence on Hattie.

* * *

Buck had always been able to awaken himself whenever he wanted. The gift had failed him very infrequently. He had told himself he wanted to be up and moving by 6:00 p.m. He awoke on time, less refreshed than he had hoped, but eager to get going. He told his cabbie, "The Wailing Wall, please."

Moments later, Buck disembarked. There, not far from the Wailing Wall, behind a wrought-iron fence, stood the men Buck had come to know as the two witnesses prophesied in Scripture.

They called themselves Moishe and Eli, and truly they seemed to have come from another time and another place. They wore ragged, burlap-like robes. They were barefoot with leathery, dark skin. Both had long, dark gray hair and unkempt beards. They were sinewy with bony joints and long muscled arms and legs. Anyone who dared get close to them smelled smoke. Those who dared attack them had been killed. It was as simple as that. Several had rushed them with automatic weapons, only to seem to hit an invisible wall and drop dead on the spot. Others had been incinerated where they stood, by fire that had come from the witnesses' mouths.

They preached nearly constantly in the language and cadence of the Bible, and what they said was blasphemous to the ears of devout Jews. They preached Christ and him crucified, proclaiming him the Messiah, the Son of God.

The only time they had been seen apart from the Wailing Wall was at Teddy Kollek Stadium, when they appeared on the platform with Rabbi Tsion Ben-Judah, a recent convert to Christ. News coverage broadcast around the world showed these two strange men, speaking in unison, not using microphones and yet being heard distinctly in the back rows. "Come nigh and listen," they had shouted, "to the chosen servant of the most high God! He is among the first of the 144,000 who shall go forth from this and many nations to proclaim the gospel of Christ throughout the world! Those who come against him, just as those who have come against us before the due time, shall surely die!"

The witnesses had not stayed on the platform or even in the stadium for that first big evangelistic rally at Kollek Stadium. They slipped away and were back at the Wailing Wall by the time the meeting was over. That coming together in a huge stadium was reproduced dozens of times in almost every country of the world over the next year and a half, resulting in tens of thousands of converts.

Enemies of Rabbi Ben-Judah did try to "come against" him during those eighteen months, as the witnesses had warned. It seemed others had gotten the point and had repented of their intentions. A lull of three to four weeks since any threats on his life had been a pleasant respite for the indefatigable Ben-Judah. But now he was in hiding, and his family and his driver had been slaughtered.

Ironically, the last time Buck had been at the Wailing Wall to watch and hear the two witnesses, he had been with Rabbi Ben-Judah. They had come back later the same night and dared approach the fence and speak to the men who had killed all others who had gotten that close. Buck had been able to understand them in his own language, though his tape recording of the incident later proved they had been speaking in Hebrew. Rabbi Ben-Judah had begun reciting the words of Nicodemus from the famous meeting of Jesus by night, and the witnesses had responded the way Jesus had. It had been the most chilling night of Buck's life.

Now, here he was, alone. He was looking for Ben-Judah, who had told Chaim Rosenzweig that Buck would know where to start looking. He could think of no better place.

As usual, a huge crowd had gathered before the witnesses, though people knew well enough to keep their distance. Even the rage and hatred of Nicolae Carpathia had not yet affected Moishe and Eli. More than once, even in public, Carpathia had asked if there was not someone who could do away with those two nuisances. He had been informed apologetically by military leaders that no weapons seemed capable of harming them. The witnesses themselves continually referred to the folly of trying to harm them "before the due time."

Bruce Barnes had explained to the Tribulation Force that, indeed, in due time God would allow the witnesses to become vulnerable, and they would be attacked. That incident was still more than a year and a half away, Buck believed, but even the thought of it was a nightmare to his soul.

This evening the witnesses were doing as they had done every day since the signing of the treaty between Israel and Carpathia: They were proclaiming the terrible day of the Lord. And they were acknowledging Jesus Christ as "the Mighty God, the Everlasting Father, and the Prince of Peace. Let no other man anywhere call himself the ruler of this world! Any man who makes such a claim is not the Christ but the Antichrist, and he shall surely die! Woe unto anyone who preaches another gospel! Jesus is the only true God, maker of heaven and earth!"

Buck was always thrilled and moved by the preaching of the witnesses. He looked around the crowd and saw people from various races and cultures. He knew from experience that many of them understood no Hebrew. They were understanding the witnesses in their own tongues, just as he was.

Buck edged a quarter of the way into the crowd of about three hundred. He stood on tiptoes to see the witnesses. Suddenly both stopped preaching and moved forward toward the fence. The crowd seemed to step back as one, fearing for its life. The witnesses now stood inches from the fence, the crowd keeping about a fifty-foot distance with Buck near the back.

To Buck it seemed clear the witnesses had noticed him. Both stared directly into his eyes, and he could not move. Without gesturing or moving, Eli began to preach. "He who has ears to hear, let him hear! Do not be afraid, for I know that you seek Jesus who was crucified. He is not here; for He is risen, as He said."

Believers in the crowd mumbled their amens and their agreement. Buck was riveted. Moishe stepped forward and seemed to speak directly to him. "Do not be afraid, for I know whom you seek. He is not here."

Eli again: "Go quickly and tell His disciples that Christ is risen from the dead!"

Moishe, still staring at Buck: "Indeed He is going before you into Galilee. There you will see Him. Behold, I have told you."

The witnesses stood and stared silently for so long, unmoving, it was as if they had turned to stone. The crowd grew nervous and began to dissipate. Some waited to see if the witnesses would speak again, but they did not. Soon only Buck stood where he had stood for the last several minutes. He couldn't take his eyes off the eyes of Moishe. The two merely stood at the fence and stared at him. Buck began to advance on them, coming to within about twenty feet. The witnesses didn't move. They seemed not even to be breathing. Buck noticed no blink, no twitch. In the fading twilight, he carefully watched their faces. Neither opened his mouth, and yet Buck heard, plain as day in his own language, "He who has ears to hear, let him hear."

9

THE INTERCOM SUMMONED Rayford to the front door of his condominium, where Hattie's driver waited. He led Rayford to the white stretch Mercedes and opened the back door. There was room on the seat next to Hattie, but Rayford chose to sit across from her. She had honored his request not to dress up, but even casually attired, she looked lovely. He decided not to say so.

Trouble was etched on her face. "I really appreciate your agreeing to see me."

"Sure. What's up?"

Hattie glanced toward the driver. "Let's talk at dinner," she said. "The Bistro OK?"

* * *

Buck stood riveted before the witnesses as the sun went down. He looked around to be sure it was still just him and them. "That's all I get? He's in Galilee?"

Again, without moving their lips, the witnesses spoke: "He who has ears to hear, let him hear."

Galilee? Did it even exist anymore? Where would Buck start, and when would he start? Surely he didn't want to be poking around there in the night. He had to know where he was going, have some sort of bearing. He spun on his heel to see if any taxis were in the area. He saw a few. He turned back to the witnesses. "If I came back here later tonight, might I learn more?"

Moishe backed away from the fence and sat on the pavement, leaning against a wall. Eli gestured and spoke aloud, "Birds of the air have nests," he said, "but the Son of Man has nowhere to lay his head."

"I don't understand," Buck said. "Tell me more."

"He who has ears—"

Buck was frustrated. "I'll come back at midnight. I'm pleading for your help."

Eli was now backing away too. "Lo, I am with you always, even to the end of the age."

Buck left, still planning to come back, but also strangely warmed by that last mysterious promise. Those were the words of Christ. Was Jesus speaking directly to him through the mouths of these witnesses? What an unspeakable privilege! He took a cab back to the King David, confident that he would, before long, be reunited with Tsion Ben-Judah.

* * *

Rayford and Hattie were welcomed expansively by the maître d' of the Global Bistro. The man recognized her, of course, but not Rayford. "Your usual table, ma'am?"

"No, thank you, Jeoffrey, but neither would we like to be hidden."

They were led to a table set for four. But even though two busboys hurried out to clear away two sets of dinnerware, and the waiter pulled out a chair for Hattie while pointing Rayford to one next to her, Rayford was still thinking of appearances. He sat directly across from Hattie, knowing they would nearly have to shout to hear each other in the noisy place. The waiter hesitated, looking irritated, and finally moved Rayford's tableware back to in front of him. That was something Hattie and Rayford might have chuckled over in their past, which included a half-dozen clandestine dinners where each seemed to be wondering what the other was thinking about their future. Hattie had been more flirtatious than Rayford, though he had never discouraged her.

Televisions throughout the Bistro carried the continuing news of war around the world. Hattie signaled for the maître d', who came running. "I doubt the potentate would appreciate this news depressing patrons who came in here for a little relaxation."

"I'm afraid it's on every station, ma'am."

"There's not even a music station of some kind?"

"I'll check."

Within moments, all the television sets in the Global Bistro showed music videos. Several applauded this, but Rayford sensed Hattie barely noticed.

In the past, when they were playing around the edges of an affair of the mind, Rayford had to remind Hattie to order and then encourage her to eat. Her attention had been riveted on him, and he had found that flattering and alluring. Now the opposite seemed the case.

Hattie studied her menu as if she faced a final exam on it in the morning. She was as beautiful as ever, now twenty-nine and pregnant for the first time. She was early enough along that no one would know unless she told them. She had told Rayford and Amanda the last time they were together. At that time she seemed thrilled, proud of her new diamond, and eager to talk about her pending marriage. She had told Amanda that Nicolae was "going to make an honest woman of me yet."

Hattie was wearing her ostentatious engagement ring; however, the diamond was turned in toward her palm so only the band was visible. Hattie was clearly not a happy woman, and Rayford wondered if this all stemmed from her getting the cold shoulder from Nicolae at the airport. He wanted to ask her, but this meeting was her idea. She would say what she wanted to say soon enough.

Though the Global Bistro had a French-sounding name, Hattie herself had helped conceive it, and the menu carried international cuisine, mostly American. She ordered an unusually large meal. Rayford had just a sandwich. Hattie small-talked until she had finished her food, including dessert. Rayford knew all the clichés, such as that she was now eating for two, but he believed she was eating out of nervousness and in an attempt to put off what she really wanted to talk about.

"Can you believe it's been nearly two years since you last served as my senior flight attendant?" he said, trying to get the ball rolling.

Hattie sat up straight in her chair, folded her hands in her lap, and leaned forward. "Rayford, this has been the most incredible two years of my life."

He looked at her expectantly, wondering if she meant that was good or bad. "You've expanded your horizons," he said.

"Think about it, Rayford. All I ever wanted to be was a flight attendant. The entire cheerleading squad at Maine East High School wanted to be flight attendants. We all applied, but I was the only one who made it. I was so proud, but flying quickly lost its appeal. Half the time I had to remind myself where we were going and when we would get there and when we would get back. But I loved the people, I loved the freedom of traveling, and I loved visiting all those places. You know I had a couple of serious boyfriends here and there, but nothing ever worked out. When I finally worked my way up to the planes and routes that only seniority could bring, I had a huge crush on one of my pilots, but that never worked either."

"Hattie, I wish you wouldn't dredge that up. You know how I feel about that period."

"I know, and I'm sorry. Nothing ever came of it, though I could have hoped for more. I've accepted your explanation and your apology, and that's not what this is about at all."

"That's good, because as you know, I am again happily married."

"I envy you, Rayford."

"I thought you and Nicolae were going to get married."

"So did I. Now I'm not so sure. And I'm not so sure I want to either."

"If you want to talk about it, I'm happy to listen. I'm no expert in matters of the heart, so I probably won't have any advice, but I'm an ear if that's what you want."

Hattie waited until the dishes were cleared, then told the waiter, "We'll be here awhile."

"I'll apply this to your tab," the waiter said. "I doubt anyone will be giving *you* the bum's rush." He smiled at Rayford, seeming to appreciate his own humor. Rayford forced a smile.

When the waiter was gone, Hattie seemed to feel the freedom to continue. "Rayford, you may not know this, but I actually had a thing for Buck Williams once. You remember he was on your plane that night."

"Of course."

"I didn't look at him romantically then, of course, because I was still enamored with you. But he was sweet. And he was cute. And he had that big, important job. He and I are closer in age, too."

"And . . . ?"

"Well, to tell you the truth, when you dumped me—"

"Hattie, I never dumped you. There was nothing to dump. We were not an item."

"Yet."

"OK, yet," he said. "That's fair. But you have to admit there had been no commitment or even an expression of a commitment."

"There had been plenty of signals, Rayford."

"I have to acknowledge that. Still, it's unfair to say I dumped you."

"Call it whatever you want so you can deal with it, but I felt dumped, OK? Anyway, all of sudden Buck Williams looked more attractive to me than ever. I'm sure he thought I was using him to meet a celebrity, which also happened. I was so grateful for Buck's introducing me to Nicolae."

"Forgive me, Hattie, but this is old news."

"I know, but I'm getting somewhere. Bear with me. As soon as I met Nicolae, I was stricken. He was only about as much older than Buck as Buck was older than I. But he seemed so much older. He was a world traveler, an international politician, a leader. He was already the most famous man in the world. I knew he was going places. I felt like a giggling schoolgirl and couldn't imagine I had impressed him in the least. When he began to show interest, I thought it was merely physical. And, I admit, I would have probably slept with him in a minute and not regretted it. We had an affair, and I fell in love, but as God is my witness—oh, Rayford, I'm sorry. I shouldn't use those kind of references around you—I never expected him to be truly interested in me. I knew the whole thing was temporary, and I was determined to just enjoy it while it lasted.

"It got to the point where I dreaded his being away. I kept telling myself to maintain a level head. The end would have to come soon, and I really believe

I was prepared for it. But then he shocked me. He made me his personal assistant. I had no experience, no skills. I knew it was just a way to keep me available to him after hours. That was all right with me, though I was afraid of what my life might become when he became even busier. Well, my worst fears were realized. He's still charming and smooth and dynamic and powerful and the most incredible person I've ever met. But I mean exactly to him what I always feared I did. You know the man usually works at least eighteen hours a day and sometimes twenty? I mean nothing to him, and I know it.

"I used to be involved in some discussions. He used to bounce an idea or two off me. But what do I know about international politics? I would make some silly statement based on my limited knowledge, and he would either laugh at me or ignore me. Then he came to where he never sought my opinions anymore. I was allowed little playthings, like helping develop this restaurant and being available to greet groups touring the new Global Community headquarters. But I'm merely window-dressing now, Rayford. He didn't give me a ring until after I was pregnant, and he still hasn't asked me if I would marry him. I guess that's supposed to be understood."

"By accepting his ring, did you not imply that you would marry him?"

"Oh, Rayford, it wasn't nearly that romantic. He merely asked me to close my eyes and stick out my hand. Then he put the ring on my finger. I didn't know what to say. He just smiled."

"You're saying you don't feel committed?"

"I don't feel anything anymore. And I don't think he ever felt anything for me except physical attraction."

"And all the trappings? The wealth? Your own car and driver? I assume you have an expense account—"

"I have all that, yes." Hattie seemed tired. She continued. "To tell you the truth, all that stuff is a lot like what flying was to me. You quickly get tired of the routine. I was drunk with the power and the glitter and the glamour of it for a while, sure. But it's not who I am. I know no one here. People treat me with deference and respect only because of who I live with. But they don't really know him either. Neither do I. I'd rather he be mad at me than ignore me. I asked him the other day if I could go back to the States for a while and visit my friends and family. He was irritated. He said I didn't even have to ask. He said, 'Just let me know and go ahead and arrange it. I've got more to do than worry about your little schedule.' I'm just a piece of furniture to him, Rayford."

Rayford was biding his time. There was so much he wanted to tell her. "How much do you talk?"

"What do you mean? We don't talk. We just coexist now."

Rayford spoke carefully, "I'm just curious about how much he knows about Chloe and Buck."

"Oh, you don't have to worry about that. Smart as he is and well connected as he is, and for as many 'eyes' as he has out there surveilling everything and everybody, I don't think he has any idea of a connection between you and Buck. I have never mentioned that Buck married your daughter. And I never would."

"Why?"

"I don't think he needs to know, that's all. For some reason, Rayford, he trusts you implicitly on some things and not at all on others."

"I've noticed."

"What have you noticed?" she asked.

"Being left out of the plans for the Condor 216, for one," Rayford said.

"Yeah," she said, "and wasn't that creative of him to use his office suite number as part of the name of the plane?"

"It just seemed bizarre to be his pilot and to be surprised by new equipment."

"If you lived with him, that would not surprise you. I've been out of the loop for months. Rayford, do you realize that I was not contacted by anyone when the war broke out?"

"He didn't call you?"

"I didn't know whether he was dead or alive. I heard him on the news, just like everyone else. He didn't even call after that. No aide let me know. No assistant so much as sent me a memo. I called everywhere. I talked to every person in the organization I knew. I even got as far as Leon Fortunato. He told me he would tell Nicolae that I called. Can you imagine? He would tell him I called!"

"So when you saw him at the airstrip . . . ?"

"I was testing him. I won't deny it. I wasn't as eager to see him as I let on, but I was giving him one more chance. Wasn't it obvious I spoiled his big appearance?"

"That's the impression I had," Rayford said, wondering if he was wise in surrendering his neutral role.

"When I tried to kiss him, he told me it was inappropriate and to act like an adult. At least in his remarks he referred to me as his fiancée. He said I was overcome with grief, as he was. I know him well enough to know there was no grief. I could see it written all over him. He loves this stuff. And regardless of what he says, he's right in the middle of it. He talks like a pacifist, but he hopes people will attack him so he can justify retaliating. I was so horrified and sad, hearing about all the death and destruction, but he comes back here to his self-made palace, pretending to grieve with all the heartbroken people around the world. But in private it's like he's celebrating. He can't get enough of this. He's rubbing his hands, making plans, devising strategies. He's putting together his new team. They're meeting right now. Who knows what they'll dream up!"

"What are you gonna do, Hattie? This is no kind of life for you."

"He doesn't even want me in the office anymore."

Rayford knew that but couldn't let on. "What do you mean?"

"I was actually fired today, by my own fiancé. He asked if he could meet me in my quarters."

"Your quarters?"

"We don't really live together anymore. I'm just down the hall, and he visits once in a great while in the middle of the night—between meetings, I guess. But I've been a fairly high-maintenance girl-next-door for a long time."

"So what did he want?"

"I thought I knew. I thought he'd been away long enough that he just wanted the usual. But he just told me he was replacing me."

"You mean you're out?"

"No. He still wants me around. Still wants me to bear his child. He just thinks the job has passed me by. I told him, 'Nicolae, that job passed me by the day before I took it. I've never been cut out to be a secretary. I was OK with the public relations and the people contacts, but making me your personal assistant was a mistake.'"

"I always thought you looked the part."

"Well, thanks for that, Rayford. But losing that job was a relief in a way."

"Only in a way?"

"Yes. Where does this leave me? I asked him what the future was for us. He had the audacity to say, 'Us?' I said, 'Yes! Us! I'm wearing your ring and carrying your child. When do we make this permanent?'"

+ + +

Buck woke with a start. He had been dreaming. It was dark. He turned on a small lamp and squinted at his watch. He still had several hours before his appointment with Moishe and Eli at midnight. But what had that dream been all about? Buck had dreamed that he was Joseph, Mary's husband. He had heard an angel of the Lord saying, "Arise, flee to Egypt, and stay there until I bring you word."

Buck was confused. He had never been communicated to in a dream, by God or anyone else. He had always considered dreams just aberrations based on daily life. Here he was in the Holy Land, thinking about God, thinking about Jesus, communicating with the two witnesses, trying to steer clear of the Antichrist and his cohorts. It made sense he might have a dream related to biblical stories. Or was God trying to tell him that he would find Tsion Ben-Judah in Egypt, rather than wherever it seemed the witnesses were sending him? They always spoke so circumspectly. He would have to simply ask them. How could he be expected to understand biblical references when he was so new at all this? He wanted to sleep until eleven-thirty before taking a cab to the Wailing Wall, but he found it difficult to fall back to sleep with the weird dream playing itself over and over in his mind. One thing he didn't want to do, especially with the news of war coming out of Cairo, was to go anywhere near Egypt. He wasn't much more than two hundred miles from Cairo as the crow flew anyway. That was plenty close enough, even if Carpathia had not used nuclear weapons on the Egyptian capital.

Buck lay back in the darkness, wondering.

* * *

Rayford was torn. What could he tell his old friend? She was clearly in pain, clearly at a loss. He couldn't blurt that her lover was the Antichrist and that Rayford and his friends knew it. What he really wanted was to plead with her, to beg her to receive Christ. But hadn't he already done that once? Hadn't he spelled out to her everything he had learned following the vanishings, which he now knew as the Rapture?

She knew the truth. At least she knew what he believed was the truth. He had spilled his guts to her, Chloe, and Buck at a restaurant in New York, and he felt he had alienated Hattie by repeating what he had said to her earlier that day in private. He had been certain his daughter was embarrassed to death. And he had been convinced that the erudite Buck Williams was merely tolerating him. It had been a shock to find that Chloe took a huge step closer to her own personal decision to follow Christ after seeing his passion that night. That meeting had also been a huge influence on Buck.

Now he tried a new tack. "Let me tell you something, Hattie. You need to know that Buck and Chloe and I all care very deeply about you."

"I know, Rayford, but—"

"I don't think you do know," Rayford said. "We have all wondered if this was the best thing for you, and each of us feels somehow responsible for your having left your job and loved ones and gone first to New York and now to New Babylon. And for what?"

Hattie stared at him. "But I hardly heard from any of you."

"We didn't feel we had a right to say anything. You're an adult. It's your life. I felt my antics had pushed you away from the aviation industry. Buck feels guilty for having introduced you to Nicolae in the first place. Chloe often wonders if she couldn't have said or done something that might have changed your mind."

"But why?" Hattie said. "How did any of you know I was not happy here?"

Now Rayford was stuck. How, indeed, did they know? "We just sensed the odds were against you," he said.

"And I don't suppose I gave you any indication that you were right, always trying to impress you whenever I saw you or Buck with Nicolae."

"There was that, yes."

"Well, Rayford, it may also come as a shock to you to know that I had never foreseen becoming pregnant out of wedlock either."

"Why should that surprise me?"

"Because I can't say my morals were exactly pristine. I mean, I was close to an affair with you. I'm just saying I wasn't raised that way, and I certainly wouldn't have planned to have a baby without being married."

"And now?"

"The same is true now, Rayford." Hattie's voice had flattened. It was clear she was tired, but now she sounded defeated, almost dead. "I am not going to use this pregnancy to force Nicolae Carpathia to marry me. He wouldn't anyway. He's not forced by anyone to do anything. If I pushed him, he'd probably tell me to have an abortion."

"Oh no!" Rayford said. "You'd never consider that, would you?"

"Wouldn't consider it? I think about it every day."

Rayford winced and rubbed his forehead. Why did he expect Hattie to live like a believer when she was not? It wasn't fair to assume she agreed with him on these issues. "Hattie, do me a big favor, will you?"

"Maybe."

"Would you think about that very carefully before you take any action? Would you seek counsel from your family, from your friends?"

"Rayford, I hardly have any friends anymore."

"Chloe and Buck and I still consider you our friend. And I believe Amanda could become your friend if she got to know you."

Hattie snorted. "I have a feeling that the more Amanda got to know me, the less she'd like me."

"That just proves you don't know her," Rayford said. "She's the type who doesn't even have to like you to love you, if you know what I mean."

Hattie raised her eyebrows. "What an interesting way to say that," she said. "I guess that's the way parents feel about their kids sometimes. My dad once told me that, when I was a rebellious teenager. He said, 'Hattie, it's a good thing I love you so much, because I don't like you at all.' That brought me up short, Rayford. You know what I mean?"

"Sure," he said. "You really ought to get to know Amanda. She'd be like another mother-figure to you."

"One is more than enough," Hattie said. "Don't forget, my mother's the one that gave me this crazy name that belongs to someone two generations older than me."

Rayford smiled. He had always wondered about that. "Anyway, you said Nicolae didn't mind if you took a trip back to the States?"

"Yeah, but that was before the war broke out."

"Hattie, several airports are still taking incoming flights. And as far as I know, no nuclear-equipped warheads landed on any major cities. The only nuclear radiation fallout was in London. You'd want to stay out of there for at least a year, I should think. But even the devastation in Cairo didn't have radiation associated with it."

"You think he'd still let me go back to the States soon then?"

"I wouldn't know, but I'm trying to get back there by Sunday to check on Amanda and to attend a memorial service."

"How are you getting there, Rayford?"

"Commercial. Personally, I think carting around even a dozen or fewer dignitaries is extravagant for the Condor 216. Anyway, the potentate—"

"Oh, please, Rayford, don't call him that."

"Does that sound as ridiculous to you as it does to me?"

"It always has. For such a brilliant, powerful man, that stupid title makes him sound like a buffoon."

"Well, I don't really know him well enough to call him Nicolae, and that last name is a mouthful."

"Don't most of you church types consider him the Antichrist?"

Rayford flinched. He never would have expected that out of her mouth. Was she serious? He decided it was too soon to come clean. "The Antichrist?"

"I can read," she said. "In fact, I like Buck's writing. I've read his pieces in the *Weekly*. When he covers all the various theories and talks about what people think, it comes out that there's a big faction who believes that Nicolae might be the Antichrist."

"I've heard that," Rayford said.

"So you could call him Antichrist, or A.C. for short," she said.

"That's not funny," he said.

"I know," she said. "I'm sorry. I don't go in for all that cosmic war between good and evil stuff anyway. I wouldn't know if a person was the Antichrist if he was staring me in the face."

He's probably stared you in the face more than anyone else over the last couple of years, Rayford thought.

"Anyway, Hattie, I think you should ask—for lack of a better title—Global Community Grand Potentate Nicolae Carpathia if it's still all right that you take a brief trip home. I'm taking a Saturday morning flight that will arrive nonstop in Milwaukee at about noon Chicago time the same day. From what I understand, there's room in the big house of a woman from our church. You could stay with us."

"I couldn't do that, Rayford. My mother is in Denver. They haven't suffered any damage yet, have they?"

"Not as far as I know. I'm sure we could book you through to Denver." Rayford was disappointed. Here was a chance to have some influence on Hattie, but there would be no getting her to the Chicago area.

"I'm not going to ask Nicolae," she said.

"You don't want to go?"

"Oh, I want to go. And I will go. I'm just going to leave word that I'm gone. That's what he said last time I checked with him. He told me I was an adult and should make these decisions for myself. He's got more important things on his mind. Maybe I'll see you on the flight to Milwaukee. In fact, unless you hear otherwise from me, why don't you assume my driver will pick you up Saturday morning. You think it would be all right with Amanda if we sat together?"

"I hope you're not being facetious," Rayford said, "because if you really wanted to talk, I'd let her know in advance."

"Wow, I don't remember your first wife being so possessive."

"She would have been if she'd known what kind of a man I was."

"Or what kind of a woman *I* was."

"Well, maybe—"

"You go ahead and check with your wife, Rayford. If I have to sit by myself, I'll understand. Who knows? Maybe we can sit across the aisle from each other."

Rayford smiled tolerantly. He hoped for at least that.

10

BUCK FOLLOWED a strong urge to take his bag when he left the King David that night. In it was his small dictation machine, his sub-notebook computer (which would soon be replaced by the mother of all computers), his camera, that great cell phone, his toiletries, and two changes of clothing.

He left his key at the front desk and took a cab to the Wailing Wall, asking the cabbie if he spoke English. The driver held up his thumb and forefinger an inch apart and smiled apologetically.

"How far to Galilee?" Buck said.

The cabbie took his foot off the accelerator. "You go to Galilee? Wailing Wall in Jerusalem."

Buck waved him on. "I know. Wailing Wall now. Galilee later."

The cabbie headed for the Wailing Wall. "Galilee now Lake Tiberius," he said. "About 120 kilometers."

Hardly anyone was at the Wailing Wall or even in the entire temple mount area at this time of the night. The newly rebuilt temple was illuminated magnificently and looked like something in a three-dimensional picture show. It seemed to hover on the horizon. Bruce had taught Buck that one day Carpathia would sit in that new temple and proclaim himself God. The journalist in Buck wanted to be there when that happened.

Buck did not at first see the two witnesses. A small group of sailors strolled past the wrought-iron fence at the end of the Wall where the witnesses usually stood and preached. The sailors chatted in English and one pointed. "I think that's them, right over there," he said. The others turned and stared. Buck followed their gaze past the fence and to a stone building. The two mysterious figures sat with their backs against it, feet tucked under them, chins resting on their knees. They were motionless, appearing to sleep. The sailors gawked and tiptoed closer. They never got within a hundred feet of the fence, apparently having heard enough stories. They weren't going to rouse the two, the way they might do to animals at the zoo for sport. These were more than animals. These were dangerous beings who had been known to toast people who trifled with them. Buck did not want to draw attention to himself by boldly approaching the fence. He waited until the sailors got bored and moved on.

As soon as the young men were out of the area, Eli and Moishe raised their heads and looked directly at Buck. He was drawn to them. He walked directly to the fence. The witnesses rose and stood about twenty feet from Buck. "I need clarification," Buck whispered. "Can I know more about my friend's location?"

"He who has ears—"

"I know that," Buck said, "but I—"

"You would dare interrupt the servants of the Most High God?" Eli said.

"Forgive me," Buck said. He wanted to explain himself but decided to remain silent.

Moishe spoke. "You must first communicate with one who loves you."

Buck waited for more. The witnesses stood there, silent. He held out both hands in puzzlement. He felt a vibration in his shoulder bag and realized his cell phone was buzzing. Now what was he supposed to do? If he wasn't to interrupt the servants of the Most High God, did he dare take a call while conversing with them? He felt a fool. He moved away from the fence and grabbed the phone, clicked it open, and said, "This is Buck."

"Buck! It's Chloe! It's about midnight there, right?"

"Right, Chloe, but right now I'm—"

"Buck, were you sleeping?"

"No, I'm up and I'm—"

"Buck, just tell me you're not at the King David."

"Well, I'm staying there, but—"

"But you're not there right now, right?"

"No, I'm at—"

"Honey, I don't know how to tell you this, but I just have this feeling that you should not be in that hotel tonight. In fact, I just have a premonition that you shouldn't be in Jerusalem overnight. I don't know about tomorrow, and I don't know about premonitions and all that, but the feeling is so strong—"

"Chloe, I'm gonna need to call you back, OK?"

Chloe hesitated. "Well, OK, but you can't take the time to talk to me for a moment when—"

"Chloe, I won't stay at the King David tonight, and I won't stay in Jerusalem overnight, OK?"

"That makes me feel better, Buck, but I'd still like to talk—"

"I'll call you back, hon, OK?"

Buck didn't know what he thought about this new level of what Bruce had referred to as "walking in the spirit." The witnesses had implied he would find who he was looking for in Galilee, which didn't really exist anymore. The Sea of Galilee was now Lake Tiberius. His dream, if he could put any stock in that, implied he should go to Egypt for some reason. Now the witnesses wanted him to use his ears to understand. He was sorry he was not "John the Revelator," but he was going to have to ask for more information. And how had they known he had to talk to Chloe first? He had been around the two witnesses enough to know that they were never too far from the miraculous. He just wished they didn't have to be so cryptic. He was here on a dangerous mission. If they could help him, he wanted their help.

Buck set his bag down and straddled it, trying to indicate that he was willing to stop anything else he was doing and simply listen. Moishe and Eli huddled and seemed to be whispering. They approached the fence. Buck began to move toward them, as he had done the last time he visited with Rabbi Tsion Ben-Judah, but both witnesses held up a hand and he stopped a few feet from his bag and several feet short of the fence. Suddenly the two began to shout at the top of their lungs. Buck was at first startled and backed up, tripping over his own bag. He righted himself. Eli and Moishe traded off quoting verses Buck recognized from Acts and Bruce's teaching.

They shouted: "And it shall come to pass in the last days, says God, that I will pour out of My Spirit on all flesh; your sons and your daughters shall prophesy, your young men shall see visions, your old men shall dream dreams."

Buck knew there was more to the passage, but the witnesses stopped and stared at him. Was he an old man already, having just turned thirty-two? Was he one of the old men who dreamed a dream? Did they know that? Were they telling him his dream was valid?

They continued: "And on My menservants and on My maidservants I will pour out My Spirit in those days; and they shall prophesy. I will show wonders in heaven above and signs in the earth beneath: blood and fire and vapor of smoke. The sun shall be turned into darkness, and the moon into blood, before the coming of the great and awesome day of the Lord. And it shall come to pass that whoever calls on the name of the Lord shall be saved."

Buck was inspired, moved, excited to get on about his task. But where should he start? And why couldn't the witnesses just tell him? He was surprised to realize he was no longer alone. The shouting of Scripture by the witnesses had produced another small crowd. Buck didn't want to wait any longer. He picked up his bag and moved toward the fence. People warned him not to advance. He heard warnings in other languages, and a few in English. "You'll regret that, son!"

Buck came within a few feet of the witnesses. No one else dared come close.

He whispered, "By 'Galilee' I can only assume you mean Lake Tiberius," he said. How was one supposed to tell people who seemed to have come back from Bible times that their geography was out of date? "Will I find my friend in Galilee, or on the Sea of Galilee, or where?"

"He who has ears to hear . . ."

Buck knew better than to interrupt and show his frustration. "How do I get there?" he asked.

Eli spoke softly. "It will go well with you if you return to the multitude," he said.

Return to the multitude? Buck thought. He backed up and rejoined the crowd.

"Are you all right, son?" someone said. "Did they hurt you?" Buck shook his head.

Moishe began to preach in a loud voice: "Now after John was put in prison, Jesus came to Galilee, preaching the gospel of the kingdom of God, and saying 'The time is fulfilled, and the kingdom of God is at hand. Repent, and believe in the gospel.'

"And as He walked by the Sea of Galilee, He saw Simon and Andrew his brother casting a net into the sea; for they were fishermen. Then Jesus said to them, 'Follow Me, and I will make you become fishers of men.'

"They immediately left their nets and followed Him."

Buck wasn't sure what to make of all that, but he sensed he had gotten all he was going to get from the witnesses that night. Though they continued to preach, and more people gathered seemingly from nowhere to listen, Buck drifted away. He lugged his bag to a short taxi line and climbed into the back of a small cab.

"Can a fella get a boat ride up the Jordan River into Lake Tiberius at this time of night?" he asked the driver.

"Well, sir, to tell you the truth, it's a lot easier coming the other way. But, yes, there are motorized boats heading north. And some do run in the night. Of course, your touring boats are daytime affairs, but there's always someone who will take you where you want to go for the right price, any time of the day or night."

"I figured that," Buck said. Not long later he was dickering with a boatman named Michael, who refused to give a last name. "In the daytime I can carry twenty tourists on this rig, and four strong young men and I pilot it by arm power, if you know what I mean."

"Oars?"

"Yes sir, just like in the Bible. Boat's made of wood. We cover the twin outboards with wood and burlap, and no one's the wiser. Makes for a pretty long, tiring day. But when we have to go back upriver, we can't do that with the oars."

It was only Michael, the twin outboards, and Buck heading north after midnight, but Buck felt as if he had paid for twenty tourists and four oarsmen as well.

Buck began the trip standing in the bow and letting the crisp air race through his hair. He soon had to zip his leather jacket to the neck and thrust his hands deep into his pockets. Before long he was back next to Michael, who piloted the long, rustic, wood boat from just ahead of the outboard motors. Few other crafts were on the Jordan that night.

Michael shouted above the wind and the sound of the water. "So, you don't really know who you're looking for or exactly where they'll be?"

They had set out from near Jericho, and Michael had told him they had more than a hundred kilometers to travel against the current. "Could take nearly three hours just to get to the mouth of Lake Tiberius," he had added.

"I don't know much," Buck admitted. "I'm just counting on figuring it out when I get there."

Michael shook his head. "Lake Tiberius is no pond. Your friend or friends could be on either shore or at either end."

Buck nodded and sat, burying his chin in his chest to keep warm, to think, and to pray.

"Lord," he said silently, "you've never spoken to me audibly, and I don't expect you to start now, but I could sure use more direction. I don't know if the dream was from you and I'm supposed to go through Egypt on the way back or what. I don't know if I'm going to find Ben-Judah with some fishermen or whether I'm even on the right track by heading to the old Sea of Galilee. I've always enjoyed being independent and resourceful, but I confess I'm at the end of myself here. A lot of people have to be looking for Ben-Judah, and I desperately want to be the first one to find him."

The small craft had just gone around a bend when the engines sputtered and the lights, fore and aft, went out. *So much for the answer to that prayer,* Buck thought.

"Trouble, Michael?"

Buck was struck by the sudden silence as the boat drifted. It seemed headed toward shore. "No trouble, Mr. Katz. Until your eyes grow accustomed to the darkness, you're not going to be able to see that I've got a high-powered weapon pointed at your head. I would like you to remain seated and answer a few questions."

Buck felt a strange calmness. This was too bizarre, too strange even for his weird life. "I mean you no harm, Michael," he said. "You have nothing to fear from me."

"I'm not the one who should be afraid just now, sir," Michael said. "I have twice within the last forty-eight hours fired this weapon into the heads of people I've believed were enemies of God."

Buck was nearly speechless. "One thing I can assure you of, Michael, is that I am in no way an enemy of God. Are you telling me you are a servant of his?"

"I am. The question is, Mr. Katz, are you? And if you are, how will you prove it?"

"Apparently," Buck said, "we will need to assure each other we are on the same side."

"The responsibility is yours. People coming up this river looking for someone I don't want them to find wind up dead. If you're the third to go, I'll still sleep like a baby tonight."

"And you justify this homicide how?" Buck said.

"Those were the wrong people looking for the wrong person. What I want from you is your real name, the name of the person you're looking for, why you are looking for that person, and what you plan to do should you find that person."

"But Michael, until I'm sure you are on my side, I could never risk revealing that information."

"Even to the point where you'd be willing to die to protect your friend?"

"I hope it doesn't come to that, but yes."

Buck's eyes were adjusting to the darkness. Michael had carefully pointed the craft in such a way that when the power had been cut it drifted back and gently nudged an outcropping of dirt and rock jutting from the shore.

"I am impressed with that answer," Michael said. "But I will not hesitate to add you to the list of dead enemies if you can't convince me you have the right motives for locating whoever it is you want to locate."

"Test me," Buck said. "What will convince you I'm not bluffing, but at the same time convince me that you have the same person in mind?"

"Excellent," Michael said. "True or false: the person you are looking for is young."

Buck responded quickly. "Compared to you, false."

Michael continued: "The person you are looking for is female."

"False."

"The person you are looking for is a medical doctor."

"False."

"A Gentile?"

"False."

"Uneducated?"

"False."

"Bilingual?"

"False."

Buck heard Michael move the huge weapon in his hands. Buck quickly added, "Bilingual doesn't say enough. Multilingual is more like it." Michael stepped forward and pressed the barrel of the weapon against Buck's throat. Buck grimaced and shut his eyes. "The man you are looking for is a rabbi, Dr. Tsion Ben-Judah." Buck did not respond. The weapon pushed harder against his neck. Michael continued: "If you are seeking to kill him, and I was his compatriot, I would kill you. If you were seeking to rescue him, and I represented his captors, I would kill you."

"But in the latter case," Buck managed, "you would have been lying about serving God."

"True enough. And what would happen to me then?"

"You might kill me, but you will ultimately lose."

"And how do we know that?"

Buck had nothing to lose. "It's all been foretold. God wins."

"If that's true, and I turn out to be your brother, you can tell me your real name." Buck hesitated. "If it turns out that I am your enemy," Michael continued, "I'll kill you anyway."

Buck couldn't argue with that. "My name is Cameron Williams. I am a friend of Dr. Ben-Judah."

"Would you be the American he talks about?"

"Probably."

"One last test, if you don't mind."

"I seem to have no choice."

"True. Quickly list for me six prophecies of Messiah that were fulfilled in Jesus Christ, according to the witnesses who preach at the Wailing Wall."

Buck breathed a huge sigh of relief and smiled. "Michael, you are my brother in Christ. All the prophecies of the Messiah were fulfilled in Jesus Christ. I can tell you six that have to do with your culture alone. He would be a descendant of Abraham, a descendant of Isaac, a descendant of Jacob, from the tribe of Judah, heir to the throne of David, and born in Bethlehem."

The weapon rattled as Michael lay it on the deck and reached to embrace Buck. He squeezed him with a huge bear hug and was laughing and weeping. "And who told you where you might find Tsion?"

"Moishe and Eli."

"They are my mentors," Michael said. "I am one who became a believer under their preaching and that of Tsion."

"And have you murdered others looking for Dr. Ben-Judah?"

"I do not consider it murder. Their bodies will be buoyed up and burned by the salt when they reach the Dead Sea. Better their bodies than his."

"Are you, then, an evangelist?"

"In the manner of Paul the apostle, according to Dr. Ben-Judah. He says there are 144,000 of us around the world, all with the same assignment that Moishe and Eli have: to preach Christ as the only everlasting Son of the Father."

"Would you believe you were an almost instant answer to prayer?" Buck said.

"That would not surprise me in the least," Michael said. "You must realize that you are the same."

Buck was spent. He was glad Michael had to go back to the outboards and busy himself with the boat. Buck turned his face away and wept. God was so good. Michael left him alone with his thoughts for a while, but then called out with good news. "You know, we're not going all the way to Lake Tiberius."

"We're not?" Buck said, moving back toward Michael.

"You're doing what you're supposed to do by heading *toward* Galilee," Michael said. "About halfway between Jericho and Lake Tiberius we will put ashore on the east side of the river. We will hike about five kilometers inland to where my compatriots and I have hidden Dr. Ben-Judah."

"How are you able to elude the zealots?"

"An escape plan has been in place since the first time Dr. Ben-Judah spoke at Kollek Stadium. For many months we thought the guarding of his family was unnecessary. It was him the zealots wanted. At the first sign of a threat or an attack, we sent to Tsion's office a car so small it appeared only the driver could fit in it. Tsion lay on the floor of the backseat, curled into a ball and covered with a blanket. He was raced to this very boat, and I took him upriver."

"And these stories about his driver having been in on the slaughter of his family?"

Michael shook his head. "That man was exonerated in a most decisive way, would you not agree?"

"Was he also a believer?"

"Sadly, no. But he was loyal and sympathetic. We believed it was only a matter of time. We were wrong. Dr. Ben-Judah is not aware of the loss of his driver, by the way."

"He, of course, knows about his family?"

"Yes, and you can imagine how awful that is for him. When we loaded him into the boat he remained in that fetal position, covered by the blanket. In a way, that was good. It allowed us to keep him in hiding until we got him to the drop-off point. I could hear his loud sobbing over the sound of the boat throughout the entire voyage. I can still hear it."

"Only God can console him," Buck said.

"I pray so," Michael said. "I confess, the consolation period has not yet begun. He has not been able to speak. He cries and cries."

"What are your plans for him?" Buck said.

"He must leave the country. His life is worthless here. His enemies far outnumber us. He will not be safe anywhere, but at least outside Israel he has a chance."

"And where will you and your friends take him?"

"Me and my friends!?"

"Who, then?"

"You, my friend!"

"Me?" Buck said.

"God spoke through the two witnesses. He assured us a deliverer would come. He would know the rabbi. He would know the witnesses. He would know the messianic prophecies. And most of all, he would know the Lord's Christ. That, my friend, is you."

Buck nearly buckled. He had felt God's protection. He had felt the excitement of serving him. But he had never felt so directly and specifically a servant of his. He was humbled to the point of shame. He felt suddenly unworthy, undisciplined, inconsistent. He had been so blessed, and what had he done with his newfound faith? He had tried to be obedient, and he had tried to tell others. But surely he was unworthy to be used in such a way.

"What do you expect me to do with Tsion?"

"We don't know. We assumed you would smuggle him out of the country."

"That will not be easy."

"Face it, Mr. Williams, it was not easy for you to find the rabbi, was it? You very nearly got yourself killed."

"Did you think you were going to have to kill me?"

"I was merely hopeful that I would not. The odds were against your being the agent of delivery, but I was praying."

"Is there an airport anywhere near that can handle a Learjet?"

"There is a strip west of Jericho near Al Birah."

"That's back downriver, right?"

"Yes, which is an easier trip, of course. But you know that is the airport that serves Jerusalem. Most flights in and out of Israel start or end at Ben Gurion Airport in Tel Aviv, but there is also a lot of air traffic near Jerusalem."

"The rabbi has to be one of the most recognizable people in Israel," Buck said. "How in the world will I get him through customs?"

Michael smiled in the darkness. "How else? Supernaturally."

Buck asked for a blanket, which Michael produced from a compartment near the back. Buck wrapped it around his shoulders and pulled it up over his head. "How much farther?" he asked.

"About another twenty minutes," Michael said.

"I need to tell you something you may find strange," Buck said.

"Something stranger than tonight?"

Buck chuckled. "I don't suppose. It's just that I may have been warned in a dream to leave through Egypt rather than Israel."

"You *may* have?"

"I'm not used to this kind of communication from God, so I don't know."

"I wouldn't argue with a dream that seemed to come from God," Michael said.

"But does it make sense?"

"It makes more sense than trying to smuggle a target of the zealots out of here through an international airport."

"But Cairo has been destroyed. Where are flights in and out of there being rerouted to?"

"Alexandria," Michael said. "But still, you have to get out of Israel somehow."

"Find me a small strip somewhere, and we can avoid customs and go from there."

"What then do you do about going through Egypt?"

"I don't know what to make of it. Maybe the dream simply meant I should take other than a usual route."

"One thing is certain," Michael said. "This will have to be done after dark. If not tonight, then tomorrow night."

"I wouldn't be able to do it tonight if the skies opened and God pointed in my face."

Michael smiled. "My friend, if I had gone through what you've gone through and seen prayer answered the way you have, I would not be challenging God to do something so simple."

"Let's just say then that I am praying God will let me wait one more day. I have to be in touch with my pilot, and we're all going to have to work together at determining the best spot from which to head back to the United States."

"There is one thing you should know," Michael said.

"Just one?"

"No, but something very important. I believe Dr. Ben-Judah will be reluctant to flee."

"What choice does he have?"

"That's just it. He may not want a choice. With his wife and children gone, he may see no reason to go on, let alone to live."

"Nonsense! The world needs him! We must keep his ministry alive."

"You don't need to convince me, Mr. Williams. I'm just telling you, you may have a selling job to get him to flee to the United States. I believe, however, that he will likely be safer there than anywhere, if he can be safe anyplace."

"Your boots will stay driest if you stand in the bow and leap out when you hear the bottom scraping the sand," Michael said. He had turned east and raced toward the shore. In what seemed to Buck the last instant, Michael cut the engines and raised them from the water. He nimbly jogged up next to Buck and peeled his eyes, bracing himself. "Fling your bag as far as you can, jump with me, and make sure you outrun the boat!"

The boat slid along the bottom, and Buck followed orders. But when he leaped, he fell sideways and rolled. The boat barely missed him. He sat up, covered with wet sand.

"Help me, please!" Michael said. He had grabbed the boat and was tugging it onto land. Once they had secured it, Buck brushed himself off, happily found his boots were fairly dry, and began following his new friend. Buck had only his bag. Michael had only his weapon. But he also knew where he was going.

"I must ask you to be very silent now," Michael whispered as they pushed their way through underbrush. "We are secluded, but we take no chances."

Buck had forgotten how long five kilometers could be. The ground was uneven and moist. The overgrowth slapped him in the face. He switched his bag from shoulder to shoulder, never fully comfortable. He was in good shape, but this was hard. This was not jogging or cycling or running on a treadmill. This was working your way through sandy shoreline to who knew where?

He dreaded seeing Dr. Ben-Judah. He wanted to be reunited with his friend and brother in Christ, but what does one say to one who has lost his family? No platitudes, no words would make it better. The man had paid one of the steepest prices anyone could pay, and nothing short of heaven could make it better.

Half an hour later, panting and sore, he and Michael came within sight of the hideout. Michael put a finger to his lips and bent low. He held aside a bundle of dried twigs, and they advanced. Twenty yards farther, in a grove of trees, was an opening to an underground shelter invisible to anyone who hadn't come there on purpose.

11

BUCK WAS STRUCK that there were no real beds and no pillows in the hideout. *So this is what the witnesses meant when they quoted that verse about having nowhere to lay his head,* Buck thought.

Three other gaunt and desperate-looking young men, who could have been Michael's brothers, huddled in the dugout, where there was barely room to stand. Buck noticed a clear view at ground level to the path behind him. That explained why Michael had not had to declare himself or give any signal to approach.

He was introduced all around, but only Michael, of the four, understood English. Buck squinted, looking for Tsion. He could hear him, but he could not see him. Finally, a dim, electric lantern was illuminated. There, sitting in the corner, his back to the wall, was one of the first and surely the most famous of what would become the 144,000 witnesses prophesied of in the Bible.

He sat with his knees pulled up to his chest, arms wrapped around his legs. He wore a white dress shirt with the sleeves rolled up and dark dress pants that rode high on his shins and left a gap between the cuffs and the top of his socks. He wore no shoes.

How young Tsion appeared! Buck knew him to be a youthful middle age anyway, but sitting there rocking and crying he appeared young as a child. He neither looked up nor acknowledged Buck.

Buck whispered that he would like a moment alone with Tsion. Michael and the others climbed through the opening and stood idly in the underbrush, weapons at the ready. Buck crouched next to Dr. Ben-Judah.

"Tsion," Buck said, "God loves you." The words had surprised even Buck. Could it possibly seem to Tsion that God loved him now? And what kind of a platitude was that? Was it now his place to speak for God?

"What do you know for sure?" Buck asked, wondering himself what in the world he was talking about.

Tsion's reply, in his barely understandable Israeli accent, squeaked from a constricted throat: "I know that my Redeemer lives."

"What else do you know?" Buck said, listening as much as speaking.

"I know that He who has begun a good work in me will be faithful to complete it."

Praise God! Buck thought.

Buck slumped to the ground and sat next to Ben-Judah, his back against the wall. He had come to rescue this man, to minister to him. Now he had been ministered to. Only God could provide such assurance and confidence at a time of such grief.

"Your wife and your children were believers—"

"Today they see God," Tsion finished for him.

Buck had worried, Buck had wondered: Would Tsion Ben-Judah be so devastated at his inequitable loss that his faith would be shaken? Would he be so fragile that it would be impossible for him to go on? He would grieve, make no mistake. He would mourn. *But not as the heathen, who have no hope.*

"Cameron, my friend," Tsion managed, "did you bring your Bible?"

"Not in book form, sir. I have the entire Scripture on my computer."

"I have lost more than my family, Buck."

"Sir?"

"My library. My sacred books. All burned. All gone. The only things I love more in this life were my family."

"You brought nothing from your office?"

"I threw on a ridiculous disguise, the long locks of the Orthodox. Even a phony beard. I carried nothing, so as not to look like a resident scholar."

"Could not someone forward the books from your office?"

"Not without endangering their life. I am the chief suspect in the murder of my family."

"That's nonsense!"

"We both know that, my friend, but a man's perception soon becomes his reality. Anyway, where could someone send my things without leading my enemies to me?"

Buck dug into his bag and produced his laptop. "I'm not sure how much battery life is left," he said. He turned on the back-lit screen.

"This would not happen to have the Old Testament in Hebrew?" Tsion said.

"No, but those programs are widely available."

"At least they are now," Tsion said, a sob still in his throat. "My most recent studies have led me to believe that our religious freedoms will soon become scarce at an alarming pace."

"What would you like to see, sir?"

At first Buck thought Tsion had not heard his question. Then he wondered if Tsion had spoken and he himself had not heard the answer. The computer ground away, bringing up a menu of Old Testament books. Buck stole a glance at his friend. Clearly, he was trying to speak. The words would not come.

"I sometimes find the Psalms comforting," Buck said.

Tsion nodded, now covering his mouth with his hand. The man's chest heaved and he could hold back the sobs no longer. He leaned over onto Buck and collapsed in tears. "The joy of the Lord is my strength," he moaned over and over. "The joy of the Lord is my strength."

Joy, Buck thought. *What a concept in this place, at this time.* The name of the game now was survival. Certainly joy took on a different meaning than ever before in Buck's life. He used to equate joy with happiness. Clearly Tsion Ben-Judah was not implying that he was happy. He might never be happy again. This joy was a deep abiding peace, an assurance that God was sovereign. They didn't have to like what was happening. They merely had to trust that God knew what he was doing.

That made it no easier. Buck knew well that things would get worse before they ever got better. If a man was not rock solid in his faith now, he never would be. Buck sat in that damp, moist, earthen hideout in the middle of nowhere, knowing with more certainty than ever that he had put his faith in the only begotten Son of the Father. With his bent and nearly broken brother sobbing in his lap, Buck felt as close to God as he had the day he trusted Christ.

Tsion composed himself and reached for the computer. He fumbled with the keys for a minute before asking for help. "Just bring up the Psalms," he said. Buck did, and Tsion cursored through them, one hand on the computer mouse and the other covering his mouth as he wept. "Ask the others to join us for prayer," he whispered.

A few minutes later, the six men knelt in a circle. Tsion spoke to them briefly in Hebrew, Michael quietly whispering the interpretation into Buck's ear. "My friends and brothers in Christ, though I am deeply wounded, yet I must pray. I pray to the God of Abraham, Isaac, and Jacob. I praise you because you are the one and only true God, the God above all other gods. You sit high above the heavens. There is none other like you. In you there is no variation or shadow of turning." With that, Tsion broke down again and asked that the others pray for him.

Buck had never heard people praying together aloud in a foreign language. Hearing the fervency of these witness-evangelists made him fall prostrate. He felt the cold mud on the backs of his hands as he buried his face in his palms. He didn't know about Tsion but felt as if he were being borne along on clouds of peace. Suddenly Tsion's voice could be heard above the rest. Michael bent down and whispered in Buck's ear, "If God is for us, who can be against us?"

Buck did not know how long he lay on the floor. Eventually the prayers became groanings and what sounded like Hebrew versions of *amen*s and *hallelujah*s. Buck rose to his knees and felt stiff and sore. Tsion looked at him, his face still wet but seemingly finished crying for now. "I believe I can finally sleep," the rabbi said.

"Then you should. We'll not be going anywhere tonight. I'll make arrangements for after dark tomorrow."

"You should call your friend," Michael said.

"You realize what time it is?" Buck said.

Michael looked at his watch, smiled, shook his head, and said simply, "Oh."

+ + +

"Alexandria?" Ken Ritz said by phone the next morning. "Sure, I can get there easily enough. It's a big airport. When will you be along?"

Buck, who had bathed and washed out a change of clothes in a tiny tributary off the Jordan, dried himself with a blanket. One of Tsion Ben-Judah's Hebrew-speaking guards was nearby. He had cooked breakfast and now appeared to roast Tsion's socks and underwear over the small fire.

"We'll leave here tonight, as soon as the sky is black," Buck said. "Then, however long it takes a forty-foot wood boat with two outboard motors and six adult men aboard to get to Alexandria—"

Ritz was laughing. "This is my first time over here, as I think I told you," he said, "but one thing I'm pretty sure about: if you think you're coming from where you are to Alexandria without carrying that boat across dry land to the sea, you're kidding yourself."

At midday all six men were out of the dugout. They were confident no one had followed them to this remote location and that as long as they stayed out of sight from the air, they could stretch their legs and breathe a little.

Michael was not as amused at Buck's naiveté as Ken Ritz had been. He found little to smile about and nothing to laugh about these days. Michael leaned back against a tree. "There are some small airports here and there in Israel," he said. "Why are you so determined to fly out of Egypt?"

"Well, that dream—I don't know, this is all new to me. I'm trying to be practical, listen to the witnesses, follow the leadings of God. What am I supposed to do about that dream?"

"I'm a newer believer than you, my friend," Michael said. "But I wouldn't argue with a dream that was so clear."

"Maybe we have some advantage in Egypt we would not have in Israel," Buck suggested.

"I can't imagine what," Michael said. "For you to legally get out of Israel and into Egypt, you still have to go through customs somewhere."

"How realistic is that, considering my guest?"

"You mean your contraband cargo?"

Now there had been an attempt at humor, but still Michael had not smiled when he said it. "I'm just wondering," Buck said, "how carefully customs officers and border guards will be looking for Dr. Ben-Judah."

"You're wondering? I'm not wondering. We either avoid the border crossings or seek yet another supernatural act."

"I'm open to any suggestion," Buck said.

\+ + +

Rayford was on the phone with Amanda. She had filled him in on everything. "I miss you more than ever right now," he told her.

"Having me come back here was sure the right idea," she said. "With Buck gone and Chloe still tender, I feel needed here."

"You're needed here too, sweetheart, but I'm counting the days."

Rayford told her about his conversation with Hattie and her plans to fly to the States. "I trust you, Rayford. She sounds like she's hurting. We'll pray for her. What I wouldn't give to get that girl under some sound teaching."

Rayford agreed. "If she could only stop through our area on her way back. Maybe when Bruce is going through some chapter on—" Rayford realized what he had said.

"Oh, Ray—"

"It's still too fresh, I guess," he said. "I just hope God provides some other Bible teacher for us. Well, it won't be another Bruce."

"No," Amanda said, "and it won't likely be soon enough to do Hattie any good, even if she does come here."

\+ + +

Late that afternoon, Buck took a call from Ken Ritz. "You still want me to meet you in Alexandria?"

"We're talking about it, Ken. I'll get back to you."

"Can you drive a stick shift, Buck?" Michael asked.

"Sure."

"An ancient one?"

"They're the most fun, aren't they?"

"Not as ancient as this one," Michael said. "I've got an old school bus that smells of fish and paint. I use it for both professions. It's on its last legs, but if we could get you down to the southern mouth of the Jordan, you might be able to use it to find a way across the border into the Sinai. I'd stock you with petrol and water. That thing'll drink more water than it will gasoline any day."

"How big is this bus?"

"Not big. Holds about twenty passengers."

"Four-wheel drive?"

"No, sorry."

"An oil burner?"

"Not as much as water, but yes, I'm afraid so."

"What's in the Sinai?"

"You don't know?"

"I know it's a desert."

"Then you know all you need to know. You'll be jealous of the bus engine and its water needs."

"What are you proposing?"

"I sell you the bus, fair and square. You get all the paperwork. If you get stopped, the tags are traced to me, but I sold the bus."

"Keep talking—"

"You hide Dr. Ben-Judah under the seats in the back. If you can get him across the border and into the Sinai, that bus should get you as far as Al Arish, less than fifty kilometers west of the Gaza Strip and right on the Mediterranean."

"And what, you'll meet us there with your wood boat and ferry us to America?"

Finally, Buck had elicited a resigned smile from Michael. "There is an airstrip there, and it's unlikely the Egyptians will care about a man wanted in Israel. If they even seem to care, they can be bought."

One of the other guards appeared to have understood the name of the seaport city, and Buck guessed he was asking in Hebrew for Michael to explain his strategy. He spoke earnestly to Michael, and Michael turned to Buck. "My comrade is right about the risk. Israel might have already announced a huge ransom for the rabbi. Unless you could beat their price, the Egyptians might lean toward selling him back."

"How will I know the price?"

"You'll just have to guess. Keep bidding until you can beat it."

"What would be your guess?"

"Not less than a million dollars."

"A million dollars? Do you think every American has that kind of money?"

"Don't you?"

"No! And anyone who did wouldn't carry it in cash."

"Would you have half that much?"

Buck shook his head and walked away. He slipped down into the hideout. Tsion followed. "What's troubling you, my friend?" the rabbi said.

"I need to get you out of here," Buck said. "And I have no idea how."

"Have you prayed?"

"Constantly."

"The Lord will make a way somehow."

"It seems impossible right now, sir."

"Yahweh is the God of the impossible," Tsion said.

\+ + +

Night was falling. Buck felt all dressed up with nowhere to go. He borrowed a map from Michael and carefully studied it, looking north and south along the waterways that divided Israel from Jordan. If only there were a clear water route from the Jordan River or Lake Tiberius to the Mediterranean!

Buck resolutely rerolled the map and handed it to Michael. "You know," he said, thinking, "I have two sets of identification. I'm in the country under the name of Herb Katz, an American businessman. But I have my real ID as well."

"So?"

"So, how 'bout we get me across the border as Herb Katz and the rabbi as Cameron Williams?"

"You forget, Mr. Williams, that even we ancient, dusty countries are now computerized. If you came into Israel as Herb Katz, there is no record that Cameron Williams is here. If he's not here, how can he leave?"

"All right then, let's say *I* leave as Cameron Williams and the rabbi leaves as Herb Katz. Though there is no record of my being here under my own name, I can show them my clearance level and my proximity to Carpathia and tell them not to ask any questions. That often works."

"There's an outside chance, but Tsion Ben-Judah does not speak like an American Jew, does he?"

"No, but—"

"And he does not look in the least like you or your picture."

Buck was frustrated. "We are agreed that we have to get him out of here, aren't we?"

"No question," Michael said.

"Then what do you propose? I am at an end."

Dr. Ben-Judah crawled to them, obviously not wanting even to stand in the low, earthen shelter. "Michael," he said, "I cannot tell you how grateful I am for your sacrifice, for your protection. I appreciate also your sympathy and your prayers. This is very hard for me. In my flesh, I would rather not go on. Part of me very much wants to die and to be with my wife and children. Only the grace of God sustains me. Only he keeps me from wanting to avenge their deaths at any price. I foresee for myself long, lonely days and nights of dark despair. My faith is immovable and unshakable, and for that I can only thank the Lord. I feel called to continue to try to serve him, even in my grief. I do not know why he has allowed this, and I do not know how much longer he will give me to preach and teach the gospel of Christ. But something deep within me tells me that he would not have uniquely prepared me my whole life and then allowed me this second chance and used me to proclaim to the world that Jesus is Messiah unless he had more use for me.

"I am wounded. I feel as if a huge hole has been left in my chest. I cannot imagine it ever being filled. I pray for relief from the pain. I pray for release from hatred and thoughts of vengeance. But mostly I pray for peace and rest so that I may somehow rebuild something from these remaining fragments of my life. I know my life is worthless in this country now. My message has angered all those except the believers, and now with the trumped-up charges against me, I must get out. If Nicolae Carpathia focuses on me, I will be a fugitive everywhere. But it makes no sense for me to stay here. I cannot hide out forever, and I must have some outlet for my ministry."

Michael stood between Tsion and Buck and put his hands on them. "Tsion, my friend, you know that my compatriots and I are risking everything to protect you. We love you as our spiritual father, and we will die before we see you die. Of course we agree that you must go. Sometimes it seems that short of God sending an angel to whisk you away, no one as recognizable and as much a fugitive as you could slip past Israeli borders. In the midst of your pain and suffering, we dare not ask you for counsel. But if God has told you anything, we need to hear it and we need to hear it now.

"The sky is getting black, and unless we want to wait another twenty-four hours, the time to move is now. What shall we do? Where shall we go? I am willing to lead you through customs at any border crossing with weapons, but we all know the folly of that."

Buck looked to Dr. Ben-Judah, who simply bowed his head and prayed aloud once more. "O God, our help in ages past—"

Buck immediately began to shiver and dropped to his knees. He sensed the Lord impressing upon him that the answer was before them. Echoing in his mind was a phrase he could only assume was of God: "I have spoken. I have provided. Do not hesitate."

Buck felt humbled and emboldened, but still he didn't know what to do. If God had told him to go through Egypt, he was willing. Was that it? What had been provided?

Michael and Tsion were now on their knees with Buck, huddled together, shoulders touching. None of them spoke. Buck felt the presence of the Spirit of God and began to weep. The other two seemed to be shivering as well. Suddenly Michael spoke, "The glory of the Lord shall be your rear guard."

Words filled Buck's mind. Though he could barely pronounce them through his emotion, he blurted, "You give me living water and I thirst no more." What was that? Was God telling him he could travel into the Sinai desert and not die of thirst?

Tsion Ben-Judah prostrated himself on the floor, sobbing and groaning. "Oh God, oh God, oh God—"

Michael lifted his face and said, "Speak Lord, for your servants hear. Heed the words of the Lord. He who has ears to hear, let him hear. . . ."

Tsion again: "The Lord of hosts has sworn, saying, 'Surely as I have thought, so shall it come to pass, and as I have purposed, so it shall stand.'"

It was as if Buck had been steamrollered by the Spirit of God. Suddenly he knew what they must do. The pieces of the puzzle were all there. He, and they, had been waiting for some miraculous intervention. The fact was, if God wanted Tsion Ben-Judah out of Israel, he would make it out. If he did not, then he would not. God had told Buck in a dream to go another way, through Egypt. He had provided transportation through Michael. And now he had promised that his glory would be their rear guard.

"Amen," Buck said, "and amen." He rose and said, "It's time, gentlemen. Let's move."

Dr. Ben-Judah looked surprised. "Has the Lord spoken to you?"

Buck shot him a double take. "Did he not speak to you, Tsion?"

"Yes! I just wanted to make sure we were in agreement."

"If I have a vote," Michael said, "we're unanimous. Let's get going."

Michael's compatriots pulled the boat into position as Buck slung in his bag and Tsion climbed aboard. As Michael fired up the engines and they started back down the Jordan, Buck handed Tsion the identification papers that carried Buck's own name and picture. Tsion looked surprised. "I have felt no leading that I should use these," he said.

"And I have a definite leading that I should not have them on my person," Buck said. "I am in the country as Herb Katz, and I'll leave the country as Herb Katz. I'll ask you for the documents back when we get into the Sinai."

"This is exciting," Tsion said; "is it not? We are talking confidently about getting into the Sinai, and we have no idea how God is going to do it."

Michael left the boat in the hands of one of his friends and sat with Buck and Tsion. "Tsion has a little cash, a few credit cards, and his own papers. If he is found with those, he will be detained and likely put to death. Shall we keep those for him?"

Tsion reached for his wallet and opened it in the moonlight. He removed the cash, folded it once, and stuck it in his pocket. The credit cards he began flipping one by one into the Jordan River. It was as close to amusement as Buck had noticed in the man since he had first seen him in the hideout. Almost everything went into the drink—all forms of identification and the miscellaneous documentation he had gathered over the years. He pulled out a small photo section and gasped. He turned the pictures toward the moon and wept openly. "Michael, I must ask you to someday ship these to me."

"I will do it."

Tsion flipped the old wallet into the water. "And now," Michael said, "I believe you should return Mr. Williams's papers to him."

Tsion reached for them. "Wait a minute," Buck said. "Should we not try to get him some phony ID, if he's not going to use mine?"

"Somehow," Tsion said, "what Michael says seems right. I am a man who has been stripped of everything, even his identity."

Buck took back his ID and began rummaging in his bag for a place to hide it. "No good," Michael said. "There's nowhere on your person or in your bag they will not search and find an extra ID."

"Well," Buck said, "I can't toss mine into the Jordan."

Michael held out a hand. "I will ship it to you along with Tsion's photographs," he said. "It's the safest."

Buck hesitated. "You must not be found with that either," he said.

Michael took it. "My life is destined to be short anyway, brother," he said. "I feel most honored and blessed to be one of the witnesses predicted in the Scriptures. But my assignment is to preach in Israel, where the real Messiah is hated. My days are limited whether I am caught with your papers or not."

Buck thanked him and shook his head. "I still don't see how we're going to get Tsion across any border without papers, real or phony."

"We already prayed," Tsion said. "I do not know how God is going to do this either. I just know that he is."

Buck's practicality and resourcefulness were at war with his faith. "But don't we at least have to do our part?"

"And what is our part, Cameron?" the rabbi said. "It is when we are out of ideas and options and actions that we can only depend upon God."

Buck pressed his lips together and turned his face away. He wished he had the same faith Tsion had. In many ways, he knew he did. But still it didn't make sense to just plunge ahead, daring border guards to guess who Tsion was.

* * *

"I'm sorry for calling now," Chloe said. "But, Daddy, I've been trying to reach Buck on his cell phone."

"I wouldn't worry about Buck, honey. You know he finds ways to stay safe."

"Oh, Dad! Buck finds ways to nearly get himself killed. I know he was at the King David under his phony name, and I'm tempted to call there, but he promised he would stay away from there tonight."

"Then I'd wait on that, Chloe. You know Buck rarely cares much about what time of the day it is. If the story or the caper takes him all night, then it takes him all night."

"You're a big help."

"I'm trying to be."

"Well, I just don't understand why he wouldn't have his cell phone with him all the time. You keep yours in your pocket, don't you?"

"Usually. But maybe it's in his bag."

"So if his bag is in the hotel and he's out gallivanting, I'm out of luck?"

"I guess so, hon."

"I wish he'd take his phone with him, even if he doesn't take his bag."

"Try not to worry, Chloe. Buck always turns up somewhere."

* * *

When Michael docked at the mouth of the Jordan, he and his fellow guards scanned the horizon and then casually walked to his tiny car and crammed themselves inside. Michael drove to his home, which had a tiny lean-to that served as a garage. That was too small for the bus that dominated the alley behind his humble place. Lights came on. A baby cried. Michael's wife padded out in a robe and embraced him desperately. She spoke urgently to him in Hebrew. Michael looked apologetically at Buck. "I need to keep in touch more," he said, shrugging.

Buck patted his pocket, feeling for his phone. It was not there. He dug in his bag and found it. He should keep in touch with Chloe more too, but for right now it was more important that he get ahold of Ken Ritz. While Buck was on the phone he was aware of all the activity around him. Silently, Michael and his friends went to work. Oil and water were dumped into the engine and radiator of the rickety old school bus. One of the men filled the gas tank from cans stored at the side of the house. Michael's wife handed out a stack of blankets and a basket of clothes for Tsion.

As Buck hung up from talking to Ritz, who had agreed to meet them at Al Arish in the Sinai, Buck passed Michael's wife on his way out to the bus. She hesitated shyly, glancing at him. He slowed, assuming she did not understand English but also wanting to express his gratitude.

"English?" he tried. She closed her eyes briefly and shook her head. "I, uh, just wanted to thank you," he said. "So, uh, thank you." He spread his hands and then clasped them together under his chin, hoping she would know what he meant. She was a tiny, fragile-looking, dark-eyed thing. Sadness and terror were etched on her face and in her eyes. It was as if she knew she was on the right side, but that her time was limited. It couldn't be long before her husband was found out. He was not only a convert to the true Messiah, but he had also defended an enemy of the state. Buck knew Michael's wife must be wondering how long it would be before she and her children suffered the same fate that Tsion Ben-Judah's family suffered. And short of that, how long before she lost her husband to the cause, worthy though it was.

It would have been against custom for her to have touched Buck, so he was startled when she approached. She stood just two feet from his face and stared into his eyes. She said something in Hebrew and he recognized only the last two words: *"Y'shua Hamashiach."*

When Buck slipped away in the darkness and arrived at the bus, Tsion was already stretched out under the seats in the back. Food and extra water and oil and gasoline had already been stored.

Michael approached, his three friends behind him. He embraced Buck and kissed him on both cheeks. "Go with God," he said, handing him the ownership documents. Buck reached to shake hands with the other three, who apparently knew he wouldn't understand them anyway, and said nothing.

He stepped onto the bus and shut the door, settling into the creaky chair behind the wheel. Michael signaled him from outside to slide open his driver's-side window. "Feather it," Michael said.

"Feather it?" Buck said.

"The throttle."

Buck put the pedal down and released it, turning the key. The engine roared noisily to life. Michael put up both hands to urge him to be as quiet as possible. Buck slowly let out the clutch, and the old crate shuddered and jumped and lurched. Just to get out of the alleyway and onto the main thoroughfare, Buck felt as if he were riding the clutch. Shifting, clutching, and, yes, feathering the throttle, he was finally free of the tiny neighborhood and out onto the road. Now, if he could just follow Michael's instructions and directions and somehow get to the border, the rest would be up to God. He felt an unusual sense of freedom, simply piloting a vehicle—albeit one like this—on his own. He was on a journey that would lead him somewhere. By dawn, he could be anywhere: detained, imprisoned, in the desert, in the air, or in heaven.

12

IT DIDN'T TAKE Buck long to learn what Michael meant by "feathering" the throttle. Any time Buck clutched to shift, the engine nearly stalled. When he came to a complete stop, he had to keep his left foot on the clutch, his right heel on the brake, and feather the throttle with the toes of his right foot.

Along with the title to the dilapidated rig, Michael had included a rough map. "There are four different places where you can cross over from Israel into Egypt by auto," Michael had told him. The two most direct were at Rafah on the Gaza Strip. "But these have always been heavily patrolled. You might rather head south directly out of Jerusalem through Hebron to Beersheba. I would advise continuing southeast out of Beersheba, though that is slightly out of your way. About two-thirds of the way between Beersheba and Yeroham is a southern but mostly western cutoff that takes you through the northern edge of the Negev. You're less than fifty kilometers from the border there, and when you come within less than ten kilometers, you can head north and west or continue due west. I couldn't guess which border would be easier to get through. I would recommend the southern, because you can then continue to a northwest route that takes you directly into Al Arish. If you take the northern pass, you must go back up to the main road between Rafah and Al Arish, which is more heavily traveled and more carefully watched."

That had been all Buck needed to hear. He would take the southernmost of the four border crossings and pray he was not stopped until then.

Tsion Ben-Judah stayed on the floor under the seats until Buck had rumbled far enough south of Jerusalem that they both felt safe. Tsion moved up and crouched next to Buck. "Are you tired?" he asked. "Would you like me to take over driving?"

"You're joking."

"It may be many months before I am able to find humor in anything," Tsion said.

"But you're not serious about sitting behind the wheel of this bus, are you? What would we do if we were stopped? Trade places?"

"I was just offering."

"I appreciate it, but it's out of the question. I'm fine, well-rested. Anyway, I'm scared to death. That will keep me alert."

Buck downshifted to navigate a curve, and Tsion swung forward from the momentum. He hung on to the metal pole next to the driver's seat, and he spun around and smacked into Buck, pushing him to the left.

"I told you, Tsion, I'm awake. You need not continually try to rouse me."

He looked at Tsion to see if he had elicited a smile. It appeared Tsion was trying to be polite. He apologized profusely and slid into the seat behind Buck, his head low, his chin resting on his hands, which gripped the bar that separated the driver from the first seat. "Tell me when I need to duck."

"By the time I know that, you'll likely already be seen."

"I do not think I can take riding long on the floorboards," Ben-Judah said. "Let us both just be on the lookout."

It was difficult for Buck to get the old bus to move faster than seventy kilometers per hour. He feared it would take all night to get to the border. Maybe that was OK. The darker and the later the better. As he chugged along, watching the gauges and trying not to do anything that might draw attention to them, he noticed in his rearview mirror that Tsion had slumped in the seat and was trying to rest on his side. Buck thought the rabbi had said something. "I beg your pardon?" Buck said.

"I am sorry, Cameron. I was praying."

Later Buck heard him singing. Later still, weeping. Well after midnight, Buck checked his map and noted that they were rolling through Haiheul, a small town just a tick north of Hebron. "Will the tourists be out at this time of night in Hebron?" Buck asked.

Tsion leaned forward. "No. But still, it is a populated area. I will be careful. Cameron, there is something I would like to talk to you about."

"Anything."

"I want you to know that I am deeply grateful that you have sacrificed your time and risked your life to come for me."

"No friend would do less, Tsion. I've felt a deep bond with you since the day you first took me to the Wailing Wall. And then we had to flee together after your television broadcast."

"We have been through some incredible experiences, it is true." Tsion said. "That is why I knew if I could merely get Dr. Rosenzweig to point you in the direction of the witnesses, you would find me. I did not dare let on to him where I was. Even my driver knew only to take me to Michael and the other brothers in Jericho. My driver was so distraught at what happened to my family that he was in tears. We have been together for many years. Michael promised to keep him informed, but I would like to call him myself. Perhaps I can use your secure phone once we have passed the border."

Buck didn't know what to say. He had more confidence than Michael that Tsion could take yet more bad news, but why did he have to be the one to bear it? The intuitive rabbi seemed to immediately suspect Buck was hiding something. "What?" he asked. "Do you think it is too late to call him?"

"It *is* very late," Buck said.

"But if the situation were reversed, I would be overjoyed to hear from him at any time of the day or night."

"I'm sure he felt—feels the same," Buck said lamely.

Buck peeked into the rearview mirror. Tsion stared at him, a look of realization coming over him. "Maybe I should call him now," he suggested. "May I use your phone?"

"Tsion, you are always welcome to whatever I have. You know that. I would not phone him now, no."

When Tsion responded, Buck knew that he knew. His voice was flat, full of the pain that would plague him the rest of his days. "Cameron, his name was Jaime. He had been with me since I started teaching at the university. He was not an educated man; however, he was wise in the ways of the world. We talked much about my findings. He and my wife were the only ones besides my student assistants who knew what I was going to say on the television broadcast. He was close, Cameron. So close. But he is no longer with us, is he?"

Buck thought about merely shaking his head, but he could not do that. He busied himself looking for road signs for Hebron, but the rabbi, of course, would not let it go.

"Cameron, we are too close and have gone through too much for you to hold out on me now. Clearly you have been told the disposition of Jaime. You must understand that the toll the bad news has taken on me can be made neither worse by hearing more, nor better by hearing less. We believers in Christ, of all people, must never fear any truth, hard as it may be."

"Jaime is dead," Buck said.

Tsion hung his head. "He heard me preach so many times. He knew the gospel. Sometimes I even pushed him. He was not offended. He knew I cared about him. I can only hope and pray that perhaps after he delivered me to Michael, he had time to join the family. Tell me how it happened."

"Car bomb."

"Instantaneous, then," he said. "Perhaps he never knew what hit him. Perhaps he did not suffer."

"I'm so sorry, Tsion. Michael didn't think you could take it."

"He underestimates me, but I appreciate his concern. I worry about everyone associated with me. Anyone who appears they might know anything of my whereabouts may suffer if they are not forthcoming. That includes so many. I will never forgive myself if they all pay the ultimate price for merely having known me. Frankly, I worry about Chaim Rosenzweig."

"I wouldn't worry about him just yet," Buck said. "He's still closely identified with Carpathia. Ironically, that's his protection for now."

Buck drove cautiously through Hebron, and he and Tsion rode in silence all the way to Beersheba. In the wee hours of the morning, about ten kilometers south of Beersheba, Buck noticed the heat gauge rising. The oil gauge still looked OK, but the last thing Buck wanted was to overheat. "I'm gonna add some water to this radiator, Tsion," he said. The rabbi seemed to be dozing.

Buck pulled far off the road onto the gravel shoulder. He found a rag and climbed out. Once he got the hood propped up, he gingerly opened the radiator cap. It was steaming, but he was able to dump a couple of liters of water in before the thing boiled over. While he was working he noticed a Global Community peacekeeping force squad car slowly drive past. Buck tried to look casual and took a deep breath.

He wiped his hands and dropped the rag into his water can, noticing the squad car had pulled over about a hundred feet in front of the bus and was slowly backing up. Trying not to look suspicious, Buck tossed the water can into the bus and came back around to shut the hood. Before he shut it, the squad car backed onto the road and turned to face him on the shoulder. With the headlights shining in his eyes, Buck heard the Global Community peacekeeper say something to him in Hebrew over his loudspeaker.

Buck held out both arms and hollered, "English!"

In a heavy accent, the peacekeeper said, "Please to remain outside your vehicle."

Buck turned to lower the hood, but the officer called out to him again, "Please to stand where you are."

Buck shrugged and stood awkwardly, hands at his sides. The officer spoke into his radio. Finally the young man emerged. "Happy evening to you, sir," he said.

"Thank you," Buck said. "Just had some overheating problems is all."

The officer was dark and slender, wearing the gaudy uniform of the Global Community. Buck wished he'd had his own passport and papers. Nothing sent a GC operative running more quickly than Buck's 2-A clearance. "Are you alone?" the officer asked.

"Name's Herb Katz," Buck said.

"I asked you are you alone?"

"I'm an American businessman, here on pleasure."

"Your papers, please."

Buck pulled out his phony passport and wallet. The young man studied them with a flashlight and pointed the light into Buck's face. Buck didn't think that was necessary with the headlights already blinding him, but he said nothing.

"Mr. Katz, can you tell me where you got this vehicle?"

"I bought it tonight. Just before midnight."

"And you bought it from?"

"I have the papers. I can't pronounce his name. I'm an American."

"Sir, the plates on this vehicle trace to a resident of Jericho."

Buck, still playing dumb, said, "Well, there you go! That's where I bought it, in Jericho."

"And you say you purchased it before midnight?"

"Yes, sir."

"Are you aware of a manhunt in this country?"

"Tell me," Buck said.

"It happens that the owner of this vehicle was detained, just over an hour ago, in connection with aiding and abetting a murder suspect."

"You don't say?" Buck said. "I just took a boat ride with this man. He runs a tour boat. I told him I needed a vehicle to just get me from Israel to Egypt so I could fly home to America. He told me he had just the rig, and this is it."

The officer moved toward the bus. "I'm going to need to see those papers," he said.

"I'll get them for you," Buck said, stepping in front of him and jumping onto the bus. He grabbed the papers and waved them as he came down the steps. The officer backed away and into the light of his own headlamps again.

"The papers seem to be in order, but it's just too coincidental that you purchased this vehicle only hours before this man was arrested."

"I don't see what buying a bus has to do with what some guy is messed up with," Buck said.

"We have reason to believe that the man who sold you this vehicle has been harboring a murderer. He was found with the suspect's papers and those of an American. It will not be long before we persuade him to tell us where he has harbored the suspect." The officer looked at his own notes. "Are you familiar with a Cameron Williams, an American?"

"Doesn't sound like the name of any friend I've got. I'm from Chicago."

"And you are leaving tonight, from Egypt?"

"That's right."

"Why?"

"Why?" Buck repeated.

"Why do you need to leave through Egypt? Why do you not fly out of Jerusalem or Tel Aviv?"

"No flights tonight. I want to get home. I've chartered a flight."

"And why didn't you simply hire a ride?"

"If you look closely at that title and bill of sale, you'll see I paid less for the bus than I would have for a ride."

"One moment, sir." The officer went back to his squad car and sat talking on the radio for several minutes.

Buck prayed he would think of something that would keep the peacekeeper from searching the bus.

Soon the young man emerged again. "You claim to never have heard of Cameron Williams. We are now determining if the man who sold you this vehicle will implicate you in his scheme."

"His scheme?" Buck said.

"It will not take us long to find out where he has hidden our suspect. It will be in his best interest to tell us the whole truth. He has a wife and children, after all."

For the first time in his life, Buck was tempted to kill a man. He knew the officer was just a pawn in a cosmic game, the war between good and evil. But he represented evil. Would Buck have been justified, the way Michael had felt justified, in killing those who might kill Tsion? The officer heard squawking on his radio and hurried back to the squad car. He returned in a moment.

"Our techniques have worked," he said. "We have extracted the location of the hiding place, somewhere between Jericho and Lake Tiberius off the Jordan River. But under the threat of torture and even death, he swears you were merely a tour guest to whom he sold the vehicle."

Buck sighed. Others might consider that mutual ruse a coincidence. To him it was as much a miracle as what he had seen at the Wailing Wall.

"Just for safety's sake, however," the officer said, "I have been asked to search your vehicle for any evidence of the fugitive."

"But you said—"

"Have no fear, sir. You are in the clear. Perhaps you were used to transport some evidence out of the country without your knowing it. We simply need to check the vehicle for anything that might lead us to the suspect. I will thank you to stand aside and remain here while I search your vehicle."

"You don't need a warrant or my permission or anything?"

The officer turned menacingly toward Buck. "Sir, you have been pleasant and cooperative. But do not make the mistake of thinking that you are talking with local law enforcement here. You can see from my car and my uniform that I represent the peacekeeping forces of the Global Community. We are restricted by no conventions or rules. I could confiscate this vehicle without so much as your signature. Now wait here."

Wild thoughts ran through Buck's mind. He considered trying to disarm the officer and racing away in the man's squad car with Tsion. It was ludicrous, he knew, but he hated inaction. Would Tsion jump the officer? Kill him? Buck heard the officer's footsteps move slowly to the back of the bus and then to the front again. The flashlight beam danced around inside the bus.

The officer rejoined him. "What did you think you were going to do? Did you think you were going to get away with this? Did you think I was going to allow you to drive this vehicle across the border into Egypt and to simply dump it? Were you going to leave it at an airport somewhere for local authorities to clean up?"

Buck was dumbfounded. This was what the officer was worried about now? Had he not seen Tsion Ben-Judah on the bus? Had God supernaturally blinded him?

"Uh, I, uh, actually had thought of that. Yes, I understood that many of the locals who try to pick up extra money helping with baggage and the like, that they, uh, would be thrilled to have such a vehicle."

"You must be a very wealthy American, sir. I realize this bus is not worth much, but it sure is a big tip for a baggage handler, wouldn't you say?"

"Call me frivolous," Buck said.

"Thank you for your cooperation, Mr. Katz."

"Well, you're welcome. And thank you."

The officer reentered his vehicle and pulled across the road, heading north back into Beersheba. Buck, his knees like jelly and his fingers twitching, slammed the hood shut and boarded the bus. "How in the world did you pull that off, Tsion? Tsion! It's me! You can come out now, wherever you are. No way you fit up in the luggage rack. Tsion?"

Buck stood on a seat and scanned the racks. Nothing. He lay on the floor and looked beneath the seats. Nothing but his own bag, the pile of clothes, the foodstuffs, and the water, oil, and gasoline. If Buck hadn't known better, he'd have thought Tsion Ben-Judah had been raptured after all.

Now what? No traffic had passed while Buck was engaged with the officer. Did he dare shout into the darkness? When had Tsion left the bus? Rather than make a scene for anyone who might happen along, Buck merely climbed aboard, restarted the engine, and drove down the shoulder of the road. After about two hundred yards, he tried to pop a U-turn and found that he had to accomplish it with a three-point turn instead. He drove down the other shoulder, clouds of dust rising behind him, illuminated by the red taillights. *C'mon, Tsion! Tell me you didn't start off walking all the way toward Egypt!*

Buck thought of honking the horn. Instead he drove another couple of hundred yards north and turned around yet again. This time his lights picked up the small, furtive wave of his friend from a grove of trees in the distance. He slowly rolled the bus to the area and opened the door. Tsion Ben-Judah leaped aboard and lay on the floor next to Buck. He was panting.

"If you have ever wondered what the saying meant about the Lord working in mysterious ways," Tsion said, "there was your answer."

"What in the world happened?" Buck said. "I thought we'd had it for good."

"So did I!" Tsion said. "I was dozing and barely understood that you were going to do something with the engine. When you raised the hood, I realized I needed to relieve myself. You were pouring the water when I got off. I was only about fifteen feet off the road when the squad car rolled by. I did not know what you would do, but I knew I could not be on that bus. I just started walking this way, praying you would somehow talk your way out of it."

"Did you hear our conversation, then?"

"No. What all was said?"

"You won't believe it, Tsion." And Buck told him the whole story as they rolled on toward the border.

As the old bus putted along in the darkness, Tsion apparently grew brave. He sat in the front seat, directly behind Buck. He was not hiding, not leaned over. He bent forward and spoke earnestly into Buck's ear. "Cameron," he said, his voice quavery and weak, "I am going nearly mad wondering who will take care of the disposition of my family."

Buck hesitated. "I don't quite know how to ask you this, sir, but what generally happens in cases like this? When pseudo-official factions do something like this, I mean."

"That is what bothers me. You never see what happens to the bodies. Do they bury them? Do they burn them? I do not know. But the mere imagining of it is deeply troubling to me."

"Tsion, far be it from me to advise you spiritually. You are a man of the Word and of deep faith."

Tsion interrupted him. "Do not be foolish, my young friend. Just because you are not a scholar does not mean you are any less mature in the faith. You were a believer before I was."

"Still, sir, I am at the end of my insight in knowing how to deal with such personal tragedy. I could not have remotely handled what you're going through in any way near how you're handling it."

"Do not forget, Cameron, that I am mostly running on emotion. No doubt my system is in shock. My worst days are yet to come."

"Frankly, Tsion, I have feared the same thing for you. At least you have been able to cry. Tears can be a great release. I fear for those who go through such trauma and find it impossible to shed tears."

Tsion sat back and said nothing. Buck prayed silently for him. Finally, Tsion leaned forward again. "I come from a heritage of tears," he said. "Centuries of tears."

"I wish I could do something tangible for you, Tsion," Buck said.

"Tangible? What is more tangible than this? You have been of such encouragement to me I cannot tell you. Who else would do this for a man he hardly knows?"

"It seems I've known you forever."

"And God has given you resources that even my closest friends do not have." Tsion seemed deep in thought. Finally he said, "Cameron, there is something you can do that would be of some comfort to me."

"Anything."

"Tell me about your little group of believers there in America. What did you call them? The core group, I mean?"

"The Tribulation Force."

"Yes! I love hearing such stories. Wherever I have gone in the world to preach and to help be an instrument in converting the 144,000 Jews who are becoming the witnesses foretold in the Scriptures, I have heard wonderful tales of secret meetings and the like. Tell me all about your Tribulation Force."

Buck began at the beginning. He started on the plane when he was merely a passenger and Hattie Durham was a flight attendant, Rayford Steele the pilot. As he talked, he kept glancing in the rearview mirror to see if Tsion was really listening or merely tolerating a long story. Buck had always been amazed that his own mind could be on two tracks at once. He could be telling a story and thinking of another at the same time. All the while he told Tsion of hearing Rayford spill his own story of a spiritual quest, of meeting Chloe and traveling back from New York to Chicago with her on the very day she prayed with her father to receive Christ, of meeting and being counseled by Bruce Barnes and mentored and tutored by him whenever possible, Buck was trying to hold at bay his fear of facing the border crossing. At the same time he was wondering whether he should complete his story. Tsion did not know yet of the death of

Bruce Barnes, a man he had never met but with whom he had corresponded and with whom he hoped to minister one day.

Buck brought the story up to just a few days before, when the Tribulation Force had reunited in Chicago, just before war erupted. Buck sensed Tsion growing more nervous as they neared the border. He seemed to move more, to interrupt more, to talk more quickly, and to ask more questions.

"And Pastor Bruce had been on the church staff for many years without having truly been a believer?"

"Yes. That was a sad, difficult story even for him to tell."

"I cannot wait to meet him," Tsion said. "I will grieve for my family, and I will miss my mother country as if she truly were my parent. But to get to pray with your Tribulation Force and open the Scriptures with them, this will be balm for my pain, salve for my wound."

Buck took a deep breath. He wanted to stop talking, to concentrate on the road, on the border ahead. Yet he could never be less than fully honest with Tsion. "You will meet Bruce Barnes at the Glorious Appearing," he said.

Buck peeked in the mirror. Clearly Tsion had heard and understood. He lowered his head. "When did it happen?" he asked.

Buck told him.

"And how did he die?"

Buck told him what he knew. "We're probably never going to know whether it was the virus he picked up overseas or the impact of the blast on the hospital. Rayford said there seemed to be no marks on his body."

"Perhaps the Lord spared him from the bombing by taking him first."

Buck considered that God was providing Rabbi Ben-Judah to be the new scriptural and spiritual mentor for the Tribulation Force, but he didn't dare suggest that. No way an international fugitive could become the new pastor of New Hope Village Church, especially if Nicolae Carpathia had his sights trained on him. Anyway, Tsion might consider Buck's idea a crazy one. Was there not some easier way God could have put Tsion in a position to help the Tribulation Force without costing him his wife and children?

In spite of his nervousness, in spite of his fear, in spite of the distraction of driving in unknown, dangerous territory with a less-than-desirable conveyance, suddenly Buck saw it all laid out before him. He wouldn't call it a vision. It was simply a realization of the possibilities. Suddenly he knew the first use for the secret shelter beneath the church. He envisioned Tsion there, supplied with everything he needed, including one of those great computers Donny Moore was dolling up.

Buck grew excited just thinking about it. He would provide for the rabbi every software package he needed. He would have the Bible in every version, every language, with all the notes and commentaries and dictionaries and encyclopedias he needed. Tsion would never again have to worry about losing his books. They would all be in one place, on one massive hard drive.

And what might Donny come up with that would allow Tsion to broadcast surreptitiously on the Internet? Was it possible his ministry could be more dramatic and wider than ever? Could he do his teaching and preaching and Bible studies on the Net to the millions of computers and televisions all over the world? Surely there must be some technology that would allow him to do this without being detected. If cell phone manufacturers could provide chips allowing a caller to jump between three dozen different frequencies in seconds to avoid static and interception, surely there was a way to scramble a message over the Net and keep the sender from being identified.

In the distance Buck saw GC squad cars and trucks near two one-story buildings that straddled the road. The buildings would be the exit from Israel. Up the road would be the entrance into the Sinai. Buck downshifted and checked his gauges. The heat was starting to rise only slightly, and he was convinced if he drove slowly and was able to shut off the vehicle for a while at the border crossing, that would take care of it. He was doing fine on fuel, and the oil gauge looked OK.

He was irritated. His mind was engaged with the possibilities of a ministry for Tsion Ben-Judah that would outstrip anything he had ever been able to accomplish before, but it also reminded him that he too could, in essence, broadcast over the Internet the truth about what was going on in the world. For how long could he pretend to be a cooperative, if not loyal employee, of Nicolae Carpathia? His journalism was no longer objective. It was propaganda. It was what George Orwell would have called "Newspeak" in his famous novel *1984*.

Buck didn't want to face a border crossing. He wanted to sit with a yellow pad and noodle his ideas. He wanted to excite the rabbi over the possibilities. But he could not. Apparently his rattletrap and its vulnerable personal cargo would have the full attention of the border guards. Whatever vehicles had preceded them were long gone, and none appeared in the rearview mirror.

Tsion lay on the floor beneath the seats. Buck pulled up to two uniformed and helmeted guards at a lowered crossbar. The one on the driver's side of the bus signaled that he should slide open the window and then spoke to him in Hebrew.

"English," Buck said.

"Passport, visa, identification papers, vehicle registration, any goods to declare, and anything on board you want us to know about before we search should be passed through the window or told to us before we raise the gate."

Buck stood and retrieved from the front seat all the papers related to the vehicle. He added his phony passport, visa, and identification. He slipped back behind the wheel and passed everything out to the guard. "I am also carrying foodstuffs, gasoline, oil, and water."

"Anything else?"

"Anything else?" Buck repeated.

"Anything else we need to see, sir! You will be interrogated inside, and your vehicle will be searched over there." The guard pointed just beyond the building on the right side of the road.

"Yes, I have some clothing and some blankets."

"Is that all?"

"Those are the only other things I am carrying."

"Very good, sir. When the bar is raised, please pull your vehicle to the right and meet me in the building on the left."

Buck slowly drove under the angled crossbar, keeping the bus in first gear, the noisiest. Tsion reached past Buck's chair and grabbed his ankle. Buck took it as encouragement, as thanks, and, if necessary, farewell. "Tsion," he whispered, "your only hope is to stay as far in the back as possible. Can you scoot all the way to the back?"

"I will try."

"Tsion, Michael's wife said something to me when I left. I didn't understand it. It was in Hebrew. The last two words were something like *Y'shua Hama-*something."

"*Y'shua Hamashiach* means 'Jesus the Messiah,'" Tsion said, his voice quavery. "She was wishing you the blessing of God on your trip, in the name of *Y'shua Hamashiach*."

"The same to you, my brother," Buck said.

"Cameron, my friend, I will see you soon. If not in this life, then in the everlasting kingdom."

The guards were approaching, obviously wondering what was keeping Buck. He shut off the engine and opened the door, just as a young guard approached. Buck grabbed a water can and shouldered his way past the guard. "Been having a little trouble with the radiator," he said. "You know anything about radiators?"

Distracted, the guard raised his eyebrows and followed Buck to the front of the bus. He raised the hood and they added water. The older guard, the one who had talked to him at the gate, said "Come on, let's go, let's go!"

"Be right with you," Buck said, aware of every nerve in his body. He made a huge noise, slamming the hood. The younger guard moved toward the door, but Buck passed him, excused himself, put one foot on the steps, and tossed the water can into the bus. He thought about "helping" the guard search the bus. He could stand with him and point out the blankets and cans of gas, oil, and water. But he had already come dangerously close, he feared, to making them suspicious. He came back off the bus and into the face of the young guard. "Thanks so much for your help. I don't know much about engines, really. Business is my game. America, you know."

The young guard looked him in the eyes and nodded. Buck prayed he would merely follow him into the building on the other side of the border crossing. The older guard was waiting, staring at him, now waving for him to come over. Buck had no choice now. He left Rabbi Tsion Ben-Judah, the most recognizable and notorious fugitive in Israel, in the hands of border guards.

Buck hurried into the processing building. He was as distracted as he'd ever been, but he couldn't let it show. He wanted to turn and see if Tsion was dragged off the bus. No way he could escape on foot as he had on the road not long before. There was nowhere to go here, nowhere to hide. Barbed wire fences lined each side. Once you got in the gate, you had to go one way or the other. There was no going around.

The original guard had Buck's papers spread out before him. "You entered Israel through what entry point?"

"Tel Aviv," Buck said. "It should all be there—"

"Oh, it is. Just checking. Your papers seem to be in order, Mr. Katz," he added, stamping Buck's passport and visa. "And you are representing . . . ?"

"International Harvesters," Buck said, making it plural because he meant it.

"And you're leaving the area when?"

"Tonight. If my pilot meets up with me at Al Arish."

"And how will you dispose of the vehicle?"

"I was hoping to sell it cheap to someone at the airport."

"Depending upon how cheap, that should be no problem."

Buck seemed frozen into place. The guard looked over his shoulder and out across the road. What was he looking at? Buck could only imagine Tsion detained, handcuffed, and led across the road. What a fool he had been to not try to find some secret compartment for Tsion. This was madness. Had he driven a man to his death? Buck couldn't stand the thought of losing yet another member of his new family in Christ.

The guard was on the computer. "This shows you were detained near Beersheba earlier this morning?"

"Detained is overstating it a bit. I was adding water to the radiator and was questioned briefly by a GC peacekeeping officer."

"Did he tell you the previous owner of your vehicle has been arrested in connection with the escape of Tsion Ben-Judah?"

"He did."

"You might be interested in this, then." The guard turned and pointed a remote control device at a television up in the corner. The Global Community Network News was reporting that a Michael Shorosh had been arrested in connection with the harboring of a fugitive from justice. "Global Community spokesmen say that Ben-Judah, formerly a respected scholar and clergyman, apparently became a radical fanatic fundamentalist, and point to this sermon he delivered just a week ago as evidence that he overreacted to a New Testament passage and was later seen by several neighbors slaughtering his own family."

Buck watched in horror as the news ran a tape of Tsion speaking at a huge rally in a filled stadium in Larnaca, on the island of Cyprus. "You'll note," the newsman said, as the tape was stopped, "the man on the platform behind Dr. Ben-Judah has been identified as Michael Shorosh. In a raid on his Jericho home shortly after midnight tonight, peacekeeping forces found personal photos of Ben-Judah's family and identification papers from both Ben-Judah and an American journalist, Cameron Williams. Williams's connection to the case has not been determined."

Buck prayed they would not show his face on television. He was startled to see the guard look over his shoulder to the door. Buck whirled to see the young guard come in, staring at him. The young man let the door close behind him and leaned back against it, his arms folded over his chest. He watched the news report with them. The tape showed Ben-Judah reading from Matthew. Buck had heard Tsion preach this message before. The verses, of course, had been taken out of context. "Whoever denies Me before men, him I will also deny before My Father who is in heaven.

"Do not think that I came to bring peace on earth. I did not come to bring peace but a sword. For I have come to 'set a man against his father, a daughter against her mother, and a daughter-in-law against her mother-in-law'; and 'a man's enemies will be those of his own household.' He who loves father or mother more than Me is not worthy of Me. And he who loves son or daughter more than Me is not worthy of Me. And he who does not take his cross and follow after Me is not worthy of Me."

The news reporter said solemnly, "This just a few days before the rabbi murdered his own wife and children in broad daylight."

"That's something, isn't it?" the older guard said.

"That's something all right," Buck said, fearing his voice betrayed him.

The guard at the desk was stacking Buck's papers. He looked past Buck to the young guard. "Everything all right with the vehicle, Anis?"

Buck had to think quickly. Which would look more suspicious? Not turning to look at the young man, or turning to look at him? He turned to look. Still standing before the closed door, arms over his chest, the rigid young man nodded once. "All is in order. Blankets and supplies."

Buck had been holding his breath. The man at the desk slid his papers across. "Safe journey," he said.

Buck nearly wept as he exhaled. "Thank you," he said.

He turned toward the door, but the older guard was not finished. "Thank you for visiting Israel," he added.

Buck wanted to scream. He turned around and nodded. "Yeah, uh, yes. You're welcome."

He had to will himself to walk. Anis did not move as Buck approached the door. He came face-to-face with the young man and stopped. He sensed the older guard watching. "Excuse me," Buck said.

"My name is Anis," the man said.

"Yes, Anis. Thank you. Excuse me, please."

Finally Anis stepped aside and Buck shakily left. His hands trembled as he folded his papers and stuffed them into his pocket. He boarded the rickety old bus and fired it up. If Tsion had found somewhere to hide, how would Buck find him now? He executed the fragile dance between clutch and accelerator and got the rig moving. Finally up to speed, he shifted into third, and the engine smoothed out a bit. He called out, "If you're still on board, my friend, stay right where you are until the lights of that border crossing disappear. Then I want to know everything."

13

RAYFORD WAS TIRED of being awakened by the phone. However, few people in New Babylon outside of Carpathia and Fortunato ever called him. And they usually had the sense not to disturb him in the middle of the night. So, he decided, the ringing phone was either good news or bad news. One chance out of two, in this day and age, wasn't bad.

He picked up the phone. "Steele," he said.

It was Amanda. "Oh, Rayford, I know it's the middle of the night there, and I'm sorry to wake you. It's just that we've had a little excitement here, and we want to know if you know anything."

"Know anything about what?"

"Well, Chloe and I were just going over all these pages from Bruce's computer printout. We told you about that?"

"Yeah."

"We got the strangest call from Loretta at the church. She said she was just working there alone, taking a few phone calls. She said she just had an overwhelming urge to pray for Buck."

"For Buck?"

"Yes. She said she was so overcome with the emotion of it that she quickly stood up from her chair. She said she thought that made her lightheaded, but something made her fall to her knees. Once she was kneeling, she realized she wasn't dizzy but was just praying earnestly for Buck."

"All I know, hon, is that Buck is in Israel. I think he's trying to find Tsion Ben-Judah, and you know what's happened to his family."

"We know," Amanda said. "It's just that Buck has a way of getting himself into trouble."

"He also has a way of getting himself out of trouble," Rayford said.

"Then what do you make of this premonition, or whatever it was, of Loretta's?"

"I wouldn't call it a premonition. We all could use prayer these days, couldn't we?"

Amanda sounded annoyed. "Rayford, this was no fluke. You know Loretta is as levelheaded as they come. She was so upset she shut the office and came home."

"You mean before nine o'clock at night? What has she become, a slacker?"

"Come on, Ray. She didn't go in until about noon today. You know she often stays till nine. People call at all hours."

"I know. I'm sorry."

"She wants to talk to you."

"To me?"

"Yes. Will you talk to her?"

"Sure, put her on." Rayford had no idea what to say to her. Bruce would have had an answer for something like this.

Loretta indeed sounded shaken. "Captain Steele, I'm so sorry 'bout troubling you at this time of the night. What is it, goin' on like three o'clock over there?"

"Yes ma'am, but it's all right."

"No, it's not all right. There's no reason to raise you out of a sound sleep. But sir, God told me to pray for that boy, I just know it."

"Then I'm glad you did."

"Do you think I'm crazy?"

"I've always thought you were crazy, Loretta. That's why we love you so much."

"I know you're sporting with me, Captain Steele, but seriously, have I lost my marbles?"

"No ma'am. God seems to be working in much more direct and dramatic ways all the time. If you were led to pray for Buck right then, you remember to ask him what was happening."

"That's just the thing, Mr. Steele. I had this overwhelming sense that Buck was in deep trouble. I just hope he makes it out of there alive. We're all hoping he can be back here in time for the Sunday service. You'll be here, won't you?"

"The Lord willing," Rayford said, stunned to hear from his own lips a phrase he had always considered silly when Irene's old friends had used it.

"We want everybody together Sunday," Loretta said.

"It's my highest priority, ma'am. And Loretta, would you do me a favor?"

"After gettin' you up in the middle of the night? You name it."

"If the Lord prompts you to pray for me, would you do it with all your might?"

"'Course I will. You know that. I hope you're not just bein' funny now."

"I've never been more serious."

* * *

When the lights of the border crossing disappeared behind him, Buck pulled the bus off the road, shifted into neutral, set the brake, turned sideways in his seat, and sighed heavily. He could barely produce volume in his voice. "Tsion, are you on this bus? Come out now, wherever you are."

From the back of the bus came an emotion-filled voice. "I am here, Cameron. Praise the Lord God Almighty, Maker of heaven and earth."

The rabbi crawled out from under the seats. Buck met him in the aisle and they embraced. "Talk to me," Buck said.

"I told you the Lord would make a way somehow," Tsion said. "I don't know if the young Anis was an angel or a man, but he was sent from God."

"Anis?"

"Anis. He walked up and down the aisle of the bus, shining his flashlight here and there. Then he knelt and shined it under the seats. I looked right into the beam. I was praying that God would blind his eyes. But God did not blind him. He came back to where I was and dropped to his elbows and knees. He kept the flashlight in my face with one hand and reached with the other to grab me by the shirt. He pulled me close to him. I thought my heart would burst. I imagined myself dragged into the building, a trophy for a young officer.

"He whispered hoarsely to me through clenched teeth in Hebrew, 'You had better be who I think you are, or you are a dead man.' What could I do? There was no more hiding. No more future in pretending I wasn't here. I said to him, 'Young man, my name is Tsion Ben-Judah.'

"Still holding my shirt in his fist and with his flashlight blinding me, he said, 'Rabbi Ben-Judah, my name is Anis. Pray as you have never prayed before that my report will be believed. And now may the Lord bless you and keep you. May the Lord make His face shine upon you and give you peace.' Cameron, as God is my witness, the young man stood and walked out of the bus. I have been lying here, praising God with my tears ever since."

There was nothing more to say. Tsion slumped into a seat in the middle of the bus. Buck returned to the wheel and drove off to the border crossing in Egypt.

Half an hour later Buck and Tsion pulled up to the entrance into the Sinai. This time, God merely used the carelessness of the system to allow Ben-Judah to slip through. The only crossing gate was on the other side of the border into the Sinai. When Buck was told to stop, one guard immediately boarded and began barking orders in his own tongue. Buck said, "English?"

"English it is, gentlemen." He looked back at Tsion. "You'll be able to go back to sleep in a few minutes there, old-timer," he said. "You've got to come in and be processed first. I'll search your bus while you're in there, and you'll be on your way."

Buck, emboldened by the most recent miracle, looked at Tsion and shrugged. He waited as Tsion made way for the guard to get past him and begin the search, but Tsion motioned to Buck that he should get going. Buck hurried off the bus and into the building. As his papers were being processed, the guard said, "No trouble at the Israeli checkpoint then?"

Buck nearly smiled. *No problem? There's no problem when God is on your side.* "No, sir."

Buck couldn't help himself. He kept looking over his shoulder for Tsion. Where had he gone now? Had God made him invisible?

This was a much easier and quicker process. Apparently the Egyptians were used to simply rubber-stamping whatever the Israelis had approved. You couldn't get to this checkpoint without going through the previous, so unless the Israelis were trying to dump their castoffs, it was usually smooth sailing. Buck's papers were stamped and stacked and handed back to him with just a few questions. "Less than a hundred kilometers to Al Arish," the guard said. "No commercial flights scheduled out of there at this time, of course."

"I know," Buck said. "I have made my own arrangements."

"Very good then, Mr. Katz. All the best."

All the best is right! Buck thought.

He turned to hurry out to the bus. There was no sign of Tsion. The original guard was still on the bus. As Buck began to board, Tsion came from behind the bus and stepped in front of him. They boarded together. The guard was going through Buck's bag. "Impressive equipment, Mr. Katz."

"Thanks."

Tsion casually moved past the guard and went back to where he had been sitting when they arrived. He stretched out on the seat.

"And you work for whom?" the guard asked.

"International Harvesters," Buck said. Tsion rose up briefly in his seat, and Buck nearly laughed. Surely Tsion appreciated that.

The guard closed the bag. "You're both all processed then and ready to proceed?"

"All set," Buck said.

The guard looked toward the back. Tsion was snoring. The guard turned toward Buck and spoke quietly, "Carry on."

Buck tried not to be too eager to drive off, but he popped the clutch when the guard was clear of the front of the bus, and soon he was out onto the road again. "All right, Tsion, where were you that time?"

Tsion sat up. "Did you like my snore?"

Buck laughed. "Very impressive. Where were you when the guard thought you were being processed with me?"

"Merely standing behind the bus. You got off and went one way, I got off and went the other."

"You're joking."

"I did not know what to do, Cameron. He was so friendly, and he had seen me. I certainly wasn't going to walk into the processing center with no papers. When you returned, I figured I had been gone an appropriate time."

"The question now," Buck said, "is how long before that guard mentions he saw *two* men on the bus."

Tsion carefully made his way up to the seat behind Buck. "Yes," he said. "First he will have to convince them that he was not seeing things. Maybe it will not come up. But if it does, they will soon give chase."

"I trust the Lord to deliver us, because he has promised he will," Buck said. "But I also think we had better be as prepared as possible." He pulled off to the side of the road. He topped off the water in the radiator and dumped nearly two liters of oil into the engine. He filled the gas tanks.

"It is like we are living in the New Testament," Tsion said.

Buck, clutching and shifting, said "They might be able to overtake this old bus. But if we can make it to Al Arish, we'll be on that Learjet and out over the Mediterranean before they know we're gone."

For the next two hours, the road grew worse. The temperature rose. Buck kept an eye on the rearview mirror and noticed that Tsion kept looking back as well. Occasionally a smaller, faster car would appear on the horizon and fly past them.

"What are we worried about, Cameron? God would not bring us so far only to have us captured. Would he?"

"You're asking me? I never had anything like this happen to me until I ran into you!"

They rode in silence for half an hour. Finally, Tsion spoke, and Buck thought he sounded as strong as he had since Buck first saw him in the hideout. "Cameron, you know I have had to force myself to eat up until now, and I have not done a good job at it."

"So eat something! There's lots of stuff in here!"

"I believe I will. The pain in my heart is so deep that I feel as if I will never do anything again only for the sake of my own enjoyment. I used to love to eat. Even before I knew Christ, I knew that food was God's provision for us. He wanted us to enjoy it. I am hungry now, but I will eat only for sustenance and energy."

"You don't have to explain it to me, Tsion. I only pray that sometime between now and the Glorious Appearing, you'll get some relief from the deep wound you must feel."

"You want anything?"

Buck shook his head, then thought better of it. "Anything there with lots of fiber and natural sugar?" He didn't know what was ahead, but he didn't want to be physically weak, regardless.

Tsion snorted. "High in fiber and natural sugars? This is food from Israel, Cameron. You just described everything we eat."

The rabbi tossed Buck several fig bars that reminded him of granola and fruit. Buck had not realized his own level of hunger until he began to eat. He suddenly felt supercharged and hoped Tsion felt the same. Especially when he saw flashing yellow lights on the horizon far behind them.

The question now was whether to try to outrun the official vehicle or to feign innocence and merely let it pass. Perhaps it was not after them anyway. Buck shook his head. What was he thinking? Of course this was probably their Waterloo. He was confident God would bring them through, but he also didn't want to be naive enough to think an emergency vehicle would be coming at them from the border crossing without Buck and Tsion in its sights. "Tsion, you'd better secure everything and get out of sight."

Tsion leaned to stare out the back. "More excitement," he muttered. "Lord, have we not had enough for one day? Cameron, I will put most of it away, but I am taking a few morsels with me to my bed."

"Suit yourself. From the looks of those cars at the border, they're small and have very little power. If I step on it, it will take them a long time to catch us."

"And when they do?" Tsion said, from beneath the seats in the back.

"I am trying to think of a strategy now."

"I will be praying," Tsion said.

Buck nearly laughed. "Your praying has resulted in a lot of mayhem tonight," he said.

There was no response from the back. Buck pushed the bus for all it was worth. He got it up to over eighty kilometers an hour, which he guessed was in the fifty mile-an-hour range. It rattled and shook and bounced, and the various metal parts squeaked in protest. He knew that if he could see the border patrol car, its driver could see him. There was no sense cutting the lights and hoping they assumed he had pulled off the road.

It seemed he might be pulling away from them. He could not judge distances well in the darkness, but they didn't appear to be coming at high speed. The lights were flashing, and he was convinced they were after him, but he pushed ahead.

From the back: "Cameron, I think I have the right to know. What is your plan? What will you do when they overtake us, as they surely will?"

"Well, I'll tell you one thing, I'm not going back to that border. I'm not even sure I'll let them pull me over."

"How will you know what they want?"

"If it's the man who searched the bus, we'll know what they want, won't we?"

"I suppose we will."

"I will holler at him from the window and urge him to deal with us at the airport. There's no sense driving all the way back to the border."

"But will that not be *his* decision?"

"I guess I'll have to engage in civil disobedience then," Buck said.

"But what if he forces you off the road? Makes you pull over?"

"I'll try to avoid hitting him at all costs, but I will not stop, and if I am forced to stop, I will not turn around."

"I appreciate your resolve, Cameron. I will pray, and you do as God leads you."

"You know I will."

Buck guessed they were thirty kilometers from the airport outside Al Arish. If he could even keep the bus close to sixty kilometers per hour, they could make it in half an hour. The border patrol car would surely overtake them before that. But they were so much closer to the airport than to the border, he was certain the officer would see the wisdom of following them to the airport rather than leading them back to the border.

"Tsion, I need your help."

"Anything."

"Stay down and out of sight, but find my phone in my bag and get it to me."

When Tsion crawled next to Buck with his phone, Buck asked him, "Sir, how old are you?"

"That is considered an impolite question in my culture," Tsion said.

"Yeah, like I care about that now."

"I'm forty-six, Cameron. Why do you ask?"

"You seem in pretty good shape."

"Thank you. I work out."

"You do? Really?"

"Does that surprise you? You would be surprised at the number of scholars who work out. Of course there are many who do not, but—"

"I just want to make sure you'll be able to run if you need to."

"I hope it does not come to that, but yes, I can run. I am not as fast as I was as a young man, but I have surprising endurance for one of my vintage."

"That's all I wanted to know."

"Remind me to ask *you* some personal question sometime," Tsion said.

"Seriously, Tsion. I did not offend you, did I?"

Buck was strangely warmed. The rabbi actually chuckled. "Oh, my friend, think about it. What would it take to offend me now?"

"Tsion, you'd better get back where you were, but can you tell me how much gasoline we have left?"

"The gauge is right there in front of you, Cameron. You tell me."

"No, I mean in our extra cans."

"I will check, but surely we do not have time to fill our tanks while we are being chased. What do you have in mind?"

"Why do you ask so many questions?"

"Because I am a student. I will always be a student. Anyway, we are in this together, are we not?"

"Well, let me just give you a hint. While you're tapping on the sides of those gas cans to tell me how much we have left, I'm going to be checking the cigarette lighter on the dashboard."

"Cameron, cigarette lighters are the first to go in old vehicles, are they not?"

"For our sakes, let's hope not."

Buck's phone buzzed. Startled, he flipped it open. "Buck here."

"Buck! It's Chloe!"

"Chloe! I really can't talk to you now. Trust me. Don't ask any questions. For right now I'm OK, but please ask everybody to pray and pray now. And listen, somehow, on the Internet or something, find the phone number for the airport at Al Arish, south of the Gaza Strip on the Mediterranean in the Sinai. Get hold of Ken Ritz, who should be waiting there. Have him call me at this number."

"But Buck—"

"Chloe, it's life or death!"

"You call me as soon as you're safe!"

"Promise!"

Buck clapped the phone shut and heard Tsion from the back. "Cameron! Are you planning to blow up this bus?"

"You really are a scholar, aren't you?" Buck said.

"I just hope you wait until we get to the airport. I mean, a flaming bus may get us there faster, but your pilot friend may just ferry our remains to the States."

+ + +

"That's all right, Chloe," Rayford said, "I long since gave up trying to sleep. I'm up reading anyway."

Chloe told him of her strange conversation with Buck. "Don't waste time on the Internet," Rayford said, "I've got a guide to all those phone numbers. Hang on."

"Daddy," she said, "it's gotta be a closer phone call for you anyway. Call Ken Ritz and tell him to call Buck."

"I'm tempted to fly over there myself, if I had a small enough craft."

"Daddy, we don't need both you and Buck endangering your lives at the same time."

"Chloe, we do that every day."

"Better hurry, Dad."

* * *

Buck guessed the border patrol car was less than half a mile behind him. He put the accelerator to the floor and the bus lurched. The steering wheel shook and bounced as they hurtled down the road. The gauges still looked OK for the moment, but Buck knew it was only a matter of time before the radiator overheated.

"I am guessing we have about eight liters of gasoline," Tsion said.

"That will be plenty."

"I agree, Cameron. That will be more than enough to make martyrs of us both."

Buck eased off the throttle just enough to smooth out the ride. Smooth, of course, was a misnomer. Buck felt it in his back and hips as they bounced along. The border patrol car had closed to within a quarter mile.

Tsion called out from the back: "Cameron, it is clear we are not going to outrun them to the airport, do you agree?"

"Yes! So?"

"Then it makes no sense to push this vehicle to its limit. It would be smarter to conserve water, oil, and gasoline to be sure we make it to the airport. If we break down, all your resolve means nothing."

Buck couldn't argue with that. He immediately slowed to about fifty kilometers per hour and sensed he had bought several miles. However, this also allowed the border patrol car to pull right up behind him.

A siren sounded and a spotlight flashed in his outside rearview mirror. Buck merely waved and drove on. Soon it was yellow flashing lights, the spotlight, the siren, and the horn of the patrol car. Buck ignored them all.

Finally, the squad car pulled even with him. He glanced down to see the very guard who had searched the bus. "Fasten your seat belt, Tsion!" Buck hollered. "The chase is on!"

"I wish I *had* a seat belt!"

Buck continued at his modest speed as the patrol car stayed with him, and the guard pointed that he should pull over. Buck waved at him and drove on. The guard pulled in front of the bus and slowed, again pointing to the side of the road. When Buck made no attempt to pull off, the car slowed even more, forcing him to swerve around it. He had no acceleration, however, and the patrol car, now on the other side of him, sped up to keep him from passing. Buck merely backed off and got behind the car again. When it stopped, he stopped.

When the guard got out, Buck backed up and drove around him, building about a hundred-yard gap before the guard jumped back in and quickly caught up again. This time, the guard pulled alongside and showed Buck a handgun. Buck opened his window and hollered, "If I stop, this bus will stall! Follow me to Al Arish!"

"No!" came the reply. "You follow me back to the border!"

"We are much closer to the airport! I don't think this bus can make it back to the border!"

"Then leave it! You can ride back with me!"

"I'll see you at the airport!"

"No!"

But Buck slid his window shut. When the guard pointed his weapon at Buck's window, Buck ducked but kept going.

Buck's phone was buzzing. He clicked it open. "Talk to me!"

"This is Ritz. What's the deal?"

"Ken, have you passed through customs there?"

"Yeah! I'm ready when you are."

"You ready for some fun?"

"I thought you'd never ask! I haven't had any real fun for ages."

"You're gonna risk your life and break the law," Buck said.

"Is that all? I've been there before."

"Tell me your position and all, Ken," Buck said.

"Looks like I'm the only plane going out of here tonight. I'm just outside of a hangar at the end of the runway. My plane is, I mean. I'm talking to you from the little terminal here."

"But you've been processed, and you're ready to leave Egypt?"

"Yeah, no problem."

"What did you tell them as far as other passengers and cargo?"

"I figured you wouldn't want me to talk about anybody but you."

"Perfect, Ken! Thanks! And who do they think I am?"

"You're exactly who I say you are, Mr. Katz."

"Ken, that's great. Hang on just a second."

The guard had pulled in front of the bus and now slammed on his brakes. Buck had to swerve almost all the way off the road to miss him, and when he pulled back on, the bus fishtailed and nearly went over.

"I am rolling back here!" Tsion said.

"Enjoy the ride!" Buck said. "I'm not stopping, and I'm not turning around."

The guard had turned off his flashing yellow lights and his spotlight. The siren was silent now too. He quickly caught up with the bus and tapped it from behind. He tapped it again. And again.

"He's afraid to hurt that squad car, isn't he?" Buck said.

"Do not be so sure," Tsion said.

"I'm sure." Buck slammed on the brakes, making Tsion slide forward and cry out. Buck heard the screeching tires behind him and saw the squad car lurch off the right side of the road and down into loose gravel. Buck punched the accelerator. The bus stalled. As he tried to start it he saw the squad car, still in the gravel, coming up along his right side. The engine kicked in, and Buck popped the clutch. He picked up the phone. "Ken, you still there?"

"Yeah, what in the world's going on?"

"You wouldn't believe it!"

"You bein' chased or something?"

"That's the understatement of the year, Ritz! I don't think we're gonna have time to go through customs there. I need to know how to get to your plane. You need to be cleared, engines running, door open, and stairs down."

"This *is* gonna be fun!" Ritz said.

"You have no idea," Buck said. The pilot quickly told Buck the layout of the airstrip and the terminal and precisely where he was. "We're within about ten minutes of you," Buck said. "If I can keep this thing rolling, I'll try to get as close to the runway and your plane as possible. What am I gonna run into?"

The squad car came up onto the road, spun, and now faced the bus. Buck swerved left, but the car cut him off. Buck couldn't avoid smashing him. The impact turned the car around in the road and knocked the hood off. Buck sensed little damage to the big old bus, but the temperature gauge was rising.

"Who's chasing you anyway?" Ritz said.

"Egyptian border patrol," Buck said.

"Then you can bet they're gonna radio ahead here. There'll be some kind of a roadblock."

"I just hit the squad car. Is this going to be a roadblock I can blast through?"

"You'll have to play that one by ear. If you're as close as you say you are, I'd better get out to my plane."

"The cigarette lighter works!" Buck hollered to Tsion.

"I am not sure I wanted to hear that!"

The smashed patrol car resumed pursuit. Buck saw the lights of the airstrip in the distance. "Tsion, come up here. We need to strategize."

"Strategy? It is lunacy!"

"And what would you call what else we've been through?"

"The lunacy of the Lord! Just tell me what to do, Cameron, and I will do it. Nothing will be able to stop us tonight."

The guard in the squad car had apparently radioed ahead not only for a roadblock but also for help. Two sets of headlights, side-by-side and covering both lanes of the road, headed toward the bus. "Have you heard the phrase 'playing chicken'?" Buck asked.

"No," Tsion said, "but it is becoming clear to me. Are you going to challenge them?"

"Don't you agree they have more to lose than we do?"

"I do. I am hanging on. Do what you have to do!"

Buck pressed the accelerator to the floor. The heat gauge was pressed to the maximum and quivering. Steam billowed from the engine. "Here's what we're going to do, Tsion! Listen carefully!"

"Just concentrate on your driving, Cameron! Tell me later!"

"There will be no later! If these cars don't back down, there's going to be a tremendous crash. I think we'll be able to keep going either way. When we get to whatever roadblock they have for us at the airport, we have to make a quick decision. I need you to pour all those gas containers into the one big water bucket, the one that's wide open at the top. I'll have the cigarette lighter hot and ready to go. If we come upon a roadblock I think I can smash through, I'll just keep going and get as close to the runway as possible. The Lear is going to be off to our right and about a hundred yards from the terminal. If the roadblock is not something we can smash through, I'll try to go around it. If that's impossible, I'm going to pull the wheel hard to the left and slam on the brakes. That will make the back end swing around into the roadblock and anything loose will slide to the back door. You must put that bucket of gasoline in the aisle about eight feet from the back door, and when I give you the signal, toss that cigarette lighter into it. It needs to be just enough ahead of the collision so it's burning before we hit."

"I do not understand! How will *we* escape that?"

"If the roadblock is impenetrable, it's our only hope! When that back door blows open and that burning gasoline flies out, we have to be hanging on up here with all our might so we don't get thrown back into it. While they're concentrating on the fire, we jump out the front and run toward the jet. Got it?"

"I get it, Cameron, but I am not optimistic!"

"Hang on!" Buck shouted as two cars from the airport closed on him. Tsion hooked one arm around the metal pole behind Buck and wrapped his other around Buck's chest, grabbing the back of the chair like a human seat belt.

Buck gave no indication of slowing or swerving and headed straight for the two sets of headlights. At the last instant he closed his eyes, fully expecting a huge collision. When he opened his eyes, the road was clear. He looked first one way then the other behind him. Both cars had gone off the road, one of them rolling. The original pursuit car was still behind him, and Buck heard gunfire.

Less than a mile ahead the small airport loomed. Huge fences of mesh and barbed wire flanked the entrance, and just inside sat a blockade of a half-dozen vehicles and several armed soldiers. Buck could see he would not be able to blast through it or go around.

He pressed in the cigarette lighter as Tsion lugged the gas cans and the bucket to the back. "It is sloshing around!" Tsion called out.

"Just do the best you can!"

As Buck raced toward the open gate and the huge blockade, the patrol car still following close behind, the cigarette lighter popped out. Buck grabbed it and tossed it back to Tsion. It bounced and rolled under a seat. "Oh no!" Buck shouted.

"I have got it!" Tsion said. Buck peeked in the rearview mirror as Tsion climbed out from under a seat, tossed the cigarette lighter into the bucket, and scrambled to the front.

The back of the bus burst into flames. "Hang on!" Buck shouted, pulling hard to the left and slamming on the brakes. The bus whirled so fast it nearly tipped over. The back smashed into the stockade of cars, and the back door burst open, flaming gasoline splashing everywhere.

Buck and Tsion jumped out and ran, low as they could, around the left side of the blockade as guards began firing into the bus and others screamed and ran from the flames. Tsion was limping. Buck grabbed the older man and dragged him around the dark side of the terminal near the runway.

There was the Learjet, ready for takeoff. Never had a plane looked like such an oasis of safety. Buck looked back twice, but no one seemed to have seen them escape. It was too good to be true, but it fit with everything else that had happened that night.

Fifty feet from the plane, Buck heard shots and turned to see a half-dozen guards racing toward them, firing high-powered weapons. When they reached the steps, Buck grabbed Tsion by the belt in the back and threw him aboard. As Buck dived into the plane, a bullet ripped through the bottom of the heel of his right boot. Pain shot through the side of his foot as he yanked the door shut, Ritz already rolling.

Buck and Tsion crawled up to behind the cockpit.

Ritz muttered, "Those rascals shoot my plane, I'm gonna be really mad."

The plane took off like a rocket and rose quickly. "Next stop," Ritz announced, "Palwaukee Airport, State of Illinois, in the U.S. of A."

Buck lay on the floor, unable to move. He wanted to look out the window, but he didn't dare. Tsion buried his face in his hands. He wept and seemed to be praying.

Ritz turned. "Well, Williams, you sure left a mess down there. What was that all about?"

"It would take a week to tell," Buck said, panting.

"Well," Ritz said, "whatever it was, that was sure fun."

An hour later, Buck and Tsion sat in reclining seats, assessing the damage. "It is only sprained," Tsion said. "I caught my foot under one of the seat supports when we first hit. I was afraid I had broken it. It will heal quickly."

Buck slowly took off his right boot and held it up so Tsion could see the trajectory of the bullet. A clean hole had been blasted from the sole to the ankle. Buck took off a bloody sock. "Would you look at that?" he said, smiling. "I won't even need stitches. Just a nick there."

Tsion used Ken Ritz's first-aid kit to treat Buck's foot and found an Ace bandage for his own ankle.

Finally settled back with their wounded limbs elevated, Tsion and Buck looked at each other. "Are you as exhausted as I am?" Buck said.

"I am ready to sleep," Tsion said, "but we would be remiss, would we not, if we did not return thanks."

Buck leaned forward and bowed his head. The last thing he heard, before he slipped into a sleep of sweet relief, was the beautiful cadence of Rabbi Tsion Ben-Judah's prayer, thanking God that "the glory of the Lord was our rear guard."

14

BUCK AWOKE nearly ten hours later, pleased that Tsion was still sleeping. He checked Tsion's Ace bandage. The ankle was swollen, but it didn't look serious. His own foot was too tender to go back into his boot. He limped forward. "How are you doing, Cap?"

"A lot better, now that we're over American airspace. I had no idea what you guys got yourselves into, and who knew what kind of fighter pilots might have been on my tail."

"I don't think we were worth all that, with World War III going on," Buck said.

"Where'd you leave all your stuff?"

Buck whirled around. What was he looking for? He had brought nothing with him. Everything he brought had been in that leather bag, which by now was charred and melted. "I promised to call my wife back, too!" he said.

"You'll be happy to know I already talked to your people," Ritz said. "They were mighty relieved to hear you were on your way home."

"You didn't say anything about my wound or about my passenger, did you?"

"Give me some credit, Williams. You and I both know your wound isn't worth worrying about, so no wife needs to hear about that until she sees it. And as for your passenger, I have no idea who he is or whether your people knew you were bringing him home for dinner, so, no, I didn't say a word about him either."

"You're a good man, Ritz," Buck said, clapping him on the shoulder.

"I like a compliment as much as the next guy, but I hope you know you owe me battle pay on top of everything else."

"That can be arranged."

Because Ritz had carefully documented his plane and passenger on the way out of the country a few days before, he was on record and easily made it back through the North American radar net. He did not announce his extra passenger, and because personnel at Palwaukee Airport were not in the habit of processing international travelers, no one there paid any attention when an American pilot in his fifties, an Israeli rabbi in his forties, and an American writer in his thirties disembarked. Ritz was the only one not limping.

Buck had finally reached Chloe from the plane. It sounded to him as if she might have bitten his head off for keeping her up all night worrying and praying, had she not been so relieved to hear his voice. "Believe me, babe," he said, "when you hear the whole story, you'll understand."

Buck had convinced her that only the Tribulation Force and Loretta could know about Tsion. "Don't tell Verna. Can you come alone to Palwaukee?"

"I'm not up to driving yet, Buck," she said. "Amanda can drive me out there. Verna isn't even staying with us anymore. She has moved in with friends."

"That could be a problem," Buck said. "I may have made myself vulnerable to the worst possible person in my profession."

"We'll have to talk about that, Buck."

It was as if Tsion Ben-Judah was in some international witness protection program. He was smuggled into Loretta's home under the cover of night. Amanda and Chloe, who had heard from Rayford the news about Tsion's family, greeted him warmly and compassionately but seemed not to know how much to say. Loretta had a light snack waiting for all of them. "I'm old and not too up on things," she said, "but I'm quickly getting the picture here. The less I know about your friend, the better, am I right?"

Tsion answered her circumspectly. "I am deeply grateful for your hospitality."

Loretta soon trundled off to bed, expressing her delight in offering hospitality as her service to the Lord.

Buck, Chloe, and Tsion limped into the living room, followed by a chuckling Amanda. "I wish Rayford were here," she said. "I feel like the only teetotaler in a car full of drunks. Every chore that requires two feet is going to fall to me."

Chloe, characteristically direct, leaned forward and reached for Tsion's hand with both of hers. "Dr. Ben-Judah, we have heard so much about you. We feel blessed of God to have you with us. We can't imagine your pain."

The rabbi took a deep breath and exhaled slowly, his lips quivering. "I cannot tell you how deeply grateful I am to God that he has brought me here, and to you who have welcomed me. I confess my heart is broken. The Lord has shown me his hand so clearly since the death of my family that I cannot deny his presence. Yet there are times I wonder how I will go on. I do not want to dwell on how my loved ones lost their lives. I must not think about who did this and how it was accomplished. I know my wife and children are safe and happy now, but it is very difficult for me to imagine their horror and pain before God received them. I must pray for relief from bitterness and hatred. Most of all, I feel terrible guilt that I brought this upon them. I do not know what else I could have done, short of trying to make them more secure. I could not have avoided serving God in the way he has called me."

Amanda and Buck each moved to put a hand on Tsion's shoulders, and with the three of them touching him, they all prayed as he wept.

They talked well into the night, Buck explaining that Tsion would be the object of an international manhunt, which would likely have even Carpathia's approval. "How many people know about the underground shelter at the church?"

"Believe it or not," Chloe said, "unless Loretta has read the printouts from Bruce's computer, even she thinks it was just some new utility installation."

"How was he able to keep that from her? She was at the church every day while it was being excavated."

"You'll have to read Bruce's stuff, Buck. In short, she was under the impression that all that work was for the new water tank and parking lot improvements. Just like everyone else in the church thought."

Two hours later, Buck and Chloe lay in bed, unable to sleep. "I knew this was going to be difficult," she said. "I guess I just didn't know how much."

"Do you wish you'd never gotten involved with somebody like me?"

"Let's just say it hasn't been boring."

Chloe then told him about Verna Zee. "She thought we were all wacky."

"Aren't we? The question is, how much damage can she do to me? She knows completely where I stand now, and if that gets back to people at the *Weekly*, it'll shoot up the line to Carpathia like lightning. Then what?"

Chloe told Buck that she and Amanda and Loretta had at least persuaded Verna to keep Buck's secret for now.

"But why would she do that?" Buck said. "We've never liked each other. We've been at each other's throats. The only reason we traded favors the other night was that World War III made our skirmishes look petty."

"Your skirmishes *were* petty," Chloe said. "She admitted she was intimidated by you and jealous of you. You were what she had always hoped to be, and she even confessed that she knew she was no journalist compared to you."

"That doesn't give me confidence about her ability to keep my secret."

"You would have been proud of us, Buck. Loretta had already told Verna her entire story, how she was the only person in her extended family not taken in the Rapture. Then I got my licks in, telling her all about how you and I met, where you were when the Rapture happened, and how you and I and Daddy became believers."

"Verna must have thought we were all from another planet," Buck said. "Is that why she moved out?"

"No. I think she felt in the way."

"Was she sympathetic at all?"

"She actually was. I took her aside once and told her that the most important thing was what she decided to do about Christ. But I also told her that our very lives depended upon her protecting the news of your loyalties from your colleagues and superiors. She said, 'His *superiors*? Cameron's only superior is Carpathia.' But she also said something else very interesting, Buck. She said that as much as she admires Carpathia and what he has done for America and the world—gag—she hates the way he controls and manipulates the news."

"The question, Chloe, is whether you extracted from her any promises of my protection."

"She wanted to trade favors. Probably wanted some sort of a promotion or raise. I told her you would never work that way, and she said she figured that. I asked if she would promise me that she would at least not say anything to anyone until after she had talked to you. And then, are you ready for this? I made her promise to come to Bruce's memorial service Sunday."

"And she's coming?"

"She said she would. I told her she'd better be there early. It'll be packed."

"It sure will. How foreign is all this going to be to her?"

"She claims she's been in church only about a dozen times in her life, for weddings and funerals and such. Her father was a self-styled atheist, and her mother apparently had been raised in some sort of a strict denomination that she turned her back on as an adult. Verna says the idea of attending church was never discussed in her home."

"And she was never curious? Never searched for any deeper meaning in life?"

"No. In fact, she admitted she's been a pretty cynical and miserable person for years. She thought it made her the perfect journalist."

"She always gave me the willies," Buck said. "I was as cynical and negative as any, but hopefully there was a balance of humor and personability there."

"Oh yeah, that's you all right," Chloe teased. "That's why I'm still tempted to have a child with you, even now."

Buck didn't know what to say or think. They had had this discussion before. The idea of bringing a child into the Tribulation was, on the surface, unconscionable, and yet they had both agreed to think about it, pray about it, and see what Scripture said about it. "You want to talk about this now?"

She shook her head. "No. I'm tired. But let's not shut the door on it."

"You know I won't, Chlo'," he said. "I also need to tell you I'm on a different time zone. I slept all the way back."

"Oh, Buck! I've missed you. Can't you at least stay with me until *I* fall asleep?"

"Sure. Then I'm going to sneak over to the church and see how Bruce's shelter turned out."

"I'll tell you what you ought to do," Chloe said, "is finish reading Bruce's stuff. We've been marking passages we want Daddy to read at the memorial service. I don't know how he'll get through all of it without taking the whole day, but it's astounding stuff. Wait till you see it."

"I can't wait."

* * *

Rayford Steele was having a crisis of conscience. Packed and ready to go, he sat reading the *Global Community International Daily* while awaiting word from Hattie Durham's driver that he was in front of the building.

Rayford missed Amanda. In many ways, they still seemed strangers, and he knew that in the little more than five years before the Glorious Appearing, they would never have the time to get to know each other and develop the lifelong relationship and bond he had shared with Irene. For that matter, he still missed Irene. On the other hand, Rayford felt guilty that in many ways he was closer to Amanda already than he had ever been to Irene.

That was his own fault, he knew. He had not known nor shared Irene's faith until it was too late. She had been so sweet, so giving. While he knew of worse marriages and less loyal husbands, he often regretted that he was never the husband to her that he could have been. She had deserved better.

To Rayford, Amanda was a gift from God. He recalled not even having liked her at first. A handsome, wealthy woman slightly older than he, she was so nervous upon first meeting him that she gave the impression of being a jabberer. She didn't let him or Chloe get a word in, but kept correcting herself, answering her own questions, and rambling.

Rayford and Chloe were bemused by her, but seeing her as a future love interest never crossed his mind. They were impressed with how taken Amanda had been with Irene from her brief encounter. Amanda had seemed to catch the essence of Irene's heart and soul. The way she described her, Rayford and Chloe might have thought she had known her for years.

Chloe had initially suspected Amanda of having designs on Rayford. Having lost her family in the Rapture, she was suddenly a lonely, needy woman. Rayford had not sensed anything but a genuine desire to let him know what his former wife had meant to her. But Chloe's suspicion had put him on guard. He made no attempt to pursue Amanda and was careful to watch for any signs coming the other way. There were none.

That made Rayford curious. He watched how she assimilated herself into New Hope Village Church. She was cordial to him, but never inappropriate, and never—in his mind—forward. Even Chloe eventually had to admit that Amanda did not come off as a flirt to anyone. She quickly became known around New Hope as a servant. That was her spiritual gift. She busied herself about the work of the church. She would cook, clean, drive, teach, greet, serve on boards and committees, whatever was necessary. A full-time professional woman, her spare time was spent in church life. "It's always been all or nothing with me," she said. "When I became a believer, it was lock, stock, and barrel."

From a distance, having hardly socialized with her after that first encounter when she merely wanted to talk to him and Chloe about Irene, Rayford became an admirer. He found her quiet, gentle, giving spirit most attractive. When he first found himself wanting to spend time with her, he still wasn't thinking of her romantically. He just liked her. Liked her smile. Liked her look. Liked her attitude. He had sat in on one of her Sunday school classes. She was a most engaging teacher and a quick study. The next week, he found *her* sitting in *his* class. She was complimentary. They joked about someday team-teaching. But that day didn't come until after they had double-dated with Buck and Chloe. It wasn't long before they were desperately in love. Having been married just a few months before in a double ceremony with Buck and Chloe had been one of the small islands of happiness in Rayford's life during the worst period of human history.

Rayford was eager to get back to the States to see Amanda. He also looked forward to some time with Hattie on the plane. He knew the work of drawing her to Christ was that of the Spirit and not his responsibility, but still he felt he should maximize every legitimate opportunity to persuade her. His problem that Saturday morning was that every fiber of his being fought against his role as pilot for Nicolae Carpathia. Everything he had read, studied, and learned under Bruce Barnes's tutelage had convinced him and the other members of the Tribulation Force, as well as the congregation at New Hope, that Carpathia himself was the Antichrist. There were advantages to believers to have Rayford in the position he found himself, and Carpathia knew well where Rayford stood. What Nicolae did not know, of course, was that one of his other trusted employees, Cameron Williams, was now Rayford's son-in-law and had been a believer nearly as long as Rayford.

How long could it last? Rayford wondered. Was he endangering Buck's and

Chloe's lives? Amanda's? His own? He knew the day would come when what Bruce referred to as "tribulation saints" would become the mortal enemies of the Antichrist. Rayford would have to choose his timing carefully. Someday, according to Bruce's teaching, to merely have the right to buy and sell, citizens of the Global Community would have to take the "mark of the beast." No one knew yet exactly what form this would take, but the Bible indicated it would be a mark on the forehead or on the hand. There would be no faking. The mark would somehow be specifically detectable. Those who took the mark could never repent of it. They would be lost forever. Those who did not take the mark would have to live in hiding, their lives worth nothing to the Global Community.

For now, Carpathia seemed merely amused by and impressed with Rayford. Perhaps he thought he had some connection, some insight to the opposition by keeping Rayford around. But what would happen when Carpathia discovered that Buck was not loyal and that Rayford had known all along? Worse, how long could Rayford justify in his own mind that the benefits of being able to eavesdrop and spy on Carpathia outweighed his own culpability in abetting the work of the evil one?

Rayford glanced at his watch and speed-read the rest of the paper. Hattie and her driver would be there in a few moments. Rayford felt as if he had undergone sensory overload. Any one of the traumas he had witnessed since the day the war broke out might have institutionalized a normal man during normal times. Now, it seemed, Rayford had to take everything in stride. The most heinous, horrible atrocities were part of daily life. World War III had erupted, Rayford had discovered one of his dearest friends dead, and he had heard Nicolae Carpathia give the word to destroy major cities and then announce his grief and disappointment on international television.

Rayford shook his head. He had done his job, flown his new plane, landed it thrice with Carpathia aboard, had gone to dinner with an old friend, gone to bed, had several phone conversations, rose, read his paper, and was now ready to blithely fly home to his family. What kind of a crazy world had this become? How could vestiges of normality remain in a world going to hell?

The newspaper carried the stories out of Israel, how the rabbi who had so shocked his own nation and culture and religion and people—not to mention the rest of the world—with his conclusions about the messiahship of Jesus, had suddenly gone mad. Rayford knew the truth, of course, and looked forward with great anticipation to meeting this brave saint.

Rayford knew Buck had somehow spirited him out of the country, but he didn't know how. He would be eager to get the details. Was this what they all had to look forward to? The martyrdom of their families? Their own deaths?

He knew it was. He tried to push it from his mind. The juxtaposition between the easy, daily, routine life of a jumbo-jet pilot—the Rayford Steele he was a scant two years ago—and the international political pinball he felt like today was almost more than his mind could assimilate.

The phone rang. His ride was here.

* * *

Buck was astonished at what he found at the church. Bruce had done such a good job camouflaging the shelter that Buck had almost not been able to find it again.

Alone in the cavernous place, Buck headed downstairs. He walked through the fellowship hall, down a narrow corridor, past the washrooms, and past the furnace room. He was now at the end of a hallway with no light—it would have been dark there at noon. Where was that entrance? He felt around the wall. Nothing. He moved back into the furnace room and flipped on the switch. A flashlight rested atop the furnace. He used it to find the hand-sized indentation in one of the concrete blocks on the wall. Setting himself and feeling the nagging sting in his right heel from his recent wound, he pushed with all his might, and a section of block wall slid open slightly. He stepped in and pulled it closed behind him. The flashlight illuminated a sign directly in front of him and six stair steps down: "Danger! High Voltage. Authorized Personnel Only."

Buck smiled. That would have scared him off if he hadn't known better. He moved down the steps and took a left. Four more steps down was a huge steel door. The sign at the landing of the stairs was duplicated on the door. Bruce had shown him, the day of the weddings, how to open that seemingly locked door.

Buck gripped the knob and turned it first right and then left. He pushed the handle in about a quarter of an inch, then back out half an inch. It seemed to free itself, but still it didn't turn right or left. He pushed in as he turned it slightly right and then left, following a secret pattern devised by Bruce. The door swung open, and Buck faced what appeared to be a man-sized circuit-breaker box. Not even a church the size of New Hope would carry that many circuit breakers, Buck knew. And as real as all those switches were, they led to no circuits. The chassis of that box was merely another door. It opened easily and led to the hidden shelter. Bruce had done an amazing amount of work since Buck had seen it just a few months before.

Buck wondered when Bruce had had the time to get in there after hours and do all that work. No one else knew about it, not even Loretta, so it was a good thing Bruce was handy. It was vented, air-conditioned, well-lit, paneled, ceilinged, floored, and contained all the necessities. Bruce had sectioned the twenty-four-by-twenty-four-foot area into three rooms. There was a full bath and shower, a bedroom with four double bunk beds, and a larger room with a kitchenette on one end and a combination living room/study on the other. Buck was struck by the lack of claustrophobia, but he knew that with more than two people in there—and being aware of how far underground you were—it could soon become close.

Bruce had spared no expense. Everything was new. There was a freezer, a refrigerator, a microwave, a range and oven, and it seemed every spare inch possible had been converted into storage space. *Now,* Buck wondered, *what did Bruce do about connections?*

Buck crawled along the carpet and looked behind a sleeper sofa. There was a bank of telephone jacks. He traced the wiring up the wall and tried to spot where it would come out in the hallway. He turned off the lights, closed the circuit-breaker door, closed the metal door, jogged up the steps, and slid the brick door shut. In a dark corner of the hallway he shined the flashlight and saw the section of conduit that led from the floor up through the ceiling. He moved back into the fellowship hall and looked out the window. From the lights in the parking lot, he could make out that the conduit went outside at the ceiling level and snaked its way up toward the steeple.

Bruce had told Buck that the reconditioned steeple had been the one vestige of the old church, the original building that had been torn down thirty years before. In the old days it actually had bells that beckoned people to church. The bells were still there, but the ropes that had once extended through a trapdoor to a spot where one of the ushers could ring them from the foyer had been cut. The steeple was now just decorative. Or was it?

Buck lugged a stepladder from a utility room up into the foyer and pushed open the trapdoor. He hoisted himself above the ceiling and found a wrought-iron ladder that led into the belfry. He climbed up near the old bells, which were covered with cobwebs and dust and soot. When he reached the section open to the air, his last step made his hair brush a web, and he felt a spider skitter through his hair. He nearly lost his balance swatting it away and trying to hang on to the flashlight and to the ladder. It was just yesterday that he had been chased across the desert, rammed, shot at, and virtually chased through flames to his freedom. He snorted. He would almost rather go through all that again than have a spider run through his hair.

Buck peeked down from the opening and looked for the conduit. It ran all the way up to the tapered part of the steeple. He reached the top of the ladder and stepped out through the opening. He was around the side of the steeple not illuminated from the ground. The old wood didn't feel solid. His sore foot began to twitch. *Wouldn't this be great?* he thought. *Slip off the steeple of your own church and kill yourself in the middle of the night.*

Carefully surveying the area to be sure no cars were around, Buck briefly shined the flashlight at the top of where the conduit ran up the steeple. There was what appeared to be a miniature satellite dish, about two-and-a-half inches in diameter. Buck couldn't read the tiny sticker applied to the front of it, so he stood on tiptoe and peeled it off. He stuck it in his pocket and waited until he was safely back inside the steeple, down the ladder, and through the trapdoor to the stepladder before pulling it out. It read "Donny Moore Technologies: Your Computer Doctor."

Buck put the stepladder away and began shutting off the lights. He grabbed a concordance off the shelf in Bruce's office and looked up the word *housetop*. Bruce's installing that crazy mini-satellite dish made him think of a verse he once heard or read about shouting the good news from the housetop. Matthew 10:27-28 said, "Whatever I tell you in the dark, speak in the light; and what you hear in the ear, preach on the housetops. And do not fear those who kill the body but cannot kill the soul. But rather fear Him who is able to destroy both soul and body in hell."

Wasn't it just like Bruce to take the Bible literally? Buck headed back to Loretta's house, where he would read Bruce's material until about six. Then he wanted to sleep until noon and be up when Amanda brought Rayford home from Mitchell Field in Milwaukee.

Would he ever cease to be amazed? As he drove the few blocks, he was struck by the difference between the two vehicles he had driven within the last twenty-four hours. This, a six-figure Range Rover with everything but a kitchen sink, and that probably still-smoldering bus he had "bought" from a man who might soon be a martyr.

More amazing, however, was that Bruce had planned so well and prepared so much before his departure. With a little technology, the Tribulation Force and its newest member, Tsion Ben-Judah, would soon be proclaiming the gospel from a hidden location and sending it via satellite and the Internet to just about anybody in the world who wanted to hear it, and to many who didn't.

It was two-thirty in the morning, Chicago time, when Buck returned from the church and sat before Bruce's papers on the dining room table at Loretta's home. They read like a novel. He drank in Bruce's Bible studies and commentary, finding his sermon notes for that very Sunday. Buck couldn't speak publicly in that church. He was vulnerable and exposed enough already, but he could sure help Rayford put together some remarks.

* * *

Despite his years of flying, Rayford had never found a cure for jet lag, especially going east to west. His body told him it was the middle of the evening, and after a day of flying, he was ready for bed. But as the DC-10 taxied toward the gate in Milwaukee, it was noon Central Standard Time. Across the aisle from him, the beautiful and stylish Hattie Durham slept. Her long blonde hair was in a bun, and she had made a mess of her mascara trying to wipe away her tears.

She had wept off and on almost the entire flight. Through two meals, a movie, and a snack, she had unburdened herself to Rayford. She did not want to stay with Nicolae Carpathia. She had lost her love for the man. She didn't understand him. While she wasn't ready to say he was the Antichrist, she certainly was not as impressed with him behind closed doors as most of his public was with him.

Rayford had carefully avoided declaring his starkest beliefs about Carpathia. Clearly Rayford was no fan and hardly loyal, but he didn't consider it the better part of wisdom to state categorically that he agreed with most Christian believers that Carpathia fit the bill of the Antichrist. Of course, Rayford had no doubt about it. But he had seen broken romances heal before, and the last thing he wanted was to give Hattie ammunition that could be used against him with Carpathia. Soon enough it wouldn't matter who might bad-mouth him to Nicolae. They would be mortal enemies anyway.

Most troubling to Rayford was Hattie's turmoil over her pregnancy. He wished she would refer to what she was carrying as a child. But it was a pregnancy to her, an unwanted pregnancy. It may not have been at the beginning, but now, given her state of mind, she did not want to give birth to Nicolae Carpathia's child. She didn't refer to it as a child or even a baby.

Rayford had the difficult task of trying to plead his case without being too obvious. He had asked her, "Hattie, what do you think your options are?"

"I know there are only three, Rayford. Every woman has to consider these three options when she's pregnant."

Not every *woman,* Rayford thought.

Hattie had continued: "I can carry it to term and keep it, which I don't want to do. I can put it up for adoption, but I'm not sure I want to endure the entire pregnancy and birth process. And, of course, I can terminate the pregnancy."

"What does that mean exactly?"

"What do you mean 'what does that mean?'" Hattie had said. "Terminate the pregnancy means terminate the pregnancy."

"You mean have an abortion?"

Hattie had stared at him like he was an imbecile. "Yes! What did you think I meant?"

"Well, it just seems you're using language that makes it sound like the easiest option."

"It *is* the easiest option, Rayford. Think about it. Obviously, the worst scenario would be to let a pregnancy run its entire course, go through all that discomfort, then go through the pain of labor. And then what if I got all those maternal instincts everybody talks about? Besides nine months of living in the pits, I'd go through all that stuff delivering somebody else's child. Then I'd have to give it up, which would just make everything worse."

"You just called it a child there," Rayford had said.

"Hmm?"

"You had been referring to this as your pregnancy. But once you deliver it, then it's a child?"

"Well, it will be *someone's* child. I hope not mine."

Rayford had let the matter drop while a meal was served. He had prayed silently that he would be able to communicate to her some truth. Subtlety was not his forte. She was not a dumb woman. Maybe the best tack was to be direct.

Later in the flight, Hattie herself had brought up the issue again. "Why do you want to make me feel guilty for considering an abortion?"

"Hattie," he had said, "I can't make you feel guilty. You have to make your own decisions. What I think about it means very little, doesn't it?"

"Well, I care what you think. I respect you as someone who's been around. I hope you don't think that I think abortion is an easy decision, even though it's the best and simplest solution."

"Best and simplest for whom?"

"For me, I know. Sometimes you have to look out for yourself. When I left my job and ran off to New York to be with Nicolae, I thought I was finally doing something for Hattie. Now I don't like what I did for Hattie, so I need to do something else for Hattie. Understand?"

Rayford had nodded. He understood all too well. He had to remind himself that she was not a believer. She would not be thinking about the good of anyone but herself. Why should she? "Hattie, just humor me for a moment and assume that that pregnancy, that 'it' you're carrying, is already a child. It's your child. Perhaps you don't like its father. Perhaps you'd hate to see what kind of a person its father might produce. But that baby is *your* blood relative too. You already have maternal feelings, or you wouldn't be in such turmoil about this. My question is, who's looking out for that child's best interest? Let's say a wrong has been done. Let's say it was immoral for you to live with Nicolae Carpathia outside of marriage. Let's say this pregnancy, this child, was produced from an immoral union. Let's go farther. Let's say that those people are right who consider Nicolae Carpathia the Antichrist. I'll even buy the argument that perhaps you regret the idea of having a child at all and would not be the best mother for it. I don't think you can shirk responsibility for it the way a rape or incest victim might be justified in doing.

"But even in those cases, the solution isn't to kill the innocent party, is it? Something is wrong, really wrong, and so people defend their right to choose. What they choose, of course, is not just the end of a pregnancy, not just an abortion, it's the death of a person. But which person? One of the people who made a mistake? One of the people who committed a rape or incest? Or one of the people who got pregnant out of wedlock? No, the solution is always to kill the most innocent party of all."

Rayford had gone too far, and he had known it. He had glanced up at Hattie holding her hands over her ears, tears streaming down her face. He had touched her arm, and she had wrenched away. He had leaned further and grabbed her elbow. "Hattie, please don't pull away from me. Please don't think I said any of that to hurt you personally. Just chalk it up to somebody standing up for the rights of someone who can't defend him- or herself. If you won't stand up for your own child, somebody has to."

With that, she had wrenched fully away from him and had buried her face in her hands and wept. Rayford had been angry with himself. Why couldn't he learn? How could he sit there spouting all that? He believed it, and he was convinced it was God's view. It made sense to him. But he also knew she could reject it out of hand simply because he was a man. How could he understand? No one was suggesting what he could or could not do with his own body. He had wanted to tell her he understood that, but again, what if that unborn child was a female? Who was standing up for the rights of that woman's body?

Hattie had not spoken to him for hours. He knew he deserved that. *But,* he wondered, *how much time is there to be diplomatic?* He had no idea what her plans were. He could only plead with her when he had the chance. "Hattie," he had said. She hadn't looked at him. "Hattie, please let me just express one more thing to you."

She had turned slightly, not looking fully at him, but he had the impression she would at least listen.

"I want you to forgive me for anything I said that hurt you personally or insulted you. I hope you know me well enough by now to know that I would not do that intentionally. More important, I want you to know that I am one of a few friends you have in the Chicago area who loves you and wants only the best for you. I wish you'd think about stopping in and seeing us in Mt. Prospect on your way back. Even if I'm not there, even if I have to go on back to New Babylon before you, stop in and see Chloe and Buck. Talk to Amanda. Would you do that?"

Now she had looked at him. She had pressed her lips together and shook her head apologetically. "Probably not. I appreciate your sentiments, and I accept your apology. But no, probably not."

And that's the way it had been left. Rayford was angry with himself. His motives were pure, and he believed his logic was right. But maybe he had counted too much on his own personality and style and not enough on God himself to work in Hattie's heart. All he could do now was pray for her.

When the plane finally stopped at the gate, Rayford helped Hattie pull her bag from the overhead rack. She thanked him. He didn't trust himself to say anything more. He had apologized enough. Hattie wiped her face one more time and said, "Rayford, I know you mean well. But you drive me nuts sometimes. I should be glad nothing ever really developed between us."

"Thanks a lot," Rayford said, feigning insult.

"I'm serious," she said. "You know what I mean. We're just too far apart in age or something, I guess."

"I guess," Rayford said. So, that was how she summarized it. Fine. That wasn't the issue at all, of course. He may not have handled it the best way, but he knew trying to fix it now would accomplish nothing.

As they emerged from the gateway, he saw Amanda's welcome smile. He rushed to her, and she held him tight. She kissed him passionately but pulled away quickly. "I didn't mean to ignore you, Hattie, but frankly I was more eager to see Rayford."

"I understand," Hattie said flatly, shaking hands and looking away.

"Can we drop you somewhere?" Amanda said.

Hattie chuckled. "Well, my bags are checked through to Denver. Can you drop me there?"

"Oh, I knew that!" Amanda said. "Can we walk you to your gate?"

"No, I'll be fine. I know this airport. I've got a little layover here, and I'm just gonna try to relax."

Rayford and Amanda said their good-byes to Hattie, and she was cordial enough, but as they walked away, she caught Rayford's eye. She pursed her lips and shook her head. He felt miserable.

Rayford and Amanda walked hand-in-hand, then arm-in-arm, then arms around each other's waist, all the way to the escalators that led down to baggage claim. Amanda hesitated and pulled Rayford back from the moving stairway. Something on a TV monitor had caught her eye. "Ray," she said, "come look at this."

They stood watching as a CNN/GNN report summarized the extent of the damage from the war around the world. Already, Carpathia was putting his spin on it. The announcer said, "World health care experts predict the death toll will rise to more than 20 percent internationally. Global Community Potentate Nicolae Carpathia has announced formation of an international health care organization that will take precedence over all local and regional efforts. He and his ten global ambassadors released a statement from their private, high-level meetings in New Babylon outlining a proposal for strict measures regulating the health and welfare of the entire global community. We have a reaction now from renowned cardiovascular surgeon Samuel Kline of Norway."

Rayford whispered, "This guy is in Carpathia's back pocket. I've seen him around. He says whatever Saint Nick wants him to say."

The doctor was saying, "The International Red Cross and the World Health Organization, as wonderful and effective as they have been in the past, are not equipped to handle devastation, disease, and death on this scale. Potentate Carpathia's visionary plan is not only our only hope for survival in the midst of coming famine and plagues, but also it seems to me—at first glance—a blueprint for the most aggressive international health care agenda ever. Should the death toll reach as high as 25 percent due to contaminated water and air, food shortages, and the like, as some have predicted, new directives that govern life from the womb to the tomb can bring this planet from the brink of death to a utopian state as regards physical health."

Rayford and Amanda turned toward the escalator, Rayford shaking his head. "In other words, Carpathia clears away the bodies he has blown to bits or starved or allowed to become diseased by plagues because of his war, and the rest of us lucky subjects will be healthier and more prosperous than ever."

Amanda looked at him. "Spoken like a true, loyal, employee," she said. He wrapped his arms around her and kissed her. They stumbled and nearly tumbled when the escalator reached the bottom.

+ + +

Buck embraced his new father-in-law and old friend like the brother he was. He considered it a tremendous honor to introduce Tsion Ben-Judah to Rayford and to watch them get acquainted. The Tribulation Force was together once more, bringing each other up-to-date and trying to plan for a future that had never seemed less certain.

15

RAYFORD FORCED himself to stay up until a normal bedtime Saturday night. He, Buck, and Tsion went over and over Bruce's material. More than once Rayford was moved to tears. "I'm not sure I'm up to this," he said.

Tsion spoke softly. "You are."

"What would you have done had I been unable to get back?"

Buck said, "I don't know, but I can't risk speaking in public. And certainly Tsion can't."

Rayford asked what they were going to do about Tsion. "He can't stay here long, can he?" he said.

"No," Buck said. "It won't be long before it gets back to Global Community brass that I was involved in his escape. In fact, it wouldn't surprise me if Carpathia already knows."

They decided amongst themselves that Tsion should be able to come to New Hope Sunday morning, possibly with Loretta, as a guest who appeared to be an old friend. There was enough difference in their ages that, except for his Middle Eastern look, he might appear to be a son or a nephew. "But I wouldn't risk his exposure any further than that," Rayford said. "If the shelter is ready, we need to sneak him in there before the end of the day tomorrow."

Late in the evening a bleary-eyed Rayford called a meeting of the Tribulation Force, asking Tsion Ben-Judah to wait in another room. Rayford, Amanda, Buck, and Chloe sat around the dining room table, Bruce's pages piled high before them. "I suppose it falls to me," Rayford said, "as the senior member of this little band of freedom fighters, to call to order the first meeting after the loss of our leader."

Amanda shyly raised her hand. "Excuse me, but I believe I am the senior member, if you're talking age."

Rayford smiled. There was precious little levity anymore, and he appreciated her feeble attempts. "I know you're the oldest, hon," he said, "but I've been a believer longer. Probably by a week or so."

"Fair enough," she said.

"The only order of business tonight is voting in a new member. I think it's obvious to all of us that God has provided a new leader and mentor in Dr. Ben-Judah."

Chloe spoke up. "We're asking an awful lot of him, aren't we? Are we sure he wants to live in this country? In this city?"

"Where else could he go?" Buck asked. "I mean, it's only fair to ask him rather than to make assumptions, I guess, but his options are limited."

Buck told the others about the new phones, the coming computers, how Bruce had outfitted the shelter for phone and computer broadcasting, and how Donny Moore was designing a system that would be interception- and trace-proof.

Rayford thought everyone seemed encouraged. He finalized preparations for the memorial service the next morning and said he planned to be unabashedly evangelistic. They prayed for the confidence, peace, and blessing of God on their decision to include Tsion in the Tribulation Force. Rayford invited him into the meeting.

"Tsion, my brother, we would like to ask you to join our little core group of believers. We know you have been deeply wounded and may be in pain for a long, long time. We're not asking for an immediate decision. As you can imagine, we need you not to just be one of us, but also to be our leader, in essence, our pastor. We recognize that the day may come when we might all be living with you in the secret shelter. Meanwhile, we will try to maintain as normal lives as possible, trying to survive and spread the good news of Christ to others until his Glorious Appearing."

Tsion rose at one end of the table and placed both hands atop it. Buck, who so recently had thought Tsion looked younger than his forty-six years, now saw him weary and spent, grief etching his face. His words came slowly, haltingly, through quivering lips.

"My dear brothers and sisters in Christ," he said in his thick, Israeli accent, "I am deeply honored and moved. I am grateful to God for his provision and blessing to me in bringing young Cameron to find me and save my life. We must pray for our brothers, Michael and his three friends, whom I believe are among the 144,000 witnesses God is raising up around the world from the tribes of Israel. We must also pray for our brother Anis, whom Cameron has told you about. He was used of God to deliver us. I know nothing more about him, except that should it come out that he could have detained me, he too may be a martyr before we know it.

"Devastated as I am over my own personal loss, I see the clear hand of God Almighty in guiding my steps. It was as if my blessed homeland were a saltshaker in his hand, and he upended it and shook me out across the desert and into the air. I landed right where he wants me. Where else can I go?

"I need no time to think about it. I have already prayed about it. I am where God wants me to be, and I will be here for as long as he wishes. I do not like to live in hiding, but neither am I a reckless man. I will gratefully accept your offer of shelter and provisions, and I look forward to all the Bible software Cameron has promised to put on the new computer. If you and your technical adviser, young Mr. Moore, can devise a way to multiply my ministry, I would be thankful. Clearly, my days of international travel and speaking are over. I look forward to sitting with fellow believers in your church tomorrow morning and hearing more about your wonderful mentor, my predecessor, Bruce Barnes.

"I cannot and will not promise to replace him in your hearts. Who can replace one's spiritual father? But as God has blessed me with a mind that understands many languages, with a heart that seeks after him and always has, and with the truth he has imparted to me and which I discovered and accepted and received only a little too late, I will dedicate the rest of my life to sharing with you and anyone else who will hear it the Good News of the gospel of Jesus Christ, the Messiah, the Savior, my Messiah, and my Savior."

Tsion seemed to collapse into his chair, and, as one, Rayford and the rest of the Tribulation Force turned and knelt before theirs.

+ + +

Buck felt the presence of God as clearly as he had during his escapade in Israel and Egypt. He realized his God was not limited by space and time. Later, when he and Chloe went up to bed, leaving Rayford alone in the dining room to put the final touches on his memorial service message, they prayed that Verna Zee would follow through on her promise to attend. "She's the key," Buck said. "Chloe, if she gets spooked and says anything to anybody about me, our lives will never be the same."

"Buck, our lives haven't been the same from one day to the next for almost two years."

Buck gathered her in, and she nestled against his chest. Buck felt her relax and heard her deep, even breathing as she fell asleep minutes later. He lay awake another hour, staring at the ceiling.

Buck awoke at eight in an empty bed. He smelled breakfast. Loretta would have already been at church. He knew Chloe and Amanda had bonded and frequently worked together, but he was surprised to find Tsion also putzing around in the kitchen. "We will add a little Middle Eastern flavor to our morning repast, no?" he asked.

"Sounds good to me, brother," Buck said. "Loretta will be back to pick you up at about nine. Amanda, Chloe, and I will head over as soon as we're finished with breakfast."

Buck knew there would be a crowd that morning, but he didn't expect the parking lots to be full and the streets lined with cars for blocks. If Loretta hadn't had a reserved spot, she might have done better to leave her car at home and walk to the church with Tsion. As it was, she told Buck later, she had to wave someone out of her spot when she got back with him.

It didn't make sense for Tsion to be seen with Buck at church. Buck sat with Chloe and Amanda. Loretta sat near the back with Tsion. Loretta, Buck, Chloe, and Amanda kept an eye out for Verna.

\+ + +

Rayford would not have known Verna if she was standing in front of him. He was occupied with his own thoughts and responsibilities that morning. Fifty minutes before the service he signaled the funeral director to move the casket into the sanctuary and open it.

Rayford was in Bruce's office when the funeral director hurried back to him. "Sir, are you sure you still want me to do that? The sanctuary is full to overflowing already."

Rayford didn't doubt him but followed him to look for himself. He peeked through the platform door. It would have been inappropriate to open the casket in front of all those people. Had Bruce's body been on display, waiting for them when they arrived, that would have been one thing. "Just wheel the closed coffin out there," Rayford said. "We'll schedule a viewing later."

As Rayford headed back to the office, he and the funeral director came upon the casket and the attendants in an otherwise empty corridor that led to the platform. Rayford was overcome with a sudden urge. "Could you open it just for me, briefly?"

"Certainly, sir, if you would avert your eyes a moment."

Rayford turned his back and heard the lid open and the movement of material.

"All right, sir," the director said.

Bruce looked less alive and even more like the shell Rayford knew this body to be than he had under the shroud outside the demolished hospital where Rayford had found him. Whether it was the lighting, the passage of time, or his own grief and fatigue, Rayford did not know. This, he knew, was merely the earthly house of his dear friend. Bruce was gone. The likeness that lay here was just a reflection of the man he once was. Rayford thanked the director and headed back to the office.

He was glad he had taken that last look. It wasn't that he needed closure, as so many said of such a viewing. He had simply feared that the shock of Bruce appearing so lifeless at a corporate viewing might render him speechless. But it didn't now. He was nervous, yet he felt more confidence than ever about representing Bruce and representing God to these people.

* * *

The lump in Buck's throat began the moment he entered the sanctuary and saw the crowd. The number didn't surprise him, but how early they had assembled did. Also, there was not the usual murmuring as at a normal Sunday morning service. No one here seemed even to whisper. The silence was eerie, and anyone could have interpreted it as a tribute to Bruce. People wept, but no one sobbed. At least not yet. They simply sat, most with heads bowed, some reading the brief program that included Bruce's vital statistics. Buck was amazed by the verse someone, probably Loretta, ran along the bottom of the back page of the program. It read simply, "I know that my Redeemer lives."

Buck felt Chloe shudder and knew she was near tears. He put his arm around her shoulder and his hand brushed Amanda just beyond her. Amanda turned, and Buck saw her tears. He put a hand on her shoulder, and there they sat in their silent grief.

At precisely ten o'clock, just the way (Buck thought) a pilot would do it, Rayford and one other elder emerged from the door at the side of the platform. Rayford sat while the other man stepped to the pulpit and motioned that all should rise. He led the congregation in two hymns sung so slowly and quietly and with such meaning that Buck could barely get the words out. When the songs had concluded, the elder said, "That is the extent of our preliminary service. There will be no offering today. There will be no announcements today. All meetings will resume next Sunday, as scheduled. This memorial service is in memory of our dear departed pastor, Bruce Barnes."

He proceeded to tell when and where Bruce was born and when and where he died. "He was preceded by his wife, a daughter, and two sons, who were raptured with the church. Our speaker this morning is Elder Rayford Steele, a member of this congregation since just after the Rapture. He was a friend and confidant of Bruce. He will deliver the eulogy and a brief message. You may come back at 4:00 p.m. for a viewing if you wish."

* * *

Rayford felt as if he were floating in another dimension. He had heard his name and knew well what they were about that morning. Was this a mental defense mechanism? Was God allowing him to set aside his grief and his emotions so he could speak clearly? That was all he could imagine. Were his emotions to overcome him, there would be no way he could speak.

He thanked the other elder and opened his notes. "Members and friends of New Hope Village Church," he began, "and relatives and friends of Bruce Barnes, I greet you today in the matchless name of Jesus Christ, our Lord and Savior.

"If there is one thing I have learned out there in the world, it is that a speaker should never apologize for himself. Allow me to break that rule first and get it out of the way, because I know that despite how close Bruce and I were, this is not about me. In fact, Bruce would tell you, it's not about him either. It's about Jesus.

"I need to tell you that I'm up here this morning not as an elder, not as a parishioner, and certainly not as a preacher. Speaking is not my gift. No one has even suggested that I might replace Bruce here. I am here because I loved him and because in many ways—primarily because he left a treasure trove of notes behind—I am able in a small way to speak for him."

+ + +

Buck held Chloe close, as much for his own comfort as for hers. He felt for Rayford. This had to be so hard. He was impressed with Rayford's ability to be articulate in this situation. He himself would have been blubbering, he knew.

Rayford was saying, "I want to tell you how I first met Bruce, because I know that many of you met him in much the same way. We were at the point of the greatest need in our lives, and Bruce had beat us to it by only a few hours."

Buck heard the story he had heard so many times before, of Rayford's having been warned by his wife that the Rapture was coming. When he and Chloe had been left behind and Irene and Raymie had been taken, at the end of himself he had sought out the church where she had heard the message. Bruce Barnes had been the only person left on the staff, and Bruce knew exactly why. He became, in an instant, an unabashed convert and evangelist. Bruce had pleaded with Rayford and Chloe to hear his own testimony of losing his wife and three young children in the middle of the night. Rayford had been ready. Chloe had been skeptical. It would be a while before she came around.

Bruce had provided them with a copy of a videotape his senior pastor had left behind for just this purpose. Rayford had been amazed that the pastor could have known in advance what he would be going through. He had explained from the Bible that all this had been predicted and then had been careful to explain the way of salvation. Rayford now took the time, as he had on so many occasions in Sunday school classes and testimony meetings, to go through that same simple plan.

Buck never ceased to be moved by what Bruce had always called "the old, old story." Rayford said, "This has been the most misunderstood message of the ages. Had you asked people on the street five minutes before the Rapture what Christians taught about God and heaven, nine in ten would have told you that the church expected them to live a good life, to do the best they could, to think of others, to be kind, to live in peace. It sounded so good, and yet it was so wrong. How far from the mark!

"The Bible is clear that all our righteousnesses are like filthy rags. There is none righteous, no not one. We have turned, every one, to his own way. All have sinned and fall short of the glory of God. In the economy of God, we are all worthy only of the punishment of death.

"I would be remiss and would fail you most miserably if we got to the end of a memorial service for a man with the evangelistic heart of Bruce Barnes and did not tell you what he told me and everyone else he came in contact with during the last nearly two years of his life on this earth. Jesus has already paid the penalty. The work has been done. Are we to live good lives? Are we to do the best we can? Are we to think of others and live in peace? Of course! But to earn our salvation? Scripture is clear that we are saved by grace through faith, and that not of ourselves; not of works, lest anyone should boast. We live our lives in as righteous a manner as we can in thankful response to that priceless gift of God, our salvation, freely paid for on the cross by Christ himself.

"That is what Bruce Barnes would tell you this morning, were he still housed in the shell that lies in the box before you. Anyone who knew him knows that this message became his life. He was devastated at the loss of his family and in grief over the sin in his life and his ultimate failure to have made the transaction with God he knew was necessary to assure him of eternal life.

"But he did not wallow in self-pity. He quickly became a student of the Scriptures and a teller of the Good News. This pulpit could not contain him. He started house churches all over America and then began speaking throughout the world. Yes, he was usually here on Sundays, because he believed his flock was his primary responsibility. But you and I, all of us, let him travel because we knew that here was a man of whom the world was not worthy."

Buck watched closely as Rayford stopped speaking. He stepped to the side of the pulpit and gestured at the coffin. "And now," he said, "if I can get through this, I would like to speak directly to Bruce. You all know that the body is dead. It cannot hear. But Bruce," he said, raising his eyes, "we thank you. We envy you. We know you are with Christ, which Paul the apostle says is 'far better.'

"We confess we don't like this. It hurts. We miss you. But in your memory we pledge to carry on, to stay at the task, to keep on keeping on against all odds. We will study the materials you have left behind, and we will keep this church the lighthouse you made it for the glory of God."

\+ + +

Rayford stepped back into the pulpit, feeling drained. But he was not half done. "I would also be remiss if I did not try to share with you at least the core thoughts from the sermon Bruce had prepared for today. It is an important one, one none of us in leadership here would want you to have missed. I can tell you I have been over it many times, and it blesses me each time. But before I do that, I feel compelled to open the floor to anyone else who feels led to say anything in memory of our dear brother."

Rayford took one step back from the microphone and waited. For a few seconds he wondered if he had caught everyone off guard. No one moved. Finally, Loretta stood.

"Y'all know me here," she said. "I've been Bruce's secretary since the day everybody else disappeared. If you'll pray I can maintain my composure, I have just a few things to say about Pastor Barnes."

Loretta told her now-familiar story, of how she was the only one of more than a hundred blood relatives who was left behind at the Rapture. "There are only a dozen or so of us in this room who were members of this church before that day," she said. "We all know who we are, and grateful as we are to have finally found the truth, we live in regret for all the wasted years."

\+ + +

Buck, Chloe, and Amanda turned in their pew to hear Loretta better. Buck noticed tissues and handkerchiefs all over the sanctuary. Loretta finished with this: "Brother Barnes was a very bright man who had made a very huge mistake. As soon as he got right with the Lord and committed himself to serve him for the rest of his days, he became pastor to the rest of us. I can't tell you the countless numbers that he personally led to Christ. But I can tell you this: He was never condescendin', never judgmental, never short-tempered with anyone. He was earnest and compassionate, and he loved people into the kingdom. Oh, he never was polite to the point where he wouldn't tell people exactly how it was. There are enough people in here who can attest to that. But winnin' people to Christ was his main, whole, and only goal. I just pray that if there's anybody here who is still wonderin' or holdin' out, that you'll realize maybe you're the reason that we'll always be able to say that Bruce did not die in vain. His passion for souls continues beyond the grave." And Loretta broke down. She sat. The stranger next to her, the dark-complected man known only to her and the Tribulation Force, gently put his arm around her.

* * *

Rayford stood listening as people from all over the sanctuary stood and testified to the impact Bruce Barnes had had on their lives. It went on and on and on for more than an hour. Finally, when there seemed to be a lull, Rayford said, "I hate to arbitrarily end this, but if there is anyone else, let me ask you to stand quickly. After one more, I'll then allow any who need to leave to do so. Staying for my summary of what would have been Bruce's sermon this morning is optional."

Tsion Ben-Judah stood. "You do not know me," he said. "I represent the international community where your pastor toiled so long and so earnestly and so effectively. Many, many Christian leaders around the globe knew him, sat under his ministry, and were brought closer to Christ because of him. My prayer for you is that you would continue his ministry and his memory, that you would, as the Scriptures say, 'not grow weary in doing good.'"

Rayford announced, "Stand if you would. Stretch, embrace a friend, greet someone." People stood and stretched and shook hands and embraced, but few said anything. Rayford said, "While you are standing I would like to excuse any who are overcome, hungry, restless, or for any other reason need to leave. We are long past our normal closing time. We will tape the rest of this service for any who have to leave. I will be summarizing Bruce's message for this morning, apologizing in advance for reading some of it to you. I am not the preacher he was, so bear with me. We'll take a couple of minutes' break now, so feel free to leave if you need to."

Rayford backed away from the pulpit and sat. En masse, the congregation sat back down and looked expectantly at him. When it was clear no one was leaving, someone giggled, then another, and a few more. Rayford smiled and shrugged and returned to the pulpit.

"I guess there are things more important in this life than personal comfort, aren't there?" he said. A few *amens* resounded. Rayford opened his Bible and Bruce's notes.

* * *

Buck knew what was coming. He had been over the material nearly as many times as Rayford had and had helped condense it. Still, he was excited. People would be inspired by what Bruce believed had happened, what he predicted would happen, and what was yet to come.

Rayford began by explaining, "As best we have been able to determine, these sermon notes were written onboard an aircraft while Bruce was returning from Indonesia last week. The name of the file is 'Sermon' with today's date, and what he has here is a rough outline and a lot of commentary. Occasionally he lapses into personal notations, some of which I feel free to share with you now that he is gone, others that I feel compelled to keep from you now that he is gone.

"For instance, shortly after outlining where he wants to go with this message, he notes, 'I was ill all night last night and feel not much better today. I was warned about viruses, despite all my shots. I can't complain. I have traveled extensively without problem. God has been with me. Of course, he is with me now, too, but I fear dehydration. If I'm not better upon my return, I'll get checked out.'

"So," Rayford added, "we get a glimpse of the ailment that brought him low and which led to his collapse at the church upon his return. As most of you know, he was rushed to the hospital, where it is our belief that he died from this ailment and not from the blast.

"Bruce has outlined a message here that he believed was particularly urgent, because, as he writes, 'I have become convinced we are at the end of the eighteen-month period of peace, which follows the agreement the Antichrist has made with Israel. If I am right, and we can set the beginning of the Tribulation at the time of the signing of the treaty between the nation of Israel and what was then known as the United Nations, we are perilously close to and must prepare for the next ominous and dire prediction in the Tribulation timeline: The Red Horse of the Apocalypse. Revelation 6:3-4 indicates that it was granted to the one who sat on it to take peace from the earth, and that people should kill one another; and there was given to him a great sword. In my mind, this is a prediction of global war. It will likely become known as World War III. It will be instigated by the Antichrist, and yet he will rise as the great solver of it, the great peacemaker, as he is the great deceiving liar.

"'This will immediately usher in the next two horses of the apocalypse, the black horse of plague and famine, and the pale horse of death. These will be nearly simultaneous—it should not surprise any of us to know that global war would result in famine, plague, and death.'

"Do any of you find this as astounding as I did when I first read it?" Rayford asked. All over the sanctuary, people nodded. "I remind you that this was written by a man who died either just before or just after the first bomb was volleyed in the global war we find ourselves in. He didn't know precisely when it would occur, but he didn't want to let one more Sunday pass without sharing this message with you. I don't know about you, but I'm inclined to heed the words of one who interprets the prophecy of Scripture so accurately. Here's what Bruce, in his own notes, says is yet to come:

"'The time is short now for everyone. Revelation 6:7-8 says the rider of the pale horse is Death and that Hades follows after him. Power was given to them over a fourth of the earth, to kill with sword, with hunger, with death, and by the beasts of the earth. I confess I don't know what the Scripture is referring to when it says the beasts of the earth, but perhaps these are animals that devour people when they are left without protection due to the war. Perhaps a great beast of the earth is some symbolic metaphor for the weapons employed by the Antichrist and his enemies. Regardless, in short order one-fourth of the world's population will be wiped out.'

"Bruce continues: 'I shared this with three close compatriots not long ago, and asked them to consider that there were four of us in the room. Was it possible that one of us would be gone in due time? Of course it was. Might I lose a fourth of my congregation? I pray my church will be spared, but I have so many congregations now around the world, it is impossible to imagine that all could be spared. Of the quarter of the earth's population that will perish, surely many, many of these will be tribulation saints.

"'Given the level of modern technology, global war will take little time at all to wreak its havoc and devastation. These three last horsemen of the apocalypse will gallop one right after the other. If people were horrified by the painless, bloodless, disappearance of the saints at the Rapture, which resulted in enough chaos of its own because of crashes and fires and suicides, imagine the desperation of a world ripped to shreds by global war, famine, plague, and death.'"

Rayford looked up from Bruce's notes. "My wife and I watched the news yesterday at the airport," he said, "as I'm sure many of you watched wherever you were, and we saw these very things reported from all around the world. Only the greatest skeptic would accuse us of having written this after the fact. But let's say that you're skeptical. Let's say you believe we are charlatans. Who then wrote the Bible? And when was it written? Forget Bruce Barnes and his present-day predictions, a week before the fact. Consider these prophecies made thousands of years ago. You can imagine the pain it brought Bruce to have to prepare this sermon. In a side note he writes, 'I hate preaching bad news. My problem in the past was that I always hated hearing bad news too. I shut it out. I didn't listen. It was there if I merely had ears to hear. I must share more bad news in this message, and though it grieves me, I cannot shirk the responsibility.'

"You'll note Bruce's turmoil here," Rayford said. "Because I'm the one who has to deliver this, I empathize totally with where he was. The next part of his outline indicates that the Four Horsemen of the Apocalypse, once they have visited their judgments on the earth, represent the first four of the seven Seal Judgments that Revelation 6:1-16 indicates will occur during the first twenty-one months of the Tribulation. According to Bruce's calculations, using as a reference point the treaty signed between Israel and the United Nations, which we now know as the Global Community, we are closing in on the end of that twenty-one-month period. Therefore, it behooves us to understand clearly the fifth, sixth, and seventh Seal Judgments predicted in Revelation. As you know from what Bruce has taught before, there are yet to come two more seven-part judgments that will carry us through to the end of the seven-year Tribulation and the glorious appearing of Christ. The next seven will be the Trumpet Judgments, and the seven following that will be the Vial Judgments. Whoever becomes your pastor-teacher will, I'm sure, carefully walk you through those as the time draws near. Meanwhile, let me, with Bruce's notes and commentary, make us all aware of what we have to look forward to just within the next few weeks."

+ + +

Rayford was exhausted, but worse than that, he had gone over and over in his mind what he was about to share. It was not good news. He felt weak. He was hungry. He was enough in tune with his body to know he needed sugar. "I'm going to ask for just a five-minute break. I know many of you may need to use the facilities. I need to get a drink. We'll meet back here at precisely one o'clock."

He left the platform, and Amanda made a beeline for the side door, meeting him in the corridor. "What do you need?" she asked.

"Besides prayer?"

"I've been praying for you all morning," she said. "You know that. What do you want? Some orange juice?"

"You make me sound like a diabetic."

"I just know what I would need if I'd been standing up there that long between meals."

"Juice sounds great," he said. While she hurried off, Buck joined Rayford in the hallway.

"Do you think they're ready for what's to come?" Buck asked.

"Frankly, I think Bruce has been trying to tell them this for months. There's nothing like today's newscasts to convince you your pastor is right."

+ + +

Buck assured Rayford he would continue praying for him. When he returned to his seat, he found that, again, it appeared not one person had left. It didn't surprise Buck that Rayford was back in the pulpit exactly when he said he would be.

"I won't keep you much longer," he said. "But I'm sure you all agree that this is life-and-death stuff. From Bruce's notes and teaching we learn that

Revelation 6:9-11 points out that the fifth of the seven Seal Judgments concerns tribulation martyrs. The Scripture says, 'I saw under the altar the souls of those who had been slain for the word of God and for the testimony which they held. And they cried with a loud voice, saying, "How long, O Lord, holy and true, until You judge and avenge our blood on those who dwell on the earth?" Then a white robe was given to each of them; and it was said to them that they should rest a little while longer, until both the number of their fellow servants and their brethren, who would be killed as they were, was completed.'

"In other words," Rayford continued, "many of those who have died in this world war, and are yet to die until a quarter of the world's population is gone, are considered tribulation martyrs. I put Bruce in this category. While he may not have died specifically for preaching the gospel or *while* preaching the gospel, clearly it was his life's work and it resulted in his death. I envision Bruce under the altar with the souls of those slain for the word of God and for the testimony they held. He will be given a white robe and told to rest a while longer until even more martyrs are added to the total. I must ask you today, are you prepared? Are you willing? Would you give your life for the sake of the gospel?"

* * *

Rayford paused to take a breath and was startled when someone cried out, "I will!"

Rayford didn't know what to say. Suddenly, from another part of the sanctuary: "So will I!"

Three or four others said the same in unison. Rayford choked back tears. It had been a rhetorical question. He had not expected an answer. How moving! How inspiring! He felt led not to let others follow based on emotion alone. He continued, his voice thick, "Thank you, brothers and sisters. I fear we may all be called upon to express our willingness to die for the cause. Praise God you are willing. Bruce's notes indicate that he believed these judgments are chronological. If the Four Horsemen of the Apocalypse lead to the white-robed tribulation martyrs under the altar in heaven, that could be happening even as we speak. And if it is, we need to know what the sixth seal is. Bruce felt so strongly about this Seal Judgment that on his computer he cut and pasted right here into his notes several different translations and versions of Revelation 6:12-17. Let me just read you the one he marked as the most stark and easily understood:

"'I looked when He'—and you'll recall that the *he* mentioned here is the Lamb, who is described in verse fourteen of the previous chapter as 'Him who lives forever and ever,' who is, of course, Jesus Christ himself—'He opened the sixth seal, and behold, there was a great earthquake; and the sun became black as sackcloth of hair, and the moon became like blood. And the stars of heaven fell to the earth, as a fig tree drops its late figs when it is shaken by a mighty wind. Then the sky receded as a scroll when it is rolled up, and every mountain and island was moved out of its place. And the kings of the earth, the great men, the rich men, the commanders, the mighty men, every slave and every free man, hid themselves in the caves and in the rocks of the mountains, and said to the mountains and rocks, "Fall on us and hide us from the face of Him who sits on the throne and from the wrath of the Lamb! For the great day of His wrath has come, and who is able to stand?""'"

Rayford looked up and scanned the sanctuary. Some stared at him, ashen. Others peered intently at their Bibles. "I'm no theologian, people. I'm no scholar. I have had as much trouble reading the Bible as any of you throughout my lifetime, and especially over the nearly two years since the Rapture. But I ask you, is there anything difficult to understand about a passage that begins, 'Behold, there was a great earthquake'? Bruce has carefully charted these events, and he believed that the first seven seals cover the first twenty-one months of the seven-year tribulation, which began at the time of the covenant between Israel and the Antichrist. If you happen to be one who doesn't believe the Antichrist has appeared on the scene yet, then you don't believe there's an agreement between Israel and that person. If that is true, all this is still yet to come. The Tribulation did not begin with the Rapture. It begins with the signing of that treaty.

"Bruce taught us that the first four Seal Judgments were represented by the Four Horsemen of the Apocalypse. I submit to you that those horsemen are at full gallop. The fifth seal, the tribulation martyrs who had been slain for the word of God and for the testimony which they held, and whose souls are under the altar, has begun.

"Bruce's commentary indicates that more and more martyrs will be added now. Antichrist will come against tribulation saints and the 144,000 witnesses springing up all over the world from the tribes of Israel.

"Hear me, from a very practical standpoint. If Bruce is right—and he has been so far—we are close to the end of the first twenty-one months. I believe in God. I believe in Christ. I believe the Bible is the Word of God. I believe our dear departed brother 'rightly divided the word of truth,' and thus I am preparing to endure what this passage calls 'the wrath of the Lamb.' An earthquake is coming, and it is not symbolic. This passage indicates that everyone, great or small, would rather be crushed to death than to face the one who sits on the throne."

\+ + +

Buck was furiously taking notes. This was not new to him, but he was so moved by Rayford's passion and the idea of the earthquake being known as the wrath of the Lamb that he knew it had to be publicized to the world.

Perhaps it would be his swan song, his death knell, but he was going to put in the *Global Community Weekly* that Christians were teaching of the coming "wrath of the Lamb." It was one thing to predict an earthquake. Armchair scientists and clairvoyants had been doing that for years. But there was something about the psyche of the current world citizen that caused him or her to become enamored of catchphrases. What better catchphrase than one from the Word of God?

Buck listened as Rayford concluded: "At the end of this first twenty-one-month period, the mysterious seventh Seal Judgment will usher in the next twenty-one-month period, during which we will receive the seven Trumpet Judgments. I say the seventh Seal Judgment is mysterious because Scripture is not clear what form it will take. All the Bible says is that it is apparently so dramatic that there will be silence in heaven for half an hour. Then seven angels, each with a trumpet, prepare themselves to sound. We will study those judgments and talk about them as we move into that period. However, for now, I believe Bruce has left us with much to think and pray about.

"We have loved this man, we have learned from this man, and now we have eulogized him. Though we know he is finally with Christ, do not hesitate to grieve and mourn. The Bible says we are not to mourn as do the heathen, who have no hope, but it does not say we should not mourn at all. Embrace the grief and grieve with all your might. But don't let it keep you from the task. What Bruce would have wanted above all else is that we stay about the business of bringing every person we can into the kingdom before it is too late."

* * *

Rayford was exhausted. He closed in prayer, but rather than leaving the platform he merely sat and lowered his head. There was not the usual rush for the doors. Most continued to sit, while a few slowly and quietly began to make their way out.

16

BUCK HELPED CHLOE into the Range Rover, but before he could get around to the driver's side, he was accosted by Verna Zee.

"Verna! I didn't see you! I'm glad you made it."

"I made it all right, Cameron. I also recognized Tsion Ben-Judah!"

Buck fought to keep from covering her mouth with his hand. "I'm sorry?"

"He's going to be in deep trouble when the Global Community peacekeeping forces find out where he is. Don't you know he's wanted all over the world? And that your passport and ID were found on one of his accomplices? Buck, you're in as much trouble as he is. Steve Plank has been trying to get ahold of you, and I'm tired of pretending I have no idea what you're up to."

"Verna, we're going to have to go somewhere and talk about this."

"I can't keep your secret forever, Buck. I'm not going down with you. That was a pretty impressive meeting, and it's obvious everybody loved that Barnes guy. But do all these people believe that Nicolae Carpathia is the Antichrist?"

"I can't speak for everyone."

"But how about you, Buck? You report directly to the man. Are you going to write a story in one of his own magazines that says that?"

"I already have, Verna."

"Yeah, but you've always represented it as a neutral report of what some believe. This is your church! These are your people! You buy into all this stuff."

"Can we go somewhere and talk about this or not?" Buck said.

"I think we'd better. Anyway, I want to interview Tsion Ben-Judah. You can't blame me for going for the scoop of a lifetime."

Buck bit his tongue to keep from saying she wasn't enough of a writer to do justice to a story like Ben-Judah anyway. "Let me get back to you tomorrow," he said. "And then we can—"

"Tomorrow? Today, Buck. Let's meet at the office this afternoon."

"This afternoon is not good. I'm coming back here for the viewing at four."

"Then how about six-thirty?"

"Why does it have to be today?" Buck asked.

"It doesn't. I could just tell Steve Plank or Carpathia himself or anybody I want exactly what I've seen today."

"Verna, I took a huge risk in helping you out the other night and letting you stay at Loretta's home."

"You sure did. And you may regret it for the rest of your life."

"So none of what you heard here today made any impact on you?"

"Yes, it did. It made me wonder why I went soft on you all of a sudden. You people are wacko, Buck. I'm gonna need some compelling reason to keep quiet about you."

That sounded like extortion, but Buck also realized that Verna had apparently stayed for the entire service that morning. Something had to be working on her. Buck wanted to find out how she could relegate the prophecies of Revelation and what had happened in the world in the last twenty months or so to mere coincidence. "All right," he said. "Six-thirty at the office."

\+ + +

Rayford and the other elders had agreed there would be no more formality at the viewing. No prayer, no message, no eulogies, no nothing. Just a procession of people filing past the coffin and paying their last respects. Someone had suggested opening the fellowship hall for refreshments, but Rayford, having been tipped off by Buck, decided against it. A ribbon was draped across the stairway, from wall to wall, to keep everyone from going downstairs. A sign indicated the viewing would last from 4 to 6 p.m.

\+ + +

At about five, while a crowd of hundreds slowly moved past the casket in a line that stretched out the front door, through the parking lot, and down the street, Buck wheeled into Loretta's parking spot with the Range Rover full of people.

"Chloe, I promise this is the last time I take advantage of your ailment and use you as a decoy."

"A decoy for what? Do you think Carpathia is here and is going to grab you or Tsion?"

Buck chuckled. Rayford had been in the sanctuary since just before four. Now, Buck, Chloe, Amanda, Tsion, and Loretta emerged from the Range Rover. Amanda got on one side of Chloe and Loretta on the other. They helped her up the back steps as Buck opened the door. Buck peeked at the parishioners waiting in line to get into the church. Nearly all ignored his little group. Those who idly watched them seemed to be concentrating on the pretty young newlywed, her ankle cast, her sling, and her cane.

As the three women made their way to the office, planning to view the body when the crowd dissipated, Buck and Tsion slipped away. When Buck entered the office about twenty minutes later, Chloe asked, "Where's Tsion?"

"He's around," Buck said.

* * *

Rayford stood near Bruce's coffin, shaking hands with mourners. Donny Moore approached. "I'm sorry to bother you with a question right here," Donny said, "but would you know where I could find Mr. Williams? He ordered some stuff from me, and I've got it for him."

Rayford directed him to the office.

As Donny and dozens of others filed past, Rayford wondered how long Hattie Durham would be with her mother in Denver. Carpathia had scheduled a meeting with Pontifex Maximus Peter Mathews, who had recently been named Supreme Pontiff of Enigma Babylon One World Faith, a conglomeration of all the religions in the world. Carpathia wanted Rayford back to New Babylon by the Thursday after next to fly the Condor 216 to Rome. There he was to pick up Mathews and bring him to New Babylon. Carpathia had made noises about headquartering Mathews and One World Faith in New Babylon, along with almost every other international organization.

Rayford found himself numb, shaking hand after hand. He tried not to look at Bruce's body. He busied himself remembering what else he'd heard Carpathia saying through that ingenious reverse intercom bugging device the late Earl Halliday had installed in the Condor. Most interesting to Rayford was Carpathia's insistence on taking over leadership of several of the groups and committees that had been headed by his old friend and financial angel Jonathan Stonagal. Buck had told Rayford and the rest of the Tribulation Force that he was in the room when Carpathia murdered Stonagal and then brainwashed everyone else to believe they'd just witnessed a suicide. With Carpathia now angling his way into the leadership of international relations committees, commissions on international harmony, and, most important, secret financial cooperatives, his motives for that murder became clear.

Rayford let his mind wander to the good old days, when all he had to do was show up at O'Hare on time, fly his routes, and come home. Of course, he was not a believer then. Not the kind of husband and father he should have been. The good old days really hadn't been so good at all.

He couldn't complain about excitement in his life. While he despised

Carpathia and hated to be in a position of actual service to the man, he had long since decided to be obedient to God. If this was where God wanted him, it was where he would serve. He just hoped Hattie Durham might come back through Chicago before he had to leave. Somehow, he and Amanda and Chloe and Buck had to pull her away from Nicolae Carpathia. It had been encouraging to him, in a perverse way, that she had found her own reasons to distance herself from Nicolae. But Carpathia might not be so easily dumped, considering that she was carrying his child and he was so jealous of his public image.

* * *

Buck was busy with Donny Moore, learning the incredible features of the new computers, when he heard Loretta on the phone.

"Yes, Verna," she was saying, "he's busy with someone right now, but I'll tell him you said Steve Plank called."

Buck excused himself from Donny for a second and mouthed to Loretta, "If she's at the office, ask her if my checks are there."

Buck had been away from both the New York and Chicago offices on paydays for several weeks and was pleased to see Loretta nodding after she had asked Verna about the checks. One thing he had seen in Bruce's printouts, and which had been corroborated by Tsion, was that he needed to start investing in gold. Cash would soon be meaningless. He had to start stockpiling some sort of financial resource because, even in the best-case scenario, even if Verna became a believer and protected him from Carpathia, he couldn't maintain this ruse for long. That relationship would end. His income would dry up. He would not be able to buy or sell without the mark of the beast anyway, and the new world order Carpathia was so proud of could virtually starve him out.

* * *

By a quarter to six, the sanctuary was nearly empty. Rayford headed back to the office. He shut the door behind him. "We can have our moment alone with Bruce's body in a few minutes," he said.

The Tribulation Force, plus Loretta and minus Tsion, sat somberly. "So, that's what Donny Moore brought you?" Rayford said, nodding at the stack of laptops.

"Yep. One for each of us. I asked Loretta if she wanted one too."

Loretta waved him off, smiling. "I wouldn't know what to do with it. I probably couldn't even open it."

"Where's Tsion?" Rayford said. "I really think we ought to keep him with us for a while and—"

"Tsion is safe," Buck said, looking carefully at Rayford.

"Uh-huh."

"What does that mean?" Loretta asked. "Where is he?"

Rayford sat in a chair on wheels and rolled it close to Loretta. "Ma'am, there are some things we are not going to tell you, for your own good."

"Well," she said, "what would you say if I told you I didn't appreciate that very much?"

"I can understand, Loretta—"

"I'm not so sure you can, Captain Steele. I've had things kept from me all my life just because I was a polite, southern lady."

"A southern belle is more like it," Rayford said.

"Now you're patronizin' me, and I don't appreciate that either."

Rayford was taken aback. "I'm sorry, Loretta, I meant no offense."

"Well, it offends me to have secrets kept from me."

Rayford leaned forward. "I'm quite serious about doing this for your own good. The fact is, someday, and I mean someday very soon, very high-placed officials may try to force you to tell them where Tsion is."

"And you think if I know where he is, I'll crack."

"If you don't know where he is, you can't crack and don't even have to worry about it."

Loretta pursed her lips and shook her head. "I know y'all are livin' dangerous lives. I feel like I've risked a lot just by puttin' you up. Now I'm only your landlady, is that it?"

"Loretta, you're one of the dearest people in the world to us, that's who you are. We wouldn't do anything to hurt you. That's why, even though I know it offends you—and that's the last thing I want to do—I'm not going to let you intimidate me into telling you where Tsion is. You'll be able to communicate with him by phone, and we can communicate with him by computer. Someday you may thank us for withholding this from you."

Amanda interrupted. "Rayford, are you and Buck saying that Tsion is where I think he is?"

Rayford nodded.

"Is that necessary already?" Chloe asked.

"I'm afraid so. I wish I could say how long it will be for the rest of us."

Loretta, clearly peeved, stood and paced, her arms folded across her chest. "Captain Steele, sir, could you tell me one thing? Could you tell me that you're not keepin' this from me because you think I'd blab it all over?"

Rayford stood. "Loretta, come here."

She stopped and stared at him.

"Come on now," he said. "Come right over here and let me hug you. I'm young enough to be your son, so don't be taking this as condescending."

Loretta seemed to be refusing to smile, but she did slowly approach Rayford. He embraced her. "Ma'am, I've known you long enough to know that you don't tell secrets. The fact is, the people who might ask you about Tsion Ben-Judah's whereabouts wouldn't hesitate to use a lie detector or even truth serum if they thought you knew. If they could somehow force you to give him up against your will, it could really hurt the cause of Christ."

She hugged him. "All right then," she said. "I still think I'm a tougher bird than you people seem to think, but all right. If I didn't think you were doin' this with my best interests in mind, misguided as y'all are, I'd throw you out of my boardinghouse."

That made everybody smile. Everybody except Loretta.

There was a knock at the door. "Excuse me, sir," the funeral director said to Rayford. "The sanctuary is empty."

+ + +

Buck was last in line as the five of them filed into the sanctuary and stood by Bruce's coffin. At first Buck felt guilty. He was strangely unmoved. He realized he had expended his emotion during the memorial service. He knew so well that Bruce was no longer there that he largely felt nothing by simply noting that his friend was, indeed, dead.

And yet he was able to use these moments, standing there with the people closest to him in the world, to think about how dramatically and specifically God had acted in his behalf even just within the last several hours. If there was one thing he had learned from Bruce, it was that the Christian life was a series of new beginnings. What had God done for him lately? What *hadn't* he done for him? Buck only wished he would feel the same compulsion to renew his commitment to the service of Christ when God didn't seem so close.

Twenty minutes later, Buck and Chloe pulled into the parking lot of *Global Community Weekly*. Only Verna's car was in the lot.

To Buck, it seemed Verna looked both surprised and disappointed to see Chloe hobbling in with him. Chloe must have noticed too. "Am I not welcome here?" she said.

"Of course," Verna said. "If Buck needs someone to hold his hand."

"Why would I need someone to hold my hand?"

They sat in a small conference room with Verna at the head of the table. She leaned back in her seat and steepled her fingers. "Buck, we both know I hold all the cards now, don't we?"

"What happened to the new Verna?" Buck asked.

"There was no new Verna," she said. "Just a slightly mellower version of the old Verna."

Chloe leaned forward. "Then nothing we've said, nothing you and I have talked about, nothing you've seen or heard or experienced at Loretta's house or at the church has meant anything to you whatsoever?"

"Well, I have to admit I appreciate the new car. It is better than the one I had. Of course, that was only fair, and the least Buck could do for me after ruining mine."

"So," Chloe said, "your moments of vulnerability, your admitting that you had been jealous of Buck, and your realization that you had been inappropriate in how you talked with him, that was all, what, made up?"

Verna stood. She put her hands on her hips and stared down at Buck and Chloe. "I'm really surprised at how petty this conversation has begun. We're not talking about office politics here. We're not talking about personality conflicts. The fact is, Buck, you're not loyal to your employer. It's not just a matter of worrying, because it isn't journalism the way it's supposed to be. I've got a problem with that myself. I even told Chloe that, didn't I, Chloe?"

"You did."

"Carpathia has bought up all the news outlets, I know that," Verna continued. "None of us old-fashioned journalists enjoy the prospect of covering news our owner is making. We don't like being expected to put his spin on everything. But, Buck, you're a wolf in sheep's clothing. You're a spy. You're the enemy. You not only don't like the man, you also think he's the Antichrist himself."

"Why don't you sit down, Verna?" Chloe said. "We all know the little negotiation hints from the books that teach you how to look out for number one. I can't speak for Buck, but your trying to tower over me doesn't intimidate me."

"I'll sit down, but only because I want to."

"So, what's your game?" Chloe said. "Are you about to engage in extortion?"

"Speaking of that," Buck said, "I'll thank you for my checks for the last several weeks."

"I haven't touched them. They're in your top drawer. And no, I'm not a blackmailer. It just seems to me your life depends on who knows or doesn't know that you're harboring Tsion Ben-Judah."

"That's something you think you know?"

"I saw him in church this morning!"

"At least you thought you did," Chloe said.

Buck flinched and looked at her. So did Verna. For the first time, Buck saw a flicker of uncertainty on Verna's face.

"You're telling me I didn't see Tsion Ben-Judah in church this morning?"

"It certainly sounds unlikely," Chloe said. "Wouldn't you say?"

"Not really. I know Buck was in Israel and that his papers were found with a Ben-Judah sympathizer."

"And so you saw Buck in church with Ben-Judah?"

"I didn't say that. I said I saw Ben-Judah. He was sitting with that woman who put me up the other night, Loretta."

"So Loretta's dating Tsion Ben-Judah, is that what you're saying?"

"You know what I'm saying, Chloe. Ben-Judah even spoke in that service. If that wasn't him, I'm no journalist."

"No comment," Buck said.

"I resent that!"

Chloe kept the pressure on. "You were sitting somewhere where we couldn't see you—"

"I was in the balcony, if you must know."

"And from the balcony you could see a man sitting in the back with Loretta?"

"I didn't say that. I meant I could tell he was sitting with her. They both spoke and it sounded like it was coming from the same area."

"So Ben-Judah escapes from Israel, apparently with Buck's help. Buck is brilliant enough to leave his official papers with some enemy of the state. When Buck gets Ben-Judah safely into North America, he brings him out in public at his own church, and then Ben-Judah stands and speaks in front of hundreds of people. This is your thought?"

Verna was sputtering. "Well, he, well, if that wasn't Ben-Judah, who was it?"

"This is your story, Verna."

"Loretta will tell me. I got the impression she liked me. I'm sure I saw him walking out the back with her. A small, kind of stocky Israeli?"

"And you could tell from behind who he was?"

"I'm gonna call Loretta right now." She reached for a phone. "I don't suppose you'd give me her phone number."

Buck wondered if that was a good idea. They had not prepped Loretta. But after the incident in the office with Rayford earlier, he believed Loretta could handle Verna Zee. "Sure," Buck said, scribbling the number.

Verna hit the speaker button and dialed.

"Loretta's phone, Rayford Steele speaking."

Apparently, Verna had not expected that. "Oh, uh, yes. Loretta please."

"May I ask—"

"Verna Zee."

When Loretta came on, she was her typical, charming self. "Verna, dear! How are you? I heard you were at the service today, but I missed you. Did you find it as moving as I did?"

"We'll have to talk about that sometime, Loretta. I just wanted to—"

"I can't think of a better time than now, sweetheart. Would you like to meet someplace, come over, what?"

Verna looked irritated. "No, ma'am, not now. Sometime, maybe. I just wanted to ask you a question. Who was that man with you in church this morning?"

"That man?"

"Yes! You were with a Middle Eastern man. He spoke briefly. Who was he?"

"Is this on the record?"

"No! I'm just asking."

"Well I'm just telling you that that's a personal, impertinent question."

"So you're not going to tell me?"

"I don't believe it's any of your business."

"What if I told you that Buck and Chloe said you'd tell me?"

"First off, I'd probably say you were a liar. But that would be impolite and more impertinent than the question you asked."

"Just tell me if that was Rabbi Tsion Ben-Judah of Israel!"

"It sounds like you've already named him. What do you need my input for?"

"So, it *was* him?"

"You said it. I didn't."

"But was it?"

"You want the honest truth, Verna? That man is my secret lover. I keep him under the bed."

"What? What? So, come on—"

"Verna, if you'd like to talk about how moved you were by our memorial service this morning, I'd love to chat with you some more. Do you?"

Verna hung up on Loretta. "All right, so you've all gotten together and decided not to tell the truth. I don't think I'll have much trouble convincing Steve Plank or even Nicolae Carpathia that it appears you're harboring Tsion Ben-Judah."

Chloe looked at Buck. "You think Buck would do something so royally stupid it would not only get him fired, but it would also get him killed? And you're going to use the threat of this news to the Global Community higher-ups in exchange for what?"

Verna stalked out of the room. Buck looked at Chloe, winked, and shook his head. "You're priceless," he said.

Verna rushed back in and slapped Buck's checks on the table. "You know your time is short, Buck."

"Truth to tell," Buck said, "I believe all of our time is short."

Verna sat down resignedly. "You really believe this stuff, don't you?"

Buck tried to change the tone. He spoke sympathetically. "Verna, you've talked with Loretta and Amanda and Chloe and me. We've all shared our stories. You heard Rayford's story this morning. If we're all wacko, then we're all wacko. But were you not in the least impressed with some of the things that Bruce Barnes garnered from the Bible? Things that are coming true right now?"

Verna, at last, was silent for a moment. Finally she spoke. "It *was* kind of strange. Kind of impressive. But isn't it just like Nostradamus? Can't these prophecies be read into? Can't they mean anything you want them to mean?"

"I don't know how you could believe that," Chloe said. "You're smarter than that. Bruce said that if the treaty between the United Nations and Israel was the covenant referred to in the Bible, it would usher in the seven-year tribulation period. First there would be the seven Seal Judgments. The Four Horsemen of the Apocalypse would be the horse of peace—for eighteen months—the horse of war, the horse of plague and famine, and the horse of death."

"That's all symbolic, isn't it?" Verna said.

"Of course it is," Chloe said. "I haven't seen any horsemen. But I have seen a year and a half of peace. I have seen World War III break out. I've seen it result in plagues and famine with more to come. I've seen lots of people die, and more will. What will it take to convince you? You can't see the fifth Seal Judgment, the martyred saints under the altar in heaven. But did you hear what Rayford said Bruce believes is coming next?"

"An earthquake, yes, I know."

"Will that convince you?"

Verna turned in her chair and stared out the window. "I suppose that would be pretty hard to argue with."

"I have some advice for you," Chloe said. "If that earthquake is as devastating as the Bible makes it sound, you may not have time to change your mind about all of this before *your* time is up."

Verna stood and walked slowly to the door. Holding it open, she said softly, "I still don't like the idea of Buck's pretending to Carpathia to be something he's not."

Buck and Chloe followed her out toward the front door. "Our private lives, our beliefs, are none of our employer's business," Buck said. "For instance, if I knew you were a lesbian, I wouldn't feel it necessary to tell your superiors."

Verna whirled to face him. "Who told you that? What business is that of yours? You tell anybody that and I'll—"

Buck raised both hands. "Verna, your personal life is confidential with me. You don't have to worry that I'll ever say anything to anybody about that."

"There's nothing to tell!"

"My point exactly."

Buck held the door open for Chloe. In the parking lot, Verna said, "So we're agreed?"

"Agreed?" Buck said.

"That neither of us is going to say anything about the other's personal life?"

Buck shrugged. "Sounds fair to me."

+ + +

The funeral director was on the phone with Rayford. "So," he was saying, "with the backlog of deaths, the scarcity of grave sites, and so forth, we're estimating interment no sooner than three weeks, possibly as late as five weeks. We store the bodies at no charge to you, as this is a matter of public health."

"I understand. If you could simply inform us once the burial has occurred, we'd appreciate it. We will not have a service, and no one will attend."

Loretta sat at the dining room table next to Rayford. "That seems so sad," she said. "Are you sure not even one of us should go?"

"I've never been much for graveside services," Rayford said. "And I don't think anything more needs to be said over Bruce's body."

"That's true," she said. "It's not like that's him. He's not going to feel lonely or neglected."

Rayford nodded and pulled a sheet from a stack of Bruce's papers. "Loretta, I think Bruce would have wanted you to see this."

"What is it?"

"It's from his personal journal. A few private thoughts about you."

"Are you sure?"

"Of course."

"I mean, are you sure he'd want me to see it?"

"I can go only by my *own* feelings," he said. "If I had written something like this, I would want you to see it, especially after I was gone."

Loretta, her fingers shaking, pulled the sheet to where she could read it with her bifocals. She was soon overcome. "Thank you, Rayford," she managed through her tears. "Thank you for letting me see that."

+ + +

"Buck! I had no idea Verna was a lesbian!" Chloe said.

"*You* had no idea? Neither did I!"

"You're kidding!"

"I'm not. You think that little revelation was of God too?"

"I'd sooner think it was a wild coincidence, but you never know. That tidbit may have saved your life."

"*You* may have saved my life, Chloe. You were brilliant in there."

"Just sticking up for my man. She rattled the wrong cage."

17

A WEEK AND A HALF LATER, as Rayford was preparing to head back to New Babylon to resume his duties, he got a call from Leon Fortunato. "You haven't heard anything from the potentate's woman, have you?"

"The potentate's woman?" Rayford repeated, trying to let his disgust show.

"You know who I'm talking about. She flew over there on the same flight you did. Where is she?"

"I wasn't under the impression I was responsible for her."

"Steele, you don't really want to withhold information about somebody Carpathia wants to know about."

"Oh, *he* wants to know where she is. In other words, he hasn't heard from her?"

"You know that's the only reason I'd be calling you."

"Where does he think she is?"

"Don't play games with me, Steele. Tell me what you know."

"I don't know precisely where she is. And I don't feel the liberty to be reporting on her whereabouts or even where I think she is, without her knowledge."

"I think you'd better remember who you work for, pal."

"How can I forget?"

"So, you want me to imply to Carpathia that you're harboring his fiancée?"

"If that's what you're worried about, I can put your mind at ease. The last time I saw Hattie Durham was at Mitchell Field in Milwaukee when I arrived."

"And she went on where?"

"I really don't think I should be sharing her itinerary if she chose not to."

"You could regret this, Steele."

"You know what, Leon? I'll sleep tonight."

"We're assuming she went to see her family in Denver. There was no war damage there, so we don't understand why we can't get through by phone."

"I'm sure you have many resources for locating her. I'd rather not be one of them."

"I hope you're financially secure, Captain Steele."

Rayford did not respond. He didn't want to get into more of a war of words with Leon Fortunato.

"There's been a slight change of plans by the way, as it relates to your picking up Supreme Pontiff Mathews in Rome."

"I'm listening."

"Carpathia will be going with you. He wants to accompany Mathews back to New Babylon."

"How does that affect me?"

"I just wanted to make sure you didn't leave without him."

* * *

Buck had already had his tongue-lashing by phone from Steve Plank about having allowed his passport and ID to fall into the wrong hands in Israel. "They tortured that Shorosh guy within an inch of his life, and he still swore you were just a passenger on his boat."

"It was a nice big, wood boat," Buck had said.

"Well, the boat is no more."

"What was the point of destroying a man's boat and torturing him?"

"Are we on the record?"

"I don't know, Steve. Are we talking as journalists, friends, or is this a warning from a colleague?"

Steve changed the subject. "Carpathia still likes the copy you're sending out from Chicago. He thinks *Global Community Weekly* is the best magazine in the world. Of course, it always has been."

"Yeah, yeah. If you forget about objectivity and journalistic credibility—"

"We all forgot about that years ago," Plank had said. "Even before we were owned by Carpathia, we still had to dance to somebody's tune."

* * *

Buck brought Amanda, Chloe, Rayford, and Tsion up to speed on their new laptop computers. Tsion had been using his secure phone to talk to everyone at Loretta's place, which they began calling their "safe house." More than once Loretta said, "That man sounds like he's next door."

"That's cellular technology for you," Buck said.

Tsion required daily visits from his fellow Tribulation Force members, just to keep his spirits up. He was fascinated by the new technology, and he spent much of his time monitoring the news. He was tempted to try to communicate via e-mail to many of his spiritual children around the world; however, he feared they might be tortured in attempts to determine his whereabouts. He asked

Buck to ask Donny how he might go about communicating widely without the recipients of his missives suffering for it. The solution was simple. He would merely put his messages on a central bulletin board, and no one would know who was accessing them.

Tsion spent much of his days poring over Bruce's material and getting it into publishable shape. That was made easier by Buck's getting it to Tsion on disk. Frequently Tsion uploaded portions and in essence broadcast them to certain members of the Tribulation Force. He was especially impressed with what Bruce had to say about Chloe and Amanda. In his personal journal Bruce frequently mentioned his dream that they work together, researching, writing, and teaching cell groups and house churches. Eventually it was agreed that Amanda would not return to New Babylon until after Rayford got back from his flight to Rome. That would give her a few more days with Chloe to plan a ministry similar to what Bruce had outlined. They didn't know where it would take them or what the opportunities would be, but they enjoyed working together and seemed to learn more that way.

Buck was glad Verna Zee was keeping her distance. Much of the staff of the Chicago office was deployed to various bombed-out cities to report on the resultant chaos. There was no doubt in Buck's mind that the black horse of plagues and famine and the pale horse of death had come galloping in on the heels of the red horse of war.

* * *

On Wednesday evening, Amanda drove Rayford to Milwaukee for his flight to Iraq. "Why couldn't Mathews fly on his own plane to see Carpathia?" she said.

"You know Carpathia. He likes to take the upper hand by being the most deferential and kind. He not only sends a plane for you, he also comes along and accompanies you back."

"What does he want from Mathews?"

"Who knows? It could be anything. The increase in converts we're seeing has to be very troubling for Mathews. We are one faction that doesn't buy into the one-world faith routine."

* * *

At six Thursday morning, Loretta's household was awakened by the phone. Chloe grabbed it. She put her hand over the mouthpiece and told Buck, "Loretta's got it. It's Hattie."

Buck leaned close to listen with her. "Yes," Loretta was saying, "you woke me, darlin', but it's all right. Captain Steele said you might call."

"Well, I'm flying through Milwaukee on my way back to New Babylon, and I purposely scheduled a six-hour layover. Tell anybody there who cares that I'll be at Mitchell Field if they want to talk to me. They shouldn't feel obligated, and I won't be offended if they don't come."

"Oh, they'll come, hon. Don't you worry about that."

+ + +

That same hour was three o'clock in the afternoon in Baghdad when Rayford's commercial flight landed. He had planned to stay onboard to wait for the short flight on to New Babylon a little over an hour later, but his cell phone vibrated in his pocket. He wondered if this would be the call from Buck, or from Carpathia about Buck, that would end the speculation and suspicion of the Tribulation Force. They all knew it couldn't be long before Buck's position was jeopardized past the point of safety.

Rayford also had a fleeting thought that this might be a call from Hattie Durham. He had waited as long as he could before heading back, hoping to connect with her before her return. Like Carpathia and Fortunato, he had no luck trying to reach her by phone in Denver.

But the call was from his copilot, Mac McCullum. "Get off that plane, Steele, and stretch your legs. Your taxi is here."

"Hey, Mac! What's that mean?"

"It means the big boss doesn't want to wait. Meet me at the helipad on the other side of the terminal. I'm coptering you back to headquarters."

Rayford had wanted to put off his return to New Babylon as long as possible, but at least a helicopter ride was a diversion. He envied McCullum's ability to easily switch back and forth between copiloting jumbo jets and flying whirlybirds. Rayford hadn't piloted a helicopter since his military days more than twenty years before.

+ + +

Global Community Weekly was released to the public every Thursday, with the following Monday's date on the cover. Buck tingled with excitement merely anticipating that day's issue.

At the safe house it was decided that Amanda and Chloe would drive up to Milwaukee to pick up Hattie. Loretta would come home from the church office in time to host a small luncheon for her. Buck would go to the office to see the first copies of the magazine and head for Loretta's house when he got the call from Chloe that she and Amanda and Hattie were home.

Buck had gone out on a limb with his cover story. Purporting, as usual, to take a neutral, objective, journalistic viewpoint, Buck started with much of the material Bruce would have preached the Sunday morning of his own funeral. Buck did the writing, but he assigned reporters from every *Global Community Weekly* office still standing in several countries to interview local and regional clergymen about the prophecies in the book of Revelation.

For some reason, his reporters—most of them skeptics—went at this task with glee. Buck was faxed, modemed, phoned, couriered, and mailed dispatches from all over the world. His cover story title, and the specific question he wanted his reporters to ask religious leaders, was "Will we suffer the 'wrath of the Lamb'?"

Buck had enjoyed this self-assigned task more than all the other cover stories he had ever done. That included his Man of the Year stories, even the one on Chaim Rosenzweig. He had spent nearly three days and nights, hardly sleeping, collating, contrasting, and comparing the various reports.

He, of course, could detect fellow believers in some of the comments. Despite the skepticism and cynicism of most of the reporters, tribulation-saint pastors and a few converted Jews were quoted that the "wrath of the Lamb" predicted in Revelation 6 was literal and imminent. The vast majority of the quotes were from clergy formerly representing various and sundry religions and denominations, but now serving Enigma Babylon One World Faith. Almost to a person, these men and women "faith guides" (no one was called a reverend or a pastor or a priest anymore) took their lead from Pontifex Maximus Peter Mathews. Buck himself had talked to Mathews. His view, echoed dozens of times, was that the book of Revelation was "wonderful, archaic, beautiful literature, to be taken symbolically, figuratively, metaphorically. This earthquake," Mathews had told Buck by phone, a smile in his voice, "could refer to anything. It may have happened already. It may refer to something someone imagined going on in heaven. Who knows? It may be some story related to the old theory of an eternal man in the sky who created the world. I don't know about you, but I have not seen any apocalyptic horsemen. I haven't seen anyone die for their religion. I haven't seen anyone 'slain for the word of God,' as the previous verses say. I haven't seen anyone in a white robe. And I don't expect to endure any earthquake. Regardless of your view on the person or concept of God, or *a* god, hardly anyone today would imagine a supreme spirit-being full of goodness and light subjecting the entire earth—already suffering from so recent a devastating war—to a calamity like an earthquake."

"But," Buck had asked him, "are you not aware that this idea of fearing the 'wrath of the Lamb' is a doctrine still preached in many churches?"

"Of course," Mathews had responded. "But these are the same holdovers from your right-wing, fanatical, fundamentalist factions who have always taken the Bible literally. These same preachers, and I daresay many of their parishioners, are the ones who take the creation account—the Adam and Eve myth, if you will—literally. They believe the entire world was under water at the time of Noah and that only he and his three sons and their wives survived to begin the entire human race as we now know it."

"But you, as a Catholic, as the former pope—"

"Not just the former pope, Mr. Williams, also a former Catholic. I feel a great responsibility as leader of the Global Community's faith to set aside all trappings of parochialism. I must, in the spirit of unity and conciliation and ecumenism, be prepared to admit that much Catholic thought and scholarship was just as rigid and narrow-minded as that which I'm criticizing here."

"Such as?"

"I don't care to be too specific, at the risk of offending those few who still like to refer to themselves as Catholics, but the idea of a literal virgin birth should be seen as an incredible leap of logic. The idea that the Holy Roman Catholic Church was the only true church was almost as damaging as the evangelical Protestant view that Jesus was the only way to God. That assumes, of course, that Jesus was, as so many of my Bible-worshiping friends like to say, 'the only begotten Son of the Father.' By now I'm sure that most thinking people realize that God is, at most, a spirit, an idea, if you will. If they like to infuse him, or it, or her, with some characteristics of purity and goodness, it only follows that we are *all* sons and daughters of God."

Buck had led him. "The idea of heaven and hell then . . . ?"

"Heaven is a state of mind. Heaven is what you can make of your life here on earth. I believe we're heading toward a utopian state. Hell? More damage has been done to more tender psyches by the wholly mythical idea that—well, let me put it this way: Let's say those fundamentalists, these people who believe we're about to suffer the 'wrath of the Lamb,' are right that there is a loving, personal God who cares about each one of us. How does that jibe? Is it possible he would create something that he would eventually burn up? It makes no sense."

"But don't Christian believers, the ones you're trying to characterize, say that God is not willing that any should perish? In other words, he doesn't send people to hell. Hell is judgment for those who don't believe, but everyone is given the opportunity."

"You have summarized their position well, Mr. Williams. But, as I'm sure you can see, it just doesn't hold water."

Early that morning, before the door was unlocked, Buck picked up the shrink-wrapped bundle of *Global Community Weeklys* and lugged them inside. The secretaries would distribute one to each desk, but for now Buck ripped off the plastic and set a magazine before him. The cover, which had been tweaked at the international headquarters office, was even better than Buck had hoped. Under the logo was a stylized illustration of a huge mountain range splitting from one end to the other. A red moon hung over the scene, and the copy read: "Will You Suffer the Wrath of the Lamb?"

Buck turned to the extra-long story inside that carried his byline. Characteristic of a Buck Williams story, he had covered all the bases. He had quoted leaders from Carpathia and Mathews to local faith guides. There was even a smattering of quotes from the man on the street.

The biggest coup, in Buck's mind, was a sidebar carrying a brief but very cogent and articulate word study by none other than Rabbi Tsion Ben-Judah. He explained who the sacrificed Lamb was in Scripture and how the imagery had begun in the Old Testament and was fulfilled by Jesus in the New Testament.

Buck had been suspicious about not having been called on the carpet by anyone but his old friend Steve Plank regarding his potential involvement in the escape of Tsion Ben-Judah. Quoting Tsion extensively in his own sidebar could have made it seem as if Buck were rubbing in the faces of his superiors his knowledge of Ben-Judah's whereabouts. But he had headed that off. When the story was filed and sent via satellite to the various print plant facilities, Buck added a note that "Dr. Ben-Judah learned of this story over the Internet and has submitted his view via computer from an undisclosed location."

Also amusing to Buck, if anything about this cosmic subject could be amusing, was that one of his enterprising young reporters from Africa took it upon himself to interview geological scholars in a university in Zimbabwe. Their conclusion? "The idea of a global earthquake is, on the face of it, illogical. Earthquakes are caused by faults, by underground plates rubbing against each other. It's cause and effect. The reason it happens in certain areas at certain times is, logically, because it's not happening other places at the same time. These plates move and crash together because they have nowhere else to go. You never hear of simultaneous earthquakes. There is not one in North America and one in South America at precisely the same time. The odds against one earth-wide geological event, which would really be simultaneous earthquakes all over the globe, are astronomical."

✣ ✣ ✣

McCullum landed the chopper on the roof of the Global Community international headquarters building in New Babylon. He helped carry Rayford's bags into the elevator that took them past Carpathia's Suite 216, an entire floor of offices and conference rooms. Rayford had never understood its address, as it was not on the second floor at all. Carpathia and his senior staff occupied the top floor of the eighteen-story building.

Rayford hoped Carpathia would not know precisely when they arrived. He assumed he would have to face the man when he flew him to Rome to pick up Mathews, but Rayford wanted to get unpacked, freshen up, and settle in at his condo before getting back on board a plane again right away. He was grateful they were not intercepted. He had a couple of hours before takeoff. "See you on the 216, Mac," he said.

* * *

The phones began ringing at the *Global Weekly* office even before anyone else began to arrive. Buck let the answering machine take the calls, and it wasn't long before he rolled his chair to the receptionist's desk and just sat listening to the comments. One woman said, "So, *Global Community Weekly* has stooped to the level of the tabloids, covering every latest fairy tale to come out of the so-called church. Leave this trash to the yellow journalists."

Another said, "I wouldn't have dreamed people still believe this malarkey. That you could dig up that many weirdos to contribute to one story is a tribute to investigative journalism. Thanks for exposing them to the light and showing them what fools they really are."

Only the occasional call carried the tone of this one from a woman in Florida: "Why didn't somebody tell me about this before? I've been reading Revelation since the minute this magazine hit my doorstep, and I'm scared to death. What am I supposed to do now?"

Buck hoped she would read deep enough into the article to discover what a converted Jew from Norway said was the only protection from the coming earthquake: "No one should assume there will be shelter. If you believe, as I do, that Jesus Christ is the only hope for salvation, you should repent of your sins and receive him before the threat of death visits you."

Buck's personal phone buzzed. It was Verna.

"Buck, I'm keeping your secret, so I hope you're keeping your end of the bargain."

"I am. What's got you so agitated this morning?"

"Your cover story, of course. I knew it was coming, but I didn't expect it to be so overt. Do you think you've hidden behind your objectivity? Don't you think this exposes you as a proponent?"

"I don't know. I hope not. Even if Carpathia didn't own this magazine, I would want to come across as objective."

"You're deluding yourself."

Buck scrambled mentally for an answer. In one way, he appreciated the warning. In another, this was old news. Maybe Verna was just trying to find some point of contact, some reason to start a dialogue again. "Verna, I urge you to keep thinking about what you heard from Loretta, Chloe, and Amanda."

"And from you. Don't leave yourself out." Her tone was mocking and sarcastic.

"I mean it, Verna. If you ever want to talk about this stuff, you can come to me."

"With what your religion says about homosexuals, are you kidding?"

"My Bible doesn't differentiate between homosexuals and heterosexuals," Buck said. "It may call practicing homosexuals sinners, but it also calls heterosexual sex outside of marriage sinful."

"Semantics, Buck. Semantics."

"Just remember what I said, Verna. I don't want our personality conflict to get in the way of what's real and true. You were right when you said the outbreak of the war made our skirmishes petty. I'm willing to put those behind us."

She was silent for a moment. Then she sounded almost impressed. "Well, thank you, Buck. I'll keep that in mind."

* * *

By late morning Chicago time it was early evening in Iraq. Rayford and McCullum were flying Carpathia, Fortunato, and Dr. Kline to Rome to pick up One World Faith Supreme Pontiff Peter Mathews. Rayford knew Carpathia wanted to pave the way for the apostate union of religions to move to New Babylon, but he wasn't sure how Dr. Kline fit into this meeting. By listening in on his bugging device, he soon found out.

As was his usual custom, Rayford took off, quickly reached cruising altitude, put the plane on autopilot, and turned over control to Mac McCullum. "I feel like I've been on a plane all day," he said, leaning back in his seat, pulling the bill of his cap down over his eyes, applying his headphones, and appearing to drift off to sleep. In the approximately two hours it took to fly from New Babylon to Rome, Rayford would get a lesson in new-world-order international diplomacy. But before they got down to business, Carpathia checked with Fortunato on the flight plans of Hattie Durham.

Fortunato told him, "She is on some kind of a multi-leg journey that has a long layover in Milwaukee, then heads for Boston. She'll fly nonstop from Boston to Baghdad. She'll lose several hours coming this way, but I think we can expect her tomorrow morning."

Carpathia sounded peeved. "How long before we get the international terminal finished in New Babylon? I am tired of everything having to come through Baghdad."

"They're telling us a couple of months now."

"And these are the same building engineers who tell us everything else in New Babylon is state of the art?"

"Yes, sir. Have you noticed problems?"

"No, but it almost makes me wish this 'wrath of the Lamb' business was more than a myth. I would like to put the true test to their earthquake-proof claims."

"I saw that piece today," Dr. Kline said. "Interesting bit of fiction. That Williams can make an interesting story out of anything, can't he?"

"Yes," Carpathia said solemnly. "I suspect he has made an interesting story of his own background."

"I don't follow."

"I do not follow either," Carpathia said. "Our intelligence forces link him to the disappearance of Rabbi Ben-Judah."

Rayford straightened and listened more closely. He didn't want McCullum to realize he was listening on a different frequency, but neither did he want to miss anything.

"We are learning more and more about our brilliant young journalist," Carpathia said. "He has never been forthcoming about his ties to my own pilot, but then neither has Captain Steele. I still do not mind having them around. They may think they are in strategy proximity to me, but I am also able to learn much about the opposition through them."

So there it is, Rayford thought. *The gauntlet is down.*

"Leon, what is the latest on those two crazy men in Jerusalem?"

Fortunato sounded disgusted. "They've got the whole nation of Israel up in arms again," he said. "You know it hasn't rained there since they began all that preaching. And that trick they pulled on the water supply—turning it to blood—during the temple ceremonies, they're doing that again."

"What has set them off this time?"

"I think you know."

"I have asked you not to be circumspect with me, Leon. When I ask you a question, I expect—"

"Forgive me, Potentate. They have been carrying on about the arrest and torture of people associated with Dr. Ben-Judah. They are saying that until those suspects have been released and the search has been called off, all water supplies will be polluted by blood."

"How do they do that?"

"No one knows, but it's very real, isn't it Dr. Kline?"

"Oh yes," he said. "I have been sent samples. There is a high water content, but it is mostly blood."

"Human blood?"

"It has all the characteristics of human blood, although the type is difficult to determine. It borders on some cross between human and animal blood."

"How is morale in Israel?" Carpathia asked.

"The people are angry with the two preachers. They want to kill them."

"That is not all bad," Carpathia said. "Can we not get that done?"

"No one dares. The death count on those who've made attacks on them is over a dozen by now. You learn your lesson after a while."

"We are going to find a way," Carpathia said. "Meanwhile, let the suspects go. Ben-Judah cannot get far. Anyway, without being able to show his face in public, he cannot do us much harm. If those two rascals do not immediately purify the water supply, we will see how they stand up to an atomic blast."

"You're not serious, are you?" Dr. Kline said.

"Why would I not be?"

"You would drop an atomic bomb on a sacred site in the Holy City?"

"Frankly, I do not worry about the Wailing Wall or the Temple Mount or the new temple. Those two are giving me no end of grief, so mark my word: The day will come when they push me too far."

"It would be good to get Pontiff Mathews's opinion of all of this."

"We have enough of an agenda with him," Carpathia said. "In fact, I am sure he has an agenda for me as well, though perhaps a hidden one."

Later, after someone switched on the TV and the three men caught up on the international coverage of the war cleanup effort, Carpathia turned his attention to Dr. Kline.

"As you know, the ten ambassadors voted unanimously to fund abortions for women in underprivileged countries. I have made an executive decision to make that unilateral. Every continent has suffered from the war, so all could be considered underprivileged. I do not anticipate a problem from Mathews on this, the way he might have protested were he still pope. However, should he express some opposition, are you prepared to discuss the long-term benefits?"

"Of course."

"And where are we on the technology for predetermining the health and viability of a fetus?"

"Amniocentesis can now tell us everything we want to know. Its benefits are so far-reaching that it is worth any risk the procedure might afford."

"And, Leon," Carpathia said, "are we at a point where we can announce sanctions requiring amniocentesis on every pregnancy, along with an abortion requirement for any fetal tissue determined to result in a deformed or handicapped fetus?"

"Everything is in place," Fortunato said. "However, you are going to want as broad a base of support as possible before going public with that."

"Of course. That is one of the reasons for this meeting with Mathews."

"Are you optimistic?" Fortunato asked.

"Should I not be? Is Mathews not aware that I put him where he is today?"

"That's a question I ask myself all the time, Potentate. Surely you notice his lack of deference and respect. I don't like the way he treats you as if he's an equal."

"For the time being, he can be as pushy as he wants. He can be of great value to the cause because of his following. I know he is having financial difficulty because he cannot sell surplus churches. They are single-use facilities, so he will no doubt be pleading his case for more of an allotment from the Global Community. The ambassadors are already upset about this. For right now, though, I do not mind having the upper hand financially. Maybe we can strike a deal."

18

BUCK WAS AMUSED that his cover story was the hottest topic of the day. Every talk show, news show, and even some variety shows mentioned it. One comedy featured an animated short of a woolly lamb going on the rampage. They called it "Our View of the 'Wrath of the Lamb.'"

Glancing at the magazine before him, Buck suddenly realized that when he was exposed, when he would have to step down, when he possibly became a fugitive, it would be impossible to match the distribution of a magazine so well-established around the world. He might have a larger audience via television and the Internet, but he wondered if he would ever have the influence again that he had right now.

He looked at his watch. It was almost time to head for the safe house and the luncheon with Hattie.

+ + +

Rayford and Mac McCullum had about an hour's break after they hit the ground in Rome and before they were to head back to New Babylon. They passed Peter Mathews and one of his aides boarding the plane. Rayford was nauseated by Carpathia's obsequious deference to Mathews. He heard the potentate say, "How good of you to allow us to come and collect you, Pontiff. I am hoping we can have meaningful dialogue, profitable to the good of the Global Community."

Just before Rayford stepped out of earshot, Mathews told Carpathia, "As long as it's profitable to the One World Faith, I don't much care whether you benefit or not."

Rayford found reasons to excuse himself from McCullum and hurry back to the plane and into the cockpit. He apologized to Fortunato for "having to check on a few things" and was soon back in his customary spot. The door was locked. The reverse intercom was on, and Rayford was listening.

+ + +

Buck had not seen Hattie Durham in real distress since the night of the Rapture. He, like most other men, usually saw her only as striking. Now the kindest term he could think of for her was disheveled. She carried an oversized purse stuffed mostly with tissues, and she made use of every last one. Loretta pointed her to the head of the table, and when lunch was served, they all sat awkwardly, seeming to try to avoid meaningful conversation. Buck said, "Amanda, would you pray for us?"

Hattie quickly entwined her fingers under her chin, like a little girl kneeling at her bedside. Amanda said, "Father, sometimes in the situations we find ourselves, it's difficult to know what to say to you. Sometimes we're unhappy. Sometimes we're distraught. Sometimes we have no idea where to turn. The world seems in such chaos. However, we know we can thank you for who you are. We thank you that you're a good God. That you care about us and love us. We thank you that you're sovereign and that you hold the world in your hands. We thank you for friends, especially old friends like Hattie. Give us words to say that might help her in whatever decision making she must do, and thank you for the provision of this food. In Jesus' name, Amen."

They ate in silence, Buck noticing that Hattie's eyes were full of tears. Despite that, she ate quickly and was done before the rest. She grabbed yet another tissue and blew her nose.

"Well," she said, "Rayford insisted that I drop in on you on my way back. I'm sorry I missed him, but I think he really wanted me to talk to you anyway. Or maybe he wanted you to talk to me."

The women looked as puzzled as Buck felt. That was it? The floor was theirs? What were they supposed to do? It was hard to meet this woman at her point of need if she wasn't going to share that need.

Loretta began. "Hattie, what's troubling you the most just now?"

Either what Loretta said or how she said it unleashed a torrent of tears. "Fact is," Hattie managed, "I want an abortion. My family is encouraging me that way. I don't know what Nicolae will say, but if there's no change in our relationship when I get back there, I'm going to want an abortion for sure. I suppose I'm here because I know you'll try to talk me out of it, and I guess I need to hear both sides. Rayford already gave me the standard right-wing, pro-life position. I don't guess I need to hear that again."

"What do you need to hear?" Buck said, feeling very male and very insensitive just then.

Chloe gave him a look that implied he should not push. "Hattie," she said, "you know where we stand. That's not why you're here. If you want to be talked out of it, we can do that. If you won't be talked out of it, nothing we say will make any difference."

Hattie looked frustrated. "So, you think I'm here to get preached at."

"We're not going to preach at you," Amanda said. "From what I understand, you know where we stand on the things of God as well."

"Yes, I do," Hattie said. "I'm sorry to have wasted your time. I guess I have a decision to make about this pregnancy, and it was foolish of me to drag you into it."

"Don't feel like you have to leave, darlin'," Loretta said. "This is my house, and I'm your hostess, and you might risk offendin' me if you were to leave too early."

Hattie looked at her as if to be sure Loretta was teasing. It was clear that she was. "I can just as easily wait at the airport," Hattie said. "I'm sorry to have put you through all this inconvenience."

Buck wanted to say something but knew he couldn't communicate at this level. He looked into the eyes of the women, who intently watched their guest. Finally, Chloe stood and walked behind Hattie's chair. She put her hands on Hattie's shoulders. "I have always admired and liked you," she said. "I think we could have been friends in another situation. But Hattie, I feel led to tell you that I know why you came here today. I know why you followed my dad's advice, though you may have done it against your will. Something tells me your visit home was not successful. Maybe they were too practical. Maybe they didn't give you the compassion you needed along with their advice. Maybe hearing that they wanted you to end this pregnancy was not what you really wanted.

"Let me just tell you, Hattie, if it's love you're looking for, you came to the right place. Yes, there are things we believe. Things we think you should know. Things we think you should agree with. Decisions we think you should make. We have ideas about what you should do about your baby, and we have ideas about what you should do about your soul. But these are personal decisions only you can make. And while they are life-and-death, heaven-and-hell decisions, all we can offer is support, encouragement, advice if you ask for it, and love."

"Yeah," Hattie said, "love, if I buy into everything you have to sell."

"No. We are going to love you anyway. We're going to love you the way God loves you. We're going to love you so fully and so well that you won't be able to hide from it. Even if your decisions go against everything we believe to be true, and even though we would grieve over the loss of innocent life if you chose to abort your baby, we won't love you any less."

Hattie burst into tears as Chloe rubbed her shoulders. "That's impossible! You can't love me no matter what I do, especially if I ignore your advice!"

"You're right," Chloe said. "We are not capable of unconditional love. That's why we have to let God love you through us. He's the one who loves us regardless of what we do. The Bible says he sent his Son to die for us while we were dead in our sins. That's unconditional love. That's what we have to offer you, Hattie, because that's all we have."

Hattie stood awkwardly, and her chair scraped the floor as she turned to embrace Chloe. They held each other for a long minute, and then the entire party moved into the other room. Hattie tried to smile. "I feel foolish," she said, "like a blubbering schoolgirl."

The other women didn't protest. They didn't tell her she looked fine. They simply looked at her with love. For a moment Buck wished he was Hattie so he could respond. He didn't know about her, but this sure would have won him over.

* * *

"I'll get right to it," Peter Mathews told Carpathia. "If there are ways we can help each other, I want to know what you need. Because there are things I need from you."

"Such as?" Carpathia asked.

"Frankly, I need amnesty from One World Faith's debt to your administration. We might be able to pay back some of our allotment someday, but right now we just don't have the income."

"Having trouble selling off some of those surplus church buildings?" Carpathia said.

"Oh, that's part of it, but a very small part. Our real problem lies with two religious groups who not only have refused to join our union, but who are also antagonistic and intolerant. You know who I'm talking about. One group is a problem that you caused yourself by that agreement between the Global Community and Israel. The Jews have no need for us, no reason to join. They still believe in the one true God and a Messiah who's supposed to come in the sky by and by. I don't know what your plan is after the contract runs out, but I could sure use some ammunition against them.

"The other bunch are these Christians who call themselves tribulation saints. They're the ones who think the Messiah already came and raptured his church and they missed it. I figure if they are right, they're kidding themselves to think he'd give them another chance, but you know as well as I do they're growing like wildfire. The strange thing is, a whole bunch of their converts are Jews. They've got these two nuts at the Wailing Wall telling everybody that the Jews are halfway there with their belief in the one true God, but that Jesus is his Son, that he came back, and that he's coming back again."

"Peter, my friend, this should not be strange doctrine to you as a former Catholic."

"I didn't say it was strange to me. I just never realized the depth of the intolerance that we Catholics had and that those tribulation saint–types have now."

"You have noticed the intolerance too?"

"Who hasn't? These people take the Bible literally. You've seen their propaganda and heard their preachers at the big rallies. There are Jews buying into this stuff by the tens of thousands. Their intolerance hurts us."

"How so?"

"You know. The secret to our success, the enigma that is One World Faith, is simply that we have broken down the barriers that used to divide us. Any religion that believes there's only one way to God is, by definition, intolerant. They become enemies of One World Faith and thus the global community as a whole. Our enemies are your enemies. We have to do something about them."

"What do you propose?"

"I was about to ask you that very question, Nicolae."

Rayford could only imagine Nicolae wincing at Mathews' referring to him by his first name.

"Believe it or not, my friend, I have already given this a great deal of thought."

"You have?"

"I have. As you say, your enemies are my enemies. Those two at the Wailing Wall, the ones the so-called saints refer to as the witnesses, have meant no end of grief for me and my administration. I do not know where they come from or what they are up to, but they have terrorized the people of Jerusalem, and more than once they have made me look bad. This group of fundamentalists, the ones who are converting so many Jews, look to these two as heroes."

"So, what conclusion have you come to?"

"Frankly, I have been considering more legislation. Conventional wisdom says you cannot legislate morale. I happen not to believe that. I admit my dreams and goals are grandiose, but I will not be deterred. I foresee a global community of true peace and harmony, a utopia where people live together for the good of each other. When that was threatened by insurrection forces from three of our ten regions, I immediately retaliated. In spite of my long-standing and most sincere opposition to war, I made a strategic decision. Now I am legislating morale. People who want to get along and live together will find me most generous and conciliatory. Those who want to cause trouble will be gone. It is as simple as that."

"So, what are you saying, Nicolae? You're going to wage war on the fundamentalists?"

"In a sense I am. No, we will not do it with tanks and bombs. But I believe the time has come to enforce rules for the new Global Community. As this would seem to benefit you as much as it would benefit me, I would like you to cooperate in forming and heading an organization of elite enforcers, if you will, of pure thought."

"How are you defining 'pure thought'?"

"I foresee a cadre of young, healthy, strong men and women so devoted to the cause of the Global Community that they would be willing to train and build themselves to the point where they will be eager to make sure everyone is in line with our objectives."

Rayford heard someone rise and begin pacing. He assumed it was Mathews, warming to the idea. "These would not be uniformed people, I assume."

"No. They would blend in with everyone else, but they would be chosen for their insight and trained in psychology. They would keep us informed of subversive elements who oppose our views. Surely you agree that we are long past the time where we can tolerate the extreme negative by-product of free speech run amok."

"Not only do I agree," Mathews said quickly, "but I stand ready to assist in any way possible. Can One World Faith help seek out candidates? train them? house them? clothe them?"

"I thought you were running short of funds," Carpathia said, chuckling.

"This will only result in more income for us. When we eliminate the opposition, everyone benefits."

Rayford heard Carpathia sigh. "We would call them the GCMM. The Global Community Morale Monitors."

"That makes them sound a little soft, Nicolae."

"Precisely the idea. We do not want to call them the secret police, or the thought police, or the hate police, or any kind of police. Make no mistake. They will be secret. They will have power. They will be able to supersede normal due cause in the interest of the better good for the global community."

"To what limit?"

"No limit."

"They would carry weapons?"

"Of course."

"And they would be allowed to use these to what extent?"

"That is the beauty of it, Pontiff Mathews. By selecting the right young people, by training them carefully in the ideal of a peaceful utopia, and by giving them ultimate capital power to mete out justice as they see fit, we quickly subdue the enemy and eliminate it. We should foresee no need of the GCMM within just a few years."

"Nicolae, you're a genius."

* * *

Buck was disappointed. When it came time to run Hattie back up to Milwaukee, he felt little progress had been made. She had a lot of questions about just what it was these women did with their time. She was intrigued by the idea of Bible studies. And she had mentioned her envy of having close friends of the same sex who seemed to really care about each other.

But Buck had been hoping there would have been some breakthrough. Maybe Hattie would have promised not to have an abortion or broken down and become a believer. He tried to push from his mind that Chloe might get the idea of taking and raising as their own the unwanted baby Hattie was carrying. He and Chloe were close to a decision about whether to bring a baby into this stage of history, but he hardly wanted to consider raising the child of the Antichrist.

Hattie thanked everyone and climbed into the Range Rover with the women. Buck implied he was going to take one of the other cars back to the *Global Community Weekly* office, but instead he drove to the church. He stopped on the way for a treat for his friend, and within minutes he had gone through the labyrinth that took him to the inner sanctum of Rabbi Tsion Ben-Judah's personal study chamber.

Every time Buck sneaked into that place, he was certain that claustrophobia, loneliness, fear, and grief would have overcome his friend. Without fail, however, it was Buck who was warmed by these visits. Tsion was hardly gleeful. He did not laugh much, nor did he offer a huge smile when Buck appeared. His eyes were red, and his face showed the lines of the recently bereaved. But he was also staying fit. He worked out, running in place, doing jumping jacks, stretching, and who knew what else. He told Buck he did this for at least an hour a day, and it showed. He seemed in a better frame of mind each time Buck saw him, and he never complained. That afternoon Tsion seemed genuinely pleased to have a visitor. "Cameron," he said, "were I not living with a heaviness of soul right now, certain parts of this place, even its location, would be paradise. I can read, I can study, I can pray, I can write, I can communicate by phone and computer. It is a scholar's dream. I miss the interaction with my colleagues, especially the young students who helped me. But Amanda and Chloe are wonderful students themselves."

He greedily joined Buck in their fast-food snack. "I need to talk about my family. I hope you don't mind."

"Tsion, you may talk about your family with me anytime you want. You should forgive me for not being more diligent in asking."

"I know you, like many others, wonder if you should bring up such a painful subject. As long as we do not dwell on how they died, I am most pleased to talk about my memories. You know I raised my son and daughter from the ages of eight and ten to fourteen and sixteen. They were my wife's children from her first marriage. Her husband was killed in a construction accident. The children did not accept me at first, but I won them over by my love for *her*. I did not try to take the place of their father or pretend I was in charge of them. Eventually they referred to me as their father, and it was one of the proudest days of my life."

"Your wife seemed like a wonderful woman."

"She was. The children were wonderful too, though my family was human just like anyone else. I do not idealize them. They were all very bright. That was a joy to me. I could converse with them about deep things, complicated things. My wife herself had taught at the college level before having children. The children were both in special private schools and were exceptionally good students. Most important of all, when I began to tell them what I was learning in my research, they never once accused me of heresy or of turning my back on my culture, my religion, or my country. They were bright enough to see that I was discovering the truth. I did not preach at them, did not try to unduly influence them. I would merely read them passages and say, 'What do you deduce from this? What is the Torah saying here about qualifications for Messiah?' I was so fervent in my Socratic method that at times I believe they came to my ultimate conclusions before I did. When the Rapture occurred, I immediately knew what had happened. In some ways I was actually disappointed to find that I had failed my family and that all three of them had been left behind with me. I would have missed them, as I miss them now, but it also would have been a blessing to me had any of them seen the truth and acted upon it before it was too late."

"You told me they all became believers shortly after you did."

Tsion stood and paced. "Cameron, I do not understand how anyone with any exposure to the Bible could doubt the meaning of the mass vanishings. Rayford Steele, with his limited knowledge, knew because of the testimony of his wife. I, above all people, should have known. And yet you see it all around you. People are still trying to explain it away. It breaks my heart."

Tsion showed Buck what he was working on. He had nearly completed the first booklet in what he hoped would be a series from Bruce's writings. "He was a surprisingly adept scholar for a young man," Tsion said. "He was not the linguist that I am, and so I am adding some of that to his work. I think it makes for a better final product."

"I'm sure Bruce would agree," Buck said.

Buck wanted to broach the subject of Tsion's helping the church, remotely of course, locate a new pastor. How perfect if it could be Tsion! But that was out of the question. Anyway, Buck did not want anything to interrupt Tsion's important work.

"You know, Tsion, that I will likely be the first to join you here on a permanent basis."

"Cameron, I cannot see you as content to hide out."

"It'll drive me crazy, there's no doubt about that. But I have begun to get careless. Riskier. It's bound to catch up with me."

"You will be able to do what I do on the Internet," Tsion said. "I am communicating with many hundreds already, just by learning a few tricks. Imagine what you can do with the truth. You can write the way you used to write, with total objectivity and seriousness. You will not be influenced by the owner of the paper."

"What was that you said about the truth?"

"You can write the truth, that's all."

Buck sat and began noodling on paper. He drew the cover of a magazine and called it simply "Truth." He was excited.

"Look at this. I could design the graphics, write the copy, and disseminate it on the Net. According to Donny Moore, it could never be traced back here."

"I don't want to see you forced into self-incarceration," Ben-Judah said. "But I confess I would enjoy the company."

19

RAYFORD WAS PROUD of Hattie Durham. From what he could gather in New Babylon, she had pulled another fast one on Nicolae and his henchman Leon Fortunato. Apparently she had flown from Milwaukee to Boston, but rather than taking her connecting flight on to Baghdad, she had stopped somewhere.

Rayford had been out of hearing range, of course, when the meetings with Peter Mathews were continued at New Babylon headquarters. All he knew was that there was great consternation around the place, especially among Nicolae and Leon, that Hattie had slipped off schedule yet again. Though Nicolae had shown indifference to her, not knowing where she was made her a loose cannon and a potential embarrassment.

When word finally arrived that she had a new itinerary, Carpathia himself asked to see Rayford in private. The new secretarial staff was in place and operational by the time Rayford entered Suite 216 and was granted audience with the potentate.

"It is good to see you again, Captain Steele. I fear I have not been as forthcoming with my thanks for your service as I used to be, before so many distractions have come about.

"Let me get straight to the point. I know that Ms. Durham once worked for you. In fact, you came to us based on her recommendation. I know also that she has at times confided in you. Thus, it should come as no surprise to you that there has been some trouble in paradise, as they say. Let me be frank. The fact is, I believe Ms. Durham always overestimated the seriousness of our personal relationship."

Rayford thought back to when Nicolae had seemed to proudly announce that Hattie was pregnant and that she was wearing his ring. But Rayford knew better than to try to catch the liar of liars in a lie.

Carpathia continued: "Ms. Durham should have realized that in a position such as the one I hold, there really is no room for a personal life that would enjoy the commitment required by a marriage and family. She seemed pleased with the prospect of bearing a child, my child. Thus, I did not discourage that or encourage some other option. Should she take the pregnancy to term, I would of course exercise my fiscal responsibility. However, it is unfair for her to expect me to devote the time that might be available to the normal father.

"My advice to her would be to terminate the pregnancy. However, due to the fact that this result of our relationship is really her responsibility, I will leave that decision to her."

Rayford was puzzled and didn't try to hide it. Why was Carpathia telling him this? What assignment was going to fall to him? He didn't have long to wait.

"I have needs like any other man, Captain Steele. You understand. I would never commit myself to just one woman, and I certainly made no such commitment to Ms. Durham. The fact is that I already have someone else with whom I am enjoying a relationship. Therefore, you can see my dilemma."

"I'm not sure I do," Rayford said.

"Well, I have replaced Ms. Durham as my personal assistant. I sense that she is distraught from that and from what she has to deduce is a relationship that has soured. I do not see it as souring; I see us both moving on. But, as I say, as she saw it as more important a commitment than I did, she is thus more upset and disappointed at the conclusion of it."

"I need to ask you about the ring you gave her," Rayford said.

"Oh, that is no problem. I will not be requiring that back. In fact, I always believed that the stone was much too large to be worn as an engagement ring. It clearly is decorative. She need not worry about returning that."

Rayford was getting the picture. Carpathia was going to call on him, as Hattie's old friend and boss, to deliver the news. Why else would he need all this information?

"I will do the right thing by Ms. Durham, Captain Steele. You may be assured of that. I would not want her to become destitute. I know she is employable, probably not as a clerical person, but certainly in the aviation industry."

"Which has been devastated by the war, as you know," Rayford said.

"Yes, but with her seniority and perhaps with some gentle pressure on my part . . ."

"And so you're saying that you will give her some sort of severance or a stipend or settlement?"

Carpathia seemed to brighten. "Yes, if that will make it easier for her, I am happy to do that."

I should think you would be, Rayford thought.

"Captain Steele, I have an assignment for you—"

"I deduced that."

"Of course, you would. You are a bright man. We have received word that Ms. Durham is back on her itinerary and is expected in Baghdad on a flight from Boston on Monday."

It finally hit Rayford why Hattie might have delayed her return. Perhaps she knew of Amanda's plans. It would be just like Amanda to arrange to meet her somewhere and accompany her back. Amanda would have had an ulterior motive, of course: to keep Hattie from visiting a reproductive clinic. She also would have wanted to continue expressing love to her. Rayford decided against telling Carpathia he was headed to the airport in Baghdad Monday anyway to pick up his own wife.

"Assuming you are free, Captain Steele, and I will make sure that you are, I would ask that you would meet Miss Durham's plane. As her old friend, you will be the right one to break this news to her. Her belongings have been delivered to one of the condominiums in your building. She will be allowed to stay there for a month before deciding where she would like to relocate."

Rayford interrupted. "Excuse me, but are you asking me to do something that you yourself should be doing?"

"Oh, make no mistake, Captain Steele. I am not afraid of this confrontation. It would be most distasteful for me, yes, but I recognize my responsibility here. It is just that I am under such crushing deadlines for important meetings. We have established many new directives and legislative encyclicals in light of the recent insurrection, and I simply cannot be away from the office."

Rayford thought Carpathia's meeting with Hattie Durham might have taken less time than the meeting they were conducting right then. But what was the sense of arguing with a man like this?

"Any questions, Captain Steele?"

"No. It's all very clear to me."

"You will do it then?"

"I was not under the impression I had a choice."

Carpathia smiled. "You have a good sense of humor, Captain Steele. I would not say your job depends on it, but I appreciate that your military background has trained you to realize that when a directive is given, it is to be carried out. I want you to know that I appreciate it."

Rayford stared at him. He willed himself not to say the obligatory, "You're welcome." He nodded and stood.

"Captain Steele, might I ask you to remain seated for a moment."

Rayford sat back down. *What now? Is this the beginning of the end?*

"I would like to ask you about your relationship with Cameron Williams." Rayford did not respond at first. Carpathia continued. "Sometimes known as

Buck Williams. He was formerly a senior staff writer for *Global Weekly*, now *Global Community Weekly*. He is my publisher there."

"He's my son-in-law," Rayford said.

"And can you think of any reason why he would not have shared that happy news with me?"

"I suppose you'll have to ask him that, sir."

"Well, then perhaps I should ask you. Why would *you* not have shared that with me?"

"It's just personal family business," Rayford said, trying to remain calm. "Anyway, with him serving you at such a high level, I assumed you would become aware of it soon enough."

"Does it happen that he shares your religious beliefs?"

"I prefer not to speak for Buck."

"I will take that as a yes." Rayford stared at him. Carpathia continued, "I am not saying that this is necessarily a problem, you understand." *I understand all right,* Rayford thought. "I was just curious," Carpathia concluded. He smiled at Rayford, and the pilot read everything in that smile that the Antichrist implied. "I will look forward to a report of your meeting with Miss Durham, and I have full confidence that it will be successful."

+ + +

Buck was at the Chicago office of *Global Community Weekly* when he took a call from Amanda on his private phone. "I got the strangest call from Rayford," she said. "He asked if I had hooked up with Hattie on her flight out of Boston to Baghdad. I told him no. I thought she was already back there. He said he thought she was on another schedule now and that we would likely be arriving at about the same time. I asked him what was up, but he seemed rushed and didn't feel free to take the time to tell me. Do you know what's happening?"

"This is all news to me, Amanda. Did your flight refuel in Boston as well?"

"Yes. You know New York is completely shut down. So is Washington. I don't know if these planes can go all the way from Milwaukee to Baghdad."

"What would have taken Hattie so long to get back there?"

"I have no idea. If I had known she was going to delay her return, I would have offered to have flown with her. We need to maintain contact with that girl."

Buck agreed. "Chloe misses you already. She and Tsion are working hard on some New Testament curriculum. It's almost as if they're in the same room, though they're at least a quarter of a mile apart."

"I know she's enjoying that," Amanda said. "I wish I could talk Rayford into letting me move back this way. I'd see less of him, but I don't see much of him in New Babylon either."

"Don't forget you can be in that 'same room' with Tsion and Chloe, no matter where you are now."

"Yeah," she said, "except that we're nine hours later than you guys."

"You'll just have to coordinate your schedules. Where are you now?"

"We're over the continent. Should be touching down in an hour or so. It's what there, just a little after eight in the morning?"

"Right. The Tribulation Force is about as spread out as it's been for a while. Tsion seems productive and contented, if not happy. Chloe is at Loretta's and excited about her study and her teaching opportunities, though she knows she may not always be free, legally, to do that. I'm here, you're there, and you'll be meeting up with Rayford before you know it. I guess we're all present and accounted for."

"I sure hope Rayford's right about Hattie," Amanda said. "It'll be handy if he can pick us both up."

* * *

It was time for Rayford to head for Baghdad. He was confused. Why had Hattie remained incommunicado in Denver for so long and then misled Fortunato about her return flight when she *did* reestablish contact? If it wasn't for the purpose of hooking up with Amanda, what was it? What would have interested her in Boston?

Rayford couldn't wait to see Amanda. It had been only a few days, but they were still newlyweds, after all. He did not relish his assignment with Hattie, especially with Amanda getting in at the same time. One thing he could justify, however, based on what he had been told about Hattie's encounter with Loretta, Chloe, and Amanda at the safe house, was that Hattie would be comforted by Amanda's presence.

The question was, would this word from Rayford be bad news for Hattie? It might make her future easier to accept. She knew it was over. She feared Carpathia might not let her go. She would be offended, of course, insulted. She wouldn't want his ring or his money or his condo. But at least she would know. To Rayford's male mind, this seemed a practical solution. He had learned enough from Irene and Amanda over the years, however, to know that regardless of how unattractive Nicolae Carpathia had become to Hattie, still she would be hurt and would feel rejected.

Rayford phoned Hattie's driver. "Could you drive me, or could I borrow your car? I'm to pick up Miss Durham in Baghdad and also my—"

"Oh, sorry sir. I'm no longer Miss Durham's driver. I drive for someone else in the executive suite."

"You know where I could get wheels then?"

"You could try the motor pool, but that takes awhile. Lots of paperwork, you know."

"I don't have that kind of time. Any other suggestions?" Rayford was angry with himself for not planning better.

"If the potentate called the motor pool, you'd have a vehicle as quick as you wanted it."

Rayford phoned Carpathia's office. The secretary said he was unavailable.

"Is he there?" Rayford asked.

"He is here, sir, but as I said, he's not available."

"This is sort of urgent. If he's at all interruptible, I'd appreciate it if you'd let me talk to him for just a second."

When the secretary came back on the line, she said, "The potentate wants to know if you could drop by his office for a moment before you finish your assignment for him."

"I'm a little short of time, but—"

"I'll tell him you'll be here then."

Rayford was three blocks from Carpathia's building. He hurried down in the elevator and jogged toward headquarters. He had a sudden thought and grabbed his phone. As he ran, he called McCullum. "Mac? Are you free right now? Good! I need a chopper ride to Baghdad. My wife's coming in, and I'm supposed to meet Hattie Durham as well. Rumors about her? I'm not at liberty to say anything, Mac. I'll be in Carpathia's office in a few minutes. Meet you on the helipad? Good! Thanks!"

* * *

Buck was working on his laptop with his office door shut when the machine signaled that he had incoming, real-time mail. He liked this feature. It was like being on a chat line with just one person. The message was from Tsion. He asked, "Shall we try the video feature?"

Buck typed, "Sure." And he tapped in the code. It took a few minutes to program itself, but then Tsion's image flickered on the screen. Buck tapped in, "Is that you, or am I looking in the mirror?"

Tsion responded, "It's me. We could use the audio and talk to each other, if you're in a secure area."

"Better not," Buck tapped in. "Did you want something specific?"

"I would like a companion for breakfast," Tsion said. "I'm feeling much better today, but I'm getting a little claustrophobic here. I know you can't sneak me out, but could you get in without Loretta suspecting?"

"I'll try. What would you like for breakfast?"

"I have cooked up something American just for you, Buck. I'm turning my screen now to see if it can pick it up."

The machine was not really built to pan around a dark, underground shelter. Buck typed in: "I can't see anything, but I'll trust you. Be there as soon as I can." Buck told the receptionist he would be gone for a couple of hours, but as he was heading to the Range Rover, Verna Zee caught him. "Where are you going?" she asked.

"I'm sorry?" he said.

"I want to know where you'll be."

"I'm not sure where all I'll be," he said. "The desk knows I'll be gone for a couple of hours. I don't feel obligated to share specifics."

Verna shook her head.

* * *

Rayford slowed as he reached the grand entrance of Global Community headquarters. The compound had been set in an unusual area where upscale residences surrounded it. Something had caught Rayford's attention. Animal noises. Barking. He had been aware of dogs in the area. Many employees owned expensive breeds they enjoyed walking and tethering outside their places. They were showpieces of prosperity. He had heard one or two barking at times. But now they were all barking. They were noisy enough that he turned to see if he could detect what was agitating them so. He saw a couple of dogs jerk away from their owners and race down the street howling.

He shrugged and entered the building.

* * *

Buck considered swinging by Loretta's house and picking up Chloe. He would have to think of a story to tell Loretta at the church office. He wouldn't be able to park or walk into the church without her seeing him. Maybe he and Chloe would just spend some time with her and then appear to be leaving the church the back way. If no one was watching, they could slip down and see Tsion. It sounded like a plan. Buck was halfway to Mt. Prospect when he noticed something strange. Roadkill. Lots of it. And more potential roadkill skittering across the streets. Squirrels, rabbits, snakes. Snakes? He had seen few snakes in the Midwest, particularly this far north. The occasional garter snake was all. That's what these were, but why so many of them? Coons, possum, ducks, geese, dogs, cats, animals everywhere. He lowered the window of the Range Rover and listened. Huge clouds of birds swept from tree to tree. But the sky was bright. Cloudless. There seemed to be no wind. No leaf even shivered on a tree. Buck waited at a stoplight and noticed that, despite the lack of wind, the streetlights swayed. Signs bent back and forth. Buck blew the light and raced toward Mt. Prospect.

* * *

Rayford was ushered into Carpathia's office. The potentate had several VIPs around a conference table. He quickly pulled Rayford aside. "Thank you for stopping in, Captain Steele. I just wanted to reiterate my wish that I not have to face Ms. Durham. She may want to talk to me. That will be out of the question. I—"

"Excuse me," Leon Fortunato interrupted, "but Potentate, sir, we're getting some strange readouts on our power meters."

"Your power meters?" Carpathia asked, incredulous. "I leave maintenance to you and your staff, Leon—"

"Sir!" the secretary said. "An emergency call for you or Mr. Fortunato from the International Seismograph Institute."

Carpathia looked irritated and whirled to face Fortunato. "Take that, will you, Leon? I am busy here."

Fortunato took the call and appeared to want to keep quiet until he blurted, "What? What?!"

Now Carpathia was angry. "Leon!"

Rayford moved away from Carpathia and looked out the window. Below, dogs ran in circles, their owners chasing them. Rayford reached in his pocket for his cell phone and quickly called McCullum. Carpathia glared at him. "Captain Steele! I was talking to you here—"

"Mac! Where are you? Start 'er up. I'm on my way now!"

Suddenly the power went out. Only battery-operated lights near the ceiling shined, and the bright sun flooded through the windows. The secretary screamed. Fortunato turned to Carpathia and tried to tell him what he had just heard. Carpathia shouted above the din. "I would like order in here, please!"

And as if someone had flipped a switch, the day went black. Now even the grown men moaned and shrieked. Those battery-operated lights in the corner cast a haunting glow on the building, which began to shudder. Rayford made a dash for the door. He sensed someone right behind him. He pushed the elevator button and then smacked himself in the head, remembering there was no power. He dashed upstairs to the roof, where McCullum had the chopper blades whirring.

The building shifted under Rayford like the surf. The chopper, resting on its skis, dipped first to the left and then to the right. Rayford reached for the opening, seeing Mac's wide eyes. As Rayford tried to climb in, he was pushed from behind and flew up behind Mac. Nicolae Carpathia was scrambling in. "Lift off!" he shouted. "Lift off!"

McCullum raised the chopper about a foot off the roof. "Others are coming!" he shouted.

"No more room!" Carpathia hollered. "Lift off!"

As two young women and several middle-aged men grabbed the struts, Mac pulled away from the building. As he banked left, his lights illuminated the roof, where others came shrieking and crying out the door. As Rayford watched in horror, the entire eighteen-story building, filled with hundreds of employees, crashed to the ground in a mighty roar and a cloud of dust. One by one the screaming people hanging from the chopper fell away.

Rayford stared at Carpathia. In the dim light from the control panel he saw no expression. Carpathia simply appeared busy about strapping himself in. Rayford was ill. He had seen people die. Carpathia had ordered Mac away from people who might have been saved. Rayford could have killed the man with his bare hands.

Wondering if he wouldn't have been better off to have died in the building himself, Rayford shook his head and resolutely fastened his seat belt. "Baghdad!" he shouted. "Baghdad Airport!"

* * *

Buck had known exactly what was coming and had been speeding through lights and stop signs, jumping curbs, and going around cars and trucks. He wanted to get to Chloe at Loretta's house first. He reached for his phone, but he had not stored speed-dial numbers yet, and there was no way he could drive this quickly and punch in an entire number at the same time. He tossed the phone on the seat and kept going. He was going through an intersection when the sun was snuffed out. Day went to night in an instant, and power went out all over the area. People quickly turned on their headlights, but Buck saw the crevasse too late. He was heading for a fissure in the road that had opened before him. It looked at least ten feet wide and that deep. He figured if he dropped into it he would be killed, but he was going too fast to avoid it. He wrenched the wheel to the left and the Range Rover rolled over completely before plunging down into the hole. The passenger-side air bag deployed and quietly deflated. It was time to find out what this car was made of.

Ahead of him the gap narrowed. There would be no going out that way unless he could start going up first. He pushed the buttons that gave him all-wheel drive and stick shift, shifted into low gear, crimped the front wheels slightly to the left, and floored the accelerator. The left front tire bit into the steep bank of the crevasse, and suddenly Buck shot almost straight up. A small car behind him dropped front first into the hole and burst into flames.

The ground shifted and broke up. A huge section of sidewalk pushed up from the ground more than ten feet and toppled into the street.

The sound was deafening. Buck had never raised his window after listening to the animals, and now the thunderous crashing enveloped him as trucks flipped over and streetlamps, telephone poles, and houses fell.

Buck told himself to slow down. Speed would kill him. He had to see what he was encountering and pick his way through it. The Range Rover bounced and twisted. Once he spun in a circle. People who had, for the moment, survived this were driving wildly and smashing into each other.

How long would it last? Buck was disoriented. He looked at the compass on the dash and tried to stay pointed to the west. For a moment there seemed almost a pattern in the street. He went down then up then down then up as if on a roller coaster, but the great quake had just begun. What at first appeared as jagged peaks the Rover could handle quickly became swirling masses of mud and asphalt. Cars were swallowed up in them.

* * *

Horror was not a good enough word for it. Rayford could not bring himself to speak to Carpathia or even to Mac. They were headed toward Baghdad Airport, and Rayford could not keep from staring at the devastation below. Fires had broken out all over the place. They illuminated car crashes, flattened buildings, the earth roiling and rolling like an angry sea. What appeared a huge ball of a gasoline fire caught his eye. There, hanging in the sky so close it seemed he could touch it, was the moon. The bloodred moon.

* * *

Buck was not thinking of himself. He was thinking of Chloe. He was thinking of Loretta. He was thinking of Tsion. Could God have brought them through all this only to let them die in the great earthquake, the sixth Seal Judgment? If they all went to be with God, so much the better. Was it too much to ask that it be painless for his loved ones? If they were to go, he prayed, "Lord, take them quickly."

The quake roared on and on, a monster that gobbled everything in sight. Buck recoiled in horror as his headlights shone on a huge house dropping completely underground. How far was he from Chloe at Loretta's? Would he have a better chance of getting to Loretta and Tsion at the church? Soon Buck found his the only vehicle in sight. No streetlights, no traffic lights, no street signs. Houses were crumbling. Above the road he heard screams, saw people running, tripping, falling, rolling.

The Range Rover bounced and shook. He couldn't count the times his head hit the roof. Once a strip of curb rolled up and pushed the Range Rover on its side. Buck thought the end was near. He was not going to take it lying down. There he was, pressed up against the left side of the vehicle, strapped in. He reached for the seat belt. He was going to unfasten it and climb out the passenger's-side window. Just before he got it unlatched, the rolling earth uprighted the Range Rover, and off he drove again. Glass broke. Walls fell. Restaurants disappeared. Car dealerships were swallowed. Office buildings stood at jagged angles, then slowly toppled. Again Buck saw a gap in the road he could not avoid. He closed his eyes and braced himself, feeling his tires roll over an uneven surface and break glass and crumple metal. He looked around quickly as he took a left and saw that he had driven over the top of someone else's car. He hardly knew where he was. He just kept heading west. If only he could get to the church or to Loretta's house. Would he recognize either? Was there a prayer that anyone he knew anywhere in the world was still alive?

* * *

Mac had caught a glimpse of the moon. Rayford could see he was awestruck. He maneuvered the chopper so Nicolae could see it too. Carpathia seemed to stare at it in wonder. It illuminated his face in its awful red glow, and the man had never looked more like the devil.

Great sobs rose in Rayford's chest and throat. As he looked at the destruction and mayhem below, he knew the odds were against his finding Amanda. *Lord, receive her unto yourself without suffering, please!*

And Hattie! Was it possible she might have received Christ before this? Could there have been somebody in Boston or on the plane who would have helped her make the transaction?

Suddenly there came a meteor shower, as if the sky was falling. Huge flaming rocks streaked from the sky. Rayford had seen it go from day to night and now back to day with all the flames.

* * *

Buck gasped as the Range Rover finally hit something that made it stop. The back end had settled into a small indentation, and the headlights pointed straight up. Buck had both hands on the wheel, and he was reclining, staring at the sky. Suddenly the heavens opened. Monstrous black and purple clouds rolled upon each other and seemed to peel back the very blackness of the night. Meteors came hurtling down, smashing everything that had somehow avoided being swallowed. One landed next to Buck's door, so hot that it melted the windshield and made Buck unlatch his seat belt and try to scramble out the right side. But as he did, another molten rock exploded behind the Range Rover and punched it out of the ditch. Buck was thrown into the backseat and hit his head on the ceiling. He was dazed, but he knew if he stayed in one place he was dead. He climbed over the seat and got behind the wheel again. He strapped himself in, thinking how flimsy that precaution seemed against the greatest earthquake in the history of mankind.

There seemed no diminishing of the motion of the earth. These were not aftershocks. This thing simply was not going to quit. Buck drove slowly, the Range Rover's headlights jerking and bouncing crazily as first one side and then the other dropped and flew into the air. Buck thought he recognized a landmark: a low-slung restaurant at a corner three blocks from the church. Somehow he had to keep going. He carefully drove around and through destruction and mayhem. The earth continued to shift and roll, but he just kept going. Through his blown-out window he saw people running, heard them screaming, saw their gaping wounds and their blood. They tried to hide under rocks that had been disgorged from the earth. They used upright chunks of asphalt and sidewalk to protect them, but just as quickly they were crushed. A middle-aged man, shirtless and shoeless and bleeding, looked heavenward through broken glasses and opened his arms wide. He screamed to the sky, "God, kill me! Kill me!" And as Buck slowly bounced past in the Range Rover, the man was swallowed into the earth.

\+ + +

Rayford had lost hope. Part of him was praying that the helicopter would drop from the sky and crash. The irony was, he knew Nicolae Carpathia was not to die for yet another twenty-one months. And then he would be resurrected and live another three-and-a-half years. No meteor would smash that helicopter. And wherever they landed, they would somehow be safe. All because Rayford had been running an errand for the Antichrist.

\+ + +

Buck's heart sank as he saw the steeple of New Hope Village Church. It had to be less than six hundred yards away, but the earth was still churning. Things were still crashing. Huge trees fell and dragged power lines into the street. Buck spent several minutes wending his way through debris and over huge piles of wood and dirt and cement. The closer he got to the church, the emptier he felt in his heart. That steeple was the only thing standing. Its base rested at ground level. The lights of the Range Rover illuminated pews, sitting incongruously in neat rows, some of them unscathed. The rest of the sanctuary, the high-arched beams, the stained-glass windows, all gone. The administration building, the classrooms, the offices were flattened to the ground in a pile of bricks and glass and mortar.

One car was visible in a crater in what used to be the parking lot. The bottom of the car was flat on the ground, all four tires blown, axles broken. Two bare human legs protruded from under the car. Buck stopped the Range Rover a hundred feet from that mess in the parking lot. He shifted into park and turned off the engine. His door would not open. He loosened his belt and climbed out the passenger side. And suddenly the earthquake stopped. The sun reappeared. It was a bright, sunshiny Monday morning in Mt. Prospect, Illinois. Buck felt every bone in his body. He staggered over the uneven ground toward that little flattened car. When he was close enough, he saw that the crushed body was missing a shoe. The one that remained, however, confirmed his fear. Loretta had been crushed by her own car.

Buck stumbled and fell facedown in the dirt, something gashing his cheek. He ignored it and crawled to the car. He braced himself and pushed with all his might, trying to roll the vehicle off the body. It would not budge. Everything in him screamed against leaving Loretta there. But where would he take the body if he could free it? Sobbing now, he crawled through the debris, looking for any entrance to the underground shelter. Small recognizable areas of the fellowship hall allowed him to crawl around what was left of the flattened church. The conduit that led to the steeple had been snapped. He made his way over bricks and chunks of wood. Finally he found the vent shaft. He cupped his hands over it and shouted down into it, "Tsion! Tsion! Are you there?"

He turned and put his ear to the shaft, feeling cool air rush from the shelter. "I am here, Buck! Can you hear me?"

"I hear you, Tsion! Are you all right?"

"I am all right! I cannot get out the door!"

"You don't want to see what's up here anyway, Tsion!" Buck shouted, his voice getting weaker.

"How is Loretta?"

"Gone!"

"Was it the great earthquake?"

"It was!"

"Can you get to me?"

"I will get to you if it's the last thing I do, Tsion! I need you to help me look for Chloe!"

"I am OK for now, Buck! I will wait for you!"

Buck turned to look in the direction of the safe house. People staggered in ragged clothes, bleeding. Some dropped and seemed to die in front of his eyes. He didn't know how long it would take him to get to Chloe. He was sure he would not want to see what he found there, but he would not stop until he did. If there was one chance in a million of getting to her, of saving her, he would do it.

* * *

The sun had reappeared over New Babylon. Rayford urged Mac McCullum to keep going toward Baghdad. Everywhere the three of them looked was destruction. Craters from meteors. Fires burning. Buildings flattened. Roads wasted.

When Baghdad Airport came into sight, Rayford hung his head and wept. Jumbo jets were twisted, some sticking out of great cavities in the ground. The terminal was flattened. The tower was down. Bodies strewn everywhere.

Rayford signaled Mac to set the chopper down. But as he surveyed the area, Rayford knew. The only prayer for Amanda or for Hattie was that their planes were still in the air when this occurred.

When the blades stopped whirring, Carpathia turned to the other two. "Do either of you have a working phone?"

Rayford was so disgusted he reached past Carpathia and pushed open the door. He slipped out from behind Carpathia's seat and jumped to the ground. Then he reached in, loosened Carpathia's belt, grabbed him by the lapels, and yanked him out of the chopper. Carpathia landed on his seat on the uneven ground. He jumped up quickly, as if ready to fight. Rayford pushed him back up against the helicopter.

"Captain Steele, I understand you are upset, but—"

"Nicolae," Rayford said, his words rushing through clenched teeth, "you can explain this away any way you want, but let me be the first to tell you: You have just seen the wrath of the Lamb!"

Carpathia shrugged. Rayford gave him a last shove against the helicopter and stumbled away. He set his face toward the airport terminal, a quarter mile away. He prayed this would be the last time he had to search for the body of a loved one in the rubble.

Epilogue

"WHEN HE OPENED the seventh seal, there was silence in heaven for about half an hour. And I saw the seven angels who stand before God, and to them were given seven trumpets. Then another angel, having a golden censer, came and stood at the altar. He was given much incense, that he should offer it with the prayers of all the saints upon the golden altar which was before the throne. And the smoke of the incense, with the prayers of the saints, ascended before God from the angel's hand. Then the angel took the censer, filled it with fire from the altar, and threw it to the earth. And there were noises, thunderings, lightnings, and an earthquake.

"So the seven angels who had the seven trumpets
prepared themselves to sound."
REVELATION 8:1-6

DEAR READER,

With the advent of the movie *2012* and an Internet full of ominous warnings (from the ancient Mayans to the ancient Egyptians), doomsday prophecies are gaining purchase. The movie trailers show *2012* to be a picture with high production value and sophisticated special effects. And the History Channel Web site carries fascinating commentary from astronomers, archaeologists, and others who agree that we are heading toward something cataclysmic. This is something Dr. Tim LaHaye has been saying for years, and he believes we have more reason now than ever before to expect that the rapture of the church (the spiriting away of true believers in an instant)—as prophesied in the Bible—could occur in our lifetime.

While it may be that God, in His mercy, will wait one more day (a thousand years in our economy of time), the Bible urges people to watch and wait . . . and be ready.

As for the predicting of a specific day or time, however, Scripture also makes it clear that this is folly. Jesus Himself told His disciples that even He did not know the day or the hour, but only His Father knew.

In our opinion, it is not ours to predict a specific date for the end of the world as we know it. And we acknowledge that our view of biblical prophecy sounds as absurd to the modern mind as do the astrological and even scientific warnings currently bandied about.

We will watch the movie. We will listen to the experts. But we respectfully ask that our interpretation of the biblical record also be carefully considered. We don't expect everyone to agree, and we expect many to scoff, but we urge all to at least be aware of what it is you are disagreeing with or scoffing at. We sincerely don't want to see anyone left behind.

Dr. Tim LaHaye and Jerry B. Jenkins

About the Authors

Jerry B. Jenkins, former vice president for publishing at Moody Bible Institute of Chicago and currently chairman of the board of trustees, is the author of more than 175 books, including the best-selling Left Behind series. Twenty of his books have reached the *New York Times* Best Sellers List (seven in the number-one spot) and have also appeared on the *USA Today*, *Publishers Weekly*, and *Wall Street Journal* best-seller lists. *Desecration*, book nine in the Left Behind series, was the best-selling book in the world in 2001. His books have sold nearly 70 million copies.

Also the former editor of *Moody* magazine, his writing has appeared in *Time*, *Reader's Digest*, *Parade*, *Guideposts*, and dozens of Christian periodicals. He was featured on the cover of *Newsweek* magazine in 2004.

His nonfiction books include as-told-to biographies with Hank Aaron, Bill Gaither, Orel Hershiser, Luis Palau, Joe Gibbs, Walter Payton, and Nolan Ryan among many others. The Hershiser and Ryan books reached the *New York Times* Best Sellers List.

Jerry Jenkins assisted Dr. Billy Graham with his autobiography, *Just As I Am*, also a *New York Times* best seller. Jerry spent 13 months working with Dr. Graham, which he considers the privilege of a lifetime.

Jerry owns Jenkins Entertainment, a filmmaking company in Los Angeles, which produced the critically acclaimed movie *Midnight Clear*, based on his book of the same name. See www.Jenkins-Entertainment.com.

Jerry Jenkins also owns the Christian Writers Guild, which aims to train tomorrow's professional Christian writers. Under Jerry's leadership, the guild has expanded to include college-credit courses, a critique service, literary registration services, and writing contests, as well as an annual conference. See www.ChristianWritersGuild.com.

As a marriage-and-family author, Jerry has been a frequent guest on Dr. James Dobson's *Focus on the Family* radio program and is a sought-after speaker and humorist. See www.AmbassadorSpeakers.com.

Jerry has been awarded four honorary doctorates. He and his wife, Dianna, have three grown sons and four grandchildren.

Check out Jerry's blog at http://jerryjenkins.blogspot.com.

Dr. Tim LaHaye (www.timlahaye.com), who conceived and created the idea of fictionalizing an account of the Rapture and the Tribulation, is a noted author, minister, and nationally recognized speaker on Bible prophecy. He is the founder of both Tim LaHaye Ministries and The PreTrib Research Center. Presently Dr. LaHaye speaks at many Bible prophecy conferences in the U.S. and Canada, where his current prophecy books are very popular.

Dr. LaHaye holds a doctor of ministry degree from Western Theological Seminary and a doctor of literature degree from Liberty University. For 25 years he pastored one of the nation's outstanding churches in San Diego, which grew to three locations. It was during that time that he founded two accredited Christian high schools, a Christian school system of ten schools, and San Diego Christian College (formerly known as Christian Heritage College).

Dr. LaHaye has written over 50 nonfiction and coauthored 25 fiction books, many of which have been translated into 34 languages. He has written books on a wide variety of subjects, such as family life, temperaments, and Bible prophecy. His most popular fiction works, the Left Behind series, written with Jerry B. Jenkins, have appeared on the best-seller lists of the Christian Booksellers Association, *Publishers Weekly*, the *Wall Street Journal*, *USA Today*, and the *New York Times*.

Another popular series by LaHaye and Jenkins is The Jesus Chronicles. This four-book novel series gives readers rich first-century experiences as John, Mark, Luke, and Matthew recount thrilling accounts of the life of Jesus. Dr. LaHaye is coauthor of another fiction series, Babylon Rising. Each of the four titles in this series have debuted in the top 10 on the *New York Times* Best Sellers List. These are suspense thrillers with thought-provoking messages.